D0045339

Also by Tom Wolfe

The Kandy-Kolored Tangerine-Flake Streamline Baby (1965)

The Pump House Gang (1968)

The Electric Kool-Aid Acid Test (1968)

Radical Chic & Mau-Mauing the Flak Catchers (1970)

The Painted Word (1975)

Mauve Gloves & Madmen, Clutter & Vine (1976)

The Right Stuff (1979)

In Our Time (1980)

From Bauhaus to Our House (1981)

The Bonfire of the Vanities (1987)

SRIPEND
CHRISTMAS 1998
DEAR DADDY –
DO PROMISE NOT TO
READ THIS ALL AT ONCE!!
ALL OUR LOVE
OLIVIA + NELL
XX

TOM

WOLFE

A Man in Full

A Novel

JONATHAN CAPE / LONDON

Published by Jonathan Cape 1998

2 4 6 8 10 9 7 5 3 1

First published in Great Britain in 1998 by
Jonathan Cape
Random House, 20 Vauxhall Bridge Road,
London SW1V 2SA

Random House Australia (Pty) Limited
20 Alfred Street, Milsons Point, Sydney,
New South Wales 2061, Australia

Random House New Zealand Limited
18 Poland Road, Glenfield,
Auckland 10, New Zealand

Random House South Africa (Pty) Limited
Endulini, 5A Jubilee Road, Parktown 2193, South Africa

Random House UK Limited Reg. No. 954009

For their help in identifying settings used in the book-jacket illustration, the publisher thanks (for research) William R. Mitchell, Jr., Mary Rose Taylor of the Margaret Mitchell House and Museum, and C. Tom Hill of the Thomas County Historical Society; and (for location photography) Brett Davidson and Pamela Scheier.

This novel's story and characters are fictitious. Certain long-established institutions, agencies, and public offices are mentioned, but the characters involved in them are wholly imaginary. One institution, the Santa Rita jail, is dealt with anachronistically. The jail was demolished not by the last major earthquake in the San Francisco Bay Area but shortly before it.

Quotations from Epictetus are drawn from *The Stoic and Epicurean Philosophers*, edited by Whitney J. Oates (1940).

Several chapters of this novel have been published, in slightly different form, in *Rolling Stone*, *The Times* and *Men's Journal*.

A CIP catalogue record for this book
is available from the British Library

ISBN 0-224-03036-1

Printed and bound in Great Britain by
Mackays of Chatham PLC, Chatham, Kent

With immense admiration

the author dedicates

A Man in Full *to*

PAUL McHUGH

whose brilliance, comradeship,

and unfailing kindness saved the day.

This book would not exist

had it not been for you, dear friend.

And the author wants to express

a gratitude beyond measure to

MACK AND MARY TAYLOR

who opened his eyes

to the wonders of Atlanta

and the Georgia plantation country

and gave him the run

of their vast storehouse of knowledge and insights,

all with a hospitality he will never forget.

The author bows deeply to

JANN WENNER

the generous genius

who walked this book along until it found its feet,

just as he did The Right Stuff, The Bonfire of the Vanities,

and Ambush at Fort Bragg.

KAILEY WONG

whose eye for the telling details of contemporary American life

is unsurpassed and whose help, once more, has been invaluable.

TOMMY PHIPPS

whose walks on the beach with the author never failed to generate

the necessary new approach and the joie de vivre *to try it.*

GEORGE AND NAN McVEY

who provided the denouement,

not to mention decades of treasured friendship.

COUNSELOR EDDIE HAYES

who stepped out of his starring role in Act III

whenever the author needed him, which was often.

You were there on the darkest night, Counselor!

The author embraces

SHEILA, ALEXANDRA, AND TOMMY

whose love has made it all worthwhile.

Contents

A Man in Full

Prologue

Cap'm Charlie

CHARLIE CROKER, ASTRIDE HIS FAVORITE TENNESSEE WALKING horse, pulled his shoulders back to make sure he was erect in the saddle and took a deep breath . . . Ahhhh, that was the ticket . . . He loved the way his mighty chest rose and fell beneath his khaki shirt and imagined that everyone in the hunting party noticed how powerfully built he was. Everybody; not just his seven guests but also his six black retainers and his young wife, who was on a horse behind him near the teams of La Mancha mules that pulled the buckboard and the kennel wagon. For good measure, he flexed and fanned out the biggest muscles of his back, the latissimi dorsi, in a Charlie Croker version of a peacock or a turkey preening. His wife, Serena, was only twenty-eight, whereas he had just turned sixty and was bald on top and had only a swath of curly gray hair on the sides and in back. He seldom passed up an opportunity to remind her of what a sturdy cord—no, what a veritable *cable*—kept him connected to the rude animal vitality of his youth.

By now they were already a good mile away from the Big House and deep into the plantation's seemingly endless fields of broom sedge. This late in February, this far south in Georgia, the sun was strong enough by 8 a.m. to make the ground mist lift like wisps of smoke and create a heavenly green glow in the pine forests and light up the sedge with a tawny gold. Charlie took another deep breath . . . *Ahhhhhh* . . . the husky aroma of the grass . . . the resinous air of the pines . . . the heavy, fleshy odor of all his animals, the horses, the mules, the dogs . . . Somehow nothing reminded him so instantly of how far he had come in his sixty years on this earth as the smell of the animals. Turpmtine Plantation! Twenty-nine thousand acres of prime southwest Georgia forest, fields, and swamp! And all of it, every square inch of it, every beast that moved on it, all fifty-nine horses, all twenty-two mules, all forty dogs, all thirty-six buildings that stood upon it, plus a mile-long asphalt landing strip, complete with jet-fuel pumps and a hangar—all of it was his, Cap'm Charlie Croker's, to do with as he chose, which was: to shoot quail.

His spirits thus buoyed, he turned to his shooting partner, a stout brick-faced man named Inman Armholster, who was abreast of him on another of his walking horses, and said:

"Inman, I'm gonna—"

But Inman, with a typical Inman Armholster bluster, cut him off and insisted on resuming a pretty boring disquisition concerning the upcoming mayoral race in Atlanta: "Listen, Charlie, I know Jordan's got charm and party manners and he talks white and all that, but that doesn't"—*dud'n*—"mean he's any friend of . . ."

Charlie continued to look at him, but he tuned out. Soon he was aware only of the deep, rumbling timbre of Inman's voice, which had been smoke-cured the classic Southern way, by decades of Camel cigarettes, unfiltered. He was an odd-looking duck, Inman was. He was in his mid-fifties but still had a head of thick black hair, which began low on his forehead and was slicked back over his small round skull. Everything about Inman was round. He seemed to be made of a series of balls piled one atop the other. His buttery cheeks and jowls seemed to rest, without benefit of a neck, upon the two balls of fat that comprised his chest, which in turn rested upon a great swollen paunch. Even his arms and legs, which looked much too short, appeared to be made of spherical parts. The down-filled vest he wore over his hunting khakis only made him look that much rounder. Nevertheless, this ruddy pudge was chairman of Armaxco Chemical and about as influential a businessman as existed in Atlanta. He was this weekend's prize pigeon, as Charlie thought of it, at Turpmtine. Charlie desperately wanted Armaxco to lease space in what so far was the worst mistake of his career as a real estate developer, a soaring monster he had megalomaniacally named Croker Concourse.

"—gon' say Fleet's too young, too brash, too quick to play the race card. Am I right?"

Suddenly Charlie realized Inman was asking him a question. But other than the fact that it concerned André Fleet, the black "activist," Charlie didn't have a clue what it was about.

So he went, "Ummmmmmmmmmmm."

Inman apparently took this to be a negative comment, because he said, "Now, don't give me any a that stuff from the smear campaign. I know there's people going around calling him an out-and-out crook. But I'm telling you, if Fleet's a crook, then he's my kinda crook."

Charlie was beginning to dislike this conversation, on every level. For a start, you didn't go out on a beautiful Saturday morning like this on the next to last weekend of the quail season and talk politics, especially not Atlanta politics. Charlie liked to think he went out shooting quail at Turpmtine just the way the most famous master of Turpmtine, a Confederate Civil War hero named Austin Roberdeau Wheat, had done it a hundred years ago; and a hundred years ago nobody on a quail hunt at Turpmtine would have been out in the sedge talking about an Atlanta whose candidates for mayor were both black. But then Charlie was honest with himself. There was more. There was . . . Fleet. Charlie had had his own dealings with André Fleet, and not all that long ago, either, and he didn't feel like being reminded of them now or, for that matter, later.

So this time it was Charlie who broke in:

"Inman, I'm gonna tell you something I may regret later on, but I'm gonna tell you anyway, ahead a time."

After a couple of puzzled blinks Inman said, "All right . . . go ahead."

"This morning," said Charlie, "I'm only gonna shoot the bobs." *Morning* came out close to *moanin'*, just as *something* had come out *sump'm*. When he was here at Turpmtine, he liked to shed Atlanta, even in his voice. He liked to feel earthy, Down Home, elemental; which is to say, he was no longer merely a real estate developer, he was . . . a man.

"Only gon' shoot the bobs, hunh," said Inman. "With *that*?"

He gestured toward Charlie's .410-gauge shotgun, which was in a leather scabbard strapped to his saddle. The spread of buckshot a .410

fired was smaller than any other shotgun's, and with quail the only way you could tell a bob from a hen was by a patch of white on the throat of a bird that wasn't much more than eight inches long to start with.

"Yep," said Charlie, grinning, "and remember, I told you ahead a time."

"Yeah? I'll tell you what," said Inman. "I'll betcha you can't. I'll betcha a hundred dollars."

"What kinda odds you gon' give me?"

"*Odds?* You're the one who brought it up! You're the one staking out the bragging rights! You know, there's an old saying, Charlie: 'When the tailgate drops, the bullshit stops.' "

"All right," said Charlie, "a hundred dollars on the first covey, even Stephen." He leaned over and extended his hand, and the two of them shook on the bet.

Immediately he regretted it. *Money on the line.* A certain deep worry came bubbling up into his brain. PlannersBanc! Croker Concourse! Debt! A mountain of it! But real estate developers like him learned to live with debt, didn't they . . . It was a normal condition of your existence, wasn't it . . . You just naturally grew gills for breathing it, didn't you . . . So he took another deep breath to drive the spurt of panic back down again and flexed his big back muscles once more.

Charlie was proud of his entire physique, his massive neck, his broad shoulders, his prodigious forearms; but above all he was proud of his back. His employees here at Turpmtine called him Cap'm Charlie, after a Lake Seminole fishing-boat captain from a hundred years ago with the same name, Charlie Croker, a sort of Pecos Bill figure with curly blond hair who, according to local legend, had accomplished daring feats of strength. There was a song about him, which some of the old folks knew by heart. It went: "Charlie Croker was a man in full. He had a back like a Jersey bull. Didn't like okra, didn't like pears. He liked a gal that had no hairs. Charlie Croker! Charlie Croker! Charlie Croker!" Whether or not there had actually existed such a figure, Charlie had never been able to find out. But he loved the idea, and he often said to himself what he was saying to himself at this moment: "Yes! I got a back like a Jersey bull!" In his day he had been a star on the Georgia Tech football team. Football had left him with a banged-up right knee, that had turned arthritic about three years ago. He didn't associate that with age, however. It was an honorable wound of war. One of the beauties of a Tennessee walking horse was that its gait spared you from having to post, to pump up and down at the knees when the horse trotted. He wasn't sure he could take posting on this chilly February morning.

Up ahead, his hunting guide and dog trainer, Moseby, was riding yet another of his walking horses. Moseby signaled the dogs with a curious, low-pitched, drawn-out whistle he somehow produced from deep in his throat. Charlie could just make out one of his two prize pointers, King's Whipple and Duke's Knob, ranging through the golden sea of sedge, trying to get wind of quail coveys.

The two shooters, Charlie and Inman, rode on in silence for a while, listening to the creaking of the wagons and the clip-clopping of the mules and the snorts of the horses of the outriders and waiting for some signal from Moseby. One wagon was a rolling dog kennel containing cages for three more pairs of pointers to take turns in the ceaseless roaming of the sedge, plus a pair of golden retrievers that had been born in the same litter and were known as Ronald and Roland. A team of La Mancha mules, adorned in brass-knobbed yokes and studded harnessing, pulled the wagon, and two of Charlie's dog handlers, both of them black, attired in thornproof yellow overalls, drove them. The other was the buckboard, an ancient wooden thing rebuilt with shock absorbers and pneumatic tires and upholstered with rich tan leather, like a Mercedes-Benz's. Two more of Charlie's black employees, wearing the yellow overalls, drove the La Manchas that pulled the buckboard and served food and drink from an Igloo cooler built into the back. Sitting on the leather seats were Inman's wife, Ellen, who was close to his age and didn't ride anymore, and Betty and Halbert Morrissey and Thurston and Cindy Stannard, four more of Charlie's weekend guests who didn't ride or shoot. Charlie himself wouldn't have been caught dead confined to a buckboard during a quail shoot, but he liked having an audience. Off to the side were two black employees on horseback, wearing the yellow overalls, whose main job was to hold the horses of the shooters or of Charlie's wife, Serena, and Inman and Ellen's eighteen-year-old daughter, Elizabeth, when they dismounted.

Serena and Elizabeth had drifted off from the rest of them and were riding side by side fifty or sixty yards away, Charlie now discovered. This he found annoying, although at first he couldn't have said why. Both were dressed with perfect propriety, in khaki—at a Georgia plantation shoot khaki was as obligatory as tweeds at a grouse shoot in Scotland—and both were mounted flawlessly on their horses, except that they were leaning slightly toward one another, chatting away softly, smiling, and then going into convulsions of stifled laughter. Oh, what great chums they had become this morning—his wife and Inman and Ellen's daughter . . . No one who saw Serena's thick, slightly wild array of black hair and her big periwinkle-blue eyes, which stood out so vividly beneath it, could help but realize how young she was. Less than half his age! Even from fifty or sixty yards away she had Second Wife written all over her! Moreover, she was making it pretty obvious that she had more in common with this teenager, Elizabeth Armholster, than with Elizabeth's mother or Betty Morrissey or Cindy Stannard or anybody else in the party. Elizabeth was a sexy little number herself . . . pale skin, a great mane of light brown hair, big sensual lips, and a chest she made sure you saw, even beneath the khaki . . . Charlie chided himself for thinking that way about his friend's eighteen-year-old daughter, but the way she flaunted it all—the way her stretch riding pants hugged her thighs and the declivities of her loins fore and aft—how could you help it? What did Ellen Armholster really make of Serena, who was much closer to being her daughter's contemporary than her own—Ellen, who had been such a pal of Martha's? Then he took a deep breath and drove Martha and all of that old business out of his mind, too.

You could hear the low voice of one of the buckboard drivers saying, "Buckboard One to base . . . Buckboard One to base . . ." There was a radio transmitter under the driver's seat. "Base" was the overseer's office, back near the Big House. Buckboard *One* . . . Charlie hoped Inman and Ellen and the Morrisseys and the Stannards got the drift of that and were reminded that he had sent out *four* shooting parties this morning, *four* sets of weekend guests, with four buckboards (Buckboards One, Two, Three, and Four), four kennel wagons, four dog trainers, four sets of outriders, four of everything . . . Turpmtine was that big and that lavishly run. There was a formula. To send out one shooting party, with one pair of shooters, half a day each week for the entire season, which ran only from Thanksgiving to the end of February, you had to have at least five hundred acres. Otherwise you would wipe out your quail coveys and have no birds to shoot the following year. To send out one party all day once a week, you had to have at least a thousand acres. Well, he had 29,000 acres. If he felt like it, he could send out four parties all day, every day, seven days a week, throughout the season. Quail! The aristocrat of American wild game! It was what the grouse and the pheasant were in England and Scotland and Europe—only better! With the grouse and the pheasant you had your help literally beating the bushes and driving the birds toward you. With the quail you had to stay on the move. You had to have great dogs, great horses, and great shooters. Quail was king. Only the quail *exploded* upward into the sky and made your heart bang away so madly in your rib cage. And to think what he, Cap'm Charlie, had here! Second biggest plantation in the state of Georgia! He kept up 29,000 acres of fields, woods, and swamp, plus the Big House, the Jook House for the guests, the overseer's house, the stables, the big barn, the breeding barn, the Snake House, the kennels, the gardening shed, the plantation store, the same one that had been there ever since the end of the Civil War, likewise the twenty-five cabins for the help—he kept all this going, staffed, and operating, not to mention the landing field and a hangar big enough to accommodate a Gulfstream Five—he kept all this going, staffed, and operating year round . . . for the sole purpose of hunting quail for thirteen weeks. And it wasn't sufficient to be rich enough to do it. No, this was the South. You had to be man enough to *deserve* a quail plantation. You had to be able to deal with man and beast, in every form they came in, with your wits, your bare hands, and your gun.

He wished there was some way he could underline all this for Inman, but of course there wasn't, unless he wanted to sound like a complete fool. So he decided to approach the subject from a wholly different direction.

"Inman," he said, "did I ever tell you my daddy used to work here at Turpmtine?"

"He did? When?"

"Aw, back when I was nine or ten."

"What'd he do?"

Charlie chuckled. "Not a hell of a lot, I s'peck. He only lasted a couple months. Daddy musta got fired"—came out *farred*—"from half the plantations south of Albany."

Inman didn't say anything, and Charlie couldn't read anything in his face. He wondered if this reference to the Cracker origins of Clan Croker had made Inman uncomfortable. Inman was Old Atlanta, insofar as there *was* any Old Atlanta. Atlanta had never been a true Old Southern city like Savannah or Charleston or Richmond, where wealth had originated with the land. Atlanta was an offspring of the railroad business. It had been created from scratch barely 150 years ago, and people had been making money there on the hustle ever since. The place had already run through three names. First they called it Terminus, because that was where the new railroad ended. Then they named it Marthasville, after the wife of the governor. Then they called it Atlanta, after the Western and Atlantic Railroad and on the boosters' pretext that the rail link with Savannah made it tantamount to a port on the Atlantic Ocean itself. The Armholsters had hustled and boosted with the best of them, Charlie had to admit. Inman's father had built up a pharmaceuticals company back at a time when that was not even a well-known industry, and Inman had turned it into a chemicals conglomerate, Armaxco. Right now he wouldn't mind being in Inman's shoes. Armaxco was so big, so diverse, so well established, it was cycleproof. Inman could probably go to sleep for twenty years and Armaxco would just keep chugging away, minting money. Not that Inman would want to miss a minute of it. He loved all those board meetings too much, loved being up on the dais at all those banquets too much, loved all those tributes to Inman Armholster the great philanthropist, all those junkets to the north of Italy, the south of France, and God knew where else on Armaxco's Falcon 900, all those minions jumping every time he so much as crooked his little finger. With a corporate structure like Armaxco's beneath him, Inman could sit on that throne of his as long as he wanted or until he downed the last mouthful of lamb shanks and mint jelly God allowed him—whereas he, Charlie, was a one-man band. That was what a real estate developer was, a one-man band! You had to sell the world on . . . yourself! Before they would lend you all that money, they had to believe in . . . *you*! They had to think you were some kind of omnipotent, flaw-free genius. Not *my corporation* but Me, Myself & I! His mistake was that he had started believing it himself, hadn't he . . . Why had he ever built a mixed-use development out in Cherokee County crowned with a forty-story tower and named it after himself? *Croker Concourse!* No other Atlanta developer had ever dared display that much ego, whether he had it or not. And now the damned thing stood there, 60 percent empty and hemorrhaging money.

The deep worry was lit up like an inflammation. Couldn't let that happen . . . not on a perfect morning for shooting quail at Turpmtine. So he returned to the subject of his father.

"It was a whole different world back then, Inman. A big Saturday night was going to the jookhouse up near the—"

Charlie broke off in the middle of the sentence. Up ahead, Moseby, the dog trainer, had stopped and looked back and lifted his cap. That was the signal. Then his low voice came rolling across the sedge:

"Poi-i-i-int!"

Sure enough, over there was Knobby—Duke's Knob—in the classic pointer's stance, his nose thrust forward and his tail sticking up at a forty-five-degree angle like a rod. He had gotten wind of a covey of quail in the sedge. Out beyond Moseby, Whip—King's Whipple—was in the same position, backing Knobby's point.

The wagons came to a halt, and everyone grew quiet, and the two shooters, Charlie and Inman, dismounted. Luckily for Charlie, when you mounted or dismounted, your left leg bore the weight as you swung yourself over the horse's back, and his right knee didn't have to go through the ordeal. He had barely dismounted when one of his boys in the yellow overalls, Ernest, arrived on horseback and took the reins of his horse and Inman's. Charlie withdrew his .410 from the leather scabbard and slipped two shells into its twin barrels and began walking through the sedge with Inman. He realized that the knee had stiffened and he was limping, but he was not conscious of the pain. The adrenaline took care of that. His heart was thumping away. No matter how many times you went hunting quail, you never became immune to the feeling that came over you when the dogs set the point and you approached a covey hidden somewhere nearby in the grass. The quails' instinct in the face of danger was to hide in the tall grass and then, all at once, to explode upward in flight with incredible acceleration. Everybody used the same term for it: *explode*. You didn't dare have more than two shooters at a time. The little birds rocketed upward in every direction, scattering in order to confound their predators. In the excitement, hunters swung their guns about so wildly that three or more shooters would pose more of a threat to each other than to the quail. It was dangerous enough with two. That was why he made his help wear the yellow overalls. He didn't want some idiot guest with buck fever cutting loose with a load of buckshot in the direction of one of his boys.

Inman took a position off to Charlie's right. The understanding was that an imaginary line ran between them, and Charlie could go after any birds to the left of it. It was so quiet, he could hear his own breathing, which was too rapid. He could feel the pressure of all the eyes now fixed upon him, the guests', the mule drivers', the outriders', Moseby's, his wife's . . . He'd brought quite a little army out here, hadn't he—*and* he'd opened his big mouth and announced he was going to shoot only the males—and bet Inman a hundred dollars, within practically everybody's hearing.

He had the stock of the .410 up near his shoulder. It seemed to take forever. In fact, it was no more than twenty seconds—

Thrash!

With an extraordinary pounding of the air the covey burst up out of the grass. The sound seemed suffocatingly loud. Gray blurs hurtled at every angle. A patch of white. He swung the .410 to the left. Keep the barrel moving ahead of the bird! That was the main thing. He fired one barrel. He thought—didn't know. Another white patch. Swung the barrel almost straight up. Fired again. A bird came peeling down out of the sky.

Charlie stood there holding the shotgun, conscious of the sharp smell of exploded gunpowder, his heart hammering away. He turned toward Inman.

"How'd you do?"

Inman was shaking his head so hard his jowls were lagging behind his chin and flopping around. "Shit—'scuse me, ladies"—his wife, Ellen, and Betty and Halbert Morrissey and the Stannards had climbed down off the buckboard and were heading toward the two shooters—"I missed the first one. Didn't lead the sonofabitch." He seemed furious with himself. "I might've gotten the second one, but I ain't even sure a that, goddamn it, 'scuse me." He shook his head some more.

Charlie hadn't even been aware of Inman's gun going off.

Inman said, "How'd *you* do?"

"I know I got the second one," said Charlie. "I don't know about the first one."

"Got both, Cap'm Charlie." It was Lonnie, one of the dog handlers on the kennel wagon.

"Better be bobs," said Inman. "Either that or you better have a picture of Ben Franklin handy."

Soon enough the retrievers, Ronald and Roland, had fetched both of Charlie's birds from the underbrush and brought them to Lonnie, who in turn brought them over to Cap'm Charlie. Quail seemed so small, once you actually had one in your hands. Their bodies were still warm, almost hot. Charlie turned up their beaks with his forefinger, and there they were, the white patches on their throats.

A surge of inexpressible joy swept through him. He had done it, just as he said he would! Shot two males from out of that rocketing bevy! It was an omen! What could go wrong now? Nothing! He didn't even dare to let himself smile, for fear of revealing just how proud and sure he was of himself.

He could hear a buzz of conversation between the mule drivers and the outriders and among the guests about how Cap'm Charlie had called his shots and made them, with a hundred dollars riding on the outcome. Inman came over and put his hand down on one bob and then the other.

Now Charlie allowed himself a smile. "Whatcha doing, Inman? You think me and Lonnie's got a couple of old birds stowed away to trick you with?"

"Well, I'll be a sonofabitch," said Inman glumly. "I didn't think you could do it."

And now Charlie let himself laugh from deep inside. "Don't do to doubt me, Inman, not where quail's concerned! Now how 'bout introducing me to that pal a yours you were talking about, Ben Franklin!"

Inman thrust his hands down into the pockets of his khakis, and a sheepish expression came over his face. "Well, hell . . . I didn't bring anything out here. I didn't come out here to *shop*, f'r chrissake, and I sure as hell wasn't gonna buy anything at that plantation *store* a yours."

"Oh brother!" said Charlie. " 'Didn't bring anything out here'! I'm gonna file that one along with 'The truck's broke down' and 'The cook took sick'! 'Didn't bring anything *out* here'?" Charlie looked around at Ellen Armholster and the Morrisseys and the Stannards and beamed. "Juh hear that? It's easy to bet blue chips when you ain't even got table stakes!"

Oh, this was rich stuff. Now he looked around at his mule drivers and outriders, all his boys in the yellow overalls, to make sure they were in on it, too, and at Moseby, who had ridden back toward them, and at Serena—

—but where was she? Then he spotted her. She was still way off, maybe seventy or eighty yards away, out in the field, Serena and Elizabeth Armholster, too, still on their horses, which were side by side. They were chatting and laughing up a storm. He couldn't believe it. The two young women, with their wild hair and loamy loins, hadn't paid the slightest attention to what had just gone on. Couldn't have cared less about what two . . . old men . . . had or hadn't accomplished with their shotguns. He was suddenly filled with a rage he didn't dare express.

Just then Serena and Elizabeth swung their mounts about and headed toward them, laughing and talking to each other the whole time. And now, still high in the saddle, they pulled up beside Charlie and Inman and Ellen and the Morrisseys and the Stannards. Their youthfulness couldn't have been more obvious . . . the high color in their flawlessly smooth cheeks . . . the imperiously correct postures of two girls at a horse show . . . the tender curves of their necks and jaws . . . the perfectly packed fullness of their cloven hindquarters . . . as compared to the sagging hides of Ellen Armholster and Betty Morrissey and Cindy Stannard's generation . . .

The ever-obliging Betty Morrissey looked up at Serena and said, "You know what your husband just did? He shot two bobs, and Inman owes him a hundred dollars."

"Oh, that's wonderful, Charlie," said Serena.

Charlie studied her face. She hadn't said it in any pointedly ironic way, but from the mischievous way her eyes, which were such a vivid blue, flashed beneath the black corona of her hair and from the little glance she flicked toward Elizabeth Armholster, he knew she *meant* it ironically. He could feel his face turning hot.

Elizabeth looked down at her father and said, "How'd *you* do, Daddy?"

"Don't ask," said Inman in a glum voice.

Teasingly: "Oh, come on, Daddy. 'Fess up."

"Believe me, you don't want to know," said Inman, twisting his lips in a way that tried, unsuccessfully, to make it seem as if he were making light of his miserable performance.

Then Elizabeth leaned way over in the saddle, causing her long, light brown hair to cascade down either side of her face, and put her hand on the back of Inman's neck and rubbed it and puckered up those full lips of hers and said in a babyish, coquettish voice she had obviously used on her father before:

"Oh, golly gee, Daddy didn't shoot *any*body in the whole quail family?"

With that she flicked a glance of her own toward Serena, who compressed her lips as if she was making a determined effort not to laugh in the two old shooters' faces.

Now Charlie's face was red hot. The *whole quail family*! What was that supposed to mean? Animal rights? Whatever it was, it was intentional heresy—the two of them peering down from the eminence of their steeds upon the old parties below and sniggering and exchanging glances of conspiratorial superiority—why, the . . . the . . . the . . . the *impudence* of it! According to a tradition as old as the plantations themselves, a quail shoot was a ritual in which the male of the human species acted out his role of hunter, provider, and protector, and the female acted as if this was part of the natural, laudable, excellent, and compelling order of things. None of this could Charlie have put into words, but he felt it. Oh, he felt it—

Just then a burst of static came over the radio on the buckboard, followed by some words in a deep voice Charlie couldn't make out.

One of the mule drivers yelled over: "Cap'm Charlie! It's Durwood. Says Mr. Stroock called from Atlanta and wants you to call him back right away."

A sinking feeling ran through Charlie. There was only one reason why Wismer Stroock, his young chief financial officer, would ever dare try to track him down in the fields of Turpmtine on a Saturday morning during a quail shoot.

"Tell'm—tell'm I'll call him later on, after we get back to the Gun House." He wondered if the quaver of concern in his voice had been detectable.

"Says it's urgent, Cap'm."

Charlie hesitated. "Just tell'm what I said."

He looked down at the patches of white on the throats of the two dead bobs, but he could no longer focus on them. The birds' bellies looked like a reddish-gray fuzz.

PlannersBanc. The mountain of debt. The avalanche has begun, thought Cap'm Charlie.

Chapter I

Chocolate Mecca

FOR A WHILE THE FREAKNIC TRAFFIC INCHED UP PIEDMONT . . . inched up Piedmont . . . inched up Piedmont . . . inched up as far as Tenth Street . . . and then inched up the slope beyond Tenth Street . . . inched up as far as Fifteenth Street . . . whereupon it came to a complete, utter, hopeless, bogged-down glue-trap halt, both ways, northbound, southbound, going and coming, across all four lanes. That was it. Nobody was moving on Piedmont Avenue; not anywhere, not any which way; not from here; not for now. Suddenly, as if they were pilots ejecting from fighter planes, black boys and girls began popping out into the dusk of an Atlanta Saturday night. They popped out of convertibles, muscle cars, Jeeps, Explorers, out of vans, out of evil-looking little econo-sports coupes, out of pickup trucks, campers, hatchbacks, Nissan Maximas, Honda Accords, BMWs, and even ordinary American sedans.

Roger Too White—and in that moment this old nickname of his, Roger Too White, which he had been stuck with ever since Morehouse, came bubbling up, uninvited, into his own brain—Roger Too White stared through the windshield of his Lexus, astonished. Out the passenger-side window of a screaming-red Chevrolet Camaro just ahead of him, in the lane to his left, shot one leg of a pair of fiercely pre-faded blue jeans. A girl. He could tell it was a girl because of the little caramel-colored foot that protruded from the jeans, shod only in the merest of sandals. Then, much faster than it would take to tell it, out the window came her hip, her little bottom, her bare midriff, her tube top, her wide shoulders, her long wavy black hair with its heavenly auburn sheen. Youth! She hadn't even bothered to open the door. She had come rolling out of the Camaro like a high jumper rolling over the bar at a track meet.

As soon as both feet touched the pavement of Piedmont Avenue, she started dancing, thrusting her elbows out in front of her and thrashing them about, shaking those lovely little hips, those tube-topped breasts, those shoulders, that heavenly hair.

RAM YO' *BOO*TY! RAM YO' *BOO*TY!

A rap song was pounding out of the Camaro with such astounding volume, Roger Too White could hear every single vulgar intonation of it even with the Lexus's windows rolled up.

> HOW'M I SPOSE A LOVE HER,
> CATCH HER MACKIN' WITH THE BROTHERS?

—sang, or chanted, or recited, or whatever you were supposed to call it, the guttural voice of a rap artist named Doctor Rammer Doc Doc, if it wasn't utterly ridiculous to call him an artist.

> RAM YO' *BOO*TY! RAM YO' *BOO*TY!

—sang the chorus, which sounded like a group of sex-crazed crack fiends. It took a Roger Too White to imagine that sex-crazed crack fiends could get together and cooperate long enough to sing a chorus, although he did correctly identify Doctor Rammer Doc Doc, who was so popular that even a forty-two-year-old lawyer like himself couldn't completely shut him out of his waking life. His own tastes ran to Mahler and Stravinsky, and he would have gladly majored in music history at Morehouse, except that music history hadn't been considered too great a major for a black undergraduate who wanted to get into the University of Georgia law school. All of that, compressed into a millisecond, blipped through his mind in this moment, too.

The girl swung her hips in an exaggerated arc each time the fiends hit the *BOO* of *BOO*TY. She was gorgeous. Her jeans were down so low on her hips, and her tube top was up so high on her chest, he could see lots of her lovely light-caramel-colored flesh, punctuated by her belly button, which looked like an eager little eye. Her skin was the same light color as his, and he knew her type at a glance. Despite her funky clothes, she was a blueblood. She had Black Deb written all over her. Her parents were no doubt the classic Black Professional Couple of the 1990s, in Charlotte or Raleigh or Washington or Baltimore. Look at the gold bangles on her wrists; must have cost hundreds of dollars. Look at the soft waves in her relaxed hair, a 'do known as a *Bout en Train*; French, baby, for "life of the party"; cost a fortune; his own wife had the same thing done to her hair. Little cutie, shaking her booty, probably went to Howard or maybe Chapel Hill or the University of Virginia; belonged to Theta Psi. Oh, these black boys and girls came to Atlanta from colleges all over the place for Freaknic every April, at spring break, thousands of them, and here they were on Piedmont Avenue, in the heart of the northern third of Atlanta, the white third, flooding the streets, the parks, the malls, taking over Midtown and Downtown and the commercial strips of Buckhead, tying up traffic, even on Highways 75 and 85, baying at the moon, which turns chocolate during Freaknic, freaking out White Atlanta, scaring them indoors, where they cower for three days, giving them a snootful of the future. To these black college students shaking it in front of his Lexus, this was nothing more than what white college students had been doing for years at Fort Lauderdale and Daytona and Cancún, or wherever they were going now, except that these boys and girls here in front of him weren't interested in any beach. They were coming to the . . . streets of Atlanta. Atlanta was their city, the Black Beacon, as the Mayor called it, 70 percent black. The Mayor was black—in fact, Roger and the Mayor, Wesley Dobbs Jordan, had been fraternity brothers (Omega Zeta Zeta) at Morehouse—and twelve of the nineteen city council members were black, and the chief of police was black, and the fire chief was black, and practically the whole civil service was black, and the Power was black, and White Atlanta was screaming its head off about "Freaknik," with a *k* instead of a *c*, as the white newspapers called it, ignorant of the fact that Freaknic was a variation not of the (white) word *beatnik* but of the (neutral) word *picnic*. They were screaming that these black *Freaknik* revelers were rude, loud, rowdy, and insolent, that they got filthy drunk and littered the streets and urinated on (white) people's lawns, that they tied up the streets and the malls and cost the (white) merchants millions of dollars, even that they made so much noise they were disrupting the fragile mating habits of the rhinoceroses at the Grant Park zoo. The mating habits of the rhinos!

In other words, these black boys and girls had *the audacity* to do exactly what white boys and girls did every year during *their* spring breaks. Oh yes, and White Atlanta was screaming everything they could think of, except for what they really thought, which was: *They're everywhere,* they're in *our* part of town, *and they're doing what they damn well please—and we can't stop them!*

Out of the other side of the Camaro popped the driver, a great lubberly lad. A snub-tailed Eclipse was practically touching his rear bumper. He put one hand on the airfoil lip on the trunk of the Camaro and—youth!—vaulted between the two cars and landed right in front of the girl. And no sooner had *his* feet touched the pavement of Piedmont Avenue than *he* was dancing.

RAM YO' *BOOTY*! RAM YO' *BOOTY*!

He was a tall fellow, slightly darker than she was, but not much. He could still pass the Brown Paper Bag Test, as they used to call it here in the Black Beacon, which meant that so long as your skin was no darker than a brown paper bag from the grocery store, you were eligible for Black Society and black debs. He had on a baseball cap, backwards. He had one gold earring, like a pirate's. He had on an orange T-shirt so big the short sleeves came down to his elbows and the neck opening revealed his clavicle; the tail came down below his hips, so that you could barely see his baggy cut-off jeans, whose crotch hung down to his knees. On his feet he wore a pair of huge black sneakers known as Frankensteins, with rubbery white tongue-like shapes lapping up the sides from the soles. Homey; that was the look. Ghetto Boy; but Roger Too White, who was wearing a chalk-striped gray worsted suit, a blue-and-white-striped shirt with a white collar crisp with stays, and a navy silk tie, wasn't buying this ghetto rags getup: the boy was big, but he was fat and happy. He didn't have those hard muscles and thong-like tendons and that wary look through the eyes of the ghetto boy—and he *did* have a Chevrolet Camaro that must have set his daddy back close to $20,000. No, this was probably the son of somebody who had inherited the oldest black bank or insurance company in Memphis or Birmingham or Richmond or—Roger Too White checked out the license plate: Kentucky—okay, in Louisville—from his daddy. Our Louisville company chairman-in-embryo, now a college boy, has come to Atlanta for three days for Freaknic, to raise hell and feel like a true blood and righteous brother.

Roger Too White looked up ahead and to his left and behind him, and everywhere he looked there were happy, frolicsome black boys and girls like this pair, out on the pavement of Piedmont Avenue, dancing between the cars, shouting to each other, throwing away beer cans that went *ping! ping! ping!* on the roadway, shaking their young booties, right at the entrance to a white enclave, Ansley Park, and baying at that chocolate moon. The very air of Saturday-night Atlanta was choked with the hip-hopped-up mojo of rap music booming from a thousand car stereos—

RAM YO' *BOOTY*!

—and then he took a look at his watch. Oh shit! It was 7:05, and he had to be at an address on Habersham Road in Buckhead, some street he had never laid eyes on, by 7:30. He had allowed himself plenty of time, because he knew Freaknic was in progress and the traffic would be terrible, but now he was trapped in the middle of an impromptu block party on Piedmont Avenue. He felt panicky. He could never say this out loud to a living soul, not even to his wife, but he couldn't stand the thought of being late for appointments—especially where important white people were concerned. And this was the Georgia Tech football coach, Buck McNutter, an Atlanta celebrity, a man he didn't even know, who had summoned him out on a Saturday night, urgently; unwilling to even go into it on the telephone. He *couldn't* be late to an appointment with a man like that. *Couldn't!* Maybe that was craven of him, but that was the way he was. Once, when he was representing the MoTech Corporation in the Atlanta Pythons stadium negotiations, he was standing around in a conference room up in the Peachtree Center with a bunch of white lawyers and executives, and they were all waiting for Russell Tubbs, whom he knew very well because he, too, was black and a lawyer. Russ was representing the city. One of these big meaty white business types, a real red-faced Cracker, is talking to another one, just as big, red-faced, and slit-eyed, and they've got their backs to him. They didn't know he was there. And one of them says, "When the hell's this guy Tubbs gonna get here?" And the other one puts on this real Cracker-style imitation of a black accent and says, "Well now, I don' rightly know de answer to dat. Counselor Tubbs, he operates on C.P.T." *Colored People's Time.* Roger Too White had used that tired old joke himself, with other brothers, but to hear it come out of the mouth of this fatback white bigot—he wanted to strangle him on the spot. But he didn't strangle him, did he—no, instead he had swallowed it . . . whole . . . and pledged to himself that he would never—*ever!*—be late to an appointment, particularly with a prominent white person. And he never had been, from that day to this—and now he was trapped in a Freaknic Saturday-night block party that could go on forever.

Desperate, Roger Too White sought a way out—*the sidewalk*. He was in the right lane, the lane next to the curb, and maybe he could drive up over the curb and onto the sidewalk and down to Tenth Street and get out that way somehow. The sidewalk was against an embankment topped by a fence with rustic stone pillars that ran up the hill of Piedmont Avenue. The embankment was like a cliff, retaining a stretch of high ground that cropped up between the avenue and Piedmont Park, which was on the other side. Right above the wall you could see a low structure that from this angle looked like a lodge in the mountain resort area of western North Carolina. There was a terrace, and up on that terrace were a bunch of white people in formal clothes. They were peering down at the Freaknic revelers.

RAM YO' *BOOTY*! RAM YO' *BOOTY*!

From where he was, he could see the white faces of the men and the shoulders of their tuxedos. He could see the white faces of the women and, in many cases, their bare white shoulders and the bodices of their dresses. They were not smiling. They were not happy. Bango! The Piedmont Driving Club! That was what this otherwise unremarkable building was: the Piedmont Driving Club! Now he recognized it! The Driving Club was the very sanctum, the very citadel of the White Atlanta Establishment. He got the picture immediately. These white swells had no doubt planned this big party for this Saturday night ages ago, never dreaming it would coincide with Freaknic. And now their worst white nightmare had come true. They were marooned in the very middle of it. *Black Freaknik!* On this side, black boys and girls were ejecting from their automobiles and shaking it to Doctor Rammer Doc Doc's "Ram Yo' Booty." On the other side, in Piedmont Park, thousands of black boys and girls were gathering for a concert featuring another rapper, G. G. Good Jookin'. All those white faces up on the Driving Club terrace could look here, and they could look there, and they could see nothing in any direction but a rising tide of exuberant young black people, utterly unfettered and unafraid.

Perfection! The perfect poetic justice was what this black traffic-jam jam session on Piedmont was! The very origin of the Piedmont Driving Club was . . . driving vehicles. The club had started up in 1887, just twenty-two years after the Civil War, when the Atlanta elite, which meant the white elite, it went without saying, had begun meeting on the weekends in what was now Piedmont Park to show off their buggies, phaetons, barouches, victorias, and tallyhos with all the custom bodywork and harnesses and tack and the hellishly expensive horses, in order to bask in one another's conspicuous consumption. So then they had bought themselves a clubhouse, and gradually they had enlarged it, and eventually it became the rambling structure up there on the high ground he was looking at right now. It wasn't all that long ago that no black man set foot in the place unless he was a cook, a dishwasher, a waiter, a doorman, a maître d' or an attendant who parked the members' cars. Lately the Driving Club had seen the handwriting on the wall, and they were looking for some black members. Roger himself had received an overture, if that was what it was, from a jolly lawyer named Buddy Lee Witherspoon. That was an example of just how Too White even white people perceived him to be, wasn't it! Well, they could just go kiss his —he was damned if he would ever set foot in that place and circulate on that terrace with all those white faces he was now staring up at—not even if they got down on their knees and begged him. Hell, no! He was going to get out of this Lexus sedan and join the party and stand in the street and raise his black fists up toward that terrace and roar out to them: "Look, you want a driving club? You want a driving club that convenes at Piedmont and Fifteenth Street? You want to see the elite meet? Then feast your eyes on this! Take a good look! BMWs, Geos, Neons, Eclipses, sports utilities, Hummers, runabouts, Camrys, and Eldorados, millions of dollars' worth of cars, in the hands of young black Americans, billions of volts of energy and excitement, with young black America in the driver's seat and shaking its black booty right in your pale trembling faces! Look at me! Listen to me, because I'm going to—"

But then he lost heart, because he knew he wasn't going to say that or anything else. He wasn't even going to get out of the car. *Got to be at Coach Buck McNutter's house in Buckhead in less than twenty-five minutes, and Coach Buck McNutter is very white.*

For an instant, as he had many times before, Roger Too White hated himself. Maybe he *was* too white . . . Too White . . . His father, Roger Makepeace White, pastor of the Beloved Covenant Church, had named him Roger Ahlstrom White II, out of his intellectual reverence for a religious historian named Sidney Ahlstrom. His father had thought that the II was the proper designation for sons who had the same first name as their fathers but different middle names. So when he was a boy growing up in Vine City and Collier Heights, all his aunts and uncles and cousins had started calling him Roger Two, and then everybody started calling him Roger Two, as if he had a double name like Buddy Lee. Then when he got to Morehouse in the seventies, his fellow students turned that perfectly harmless nickname on him like a skewer through the ribs and started calling him Roger Too White instead of Roger White II. He had come to Morehouse, the crown jewel of the four black colleges that made up the Atlanta University Center, with the misfortune of being deeply influenced in all matters political (and moral and cultural and pertaining to personal conduct, property, dress, and etiquette) by his father, an ardent admirer of Booker T. Washington. Booker T. had made the most important pronouncement of his life right over there in Piedmont Park, his so-called Atlanta Compromise speech of 1895 at the Cotton States Exposition, in which he said black people should seek economic security before political or social equality with whites. Alas, the late seventies were a time when, especially at Morehouse, the number-one elite blueblood black college in America, molder of the much-vaunted Morehouse Man, you had to be for the legacy of the Panthers and CORE and SNCC and the BLA and Rap and Stokely and Huey and Eldridge, or you were *out of it*. Black Atlanta's own Martin Luther King had been murdered not even ten years before, and so obviously gradualism and Gandhiism and all that were finished. If you were a proponent of *Booker T. Washington*, then you were worse than out of it. The way people acted, you might as well have been waving a placard for Lester Maddox or George Wallace or Eugene Talmadge. But damn it all, Booker T. was no Uncle Tom! He never kowtowed to the white man! He didn't even want integration! He said the white man will *never* like you! He said he'll never treat you fair out of the goodness of his heart! He'll treat you fair only after you've made something out of yourself and your career and your community and he's dying to do business with you! But nobody at Morehouse, and certainly nobody in Omega Zeta Zeta, wanted to even hear about all that. They wanted to hear about confrontations with the White Establishment and gunfights with the cops that brothers had had in the sixties. Booker T. *Wash*ington? Roger Too White they started calling him, and he hadn't been able to shake it in the whole three decades since then.

And maybe they were right . . . maybe they were right . . . In this very moment, as he looked up through the windshield of his Lexus at the Piedmont Driving Club, in this very moment when he felt the urge to get out of the car and lift his fists to the heavens and announce the new dawn, he was pulled in two directions. Part of him was so proud of these boys and girls all around him on the street, these young brothers and sisters who didn't hesitate for a second to claim the streets of Atlanta, *all* the streets, as their own, with just as much Dionysian abandon as any white college students—while another part of him said, "Why can't you put on a classier show? If you can afford the BMWs and the Camaros and the Geo convertibles and the Hummers"—he could see one of those monsters, a Hummer, four or five cars ahead of him—

He turned his head to take another look at the Deb dancing in the street—

What?

He couldn't believe it. She was now up *on top of* the Camaro, dancing as if she were on top of a bar, like the bar of the Sportsman's Club downtown on Ellis Street. And there wasn't just her lubberly boyfriend staring up at her, there was a whole *mob* of boys, college boys, the *jeunesse dorée* of Black America, all of them wearing *their* ghetto rags and jumping around like a bunch of maniacs and grinning and shrieking, "Take it off! Take it off! Take it off!"

RAM YO' *BOO*TY! RAM YO' *BOO*TY!

The Deb, this beautiful, exquisite young woman, was merrily teasing them on, grinding her booty and projecting her breasts, and touching the top of the fly of her jeans with both hands, as if at any moment she was about to unzip them, slip them down off her hips, all with a salacious leer on her lips and a lubricious look in her eyes.

"TAKE IT OFF! TAKE IT OFF! TAKE IT OFF!"

There must have been thirty berserk boys around that Camaro, wild with anticipation. Some were thrusting money up toward her. She looked at them with a grin of concupiscent mockery and continued to grind her hips.

Roger Too White's heart was pounding, partly because he feared what a terrible turn this exhibition might take—but also—and he felt this immediately, in his very loins—because he had seldom been so aroused by any sight in his life—he didn't want her to—and yet he *did*—

—when suddenly Circe, the Deb, the golden tan daughter of some Ideal Black Professional Couple of the 1990s, stretched her right arm straight out, pointing upward—and grinned.

Stunned, astonished, her besotted subjects on the pavement swiveled their heads in that direction, too. Now they were all looking upward, obedient drones of Circe, the great tubby lubberly Louisville company chairman-in-embryo among them. They had all spotted the white people up on the terrace of the Driving Club peering down from the formal eminence of their tuxedos and cocktail dresses. All the boys and girls, the whole street full of them, began laughing and shouting.

RAM YO' *BOO*TY! RAM YO' *BOO*TY!

Then they all started dancing, all those black boys and girls out in their shiny screaming sea of cars, with the Deb up on top of the Camaro like the Queen of the Rout, all facing in one direction, toward the Piedmont Driving Club, shaking their booties and thrashing their elbows. Did they know that this was the Piedmont Driving Club and what the Piedmont Driving Club was? Not one chance in a thousand, thought Roger Too White. All they saw was a clutch of bewildered white people clad in their evening clothes. The dance in the street became a good-natured mockery. You want to see Freaknic? Then we'll show it to you! We'll give you a real eyeful! We're loose! We're down! You're dead! You're rickety!

GONNA SOCK IT TO MY BABY!
LIKE A ROCKET, DON'T MEAN MAYBE!

—Suddenly a new rap song was pounding from the Camaro—

GIRL, CAN'T KNOCK IT, SAY BE
LIMBO!
SHANKS AKIMBO!
HEY! YO! BIMBO! YOU UNLOCK IT!
GONNA TAKE IT OUT MY POCKET!
AN' THEN I'M GONNA COCK IT IN—
CHOC-OLATE MECCA! UNNHHH!
CHOC-OLATE MECCA! UNNHHH!
CHOC-OLATE MECCA! UNNHHH!
CHOC-OLATE MECCA! UNNHHH!

With each CHOC of CHOCOLATE MECCA the Black Deb on top of the Camaro thrust her hips this way, and with each UNNHHH! she thrust them that way. And now the whole block party was doing the same thing, grinning and laughing at the stricken white people on the terrace.

CHOCOLATE MECCA! UNNHHH!
CHOCOLATE MECCA! UNNHHH!
CHOCOLATE MECCA! UNNHHH!

Suddenly the tubby boy, the company chairman-to-be, stopped dancing, wheeled about, and walked up close to his Camaro, facing the passenger-side door. What was he doing? The Black Deb apparently wondered the same thing, because she stopped dancing, too, and looked down at him. He was so close to the Camaro, you couldn't see anything but his back, but he seemed to be fumbling with the fly of his cut-off jeans. Roger Too White had a disheartening premonition . . . Surely he wouldn't . . . right there in the middle of Piedmont Avenue . . . Now the boy reached down under the tail of his long, floppy T-shirt and lifted it as high as his waist and hooked his thumbs over the top of his cut-off jeans and, in a single motion, pulled his jeans and his undershorts down around his knees and leaned over and stuck out his big fat bare bottom.

The Black Deb shrieked and exploded with laughter. Boys and girls all over the street shrieked and exploded with laughter.

Mooning!

Mooning!

He was mooning the very Piedmont Driving Club itself!

Roger Too White, encased in his fancy Lexus and his $2,800 custom-made suit and $125 shirt and crêpe de chine necktie, was appalled. He wanted to cry out: "Brothers! Sisters! Is *this* why you've become the *jeunesse dorée* of Black America? Is *this* why we've finally scaled the heights educationally and professionally? Is *this* why your parents struggled to accumulate the capital to give you those cars you're cruising around Atlanta in tonight? Is *this* why they made sure your generation went to college? So you brothers could act like *this*? Wearing ghetto rags and snorting and squealing like rutboars and turning that beautiful sister into a common Ellis Street hootchy and throwing money at her? And you sisters—why would you do something like this? You veritable flowers of black womanhood—why would you let the brothers turn you into the very same stereotypes that the hip-hop videos make you out to be? Why don't you say no to such sexist disrespect? Why don't you insist, as you should, as you easily *could,* upon the love, affection, and genuine respect you deserve? Brothers, Sisters, listen to me—"

At the same time another feeling entirely was sweeping through his loins. Deep inside he was . . . exhilarated. The *freedom* of these young brothers and sisters, the abandon, the Dionysian *fearlessness* on the very threshold of the Piedmont Driving Club—

Oh my God, oh my God—

Oh, Chocolate Mecca!

MIRACULOUSLY, THE TRAFFIC started moving again, and the girls and boys popped back into their cars as fast as they had ejected from them, and the Freaknic traffic began inching up Piedmont Avenue once more. Not a moment too soon, either. The Black Deb had managed to take advantage of the brief interlude of mocking the stuffed white shirts on the terrace of the Driving Club to scramble back down into the Camaro, alongside her fat moon-happy friend, and now the traffic was moving again, and it was all over.

Roger Too White's heart was still pounding, from a fear of what the scene might have turned into—and from a sexual stimulation that made him wonder all over again about his proper forty-two-year-old self—but he managed to keep his wits about him long enough to peel off from Piedmont Avenue at Morningside Drive.

He sped over to Lenox Road and then headed north and made a big loop around the Lenox Square area, which he knew would be clogged with Freaknickers. By driving much too fast, he managed to get over to Habersham Road, near West Paces Ferry, only eleven minutes late.

Aw, man . . . Habersham Road . . . It was dusk, but it was still light enough to see what Habersham Road was . . . Georgia Tech was treating Coach Buck McNutter like a king. The Stingers Club, the new group of alumni football boosters, had raised enough money to top off the university's regular football coach's pay enough, and guarantee the great McNutter $875,000 a year, thereby wooing him away from the University of Alabama. As a bonus on a bonus, they guaranteed him a house in Buckhead, gratis. Not only that, Habersham Road was obviously in the very best part of Buckhead. The lawns rose up from the street like big green breasts, and at the top of each breast was a house big enough to be called a mansion . . . Trees everywhere . . . reaching up so high it was obvious they were virgin timber . . . boxwood bushes so big and dense and well clipped, you could *hear* all those gardeners snicker-snacking away just by looking at them . . . and, above all, the dogwood. It was a late spring, for Georgia, and the dogwood had just burst out in all their glory. Here in the gloaming, the white blossoms, arranged in their distinctive planes, swept from green breast to green breast, from mansion to mansion, estate to estate, as if some divine artist had adorned the heavenly air itself with them to show that the residents of Buckhead, off West Paces Ferry Road, were the elect, the anointed, the rightful white hard grabbers of whatever Atlanta, Georgia, had to offer. In Cascade Heights and at Niskey Lake, where Roger Too White lived, way down in Southwest Atlanta, he and a lot of other successful black people, the lawyers, the bankers, the insurance company executives, had big houses—some with white columns—and big lawns and, for that matter, dogwood. But it just wasn't the same. Niskey Lake didn't have those big green breasts, and the dogwood blossoms didn't seem to exist in such divine clouds . . .

Roger Too White drove his Lexus up a driveway that ascended the lush swell of the lawn McNutter. As seen through the planes of dogwood blossoms, the house appeared to have been done in the French Maison Lafitte style, with lofty casement windows from which came a soft, mellow light, upstairs and down. At the top of the hill, the driveway made a showy loop, bordered with liriope, in front of the house. Roger Too White parked near the front door. As he walked toward it, he remembered all the stories he had heard of the black men who had been hassled and detained by not only the police but also the Buckhead private security patrols . . . just for being black and setting foot on this hallowed earth near the holy white corridor of West Paces Ferry Road.

The doorbell was answered by Coach Buck McNutter himself. Oh, there was no mistake about that. Roger Too White had never met the man before, but he knew that face. He had seen it God knew how many times on television and in the pages of *The Atlanta Journal-Constitution*. It was the real loose-sausage-eating, brown-liquor-drinking Southern face of a white athlete turned forty and covered with a smooth well-fed layer of flesh. His neck, which seemed a foot wide, rose up out of a yellow polo shirt and a blue blazer as if it were unit-welded to his trapezius muscles and his shoulders. He was like a single solid slab of meat clear up to his hair, which was a head of hair and a half, a strange silvery blond color, coiffed with bouncy fullness and little flips that screamed $65 male hairdo. Not a single cilium was out of place. Amid the vast smooth meat of his head and neck, his eyes and his mouth seemed terribly tiny, but they were both going all out to register pleasure at the sight of Counselor Roger White, this black man who had arrived at the door at 7:42 on Freaknic Saturday night.

"Hey, Mr. White!" exclaimed Coach Buck McNutter. "Buck McNutter!"

With that, he extended an enormous right hand. Roger Too White put out his own hand and felt it disappear, knuckles and all, inside a grip that made him wince.

"Sure do 'preciate you doing this! Particularly"—P'tickly—"on a Saturday night!"

"Not at all," said Roger Too White. There was something so desperate about the man's show of gratitude, he didn't bother apologizing for being twelve minutes late.

"Come on in and make yourself comfortable!" Then, over his shoulder: "Hey, Val, Mr. White's here!"

Val turned out to be a blond woman, in her late twenties, if Roger Too White was any judge. Everything about her, especially the provocative way she lowered her eyebrows when she smiled, gave off whiffs of frisky trouble. She came into the entry hall from some side room with the same desperate delight in her eyes as the coach.

"Hi!" She really sang it out.

"Mr. White, I want you to meet my wife, Val!"

So they shook hands, too. There was so much frenzied grinning going on that Roger Too White couldn't help grinning himself. He understood part of it. He saw this type of prominent white person all the time in Atlanta. Buck McNutter was a prototypical Southern white boy, from Mississippi, which was an even harder case than Georgia, a real hardtack Cracker in his heart but one who had decided that if he had to deal with these nigras, then the better part of valor was to put on a good show of being civil about it. (Proving Booker T. absolutely right, of course.)

"Let's go on in the library, Mr. White," said Buck McNutter.

With this, he dropped the grin. In fact, his beefy face grew long, verging on sad. Obviously the pertinent part of Counselor White's house call on Habersham Road was about to begin.

"Can I get you something to drink?" said young Mrs. McNutter. She said it with such an animated grin that for an instant it looked like a leer and made Roger Too White wonder what on earth she had in mind.

"Oh, no thanks," he said.

"You sure? Then I'll just let you two take care of yourselves."

The library was paneled in a dark wood, mahogany or perhaps walnut, and lined with shelves that seemed to contain far more silver bowls, trophies, and pieces of blown-glass sculpture than books. The combination of the dark wood, the soft light, and the gleaming *objets* was such that at first Roger Too White failed to notice the figure sprawled back on a tufted leather sofa. The long legs were utterly ajar. The long arms rested slackly on the sofa's seat. The milky-white eyes, set in a dark brown face beneath the brow of a shaved head, stared with utmost sullenness. Roger Too White knew that face immediately because it was even more famous in Atlanta than Coach Buck McNutter's. It was the face of Georgia Tech's all-American football star, a running back named Fareek Fanon, constantly referred to in the newspapers and on television as Fareek "the Cannon" Fanon, a local boy, the proudest product of one of Atlanta's most run-down areas, the Bluff, in a neighborhood known as English Avenue. Even slouched back the way he was, with dreadful posture, in this dim room, the young black man radiated physical power. He wore a black polo shirt with red stripes on the collar, wide open at the throat, revealing the long, thick pair of muscles that came down the sides of his neck and inserted at the clavicle. Adorning his neck was a gold chain so chunky you could have used it to pull an Isuzu pickup out of a red clay ditch. In his forearms and in his elbows and wrists you could see the dense muscles and cable-like tendons of the real ghetto boy (not to mention a massive gold Rolex watch with diamonds set in the face), and above all, you could see that wary, hostile look through the eyes. The polo shirt hung out over his hips, which were engulfed in a pair of ridiculously voluminous black homey jeans that bunched up at his ankles where they met a pair of black Frankensteins, just like those the college boy had been wearing on Piedmont Avenue. In each of his earlobes, which seemed small for so big a man, was imbedded a tiny diamond-bright gem. They may have been diamonds and they may have been rhinestones, but Roger Too White wouldn't have put it past a kid like this to insist on diamonds.

"Mr. White," said Buck McNutter, "I want you to meet Fareek Fanon."

Fareek "the Cannon" Fanon didn't budge. He waited a couple of beats, then gave Roger Too White a barely perceptible nod and a little shrug of the lips that seemed to say, "So you're here. So what?"

McNutter glowered, clenched his teeth, mouthed the words "Get up!," then pantomimed *Get up!* with his chin.

The Cannon gave McNutter the little lip shrug, which now seemed to say, "Why've I got to put up with this Good Manners shit?"

Slowly, with a great show of world-weariness, the Cannon got up. Even with his abysmal posture he towered over Roger Too White. Roger Too White extended his hand, and the Cannon deigned to shake it, albeit with a gloriously bored limpness.

"Fareek is a member of our football team," said Coach McNutter.

"Oh, I know that very well," said Roger Too White, smiling, looking the young man in the eye, hoping to establish some rapport with this hard case. "I expect everybody in Atlanta knows that. I've been following your adventures, along with everybody else."

The Cannon said nothing. Instead, he gave Roger Too White a quick look up and down, a dubious look, as if to say, "Why would I care what some bitch in a suit like you thinks about me?"

There was an awkward silence, and then McNutter said, "Mr. White, I've asked you to come over here tonight because Fareek has a problem. I have a problem. Georgia Tech has a problem. It happened last night, at a Freaknik party. Fareek's being accused of—he's being accused of rape. Actually, it's a kind of a date-rape thing, I suppose you might say. Fareek swears he didn't do anything improper, but he's in a real bind. So am I. So is Georgia Tech."

The Cannon looked away and did that little disdainful shrug with his lips again. This time it looked almost like a smirk.

McNutter's eyes blazed with reproach. He'd had enough of this ghetto-boy cool attitude. "All right, Fareek—tell Mr. White who the young woman is!"

In a bored, barely audible voice the Cannon said, "Some white girl goes to Tech."

" 'Some white girl goes to Tech'!" said McNutter. "Tell Mr. White what some-white-girl-goes-to-Tech's name is, Fareek! Tell him her *name*!"

"I 'unno."

"In a pig's eye you don't know!" roared McNutter. Then he turned to Roger Too White. "I'll tell you who it is, Mr. White. Her name is

Elizabeth Armholster. She's Inman Armholster's daughter, that's who she is."

"You're kidding!" said Roger Too White, in spite of himself, realizing too late that this was not a very professional response from anyone who fancied himself a high-powered lawyer.

"I'm *not* kidding," said McNutter, "and he wants Fareek's ass, and he wants Georgia Tech's ass, and if we lose Fareek, then it's my ass, too."

Inman Armholster. Inman Armholster was one of the first five names you'd think of if the subject was the White Establishment in Atlanta. He was in every network worth networking with in this whole town. He was Old Family and Piedmont Driving Club all the way, and he was rich as Croesus. He could have been up on that terrace tonight, and even if he wasn't, you could be sure he was invited. *Inman Armholster.*

Roger Too White looked at McNutter and then he looked at Fareek Fanon. Questions came flooding into his mind faster than he could sort them out, but the first one was obvious enough. Why had this big white side of beef, McNutter, called him in? He wasn't a criminal lawyer, and he wasn't a negligence lawyer. He wasn't even a litigator. He was a corporate lawyer, and his specialty was contracts. Inman Armholster wasn't going to be out for money. He was going to be out for blood.

Roger Too White looked at the young athlete again, standing there behind his smug shield of coolness, clad in his ridiculous ghetto rags, the little jewelry in his ears and the big jewelry on his neck and wrist catching the light. The football star. Roger Too White had never seen one of these people up close before, but here stood an example of one of the worst role models black youth could emulate: the big-time athlete, the mercenary for hire who assumes that the world owes him money and sex, and lots of both, whenever he wants it, and that he will be immune, whatever happens. The code of the mercenary! Rape, pillage, and loot! With no one to answer to! And this sucker has to pick Inman Armholster's daughter. Whether he knew it or not, and he didn't seem to know much, the Cannon was now a stick of dynamite.

Oh, Chocolate Mecca.

Chapter II

The Saddlebags

ALMOST EXACTLY THIRTY-SIX HOURS LATER, WHICH IS TO SAY, at 7:30 a.m., Monday, it was one of those brutally bright April mornings you sometimes get in Atlanta. Even up here on the thirty-second floor of the PlannersBanc Tower, behind a sealed inch-thick thermoplate glass wall, with a ten-ton HVAC system chundering cold air down from the ceiling, you could sense the heat that would soon oppress the city. The conference room faced east, making the glare from the sun unbearable. There was nothing in front of all that plate glass to reduce it, either, no curtains, no blinds, no screens, not one shred, not one slat. Oh no; the whole thing had been carefully thought out, and everybody at the PlannersBanc end of the table knew exactly what the game was.

Everybody, not just the senior loan officer Raymond Peepgass, knew this breakfast meeting was an elaborate practical joke, starting with the word "breakfast." Peepgass had made sure the whole lot of them had been advised that if they wanted breakfast, they had better attend to it before they got here. And that they had done, apparently. Nobody was even looking at the "breakfast." They were all settling back and eyeing the mark, the quarry, the prey, or whatever you should call the butt of a practical joke involving half a billion dollars. It was the old man at the other end of the table, the Croker Global Corporation's end. To Peepgass, who was a mere forty-six, any man sixty years old was an old man, even a man as burly and physically intimidating as Charlie Croker was.

Obviously Croker did not realize he was *it.* He was reared back confidently in his chair with his suit jacket thrown open. The fool seemed to think he was still one of those real estate developers who own the city of Atlanta. He was grinning at the underlings on either side of him, his lawyers, financial officers, division heads, his aging Banking Relations preppies, and his so-called executive assistants, who were a couple of real numbers with skirts up to . . . here . . .

Christ, he was a brute, for a man sixty years old! He was an absolute bull. His neck was wider than his head and solid as an oak. (Fleetingly it occurred to Peepgass that he, a member of the first Amped-Up Audio generation, raised in a treeless spec-house development outside of San Jose, California, had never, so far as he knew, seen an oak, much less a bull.) Croker was almost bald, but his baldness was the kind that proclaims *masculinity to burn*—as if there was so much testosterone surging up through his hide it had popped the hair right off the top of his head.

Look at him . . . the way he's beaming at the two numbers with the legs. They're standing, hovering over him . . . so gorgeous! . . . a pair of real model-girls! . . . Miles of blond hair, both of them, down to their shoulder blades . . . long legs glistening with youth, lubricity, and panty hose . . . That one . . . the taller one . . . such a lovely long neck . . . pale skin . . . a slender face, a full-budding lower lip, a demure high-necked silk blouse with a floppy bow tie of the same wan and vulnerable fabric . . .

Croker looks up at her with a broad grin and says something, and Peepgass can make out only one thing clearly, a name: "Peaches." *Peaches.* He couldn't believe it. Only in Atlanta would you actually come across some blond bombshell named Peaches.

A cloud rose up Peepgass's brainstem. Sirja was blond and sexy, too, wasn't she . . . That little Finnish hooker—a notions buyer for a Helsinki department store! How had he ever let a 105-pound Helsinki notions buyer do what she was now doing to him . . . With a sinking feeling, more of a nervous intuition than a thought, he realized that the

Charlie Crokers of this world would never let any such thing happen to them . . .

Just then Croker's gaze wandered toward a far corner of the room and a doubtful, puzzled look came over his face.

Peepgass's colleague, Harry Zale, the workout artiste, leaned his huge head over and said out of the corner of his mouth:

"Hey, Ray, check out the big boffster. He just noticed the dead plant."

It was true. Croker's eyes had drifted over to the corner where, in a dismal gloaming, there stood a solitary tropical plant, a dracaena, in a clay pot, dying. Several long, skinny yellowish fronds drooped over like the tongues of the dead. The pot rested on an otherwise empty expanse of Streptolon carpet pocked with the mashed-in depressions of desk feet, chair casters, and office machines that had been moved somewhere else. The old man had to squint to make it out. He was puzzled. He could hardly see a thing. From where he was sitting, he should have been able to look out through the plate-glass wall and seen much of Midtown Atlanta . . . the IBM tower, the GLG Grande, Promenade One, Promenade Two, the Campanile, the Southern Bell Center, Colony Square, and three of his own buildings, the Phoenix Center, the MossCo Tower, and the TransEx Palladium. But he couldn't . . . It was the glare. He and his contingent had been seated so that they had to look straight into it.

Oh, everything about this room was cunningly seedy and unpleasant. The conference table itself was a vast thing, a regular aircraft carrier, but it was put together in modular sections that didn't quite jibe where they met, and its surface was not wood but some sort of veal-gray plastic laminate. On the table, in front of each of the two dozen people present, was a pathetic setting of paperware, a paper cup for the orange juice, a paper mug with foldout handles for the coffee, which gave off an odor of incinerated PVC cables, and a paper plate with a huge, cold, sticky, cheesy, cowpie-like cinnamon-Cheddar coffee bun that struck terror into the heart of every man in the room who had ever read an article about arterial plaque or free radicals. That, in its entirety, was the breakfast meeting's breakfast.

To top it off, on the walls a pair of NO SMOKING signs glowered down upon the Croker Global crew with the sort of this-means-you lettering you might expect to find in the cracking unit of an oil refinery, but not at a conference of twenty-four ladies and gentlemen of banking and commerce in the PlannersBanc Tower in Midtown Atlanta.

On second thought, Peepgass decided, to say that Croker or any other shithead actually *noticed* all these things at first was probably overstating the case. At first they merely sensed them, stimulus by stimulus, through their antennae, through the hair on their arms. It was the central nervous system that finally informed the tycoons that they had descended to the status of shithead at PlannersBanc.

Shithead was the actual term used at the bank and throughout the industry. Bank officers said "shithead" in the same matter-of-fact way they said "mortgagee," "co-signer," or "debtor," which was the polite form of "shithead," since no borrower was referred to as a debtor until he defaulted. Why did bankers turn so quickly to scatology when loans went bad? Peepgass didn't know, but that was the way they were. At the Harvard Business School, back in the 1970s, he had taken a course called Structural Ethics in Corporate Culture, in which the teacher, a Professor Pelfner, had talked about Freud's theory of money and excrement . . . How did it go? . . . Dr. Freud, Dr. Freud . . . He couldn't remember . . . When people at the bank now referred to Croker as a shithead, they truly meant it. They truly *felt* it. His botching things was malfeasance. It made them look so goddamned bad! Half a *billion*! Now his heedless deadbeat squandering was making them all look like fools!—suckers!—patsies! And he, Raymond Peepgass, was one of the patsies who had signed off on those foolish loans! Fortunately, others up the chain of command had also. Still, he was a senior loan officer, and the banking industry was shrinking, and there were plenty of former senior loan officers of Atlanta banks who were now sitting in their dens in Dunwoody, Decatur, Alpharetta, and Snellville, middle-aged and hopelessly unemployed, staring out the window at their sons' basketball backboards in their driveways. At PlannersBanc today, the watchwords were "lean and mean" and "mental toughness." For seventy-five years the bank had been called the Southern Planters Bank and Trust Company. But now that seemed too stodgy, too slow-footed, too old-fashioned, and, above all, too Old South. *Planters* was a word humid with connotations of cotton plantations and slavery. So Planters had been sterilized and pasteurized into Planners. Nobody could object to Planners; even the most dysfunctional welfare case in the Capital Homes could be a planner. Then the two words, Planners and Banc, were fused into PlannersBanc in keeping with the new lean, mean fashion of jamming names together with a capital letter sticking up in the middle . . . NationsBank, SunTrust, BellSouth, GranCare, CryoLife, CytRtx,

XcelleNet, 3Com, MicroHelp, HomeBanc . . . as if that way you were creating some hyperhard alloy for the twenty-first century. The French *banc* was supposed to show how cosmopolitan, how international, how global, how slick you had become. Obviously PlannersBanc hadn't exercised sufficient slick steely Mental Toughness with Charlie Croker, and Croker's troubles remained a live threat to Peepgass's position. He was eager to see Harry Zale go to work on that big arrogant egomaniacal shithead down there at the end of the table.

He leaned over toward Harry and said, "Well . . . you about ready?"

"Yep," said Harry. And then he smiled and winked and said, "Let's take the safeties off the ring binders."

Peepgass's heart jumped inside his rib cage. The Male Battle was about to begin! But even that much explanation would have been beyond him. (He could have used Dr. Freud's help on this one, too.)

There were a dozen men at the PlannersBanc end of the table. But the show was all Harry Zale's. Harry, who was about forty-five, had a big jowly round head with a thin top dressing of black-and-gray hair combed straight back and a chin that swelled out like a melon. He was one of those mesomorphs who have short arms and thick chests and torsos. Just now Harry was jotting down a note, and you couldn't help but be aware that he was left-handed, because he was the type of awkward left-hander who hunches way over and curls his shoulder, arm, wrist, and hand into a pretzel shape as he writes. But for what he did, Harry Zale looked perfect. He was a workout artiste, and the workout artistes were the Marines, the commandos, the G.I. Joes of commercial banking. Or maybe the term should be D.I., for drill instructor, since Harry liked to refer to what was about to take place not as a workout session but as "boot camp."

The time had come, and so Peepgass drew himself up in his seat and raised his voice and announced to the entire table, "All right, ladies and gentlemen—" And then he paused. What he meant to say next was a brusque "Time to get started." But that was close to being an order, and he was not sure he could look Charlie Croker in the face and bark out an order. And so he said, "Why don't we get started?"

The Croker Global people who had been standing now took their seats. The fabulous bird, Peaches, sat right next to Croker. The other sat several seats away.

Peepgass had no intention of referring to Croker by name. Or, if he had to, he wouldn't call him Charlie. He'd call him Mr. Croker as coldly as he could, by way of letting him know that *things have changed,* that he was no longer a star customer, a priceless pal, and an Atlanta business giant; he was just another shithead. But as he looked at Croker's square-jawed face and massive neck, the memory of how fawningly, how ingratiatingly, how constantly he had called him Charlie, of how many times he had charlied him within an inch of his life, came flashing back to him; and contrary to every conscious intention, he heard himself saying:

"Charlie, I believe you met Harry on the way in." He gestured toward the workout artiste. "Harry's the head of our Real Estate Asset Management Department"—eventually, although not immediately, the shitheads always figured out the acronym—"and so I've asked Harry—" He paused again. He couldn't think of how to say what it was Harry was about to do. "—I've asked Harry to get things under way."

Harry didn't even look up. He just kept on writing on a yellow legal pad, with his left arm and hand all curled around it. Silence commandeered the room. It was as if Harry had more important things than Mr. Charles E. (for Earl) Croker on his mind. Presently he lifted his big chin. He sighted Croker down his nose and let his gaze linger . . . and linger . . . and linger . . . without saying a word . . . the way a father might lead into a man-to-man talk with a boy who knows he's been bad.

And then he said in a high-pitched, rasping voice, "Why are we here, Mr. Croker? Why are we having this meeting? What's the problem?"

Oh, Peepgass loved this part of Harry's workout sessions—the rude, grating, condescending way they started off! This was why a workout artiste like Harry Zale was known as an artiste! This was artistry. This was boot camp in the PlannersBanc Tower.

Croker stared at the artiste. Then he turned and looked past Peaches toward his chief financial officer, a young but dour presence named Wismer Stroock, probably not much more than thirty, who wore glasses with rectangular titanium frames and had pale skin, a heavy five o'clock shadow, and the sunken cheeks and stringy neck peculiar to compulsive joggers. Croker smiled at Stroock in a smirking way, and this smile said, "Hey, what kind of cute little stunt is this supposed to be? Who is this character? What is this *why are we here* bullshit?"

Harry kept staring at Croker, never once blinking. But Peepgass had to give Croker credit; he didn't blink, either. How long would it take Harry to get the saddlebags this time? Everybody rated Harry's performance that way, according to how long it took him to get the saddlebags.

Finally Croker said, "*You* called this meetin', my friend."

Muh frin; he spoke with a South Georgia drawl. Croker had lived in Atlanta for forty years, but his act—Peepgass regarded it as an act—was Baker County. Peepgass had never set foot in the place, of course, but he took Baker County to be about as Redneck as it got in Georgia. It was in Baker County that one of the first big civil rights protests of the 1960s had been ignited. A sheriff known as Gator Johnson had shot a black man named Ware after Ware had made a pass at the black mistress of the white overseer of a plantation belonging to Robert Woodruff, the president of Coca-Cola. *Gator Johnson!* thought Peepgass . . . and if you read all the articles about Charlie Croker in *The Atlanta Journal-Constitution* and *Atlanta* magazine and the profiles that had run in *Forbes* and *The Wall Street Journal*, you had to endure constant references to the piney woods, the swamps, hunting, fishing, horses, snakes, raccoons, wild boars, infantry combat, football, and a lot of other Southern Manhood stuff; but above all, football. Back in the late 1950s, when Georgia Tech was a national football power, Charlie Croker had been not only a star running back but a linebacker, one of the last players on any major football team to play both offense and defense, earning him the title, on the Atlanta sports pages, of "the Sixty-Minute Man." The Sixty-Minute Man became a local legend his senior year in the closing seconds of the big game with Tech's arch rival, the University of Georgia. With forty-five seconds left on the clock, Tech was losing, 20–7, when Croker ran forty-two yards for a touchdown. The score was now 20–14. Following the kickoff, with twenty-one seconds remaining, Georgia was trying to eat up the clock with routine running plays when the Georgia quarterback attempted yet another handoff to his fullback—and Croker blitzed through the line from his linebacker position and took the ball out of the quarterback's hand before his own fullback could reach it, knocked the fullback to the ground like a bowling pin, and ran forty yards for another touchdown, and Tech won, 21–20. To this day old-timers recognized him in malls or lobbies and yelled out, "The Sixty-Minute Man!" *Atlanta* magazine had asked him what kind of exercise regimen he followed now, almost fifty years later, and Peepgass had always remembered Croker's answer: "*Exercise* regimen? Who the hell's got time for an exercise regimen? On the other hand, when I need firewood, I start with a tree." Croker was the kind who liked to be known as Charlie, not Charles, because it was earthier. On his own plantation in Baker County he actually had his black employees call him Captain

Charlie, or just Cap'm. But he was the kind of Cap'm Charlie who always had to let you know he was a self-made Cap'm Charlie.

"And since it's your meeting," the Captain continued, "I s'peck *you're* gettin' ready to tell *us* why."

He said it with such a relaxed smile, Peepgass began to wonder if Harry was going to get any saddlebags at all.

"No, I wanna know if *you* know," said Harry. "Think of this as an AA meeting, Mr. Croker. Now that the spree is over, we wanna see some real self-awareness here. You're right, we called this meeting, but I want you to tell me *why*. What's it all about? What's the problem here?"

Peepgass watched Croker's face. Oh, he loved this part, too, the moment when the shitheads finally realized that *things have changed*, that their status has taken a header (into the excrement).

Croker eyed Harry, really sizing him up now, not sure how to play it. (They never were.) Every manly fiber in his being—and Charlie Croker's being was positively thick with manly fiber—wanted to put this condescending asshole in his place, firmly and rapidly. But if the session turned into a personal pissing match, he was at a distinct disadvantage. The condescending asshole could cause him severe grief. PlannersBanc held all the cards. PlannersBanc could bring six other banks and two insurance companies piling in on top of him. Croker Global owed the other lenders an additional $285 million, making a total of $800 million, of which $160 million were notes he, Croker, was personally liable for.

"Well, *we're* here," said Croker at last, "*we're* here"—(and if you don't know why *you're* here, then *we* can't help you out)—"to see about restructuring this thing, and we've come here with a good solid business plan, and I think you're gonna *love* it."

With that he reared back in his chair again, mighty pleased with himself, and Wismer Stroock and the rest of the financial types and lawyers and division heads and the Banking Relations preppies and Peaches and the other model-girl reared back also, looking mighty pleased with Himself, too.

"But what is 'this thing'?" asked the Artiste. "You're talking about solutions, about a way out. First we gotta know what we're *in*, because it's getting deep, and it's thick, and it's slimy. The Croker Global Corporation is sinking into the ooze. You're disappearing on us, Mr. Croker, like the Lost Continent. Before we lose you, you gotta tell me what this ooze *is*."

At this point Croker did something Peepgass had never seen a shithead do before. Quite nonchalantly he stood up, looking neither this way nor that, as if there was no one else in the room. He was a mountain! He took off his jacket—and as he did so, his chest flexed into a couple of massive hillocks. He undid his cuff links and rolled up his sleeves—and his forearms looked like a pair of country hams. (Peepgass had seen pictures of country hams in the Christmas mail-order catalogues that every credit-card holder in metropolitan Atlanta received.) He loosened his necktie and unbuttoned his shirt at the collar—and his mighty neck swelled out until it seemed to merge with his trapezii in one continuous slope to the shoulders. And then he arched his back and stretched and preened and showed the room his omnipotent deltoids and latissimi dorsi, which bulged beneath his shirt. Then he sat down again. His minions, Peaches and the rest, rose in their seats and then settled back with him.

"Now," said Charlie Croker, narrowing his eyes, lifting his chin, and putting on the grimace that signifies tolerance stretched just about to its limit, "you said something about . . . ooze?" *Sump'm 'bout . . . ooze?*

Peepgass's heart tripped faster still. The Male Battle was now surely joined.

Harry was a bulldog. He wouldn't let go, and he wouldn't let the big boffster break up his routine.

"That's right, Mr. Croker, ooze." Harry threw in a lot of *Mr. Crokers*, but Croker wouldn't lower himself to utter Harry's name, if, indeed, he knew it. "Ooze . . . as in Ooze Creek. It seems to me we're drifting up Ooze Creek without a paddle."

Now began a round of verbal fencing in which the Artiste kept cutting off Croker's evasions, blusters, rambles, tangents, until finally Croker was in a corner where there was nothing to do but come forth with the damning information. Even so, he sidestepped at the last moment and made his grim young sidekick, Wismer Stroock, say the actual words. Stroock was very nearly Croker's opposite. Croker was all heartiness and manly charm and bluster and Down Home Drawl and cagy Old Dawg of the South; Stroock was all MBA Youth and Low Cholesterol and High Density Lipids and Semiconductor Circuits, and by his voice you couldn't tell where he was from, unless it was the Wharton School of Business and Economics. Yes, he said, Croker Global had borrowed a total of $515 million from PlannersBanc; and yes, Croker Global had now failed to come up with $36 million in scheduled interest payments and a scheduled $60 million repayment of principal.

"But this situation is not acute," said Wismer Stroock.

Peepgass cut a glance at Harry, and they both smiled. The developers and their minions never used the word *problem*; to these shitheads there were only *situations*.

"The underlying assets remain sound," Stroock continued. "After the market saturation of 1989 and 1990, the absorption rate of commercial space in metro Atlanta has steadily increased, and vacancies have dropped below 20 percent, making Croker Concourse, as a prime outer perimeter property, perfectly positioned for the inevitable upswing in demand. As for Croker Global Foods, our facilities are mainstays in fourteen key markets, from Contra Costa County, California, to Monmouth County, New Jersey. It just so happens that all our divisions have been hit simultaneously by the same cyclical downturn, that's all. What we're talking about here is a cash-flow situation. All our divisions have potential for tremendous growth in the near term, once the general climate improves. Now, you take Global Foods—"

Oh, he was very smooth in his modem-mouth fashion, this Wismer Stroock. He commenced a disquisition about Croker Global Foods and its wholesale food distribution centers and about "emerging pockets of regional restaurant strength" and "food deflation" and "dampened margins" and "the enhanced pricing of crop packs" . . .

Harry let Stroock have his head until he said, "Anyway, what we're really looking at here is the prospect of a significant uptick in cash flow over the next two quarters. This is not a stagnant situation by any means. All we really need is a temporary freeze on these big principal payments, and—"

"Whoa!" said Harry with a grating whine, "whoa, whoa, whoa. Did I hear the word *freeze*?" Then he looked at Charlie Croker. "Mr. Croker, did Mr. Stroock just say something about freezing the principal payments?"

He kept staring at Croker with his chin lifted and his head cocked, as if his credulity was being put to a severe test. "Let me tell you two gentlemen something about loans. A loan is not a gift. When we make a loan, we actually expect to get paid back."

"Nobody's talkin' about not payin' you back," snapped Croker. "We're talkin' about something very simple." *Sump'm veh simple.*

"Simple I like," said the Artiste. "I'd like to hear some simple proposals as to how we're gonna get paid back. Simple, no assembly necessary, batteries included."

Peepgass noticed that the first little dark crescents of sweat were beginning to form on Croker's shirt, beneath his arms.

"That happens to be precisely what we been showin' you," he said.

"All I've heard so far are some projections concerning office leasing in Atlanta and the American food service industry," said the Artiste. "We're talking about half a billion dollars here."

"Look," said Charlie Croker, "you may recall that one of your own people, Mr. John Sycamore, assured us over and over again that if—"

"Mr. Sycamore's no longer on the case."

"That may be, but—"

"Mr. Sycamore is no longer a factor here."

"Yeah, but the fact is, he was your representative, and he practically got down on his knees and—"

"Mr. Sycamore's hopes—"

"—begged us to take that last $180 million loan and assured us—"

"Mr. Sycamore's hopes—"

"—if any situation arose regarding the payback schedule, he—"

"Mr. Sycamore's hopes and dreams, whatever they were, no longer exist so far as the obscene mess we have now is concerned. They disappeared down the memory hole."

Charlie Croker stared, steaming. Peepgass smiled to himself, albeit morosely. If John Sycamore had any sense, he was at this moment busy sending out résumés. A dapper and ebullient little fellow, Sycamore had been the salesman, the line officer, who had opened the door to Charlie Croker and Croker Global's half a billion dollars' worth of debt. At the time that had made Sycamore a star, a real "first-tier" operator, to use the PlannersBanc parlance. Back then big loans were spoken of as "sales," and hotshots like Sycamore worked for the "Marketing Department." Now that the huge debt had gone bad, Sycamore's career at PlannersBanc was a shambles. He was officially a shithead, too.

Seeing that Croker was once again speechless, Harry chose this moment to take off *his* jacket. He stood up and removed it very slowly. Peepgass knew what was coming. This was always a great touch.

In the process of taking his jacket off, the Artiste thrust his thick chest forward. Running down it were a pair of suspenders. They were broad and black, these suspenders, and even at the other end of the table you couldn't miss the motif embroidered on them in dead white: the skull and crossbones, repeated over and over.

As for Charlie Croker—the shitheads, Peepgass had observed, always pretended they hadn't noticed the damnable death's-head suspenders; although later, if they were in any mood to reminisce, they would invariably ask about the suspenders and inquire if this had been a calculated gesture on the Artiste's part or if he just happened to be wearing a pair of skull-and-crossbones suspenders. Croker did the usual. He tried to act as if he hadn't noticed. He looked away and scanned the room . . . but of course there was no relief there, just more of the cheap and seedy details, the Streptolon carpet, the synthetic furniture, the NO SMOKING signs, the glare, the dying dracaena, the vile cinnamon-Cheddar coffee buns on the paper plates . . .

The little crescents of sweat under the tycoon's arms, Peepgass now noticed, had become full half-moons.

An elaborate practical joke! Yet none of it was designed simply to humiliate the shitheads and punish them for their sins. What would be the point of that, when you needed them to help you recover hundreds of millions of dollars? No, this was boot camp, in Harry Zale's formulation. The main purpose of a boot camp, like the Marine boot camp at Parris Island—Harry had been in the Marines during the war in Vietnam—the main purpose of a boot camp was psychological conditioning. The idea was to strip away the recruit's old habits, soft comforts, and home-turf ties and turn him into a new man, a U.S. Marine. Well, your typical shithead was a business executive who arrived at a workout session with bad habits, creature comforts, regal ties, a layer of fat, and an ego that would have made the Sun King flinch. The word *tycoon*, from the Japanese, meaning "mighty ruler," might be a cliché, but it was no exaggeration in the case of your typical chief executive officer of an American corporation here at the turn of the century. He was surrounded by people who jumped whenever he crooked a finger or cut a glance. They performed all onerous chores for him, no matter how slight. Your typical big shithead like Charlie Croker had not had to stand in line at an airport, walk through a metal detector, or utter his name to someone at a counter for years, unless it was to board the Concorde. He lived a life of private planes, private elevators, hotel suites, Lucullan meals, golf weekends, ski weekends, ranch weekends, and cutie-pie weekends, as in "boffing bimbos in the Caribbean," which was one of Harry's favorite phrases. A "big boffster" like Charlie Croker was an executive who used the company airplane to go boffing bimbos in the Caribbean and kept the executive offices positively awiggle with cutie pies, such as the pair who were seated with him at this very table right now. To see this shithead go on in these magazine articles about what a son of the Down Home sod he was was ludicrous.

At the outset, Peepgass had to admit, PlannersBanc had only made things worse. In the quest for "big sales," line officers like John Sycamore had catered to the tycoon's every lordly vice. The bank had treated Croker to enough food at the PlannersClub, up on the fiftieth floor of the PlannersBanc Tower, and at the dining room of the Ritz Carlton Buckhead to keep half of Ethiopia alive for a year. And Cap'm Charlie, no dummy, had buttered up his lenders as well. A real "first-tier" officer was one who maintained a close personal tie with the big borrower. So when Charlie Croker had telephoned Sycamore to say he had an extra ticket to the Masters golf tournament in Augusta, Sycamore had risen from his dying mother's bedside at Piedmont General Hospital and left her a number at the clubhouse where she could reach him if she felt she was departing this trough of mortal error for good. In those, the palmy days, when Croker visited PlannersBanc, he was taken straight to the executive floor, the forty-ninth, where there was a reception room with a $270,000 custom-made rug the size of a tennis court, and he had sat only at conference tables of mahogany with fruitwood bandings, amid walnut-paneled walls and more custom carpeting, and was served only viands by the in-house chef and coffee from New Orleans in bone chinaware bearing PlannersBanc's logo (a highly stylized Creative Director's phoenix with outstretched wings) beneath white ceilings fitted with pinhole spotlights that lit up pictures so baffling they were bound to be worth a fortune. And beyond the glass window walls, always exquisitely curtained against glare, all of Atlanta, with its new glass towers rising up like the Emerald City of Oz, was laid out before him. *(It's all yours, Charlie.)*

There was one more thing about the shithead's relationship with the bank . . . something Peepgass never talked about to anybody at the bank, even though he was sure that plenty of his colleagues were aware of it and *felt* it. There were believed to be—he knew very well what people outside banking thought, had known it ever since his days at the Harvard Business School—there were believed to be two kinds of males in American business. There were the true Male Animals, who went into investment banking, hedge funds, arbitrage, real estate development, and other forms of empire building. They were the gamblers, plungers, traders, risk takers; in short, the Charlie Crokers of this world. And then there were the passive males who went into commercial banking, where all you did was lend money and sit back and collect interest. At Harvard the only thing considered duller, safer, and less adventurous than working for a bank was working for some old-line can't-miss industrial firm like Otis Elevator, which only needed caretakers. The Charlie Crokers were convinced that if they got in a tight corner, they could always manipulate the banking types—such as Raymond Peepgass. Using their stronger wills, greater guile, and higher levels of testosterone, they could always get them to roll over their out-of-control loans, restructure them, refinance them, or otherwise push trouble off into an open-ended future.

But lo!—somewhere in the shallows of the PlannersBanc hormone pool the bank had found the likes of Harry Zale, the workout artiste, the bank's own Marine drill instructor. Harry was here to make the shitheads pop to, to render the fat, melt down the ego, separate the soul from its vain props, and create a new man: a shithead who actually focuses on paying back the money.

Still standing, Harry took a deep breath, which thrust his chest out and flaunted the skull-and-crossbone suspenders even more flagrantly. Then he sat down and raised his big chin and looked down his nose once more and gave Charlie Croker another lingering stare and said:

"Okay, Mr. Croker, we're all waiting. The floor is now open for concrete proposals for paying back money. As I said, simple we like, no assembly necessary, batteries included."

It was probably the Artiste's infatuation with this little metaphor of his that finally did it. Croker had been no-assembly-necessary'd, batteries-included'd, why-are-we-here'd, dead-dracaena'd, coffee-burned, lectured at, and trifled with long enough. He leaned forward with his huge forearms on the table and the testosterone flowing. His shoulders and neck seemed to swell up. He thrust his own square jaw forward, and the lawyers and the accountants all hunched forward with him; and so did Peaches.

A small and ominous smile was now on Croker's face. His voice was low, controlled, and seething: "Well now, friend"—*frin*—"I wanna ask you sump'm. You ever been huntin'?"

Harry said nothing. He just put on a smile exactly like Croker's.

"You ever headed out in a pickup truck early inna moaning and lissened t'all'ose'ol' boys talking about alla *buds* 'ey gon' shoot? People, they shoot a lotta buds with their mouths onna way out to the fields . . . with their mouths . . . But comes a time when you finally got to stop the truck and pick up a gun and do sump'm with it . . . see . . . And down whirr I grew up, in Baker County, theh's a saying: 'When the tailgate drops, the bullshit stops.' "

He eyed Harry even more intently. Harry just stared back without blinking, without altering his little smile so much as an eighth of an inch.

"An'eh's been a certain amount a bullshit in 'is room 'is morning," Croker continued, "if you don't mind the introduction of some plain English into these proceedings. Well, now the tailgate's dropped. We're here with a serious business plan and a serious proposal for restructuring these loans and straightening out this situation. But we're not here for a lecture about the nature of loan obligations . . . see . . . I'm not sure who the hale you think you're talking to, but—"

"I know exactly—"

"—you need to be straightened out—"

"I know exactly—"

"—on a coupla things, my—"

"I know exactly—"

"—frin, because—"

"I know exactly who I'm talking to, Mr. Croker." Croker's voice was low and strong, but Harry's high grinding whine cut through it. "I'm talking to an individual who owes this bank half a billion dollars and six other banks and two insurance companies two hundred and eighty-five million more, that's who I'm talking to. And you know, there's an old saying here in Atlanta, too, and that saying is 'Money talks, and bullshit walks,' and the time has come to talk with money, Mr. Croker. All I'm telling you is what's already obvious. All I'm telling you are some home truths in the privacy of this room. You wanna throw this thing open to all seven banks and the two insurance companies and have a *real* workout session? We can *do* that! Happens all the time. It'll have to be in an auditorium. Nine different lenders? We're talking about more than a hundred people sitting in an auditorium, with an audio system and microphones, and it'll be incumbent upon every one of those lenders to pick up a microphone and tell you something over the wall speakers that I'm gonna tell you right now, very quietly, in this little room, across this table, on behalf of only one lender, PlannersBanc, and it's this, Mr. Croker . . ." Seeing that Croker was suitably stunned by his belligerence, the Artiste paused for maximum effect and then said in a menacingly calm voice, "This is one of the worst cases of corporate mismanagement . . . one of the grossest violations of a fiduciary obligation . . . I've ever seen . . . And in my job I look down the gullet of mismanagement and malfeasance every day. You and your corporation have taken *five hundred million* dollars from this bank, Mr. Croker, and treated it like your own private Freaknik, like you could take *five hundred million* dollars from us and do anything you wanted with it, go hog-wild, go *Freaknik,* because nobody could touch you, because this was *Freaknik* time for Croker Global and the town was yours. Well, I got news for you, Mr. Croker. This ain't Saddy night no mo'. Freaknik's over, baby. You know what I'm sayin'?" Peepgass's heart was pounding. He couldn't tell whether Harry was imitating Croker's Down Home accent or a black accent or both. "This here's the morning after, bro, and Croker Global's got the biggest hangover in the history of debt defalcation in the southeastern *Yew*-nited States."

Now Peepgass's eyes were fastened on Charlie Croker. Croker looked as if his breath had been knocked out. He no longer looked furious. The smoke was no longer coming out of his ears. He still stared at Harry, but his stare was frozen and opaque.

The Artiste! Oh yes, this was artistry!

It wasn't that the Artiste was tougher than the tycoon, more of a man, and had dominated him in a fair fight. No, it was the *tone,* the stance the Artiste dared assume, the insolence he so cavalierly brandished as his natural prerogative, the way he lifted his big chin and looked down his nose and, with every twist of his body and his grating whine, announced: "Behold! Nothing but another shithead." With a few arcs of that chin he had knocked the vain props out from under the great man, ripped away the insulation and the princely protocol, and left him sitting white and plump in his birthday suit, a sinner, a debtor, a deadbeat minus his dignity, naked before an unsparing dun.

Peepgass noticed that the tycoon's half-moons had begun to enlarge and had spread across his shirt along the curves on the underside of his mighty chest muscles.

Harry began speaking in a softer, lower voice. "Listen, Mr. Croker, don't get me wrong. We're on your side here. We don't want this to turn into a free-for-all with nine lenders, either. And we wouldn't particularly look forward to the press coverage." He paused to let that terrorist threat, the press, stalk the room. "We're the agent bank in this setup, and that gives us the privilege of looking out for PlannersBanc first of all. But we gotta come up with something *concrete*." He extended his right fist up in the air as high as it would go and said, "Where's the money gonna come from? It ain't gonna come . . . *poof!*"—he sprung his fist open—"from outta the air! Mr. Stroock assures us you got a lot of sound assets. Okay . . . good. The time has come to make them liquid. The time has come to pay us back. The time has come to sell something. I'm with you—the tailgate has dropped."

At that point young Stroock jumped in, evidently to give his boss, Croker, time to get his breath back and his battered wits together. Just "selling something," said Stroock, was not such an easy proposition. Croker Global had considered this particular option. But in the first place there was a complex of interlocking ownerships. Certain corporate structures within Croker Global's real estate portfolio actually owned certain independently structured divisions of Croker Global Foods, each of which was a corporation in its own right, and—

"I'm aware of all that," said the Artiste. "I've got your organization chart. I'm entering it in the Org-off."

"The Org-off?" said Wismer Stroock.

"Yeah. That's a contest we have at PlannersBanc for the worst-looking organization chart. I thought nobody was gonna be able to beat Chai Long Shipping, out of Hong Kong. They got three hundred ships, and each ship is a separate corporation, and each corporation owns a fraction of at least five other ships, and each ship has a color code, and the chart is ten feet long. Looks like a Game Boy semiconductor panel, blown up. I thought Chai Long was a sure thing in the Org-off until I saw yours. Yours looks like a bowl of linguine primavera. You just gotta untangle it and sell something."

"Unh-huh. I see. Do you mind if I finish?"

"No, I don't mind, but why don't we entertain a few modest proposals first."

The Artiste turned to an assistant on his other side and said in a low voice, "Gimme the cars, Sheldon." The young man, Sheldon, snapped open a ring binder and handed Harry a sheet of paper.

The Artiste studied it for a moment, then looked up at Croker and said, "Now, in your last financial statement you list seven company automobiles, three BMW 750:L's valued at . . . What's it say here? . . . $93,000 each . . . Two BMW 540:A's valued at $55,000 each, a Ferrari 355 valued at $129,000, and a customized Cadillac Seville STS valued at $75,000 . . . By the way, how'd you get here this morning?"

Croker gave the Artiste a long death-ray stare, then said, "I drove."

"What'd you drive? A BMW? The Ferrari? The customized Cadillac Seville STS? Which one?"

Croker eyed him balefully but said nothing. The steam was coming back into his system. His mighty chest rose and fell with a prodigious sigh. The dark stains were inching closer, from either side of his chest, toward the sternum.

Harry said, "Seven company cars . . . Sell 'em."

"Those cars are in constant use," said Croker. "Besides, suppose we sold 'em—to the distinct disadvantage of our operations, by the way. What are we talking about here? A couple of hundred thousand dollars."

"Hey!" said the Artiste with a big smile. "I don't know about you, but I have great respect for a couple of hundred thousand dollars. Besides, your arithmetic's a little off. It's five hundred and ninety-three thousand. A thousand more insignificant items like that and we've got half a billion and plenty to spare. See how easy it is? Sell 'em."

He turned to his assistant again and said, "Gimme the airplanes." The ring binder snapped open, and the assistant, Sheldon, gave him several sheets of paper.

"Now, Mr. Croker," said Harry, looking at the pages, "you also list four aircraft, two Beechjet 400A's, a Super King Air 350, and a Gulfstream Five." Then he looked up at Croker and, in a voice like W. C. Fields's, repeated: "A Gulfstream Five . . . a Gee-Fiiiiiiive . . . That's a $38 million aircraft, if I'm not mistaken, and I see here that yours has certain . . . en*hance*ments . . . a Satcom telephone system, $300,000 installed . . . A Satcom telephone enables you to telephone, while you're alofffffft, from anywhere in the world, isn't that correct?"

"Yeah," said Croker.

"How many of Croker Global's operations are overseas, Mr. Croker?"

"As of now, none, but—"

"And I see you've also got a set of SkyWatch cabin radar display screens, worth $125,000 installed, and a cabin interior custom designed and furnished by a Mr. Ronald Vine for $2,845,000. And it says here there's a *painting* installed on that airplane worth $190,000." The Artiste raised his great chin and looked down his nose at Croker with a mixture of incredulity and disdain. "Are those figures correct? They come straight from your financial statement. You presented these items as collateral."

"That's right."

"That's $40 million tied up in that one aircraft." He turned to his assistant. "What's the total value of the other three planes, Sheldon?"

"Fifteen million, nine hundred thousand."

"Fifteen million, nine hundred thousand," said Harry. "So now we're talking about $58 million worth of airplanes. Where do you keep those airplanes, Mr. Croker?"

"Out at PDK," said Croker, referring to the airport for private aircraft in DeKalb County, just east of the city. PDK was short for Peachtree–DeKalb.

"You lease hangar space there?"

"Yeah."

"How many pilots do you employ?"

"Twelve."

"Twelve . . ." The Artiste arched his eyebrows and whistled through his teeth in mock surprise. He smiled. "We're gonna save you a whole *lotta* money." He smiled again, as if this was all great fun. Then the smile vanished, and he said with a toneless finality, "Sell 'em."

"That we could always do," said Croker, "but it would be totally self-defeating. Those aircraft are not used in a frivolous manner. In Global Foods we got seventeen warehouses in fourteen states. We got—"

"Sell 'em."

"We got—"

"Sell 'em. From now on we're gonna be like the Vietcong. We're gonna travel on the ground and live off the land."

He now turned to Sheldon and said something out of the side of his mouth that Peepgass didn't catch. The young man's binder popped open, and he handed the Artiste three or four sheets of paper.

Harry studied them for a moment and then said, without looking up, "The experimental farrrrrrrm." He sounded like W. C. Fields again. "Twenty-nine thousand acres in Baker County, Georgia . . . We got the correct spelling here, T, U, R, P, M, T, I, N, E?"

"That's right," said Croker.

"The place is called Turp-um-tine?"

"Turpmtine," Coker said with an edge to his voice. "It's always been called that. Turpmtine's been in operation since the 1830s. For the first fifty or sixty years the only crop they had there was turpentine, and that was the way the—the farm workers pronounced it, 'turpmtine.' As a matter of fact, they called themselves the Turpmtine Ni—the Turpmtine

People. That was all they did, for generations, they harvested turpentine from the pine trees. We got descendants of the—of these people—working there right now."

Peepgass wondered why Croker was suddenly so forthcoming, informative, and reflective.

"It's listed here," said Harry, "as an 'experimental farm.' My information is that it's a plantation."

"Well, down 'eh below the gnat line," said Croker in an amiable voice, "anything much over five hundred acres, they're liable to call it a plantation."

"Yeah," said Harry, "but my impression is that Turpmtine is known specifically as a quail plantation. Do you shoot quail at Turpmtine?"

"It's quail country. Certainly we shoot some quail there. Be hard to resist."

"But would you say that's the main enterprise at Turpmtine, shooting quail? Mr. Sycamore visited Turpmtine several times, I believe, and that was *his* impression."

Croker's huge chest delivered another labored sigh. Peepgass knew exactly what he was thinking. *First they tell me Sycamore's out of the picture, and now they're quoting him as an authority.* But what he said was "Turpmtine's been a workin' farm for more'n a century and a half, and it's still a workin' farm. In fact, now more'n it's ever been. It's the main testin' ground for our food division." He was now dropping g's by the bushel. "We got more'n a thousand experimental plats"—*spearmental plats*—"at Turpmtine where we're runnin' experiments on crop production and rotation and tillin'—we got experiments with robots that'll level an acre of—"

"And you also got fifty-nine horses, valued at $4,700,000, according to this," said the Artiste. He held up one of the sheets of paper Sheldon had handed him. "Whatta these fifty-nine horses do? They don't pull plows, do they?"

"The horses are a profitable business in their own right," said Croker, managing to control his temper. "The market for good horses is fireproof. Besides that, we got a good stud business."

"That's what I understand," said the Artiste, studying a sheet of paper. "It says here you got a stud named First Draw, and he's worth three million dollars." He lifted his big chin and peered down his nose at Croker.

"That's true," said Croker.

Harry said, "First Draw . . . Does that horse's name by any chance allude in some way to the proceeds of a real estate construction loan?"

Sniggers and guffaws from the PlannersBanc end of the table; and not even Croker's somber young Wismer Stroock could resist a small smile.

Croker paused, then said with a sudden burst of joviality, "It's a gamblin' term. Refers to the game of draw poker."

"I'm sure it's a gambling term," said the Artiste, "but I'm not so sure the game is poker."

More sniggers and guffaws. Everybody at both ends of the table knew that when a developer obtained a loan commitment from a bank, the bank released the money to him in stages, and the first stage was known as "the first draw." There was a motto among the developers in Atlanta: "Buy the boat with the first draw," which meant, Buy the seventy-four-foot Hatteras motor yacht you've always wanted, the house on Sea Island you've been dreaming of, the condominium in Vail, the ranch in Wyoming, with that first release of money, just in case something goes wrong and you don't make any profit on the project. Strictly speaking, using the first draw that way was illegal—fraudulent, in a word—since in the loan agreement the developer promised to devote every nickel to the project. But in the heady days of the late 1980s and then again in the late 1990s the banks had winked and looked the other way, and there were, in point of fact, quite a few boats named *First Draw* moored on Sea Island and at Hilton Head, and there was a stallion down in Baker County . . .

"First Drawwwwwwww," said the Artiste in his W. C. Fields voice. "Yowza, yowza. Is it also a fact, Mr. Croker, that you ride some of those fifty-nine horses while you shoot quail at Turpmtine?"

"Well, you best get off *uv*'em first, before you shoot a shotgun, or you'll regret it. But cert'ny, you ride out to the fields. And it's good for the horses."

The Artiste eyed the shithead dubiously. "Fifty-nine horses . . . $4,700,000." Then he looked down at the sheets in front of him. "Twenty-nine thousand acres . . . land, improvements, and equipment . . . a 5,000-foot concrete runway capable of accommodating a Gulfstream Five jet aircraft . . . Total value, $32 million . . . All told, with the horses, that's $37 million right there." He paused, then said in his dead-even voice, "Sell 'em."

"Sell . . . what?"

"The plantation and the horses. The works."

Now Croker paused. He squinted into the glare, as if to see the Artiste better. "For the moment I'm gonna leave aside the importance of Turpmtine to the future of our corporation, and I'm gonna mention two other things." The old man seemed to have decided to take the reasonable approach. "First, this is not the time in the real estate cycle"—*sackle*—"to put a 29,000-acre farm on the market. But I'm sure you know that. Second, Turpmtine is not just a farm. It's an institution . . . a veh remarkable institution."

The old man's voice was suddenly warm and resonant. He launched into a passionate account of Turpmtine's history, with some more about "the Turpmtine People." He told of how Croker Global was today one of the biggest employers of unskilled black labor in that part of Georgia. He told of black workers tending the plats, black workers tending the horses, black workers tilling the soil, black workers preserving the ecology of Turpmtine's eight thousand acres of swamp. You could hear his voice welling up toward a peroration.

"Nobody else is gonna employ these people the way we do. Nobody but Croker Global is gonna have experimental plats and agrochemical experiments and a horse operation and peanuts, cotton, timber, and an ecological program—"

"And quail shooting," said the Artiste.

"Yeah, all right, quail shooting. That provides employment for these people, too. We got some black dog trainers, and they're damned good at it. We got—we got people tendin' the dogs and the horses and the copses and the wagons and . . . and everything else. Now, if Croker Global pulled out, *sold* out, where would these people go? I'll tell you. *On welfare.* We're talkin'bout southwest Georgia here, out in the country, the real *country*, and these folks don't just go off to some . . . *other job*. These are good, proud folks who don't wanna be on the dole. These are good country folks who see welfare as a stigma. These are Turpmtine folks who count on Croker Global as the one steady rock in their lives. So there's no way you or me or anybody else can look at Turpmtine as just some asset to be capitalized or liquidated. There's a dimension here you can't put in a financial statement, a dimension that involves pain and suffering, that involves a human cost."

"Hey, wait a minute," said Harry, lifting both hands, palms outward, and casting his eyes down in the gesture that says, *Please, no more.* "I understand pain. I understand suffering. I understand the human cost." Now he looked up, straight at Croker, with a gaze that bespoke the utmost sincerity. "I've been there. I was in the war . . . I lost four fingers . . ."

With that he raised his right fist above his head as high as it would go, with the back of his hand twisted toward Croker, so that it looked like a stump of a hand with only the ridges of the four big knuckles remaining. Then he extended a single finger upward, his middle finger, and kept it that way, a look of quizzical sadness on his face.

"Sell it," he said.

Croker stared at the upright middle finger and squinted and stared some more, and his face grew red. And then Peepgass saw them . . . the saddlebags! The saddlebags! The saddlebags had formed! They were complete! The great stains of sweat on the tycoon's shirt had now spread from both sides, from under the arms and across the rib cage and beneath the curves of his mighty chest until they had met, come together, hooked up—two dark expanses joined at the sternum. They looked just like a pair of saddlebags on a horse.

Oh, Peepgass loved it! Harry had done it again!—gotten his saddlebags—even with a tough old bird like Charlie Croker!

Fellows here at the PlannersBanc end of the table were nudging each other and smiling. They'd noticed it, too. Peepgass was elated. Somehow Harry had redeemed them all. He turned toward the Artiste and said, behind his hand, "Saddlebags, Harry! Saddlebags!"

He meant it to be *sotto voce*, little more than a whisper, but it came out much too loud. He hadn't meant to grin, either, but he did. He couldn't hold back. He could see Croker staring at him.

The Artiste lowered his arm, and Croker began to sputter. His voice was low and deep in his throat. "Now, listen . . ." he began.

In a perfectly pleasant voice Harry Zale said, "Just a moment, Mr. Croker," and he leaned over toward Peepgass and said in a low voice, "Time for a little lender's cactus, wouldn't you say?"

Peepgass chuckled. "Perfect," he said. Oh God, this would be rich.

Harry straightened up and looked at Croker and arched his eyebrows.

"Now you listen . . ." Croker resumed, his voice lost somewhere deep in his trachea.

"Excuse me, Mr. Croker," said the Artiste, "but we're gonna have a lender's cactus now. So we're gonna ask you gentlemen and you ladies to step outside the room so we can cactus."

"You're gonna what?" asked Croker.

"We're gonna have a lender's cactus."

"Did you say *cactus*?" asked Croker.

"Right," said the Artiste. "So if you'll just step outside for a little while, we'll appreciate it."

"Are you trying to say *caucus*?" Croker was all but snarling.

"No, *cactus*," said the Artiste with a merry smile. "This time we want all the pricks on the outside."

The Artiste kept the smile spread across his face, as if this was all good Boys' Locker Room fun. The tycoon stared with as furious a scowl as Peepgass had ever seen on a man's face. All that the Artiste gave him was the big unblinking grin. Ten kinds of mayhem must have been going through Croker's mind, but he said nothing. Slowly he rose, and Wismer Stroock and the rest of his retinue rose with him. The long-legged bird, Peaches, now standing beside him, stared at the old man's shirt. For the first time Croker seemed to be aware that it was a sopping mess. He glanced down morosely at his saddlebags, then picked up his jacket and wheeled about and started walking out of the room.

He took a step, and then when he took a second step, his entire huge body seemed to buckle and collapse to starboard before he could right himself. Then he took another step and then another, and the same thing happened again. Evidently something was terribly wrong with his right knee or his right hip. The whole room was watching. On he walked toward the door, taking a normal step and then buckling, taking a normal step and then buckling. It made it seem as if the drubbing he had just suffered at the hands of Harry Zale had taken some terrible physical toll on his body.

Then he stopped and paused for a moment. Slowly he turned about. He stared, balefully, but not at Harry Zale. He stared at Peepgass himself, and with a hissing stage whisper he said:

"Asshole."

All at once Peepgass was aware that now everybody in the room, at both ends of the table, was looking at *him*. They were waiting for him to respond. But he was stunned, speechless. And more than that—he was afraid. What did he dare say to this enraged bull down at the other end of the table? A moment ago he had been so elated!—reveling as the Artiste had reduced the great tycoon to a sweating, sputtering, groggy, humiliated shithead. A moment ago he had felt redeemed, avenged against Croker and his entire saber-toothed ilk! And now he stood here paralyzed while a scalding realization spread through the very lining of his skull: I can't take this man on! Not even verbally! Not even when he's thrown such an insult—"Asshole"—right in my face in front of my own people! And he stood there, unable to make a sound, while his face burned and his heart pounded.

Croker shook his head disdainfully and turned away and continued his gimp-legged retreat from the room, taking a step and buckling, taking a step and buckling, taking a step and buckling, taking a step and buckling.

Peepgass just stood there, frozen, speechless, afraid to look into the eyes of anybody else in the room.

Chapter III

Turpmtine

BY NOON CHARLIE CROKER WAS SITTING IN HIS FAVORITE SEAT in the forward cabin of his Gulfstream Five as the two BMW/Rolls-Royce engines roared and the aircraft lifted off from PDK.

His right knee still hurt, and he was burning up, but he kept his jacket on because he didn't want the ship's only other passenger, Wismer Stroock, looking at his shirt. *"Saddlebags!"* Ray Peepgass had exclaimed, and by now Charlie had figured out that insolent wisecrack. The shirt was still wet beneath the arms and across the ribs. The saddlebags wouldn't go away.

Wismer Stroock was seated facing him. Between the two of them was Charlie's pride and joy, a desktop that had been custom-made out of a slab of tupelo maple from Turpmtine Plantation and cantilevered from the G-5's wall by stainless-steel supports. The Wiz was only thirty-two, but he had a bony neck and a bony jaw and sunken cheeks and cadaverous cheekbones from getting up every morning, *every* morning, before dawn and running six miles through the streets of a Dunwoody subdivision called Quail Ridge. The rectangular titanium frames of the Wiz's eyeglasses made his eyes look like a pair of bar-code scanners. At this moment the bar-code scanners were aimed out the window, as if the Wiz were absorbed in the process of takeoff or the G-5's distinctive white wing with its rudder-like upturned tip. In fact, Charlie could tell that his young chief financial officer was embarrassed for him and didn't want to humiliate him any further by even so much as contemplating his face. That meant he must have *really* looked bad over at PlannersBanc.

The head remained in profile, but the two bar-code scanners rotated toward him for an instant, and so Charlie decided to put an end to the tension.

"Okay, Wiz, got any good ideas?" He tried to boom his voice out over the noise of the engines.

Now the Wiz looked straight at him and opened his mouth, but no words came out. Instead, he held his fingertips up to his ears, as if it was too noisy to hear, and looked away again.

So Charlie looked away, too, and tried to buck himself up by considering the glories of his surroundings, namely, the G-5 and its wonderful appurtenances. The cabin's dozen seats were big as thrones and upholstered in the richest tan leather imaginable and placed at conspicuously wasteful intervals, like chairs in a club lounge. There were curtains and carpeting woven with Croker Global's navy-and-gold globe logo and custom-made consoles with the logo carved on the doors in relief so deep people couldn't resist running their fingers over it. There were SkyWatch screens they could see from any seat they sat in . . . as a tiny white airplane shape moved across an electronic map and showed them precisely where they were flying, anywhere in the world.

But what really got them was Charlie's desktop. It had been fashioned from a single slab of wood, four or five inches thick, cut from the knee of a black tupelo maple tree from Jookers Swamp at Turpmtine, the knee being the part of the tree that swelled out just above the waterline. The desk retained the irregular shape and rugged edge of the slab as it was originally cut, although it was all highly polished and the top was like glass, with the burled swirls of the grain creating an extraordinary design. The desk was actually the brainchild of Ronald Vine, the decorator Serena had insisted he bring down to Atlanta from New York to do the G-5's interior; but Charlie loved that desk so much, there were days when he believed the original idea, the germ of the inspiration, must have been his. He loved it so much, he had had Ronald—Charlie had actually grown to admire and enjoy the guy—make a much larger version of it as a dining table for the new hunting lodge at Turpmtine, the Gun House, that Ronald had designed and built last year . . . at a cost (to Croker Global Foods) of $3.6 million by the time it was all over. Ronald had also paneled the bulkheads of the G-5 with tupelo maple. It was lighter and warmer and livelier than the usual stiff-necked mahogany. On the bulkhead facing Charlie, the one right behind the Wiz's seat, Ronald had affixed the ornate gold frame of the greatest work of art in the history of the world, so far as Charlie Croker was concerned, and Charlie was staring at it right now.

It was a painting by N. C. Wyeth of Jim Bowie rising up from his deathbed to fight the Mexicans at the Alamo. Wyeth had done it in reds, oranges, tans, blacks, and whites as the frontispiece for *Lone Star*, a child's history of Texas that was the only book, the *only book*, Charlie could remember his father and mother ever possessing. The day in 1986 when he bought that painting, the one he was staring at right now, for $190,000 at an auction at Sotheby's up in New York City had been one of the happiest days of his entire life.

And this was already one of the worst days of his entire life, and it was only twelve noon. *Humiliation* . . . well, let's face facts. The whole thing had been humiliating, from start to finish. That sonofabitch Zell or Zale, or whatever his name was, the smart guy with the big chin, had humiliated him in a whole room full of people, including eleven of his own people, from his own office. He had given him *the finger*! He had called him *a prick*! He had compared him to some drunk fool peeing in the street during *Freaknik*! And he had had to grit his teeth and take it!

On the way out, gimping along on his bad knee like an old man, he had annihilated this Zell or Zale four or five times. On the elevator going down he had thrown both hands up toward the sonofabitch's face in a feint, and when the sonofabitch had lifted his own hands in defense, he had grabbed him around the waist in a bear hug and squeezed with every ounce of the strength of his mighty arms and his massive back—*I've got a back like a Jersey bull*—until the sonofabitch's backbone cracked and he started whimpering for mercy—

Lost four fingers in the war, did you, you pansy, you cow, you gladiola! Now how about a little joke about losing your very life—

Between PlannersBanc's marble mausoleum of a lobby and his car, which was in the tower's parking garage, he had destroyed the sonofabitch three or four more times in various ways, until he ran out of ideas for committing homicide with his bare hands; and truly, if the sonofabitch had been so unwise as to turn up at that moment, something violent surely would have taken place.

As soon as he and Wismer Stroock reached the car, Charlie had decided not to go back to the office and, instead, told the Wiz to get on the telephone and call the office and have Marguerite get hold of Lud and Jimmy and Gwenette and have them get the Gulfstream ready to fly to Turpmtine immediately and call Durwood to pick them up at the landing strip and have lunch ready in the Gun House. He wanted to get away to someplace quiet to work out a little strategy with the Wiz. Or that was what he told the Wiz—and, for that matter, himself. He insisted on doing the driving out to PDK himself, even though it hurt his knee just to press his foot on the gas pedal. He didn't want the Wiz—or himself—to think he was a totally helpless case. On the way out on the Buford Highway, heading for PDK, he put the car on cruise control as much as he could. His knee hurt that much.

And so now, as the aircraft roared and strained to gain altitude, Charlie concentrated on the painting of Jim Bowie and tried to draw strength from it, as he had so many times before in moments of stress. The knee was aching so goddamned much—oh, he was like a lot of old football players . . . It had been great and glorious stuff, playing football for Tech, for the Ramblin' Wreck back in the fifties and early sixties . . . and now he was a worn-out arthritic wreck himself . . . But that wouldn't have stopped a Jim Bowie. In the painting, Bowie, who was already dying, lay on a bed with a cheap metal bedstead, an old-fashioned infirmary bed. He had propped himself up on one elbow. With his other hand he was brandishing his famous Bowie knife at a bunch of Mexican soldiers who had burst into the room with rifles and bayonets and were heading for him. It was the way Bowie's big neck and his jaw jutted out toward the Mexicans and the way his eyes blazed, defiant to the end, that made it a great painting. Never say die, even when you're dying, was what that painting said. Charlie always wished he could have met N. C. Wyeth and shaken his hand. He stared at the indomitable Bowie and waited for an infusion of courage. Instead, he felt some sort of disturbing electrical field forming beneath his sternum, around his heart. For an instant he didn't know what it was—but then he did. Its name was panic.

The ship had taken off to the northeast, and the two pilots, Lud Harnsbarger, the captain, and Jimmy Kite, the co-pilot, were executing a big lazy turn to the northwest in order to head back south for the trip down to Turpmtine. Gwenette, the stewardess, must have already gotten up from her seat in the rear, because Charlie heard a refrigerator cabinet or the microwave, or something, slam shut back in the galley. Gwenette probably figured she ought to move fast, since it didn't take much more than thirty minutes' flying time to reach the plantation.

In the distance the sun was exploding off the towers of Downtown and Midtown Atlanta and the commercial swath on the eastern side of Buckhead. Charlie knew them all by sight. He knew them not by the names of their architects—what were architects but neurotic and "artistic" hired help?—but by the names of their developers. There was John Portman's seventy-story glass cylinder, the Westin Peachtree Plaza, flashing in the sun. (Portman was smart; he was his own architect.) There was Tom Cousins's twin-towered 191 Peachtree. There was Blaine Kelley's Promenade Two, with all the little neon fins on top. There was Lars Gunsteldt's GLG Grande Tower. There was Charlie's own Phoenix Center; and, over there, his MossCo Tower; and over there, his TransEx Palladium. (Palladium! What an innocent time the 1980s had been!) There was Mack Taylor and Harvey Mathis's Buckhead Plaza. There was Charlie Ackerman's Tower Place. Downtown, Midtown, and Buckhead were like islands rising from an ocean of trees. Many was the time that the view from up here in the G-5, looking down upon the towers and the trees, had filled him with an inexpressible joy. *I did that! That's my handiwork! I'm one of the giants who built this city! I'm a star!* Total strangers used to say hello to him in restaurants, in malls, at sports events, with a certain glistening look in their eyes, because they knew he was . . . the fabled Charlie Croker!—which made it all the more unbelievable, this thing that had just happened at PlannersBanc . . . *Saddlebags!* Such contempt!

He looked away from the buildings and out over the ocean of trees. Since Atlanta was not a port city and was, in fact, far inland, the trees stretched on in every direction. They were Atlanta's greatest natural resource, those trees were. People loved to live beneath them. Fewer than 400,000 people lived within the Atlanta city limits, and almost three-quarters of them were black; if anything, over the past decade Atlanta's population had declined slightly. But for the past thirty years all sorts of people, most of them white, had been moving in beneath those trees, into all those delightful, leafy, rolling rural communities that surrounded the city proper. By the hundreds of thousands they had come, from all over Georgia, all over the South, all over America, all over the world, into those subdivided hills and downs and glens and glades beneath the trees, until the population of Greater Atlanta was now more than 3.5 million, and they were still pouring in. How fabulous the building booms had been! As the G-5 banked, Charlie looked down . . . There was Spaghetti Junction, as it was known, where Highways 85 and 285 came together in a tangle of fourteen gigantic curving concrete-and-asphalt ramps and twelve overpasses . . . And now he could see Perimeter Center, where Georgia 400 crossed 285. Mack Taylor and Harvey Mathis had built an office park called Perimeter Center out among all those trees, which had been considered a very risky venture at the time, because it was so far from Downtown; and now Perimeter Center was the nucleus around which an entire edge city, known by that very name, Perimeter Center, had grown. Taylor and Mathis had proved to be geniuses.

Edge city . . . Charlie closed his eyes and wished he'd never heard of the damn term. He wasn't much of a reader, but back in 1991 Lucky Putney, another developer, had given him a copy of a book called *Edge City* by somebody named Joel Garreau. He had opened it up and glanced at it—and couldn't put it down, even though it was 500 pages long. He had experienced the *Aha!* phenomenon. The book put into words something he and other developers had felt, instinctively, for quite a while: namely, that from now on, the growth of American cities was going to take place not in the heart of the metropolis, not in the old Downtown or Midtown, but out on the edges, in vast commercial clusters served by highways. The commercial part of Buckhead, which not so long ago had seemed like the suburbs, was precisely that: an edge city, Atlanta's first. Then came Perimeter Center. Then Don Childress developed the Galleria out where Highways 75 and 285 crossed, and Frank Carter developed the Cumberland Mall, and another edge city grew up around them. All the edge cities were north of Downtown and Midtown Atlanta, and they were being built deeper and deeper into the immense ocean of trees. Already a new edge city was forming around Spaghetti Junction and another one northeast of there, out in Gwinnett County, known as the Gwinnett Place Mall. Already Forsyth County, farther north still, had turned from a sleepy Redneck Redman Chewing Tobacco rural outback into Subdivision Heaven, and one of the three fastest-growing counties in the United States. Bango! Charlie had envisioned a new edge city, due west of Forsyth and north of the Galleria, in Cherokee County. It would be an edge city bearing his name: Croker.

Did he dare open his eyes and look down? He didn't want to, but he couldn't help himself. Just as he feared, the G-5 was in the perfect spot for an aerial view of Croker Concourse. There it was, the tower, the mall, the cineplex, the hotel-and-apartment complex, the immense swath of asphalt (conspicuously empty) for parking—a preposterously lonely island sticking up out of that ocean of trees. Croker's folly! Had to leapfrog the future, didn't you, Charlie! A few years down the line somebody would make a fortune off what he had put together there, once the outer perimeter highway was built, but for now—*too far* north, *too far* from the old city, Atlanta itself. For now—

Saddlebags! His shirt felt sopping wet against his skin all over again, and his eyes, although he tried to avert them, stayed fixed upon Croker Concourse. Had to build a tower, didn't he . . . had to take the name Croker soaring up forty stories into the sky . . . with a dome to top it all off. You couldn't very well miss it, the dome, out in its splendid leafy loneliness . . . The dome contained a planetarium and housed the Cosmos Club. Atlanta was big on private dining clubs in fancy high-rises, but there had never been one quite like this one. Into the club's domed ceiling he had put a state-of-the-art astronomical light-show apparatus developed by the Henry Beuhl, Jr., observatory at Carnegie-Mellon University in Pittsburgh . . . Croker Global . . . Croker of the Cosmos . . . He had sunk $8.5 million into the thing, but it had turned out that nobody wanted to drive all the way out to Cherokee County for lunch and look up at a bunch of fake stars twinkling in the blackness of space while they ate their grilled yellowfin tuna on a bed of kale and Moroccan couscous or whatever it was Greater Atlanta yuppies ate for lunch. The Cosmos Club had been a hideously expensive bomb. Cosmos Club . . . cosmic pinnacle of the great Croker Concourse . . . And there it was, right down there . . .

When the G-5 finally completed its turn and cleared the city and headed south over the green woods and farmlands of the Georgia Piedmont, he wasn't sorry. There was no more joy in looking down at Atlanta and its edge cities. *Saddlebags!* That they would have the gall, the temerity, the audacity to treat him, Charlie Croker, with such—such—such—

Wismer Stroock was no longer looking out the window but straight at him, through his titanium frames. Charlie sighed and gave him a resigned smile, as if to say, "You know what's going through my mind, and I know you know it." And then, aloud:

"Like I was saying, Wiz, got any good ideas?"

Thanks to the G-5's exquisitely muffled engines, a soft surf of sound, nothing more, enveloped the aircraft. The Wiz didn't even have to raise his voice. When he became intense, his voice didn't go up; instead, a ditch formed down the middle of the forehead of his gaunt face. Wismer Stroock was of the new breed of financial officers who came out of the business schools. Technogeeks was what Charlie called them. But the Wiz could "run the numbers" and he was a genius at the "cross-functional integration" of the different divisions of the Croker Global Corporation—two expressions he used all the time—and Charlie had become highly dependent on him.

"Good ideas vis-à-vis who, Charlie? Or vis-à-vis what?"

That was another thing Wiz said all the time, "vis-à-vis." You never could figure out why.

"How do I deal with these people?" said Charlie. "How do I approach them? Before, there was always Sycamore, who was a reasonable human being. But these people . . ." He gave his hands a little upward toss. "When I think of all the money we spent on Sycamore, all the times we flew him to Turpmtine on this goddamned airplane, all the ball games, that weekend in Augusta, all the dinners we treated him to . . . him and Peepgass, for that matter. Peepgass—" He decided not to finish the sentence. He grew silent.

"I'm afraid that's a sunk cost, Charlie," said Wismer Stroock. "At this point the whole paradigm has shifted."

Charlie started to remonstrate. Most of the Wiz's lingo he could put up with, even a "sunk cost." But this word *paradigm* absolutely drove him up the wall, so much so that he had complained to the Wiz about it. The damned word meant nothing at all, near as he could make out, and yet it was always "shifting," whatever it was. In fact, that was the only thing the "paradigm" ever seemed to do. It only shifted. But he didn't have the energy for another discussion with Wismer Stroock about technogeekspeak. So all he said was:

"Okay, the paradigm has shifted. Which means what?"

"Except for Peepgass," said the Wiz, "those were the bank's workout people, Charlie. Peepgass is a loan officer, and Sycamore was in marketing. In marketing they're incentivized to think of charm and customer satisfaction as value-adding strategies, but not in the workout department. What we're dealing with now is a division of the bank that has a very narrow niche focus."

Niche focus? But he got the drift of it.

"At the end of the day they know they're going to be judged by only one thing: how much money they recover for the bank. Their orientation is post-goodwill. Down in Texas after the oil crash and all the bankruptcies, the workout people the banks sent in were so niche-focused on that one thing, they started getting death threats. They'd call them up at their hotels in the middle of the night and threaten to execute them."

A tired smile. "Do any good? Worth trying?"

"I don't think it was a value-creating exercise," said the Wiz.

No doubt the Wiz was making his little joke, but you never really knew with this dour young man, because he always talked that way. Suddenly Charlie felt very angry.

"I don't give a damn about their orientation, Wiz. That fat little sonofabitch, he gave me the finger, he called me a prick, and did you see the way Peepgass—did you see the way that little . . . that little . . . *pussy—*"

He gave up on that line of thought, too. A sixth sense told him it was useless to try to get into a discussion of Ray Peepgass's character with the Wiz. Peepgass wasn't a bad-looking guy, and he was probably bright, but he was soft. His head of thick, thatchy, sandy hair made him look ten years younger than he was, but in a weak, boyish way. His neck and his chin and his cheeks and his hands were soft. To see that soft, weak face grinning at his expense—it had been infuriating. Peepgass was not strong, not fit, not manly. But the point would be lost on the Wiz. The Wiz was young and fit, but he was neither manly nor unmanly. He was a financial officer and a technogeek. He ran six miles before dawn every morning solely to keep the Wismer Stroock cardiovascular system lubricated and tuned up for the long-term project, which was to live forever. As to whether Ray Peepgass was or was not a sad specimen of contemporary Georgia manhood, the Wiz would be completely uninterested.

Sure enough, the Wiz ignored the reference to Peepgass and said, "The good news is, they don't have many branches on their decision tree at PlannersBanc. I don't see that foreclosure is a viable strategic alternative for them. They've done a DFC, the same as we have, and if they foreclose, *our* operating losses become *their* operating losses. Cash flow is king."

By now Charlie knew that a DFC was a "discounted cash flow," but exactly how you picked a number to discount it at, he never could figure out.

"At the end of the day," the Wiz continued, "PlannersBanc will be willing to do anything other than be left having to manage Croker Concourse and seventeen wholesale food warehouses. The net-net is, they'll have to restructure the loans. But we can't stonewall them, either. We'll have to give them something reasonably substantial, Charlie, just to buy some breathing space and get the best deal we can and recapture some goodwill. We lost a lot of goodwill because we didn't let them know about our situation soon enough."

Charlie knew the Wiz wanted to say *I told you so.* For months he had been urging him to "make a preemptive strike" by alerting PlannersBanc to the cash-flow situation, but he, Charlie, had been sure he could come up with something and pull it all out, as he always had in the past.

After a pause Charlie said, "Okay, we give them something reasonably substantial. Like what?"

The Wiz looked at him through the titanium rectangles with his bar-code-scanner stare, and his lips parted, and the words didn't come out. He had withheld them.

"Go ahead," said Charlie. He gestured encouragingly.

"Well," said the Wiz, "I'm just thinking out loud—I'm not anticipating that you're going to like it—it's not something I want to see happen—I'm only considering our strategic alternatives—but what *about* the plantation?"

Incredulous: "Turpmtine?"

"Well, I mean, only in the sense that here we have a non-core asset, not functionally integrated into the rest of the corporation and not creating any particular synergies, or at least not resulting in any strategic advantage, not in any zero-sum sense—and it's worth a great deal of money." The Wiz's diction was beginning to degenerate into sheer technogeekspeak gibberish . . . out of fear. He knew he had blundered onto dangerous ground with his boss. He tried to extricate himself. "I wouldn't want to see Turpmtine go, either, but it's already a red flag as far as these people are concerned. You saw that. I mean, what do you suppose these people make a year? I bet that fellow Zale doesn't make $150,000, and he knows you've got a 29,000-acre quail plantation."

That was evidently supposed to make him, Charlie, feel better, feel superior; but the very mention of the name Zale did the opposite. It sent a sickening wave of shame through his nervous system. This Zale, with his big jaw and contemptuous stares, had *humiliated* him!—in front of his own people!—and obviously that fact was very much on the Wiz's mind.

"Wiz," said Charlie, "I wouldn't give 'em the satisfaction. There's a lot of other reasons not to sell Turpmtine, but that's enough for now. They're not gonna get the fuckin' satisfaction."

"As I said, Charlie, I'm only trying to offer some constructive feedback. I'm only considering strategic alternatives. What about the planes?"

"I don't mind selling some of the planes . . . but we keep this one."

The Wiz exhaled and pulled in his chin. "That'd give them something, I guess. A bone, anyway, although I'm not sure they'd be terribly impressed. You saw what got them so aggravated." He lifted his hand up to eye level and then pointed his forefinger down several times toward the floor of the aircraft.

Of course, the Wiz was right. Charlie knew that. And now he realized something else: exactly why he was on this airplane at this moment, making a largely pointless flight to a South Georgia plantation on a Monday afternoon in April. He was damned if *they* (those insolent bastards at the bank) could tell *him* (one of the Creators of Greater Atlanta) he couldn't have the G-5 and Turpmtine or, for that matter, the Cadillac SLS he had just driven himself and the Wiz out to the airport in. It was utterly, blatantly wasteful to crank up a ship like the G-5 and have two pilots and a stewardess hop to it in order to take two men down to Baker County, where they weren't going to do anything but talk, and then fly back. Well—so what! It underscored his rights, his power, his refusal to cave in to a lot of impudent threats . . .

But there was something else also, something he fought to keep from becoming a conscious thought. The truth was, he had been *afraid* to return to the office immediately. He didn't dare return in a state of . . . of . . . of . . . agitation (he avoided the word *panic*) . . . to that grand space he had set aside for himself and Croker Global up on the thirty-ninth floor at Croker Concourse.

Why had he taken an army with him over to PlannersBanc? Eleven people he had brought along! Christ! By now the word was all over the office! Cap'm Charlie has just been humiliated! They ripped his eyeballs out and made him swallow them! Nothing like this had ever happened to Charlie Croker before. They had punched holes in his *charisma* and now it was hemorrhaging all over the place. If he didn't pull himself together, the whole office would smell the blood immediately. They would detect it in the way he walked in, hobbling on his bad knee . . . Step, *gimp*, step, *gimp*, step, *gimp* . . . They would see it in the look on his face. They would suddenly see him as . . . an old man . . . a toothless, eyeless, limping, gimping alpha lion. He had hired a lot of young hotshots over the past few years. The Wiz was one of them. He wanted to feel and look wired into the new generation. But the new generation wouldn't waste an ounce of sympathy. They'd start making telephone calls and drafting résumés. A real estate developer was not like an industrial CEO or an investment banker. No, you either had *the aura*, the aura of magic, fireproof confidence, and invincibility—or you had nothing. And right now he felt as if he was leaking fast, right down to charisma zero. He couldn't let them see him in this state. He had to regroup. He had to stop gimping around on an old rusting football knee. Tomorrow morning, when he took the elevator up to the top of Croker Concourse, he had to look, sound, make every move of his alpha lion body, as if nothing had happened.

Why hadn't he told the bastards off right then and there in that insultingly seedy excuse for a conference room? How could he have let them abuse him like that? What had happened? Was he truly *getting old*? Or maybe the explanation was more obvious. He was in a terrible jam! He had guaranteed $160 million in loans himself! It was madness! The Wiz had warned him against it. The cardinal rule of real estate development was: Other people's money!—non-recourse loans only!—never guarantee a loan yourself! But he had been so desperate to get financing for his edge city, he had crawled way out on the forbidden limb . . . and he didn't have a single friend left at PlannersBanc. A hundred and sixty *million* dollars! They could seize everything he possessed on this earth, right down to the house he lived in and the cars he drove. Never in his entire life had he been in such deep water, deep slime, deep ooze, Ooze Creek, up Ooze Creek without a paddle . . . All of that smart guy's wisecracks started ricocheting around in his skull . . . Why hadn't he put that Zale or Zell, or whatever his name was, in his place, even if it meant walking around the table and breaking his fat jaw for him?

Aw, this was *esprit de l'escalier* stuff, as the French say, the *shoulda dones* you think of on the stairs at night after it's all over. He opened his eyes.

"What kin I gitcha, Cap?"

Gwenette, the stewardess, was standing beside the desk, smiling. She had no idea what had gone on, of course. She wore a short-sleeved blouse with a repeat pattern of navy-and-gold Croker Global globes and a navy skirt, but beneath this corporate getup she was a real country girl, young, plump, hearty, plain, no matter what she tried to do with her hair or her makeup. *Plain* was what he had been looking for this time. He had made a real fool of himself when Peaches was the stewardess on the G-5 . . .

"I don't know, Gwenette," he said. In fact, he was dying for a good stiff jolt of Jack Daniel's in a short glass with ice and a little water—but at noon? He didn't want the Wiz to know how much he needed a drink—how much he *craved* it! But why the hell shouldn't he have it, if he wanted it? So he said, "We got any a Auntie Bella's biscuits on board? And maybe a little glass of Jack Daniel's?"

Auntie Bella was the cook at Turpmtine, a real Baker County colored woman, of the old school—and suddenly he had a terrible, sickening vision. How could he possibly look Auntie Bella in the eye one day and inform her that Cap'm Charlie was no more, Cap'm Charlie had blown it, he was flat as a tick, he'd lost Turpmtine, and she was out of a job and would have to find a new home?

"We got 'em froze," said Gwenette, "but they heat up pretty good."

"We got any a Uncle Bud's ham?" Uncle Bud was Auntie Bella's husband, who never had done anything but loaf around the kitchen and cure hams out in the smokehouse. He was an old man, but so erect and lordly that Charlie had always wondered if he wasn't the descendant of some African chief or something.

"We always got some a the ham, Cap," said Gwenette.

Not only Gwenette but also the two pilots, Lud and Jimmy, called him "Cap." They'd picked that up from the employees at Turpmtine. The full "Cap'm Charlie" was a little too servile for Gwenette, Lud, and Jimmy, he reckoned, but at the same time they admired him and felt too warmly toward him to use a cold, formal "Mr. Croker." So they'd settled on "Cap" as the middle ground. He liked that.

"Well, then, let me have a coupla ham biscuits, too."

"How 'bout yew, Mr. Stroock?"

"Oh . . . I'll just have a glass of Quibelle."

That was the Wiz for you, working twenty-four hours a day on Project Wiz, whose object was eternal life. Quibelle was one of those bottled carbonated waters. Why anybody would want to drink carbonated water,

Charlie didn't know, except that it was a New York fad that had seeped into Atlanta.

Gwenette headed back to the galley, and he had another sickening vision . . . of having to look Gwenette and Lud and Jimmy in the eye and inform them that their Cap . . . had been grounded . . . From now on he'd have to be like the Vietcong and travel on the ground and live off the land . . .

He looked at the Wiz and said, "Naw, Wiz, they're not gonna git Turpmtine and they're not gonna git this airplane."

Suddenly he had an inspiration. He cocked his head and gave Wiz a long, fixed stare, the way you do when you're about to say something of far-reaching importance.

"I got an idea, Wiz. If we're gonna sell something"—*sump'm*—"to satisfy these bastards, why not do it up right? What if we sell the food division, the whole damn thing?"

To his surprise and disappointment, the Wiz smiled indulgently; and the Wiz was not a smiler. "I know it's never exactly captured your imagination," he said.

"It's worse than that," said Charlie. "The whole goddamn business is depressing. I can't stand going in those warehouses. They're so fuckin' gloomy. You wanna know what's really depressing? It's seeing those poor bastards—whatta they call 'em?—the freezer pickers?—coming out of those freezer units. I don't know if I ever told you. I was in the warehouse in St. Louis once, showing it to Harvey Morehead, and this guy comes out of the freezer unit, and he's got two icicles hanging out of his nose. *Icicles*—hanging out of his nose." He shook his head. "I can't understand how I ever got involved in a business like that."

In fact, he understood very well. He had bought the old Maws & Gullett Food Service Corporation in 1987 and renamed it Croker Global Foods at a time when many big developers, like John Harbert in Birmingham, were branching out into other businesses. Harbert had become a real tycoon. Everything was booming, and Maws & Gullett was on the market for a reasonable price, and along with the wholesale food operation he would be acquiring a lot of good real estate, where the warehouses were located, and the name Croker—CROKER GLOBAL FOODS—would be on the sides of trucks and be spread all over the country. Terrific . . . but the business had no sex appeal. There was no way you could show a wholesale food warehouse to somebody and expect him to say *Wow*. You could take somebody into the lobby of the tower at Croker Concourse, and even though the damned building was more than half empty and bleeding to death financially, the sheer "curb flash" would bowl him over . . . the Henry Moore sculpture out front, the marble arch over the doorway, the fifty-foot-high ceiling in the lobby, the tons of marble on the floor and the walls, the Belgian tapestries, the piano player in a tuxedo playing classical music from 7:30 a.m. on . . . Whereas you take somebody like Harvey Morehead to one of those warehouses, and he can't wait to get out of there.

"Well, Charlie," said the Wiz, "in my opinion we have to learn to love it. Food service is not a business we can afford to get out of right now."

"Whaddaya mean?"

"I mean that Croker Global Foods is the one part of the corporation where—well, first let me give you a kind of executive summary of where we are now. Okay?"

"Go ahead."

"Okay," said the Wiz. "If you've got assets with a market value of $2.2 billion and debts of $1.3 billion, then your net worth is $900 million, and you're rich, right? That's where we were in late 1989, 1990, and early 1991 even. Okay? But if you wake up one day and the market value of your assets has declined to $1.1 billion, and you still owe the $1.3 billion, then suddenly the paradigm has shifted and your net worth is minus $200 million, and it's a serious issue. And that's where we are today. All right? In the real estate business, market values can move up and down very fast. They're agile, they're flexible, they're terpsichorean." The Wiz made an awkward little flutter with his fingers to indicate *terpsichorean*. "But debt just sits there, like a rock formation, like a mountain. It doesn't budge. We're not in a cyclical downturn, Charlie, we're in a . . . special situation."

"Awright, but what's that got to do with the food division? It's losing money, too."

"That's true," said the Wiz. "But there are two serious impediments to selling it. First of all, it's so encumbered with debt that if we sold it now, in this market, we wouldn't see a nickel of it. It would all go to the banks, and we'd still owe a hundred million or so on it."

"Yeah, but the banks would get some cash, and maybe they'd leave us alone for a while and give us some room."

"Perhaps," said the Wiz, "but that brings me to impediment number two. The food division has lost value because the restaurant business is in a slump right now. But that *is* a cyclical downturn, and the industry will recover. Our warehouses are solidly positioned for the eventual upturn. People don't have to lease expensive office space in top-end buildings like Croker Concourse, but they can't defer their food consumption function."

"Can't defer their food consumption function?"

"They have to eat. Every day."

"All the same—"

"Charlie! What's the personal dividend you're taking out of this corporation each year? Seven million dollars?"

Charlie nodded glumly. It was true. The annual outflow of what he spent personally had become a form of madness. After taxes, after the $50,000 a month to his first wife, Martha, after the endless fantasies in furniture, clothes, travel, servants his second wife, Serena, managed to come up with, after the house on Sea Island, the house on Blackland Road, the stable and forty acres in Buckhead up near the Cobb County line where he went riding—he couldn't figure out where it all went. It sure as hell didn't go into stocks, bonds, municipals, treasuries, or the mattress. And that didn't even include Turpmtine, most of which was billed to Croker Global Foods. Shit! He hadn't even thought of that. Without the food division, he'd have to swallow the cost of Turpmtine himself. He couldn't very well bill a plantation to Croker Concourse.

"And of that seven million, do you know how much comes from Croker Global Foods, Charlie? Four. The cash flow of the food division is more than Croker Concourse and our other buildings put together. The food division is the engine that drives the cash flow of the whole corporation."

"Awright," said Charlie, "you've made your point."

The engine that drives the cash flow. Give me a break . . .

Oh, he understood the Wiz a lot better than the Wiz thought he did. The Wiz looked upon him as an aging, uneducated, and out-of-date country boy who had somehow, nonetheless, managed to create a large and, until recently, wildly successful corporation. That the country boy, with half his brainpower, should be the lord of this corporation and that he, a Wharton MBA and financial genius, with "an excellence that cuts across disciplines," to use a Wizism, should be his vassal was an anomaly, a perversity of Fate, that would in the long run be corrected. He had youth on his side. In the meantime, his resentment rose and fell, and he took a sharp pleasure in rubbing in the old man's ignorance with these little lectures. Or part of him felt that way. The other part of him was in awe, in unconscious awe, of something the old boy had and he didn't: namely, the power to charm men and the manic drive to bend their wills into saying yes to projects they didn't want, didn't need, and never thought about before. The common word for this was *salesmanship*, a term the Wiz probably looked down his nose at. Yet the Wiz was in awe of something that was at the heart of salesmanship when the game got up into the hundreds of millions of dollars and it was time to make a decision and act, *make your move*, even though you could run the numbers all day and they added up only to imponderables and the decision tree was so full of branches, twigs, sapsuckers, and leaves, a mere Wiz couldn't find the paradigm no matter how hard he looked . . . And that thing was manhood. It was as simple as that.

Charlie looked at the Wiz, sitting there on the other side of the tupelo desk, beneath N. C. Wyeth's painting of Jim Bowie at the Alamo, and he said to himself, "My motto is 'Ready, fire, aim,' and you give me lectures and make sly fun of me about that. But yours is 'Ready, aim, aim, aim, aim, aim, aim, aim . . .' "

He turned away and looked out the window and let the surf of the engines roll over his nerve endings. Down below . . . Startled, he put his nose up against the window and stared. It was breathtaking! A glorious cloud of pink seemed to cover the earth. A peach orchard . . . in full blossom . . . a huge one, gorgeous beyond belief . . . We must be down around Thomaston . . . Wonder who owns it? . . .

Gwenette reappeared with his glass of Jack Daniel's and his two ham biscuits and the Wiz's glass of carbonated water and set them down on the desk. Charlie noticed the way her plump lower abdomen, which was about at his eye level, swelled out against her navy skirt. How old was she? Twenty-four or -five, he figured.

As soon as she headed back to the galley, he said to the Wiz, "How many warehouses we got in the food division? Seventeen?"

"That's correct. Seventeen."

"What's the payroll?"

"For all the warehouses? For the entire division?"

"Yeah, the entire division."

"I don't have the number on the tip of my tongue, but I can do a back-of-the-envelope calculation."

He produced an HP-12C calculator from the side pocket of his jacket, and the ditch down the middle of his forehead deepened, and he began pecking away. That damned HP-12C was the Wiz in hardware form. It was the wizard's wand of the technogeeks. Charlie couldn't stand the sight of it, because it utterly baffled him and made him feel how cut off he was from the new generation coming out of the business schools. Curious about the thing, he had once asked the Wiz to let him try it for a second. He tried to enter 2+2. He couldn't get 4! Couldn't get 2+2=4! Turned out that with this damned machine, you had to enter +2 plus +2. It worked backwards or something. Only people with MBA's from Wharton could even get it to function.

In no time the Wiz looked up and said, "Two hundred and seven million, three hundred and seventy-five thousand, in round numbers, give or take twenty-five thousand."

"Jesus, that's a lot of money. Am I right?"

"That's true."

"What if we cut the payroll by 20 percent?"

"How? What type of initiatives? Across-the-board layoffs?"

"Right. What would we save?"

"Well, $40 million. But I don't see how we could do it. I'm not aware of any inefficient fits in the employment situations in the warehouses, and the Teamsters would go crazy. They're all Teamster shops."

"I can deal with the Teamsters. They have a practical streak."

"Are you serious? Twenty percent? I don't know, that's an awfully deep cut, Charlie."

"The restaurant business is way down, volume is way down, and I don't recall any layoffs to speak of."

"Maybe, but I've never gotten any indication there was any real slack at the warehouses."

"Well, let's find out. Let's try it."

"I don't *know*, Charlie. Twenty *percent*. That's twelve hundred people."

The word *people*, as opposed to the words they had been using, *payroll* and *employment situations*, jarred Charlie for a moment. "You're probably right," he said. "That is a lot. What about 15 percent? We'd still save $30 million—right?—and we'd be talking about only nine hundred layoffs, which is fewer than a thousand. It won't look so drastic, and it'll impress the hell out of the bank. You know why?"

"Why?"

"Because banks can't stand paying money to employees. To them, giving money, that sacred thing, money, giving money to people, just to spend on themselves, that's practically immoral. Layoffs are right on their wavelength."

The Wiz arched his eyebrows and rolled his eyes but said no more. He looked out the window, and Charlie followed his gaze. Down below, amid a swath of orchards, you could see a house on a low rise with a long, long, long curving driveway leading up to it. The driveway was bordered on both sides by a parade of dogwood trees, planted so close together that their profusions of blossoms created two glorious trains of white, stretching on for what must have been half a mile. Christ! Must cost a fortune to keep up a place like that, and—bango!—you could lose it all before you knew it!—and then where would all those heavenly bowers be?

Now, while the Wiz continued to stare out the window, Charlie looked at N. C. Wyeth's painting of Jim Bowie, which made him think about his mama and his daddy and the shack he'd grown up in . . . Baker County had been so rural, there had been only one town, Newton, big enough to make it onto the Esso road map . . . There hadn't been many places for poor white people to work in Baker County other than the plantations and the pulp mill. His daddy had worked at Ichauway, the plantation owned by Robert Woodruff, the president of Coca-Cola, right there on the Flint River, and at Turpmtine and two or three other places, none of them stayed for very long, and then he went to work at the pulp mill. He'd lost the index finger of his right hand working in the pulp mill. That was the worst job in Georgia. Just going over to the mill to see his daddy was like going to see a horrible freak show of men with fingers and eyes missing. A bunch of Teamsters working in a modern warehouse for twelve or fourteen dollars an hour, with forklifts to do the heavy lifting and OSHA regulations and God knows what else—Croker Global Foods was a country club compared to real work. Just as if it were yesterday, he could see that godforsaken pulp mill, and he could hear it, with the saws and the rippers screaming and whining and the geysers of sawdust spewing up from the blades and the chips flying and those poor crippled bastards working like dogs, his daddy among them. Some of them had an eye *and* a finger or two missing. He could see the pitiful stumps—

Aha! Was *that* the real reason he had suddenly thought of his daddy and the pulp mill—the missing fingers? He could feel his lips compress and his face turn red just thinking about the insolent sonofabitch with the chin giving him the finger and making the crack about losing four fingers in the war. He had *seen* men with missing fingers, his own daddy for a start, and he'd actually *been* in a war . . . In the early years of the war in Vietnam he'd won the Purple Heart and the Bronze Star with a combat V, and he was willing to bet money that the cute guy with the big chin had never even served in the armed forces. He'd have the Wiz or Marguerite or somebody check the guy out. He was tempted to say something to the Wiz right now about that sonofabitch and who had or had not experienced combat, but he restrained himself. Nobody wanted to hear war stories from a sixty-year-old man.

The two of them sat in silence a moment longer, ruminating. Just then the door to the cockpit opened, and the chief pilot, Lud Harnsbarger, came out and beamed at Charlie and said, "Well, Cap, everything okay? 'Bout to begin the *de*scent."

"Yeah, everything's fine, Lud."

Charlie liked everything about Lud Harnsbarger. He was from over in Cobb County, near Marietta, which he pronounced "May-retta." He was one of those big, tall, blond Georgia boys who are lean and strong but have such thick, fair Anglo-Saxon skin you don't see any muscular definition. He was wearing a short-sleeved white shirt and a navy necktie with the Croker Global logo embroidered on it in neat rows, and the sunlight lit up a furze of reddish-blond hair on his big forearms. Charlie always liked that, the way that ever-so-delicate furze of hair lit up like spun candy on his pilot's big, thick forearms; although it was the kind of thing you couldn't mention to anybody. Lud had spent four years in the Air Force flying transports. Fighter planes would have been better, but the main thing was that he was a good old Georgia boy who had put in his time in the armed services. Charlie liked the way Lud looked at him and spoke to him. Lud didn't fawn, but Charlie could always tell that he respected him as . . . a man, not just an employer.

"I jes talked to Durwood on the radio, Cap. The Range Rover's broke down. So he's gon' come on out to the strip and pick y'all up in the Suburban. Auntie Bella's gon' have some kale and sausage soup and some hot biscuits ready when you git there."

"Well, that's great, Lud," said Charlie.

And now Gwenette was standing beside him again. "Git you something else before we land, Cap?"

"No thanks," said Charlie.

"How 'bout yew, Mr. Stroock?"

The Wiz just shook his head no.

Gwenette's hips and forearms were at Charlie's eye level, and once more he was aware of the way her lower abdomen swelled out against her skirt. She was pretty plump, but her skin was lovely, absolutely smooth and flawless. It looked like milk, the way milk looks when you milk a cow and it comes right out of the udder. He had never noticed that before. She was stout . . . a real country girl . . . There had been an animal vitality about these broad-beamed country girls when he was growing up . . . something marvelous and robust . . . The juice really flowed . . .

Pop. He forced himself off that train of thought. What the hell did he think he was doing? Suppose he made a play for the likes of Gwenette? How long could that last? Twenty-four hours? Twenty-four minutes? And then he would have lost a good stewardess . . . Gwenette was heavyset, like Martha . . .

A little wavelet of guilt and remorse . . . Twenty-nine years he'd been married to Martha . . . before Serena . . . Christ! Serena . . . not even thirty yet and already tough as whit leather . . . Tough as whit leather . . . How the hell had that expression floated into his head? . . . His daddy used to say it all the time . . . Never could figure out what whit leather was . . .

He closed his eyes and thought about Peaches and hoped he'd feel a tingle in his loins. He had a theory . . . If you lost your sexual drive, you lost everything, your energy, your daring, your imagination. He kept waiting for the tingle . . . Instead, he felt an electrical jolt in his solar plexus. Suppose it happened! Suppose they took everything from him! They could wipe him out. He was sixty years old, and this time they could wipe him out—*utterly*!

Desperately he looked up at the bulkhead again, at Jim Bowie on his deathbed . . . A brave, brave man, brave as they come, and he never said die . . . Yeah!—and a few minutes later he was dead as they come, with a Mexican bayonet through his heart. And no doubt they took everything he had, including the Bowie knife, while they were at it.

Beneath his sternum, Charlie Croker's heart was hurrying as if it had an urgent appointment somewhere else.

Lud was banking the ship toward the east. They were coming in to Turpmtine. Down below, for as far as you could see . . . stands of soaring longleaf pines with riots of white dogwood blossoms running through them . . . tawny fields of sedge, just beginning to turn green, interspersed with copses of already brilliant green spreads of beggarweed, Egyptian wheat, rye, oats, peas, and corn . . . huge groves of live oak, only just beginning to burst into leaf, so that you could make out the arthritic trunks and branches and the shaggy garlands of Spanish moss strung through them in immense ghostly gray strands . . . and, in the middle distance, a swamp, eight thousand acres of it, glistening in the sun where the water broke clear of the stands of cypress and tupelo maples and the tangled thickets of cane, holly, greenbriar, and God knew what else . . . Even from up here, at this altitude, looking out the window of an airplane, you could tell that it was spring and that the swamp was . . . *coming alive* . . . The branches of the cypress and tupelo maples were swollen with buds about to explode into foliage . . .

He glanced at the Wiz. The Wiz was looking down, too . . . through his titanium frames . . . Just what the bar-code scanners must have seen down there he couldn't imagine . . . The outdoors . . . home of insects, snakes, and other irrational and undependable elements . . . Probably left him feeling nothing, except a dermatitic itch . . . Charlie wanted to reach across the tupelo desk and take him by the shoulder and say, "Wiz! Look at it! Twenty-nine thousand acres, and it's all coming alive! The sap is rising! The eggs are hatching! The seeds are germinating! Snakes, puppies, foals, and little babies are being born! You think you're such a realist—well, *that's* real life, what you see down there!"

Now the G-5 turned south again and came down even lower, and he could see the pale, sandy dirt roads running through the pines . . . He could see the sheds . . . there . . . there . . . and way over there, deep in the plantation . . . the ones he built for feeding and sheltering the mules and the horses during the quail shoots . . . And now he got his first glimpse of the white fences, miles of them it looked like, enclosing the vast clearing where the horses were turned out . . . fifty-nine horses, and they all had to be turned out every day, and some had to be segregated to keep the troublemakers, particularly the stallions, from kicking or biting each other to bits . . . The pastures were that same brilliant green . . . And over there! Two foals, no more than two weeks old, kicking up their heels!

He couldn't resist any longer. "Hey, Wiz! Take a look right over there. See what I'm talking about, those two foals? I bet they're not more than two weeks old! I think one of them's"—one *uv*'em's—"First Draw's!"

You could just begin to make out the Big House in the middle of a grove of live oaks, pin oaks, and Southern magnolias, some of the oldest of them eighty feet high, which would put out such a towering profusion of white blossoms two months from now, he sometimes traveled to Turpmtine in the middle of the summer just to see them. The house itself was not the sort of Greek Revival palace with the Ionic columns and the entablatures that the plantation parvenus had built just before the Civil War. The Big House at Turpmtine had been built in the early 1830s, with the low lines and deeply shaded wraparound porches and white clapboard siding and floor-to-ceiling double-hung windows of the true antebellum Old South. It wasn't even on high ground, because hills scarcely even existed in this part of Baker County. But what a show it was! The driveway, a broad dirt road with a sandy composition so fine and pale it looked almost white, curved for a mile through the pines before entering an avenue of live oaks planted so closely on either side that a month from now they would create a cool, dark, dense, green tunnel of foliage. Then it emerged into the clearing and made a grand loop, bordered by ancient boxwood, in front of the house. The flower beds were ablaze with vivid red horseshoe geraniums, yellow bayberry bushes, violet-mauve masses of Ithuriel's spear, orange Kaffir lilies, crimson-and-yellow Japanese quince, and the flower he loved above all others, the early-blooming Confederate rose, which now, in the afternoon, was still white but which by nightfall would be a deep rose, in mourning, folks said, for the blood shed by brave Confederate lads in the Lost Cause.

It was breathtaking—*breath*taking! Charlie felt a catch in his throat.

The G-5 was now beyond the Big House. Lud was bringing it down close to Jookers Swamp before swinging about and heading into the glide path to the landing strip. Down this low, and with so little foliage on the trees, you could clearly see the stands of cypress and black tupelo maple rising out of the water . . . You could see their huge swollen knees just above the waterline . . . And there was the Jook House, a big white clapboard structure on stilts, cantilevered out over the water, which he had built as a twelve-bedroom guest house . . . Cost $2.4 million . . . Oh, how flush he had felt! . . . way back then . . .

The landing strip was an alley of asphalt cut through a pine forest. It was almost a mile long, so as to accommodate a jet this big . . . What with the landing lights, the maintenance hangar and its asphalt apron, the fuel pumps, and the access roads that had to be built, the whole thing had cost him $3.6 million. He thought about that as the pines whizzed by in a blur on either side, and they glided in and touched down for the landing.

When they reached the hangar apron, Durwood was out there with the big Chevrolet Suburban, as promised, and Rufus Dotson, the black man who was in charge of the crew that maintained the runway and the hangar, was standing beside it. As soon as Charlie slid himself out from under his tupelo desk, he could tell his right knee had stiffened. He didn't want to be seen hobbling down the stairs, not even in front of Durwood and Rufus, but it couldn't be helped. His knee hurt so much he had to hold on to the cable that served as a railing. When he reached the bottom, Rufus was right there waiting. He was a short, squarely built man, in his fifties—or his sixties—Charlie never had known his age for sure—with dark skin and gray hair that stuck out on either side of his head. He wore an old-fashioned cap, like a golfer's cap, that covered the top of his head, which was bald. He touched the cap's little visor, respectfully, with the thumb and forefinger of his right hand and said:

"How you doing, Cap'm Charlie? Lemme give you a hand." He reached out with his big, powerful right hand. He was wearing a long-sleeved gray work shirt of a sort you seldom saw anymore, buttoned at the wrist, and a pair of jeans.

"Aw, 'at's all right, Rufus," said Charlie, who would rather have died than be helped down those stairs, "it's jes'at damn knee a mine, from playin' football."

Rufus chuckled deep in his throat and said, "You don' have to tell me 'bout the rheumatiz, Cap'm Charlie."

Mine's not rheumatism, damn it, Charlie wanted to say, mine's from *football*!

All around were the deep cooling shadows of the pines, which reached up a hundred feet or more, but out here on the hangar apron it was painfully bright. Charlie squinted. Mirage slicks flared up in front of your eyes when you looked back down the runway, and caloric waves rose from the asphalt. It made him feel hot and tired and weak. Durwood was ambling over from the Suburban.

"Hey, Cap'm," said Durwood. "Mr. Stroock."

Every time Charlie saw this big man and heard his deep Baker County voice, he just knew that he was the archetype of what the overseers had been back when overseers rode herd on the field hands who were slashing pine out in that murderous heat ten or twelve hours a day, not only before the Civil War but for a good fifty years afterward. Slashing pine was as hellish as working in the pulp mills, the way Uncle Bud told it. It drove men so close to the ragged edge, the overseers used to sleep with loaded shotguns by their beds. That Durwood could have lived such a life Charlie had not the slightest doubt. He was stone-cold Georgia Cracker, top to bottom. He was one of those big men who are more intimidating in middle age than ever before, because their hide has gotten tougher and they've learned what it takes to be mean in a calculating way, which is the meanest way of all. He was about Charlie's height, a few inches over six feet. His head and neck were huge, and everything seemed to droop, his eyes, his cheeks, his nose, his mouth, which gave him a perpetual scowl. His beefy shoulders drooped, his huge chest drooped, and his belly drooped over his belt, and some sort of horrible and irresistible power seemed to be packed inside all that flesh. He wore a khaki-colored shirt with the sleeves rolled up over his immense forearms and khaki balloon-seat twill pants whose cuffs rested on top of a pair of old battered calf-high boots of the sort that anybody in Baker County who spent time in the fields wore as protection against the rattlesnakes, which usually went for the ankles. Riding on top of his big hips was a gunbelt and a holster with the handle of a huge .45-caliber revolver showing. The revolver was for shooting snakes.

"Hey, Durwood," said Charlie, " 'zat First Draw's foal I saw ovair kickin' up his heels when we was comin' down?" He said it mainly to get some conversation going, to keep everybody thinking about something else while he step-*gimped*-step-*gimped*-step-*gimped*-step-*gimped*-step-*gimped*-step-*gimped* the twenty or thirty feet to the Suburban.

"S'peck hit was, Cap," said Durwood. "Tale you what. If you'n Mr. Stroock ain't too hongry yet, ahmoan swing on ovair fo' we git to the Gun House. 'At's the biggest, kickin'est dayum foal—I ain' never seed one 'at big, not fer no dayum two days old, anyhows."

So the three of them, Charlie, Durwood, and Wismer Stroock, got in the Suburban, and they swung on over there by the stables and the enclosure where First Draw's big foal was kicking up his heels. No sooner did they get out of the vehicle than they saw five or six of the black stablehands and the two little Australians, Johnny Groyner, the stud manager, and Melvin Bonnetbox, his steerer, standing in a semicircle out on a whitish sandy road where it emerged from the palmetto scrub and wire grass into the open space by the stable. They were so absorbed in whatever it was they were looking at, they barely even noticed that the Suburban had pulled up with their overseer, Durwood, and the master of Turpmtine, Cap'm Charlie Croker.

Durwood didn't take that too well, not with his boss having just arrived. "Hey!" he yelled out. "Cain chew boys think a nuthin' to do 'cep clusterfuckin' inna ballin' sun?" *Clusterfucking* was a term Durwood had picked up in Vietnam, where soldiers in the field weren't supposed to gather in clusters, lest all be wiped out by a single strike.

To Durwood's—and Charlie's—surprise, Johnny Groyner, a chesty elf with a close-cropped ginger-red beard, turned toward them and put his forefinger to his lips and motioned with his other hand as if to say, "Come on over and take a look at this."

So Durwood, the Wiz, and Charlie, limping worse than ever, walked on over, and right away they saw what all the fuss was about. On the edge of the road, next to a clump of palmetto scrub and wire grass, out in the boiling sun, was a diamondback rattlesnake, a huge one, six feet long if it was an inch, maybe seven . . . motionless . . . torpid . . .

A cold-blooded creature, it had found that toasty stretch of sandy road out in the sunshine of an April afternoon . . . and was soaking it up, oblivious of the growing audience. It was a monster, even for a part of Georgia notorious for big rattlers. It had such girth that you could see its skin's entire pattern of big and small brown diamonds outlined in black against a tan field. The stablehands stood a respectful distance to the rear. No one dared approach the head. Rattlers had no lids over their eerie vertical slits-for-eyes, and no one knew whether they actually slept or not.

One of the black stablehands, Sonny Colquitt, said, "Hey, Cap'm Charlie! What you want do with that big sucker? Want me git a hoe?" He meant a hoe to chop the head off with.

Charlie stared at Sonny. Then he stared at the snake, which was a magnificent brute. And then he was aware that everybody else, including Durwood and the Wiz, was staring at him, Cap'm Charlie.

So he said to Sonny, "Go git me a croker sack."

He motioned toward the stable, and Sonny hightailed it toward the stable to get a croker sack, that being the local term for a burlap bag. While Sonny was gone, Charlie took off his jacket and loosened his necktie. He didn't care if they saw his saddlebags, because they wouldn't know what they came from, and nobody in Baker County was surprised to see a man sweating in the first place. Mainly he wanted to give them a proper eyeful of his huge chest, his broad back, his massive neck. Gimp or no gimp, he was still Cap'm Charlie Croker.

In no time Sonny was back with the croker sack. He handed it to Charlie. Charlie held the sack in his left hand and stepped through the semicircle of gawkers, right between the other Australian elf, Melvin Bonnetbox, and one of the new black employees, Kermit Hoyer, and advanced toward the snake. Step-*gimp*-step-*gimp*-step-*gimp*-step-*gimp* . . . he walked as slowly and softly as he could . . . pausing by the row of rattles . . . eight of them . . . still had the original button, or so it looked like . . . And now he crept on toward the head, and a strange and wondrous thing happened. The pain began to recede from his knee. He was now close enough to the beast's head to see its graceful heart shape and the sinister but beautiful mask of black that ran across its face and eyes. And now he stepped across its body, so that he was straddling the great somnolent brute.

He knew that what he was about to do was foolhardy—and he knew he would do it anyway. The only sane way to go about it would be to get a sapling branch and whittle it into a forked stick and pin the snake's head down first. But by the time he managed to get a forked stick made, the beast might come to and retreat into the underbrush, and everybody would just be staring at poor, feckless, gimped-up Cap'm Charlie. No, there was no other choice but the foolhardiest possible way.

He could no longer hear a thing from the outside world. A rushing sound, like steam, filled his skull. He was no longer aware of telling his sixty-year-old body what to do. He crouched, he leaned over at the waist, and—

—a flash of white filled his brain, and he thrust his right hand down and grabbed the rattlesnake around the neck at the base of its skull. With a single motion he straightened up and swept the reptile off the ground and held its head out in front of himself at arm's length.

He had done it! He had done it right! Right behind the jaws he had him! One inch off in either direction—one slip of the fingers—and the brute would have sunk its fangs into his forearm—but *he had done it!*

The snake was now six or seven feet of writhing bestial anger. Its huge mouth was wide open, and its two fangs, which were truly like hypodermic needles, were erect, and it bit at the air, and great gouts of yellowish venom spurted from the fangs, and its forked black tongue flicked in every direction, and a hissing sound burst from its throat. The beast was more than six feet of muscle, vertebrae, and ribs, literally hundreds of ribs, and it lashed about until Charlie wondered if he could maintain his grip much longer. A heavy musk, like a skunk's, spewed from the snake's body and choked the air, and to Charlie in that moment it was as rich as frankincense and myrrh. But above all, there was the sound of the rattles.

A chattering terror fills the place!

That was from a poem about rattlesnakes by somebody—Somebody Harte?—that Charlie had read in high school. It was one of the few poems he had ever willingly memorized.

> *The wild bird hears; smote with the sound,*
> *As if by bullet brought to ground;*
> *On broken wing, dips, wheeling round!*

Smote with the sound! Full-grown, one-ton horses would bolt on you when they heard the terrible castanet of the rattlesnake. That sound seemed to be a trigger of terror built into the nervous system of every creature possessing the sense of hearing, including, above all, man.

Charlie turned and held out the rattling beast toward everyone in the semicircle, and they all shrank back, even Durwood, as if the incredible Cap'm Charlie were about to march upon them and cram the venomous serpent down somebody's windpipe.

In fact, Charlie wondered how much longer he could hold the damned thing. Seldom did a rattler weigh more than five pounds, but this one did, and it was thrashing with tremendous jerks and spasms. On the other hand, as Charlie well knew, it couldn't thrash like a buggy whip, and it couldn't wrap itself around his arm. It could only thrash from side to side, in a lateral plane, and once its belly lost contact with the ground it was disoriented. The Wiz, he noted with grim satisfaction, had now drifted back a full twenty feet. He Who Would Live Forever had done an instantaneous back-of-the-envelope calculation and decided that the vicinity of the Chevrolet Suburban was a better strategic alternative than anyplace anywhere near that whitish sandy road above which a gigantic terror-chattering rattlesnake now thrashed in the grip of his boss gone berserk.

Charlie gave them all one more terrible look down the gaping, venom-spouting gullet, and then he flopped the mouth of the croker sack open with his left hand and thrust the head of the rattler down into the bottom of it. Then he released his grip on the snake and jerked his right hand and arm out of the sack and drew the drawstring tight and held the sack aloft by the strings. The sack was now a hive of primal anger. The burlap thrashed about furiously, the clattering terror filled the place, and you could see the beast's fangs knifing through the fabric's loose weave and squirting its seemingly inexhaustible supply of venom into the air.

"Awright, y'all," said Charlie in a tone of coldest command, "c'mon ov'ere."

He started walking toward the Snake House, which was about fifty yards beyond the stable. He held the croker sack far out from his shoulder, suspended by the drawstrings. He'd known of cases where men had got bitten by diamondbacks because they let the bag get too close to their bodies. The strain on his arm was fierce, but he was damned if he was going to ask anybody else to help him; not now he wasn't, not after having gone this far. Out of the corner of his eye he could see the others forming behind him in a straggling line . . . with the Wiz bringing up the rear. He could hear a couple of the stablehands going, "Unnnh-unnnhhh-*unnnnnhhhhhhh*." It was music to his ears.

Charlie's body was gimping on him a little bit, but he didn't feel a thing. He felt light on his feet. He felt as if he was floating. He had . . . *done it*. And he was about to . . . *do more*.

Inside, as well as outside, the Snake House was an absolute jewel of a little building; or that was the way Charlie saw it. Outside, its octagonal, almost circular, shape and its ancient red brick (meticulously hunted down by Ronald Vine) and its white wooden trim and its heavy slate roof made it look like one of those little buildings Charlie had seen when he was in Virginia and had visited Monticello and Colonial Williamsburg. Up on top, where the eight sides of the roof came to a point, instead of a weather vane or anything like that, there was the bronze sculpture of a coiled rattlesnake. Inside—and this had been Ronald Vine's true stroke of genius—the Snake House's tiny interior was lined with what at first looked like some sort of lurid wallpaper. But then you realized the stripes were in fact rattlesnake skins, flattened out and stretched up vertically and touching, edge to edge, so that they created a vast field of rough, scaly diamonds. Around the lower part of the little eight-sided room ran an ornate white wainscoting, and at the top of the wainscoting was a wide white counter, and in the center of the counter on each of seven wall sections of the octagon—the eighth was devoted to the doorway—was a big glass aquarium, or, better said, terrarium, and in each terrarium were live snakes from the fields and swamps of Turpmtine: rattlers, copperheads, cottonmouths, and corals . . . all of them poisonous and all of them deadly.

There were plenty of Turpmtine employees, black and white, who didn't even like to *go inside* the Snake House. They had a sound instinct: you steer clear of snakes, and when you see them, you kill them. Some of the boys believed snakes were the Devil's agents. So the little band that followed Cap'm Charlie into the Snake House—they were quieter than they would have been if they were going into a Methodist church.

Charlie carried his croker sack over to the far wall, where there was a terrarium with six huge rattlesnakes, each one almost as big as the one in the sack, slithering around one another like the Devil making his appearance on earth in a slimy moving knot of coils bristling with fangs and swollen with pent-up venom. Sonny, Durwood, Kermit, Johnny, and Bonnie, as Melvin Bonnetbox was called—all of them hung back. The Wiz *truly* hung back; he made sure he was nearer the door than the terrarium.

Charlie shifted the croker sack from his left hand to his right hand, and then, without asking anybody's help or looking at a soul, he lifted up one end of the wire-mesh grille over the terrarium and laid the mouth of the croker sack on the lip of the glass. Then he lifted the bottom of the croker sack up to about a 60-degree angle. You could see the snakes in the bottom of the terrarium looking up at the croker sack and Charlie's bare left hand and wrist. Then you could see the head of the rattler in the croker sack beginning to protrude from the sack's mouth. That head and those fangs and that venom were no more than six inches from Charlie's left hand, which held up the lid. Now more and more of the snake's huge body began to slither out the mouth of the sack. Suddenly the serpent thrust its entire body, all six or seven feet of it, out of the croker sack and flopped down among its brethren in the bottom of the terrarium and joined the moving knot of slithering coils.

Ever so gingerly, Charlie lowered the lid and withdrew the croker sack. For a moment he just stood there and stared at the seven rattlesnakes inside the terrarium. The biggest of them all, the newcomer, the monster he had picked up with his bare hand, slithered about among all the deadly coils in a state of high agitation.

Then Charlie stepped back about two feet and stared some more. Out of the corners of his eyes he noticed that the boys, including even the Wiz, had now stepped forward to get a closer look. So he reached in his pants pocket withdrew his car keys, concealing them in his fist. He stared at the serpents a few beats longer—then suddenly threw the keys against the side of the terrarium. The angry newcomer struck the spot first, his fangs smashing into the glass, but the other six hit the same spot, fangs bared, within the next fraction of a second. Everybody in the room, except for Charlie, jumped back, as if rocked by an explosion. Even Durwood; even Sonny; and the Wiz, He Who Would Live Forever, was almost out the door.

Charlie turned around and let his gaze run over the whole bunch of them, one by one, and then he said, in the calmest voice imaginable, "Boys, that's one damn fine snake."

OUTSIDE THE SNAKE HOUSE, as they dispersed, the others were conversing excitedly with one another. But not the Wiz; he was standing alone, his hands in his pockets. Charlie walked over to him, and he wasn't conscious of any gimp at all in his right leg. He put his arm around the young man's shoulders, and he said:

"Wiz, I been thinking it over. I've made up my mind. We're gonna do it. We're gonna lay off 15 percent of the food division."

The Wiz didn't look at his boss. He just nodded yes and looked straight ahead. Behind the titanium frames his bar-code-scanner eyes were open wide enough to take in the world.

Charlie Croker felt almost whole again.

Chapter IV

Beige Half Brothers

THE OFFICE OF THE MAYOR OF ATLANTA, ROGER WHITE'S OLD Omega Zeta Zeta fraternity brother at Morehouse, Wesley Dobbs Jordan, was up on the second floor of the 1989 addition to City Hall, the new part of City Hall, the part you entered from Trinity Avenue. You found yourself in a lobby, a rotunda that struck Roger as very modern but at the same time very grand, which was a big admission for Roger to make to himself, because he didn't have much patience with modern architecture and decor. His own taste had never tolerated much that came after Edwin Lutyens. But this rotunda wasn't bad. It was all gray Georgia marble, which rose three stories to a fabulous dome with a skylight that flooded the place with a sunlit radiance, even on a dreary day like this one. On either side, marble stairways led up to a balcony on the second floor whose immense brass railing ran clear around the rotunda like a crown.

God, Roger thought, with a stab of envy, Wes Jordan has *made* it, if he runs this kingdom! Well, there was no use being envious of Wes, was there. Wes was unique. Wes had always had a twelve-month supply of confidence. He was a short, somewhat pudgy little guy, but at Morehouse he had been more than just an exemplar of the Morehouse Man.

He had been the Morehouse Man and a half. He had been president of Omega Zeta Zeta and president of the student body. He was a light-skinned blueblood, related to many important figures of the old Sweet Auburn black elite, and from the start he had been a leader because he was . . . *going to be a leader*. Roger was a light-skinned blueblood himself and kin to perhaps as many prominent people as Wes was, but he had never had the implacable *confidence* that Wes had or the withering cynicism with which Wes cut all enemies down to size. You couldn't pull any of that Authentic Black business on Wes. With a few words he'd take some blacker-than-thou fool's own words and stick them between his ribs and into his gizzard before the sucker knew what was happening. And now Wes was Mayor of Atlanta, and he, Roger, was approaching the throne of the Monarch of the Marble Rotunda, seeking, like everyone else, a favor. Well, at least I know him on a first-name basis, thought Roger. I won't have to stand there murmuring Mr. Mayor with my hat in my hand. Not, it occurred to him, that he was wearing a hat; but he *had* gone to the trouble of putting on the richest-looking ensemble he possessed: a navy hard-finished worsted suit with pinstripes, nipped in at the waist, a tab-collared shirt with a white collar and spaced-out pale-blue stripes on the shirtfront, a solid French-blue crêpe de chine silk necktie from Charvet in Paris, and a pair of close-soled, cap-toed, highly polished black shoes that fit him in the insteps like a pair of gloves. Debouching from the breast pocket of his jacket was a white silk handkerchief selvaged with French blue.

Once you walked up the stairs and went through the doors of the mayoral domain, you found yourself before a long modern counter, behind which sat a pretty black receptionist, late twenties if Roger had to guess, with medium-dark skin and carefully coiffed, relaxed hair. As soon as he announced his name, she said brightly:

"Oh, Mr. White! Have a seat. It'll only be a minute." *Very* brightly, in fact, and with such a warm smile that Roger turned off his status radar, which had been dialed up to detect even the slightest sign that he was being treated like any other humble petitioner before His Eminence.

In the rear of the reception area a huge white policeman sat at a desk, eyeing him with a neutral expression that changed into a small polite smile when Roger looked directly at him. Security . . . white . . . Receptionist . . . black . . . A white cop and a black receptionist . . .

Roger wondered if Wes always arranged it this way, black and white, one of each; since the petitioners who arrived in this place would be white as well as black. In fact, the only other person waiting in the reception area, sitting on a couch, was a white businessman, about fifty; or Roger took him to be a businessman. He had on the typical Atlanta white businessman's garb of the moment: a nondescript, shapeless, mall-men's-store, off-the-rack dark suit, a striped shirt, and a Pizza Grenade necktie, as Roger called the current necktie genre. It was the sort of tie that looked as if a pepperoni-and-olive pizza had just exploded on your shirtfront. Even *black* businessmen were wearing them!—and Roger had always just naturally assumed that black businessmen dressed more subtly, as well as more stylishly, than their white counterparts. And the shoes . . . white businessmen just didn't understand about shoes. They didn't wear close-soled shoes. They wore them with soles that stuck out like sidewalks.

Roger Too White took a seat across from him in a leather easy chair that made a luxurious whooshing sound as he sank into it. Idly he looked about . . . a lot of English furniture of the sort Wes had always liked, Sheraton and Hepplewhite; Wes had it in his home in Cascade Heights, too. The place looked like an old-line men's club, such as the Commerce Club or the Capital City, which Roger had been inside a few times for lunch . . . and yet—

—something was jarring the pattern, the mental atmosphere of the room . . . Then Roger noticed the curtains on either side of the window. Enormous things, these curtains were, heavily pleated and draped . . . Yoruban cotton . . . *Yoruban!* . . . The bold black, red, and yellow Yoruban designs were unmistakable, even with the material so heavily pleated and folded in upon itself. And up there on the wall above the couch, set against the dark paneling . . . fantastic African carvings, in stone and ivory . . . antelopes, wildebeests, lions, cheetahs . . . plus fabulous creatures that came from out of Yoruban myths. . . . and over there on the adjoining wall . . . two lurid but stunning and probably very valuable witch-doctor masks and a pair of crossed spears with distinctive Yoruban tassels hanging from the metal necks just below the spearheads.

Oh, Roger recognized it all, because during his junior year at Morehouse he had been one of the students chosen to go on a tour of Yorubaland during spring break—why couldn't those wallowing Freaknickers of today think of something *constructive* like that!—he had gone on a tour of Yorubaland, in the hinterlands of Lagos, Nigeria, with a group led by Dr. Michaels and Dr. Pomeroy. And why? *Roots!* It was generally believed, by scholars, that a high percentage of the slaves who had come to America had been seized in Yorubaland, which had been the seat of a great civilization, perhaps the greatest civilization in all of Africa. The houses of the chiefs were magnificent structures. Some of them had as many as fifty rooms, richly decorated with carvings and symbolic devices *just like the ones on these walls.* And then Roger remembered: Wes had been on that trip. Wes would remember all this stuff as vividly as he did.

He got up from the chair and approached the receptionist.

"Excuse me," he said. Her lovely smiling face turned toward him. "I was just wondering"—he gestured toward the carvings on the wall above the couch—"how long have these carvings been here?"

"About two and a half weeks, I guess."

"And these?" He gestured toward the mask and the spears.

"Same thing," said the receptionist. "The Mayor brought them in. I think he brought them from home."

"No kidding!" said Roger. And then he realized the expression sounded almost as silly as it had when he had said it to Coach Buck McNutter the other night. Then he said, "They're stunning."

He repeated the phrase several times on the way back to his chair, in a slightly narcoleptic fashion, talking to himself. "Yes, they're stunning . . . they're stunning . . ." All the while he was thinking, From *home*? Wes Jordan's been collecting Yoruban art?

He was still puzzling over this fact—Wes Jordan had never shown the slightest interest in African art after their return from Yorubaland, not even during the height of Afrocentrism in the late 1960s and early 1970s—he was still puzzling over it when a woman came bustling out of a door on the side wall slightly behind the receptionist and said, with much heartiness and a big smile:

"Mr. White? I'm Gladys Caesar. If you'll come with me—the Mayor's been looking forward to seeing you!"

Roger sized up Gladys Caesar immediately. She was the sort of chunky, highly energetic, relentlessly well-organized middle-aged woman, neither light-skinned nor terribly dark, either, who, since time was, *had gotten things done* in the community. He followed her down a long hallway lined on one side by glassed-in shelves bearing an astonishing array of *objets*: two Japanese ceramic dolls clad in real cloth kimonos of fabulous richness and complexity, adorned with some sort of large lake-red disks, a Lalique glass bowl with an Art Deco nude rising from the rim, a fragment (but a big one) of an apparently ancient Italian bas-relief, a fifteen-or-sixteen-inch-high bronze figure of a mustachioed New York City policeman from the turn of the century mounted on a horse and wearing a capelet over his shoulders, an exquisite model of a nineteenth-century ship inside a big bottle with a narrow neck—these *objets*, each one more expensive-looking than the previous one, stretched on and on, behind glass. Before Roger could ask the question, Gladys Caesar answered it for him:

"Gifts from visiting dignitaries. The Japanese never come without a gift. They'd consider that bad manners."

The hallway led past a couple of small offices and down toward two big mahogany doors. When they reached the door on the left, Gladys Caesar produced a key and unlocked it, pushed it open, gestured toward a big couch upholstered in white tweed, and said softly, with the warmest possible smile, "Have a seat. He'll be right in."

Roger looked about. He was in what looked like a living room, a modern living room but a spectacular one. There was a single, wide, floor-to-ceiling window, which also served as a sliding door, that looked out onto a balcony. The balcony, like the rest of the building, was made of a pale pre-cast concrete, but a modernistic dark metal railing and balusters created a pattern that gave it high style. The back of the couch was within four or five feet of the window, and in front of the couch was a glass coffee table with a beveled top that looked two inches thick, at least, supported by a simple but magnificently forged brass frame. The floor was covered by a thick rug with a dark brown geometric shape repeated against a white background; upon closer inspection Roger could see that the shape was that of a phoenix, the mythical bird that rises from the ashes, the symbol of Atlanta, which had twice burned to the ground and sprung back up. On one end of the coffee table was a stack of oversized picture books, and in the center of the table . . . a superlative Yoruban divination cup resting atop the foot-high figures of a horse and rider carved in a reddish wood in the ancient Oyo style . . . Stunning! . . . Yes, stunning . . . and then he noticed the walls, which at first glance he had assumed were more mahogany, because they were so dark. But now he could see what they really were . . . *ebony* . . . from floor to ceiling . . . without any bevels or other decorative incisions . . . Displayed on the wall opposite where he stood . . . a massing of what must have been at least a dozen Yoruban ceremonial swords, each one eighteen inches or so in length, carved in ivory in the most intricate detail . . . The ebony behind them brought out all the lacelike apertures in the swords' blades . . . *Stunning! Stunning!*

Roger was still staring, agape, when he heard a door open off to the side. Coming toward him, across the phoenix rug, from out of what appeared to be a smallish office, was Wes Jordan, all five feet, seven inches of him, beaming.

He opened his arms and held his hands up as if preparing for an embrace, and said in a deep voice, "Brother White! Brother White!"

Roger immediately recognized this as Wes's put-on voice, his ironic Authentic Black voice, and he knew "Brother" to have two meanings, both of them ironic: Brother White, as in Omega Zeta Zeta fraternity brother, and Brother White, as in my African-American soul brother.

When he drew close, Wes didn't embrace him, as Roger thought he was about to. Instead, he raised his left hand, palm open, and said, "Hey, blood, gimme five."

Roger slapped the Mayor's palm with his own, obligingly, even though he knew this was a put-on, too. Then the Mayor raised his right palm and said, "Gimme high, blood!"

Roger slapped his palm up high. Then the Mayor lowered his left hand, palm up, almost down to knee level, and said, "Gimme low, blood!"

Roger slapped the palm down low. Then, to his surprise, the Mayor *did* embrace him. He threw his arms right around him and rested his head cheek-by-jowl to Roger's and said in a perfectly normal voice, with evident sincerity, "It's good to see you, brother. I don't know where the time goes."

Then he stepped back abruptly and looked Roger up and down, from his gleaming sweet close-soled black shoes up to his white tab collar and Charvet necktie and back down to his feet again.

"Unnh-unnh-*unnnnhhhhhhh*!" A deep voice, back in the mock Authentic Black mode once more. "Ain't we da buttas, baby! Ain't we da . . . *buttas*! Was up, bro?"

Da buttas was current street slang, the hip-hop pronunciation of "the butters," which was the latest term for *smooth* or *slick* or *cool*, particularly in matters of clothing. Roger was surprised that Wes Jordan even knew the term. He had only just heard of it himself.

"How you know 'bout *da buttas,* brudda?" said Roger, slipping into Wes's put-on diction in spite of himself.

"Aw, baby," said the Mayor, "you didn't know you was lookin' at a *down* cat? You didn't know you was lookin' at Mr. Mean Streets of Atlanta? The question *is,* how does a Wringer Fleasom & Tick bitch in a suit like *you* know 'bout da buttas!"

" 'Case you didn' *know,*" said Roger, once more mimicking the Mayor's jive voice, "I got a 'leven-year-old *boy* in the house. Whatever trash you got lyin' out there litterin' the streets a this *town* you runnin', he's gon' bring it home, 'long's it's homey, cool, and straight from the ghetto."

They both started laughing, and Roger took this moment to look his old fraternity brother up and down. In contour he was the same old Wes Jordan, a little too round, a little too chubby, wearing a perfectly good but not striking dark gray suit, a white shirt—and a Pizza Grenade necktie. Him, too. But his light tan face looked harder and squarer than Roger remembered it, and his hair was receding pretty deeply; all to the good, actually, it occurred to Roger; after all, his old pal was now the Mayor of Atlanta. As it had always been, Wes's hair was naturally straight enough for him to comb it back in waves. In fact, it occurred to Roger at that moment, Wes Jordan could probably have passed for white if he had ever wanted to work on it, if he had ever wanted to move to another city somewhere and start out from zero. But what did a man like Wes need with *white* and *zero*? He was forty-three years old and already mayor of one of the four or five most important cities in the United States.

No, Wes didn't need a thing to improve himself in the credentials department. He was a true Sweet Auburn blueblood. In fact, his blood was about as blue as black blood got. His whole act, ever since he'd emerged from his office and come toward Roger, had been vintage Wes Jordan irony, which he had perfected more than two decades ago, way back in their Morehouse College days. Wes was the first in their group—or the first Roger was aware of—to isolate and make fun of the custom among black professionals and intellectuals of greeting each other with an exchange of some form of Authentic Black street talk. It was an unconscious way of expunging guilt, guilt over being so many fortunate levels above one's black brethren who truly *were* denizens of the streets—of expressing solidarity, of symbolizing an eternal awareness and vigilance in the face of a white society that, in point of fact, did not distinguish between those different levels of black males and did not even want to.

But to Wes Jordan it had always seemed phony, nonetheless, and when he engaged in it, he made it so ironic that you had to be a pretty dim bulb not to get the point. Wes might have his faults, but being insecure about his status in this life had never been one of them.

Roger said, "You'll never guess who I started thinking about soon as I walked into your waiting room out there."

"Who?"

"Professor Milford Pomeroy."

"Ahhhh," said the Mayor, "Pom-Pom Pomeroy."

"Can you guess why?"

"I'll take a wild guess, I'll take a wild guess. Could it be that you spied a few treasures of the Oyo and the Owo out there on the walls?"

"You got it," said Roger, "but I was really surprised. *You* . . . and Yoruban art?"

"Oh, we've gone to some pains to put down some . . . *Yoruban roots* in this office."

"Your receptionist—"

"Miss Beasley." The same smile.

"A very attractive young lady," said Roger.

"Yes, she is," said the Mayor.

"Miss Beasley told me *you* brought all these pieces in here. I never knew you collected Yoruban art. I hope you don't mind me saying so, Mr. Mayor, but collecting Yoruban art doesn't strike me as very Wes Jordan."

"Miss Beasley said I *collected* Yoruban art?"

"Well, no, she didn't exactly say that. You brought them in was what I think she said."

"In that she is correct," said Wes, "in that she is correct. In that she is, indeed, correct." That was another Wes Jordan mannerism, repeating a phrase over and over, until it finally seemed totally ironic or else mysteriously significant. "I *did* bring them in, at least in the sense that if it weren't for me, they wouldn't be here. I'll tell you something, Roger. Sometimes it really is fun, being the Mayor of Atlanta. I got all these pieces or got them on loan, with about a dozen telephone calls, and for half of them I didn't even have to get on the telephone myself. Everybody's looking ahead. I called the National Museum in Lagos, Nigeria,

I called the Hammer Collection—you know, Armand Hammer? I called the Linden Museum in Stuttgart, Germany, I called the Pace Gallery in New York City—by the way, Brother Roger, this is just you and me talking, right, Brother Wes and Brother Roger?"

"Oh, sure," said Roger.

"I mean, I don't even know why you're here. You were very mysterious on the telephone with Gladys, I gather, very mysterious, very mysterious." The smile again.

"Well, you'll see why in a minute. But go ahead, tell me about all this." He gestured toward the divination cup and the ivory swords again.

"I told all these people exactly what I was doing. I told them their stuff would be on loan and displayed prominently in the Mayor's office. I didn't say for how long, and they didn't ask. Well, that's not really true. They did ask, but only barely."

"But *you*, Wes? As I remember, you used to *laugh* at all this Afrocentric business. I remember one night—when was it?—'87?—'88—you made so much fun of Jesse Jackson and his 'African-American' pronouncement at that press conference—you remember?—wherever it was—Chicago, I think—that press conference where he started everybody using 'African-American' instead of 'black'?—you remember that night—you had Albert Hill laughing so hard, I thought he was going to die, and he *liked* Jesse."

"Well," said the Mayor, cocking his head and smiling more knowingly than ever, "times change. Times change, times change, and the polls change."

"The polls?"

"The polls and the focus groups."

"You use focus groups?"

"That we do, but don't get me started on all that. Have a seat"—he indicated the white couch—"and tell me what I have to thank for the honor of this visit."

So Roger took a seat on the couch, and Wes Jordan pulled up a big armchair on the other side of the coffee table and sat down and sank back comfortably.

Roger said, "Wes—do you by any chance know Fareek Fanon, the football player?"

"Oh yes," said Wes, rolling his eyes, "I know him. I shared the dais with him at a Special Junior Olympics event, I believe it was." The smile on his face had a distinctly sardonic twist. "What about him?"

Roger said, "I represent him."

"You? What on earth for?"

Roger took a deep breath and launched into the narrative of Fanon and the Freaknic party and the white student who somehow ended up in the Cannon's room at 2 a.m. and now claimed she was raped.

When he said, "Her father is Inman Armholster," the Mayor sat bolt upright and slid forward to the edge of the chair and leaned toward Roger and exclaimed:

"You're kidding!"

"That's exactly what I said when McNutter told me who she was," said Roger. "It wasn't a very lawyer-like response, but that's exactly what I said: 'You're kidding.' He wasn't kidding."

"And they want *you* to represent him? Isn't this a little outside your field?" The Mayor was now leaning so far forward, with his hands clasped and his forearms resting on his thighs, his weight seemed to be centered over the balls of his feet.

"Oh, I wondered the same thing," said Roger. "They've got two other lawyers on the case, Julian Salisbury, who's a very good white litigator, and Don Pickett, who's a very good black litigator, and they've got me."

"Yeah, I know them both," said the Mayor.

"They've got me because—well, just a minute ago you asked me if I was Brother Roger and you said you were Brother Wes. Does that still stand?"

"Sure."

"Well then, I'll tell you exactly why they've hired me. I won't put any spin on it at all. They've hired me because they know I know you. They know we went to grade school and high school together and, for that matter, Sunday school. They know we were fraternity brothers at Morehouse. They think you'll listen to me in a way you wouldn't listen to someone who hasn't known you from way back. It's as simple as that, and that's all I know."

Wes Jordan rose to his feet. He began to pace back and forth with a bemused look on his face, massaging the knuckles of his left hand with the fingers of his right.

Then he stopped and said to Roger, "Okay, let's assume that's sound thinking on their part. Just what do they think you're going to get me to do? Inman Armholster. *Jesus Christ!* And just who is 'they'? Who's paying for all this?"

"It's this new group of football boosters they've got, the Stingers."

"All of whom are white and know Inman Armholster, no doubt. Do you have any idea—" The Mayor broke off the sentence and started pacing again. "Okay. As I was saying, what are you supposed to be persuading me to do?"

"Well, they—we—whatever—we want—"

Interrupting in a distracted way, as if unaware that Roger had said anything, all the while gazing out toward the murky clouds beyond the balcony, the Mayor said, "Do you have any idea of the . . . *potential* of this thing? One of the greatest athletes to ever come out of South Atlanta, out of *black* Atlanta, and the daughter of one of the richest and most prominent men in North Atlanta, in white Atlanta, in Buckhead . . ." Then he looked at Roger and said with the faintest of smiles, "So what does your client want me to do?"

"Well, Wes—what we want, above all, is to keep this thing quiet. Julian Salisbury and Don Pickett may be terrific litigators, but this is a case we can't *win* in any court. All that has to happen is for the whole thing to get out in public and the damage is done. But it can't be kept quiet just by saying nothing. Somebody has to step in and mediate . . . mediate with Inman Armholster. Somebody has to calm a lot of very ruffled feathers, and they—and I happen to agree with them one hundred percent—they can't think of anybody who could do it better than you. You have the *trust* of the Inman Armholsters of this city."

Wes stood still and gazed out through the big plate-glass window and began to smile, as if he had just seen something terribly amusing way over in Paulding or Douglas County. Then he looked at Roger with the same smile on his face.

"Roger," he said, "do you happen to know what 'get-out-the-vote money' is? Sometimes it's called 'walking-around money.' "

"In a general way," said Roger. "I've heard the term. Why?"

"Well," said Wes Jordan, "what would you say it meant, in a general way?"

"I gather it refers to the money you have to spend on election day, or maybe starting a few days before, to alert your supporters in the poorer neighborhoods—I don't know . . . send sound trucks through and pay those people who stand on the corners near the polling places handing out leaflets and get people to drive vans to take people to the polls, things like that. Why?"

Wes smiled, a bit too superciliously in Roger's estimation. "That's what I always thought, too, Roger. But right after I announced my candidacy for mayor, Archie Blount—remember Archie?—congressman from the Fifth District?—Archie drops by, and he says, 'Wes, this is the first time you've ever run in something this big, a citywide election. In the first month of the campaign, your knowledge of how politics actually work will increase by 100 percent. In the second month it'll increase 200 percent, and in the third it'll increase 400 percent—and you'll still be in kindergarten.' I thanked him, in a patronizing way, probably—I liked him, but I didn't consider him very bright—and I continued my preparations to run on the merits, which were all in my favor, I figured.

"The very next morning I got my first surprise. There on my desk is a stack of letters this high. Clipped to each letter is a check made out to my campaign. The letter itself is a contract between me and the organization that sent it. One, I remember, was from some 'gay rights' organization. All I had to do was sign off on this letter saying that I would come out in favor of same-sex marriages, survivor's rights for same-sex couples, gay-sex education starting in elementary school, criminal sanctions against anti-gay bigotry, I can't even remember it all, and I could have the check, which was for $20,000. I disdained it, on the merits, and had my secretary send it right back. First, it was absolute rubbish, and second, my core constituency, our brothers and sisters, couldn't care less about making life easier for homosexuals, black or white. And when these gay-rights groups, who are all white boys, of course, start trying to compare their 'struggle'—it's always 'struggle'—with our folks'—I mean, they're comparing a lot of white boys hugging and kissing each other with a people rising up from slavery—it makes the smoke start coming out of your ears. So I figure I've made a can't-miss decision. I've returned the letter and the check with a polite note saying thanks but no thanks, and I think that's the end of it. Then, four days later, I see a front-page headline on this weekly, *The Five Pointer* it's called. I'm denounced as a homophobe opportunist who won't support even the most fundamental gay rights. You might say, 'Well, so what?' *The Five Pointer*'s circulation is 15,000 at the most. It's a so-called alternative newspaper. But it's very popular among white homosexuals—and so I've just lost the gay vote without even opening my mouth on the subject.

"Every letter in that stack proposed the same deal. 'Bind yourself to our agenda, and you can keep the money.' After a couple of months you're beginning to pant for money. You're beginning to need it the way you need food and air. These campaigns *devour* money, and by now the vendors are all too smart to sell you anything on credit. You start thinking back to all those checks you turned down in such a high-minded way. You start wondering if you couldn't review your positions and find room under your umbrella for some of these . . . really not so terrible . . . special-interest organizations and their . . . $20,000 checks . . . because you have now learned an elemental lesson, which is: Nobody—*nobody*—wins a citywide election strictly *on the merits.* You must have two things: money and organization. And by organization I mean you've got to have people who know every single neighborhood, particularly in South Atlanta.

"Which brings me to 'get-out-the-vote money.' In the closing days of the election you're going to be approached by people claiming they can deliver X number of votes. Some guy wearing a shirt with no collar and a Braves warm-up jacket will come up to you and say, 'I got Mechanicsville, but I gotta know right now. It's $10,000.' You hesitate, partly because he has such a belligerent, disrespectful tone in his voice, whereupon he says, 'You don't want it? Fuck you! This is the deal! I didn't come here to negotiate! Ten thousand up front or fuck you, pal!' Here's some red-eyed moron screaming 'Fuck you' in your face—the face of the next Mayor of Atlanta—but by now you know there's no use getting on your high horse. So you stand there and take it. Maybe this *is* a guy who can deliver Mechanicsville. That's where organization comes in. You've got to have people who *know* these neighborhoods, who know who can or can't deliver a neighborhood or part of a neighborhood, and who can talk their language and who's willing to get his hands dirty."

"His hands dirty?" said Roger.

"Oh yes," said Wes. "After you've made your decision who to pay off, you've got to have somebody—you can't do it yourself—somebody who delivers the $20,000, $30,000, $40,000, whatever, to these operators. In cash. After you deliver the money, you've got no control over what happens to it, and no redress. You've made a verbal agreement with some character who doesn't speak English beyond 'Take it or leave it' and 'Fuck you.' "

"What does happen to it?"

"Assuming the guy can do what he says he can, he gets on the telephone early the morning of the election and he starts calling all the people on his list, all the potential voters, and he says,

" 'Whatcha say, baby? How 'bout getting your ass out of bed and coming on out here and fulfill your civic duty? I'm talking about voting, baby.'

"And the guy'll say, 'I don't know, man. What I got coming from it?'

"And your newest ardent supporter will say, 'Thirty dollars.'

"And the guy'll say, 'Can't you do no better'n that?'

"And your vote-getter-outer says, 'Thirty's top dollar this year, bro.'

"And the guy'll say, 'Okay . . . shit . . . Who I supposed to vote for?'

" 'Wesley Dobbs Jordan.'

" 'Say who? Wesley Dobbs Who da fuck?'

" 'Ne'mind, baby, just come on down here and I'll tell you.'

" 'Ohhhhhhkay. Shit. I'll see you down'eh. You *sure* you can't do no better'n thirty?' "

"When does he get paid?" asked Roger. "*How* does he get paid?"

"He gets paid after he votes," said the Mayor of Atlanta. "As for precisely *how*, that I can't tell you, because I've never seen it done and I don't intend to. But you can be sure of one thing: it's paid in cash."

Roger said, "What exactly does the . . . operator, or whatever he's called, what does he get out of it?"

"That I don't know, either, but judging by how much you give one of these people and how many votes you get in his district, I'd say he keeps about half or maybe a little more than that. Little enough to pay for such a vital service, is what everybody figures."

"But isn't that illegal?" asked Roger. "Isn't that buying votes?"

"That it is, Brother Roger, that it is, and except in the rare case there's no other way to win a citywide election. And today you'd better have half a million dollars set aside just for that, just for handing out cash to voters, and the more you can devote to that, the better your chances. A full million dollars increases your chances by 50 percent. And would you like to know who's guaranteeing André Fleet a million in get-out-the-vote money when the time comes?"

"Guaranteeing who?"

"André Fleet."

"The Operation Higher guy? He's going to run against you?"

"He's already running against me. He's making the rounds of the 'hoods, talking to every group that's willing to sit still to hear a speaker. He actually calls 'em that, *the 'hoods*. I'm not kidding! He must think this is a made-for-TV movie. The . . . *'hoods* . . ." Withering sarcasm.

"He's calling me everything in the book. I'm a blueblood, I'm part of the 'Morehouse elite.' I'm in the back pocket of the white Chamber of Commerce. I'm an Oreo, black on the outside and white on the inside, only I ain't even very black on the outside. I'm a 'beige half brother.' Direct quote. 'It's time Atlanta had its "first black Mayor."' Maynard Jackson, Andy Young, Bill Campbell, and me—we've all been 'high yella.' I'm not making this stuff up. You ought to hear him, Roger. People bring me tapes. You know what he looks like?"

"I've seen pictures of him."

"Well, he's tall, six-five or something, he's young, five years ago he was still playing in the NBA, he's got a lot of muscles, and the ladies love him, and he's *dark*, brother." The deep put-on voice. "He's strong coffee. He's from *the streets*, brother, from the 'hood. I'd like to know what *streets* he thinks he grew up on. His father owned a service station in West End, and his mother owned a beauty parlor called Rita's Beauty Box, and he grew up in Collier Heights. *Collier Heights.* What kind of real life does he think he grew up with in his *'hood*, squirrels and robins and lightning bugs? He's too much, Mr. André Fleet is, but people are listening to him. He's saying that ever since Maynard Jackson became the first black Mayor of Atlanta, the black political leadership has been in the hands of a light-skinned elite, the *Morehouse* elite, he keeps calling it, and somehow we're in league with the White Establishment—the Piedmont Driving Club elite, he calls it—to enrich each other at the expense of the ordinary people of the streets. All of us, Maynard Jackson, Andy Young, Bill Campbell—we're all the Morehouse elite, even Andy, who grew up in Louisiana and went to Dillard, in New Orleans, and Bill Campbell, who grew up in North Carolina and went to Vanderbilt, in Nashville, Tennessee. It's one of those situations in which the truth doesn't matter, because deep down we're all Morehouse bluebloods, no matter what the facts are. We're not really black. It's the worst kind of demagoguery, Roger, the worst kind of pandering—but he's scoring. Oh, he's scoring. We run our own polls, and we run our own focus groups out in his beloved 'hoods, and he's scoring. If the election was held today, I'd be in a lot of trouble. For one thing, he has a really solid commitment for a million dollars in get-out-the-vote money."

"You mentioned that," said Roger. "From whom?"

Wes Jordan cocked his head to one side and put on a cold smile. "Inman Armholster."

Roger was dumbfounded. He fought back the impulse to say "You're kidding." He ransacked his brain to try to figure out the logic of where this put or didn't put Wes in dealing with Armholster in the matter of Fareek Fanon. Finally he shook his head and said, "I'll be damned."

"Atlanta's a small world," said the Mayor. "If you look closely, there's a handful of people who do everything."

"How does that alter your position when it comes to . . . my client?"

"It doesn't," said Wes Jordan. "That's a completely separate matter." His face took on a familiar ironic smile. "What you've tossed in my lap this morning is something that could blow this city apart. I just wanted to make sure you had the full measure of Mr. Inman Armholster."

"Why would a man like that be backing someone like André Fleet?"

"Oh, it's not very complicated," said Wes. "He thinks he's going to win. In these all-black elections, I don't see white businessmen wasting time on ideology and issues. It's more like 'Can I do business with him or not?' and I'm sure Armholster is all ready to do business with André Fleet. That's what is known as 'the Atlanta Way.' "

"The Atlanta Way?"

"Exactly," said Wes Jordan, "the Atlanta Way. Did you ever unravel a baseball?"

"No."

"It's not a particularly illuminating exercise, but I used to enjoy doing it when I was ten or eleven years old. After you take the white horsehide cover off, you come across a ball of white string, or it's like string. There's about a mile of the stuff, once you start unraveling it, all this white string. Finally you get down to the core, which is black, a small hard black rubber ball. Well, that's Atlanta. The hard core, if we're talking politics, are the 280,000 black folks in South Atlanta. They, or their votes, control the city itself. Wrapped all around them, like all that white string, are three million white people in North Atlanta and all those counties, Cobb, DeKalb, Gwinnett, Forsyth, Cherokee, Paulding . . . So how do those white millions deal with that small black core? That's what leads to the Atlanta Way. Remember that billion-dollar expansion of the airport back when Maynard was Mayor? Well, Maynard got the 'business interests' together and said, 'Boys, here's a billion-dollar project.' So they're salivating, of course, and then he says, 'And 30 percent of it's going to minority contractors.' They gulped—but only for a moment. Seven hundred million was nothing to look down your nose at, either, and in no time they were salivating all over again, and they figured they'd just make do with the minority contractors some way or other. Later on Maynard said, 'That airport created twenty-five black millionaires.' He was proud of it, and he had every right to be. That's the Atlanta Way."

Roger said, "Where does my client figure in all this?"

"I don't know yet," said Wes Jordan. "Maybe not at all. I need to look into a few things and talk to some people."

"For God's sake, Wes, be careful who you talk to about this. All this thing has to do is get out on the rumor circuit and we might as well give up on containing it. It'll blow the city apart, as you say, on its own power."

"I'm mindful of that."

"What can I tell my colleagues?"

"You can tell them that I'm fully aware of the explosive nature of the situation, that I will try to think of the best way to approach Inman Armholster, and that I will do . . . something . . . quickly. You know, Roger, you and your *dream team* had better face up to the fact that an awful lot of people, it seems to me, already know about this thing. There's McNutter and his wife, who doesn't strike me as any taciturn pillar of discretion, and there are people at Tech, people in this Stingers organization, there's the dream team and all your families."

Roger was annoyed by the "dream team" crack, but all he said was, "I haven't said a word to Henrietta."

"Yeah, and she'll probably never forgive you later on. And there's Fareek Fanon and his buddies. The Cannon doesn't strike me as any rock of restraint, either. That kid is such a jerk."

"What do you mean?"

"What do I *mean*? That cretin thinks he's doing you a terrific favor by allowing you to get close enough to see the little diamonds in his ears."

Roger was alarmed. "Well, I'll grant you—"

"Don't worry," said the Mayor, "don't worry. At City Hall we don't subtract points from anybody for being a jerk. I just want you to understand that I don't know how long you can realistically count on this thing remaining secret. There's also the girl—what's her name?—Elizabeth, Elizabeth Armholster. She's got friends, no doubt. And Armholster—he's a hotheaded old tub of lard. I can't imagine him keeping this thing to himself for very long."

"All the more reason to talk to him sooner rather than later, Wes."

Wes Jordan eyed him from above a cynical and reproachful smile. "Kindly tell your colleagues that what I do I will do quickly. Tell them that you, the Mayor's old pal, have successfully engaged the Mayor." Then his face grew as hard and serious as Roger had ever seen it. "And tell them that whatever I do, it will not be with the interests of your client or of the House of Armholster in mind. I will act solely in the interests of the city."

Roger waited for a telltale twist of the lips . . . that never came.

Chapter

The Suicidal Freezer Unit

THE CROKER GLOBAL FOODS WAREHOUSE IN THE SAN FRANCISCO Bay Area is not in any part of the fabled Bay Area that ever stole the heart of a songwriter. Or, as far as that goes, a travel writer, not even a travel writer desperate for something different to write about. No, the Croker warehouse is on the wrong side of the bay, the east side, not the San Francisco side but the Oakland side, up toward El Cerrito, in Contra Costa County, just off the marshes, in the flatlands.

On those magical evenings in San Francisco when the fog rolls in from the Pacific Ocean and people emerge from the hotels on Nob Hill and go for brave walks down the staggeringly steep slopes of Powell Street and shiver deliciously in the chilly air and listen to the happy clapper clangor of the cable cars and the mournful foghorns of the freighters heading out to sea, and all at once life is a lovely little operetta from the year 1910—at that moment, likely as not, barely five miles to the east, a brutal sun has been roasting Contra Costa County for thirteen or fourteen hours, and the roof of the Croker warehouse is still swimming in caloric waves, even though the stars are out and the mercury remains swollen up to 90 degrees, down from 104 at 3 p.m., and the employees' parking lot, which is dirt, has been cooked to cinders until it's as parched, pocked, dusty, and godforsaken as the surface of Mars.

In short, Croker Global Foods is part of the engine room, the heavy plumbing, the industrial hardpan of this Elysian littoral known as the San Francisco Bay Area.

At about 8:45 on just such an evening a young man named Conrad Hensley drove into the employees' parking lot at Croker behind the wheel of a Hyundai hatchback family wagon. Since he was wearing a full set of long johns beneath his flannel shirt and jeans, he had the air conditioning roaring away on the high setting. He cruised up and down six or seven rows of cars, churning up quite a swirl of dust as he went, and finally found a spot over by a Cyclone fence with razor wire on top. Beyond the fence, against a vast California sky bursting with stars, he could see the silhouettes of a sewage substation, the smokestack of the Bolka Rendering works, the pilings of a freeway spur that was under construction, and coming toward him, overhead, low enough to touch, it seemed like, the big belly of an airplane grumbling along the glide path to the Oakland International Airport. Such was the view on this side of the scenic San Francisco Bay.

He opened the door of his little car, slid out, stood up, and turned his eyes away from the raw floodlights on the roof of the warehouse. He put his hands on his hips and rocked his torso, like an athlete loosening up before a match. At a glance he might have passed for an athlete. He was tall enough and young enough, and he looked strong enough, despite his slight build. The sleeves of his shirt were rolled up, and his forearms bulged beneath the long johns, tapering down to hands with long fingers that had been delicate just six months ago but were now so muscular, his wedding ring bit into the flesh like a cinch. How he would ever get it off, if he had to, was a good question. With his dark eyes and long dark eyelashes, his fair skin and delicate lips, he had the sort of face that made people wonder if he wasn't French or Spanish or Italian or Portuguese or Greek or something else sort of Mediterranean. Or to put it another way, he looked almost too pretty.

For that reason he had grown the droopy mustache that young men grow in hopes of appearing older and graver and . . . well, tougher. His shirt and faded jeans were the standard uniform of vast legions of young California males who work down below the managerial level, but his were so meticulously pressed you could see the creases, even in the shirt. Obviously Conrad Hensley was a young man who wanted order in his life.

In the next moment, however, this vision of clean-cut athletic sort-of-Mediterranean orderliness began to wilt. With his flannel shirt and his long johns on, he was already burning up. At least twenty trucks, perhaps as many as thirty, were over at the loading dock, big white trucks with CROKER in enormous letters on the sides, and the rage of the engines and the air brakes hurt his head. The flatulent sighs of the air brakes were what bothered him most of all . . . but he only needed a little push . . .

He slumped back into the Hyundai, into the driver's seat. His shoulders and his lower back began to ache. His sinuses felt congested, and so he snuffled and spit out the open door of the car. This was his central nervous system rebelling against the immediate future, which was eight more hours in the Suicidal Freezer Unit.

His mouth fell open slightly, and his eyes began to gaze far beyond the Cyclone fence, far beyond the Bolka Rendering works and the freeway pilings and the San Francisco Bay and the California littoral. It was the sort of look people get when they are about to consider what insignificant specks they are in the immense and incomprehensible scheme of things, if, indeed, there is any scheme at all.

You baby havee baby.

No doubt Sukie had forgotten she ever said it, but Conrad couldn't get it out of his mind. *You baby havee baby.* Before supper he and Jill had gone over to Sukie's 24-Hour Mini-Mart with the children. Jill had Christy in her arms and he was walking with Carl, and Sukie herself, who was at the checkout, had broken into a big smile and exclaimed, "You baby havee baby!" It took a moment before he realized what she was saying, which was: "You're babies having babies!"

His face had turned hot, he was so embarrassed, but what could he say? Here was a Cambodian woman who could barely speak English, a hearty woman who liked him—seemed to like him a great deal, in fact. Then why did he feel so insulted? Because she was so close to the truth! *You're babies having babies.* He and Jill were both twenty-three, and Jill looked about sixteen, and they had no business having two children, not in this day and age, and half the time Jill was like a third baby—but he chided himself for even thinking that. It was no use bringing Jill down. What would he have left? There was nobody else in the world he could fall back on, not a single solitary soul. Other people had their mom or dad or some relative somewhere, but he—*they* hit up on *him*! In the six months since he'd had this job at Croker Global Foods, both his mom and his dad—separately—they hadn't spoken to each other for seven years—both of them had tried to hit him up for loans. "Loans." They talked about his fourteen dollars an hour in a wholesale food warehouse as if it were all the money in the world.

Well, in a way it was—for somebody in his position. Even though he knew it was a pointless exercise, he sat there in his rattling old Hyundai tallying his mistakes all over again. *If* he hadn't gotten Jill pregnant when they were both eighteen; *if* he hadn't insisted—*insisted!*—on marrying her, *if* they hadn't gone ahead and had two children, he could have gone on to San Francisco State or perhaps even Berkeley instead of having to settle for two years at Mount Diablo Community College . . . By now he could have been embarked on a real . . . career . . . The one dream he had left now was that they, Conrad Hensley & Family, were going to live in a home they owned themselves . . . a condo in Danville . . . In his mind, as he sat here in the Hyundai, he could *see* Danville . . . a lovely leafy little town with pretty houses and pretty shops, an oasis not all that far from the dump they were renting now . . . Today, being payday, meant another $150 he could put aside, bringing the total to $4,622.85. The figures were already in his head, down to the penny. Another twelve months and he'd have a shot at a down payment . . . A condo in Danville . . .

He looked over at the warehouse. At night, like this, it was an enormous silhouette hulking behind the lights . . . a monster . . . His dad had no idea what he did in the warehouse for his fourteen dollars an hour. He hadn't even asked. His dad had never had a real job in his life. His father's face came bubbling up into his brain . . . the beard, the ponytail, both shot through with gray . . . the soft, sallow flesh . . . His dad wouldn't last ten minutes in the freezer unit at Coker Global Foods.

With that, Conrad had a terrible premonition. Suppose something happened in there tonight . . . Suppose he was crippled . . . Then what? . . . The big Japanese from San Francisco, the one they called Sumo, had wrenched his back doing practically nothing, and now he couldn't walk . . . Last week one of the Okies, Junior Frye, had had his ankle crushed by a pallet sliding across a patch of ice . . . A steady pain seized Conrad's lower back, and his sinuses became so congested they began to ache. He had never felt this bad at the start of the shift . . . Something was definitely wrong . . . Why didn't he just drive to a pay phone and call in sick . . . and blow it off . . . Pickers did it all the time . . .

Awwwwwwwww pull yourself together! Be a man—

Bot THOMP bot THOMP bot THOMP bot THOMP—a beat came pounding across the parking lot. Conrad glanced into the rearview mirror and saw a tornado of dust tearing along one of the rows of cars near the entrance. In a moment the higher frequencies reached him . . . a crazy skirl of electric guitars and a chorus of raw-throated young male voices screaming—*what*? Sounded like "Brain DEAD brain DEAD brain DEAD brain DEAD!" In no time the tornado seemed to be right on top of him, and there was no mistaking the insane screams: "Brain DEAD brain DEAD brain DEAD brain DEAD!"

The funnel of dust, lit a feverish yellow by the floodlights, came roaring around the last line of cars at a crazy speed . . . a terrific yowling . . . bot THOMP "Brain DEAD!" . . . Conrad twisted about in his seat just in time to see the car fishtail in the dirt behind him with a tremendous shower of dust—and then shoot straight at him and his open door. Terrified, he doubled up and recoiled into the seat. In the next moment it was all over, with the car parked right beside his somehow, just inches from his door's outer edge. The engine shut off, the yowling music was shut off, and a great illuminated dirty yellow cloud of dust was settling over everything.

His ears were ringing. His heart was flailing away. What idiot—

Emerging from the car, a very low bright red car with a rakishly swept-back windshield in front and an airfoil wing in the rear, was a creature with a long neck, a bulging Adam's apple, and a baseball cap. The filthy silhouette straightened up in the haze. It was one of his mates in the freezer unit.

Furious, Conrad sprang out of the little Hyundai and yelled, "Hey—*Kenny*!"

"Ayyyyyyyyyyyyyyy, Conrad!" A huge grin. "Crash'n'burn, old buddy!"

"Crash and *burn*? You're crazy, Kenny! You're gonna kill somebody!"

The great gangling youth, Kenny, seemed to enjoy that immensely. "Aw, come on, Conrad. 'At wasn't nothing but a little four-wheel drift."

"Yeah, right. *You're* a four-wheel drift. You're a lunatic."

Kenny cackled with delight. He was one of those rawboned young California Okies, to use the local term for Redneck, with a neck so big and long his Adam's apple seemed to bob up and down a foot every time he swallowed. His eerily pale blue eyes looked as wild as an Arctic dog's, an impression magnified by his scraggly mustache and two-week growth of beard. He wore a T-shirt advertising an Oakland radio station, KUK: "I DON'T GIVE A KUK . . . fuh nuthun but Kuntry Metal 107.3

FM." Around his midsection was the sort of six-inch-wide leather belt weight lifters use. His body was all bones and joints and sharp angles, except for his forearms and hands, which were huge, even bigger than Conrad's. The bill of his baseball cap was turned up, revealing the undersurface, upon which was inscribed, in felt marker, SUICIDE.

"*Brain* dead," said Conrad, shaking his head in disgust but also beginning to smile the reluctant smile you give a child who is naughty but has a certain roguish charm and knows it. "Now, that's sick."

"You heard it?"

"*Heard* it? Did I have a choice? I could've stayed home in Pittsburg and heard it."

Kenny started cackling again, and the cackle threw him into a cough, and the cough started him snuffling and hawking, and then he spit on the ground and began hopping about and pumping his arms in a type of jerky dance that was in vogue among the Country Metal headbangers, as they were called. He started singing or, rather, singsonging, rapping, in a nasal voice:

Gon' put my jimbo
Up yo' shanks akimbo!
Without no shuckin' words,
No mind-suckin' words!
You get my meanin'?
Or you want a skull cleanin'?
Gon' peel yo' cap, I said
Peel yo' cap, I said
Peel yo' cap, I said
Peel yo' cap, I said
Peel yo' cap, I said said said said said
Brain DEAD *brain* DEAD *brain* DEAD *brain* DEAD!

"*Peel yo' cap?*" said Conrad. "What's *peel yo' cap* supposed to mean?"

"You don't know *peel yo' cap*? 'At's like what they do in a autopsy. They cut the top a your skull off, so they can get at your brain. That's called peeling your cap. That's jailhouse talk. They'll say, 'Don' try to git over on me, motherfucker, or I'll peel yo' cap for you.' "

"Oh, that's terrific," said Conrad, sniffling and then hawking deep in his throat. "You got any idea how sick that is—I mean, a *song* about that? That's *very* sick, Kenny. And you wanna know what's even sicker? The fact that you know that piece a garbage by heart."

"Whaddaya talking about? That's by the Pus Casserole! That's their new one! Hey, lemme show you something."

"The *Pus Casserole*," said Conrad, shaking his head.

Kenny motioned toward his bright red car and then coughed again and began a snuffling and scuffling so deep in his throat it seemed to reach down into his very lungs. The car was a snub-tailed two-door sports model with RAPIER XSI written like a speed blur across the side.

"When'd you get *this*?" asked Conrad, sneezing, snuffling, hawking, and spitting again.

"Just got it. Lemme show you something."

He opened the door, collapsed the back of the front seat forward, and motioned toward the interior. Conrad stuck his head in. There was no back seat; it had been removed. In its place was a sheet of plywood that ran from the base of the front seat to the rear window. Set in the plywood were two enormous stereo speakers.

"Twenty-inch speakers, man. Those things got so much tympanum, you're sittin' there in the front seat and they'll blow the hair around on your head and make your ears flap. God's honest truth. Your ears'll *flap*, and your ribs'll rattle. Those speakers pull so many amps—lemme show you this."

Now he took Conrad around to the rear of the car and opened the trunk. The two young men coughed, snuffled, hawked, and spit in unison. Mounted in the floor of the trunk were a pair of big fans aimed in toward the backs of the speakers and a tangle of wires and equipment.

"See those fans? That's to cool 'em off. They pull so many amps, without the fans they'd burn up. I'm talking about *catch fire*."

Conrad stood up and gave Kenny a long, level look. "How much'd that cost you, Kenny?" *Cost you, Kenny* came out in a wheeze; so he cleared his throat.

"The fans?"

"Everything. The fans, the speakers, the car . . ." He made a motion with his hand. "The whole thing."

"Awwwww, AGT paid for it." He snuffled deeply and spit and rubbed his eye sockets with his fingers. AGT was a finance company well known in Alameda and Contra Costa Counties. His watery eyes lit up. "These speakers, you can go boom-bombing with 'em. I already done it."

"*What* bombing?"

"You know. *Boom*-bombing. That's like when you drive past a buncha cars and you turn up your sound system to max-q and like the vibrations set off the car alarms?" The way he said it, Okie-style, it sounded like a question. "I was going through Danville coming over here, and you know that section over there with the houses with those big old roofs, slate or tile or whatever it is? I betcha I boomed off six or eight cars. People running out the doors . . ."

Conrad was appalled. "Not with 'Brain Dead,' I hope. Danville's a nice town."

Kenny smiled and nodded toward Conrad's Hyundai hatchback. "Whyn't you fix yours up?" He had a frog in his throat and scuffled it out. "You can fit a couple of twenty-inchers in the back a yours, no trouble at all."

"Yeah, that'd be real great, Kenny. Why'd I want to take the back seat of my car out? I got a wife and two children."

"Ummmm. Yeah, well, that's cool."

"And why would I want to go *boom*-bombing in Danville? I *like* Danville. I want to *live* in Danville. I'm gonna buy a *condo* in Danville." He snuffled, swallowed, and gave Kenny's car a wave of dismissal. "Here's *thousands of dollars* you're spending, and for what, Kenny? The only reason I'm working in there in that freezer is to get the down payment on a condo. Soon as we get a condo in Danville, me and Croker Global Foods're history. I'm not even gonna come near this place."

"Yeah, well . . . like I say, that's cool. But you oughta loosen up, Conrad, loosen up and lighten up."

"No, you're wrong," said Conrad. "I oughta *tighten* up. So should you. You ever listen to yourself? Or listen to me? Or anybody else who works in the freezer? Everybody's coughing and sneezing and taking pills all night. Everybody's *nose* is running, and this is Contra Costa County, California, one beautiful, hot, dry day after another, and the whole bunch of us, we sound like—well, whyn't you sit back and listen sometime."

"That's nothing but freezer flu, man. Don't mean a thing."

"Nothing but freezer flu, hunh? Just because there's a little name for it, don't think that makes it any better."

"Look," said Kenny, "the pay is good, fourteen dollars an hour.

Where else you gonna get that? Where else you even gonna get a job? There's no *jobs* out there, Conrad! Shit. Be happy. Crash and burn."

"No, Kenny, *not* crash and burn. You got to start thinking about where you're gonna be five years from now."

"Five *years* from now . . ." Kenny shook his head. "You say you're gonna get a condo in Danville. Well, lotsa luck, old buddy. I hope you do. But it iddn' gonna happen from working a job and saving money. Maybe your folks're gonna help you out."

Conrad laughed without smiling. "That's a joke. They hit *me* up for money. What makes you think I can't do it?"

"You ever know anybody did it? It don't happen. Sooner or later you run into the bald man with the necktie."

"What bald man with the necktie?"

"You don't know 'Easy Payments'? By Snuff Out?"

"No, I don't know 'Easy Payments' by Snuff Out."

"Jesus Christ, Conrad! You never even *heard* it? You never heard

"Nine to five you park yo' butt
Beneath the bitch box on the wall
And lap up all that crap inside
The rut they make you crawl.
So, yo, go buy yo' own death, bro,
And die on the in*stall*ment plan,
'Fo' they cut yo' nuts and hang you
From the necktie on the bald man."

Conrad sighed and gave Kenny a long, serious look. "You know your problem?" said Conrad. "You actually believe that stuff. You actually take it seriously."

"Aw, for Christ's sake, Conrad."

"Who do you think writes these songs?" said Conrad. "It's people with neckties and suits and big houses in places like Danville, that's who, and they make their money off people like you, and you just let them put all this stupid *poison* in your brain. You let them put *No!* in your heart. Take my advice, Kenny. You oughta forget about the Pus Casserole and Snuff Out and Crash'n'Burn and what was that other one?—the Child Abusers? You oughta stop listening to all that . . . *garbage*!"

"And like I said, you oughta lighten up."

"And like *I* said, you oughta tighten up." Conrad tapped his forehead. "Lotta screws loose in there, Kenny."

Conrad turned his back and went over to the Hyundai to pick up his lunch bag from the front seat, and Kenny howled, and the laughter made Conrad realize how many nights had begun this way. Kenny would recite some sick Country Metal lyrics or recount some vile marauding adventure he'd had, and Conrad would register his shock and disapproval and turn his back, and Kenny would find it all enormously amusing. With his determination to lead a serious and orderly life, he was Kenny's perfect straight man, as he knew very well. Here at the warehouse Kenny was the king of the crash'n'burners, and the crash'n'-burners sure did outnumber the straightforward strugglers like himself. He would've liked to bring Mr. Wildrotsky, who taught the American history course at Mount Diablo, a real old sixties type who wore muttonchops and wire-rim glasses and was always talking about the "working class" and the "bourgeoisie" and showing them pictures of coal miners with dirty faces—wouldn't it be funny to bring old Mr. Wildrotsky over to Croker one night and show him what the "working class" looked like today, in real life . . . bring him over and introduce him to Kenny and the crash'n'burners . . .

THE FREEZER WAS a warehouse within a warehouse, a vast refrigerated chamber down at one end of the building behind a wall covered in sheets of galvanized metal studded with rivets. A door, big as a barn's, covered in the same galvanized metal and battered as an old bucket, hung from a track. It had been opened for the start of the shift, revealing a curtain of heavy-gauge vinyl clouded by oily smears and shales of ice. The curtain had a slit up the middle so that the workmen could go in and out without too much of the cold air escaping. The freezer was maintained at dead zero Fahrenheit.

Inside, there were no windows. The chamber remained in an eternal frigid gray dusk, twenty-four hours a day. Stacks of cartons, tons of them, many of them packed with meat and fish, reached up three stories high on metal racks. Way up on the ceiling you could make out lengths of gray galvanized metal air-conditioning ducts doubling back and forth upon themselves like intestines. Between the ducts strips of fluorescent tubing emitted a feeble bluish haze. The extreme cold seemed to congeal the very light itself and remove every trace of color.

Kenny, Conrad, and some thirty other pickers stood about just inside the entryway, waiting for the shift to start. They were clad in the lumpish, padded metal-gray Zincolon gloves and freezer suits with Dynel fur collars the warehouse issued. On the backs of the jackets was written CROKER in big yellow letters that looked lemony in the fluorescent light. Beneath the freezer suits they wore so many combinations of long johns, shirts, jerseys, sweaters, insulated vests, and sweatsuits, they were puffed up like blimps or the Michelin Tire Man. Kenny had the hood of a sweatshirt pulled up over his head, with just the bill of his baseball cap sticking out, upturned and emblazoned SUICIDE. His wild eyes seemed to be beaming out from within a shadowy hole. Three of the freezer pickers were black, three were Chinese, one was Japanese, and one was Mexican, but most were Okies, like Kenny, and half the Okies had adopted Kenny's SUICIDE regalia. They were known as the crash'n'-burners, and they called the freezer the Suicidal Freezer Unit, a term Conrad couldn't get out of his head.

The way the jets of breath fog streamed from their noses and mouths was the first indication of how cold it actually was, but any picker foolish enough to try to work without his gloves on would soon have another. Each of them operated a pallet jack, a small but heavy electric vehicle with which you could jack up a loaded pallet and move it to another part of the warehouse. You stood on the back of the jack, behind its metal motor housing. It was simple to use. But if you touched the levers or handlebars with your bare hands in this ice box, your flesh would freeze to the metal. (And just try pulling it loose.)

To one side of the entrance was a wooden table manned by the night foreman, Dom, an old fellow—in the freezer, forty-eight was old—who looked a mile wide in his plaid Hudson Bay jacket. He wore a navy watch cap pulled down over his forehead and ears, which made the top half of his big round head look ridiculously tiny. Bursts of mouth fog pumped out of his mouth as he studied the printout order sheets in front of him. He had a little cylindrical remote microphone clipped to the collar of his jacket.

The boys were beginning to feel the cold creep in. It made your nose run even more. A chorus of sniffles, sneezes, snufflings, hawkings, coughs, and spitting welled up. Every now and then some picker would spit right on the floor, which made Conrad's flesh crawl.

Dom's deep voice sounded out over the wall speaker system:

"Okay, men! Before we get started, just a couple things. There's good news and bad news. First, the bad news. We been getting complaints from over at Bolka Rendering that somebody here's been using their parking lot for tailgate parties . . . Kenny."

"Ayyyyyyyyyyyy," said Kenny. "Why you looking at me?"

"Why?" said Dom. "Because two nights ago—or it was in the morning—the sun was up—and they're coming to work over there, and not only's there a buncha guys sprawled shit-faced all over their parking lot, but there's some kinda boom box playing this song where they're screaming, 'Eat shit.' Guy tells me that's all you could hear over half a Contra Costa County, 'EAT SHIT, EAT SHIT, EAT SHIT.' That's really terrific, that's very high class."

"Oooooooo, ooooooooo, ooooooooo!" whooped the crash'n'burners.

" 'Eat Shit'?" asked Kenny in a pseudo-startled voice. "Iddn'at by the Child Abusers?"

"Whoever it's by, it's disgusting," boomed Dom's voice over the speaker system. "There's a lotta women go to work at Bolka in the morning. I hope you realize that."

"Ooooooooo, ooooooooooo, ooooooooooooooo!" Now the pickers really let out whoops. Dom's concern for the tender sex, especially in the form it took at the Bolka Rendering works, struck them as a howl, worthy of maximum derision.

Dom shook his head. "Okay, you can laugh, but if it don't stop, somebody over *here's* gonna get child-abused. Capeesh? . . . Okay?" Lest the whoops start again, he hurried on. "All right, now here's the good news. We got a good turnout, and this is the end a the month, and so it looks like a light night. So whenever you men complete the orders, you can get outta here." Dom always said "you men" when he was appealing to their better natures.

More whoops, only now with a note of honest elation. Light nights they loved. Toward the end of the month, many of the hotels and the institutional kitchens that operated on monthly budgets—the prisons, hospitals, nursing homes, company cafeterias—cut back on their orders. On top of that, there had been a general falling off of business. The result was nights like tonight, on which the pickers could work five, six, seven hours and get paid for eight, so long as they got the orders out.

The boys converged on the foreman's table to pick up the order printouts, which were stacked in a wire basket. Now the great dreary chamber was filled with the squeals of rubber-soled boots pivoting on the concrete slab, the whines of the pallet jacks' electric motors starting up, the jolts of power hitting the driveshafts, the rumble of the wheels rolling over the concrete floor.

Conrad had slipped his order sheet onto the clipboard on his handlebars before he actually focused on what it was . . . Santa Rita . . . He ached a little more and rubbed his nose with the back of his glove. Santa Rita, down near the town of Pleasanton, was the Alameda County jail, one of eight prisons Croker supplied. Santa Rita orders always went on and on and included a lot of heavy cases of cheap meat. He scanned the sheet . . . twelve cases of beef shanks, Row J, Slot 12 . . . Each case weighed eighty pounds. In loading up a pallet the trick was to put the heaviest cases on the bottom and build up to the lightest. So that was how he'd have to start the night—lifting half a ton of frozen beef shanks in eighty-pound bricks.

He stood on the back of his pallet jack and squeezed the accelerator levers. With a whine and a jolt the machine came to life, and he headed down the aisle bearing an empty pallet on the blades before him. The boys were already plunging full-decibel into the frenzy of the light night . . . All over the freezer you could hear whining motors, squealing boots, cries, shouts, oaths, the crashing sound of pickers slinging heavy frozen cartons onto the pallets . . . They leaned into the racks' icy slots, waddled in, crawled in, swollen gray creatures with Dynel fur collars, and then they crawled back out, waddled back out, slithered back out, bearing frozen cartons of food, fat gray ice weevils swarming over the racks in a terribly diligent frenzy; and he was one of them.

His destination, Row J, Slot 12, was deep in the gloom of the freezer. He looked into the slot at floor level and sighed a long jet of breath fog. It was empty. He looked into the slot above it. It was about a quarter full, with the cartons stacked at the rear of the two pallets that formed the slot's floor. So he did the usual. He hopped up on top of the jack's motor housing and hoisted himself into the upper slot on his haunches. The slots were only four feet high. He duck-walked across a pallet toward the cartons stacked in the rear. The pallet's slats sagged in a weary, spongy way beneath his feet. He sank to his knees, hooked his hand over a carton in the uppermost row, let his body flop down on the icy blocks beneath him, and started pulling. It wouldn't budge; it seemed to be frozen fast between the cartons on either side. He started yanking on it . . . grunts . . . bursts of mouth fog . . . It was dark in here . . . inside this cliff of ice. He struggled to rock the carton free. The pressure on his fingers, his forearm, his elbow and shoulder was tremendous. His eyes started watering, and the rims of his eyelids began to burn.

Finally, with a hot burst of fog, he yanked the carton loose and began pulling it toward him. He got off his knees and rose up in a crouch once more. Then he went into a deep squat and tried to pick up this frozen eighty-pound dead weight without straining his back. Since he couldn't straighten up, he had to pull the carton in toward his midsection and duck-waddle to the mouth of the slot. Eighty pounds, frozen solid, more than half his own weight—already his shoulders, his arms, his hands, his lower back, the big muscles of his thighs were in agony. Despite the frigid temperature, his cheeks and forehead were hot from the exertion. At the edge of the slot he set the carton down, slid the four feet to the floor below, and grabbed the carton in a bear hug. For an instant he staggered before getting his feet squarely under the weight. Then he squatted again and lowered the carton onto the pallet on the front of his jack. When he stood up, a jolt of pain went through his lower back. He glanced down—

Blearily, in the periphery of his vision, he could see little glints and sparkles. Ice crystals were forming in his mustache. Sweat had run off his face, and mucus had flowed from his nose, and now his mustache was beginning to freeze up. He took the glove off his right hand and ran his fingers through his hair. There were little icicles in the hair on his head and in his eyebrows, and a regular little stalactite had formed on the end of his nose. He looked at his hand. He made a fist. Then he undid it and splayed his fingers out and turned them this way and that. They were extraordinarily broad, his fingers. From yanking, and carrying the eighty-pound carton, they were pumped up, bulging with little muscles. They were . . . stupendous . . . and grotesque at the same time. His hand looked as if it belonged to someone twice his size.

He stood still for a moment. The noise in the freezer had risen to a merry old ruckus. The whines of the jacks came from every direction . . . the crashes of product hitting the pallets . . . the shouts, the cries.

"Crash'n'burn!"—the unmistakable high nasal cry of Kenny himself somewhere a few rows away.

"Crash'n'burn!" sang Kenny's boys with the SUICIDE caps in a choral response.

Backing out of a slot nearby, here came a fat gray ice weevil wearing a Panzer helmet . . . Herbie Jonah was his name . . . He had a huge carton hugged into his abdomen. Jets of fog came out of his mouth with a regular beat. Conrad couldn't hear him, but he knew exactly what he was saying, because Herbie said the same thing all night long as he struggled with the frozen blocks: "Mother*fuck*er, mother*fuck*er, mother-*fuck*er." Over there, on the aisle, sailing past on his pallet jack at a real crash'n'burn clip came a wiry little crash'n'burner known as Light Bulb, his SUICIDE cap jammed down practically over his eyes, the hood of his sweatshirt sticking up with a funny point above the top of his head, as if he were an elf. For someone so small, he was amazingly strong. The pallet on the front of his jack was already piled high with product.

"Crash'n'burn!" Kenny sang out from somewhere, this time in falsetto.

And Light Bulb, perched on the back of his pallet jack, threw back his head and gave a falsetto yodel of his own—"Crash'n'burn!"—and zipped past.

Suddenly Dom's deep voice was bellowing over the speakers: "Cleanup! Cleanup! Betty 4! Betty 4! Cleanup! Chop chop!"

This meant a spill had occurred. "Betty 4" was Row B, Slot 4. Some product had slid off a pallet as it went around a curve; or some picker had dropped something from an upper slot; or an entire jack—picker, pallet, and all—had turned over, and product was spilled on the floor. Cleanup was not a verb but a noun, a job category. There were two cleanups, two Filipinos, known as Ferdi and Birdie, both of them too small to be pickers, who did nothing but clean up product that spilled or got smashed on the concrete slab. There would be plenty of spills tonight. There were plenty of them every light night, as the boys ya-hooed through the frozen phosphorescent haze in the name of the god of the Suicidal Freezer Unit, testosterone.

Conrad listened to the crazy din of his mates—and then caught him-self. He was letting *No!* creep into his heart. What he was doing in this place had nothing to do with jacks and slots and pallets and product or with crashing and burning. It had to do with a new life for his young family. With a deep breath, a sigh, and a long jet of breath fog, he hopped back up on the motor housing of his pallet jack and hoisted himself back into the upper slot. A weevil with *Yes!* in his heart, he burrowed back into the cliff for eleven more eighty-pound blocks of frozen beef shanks. The evening had just begun.

BY THE TIME he had loaded all twelve cartons onto the pallet on the front of his jack, his face was burning up, and his mustache was so full of ice he could feel its weight pulling at his skin. Quickly he scanned the printout again . . . Twenty-four cases of beef patties . . . Hadn't even noticed that . . . Row D, Slot 21 . . . fifty pounds apiece . . . Didn't help to dwell on it . . . He headed off on the jack, bearing the twelve cases of beef shanks on the pallet before him.

Down the aisle sailed Kenny, standing up on the back of his pallet jack. His eyes burned crazily in the shadow beneath his SUICIDE brim and the sweatshirt hood. The pallet on the front of his jack seemed to be more than half loaded already. As soon as he saw Conrad coming toward him, he broke into a big grin and yelled out, "Yo! Whoa!"

Conrad released his accelerator lever and drifted to a stop, and Kenny pulled up beside him. "Yo! Conrad! What the hell's happened to your *mus*tache?"

"Whattaya mean?" said Conrad. Kenny's own mustache was heavily flecked with frost.

"It's fucking turned to ice!" said Kenny. "You look like you got a couple a icicles hanging out your nose!"

Conrad pulled the glove off his right hand. It was true. His mustache was frozen solid from his nostrils to where it dropped down on either side of his mouth.

"I swear to God," said Kenny. "Looks exactly like a couple icicles hanging out your nose. Whattaya been doing?"

Conrad gestured toward the cartons of beef shanks on his pallet. "Santa Rita," he said.

Kenny said, "Like lifting the *QE2*, iddn'it?"

With that he shot a whining jolt of electricity to his driveshaft and sped on down the aisle.

Conrad burrowed on, a weevil with the best of them, into the Salisbury steaks, fishburgers, gravy stock, ice cream, orange juice, cut fava beans, American cheese, margarine, pepperoni pizza, chipped beef, bacon, and waffles, and the ruckus rose, and the cries rang out—*Crash'n'burn!*—and the product crashed, and the pickers yahooed, and Dom's big voice bellowed over the speakers: "Cleanup! Cleanup! Kilo

9! Kilo 9! Come on, Ferdi! You, too, Birdie! On the double!"—and the light-night frenzy ran through the chamber like a rogue hormone.

As soon as he retrieved the final item on the Santa Rita printout (a dozen cases of frozen buckwheat waffles), Conrad rubbed his nose with his glove to break up the rings of ice that had formed inside his nostrils. A thick, restless fog was beginning to roil around the tops of the racks from the heat of the machinery and the bodies of the struggling human beings. The fluorescent tubing gave off a wan tubercular-blue glimmer behind it. Conrad's pallet was piled perilously high with product. He eased the jack toward the freezer door. He pulled a handle hanging from a chain, and the door rolled open hydraulically. Slowly he drove through the slit in the vinyl curtain and out onto the dock's concrete apron.

As soon as he emerged from the freezer, he was engulfed, overwhelmed, by heat. The temperature out here was still well up into the eighties. The trucks were roaring and sighing; a few were already pulling out for the nightly delivery runs. All up and down the platform were great heaps of cartons, drums, canisters, sacks, resting on pallets the pickers had deposited. He could feel the ice melting from his hair and his eyebrows and his mustache and streaming down his face. What must he look like to the loaders and the drivers and everyone else out here in the real world? A poor encrusted weevil emerging from the polar depths, a mutant, bleary-eyed, blinking its way into a sweltering California night . . . He straightened up in an instinctive bid for dignity.

And yet when he deposited the pallet and its prodigious load at Bay 17, neither the checker nor the loaders nor the driver seemed to take any special notice of him. They were used to such creatures, the gray weevils who came crawling out from under the ice . . .

Before heading back into the freezer, Conrad got off the jack and stood and stretched. His long johns were soaked clear through from humping product for so long without a break.

He gazed out beyond the big white Croker trucks and the glare of the loading platform, out beyond the parking lot and the flatlands and the marshes. There was such a profusion of stars, they seemed to be swelling and surging in the sky. Below them, near the horizon, he could see other lights twinkling . . . San Francisco . . . Sausalito . . . Tiburon, he guessed it was . . . just across the bay . . . and so far off. Might as well be another continent. What were people his age, twenty-three, doing over there at this moment beneath that exuberant, starry sky? He couldn't even imagine it, and he steeled himself against submitting to such an idle exercise, for that would be inviting *No!* into his heart. The leafy town of Danville, in Contra Costa County, was as near to the fabled coast of California as he cared, or dared, to aspire.

With a great effort he beckoned *Yes!* back into his heart. It was slow in coming.

JUST BEFORE CONRAD reached the entrance to go back into the freezer, there was a tremendous clatter. A picker from the warehouse's main section, Dry Foods, pulled up ahead of him driving an electric truck known as a tugger, pulling three metal wagons piled high with product . . . drums of detergent, canisters of tomato paste, sacks of pinto beans, huge jugs of red food dye . . . There was no end to it. The tugger had a seat like a golf cart's, and perched on it was a chubby redheaded fellow, no older than Conrad himself, wearing a short-sleeved sport shirt, work gloves, and crepe-soled boots. The Dry Foods pickers sometimes drew orders with one or two frozen items and were told to just go into the freezer and get them. They weren't dressed for it, but they could take it for the few minutes they might have to be in there.

This one, the chubby redhead, was studying the freezer's huge door. He couldn't figure out how to open it. Conrad drove up beside him and pointed to the chain and then pulled it for him. As the door rolled open, he gestured toward the slit in the vinyl curtain as if to say, "After you."

The redhead eased his tugger and his wagons on through, and Conrad entered behind him. The light-night ruckus had not died down for a moment. Shouts, oaths, crashing sounds, whines . . . and Kenny's voice singing out through the icy haze and the roiling fog:

"Crash'n'burn!"

"*Crash'n'burn!*" answered the crash'n'burners from every aisle, every row, every rack, every icy, hazy, fogbound corner.

Baffled, the boy on the tugger swiveled his head this way and that. All at once he took off for the racks, his tugger whining shrilly from all the juice he was feeding it.

Conrad drove his jack over to the foreman's desk. Kenny was standing there beside his jack studying a printout he had just picked up.

"Shit," he said to nobody in particular. Then he caught sight of Conrad and held up the sheet and said, "Nat'n'Nate's," and made a face.

Nat'n'Nate's was a big old delicatessen in San Francisco just south of Market Street. The pickers hated Nat'n'Nate's orders because of the heavy cases of processed meat.

Conrad pulled a printout from the wire basket . . . Morden Rehabilitation, up in Santa Rosa . . . He scanned the sheet . . . Shouldn't be too bad an order. He got up on the pallet jack and drove into the canyons amid the ice cliffs.

He soon found himself humping product just one slot away from Kenny. He could hear Kenny grunting and swearing to himself. Conrad was loading a case of spareribs on his jack when Kenny emerged from the cliff embracing an eighty-pound carton of processed turkey. All at once, there was a sharp whine and a terrific clattering. Here came the redheaded Dry Foods picker, barreling out of a row on his tugger and pulling his three wagons full of product. He turned to go up the aisle. He was turning too fast. Instead of straightening out, he kept on turning in a huge crazy arc. The centrifugal force sent the wagons up on two wheels. They were going over. A massive gush of product hit the slick concrete of the aisle. A huge sack split open. *Pellets!* No, pinto beans, streaming in every direction. Hard and smooth and slippery as ball bearings they were. A loaded pallet jack came speeding up the aisle from behind . . . Panzer helmet . . . Herbie Jonah . . . Herbie veered to keep from crashing into the spill. His jack hit the streaming pinto beans, skidded, then went into a ferocious spin. Herbie, the jack, the loaded pallet—spinning, flinging frozen product in every direction, careening straight toward Kenny, who had his back turned with an eighty-pound block of frozen meat clutched to his midsection—

"Kenny!"

—Herbie, screaming, trying to keep his grip on the handlebars of the jack. Bango! He was thrown off. He hit the floor. The floor turned red. *Red!* Kenny turned his head. He could see Herbie's jack coming straight at him, but he was frozen by his own compulsive grip on the carton. Conrad sprang forward, dove at Kenny headfirst, bowled him over. A tremendous suffocating crash enveloped their bodies . . . a sea of red . . . They went sliding through a blood-red muck on the pinto beans . . . Kenny and Conrad . . . a tangle of arms and legs . . . racks and cartons wheeling overhead in the roiling fog . . . The moment stretched out endlessly and then stopped.

Conrad was upside down on his head and his right shoulder, looking up at his legs—which were *red!*—jackknifed over Kenny's body—*covered in—my blood?* Slowly, not at all sure that he could, he rolled his legs off Kenny. Everywhere—*red!* Hemorrhaging!—but he couldn't figure out where he was cut.

Kenny, lying next to him, contorted, seemed to be trying to roll over on his back. Cartons, drums, canisters, sacks were strewn about in the horrible red muck . . . A Panzer helmet, a body, a gray weevil, Herbie Jonah, smeared red . . . Herbie tried to sit up, but the heel of his hand skidded on the pinto beans, and he flopped back down into the red muck again. There was Herbie's pallet jack, smashed into Kenny's. The motor housing of Kenny's was ripped off its base. The levers of the two machines were twisted about each other. The slats on the two pallets were snapped into huge splinters. Both machines were jammed against one of the black metal uprights of the racks.

Out in the middle of the aisle all three of the Dry Food picker's wagons were turned over, but the tugger itself was still upright, nosed into the row on the other side, and the chubby redhead was still on his seat, slumped over toward his handlebars and moaning.

One of the black pickers, Tony Chase, came running toward Conrad and Kenny. Suddenly his legs went out from under him. The pinto beans. He landed in the red muck. Conrad managed to get up to a kneeling position. He could feel the pinto beans, hard as marbles, rolling underneath his knees. His Zincolon suit was dripping red—*blood!*

But wait a minute . . . Blood wouldn't look like this, couldn't possibly remain this bright . . . Then he saw them, two shattered ten-gallon jugs . . . red food dye . . . The jugs and the pinto beans . . . a flash flood of the stuff . . .

"Can't get my hand . . . can't get my hand . . ."

It was the Dry Foods picker, still hunched over the handlebars of his tugger, moaning, "Can't get my hand."

Somehow the boy had taken the glove off his right hand and neglected to put it back on before he took hold of the handlebars to steer his tugger into the turn, and his fingers and his palm had frozen to the metal.

Kenny was sitting up, staring at the wreckage of the two jacks. It was pretty obvious. If he had stayed where he was, squatting down beside his jack with the carton of frozen turkey in his arms, he would have been crushed. Conrad's diving tackle had knocked him toward the aisle. Conrad had thrown his own body directly into the path of Herbie's careening jack. Had his legs been six inches higher as he dove, they would have been crushed as the two motor housings smashed together. Had they been six inches lower, they would have been crushed by the scythe-like swing of Herbie's pallet.

The manic light had gone out in Kenny's wild blue eyes. Pickers were converging upon the spill. Kenny opened his mouth, but no words came out.

From above, Dom's voice, over the speakers: "Cleanup! Cleanup! Whiskey 8! Whiskey 8! Chop chop! Birdie! Ferdi! Both a you! On the double! Got a whole aisle out over here! Whiskey 8! Whiskey 8!"

And then Kenny, still sitting in the red muck, spoke more softly than Conrad had ever heard him speak before. "Jesus Christ, Conrad . . . you just saved my life."

THE TWO CLEANUPS, Ferdi and Birdie, earned their pay this time all right. There must have been a ton of product strewn about in the aisle and Row W, split open, staved in, mashed, crushed, all of it beginning to freeze to the floor in an icy red slush. It was a miracle that no one was badly hurt. The padded freezer suits saved them, probably, the suits and all the other stuff they swaddled themselves in. The worst off was the chubby redhead from Dry Foods who, sure enough, had ripped a chunk of flesh off his hand trying to remove it from the handlebar. The pickers who had hit the deck looked a lot worse than he did, however. They looked like survivors of a bomb explosion. There was red dye smeared all over their Zincolon jumpsuits, their gloves, their heads, their faces. Half of Conrad's hair was soaked with the dye; so was Herbie's. One side of Kenny's mustache was a sopping red. It looked as if he had been shot in the nostril.

Dom came over and took the whole bunch of them out to the loading platform to give them a break, let them warm up, and see if they were okay. Godalmighty! The checkers and the loaders looked at them now, all right! The muck had frozen to their freezer suits, and it was melting. The suits seemed to be oozing and festering blood. Every now and then a pinto bean would fall off, looking like a bloody clot. Conrad began to shiver, right out here in the stifling heat. He'd almost gotten killed, or maimed, him and Kenny both.

Kenny was abnormally quiet. He stuck by Conrad's side. He'd start to talk about what had happened, and he'd say, "I guess . . . I guess . . ." or something equally vague, and his eyes would look as if they were pinned on something a mile away.

And then Herbie came over and told Kenny he was truly sorry, but there had been no way he could control his jack once it hit the pinto beans. It seemed so strange, because nobody had ever heard Herbie express anything approaching a tender sentiment before.

"Oh, I know that," said Kenny. "I heard you yell, and I saw the goddamn thing coming at me, and I just froze. I had'at goddamn carton a processed turkey in my hands, and I couldn't even drop it or nothing. I just froze. If this character here . . ." He nodded toward Conrad and smiled faintly and then that smile, too, died on his lips, and he got the far-off look again.

Dom came over and told the boys that the lunch break was coming pretty soon and they might as well stay out here until the horn sounded and go straight in to lunch. Then he drew Conrad aside and put his arm around his shoulders and said, "You okay? You showed us something in there, kid."

Conrad didn't know what to say except that he was, in fact, okay. He was still too shaken to take any pleasure in the compliment.

The lunch break was at 12:30 a.m. in what was known as the break room, which was nothing but a clearing in the main work bay, Dry Foods, with 4-by-8-foot sheets of raw plywood serving as walls. The freezer pickers had taken off their Zincolon freezer suits, the thermal vests, the hats and gloves and wadding and swaddling, and were sitting in plastic chairs at the break room's heavy-duty folding tables. Stripped down to shirts and jeans again, they looked whipped and clammy from lifting so much product at such a furious pace and sweating so much inside their insulation. Kenny was slumped back in a chair right across the table from Conrad. Conrad had just opened his paper bag and taken out one of the two meat-loaf sandwiches Jill had fixed him. A couple of dozen pickers, carrying their Igloo coolers, were lined up waiting to cook their lunches in the microwave ovens over by the plywood walls. They kept turning their heads and looking at him. He figured it was because he and Kenny presented such a spectacle, smeared red the way they were.

Light Bulb came over from the microwave with a steaming plastic picnic plate and sat down and said, "Jeeeeeesus Christ—how you guys dooooin'? You okaaaaaay?" Light Bulb stuttered, but he stuttered on the vowels rather than the consonants. By the time he reached the *okaaaaaay*, the little crash'n'burner was no longer looking at both of them but squarely at him, Conrad. He had a glistening look on his face. Conrad could feel himself blushing. For the first time he let the thought form in his mind: They all think I'm some kind of hero.

The notion was not exhilarating. On the contrary, he felt like a fraud. When he dove at Kenny, it had not been an act of calculated bravery in the teeth of dreadful, well-known odds. He had just . . . *done* it, in a moment of terror. And he was still terrified! *I could have been killed in there!* That he shared these guilty, submerged, utterly inexpressible feelings with most of the heroes of history, he had no way of knowing.

Just then, to his great relief, the warehouse's assistant night manager, Nick Derdosian, came into the break room with a burnt-orange manila folder cradled in his arms. In the folder would be the paychecks, and everybody would have something else to think about.

Derdosian was a swarthy man in his mid-thirties. The top of his head was bald, but the rest of him was remarkably hairy. A heavy crop of black hair emerged from the short sleeves of his shirt and ran all the way down his arms and out onto the backs of his hands. Thanks to Kenny, the freezer pickers all called him Nick Necktie. He and the other supervisory personnel and salesmen had offices up in the front of the warehouse, overlooking East Bay Boulevard. Kenny referred to them collectively as "the neckties." Most of the men up in the front office did, in fact, wear neckties, as did Derdosian—until recently. Every time he turned up in the break room or the work bays, Kenny had taken to yelling out, "Nick Necktie!" and some crash'n'burner or other would echo the cry in falsetto: "Nick *Neck*tie!" This finally so rattled Derdosian, a quiet, stolid man whom God had not designed for dealing with crash'n'burners, he had lately abandoned his necktie and started wearing open-necked shirts. But he was so hairy, a carpet of crinkly chest hairs was visible in the V of the open neck, and Kenny and the crash'n'burners had started calling him Harry No Tie. "H*arreeeeee No* Tie!" So this week he had put the necktie back on and taken to approaching the crew with a necktie and a tense, ingratiating grin.

Tonight, however, he came into the break room without any smile at all. Tonight he looked gloomy and wary, as if he thought perhaps

Kenny had dreamed up some new way of making his life miserable.

Instead, Kenny merely nodded and said, "Hi, Nick." He looked every bit as glum himself.

Derdosian set the manila folder down on a nearby table, removed the stack of paychecks, and started calling out the names in alphabetical order. Conrad took his envelope without bothering to open it, folded it in two, put it in the pocket of his plaid shirt, and went back to the table.

Just then voices erupted at the next table. It was Tony Chase and the other two black pickers. Tony was showing them a white slip of paper and talking angrily. Light Bulb swung around to listen, then leaned forward again.

"Jesus Christ," he said, "Tohohohohohony just got nohohohohohotified. He's been laid off."

Conrad sat upright. Tony had been hired the same week he was.

Kenny and Light Bulb already had their envelopes out and were going through them to see if there was anything other than a check inside. Evidently they were safe. They hadn't been laid off. The same thing was going on all over the break room. From somewhere behind him Conrad heard a voice gasp out, "Fuck a *duck*!"

Slowly Conrad withdrew his envelope from his shirt pocket and slipped his big forefinger under the flap and ripped it open. There was the salmon-colored paycheck, as usual. Behind it was a white slip of paper.

He read the first few words: "Due to a necessary capacity reduction in this facility, your services . . ." Then he looked up. Kenny and Light Bulb were staring at him. He couldn't make himself speak. He could only nod up and down to tell them, "Yes, it's true."

"I don't fucking believe this," said Kenny. Lunging, he stretched his arm across the table and said, "Lemme see that," and snatched the slip of paper from Conrad's hand and studied it for a moment.

Then he bolted out of his seat. The chair hit the floor behind him with a loud plastic smack. Glaring at the retreating figure of Derdosian, he called out, "Yo! Nick!"

Derdosian stopped in the entryway to the break room. Immediately his head began to jiggle from side to side, as if to say, "I had nothing to do with it."

"What the hell's going on, *Nick*!"

Kenny's huge hands were pressed down on the surface of the table, supporting the weight of his upper body. His chin jutted forward. Every striation of the muscles of his great long neck stood out. He looked as if he were about to spring all the way from there to the opening in the plywood wall where the cowering assistant night manager stood. His wild-dog eyes bored in, demanding a response, and then they opened wide, and he screamed out:

"WHO'S THE BRIGHT BOY THOUGHT THIS UP, NICK?"

You could still hear the clatter and banging of the Dry Foods bay beyond, but here in the break room there wasn't another sound. The crew froze stock-still, riveted by this outburst of crash'n'burner fury.

"WHO'S THE SHIT FER BRAINS, NICK? YOU'RE LAYING OFF *CONRAD*? YOU'RE LAYING OFF THE BEST MAN IN THIS WHOLE FUCKING *PLACE*?"

Derdosian, transfixed, slowly lifted his shoulders and then the palms of his hands and lowered his head, in the gesture that pleads, "It wasn't me! I don't make these decisions!"

"HE WAS GONNA BUY A CONDO, NICK! HE'S GOT A WIFE AND TWO KIDS! HE'S GOT HEART, NICK, HE'S GOT HEART! HE'S WORTH MORE'N THE WHOLE BUNCHA YOU FUCKIN' NECKTIES PUT TOGETHER!"

The assistant night manager now had his palms up so high, and his head down so low, he looked as if he were trying to disappear into his own thoracic cavity.

"AW, I KNOW, NICK! YOU ONLY WORK HERE! YOU'RE SO FUCKIN' PATHETIC! YOU KNOW THAT? SO WHYN'T YOU FUCKIN' GO GET LOST! WHAT'S THE NAME A THE ASSHOLE THAT OWNS THIS FUCKIN' COMPANY? SOMEBODY CROKER? IS HE THE BRIGHT BOY? THEN HE'D BETTER FUCKIN' GET LOST, TOO, OR I'M GONNA—"

Kenny's voice broke, and he lowered his gaze and looked not at Nick Derdosian but at Conrad. He compressed his lips, which began to tremble, as did his chin. His eyes opened wide, and then he closed them slowly. When he opened them again, they were brimming with tears, which began to roll down his cheeks. Still supporting himself on the table with one hand, he raised the other and covered his face. He lowered his head, and his bony frame began convulsing all the way from his shoulders down to his weight lifter's belt.

Conrad's eyes fastened on the most insignificant thing: Kenny's pale blond hair, wet, stringy, matted down, was already thinning badly in the crown. All at once the indomitable crash'n'burner looked so weak and weary.

Kenny raised his head and tried to wipe his tears away with his hand and then with his forearm. He forced a smile.

"See? I was right, wasn't I, old buddy? They just ain't gonna let you do it. And you were right, too. You said I got *No!* in my heart. And that's the truth. I got *No!* in my heart." He clutched his throat with his forefinger and thumb. "I got it up to here . . . from lapping up all that crap inside the rut they make you crawl in."

Chapter

In the Lair of the Lust

AT THAT MOMENT, TWENTY-EIGHT HUNDRED MILES AWAY, THE bright boy who thought it up, Charlie Croker, layer-offer of freezer pickers, woke up with a start. His eyes popped open like a pair of umbrellas. He couldn't see a damn thing, it was so dark in here. The neck of his nightshirt was wet with perspiration. The big rabbit, his heart, was thumping away in his chest. The Wiz's latest numbers were already churning through his head, and he hadn't been awake five seconds. It was bad enough having PlannersBanc checking in practically every day with new demands, new threats . . . to seize this, attach that, encumber the other thing . . . but this afternoon the Wiz has to come hustling into his office to inform him of some horror the IRS has dreamed up called phantom gains . . . phantom gains . . . The bank forecloses, you lose your shirt, *and* the IRS hits you with a whole ton of taxes for your "phantom gains" . . . and now, as he lies here in bed in the dark, his heart starts thumping in a funny way, as if fluttering to the rhythm of the words themselves . . . phantom gains . . . phantom gains . . . and then—*galumph*—a palpitation—*twang*—it snaps back to its regular beat—

The insomnia factory was open for the day, heading toward peak production.

He looked at the clock by the bed. Its feverish little green digits said 3:20. He turned toward Serena. There was barely enough ambient light to make out her silhouette. She was lying on her side, turned away from him. He could see one of her haunches welling up beneath the covers. It was a wonder he could see that much. Must be thanks to the tiny light from the clock. Sure as hell couldn't be from the windows. He stared toward them, three tall windows overlooking the rolling, big-breasted lawns of Buckhead, but he couldn't even locate them in the dark. Not a glimmer of light seeped through. Serena had had Ronald Vine load them down with enough fabric, enough shades, enough undercurtains, inner curtains, outer curtains, whatever it all was, to smother an army.

You must be crazy, Croker! He had let her sink more than three and a half million dollars into the interior of this house! Three and a half million he'd like to get his hands on right now! And just try! He had paid $2,750,000 for the property itself, which had been a huge price for Atlanta, even for the Buckhead area in the final swell of the last real estate bubble, which was when he had bought it. He had already sunk a fortune into one extravaganza in Buckhead, over on Valley Road, which had gone to Martha in the divorce. So now he had bought a second one, barely a half mile away, here on Blackland Road.

Irritably, Charlie propped himself up on one elbow, halfway hoping the deflection of the mattress would wake Serena . . . Not a chance . . . Her slumbering young loins and lamb chops rose and fell. She was breathing regularly in the blissful sleep of youth. He felt a stab of nostalgia for Martha, or not for Martha herself exactly, but for life with Martha. Martha he could have reached over to and shaken by the shoulder, and she would have put up with it and woken up and asked him why he couldn't sleep.

Your first wife married you for better or for worse. Your second wife, particularly if you were sixty and she was a twenty-eight-year-old number like Serena—why kid yourself?—she married you for better.

Charlie could suddenly see the prissy face of Martha's daddy, Dr. Bunting Starling, president, back then, of the Commonwealth Club in Richmond, Virginia, where he had hosted the wedding reception. Charlie's own daddy, Mr. Earl Croker, lately of a hole in the ground in Baker County, Georgia, had gotten so drunk at that reception he had jumped on the bandstand and put his arm around the waist of the pretty singer for the Lester Lanin Orchestra and done the dirty boogie, all the while waving the shiny knob of the stump where his right index finger used to be. Christ, that had just about finished off any social standing his son might have had, which hadn't been much to start with, other than the fact that he had been the fullback on the Georgia Tech football team at a time, more than forty years ago, when Tech was a power in national football, a matter that seemed to cut more ice in Atlanta, Georgia, than Richmond, Virginia. Otherwise he had been nothing but a big old boy from down below the gnat line who was selling a lot of commercial real estate in Atlanta for Hedlock & Co. and had a way with the girls. He certainly had had a way with Martha. She was a graduate of Sweet Briar College who was in her first year of medical school at Emory University in Atlanta, and with scarcely a second thought she gave up her plans to be a doctor (like her father) in order to be Mrs. Croker. For a time there was no happier couple in the state of Georgia. He had to give himself credit for one thing. He had married well, but he was not a social climber. In point of fact, he had been far more captivated by Martha's sunny, flirtatious disposition and her fair white body than anything the Starlings-of-Virginia connection could possibly do for him. The connection did something for him, all the same, when he went out on his own as a developer in the 1970s, inasmuch as Martha added a certain polish and tone to the enterprise. In the meantime, she had borne him three children, Martha, whom they called Mattie; Catherine, whom they called Caddie; and the youngest, Wallace, born when Martha was thirty-seven.

Wallace. Wally. At this very moment, as he lay propped up on one elbow in bed with his new wife, feeling his pangs in the dark, Charlie was well aware that Wally was asleep in a bedroom in the other wing. Wally was sixteen now. Charlie called him Wally. Nobody else did; to the rest of the world he was Wallace. Charlie kept waiting for some robust, zestful spirit to break loose in the boy, so that people just couldn't resist calling him Wally. It hadn't yet. Wally was home for a week in some sort of "independent project" they had dreamed up at the boarding school in Massachusetts he went to, Trinian, and was staying with him for three days before he went back to his mother's. With another pang he realized he didn't even know what kind of project Wally was supposed to be working on. He was grateful that Wally had elected to stay a few days with him, and yet in the past two days he had spent a grand total of about thirty minutes with his son, despite promising himself that this time they would do something "significant" together. This whole situation with PlannersBanc was eating up every spare moment he had—and besides that, if he was going to be honest with himself, he had to admit that something about Wally disturbed him. Wally always gave him a certain look, a certain lost, blank look. Charlie couldn't tell if it was a look of accusation, longing, or bewilderment. Wally had sufficient cause to be bewildered, of course. Mattie and Caddie had been grown and out on their own when all the turmoil over Serena had started four years ago and he and Martha had separated, but Wally had been only twelve. What was Wally supposed to think of Serena, who was younger than his sister Mattie? What was he supposed to think of his new eleven-month-old half sister, Kingsley, who was at this moment up in the third-floor nursery with this month's nanny, Heidi? . . . A fifty-or-sixty-year-old Filipino named Heidi . . . Kingsley was some name, too. Charlie had argued with Serena about it, but she was determined to add a little yuppie grandeur to the premises: Miss Kingsley Croker . . . Serena and Kingsley and Heidi and Wally, and up on the third floor of the other wing was the Woo Dynasty: his cook, Nina Woo, and her sister, Jarmaine, the housekeeper, and Jarmaine's son, Lin Chi.

Jesus Christ! What a menagerie! All these people to look after, support, pay for—all of them sleeping like tops, no doubt—while he has to wake up in the middle of the night with insomnia and go to the mat with phantom gains and a lot of other horrible nonsense.

The house was deathly quiet. All he could hear was a muffled flow of air from the central air-conditioning vents. Outside, it was one of those merciless muggy nights in Georgia. What a racket the cicadas used to make at night in the summer when he was growing up . . . In those days you just used to listen to the bugs and sweat it out . . . Serena was so young, she probably couldn't even imagine human life without air conditioning. He stared at her haunches again. She gave a little sigh from beneath a deep layer of sleep and moved one of her arms, but that was it.

He became aware of an overwhelming urge to urinate. Gingerly he pulled the covers back. Slowly he swung his legs off the bed. Ever so stealthily he stood up and began stealing across the carpet, a Wilton weave, or whatever Ronald called it, which had set him back $225 a yard, and—*bango!*—stubbed his toe on that spindly piece of whatever-century wooden junk of a chair that Serena had placed by the door to the bathroom, and his knee started aching. Why the hell did he have to creep around in the dark like a goddamned mouse in his own goddamned house so that a twenty-eight-year-old woman worn out from shopping and driving her Jaguar XJ6 could have her precious rest?

Nevertheless, Creepy Mouse limped into the bathroom and shut the door without letting the latch so much as click in its slot. He switched on the light—and was practically annihilated by Ronald Vine's overkill of wall sconces, downlighters, beveled mirrors, and glistening marble surfaces. It was blinding. He felt so damned tired. The day was already wrecked. He stared at a big bleary bald-headed sixty-year-old man in the mirror. He turned on the cold water at one of the basins and cupped his hands and rubbed water over his face. The water really made him want to urinate, and so he went over to the toilet, which was some streamlined, low-slung beige thing, and he urinated. Was this a bad sign, this urge he always had to urinate in the middle of the night? Was it the prostate or some other old man's problem?

He would read a little, that was what he would do. It would be better than a pill. He wasn't the world's greatest reader, and trying to read before he went to bed at night usually put him right under. He noticed his half-glasses, another barnacle of advancing age, sticking out of the breast pocket of his bathrobe, which was hanging on the door, and so he put on the bathrobe and went out the far side of the bathroom and into his dressing room and turned on the light in there. It was a big room lined with closets and built-in bureaus and mirrors and bookshelves, a regular extravaganza of mahogany and ogeed moldings and beveled glass.

He went over to the bookshelves and took down a book he'd been meaning to read anyway, *The Paper Millionaire*, by some Arab-turned-Englishman named Roger Shashoua. He sat down in the lounge chair and put on the glasses and turned on the little brass reading lamp, which had cost a truly unbelievable amount—Ronald had ordered it from *Nebraska*—and opened the book. His eye fell on the inside jacket flap:

> In the course of his astonishing career, Roger Shashoua made it, lost it, made it, lost it, made it yet again and then, with impeccable timing, walked away from it all.

Charlie closed the book, turned it over, and looked at the photograph of this Roger Shashoua on the back . . . Cocky-looking little devil . . . An Arab, but with a typical Brit half-a-smirk on his face . . . ferocious head of hair, turning gray but with every hair he ever had in his head still nailed in . . . all of forty-six or forty-seven years old . . . Then he turned back to the jacket flap again:

. . . made it, lost it, made it, lost it, made it yet again . . .

He lowered the book and stared at the mahogany closets without really seeing them. He had always thought of himself that way. He was a player. He wasn't greedy, he wasn't acquisitive. He was a player, a plunger, a risk taker who loved the great game more than the rewards. If he lost everything—hell, what would it matter? He was a good old Baker County Georgia boy who started off down in the dirt, and so the idea of rolling over in the dirt once more didn't scare him. He'd dust himself off and *make it yet again.* Hadn't he done that after the real estate debacle of the 1970s? . . . Yeah, but he hadn't had all that much to lose in the first place back then, had he . . . and he had been only thirty years old. Chronological age didn't really mean anything, but . . . Jesus . . . he was *sixty* now . . . The thought weighed down his very bones. He tried to conceive of picking himself up from out of the dirt again . . . flat broke but indomitable . . . indomitable . . . The notion of having to get up every day and show a flat-broke but indomitable face to the world sent him sinking so deeply into the lounge chair, he wondered if he could even stand up . . . He gave in . . . He began to feel immensely sorry for himself . . .

The hell with that!

He sprang up out of the chair, as if escaping from the deadly caresses of self-pity. That played hell with his knee, and the sudden exertion made him light-headed. He caught a glimpse of himself in the mirror. He was in a crouch, clad in a nightshirt and a bathrobe with a pair of half-glasses teetering on the tip of his nose. He stuffed the glasses back into his pocket and put his hands on his knees and bent over and lowered his head in order to get some blood to his brain, and then he stood upright and made a fierce face in the mirror. Charlie Croker—brute! Charlie Croker—force of nature! The hell with *sixty years old* and whatever that was supposed to mean!

Enough sitting here stewing . . . Action was called for . . . Go riding! That was it. He'd go out to the Spread. The Spread, as he had taken to calling it, was forty acres off Crest Valley Road, not far from the Chattahoochee River National Park. It was like the Chattahoochee County countryside out there, and yet it was part of Atlanta, part of Buckhead, for that matter, loosely defined. He kept three horses at the Spread, one of them being Jugsy, the big jumper he had just had vanned up from Turpmtine. Hell, he really ought to ride Jugsy every day . . . It was too early just yet. Dodson, the caretaker, and his wife, Fanny, who lived in the little house near the stable—their dogs would start barking if they heard the stable opening up when it wasn't even light yet . . . Well—what he'd do was, he'd get dressed and go downstairs and fix himself breakfast, a big *country* breakfast . . . eggs, grits, biscuits, smoked ham . . . a *trout* . . . He'd always loved it when his daddy cooked himself a trout for breakfast. That sharp, almost sweet, grilled smell came back to him as he stood in this froufrou dressing room in the most expensive part of Buckhead . . . except that there wouldn't be any trout in this establishment . . . But it would be a pleasure just to fix breakfast all by himself . . . Nina Woo wasn't a bad cook, but this morning he didn't need the presence of the Woo Dynasty fluttering about him in all their insincere solicitude . . . No, he'd fix a big breakfast all by himself and eat it at his leisure and drink some good New Orleans coffee with chicory and clear his head and recharge the batteries and go for a ride.

He went over to one of the mahogany closets, his Sports Closet, Ronald called it, and took out his riding clothes, the high black boots, the tan pants, the polo shirt, a tweed hacking jacket, and the rest of it, and got dressed. The boots . . . so goddamned hard to put on . . . custom-made . . . fit like a corset around the calves . . . hurt his knee so much he groaned as he tugged on the handles of his metal boot pulls . . . He stood up . . . Ahhhhhh, but what a fabulous figure he cut now! . . . The boots were a dream in creamy black leather with glossy highlights. He could forgive the Woo Dynasty a lot for the mule's work they always did on the boots. The riding pants were made of an elasticized twill that brought out the powerful curve of his thigh muscles, and the polo shirt showed off the massive hillocks of his chest and the prodigious girth of his upper arms. More than satisfied with himself, he hooked his jacket over his thumb and tossed it over his shoulder, threw his head back, struck a jaunty pose in the mirror, and went out into the hallway. He snapped on the staircase lights and headed down toward the kitchen. The scrambled eggs (well done), the steaming grits (with a little butter), the hot biscuits (made from scratch by Auntie Bella down at Turpmtine and frozen and flown up here on the G-5), the ever-so-thin slices of smoked country ham (slaughtered, cured, and aged by Uncle Bud down at Turpmtine), the New Orleans coffee with chicory—every nerve in his body was primed for the ambrosial aromas soon to come.

The stair hall was a real piece of work, a symphony of big-bellied curves, with a balcony that swooped this way and a staircase that swooped down that way and a walnut banister that swooped all over the place upon balusters of delicate and highly ornate ironwork. Charlie noticed none of that, however. Only one thing was on his mind: a real country breakfast, starring Charlie Croker, a Baker County boy who knew what life boiled down to, once all the fat was rendered away. Now he was at the final flamboyant curve of the staircase, where it headed down to the marble floor of the entry foyer, when—*Brannnnng! Brannnnng! Brannnnng! Brannnnng!*

Holy shit! All hell broke loose. *Brannnnng! Brannnnng! Brannnnng! Brannnnng!* The sound hammered his head in relentless waves. *Brannnnng! Brannnnng! Brannnnng! Brannnnng!*

The burglar alarm! He'd totally forgotten about it! Forgot to push the bypass switch! The motion detectors! On the ground floor, which was full of French doors, Serena didn't want sensors sitting there on every pane and had insisted on motion detectors—and anything that moved could set them off. He'd set off the alarm by walking down the stairs!

Brannnnng! Brannnnng! Brannnnng! Brannnnng!

There were alarm gongs all up and down the staircase, and outside the house, too. They were hammering their metal heads off. The noise was enough to cave your skull in.

Goddamn you, Serena!

Like any man who has just committed a blunder of elementary stupidity, Charlie racked his brain to find the malefactor who had made him do it. It was Serena who had insisted on this totally useless burglar alarm system! Charlie Croker was from Baker County, where you defend your own goddamn house your own goddamn self! You don't wire yourself into some goddamn company manned by a bunch of half-wits who aren't much above burglars themselves! He had his bare hands and a short-barreled .20-gauge shotgun in the closet in the bedroom! He didn't need some armed minimum-wage winos from Radartronic Security—*Radartronic Security!*—poking around his house in the middle of the night!

Brannnnng! Brannnnng! Brannnnng! Brannnnng!

The whole menagerie—Serena, Heidi Filipino, Miss Kingsley Croker, Wally, the Woo Dynasty—they'd all be ricocheting off the walls and descending upon him. Shut off the gongs! That was the main thing. The control box was in a closet in the bedroom. He went charging up the stairs in his riding boots. *Clomp clomp clomp clomp clomp.* Knee hurt like hell—no time to worry about that. As he reached the second floor, he heard a clicking sound. That would be the telephone automatically dialing Radartronic Security, which was located somewhere down around the old Southern Railway yards. They, in turn, would telephone the house, and unless you answered and gave them your code number, they would call the police and dispatch their own so-called agents, who had keys to your house.

Serena! That's so stupid, letting a bunch of jack-legged, barely employable bums have the keys to your home! What's the matter with you!

On he charged. In no time, breathing stertorously, he was at the bedroom door. He turned the handle. Damn! It was locked. What idiot locked it? Who else? Serena.

Now he could hear the telephone ringing. *Trrrilllll . . . Trrrilllll . . . Trrrilllll . . .*

That would be the burglar alarm company calling back. Naturally nobody in the whole menagerie answered it. He ran to the door of the dressing room. Thank God, it opened. He dashed for the bathroom, went in, and opened the door to the bedroom.

Brannnnng! Brannnnng! Brannnnng! Brannnnng!

Trrrilllll . . . Trrrilllll . . . Trrrilllll . . .

Pitch-black in the bedroom, just the way he'd left it. He felt around on the wall for the light switch. The wall was lined with a padded fabric. It was like feeling around for a light switch in a mattress. Finally he found it and switched it on. The bedroom rose up in the glow from tawny, peachy, pink-lined little silk lampshades atop wall sconces. The carved Victorian mantelpiece with its bevels and escutcheons, the billowing yards of chintz curtains and silk undercurtains, the fretwork radiator covers, the vast bed with its bombastic upholstered headboard—all of it popped out in a luxurious play of highlights and deep shadows. But no Serena. Not a trace of her.

"Serena! Where are you!"

From behind the bed rose a tousled head of long black hair. A pair of extraordinary periwinkle-blue eyes blazed away. Then the shoulders, bare except for a pair of salmon-pink straps that held up a little salmon-pink chemise so low cut that he could see all but the very tips of her breasts as she came out of her crouch. Young, fabulous, perfect breasts they were. It was a sight that had stirred Charlie Croker, brute, many times, but now he was possessed by another passion entirely: the urge to blame.

"Jesus, Serena! Answer the phone! What's that damned code number?"

Then he took in the look on her young face. Her eyes were wide-open and her lips were slightly parted, but it was not an expression of pure fear. There seemed to be a delicate balance between fear and panic, on the one hand, and disbelief and hostility on the other.

She put her hand to her sternum, as if to steady her heart. "Charlie! What on *earth*!"

"Your goddamned motion detectors, Serena! I was goin' downstairs to the kitchen—and I mean, shit! Can't you pick up the telephone, for Christ's sake? That's the alarm company. What's 'at code number?"

Brannnnng! Brannnnng! Brannnnng!

Trrrilllll . . . Trrrilllll . . . Trrrilllll . . .

Then it dawned on him that the telephone was, in fact, on the table on the other side of the bed. He pointed toward the closet where the control box was. "I'll get the telephone. See if you can't turn that goddamned thing off!"

She gave him a look. The balance was slipping rapidly toward disbelief and hostility. But she said nothing. As she went into the closet, he could see the cups of her buttocks where they showed beneath the little salmon-pink chemise.

Brannnnng! Brannnnng! Brannnnng!

Trrrilllll . . . Trrrilllll . . . Trrrilllll . . .

With a bound Charlie reached the bedside table and picked up the telephone. Belligerently: "Hel*lo*!"

"This is Sur*veil*lance. We have an *alarm* signal." It was a man's measured, carefully modulated, almost singsong voice. It struck Charlie as a parody of someone trying to instill calm during an emergency. It infuriated him.

"It's a *false alarm*," said Charlie. He made it sound like an accusation. "Everything's okay."

The man's voice said, "Your name . . . *please*?" The way the voice went up two or three notes on the *please* irritated Charlie enormously. Besides, he wasn't used to having to tell people his name. By the time you spoke to Charlie Croker you were supposed to *know* who he was.

But he reined himself in. "Charles Croker," he said in an even voice, but it was run over by the relentless *Brannnnng! Brannnnng! Brannnnng!*

"Say again . . . *please*?" said the voice of Radartronic Security.

"I said *Charles Croker*! Can't you hear, for God's sake?"

The studiously imperturbable voice merely said, "Your ID number . . . *please*?"

"What?"

"Your ID number . . . *please*?"

"It's, uh, 2-2-8 . . . uh . . . Oh, for Christ's sake." He looked toward the closet, toward Serena. The closet was full of clothes, and the control box was on a side wall, so that Serena had to lean in to get at it. Charlie could see her firm young legs, bare right up to her perfect little bottom. There had been many times when this sight, too, had driven him wild. But now he saw a half-nude nitwit.

Brannnnng! Brannnnng! Brannnnng!

"Serena, what's 'at number! And for Christ's sake, can't you turn those damn gongs off? It's a little toggle switch!"

In fact, as Charlie realized from the last time he'd set off the alarm by mistake, when you opened the control box, you were presented with a baffling profusion of fuses, colored wires, buttons, switches, a veritable electronic goulash. He was in no mood to be reasonable, however.

"Serena!"

The gongs hammered on, but Serena's head emerged from the closet. She didn't say anything at first. She looked him up and down, from his bald pate and angry face down to the toes of his boots and back up again, before saying, "It's taped to the bottom of the telephone."

Charlie picked up the telephone cradle and turned it over and then spoke into the receiver: "Okay . . . you listening?"

The voice: "Yes, we *are*." Up two infuriating patient notes on the *are*.

"Okay . . . it's 2-2-8-6-8."

"Thank you. Have you ascertained the origin of the signal?"

Ascertained the origin? He found the wording ludicrously pretentious, but all he said was "Yes. It was a false alarm."

"Would you like the assistance of our agents?"

"Agents? Spare me—nawwww, I don't need any a your agents."

The voice bade him goodbye with the same stenciled calm with which it had begun.

Brannnnng! Brannnnng!—suddenly the dreadful hammering noise stopped. Serena had finally found the switch. An after-ring filled Charlie's skull as he turned back toward the closet. Serena emerged, popping out of her little chemise. She was breathing hard and looking holes through him.

"I'm gonna call upstairs to Heidi," she said. She was breathing so rapidly, it made her voice tremulous. She sat down on the edge of the bed and picked up the telephone receiver and pressed an intercom button.

Just then—a banging on the bedroom door. "Dad! Dad! You in there?"

Charlie walked over, unlocked the door, and opened it about a foot.

There was Wally, looking confused, sleepy, wilted, thin, gawky. He had a plaid bathrobe pulled over the T-shirt and boxer shorts he slept in. Wally was already six feet tall, and he had his father's curly blond hair, or the same sort of hair Charlie had enjoyed when he was young, and the beginning of his handsome features. But he was not Charlie Croker or close to becoming Charlie Croker. That was what crossed Charlie's mind the first time he saw him on any given day.

"What happened?" asked Wally.

"Nothing to worry about," said Charlie. "Just Serena's—just the burglar alarm system having another one of its little fits."

"The *burglar* alarm system had a little fit?" It was Serena. Charlie turned away from the door and looked at her. She was still sitting on the edge of the bed. She had her head cocked and a dubious little smile on her lips in the expression that asks, "Is anybody actually supposed to believe what you just said?"

Wally stuck his head through the door. What he saw was his father's new wife, sitting on the edge of his father's big bed with her long, bare legs crossed. Her hair tumbled down wildly over her bare shoulders. She had her arms crossed over her bosom, modestly enough, but there was no way that this girl and her young body could be modest in that tiny chemise. Wally's eyes stuck out like the hat pegs in a Baker County country church. Charlie was mortified, and for reasons that went well beyond modesty. His sixteen-year-old son was getting a look, a forbidden look, in the very lair of the lust, the master bedroom, on the edge of the master's bed itself, at what his father had left his mother for. Charlie looked at Wally. Charlie looked at Serena. He wanted to say, "Wally! Don't look! Get out of here!" He wanted to say, "Serena! For God's sake! Vanish! Cover yourself!" But he couldn't get a word out.

As if reading his mind, Serena stood up and said, "Excuse me," and walked over to the closet and took the matching salmon-pink silk bathrobe off a door hook and slipped into it and wrapped it about her and tied the sash. It took no more than fifteen seconds, but in those fifteen seconds Wally, sixteen years of age, drank in a lifetime supply of lubricious crevices and undulating lamb chops and *those* and *them* and *these* and *that*.

And Croker had never even had that talk with Wally, the most important talk a father could have with a son, not the one about the birds and the bees, but the one about how things really are, actually are, in real life, between men and women.

At last Wally averted his eyes and asked his father, "Are the police coming?"

"Naw," said Charlie, "the police aren't coming, and neither's those scarecrows from the burglar alarm company. I'd rather have a burglar in the house than one a those *homeless* with *pistols* they send over here."

Now Wally was looking at him with his blank, bewildered expression. He was looking him up and down, from the top of his head to the toes of his spiffy boots, the same way Serena had the moment before.

"What are you *wearing*, Dad?"

Since it was perfectly obvious what he was wearing, Charlie found the question impertinent. At the same time he didn't want to be antagonistic to Wally, whom he so seldom saw, and so he put on the beginning of a smile and said, "Well . . . what's it look like?"

"You're going *riding*? *Now*?"

"I sure am, if I can ever get outta here. Out at the Spread. I brought Jugsy up from Turpmtine. You remember Jugsy, don't you? The big bay jumper?"

Wally nodded yes with blank, unbelieving eyes, as if humoring a lunatic.

Charlie detected some of that and said, "It's a great time to go riding. The dawn comes up—nobody ever gets to see a real dawn in Atlanta anymore. You oughta come with me, Wally. You can ride Bird. You rode her once, didn't you?"

For half a second he figured it just might work out. It could be the significant experience he had been promising himself . . . Father and son riding side by side over the rolling hills of the Spread at dawn as the sun rises up behind the distant towers of the city . . . It would be something Wally would never forget. This burglar alarm fiasco might turn out to be all for the best. And then he saw the look on Wally's face.

The boy was smiling gamely and his head was nodding yes, and his eyes, which were as big around and blank as a pair of clay pigeons, were saying, "Not in a million years." It was what was known in the coarse argot of real estate development as a grin fuck.

Serena walked toward them. Wrapped in her robe of the finest charmeuse, she looked gorgeous. Her black hair was full and rich and bouncy. Her skin was fair. Her neck was long, bare, and lovely.

"Charlie," she said, speaking all too calmly now, "did I hear you say riding? Do you have . . . any idea . . . whatsoever . . . what time it is?" Then she extended an uplifted palm toward the clock on the bedside table. It was the patronizing gesture that says, *Please, be my guest.*

Against his better instincts he looked at it. Damn!—3:55 a.m. Desperately he wished for the psychokinetic power to make it blip forward six minutes, so that it would at least be after four o'clock.

Her arm still extended, Serena demanded, "What time does it say?" It was the tone you would use on a child.

Now it was Charlie who was bewildered. The impudence! A twenty-eight-year-old girl standing here in next to nothing, trying to make him look like a doddering idiot in front of his son! Frantically he ransacked his brain for the proper strategy. He couldn't just let her have it, tell her to mind her goddamn mouth—not in front of Wally. He couldn't just laugh it off—he'd look weak, since she was clearly trying to put him in his place. No—he'd—he'd tell her about the country breakfast—the country breakfast—how he was going to fix himself a real country breakfast with all the trimmings, how he was going to relax and enjoy it, how it would take more than an hour, and then it would be after five, which would be a good time to head out to—

—aw hell, that would really sound like a confused old man—a man with three servants in the house who's getting ready to go down to the kitchen by himself to fix a real country breakfast on one of the most expensive streets in Buckhead at 3:55 in the morning—and besides, every true leader of men knew that when challenged by an underling, you don't stop to explain. You squash that underling and explain later, if you have to. But suppose the underling is your barely clad new wife, and your sixteen-year-old son by your old wife is standing there—what do you do then?

Around and around his brain whirled and he was aware that his lips were parted and no words were coming out—

Loud whispering and giggling out in the hallway. He knew who that would be: the Woo Dynasty. Grateful for an interruption, he held up his forefinger and said, "Just a second!"—and ducked out into the hall, pulling the bedroom door almost shut.

Sure enough, there were Jarmaine and Nina, a pair of plump, fortyish-looking figures in bathrobes. He had never seen them in such a state before. Their thick black hair was sticking out every which way, like a pair of dove's nests. Their legs were bare and not terrific to look at, being stumpy and slightly bowed. A few feet behind them, hanging on to the stairhall banister, for the fun of it, was Lin Chi, who was eight. He was in a T-shirt and little undershorts. Jarmaine and Nina were smiling mightily.

"Mr. Croker!" said Nina through her big smile. "Burglar alarm go off!"

Both women looked at Charlie and giggled. Charlie did not find this at all unusual, however. They never laughed in his presence out of amusement. It was always out of embarrassment—in this case probably over the fact that they had had the temerity to venture so close to the master bedroom in the middle of the night.

Croker explained what had happened, providing a version of the facts that would make it easy to conclude that the system had malfunctioned.

"Ohhhhhhhhhhhh," said Nina, changing to a serious expression. The *Ohhhhhhhhhhhh* came out as a wail of revelation.

Meantime, Lin Chi, the eight-year-old, gripped a baluster with both hands and let his body hang sideways, like a sailor clutching a railing in the wind, all the while staring fixedly at Charlie.

Charlie had come to like Lin Chi. He was a real boy. In a few years he'd be a handful. He was more like what he wanted to see in a son than Wally was.

He smiled at Lin Chi. "Makes a lotta noise, don't it, Lin Chi, that burglar alarm?"

"You can say that again!" said Lin Chi, still hanging sideways. He had no accent at all.

Terribly embarrassed, Jarmaine and Nina reddened, giggled, glared at Lin Chi, and then beamed at Charlie and giggled some more.

Charlie laughed heartily to show them he hadn't found Lin Chi impertinent, and then he said, "Well, you ain't gotta worry about it anymore, Lin Chi. We're gettin' rid of it. It ain't good for nothing but false alarms, is it." Unconsciously the *ain'ts* were a great Charlie Croker compliment. They meant: "You're a real boy. You're my kind."

What the hell had happened to all these sons of the rich in Wally's generation, these well-brought-up boys who went off to the private schools? These damned schools were producing a new kind of scion of the elite: a boy utterly world-weary by the age of sixteen, cynical, phlegmatic, and apathetic around adults, although perfectly respectful and maddeningly polite, a boy inept at sports, averse to hunting and fishing and riding horses or handling animals in any way, a boy embarrassed by his advantages, desperate to hide them, eager to dress in backward baseball caps and homey pants and other ghetto rags, terrified of being envied, a boy facing the world without any visible signs of the joy of living and without . . . balls . . .

Now down the stairs came another figure, walking past the Woo Dynasty, a small thin woman in a white uniform she'd obviously just jumped into. She had made a stab at pushing her black hair back from her face, but it was almost as big a mess as Jarmaine's and Nina's. She was barefoot. She was carrying a little bundled armful. It was Heidi, the Filipino nanny, carrying Miss Kingsley Croker.

The bare feet were not the result of haste, however. Heidi was the most proper nanny they had had in the house in eleven months of hiring and firing nannies, but she always went about in bare feet. That detail Charlie always noticed. It reminded him of a book he'd seen once in the library at Tech. It was a picture book of the kilts and full regalia of the Scottish clans. It was full of lovingly colorful illustrations of Scottish lairds dressed up to beat the band—all of them with bare legs, big knotty calves, and bare feet. It was as if there was something Down Home, hog-stomping, and primeval in their makeup that you couldn't remove, no matter how fancy the clothes became. Charlie loved that, since he always assumed he was the same way. Whether this was a desirable attribute in a nanny or not, he couldn't decide.

As she rounded the last bend in the flight of stairs, Heidi looked at him and said brightly, "Hello, Mister. Everything okay?"

"Yep," said Charlie, "everything's okay. Just a false alarm. She get scared?" He motioned toward Kingsley, a pale little creature curled up in the nanny's arms, apparently dead to the world. *She.* He disliked the name Kingsley so much, he avoided using it.

"Oh no, Mister. She don't wake up."

The little girl's eyes were shut tight. She tucked her head and buried it in Heidi's bosom. Jarmaine and Nina made a polite fuss over the heiress apparent and turned back toward Charlie and did some more giggling. Their eyes were trained on his face, but then they lowered and drifted down, down over his polo shirt and his tight twill riding pants and his boots with all the glossy highlights and then back up to the riding pants and the polo shirt and up to his face. Lin Chi was doing the same thing, except that his eyes remained fixed on the fabulous boots. Heidi's, too . . . she took in all of him, but the boots were what really got her. All of them, save the infant, had been blasted out of their REM sleep by a burglar alarm and blown into the hallway to find Cap'm Charlie dressed up in his high black boots as if he's about to hop on a horse at 3:55 a.m. *I can explain!*—but he fought off the urge. Real leaders didn't explain.

Now he was aware of voices behind him, inside the bedroom, low voices, confidential voices; and not just voices, either, but also chuckles. *Wally. Serena.* He couldn't believe it. They sounded like the merriest young pals you ever encountered. He couldn't believe it, and he didn't like it. They barely knew each other, and their relationship, such as it was, had always seemed awkward and strained. What could they possibly be chuckling over? What little joke were they sharing? . . . *Him* . . . Charlie . . . It had to be at his expense.

Just then the bedroom door opened and Wally emerged. His head and his eyes were downcast, thanks to poor posture and apathy, no doubt, but a smile was spread on his lips, the afterglow of his conversation with his father's wife in the next-to-nothing outfit. Then he looked up and saw his father standing there, and the smile vanished, and he clamped his blank look back on.

Charlie was furious. But what could he say?

So he swept his eyes over the whole menagerie, Wally included, and said, "Awright, whyn't you all go back to bed now. Get some sleep." He said it so sharply, it was like a rebuke. An inexplicable rebuke; but that was all right. Every real leader knew that the occasional outburst of unexplained anger was good for discipline. It set the troops to searching their own conduct for flaws.

They all started trudging back to their quarters. Wally, his head lowered, his shoulders stooped, lugged his sixteen years off the most wearily of all.

Charlie went into the bedroom . . . to set a few things straight. He shut the door behind him. Serena was sitting on the edge of the bed again, facing him. She lowered her head, dug the fingers of both hands in under her hair at the scalp line, threw her tangled black mane back over her shoulder, raised her head, and looked him right in the eye. There was a hint of a smile on her face. Well, she was certainly in a good mood all of a sudden. . . . after joking with Wally about his sixty-year-old father.

He glowered at her for a couple of beats, then gestured behind him toward the hallway. "You missed the town meeting." It wasn't uttered as a little witticism. It was sarcasm incised on a tablet brought down from on high by the patriarch, blame.

"Oh?" If anything, Serena's trace of a smile grew a bit bolder.

"Yeah, they were all there. Your burglar alarm brought the whole gang. The whole Woo Dynasty, including Lin Chi. He was hanging off the spindles. *And* Heidi Filipino. Barefoot." All Serena did was change her suggestion of a smile into a suggestion of a sneer. So Charlie said, "Heidi brought your daughter down, in case you're interested. She was fine. She slept through the whole thing—if you were wondering."

"I know. I talked to Heidi on the intercom." She didn't even sound defensive, which annoyed him still more.

"Serena—you realize that's the third false alarm in the past month or so?"

"Past *six* months or so."

"Well, whatever, it's ridiculous. What earthly good is it? The police, they get so many false alarms, they don't even bother to respond. And *Radartronic Security*? I hope you don't honestly believe *Radartronic Security's* actually gonna protect anybody. Who do you think works for these companies? Who do you think you get for minimum wage, or whatever they pay? You get drifters, winos—and then they let 'em carry sidearms—and they've got the keys to the house! It's ludicrous! We're sayin' goodbye to the burglar alarm system."

"Well, well, well. I hadn't noticed you were so well informed about burglar alarms and burglar alarm companies."

The impudence! "I'm informed enough"—*infawmed*—"and even if I wasn't, I'm from Baker County, Georgia, and I kin take keer my own house. If these ain't enough"—he held up his hands—"I got a .20-gauge shotgun in the closet. If I have to shoot a man, I kin do it. I've done it before."

"In Vietnam, you're talking about."

As a matter of fact, he was—but was she really saying what he thought she was saying?—which was: "You've already bragged to me about what a holy terror you were in the war in Vietnam thirty-odd years ago."

"I'm talkin'bout how it's gonna be in this house from now on, 'at's what I'm talkin'bout! There ain't gonna be any more burglar alarm! Is 'at clear enough?"

Serena put both palms down flat on the bed and stiffened her arms and leaned back and uncrossed her legs and let them fall open in a pose of insouciance. Her breasts welled up under the layers of salmon-pink charmeuse. He could see the insides of her thighs where the robe had parted. Her little half-smile, half-sneer intensified. She looked him right in the eye.

She said, "Who's supposed to shoot the man when you're not here?"

"Whattya talkin'bout? What man?"

"You said if you have to shoot a man. Suppose you're outta town or off riding a horse at three o'clock in the morning. Who's supposed to shoot the man then? Me? Heidi? Nina? Jarmaine? They're not from Baker County, Georgia, far as I can tell, and I doubt if they've been to war, although we can always ask them."

"Now, you listen, goddamn it—"

"Don't you swear at me." With a single angry thrust of her arms she was up off the edge of the bed and walking toward the bathroom. Her little expression had vanished. She wasn't even looking at him any longer. She was turning her back on him and walking out of the room.

He tried to grab her by the arm. With a furious wrench she broke free and confronted him, her eyes ablaze.

"Now *you* listen, Charlie. You don't even know what's just happened in this house, do you. You don't understand the first thing."

"I know one thing 'at's happened, and I know one thing 'at's *about* to happen."

"Oh, kindly spare me the caveman stuff. Whyn't you do yourself a favor and go in the bathroom?" She extended her arm and pointed a finger toward the bathroom door, like a parent ordering a child to march. "Take a look at yourself in the mirror, in the full-length mirror. Just take a good look. Make sure you can see the boots, too."

And in that moment what struck Charlie even more than the outright insolence was her face. It wasn't contorted, there was no furious scowl, her chin wasn't trembling, she wasn't about to sob or shake or come to pieces in any fashion. Oh no, not her. She was the very picture of icy superiority, a twenty-eight-year-old girl laying down a lecture to Charlie Croker himself. He didn't know what to say.

"You're so busy being the big stuff," she was saying, "you don't even wanna think how it might affect anybody else in the house."

"Such as you, I suppose."

"Such as me, for a start. All of a sudden I wake up? The burglar alarm is ringing? I turn toward my husband, who's supposed to be beside me in bed, and he's not there? I look at the clock, and it's *three*-something? I call out your name? You don't answer? I look in the bathroom? You're not in there, either? For all I knew, somebody'd broken into the house, and you were lying in a pool of blood. Just then I hear this terrific racket. You never heard such a commotion. Sounds like somebody's charging up the stairs in army boots, some maniac or something. I run over and lock the bedroom door—just in time, because the next thing I know, somebody's turning the handle of the door this way and that, trying to get in, and throwing his weight against the door, like he's gonna push it in, and grunting and groaning—doesn't even sound like a human being. Sounds like a—a—a—a *bear*—or a *monster*. It's going *Ungggghhhhh unggggghhhhh unggggghhhhh*, like that. So I hide behind the bed. When it breaks down the door, maybe it won't see me. Then I hear it coming through the bathroom. Then I hear it fumbling around on the wall for the light. I figure, 'This is it. It's coming after me.' And then I hear this *ang*-ry, bel-*lig*erent voice say, 'Serena'—"

"I was only trying to get to the control box to—"

"Let me finish—"

"—turn the thing off before—"

"Let me finish—"

"—it woke the whole house up, and—"

"Let me finish! Good. Thank you very much. Then the light comes on, and it's standing there. It's got on *riding* boots, right up to its knees. It's got on riding *pants*. It's got on a *polo* shirt. Three o'clock in the morning; and it's going riding."

"Three fifty-five," said Charlie, immediately realizing how lame it sounded.

"Ohhhhh! Three fifty-*five*! Excuse me. All right, 3:55. *You* set off the alarm, even though you know very well you have to turn it off before you go down downstairs, and what's your first instinct? To blame somebody else. To blame me."

"I never *blamed* you."

"No? *No?* I wish you could've seen the look on your face. *Goddam*n this and *Jesus Christ* that and *shit-look-what-you-did-Serena* and *get-in-that-closet* and *what-the-hell's-the-matter-with-you-Serena* when I couldn't find that little switch right away. You weren't *blaming* me? What would *you* call it?"

"The alarm was ringing, the phone was ringing, all hell was breaking loose—I was only tryin' to get things under control."

"You were only trying to shift the blame, was what you were only trying to do, Charlie. I still haven't heard a single *Gee, I'm sorry* or anything else. I know what you told your son. I hate to think what you told Nina and Jarmaine and Heidi."

Charlie was angry all over again. "Awright—you finished now?"

"No," said his wife, "I'm not. I really do think you oughta go in the bathroom right now and take a look at yourself. It's the middle of the night, Charlie, and you're up and dressed in this . . . this . . ."—while she searched for the word, she waved her hand at him dismissively—"this . . . *getup* of yours. The barn isn't *open* in the middle of the night. Maybe Jugsy's only a stupid horse, but he's not so stupid that he's standing around ready to *go* in the middle of the night." She jutted her chin forward slightly and cocked her head and gave him a look of mock solicitude. "What are you *doing*? Anybody who didn't know you would think you were gaga."

With that she turned and headed straight into the bathroom and shut the door and locked it. *Gaga.* The impudence! Charlie was furious, and yet in that very moment he realized that it wasn't that good, keen, pure, all-out male fury that had served him so well over the years. He was going to make her feel six kinds of sorry when she came out of that bathroom . . . but in fact he felt so damned tired . . . His head felt like a husk . . . He walked over and sat down on the side of the bed. He closed his eyes and massaged his temples with his fingertips. Maybe the good old country breakfast would revive him. . . . He'd haul out the pans and thaw the biscuits and the grits—or were the grits frozen?—and where were the pans, for that matter? . . . and the butter and the coffee . . . It dawned on him that he didn't have a ghost of an idea where any of it was kept . . . Well, he'd figure it out . . . He pivoted on his hip and brought one leg up onto the bed, boot and all. The boot wasn't going to do much for the bed's white coverlet, which had a little waffle design on it and came from—what the hell was the name of it?—someplace where they sold sheets for $500 apiece was all he knew . . . Well—he was the one who had paid for all this stuff in the first place, and so he could put his damned boots any damned place he felt like. So he brought the other leg and the other boot up and let his upper body sink back on the bed and his head sink back on the pillow. He closed his eyes. He'd catch forty winks and then go downstairs and get some breakfast and head on over to the Spread and the hell with what Serena or anybody else had to say about the middle of the night. He could hear her running the water in the bathroom. He hoped she'd keep it on for a while. It was a soothing sound, and as long as he could hear it he wouldn't be having to deal with her unbelievable impudence . . .

Christ . . . Who was this woman? How the hell did she get here? The questions startled him. Then he realized they had been forming in his mind for the past thirty months at least, and he had only been married to her for thirty-six. But never before had they just popped into his head in so many words. Who was she? What was she doing here? And the terrible thing was, once he finally asked the questions, he knew the answers. Sex and vanity; it was as simple as that; and maybe vanity even more than sex. Martha had gotten *older*, that was all . . . And as he lay there stretched out on the bed, a vision of Martha's shoulders and neck, just her shoulders and neck, floated into his head. That was what he had noticed, once she reached her forties, he guessed it was. Martha had always been a big girl, a big, sunny, lovely girl, but as she got older, she got *thicker*. Her midsection got thicker, and her skin got thicker, and her shoulders and her upper back began to round over a little bit and get *thicker*. One night at a big Tech reunion at the Hyatt Regency, she was wearing some kind of bare-shouldered dress, and he happened to come up behind her from a certain angle, and Jesus Christ, she had shoulders like a middle linebacker for the Dallas Cowboys, his wife did. He couldn't get that image out of his mind. *Like a middle linebacker*—and how often could you get aroused by a forty-some-year-old woman with that much beef in her neck and her shoulders and her upper back? He hated himself for even thinking it. But that was the way the male animal was constituted, wasn't it . . .

Involuntarily he sighed, just lying here with his eyes closed. A wavelet of guilt washed over him. Martha's beefy shoulders lingered behind his eyelids for a moment, and then he could see Serena the way she had looked the first time he had ever laid eyes on her. She was standing in front of a meeting room at PlannersBanc conducting some kind of "art investment seminar" the bank had cooked up. John Sycamore and Ray Peepgass had talked him into attending it. They had these young women from some kind of graduate school in New York conducting these goddamned things, these "seminars," and Serena was standing up there giving a talk with slides and a laser-light pointer she held in her hand. She had on a little black dress that made her seem more naked than if she had been wearing nothing at all. She was so sexy that if she had pointed that little laser thing at him and hit the button, he would have risen up right then and there and done something silly. The lecture was pure bullshit, something about some German artists named Kiefer and Baselitz and Something-or-other and how much their totally sick paintings would be worth in five years if you invested in them now. But the lecturer—the lecturer he had gone for all the way. At the time it had seemed like nothing more than the usual thing. In Atlanta a real estate developer was a *star*!—and some of the others, like Lucky Putney, Dolf Brauer, and his old buddy Billy Bass, were out tomcatting around so openly, so outrageously, that his little fling with Serena seemed like nothing at all. She made him feel like a kid, like a twenty-year-old in the season of the rising sap. She liked it good and reckless, like that time they went off for a weekend to Myrtle Beach—another wavelet of guilt . . . The terrible lies he dreamed up to tell Martha in order to arrange these things . . .

—and they were walking along the beach, and then they went over behind some sand dunes, and he couldn't believe it—she had a funny look on her face, and she took off her bikini and he took off his swimming trunks—in the middle of a bright sunny day!—with a lighthouse or observatory, or whatever it was, not three hundred yards away!—they could have been caught at any moment!—him!—the great *star*!—fifty-six years old!—rutting away in the sand!—sex-crazed, like a dog in the park! But that was the thing . . . At fifty-five or fifty-six you still think you're a young man. You still think your power and energy are boundless and eternal! You still think you're going to live forever! And in fact, you're attached to your youth only by a thread, not a cord, not a cable, and that thread can snap at any moment, and it *will* snap soon in any case. And then where are you?

Vengeance is mine, saith the Lord, and I shall be paid. Nobody ever warned anybody about this, did they! All those experts, all those people who wrote the books and articles and ran the talk shows on television or whatever—when they talked about marriage, they were always talking about the first marriage, the original marriage. But by now, he figured, there must be thousands of men like him, rich businessmen who over the past ten or fifteen years had divorced their old wives of two to three decades' standing and taken on new wives, girls a whole generation younger. And what did all the experts have to say about these irresistible little morsels? Nothing! What if a man goes through all that, the separation, the divorce, all that agony, that struggle, that hellish expense, that . . . that . . . that *guilt* . . . and one day, or one night, he wakes up and wonders, Who the hell is this in the bed next to me? Why is she here? Where did she come from? What does she want? Why won't she leave? That they don't tell you about.

The thought made him tired . . . so tired . . . so tired . . . so tired . . . In the bathroom the water continued to rush and rush . . . Charlie Croker lay stretched out on the bed, in his big glossy black riding boots, with all the lights on, surveying the world from behind his eyelids. In no time, in far fewer than forty winks, he rode off into the Land of Nod.

Chapter VII

Hello Out There, 7-Eleven Land

IT WAS THE TIME OF DAY RAYMOND PEEPGASS DREADED MOST. It was after 9 p.m. this warm April night, and dark outside, and he was alone in his mean little rental unit—*rental unit!*—$625 a month—apartment number XXXA—*XXX!*—at the bottom of the steep asphalt slope of the Normandy Lea Apartments at the base of the concrete-walled cliff that supported Highway 75 some seventy or eighty feet overhead.

Terribly warm and muggy tonight, for late April in Atlanta . . . But if he kept the two little windows in the little living room open, to get some air, he could hear the merciless hum of the eight lanes of traffic up on the expressway, plus the gear changes and diesel horns of the trucks, and the crabby sounds of the young couples, already fed up with marriage, buckling and unbuckling their bawling children into and out of the Streptofoam-lined plastic child-safety seats in their Toyotas and Hondas out on the asphalt in front of the building. On the other hand, if he closed the windows he had to turn on the incremental room air conditioner, which made a grinding noise whenever the compressor came on.

So he kept the windows open, and now he could hear one of the young wives screaming at her husband—it was mostly the young wives who screamed—sometimes the husband, but mostly the wife—he could hear one of the wives screaming:

"Oh, that's just *great*! How many times did I tell you? Your attitude toward your own child *stinks!* It just stinks the whole place up! Uccccchhhh!" A child began howling.

Stinks! That was the sort of thing young wives yelled at their husbands these days! *Stinks!*

Normandy Lea . . . *Lea* . . . Peepgass had looked it up. A *lea* was a grassy meadow. Normandy Lea consisted of three two-story buildings, parallel to one another, each containing twenty apartment units. For some eccentric reason, each unit bore a roman numeral plus an arabic letter from IA and IB to XXXA and XXXB. The lea was a three-foot-wide swath of grass that fringed each building. Normandy came in the form of three astonishing steeply pitched roofs made to look like the roofs of dairy barns in northern France. The fact that Peepgass had drawn an XXX unit—*XXX!*—down at the bottom of the ravine, at the base of the highway cliff—this he found frighteningly, but perfectly, in keeping with his general run of fortune. Technically the Normandy Lea was in Collier Hills, and technically Collier Hills was the southernmost part of Buckhead; beyond that there wasn't much you could say about this poor little apartment.

Christ God, he was lonesome! The hums, thrums, and belches of Highway 75 only made it worse. All those people, hundreds of them, thousands of them, roaring past up there on top of the cliff, going somewhere, probably to *see* somebody, and he sat here alone at 9:15 p.m. looking out the window here in unit XXXA into the window of unit XIXA in the next building. Whoever lived there had tilted a mattress up against the wall and hung a bunch of plastic hangers with skirt clips on the edge of the mattress for some unfathomable reason . . .

And he had thought Snellville was Low Rent living! Jesus, the house in Snellville, a two-story, four-bedroom Williamsburg Colonial with a mock Jack'n'Jill slate-roofed well in the front yard, coach lights by the front door, and an NBA Products glass basketball basket on a stanchion out by the little backaround in front of the garage—despite the way he used to complain about the hour's drive down to Atlanta every morning in all that hellish traffic, the house in Snellville had been San Simeon compared to . . . this . . . At least there were *people* there! Betty, heavy and overbearing as she was—at least she was someone to talk to! Brian and Aubrey, only eleven and nine but fellow human beings all the same, little souls who at least filled up the void of the night!

"Now you've done it! Sometimes you really make me wanna *puke*! You really do!" The husband this time.

Peepgass went to the window, to get closer to humanity, if only as a voyeur. The husband had parked one baby, strapped into its child seat, up on top of the roof of the Toyota, and the child was yowling. The husband was wearing a white T-shirt with a shaggy, shapeless, much-too-big sleeveless sweater and jeans, plus a baseball cap. The wife wore jeans, hideously gaudy sneakers, and a black-and-red-plaid logger's shirt with the tail hanging out. She was holding the other baby, which was also yowling, in another child-safety seat with a lot of veal-colored straps hanging down.

Peepgass waited for more dialogue. Humanity! Please, God! Human voices!

But the unhappy young couple, fed up with marriage, fed up with children, fed up with the Normandy Lea, just glowered at one another.

Peepgass himself felt not so much fed up with marriage as stripped of it, as if he had been snuggled up in a nice warm bed and someone had snatched all the covers off. That someone was Betty. As soon as she had learned about Sirja, she had thrown him out. *Just like that!* No long, agonizing discussions, no visits to the marriage counselor. Just . . . *Out, Bozo!* Betty was more Old Boston than he had ever realized; none of your late-twentieth-century therapeutic mewling and puling for Betty Pierce Peepgass of the Boston Pierces. Oh no. She was tall, wiry, raw-boned, and tough, Betty was, the tennis-playing type. She had been tall, lean, fit, hearty, sunny, blond, fair-skinned Betty Pierce when he had met her twenty-one years ago in Cambridge. She was in graduate school getting her Ph.D. in English after four years at Princeton, and he was a U.C. Berkeley boy in the Harvard Business School, and they were engaged before he even got his MBA, and they had married soon thereafter. Betty had intimidated him a little, and her family, the Pierces, who had a house in Brookline and spent their summers in Maine, had intimidated him a lot. Betty had pressured him to get a job in the Northeast or, better still, become some sort of entrepreneur—she was very strong on this word *entrepreneur*—even though her own father, John Codd Pierce, was a typical Boston corporate time-server, a real vest-pocket watch-chain club man (*Porcellian* at Harvard, as she often just happened to mention). Peepgass's own father had been something close to a genius, a thermodynamics physicist at the Ames Research Center near San Jose; and his, Peepgass's, SAT and GMAT scores for Berkeley and the Harvard Business School had been way up in the ninety-something percentile. At the Business School, even back in the late 1970s, when he was there, only MBAs in the lower half of the class went into banking—and he had been near the *top* of the class. But back then he, Peepgass, had been about to get married . . . and everything . . . and the job offer from PlannersBanc . . . or the Southern Planters Bank and Trust Company, as it was then called . . . had been so indisputably *solid* . . . and it *was* a huge bank, even though it was in Atlanta, Georgia . . . Not a bad place to start out, anyway . . .

Betty Pierce Peepgass had never really adjusted to Atlanta. She detested Southern Girls with "their incessant how-yew smiles and throat-slitter sniggers," as she put it. She never got used to being away from her beloved Boston, where Pierces were Pierces. But she wasn't so depressed that she ever started to fade away . . . Oh no . . . She never suffered in the Amazon department. She had grown steadily stronger, louder, bossier, and grimmer over the years; not to mention prematurely gray, which she refused, in typical Old Boston fashion, to do anything about; and more scornful of his indecisiveness and his "umbilical attachment" (her term) to PlannersBanc. He couldn't imagine summoning up the fortitude to leave her . . . or the bank.

Nevertheless, the great flame of the 1980s, which was known as the Sexual Revolution, had been lit in Raymond Peepgass—and *shit!* He realized, as he stood here at the window of his little flat in Normandy Lea, listening to the overhead hum of Highway 75, staring out at the nighttime asphalt, inwardly crying, "Hello, out there! Any fellow humans?"—he realized that the damnable Charlie Croker even had a hand, without ever knowing it, in lighting the holocaust of 1980s Sex in him. But he shut that out of his mind, refused to think about it. The Ice Queen and her Art Geishas, Jenny and Amy Phipps-Phelps . . . He was damned if he was going to let himself dwell on all that again . . . but *Sirja*—there was no way in God's world he could help but think about Sirja . . .

Two years ago he had begun traveling to Helsinki, Finland, to monitor a $4.1 billion loan package PlannersBanc had put together for the purchase of Finnish government bonds. Helsinki had to be the dullest capital in Europe, even worse than Bonn, but Miss Sirja Tiramaki was

105 pounds of joy. He had literally bumped into her, shank to flank, Sirja with her smiling face, her super full and bouncy pale blond hair, her big brilliant blue eyes, her tenderly curved little neck, and the swollen suggestion of her surprisingly big bosom, in an aisle of the first-class cabin of a Finnair flight to Helsinki. Peepgass was in first class thanks to tens of thousands of Atlanta/Helsinki frequent-flier miles. Sirja was in first class as a trespasser from Coach in search of a vacant lavatory. Enchanted by the twinkle in her eyes, he didn't want to deflate his first-class bearing by telling her about the frequent-flier miles, and so he didn't. She was merely a notions buyer for Ragar, the Finnish department store chain, who came to the United States four to six times a year to scout the American market. But the way she spoke English, with her strange, clipped, hippety-hop Arctic Circle accent—it was so exotic—so erotic! Soon they were snuggling in his hotel in Helsinki every time he came to town on a PlannersBanc bond mission. Raymond Peepgass, senior loan officer, had never known such joy.

His exotic, erotic little flower of Scandinavia had a rather grossly inflated notion of his place in the international banking community. He flew first class, stayed in the finest hotel in Helsinki, the Grand Tatar, took her to the most famous restaurants, and, as a senior officer of the great American banking giant, PlannersBanc, had meetings with the Finance Minister himself. "Raymond!"—it was so exotic, so erotic, the way she pressed his name with her tongue against the roof of her mouth. He couldn't bring himself to puncture the lovely bubble of her conception of him as a fabulously wealthy American banker. As for the other inevitable question—"But, Raymond, you are married"—the great banker allowed as how his marriage had been dead for many years, was disintegrating rapidly, and would need merely a push . . .

The great banker assumed that his little Finnish bundle was in it for what he was in it for, namely, the revolution in the loins. In that assumption, as he now realized, he had been even more naïve than she. One day, after months of international snuggling and bundling, the no-longer-smiling little Sirja informed him that she was pregnant. No problem, he said; in America abortions were quick, legal, inexpensive, and absolutely safe: outpatient stuff. You don't understand, Raymond, said Sirja. I am Roman Catholic. I will have my child, and you will be its father. His response, as he had to admit on a long and gloomy reflection, was pure Raymond Peepgass. He was petrified. He tried to avoid her; and when he couldn't, he tried to double-talk her. Here at the office he took about one of every forty calls she made and kept telling her he had to think things through. This was not a smart strategy. She turned up at his office one day, visibly pregnant, and announced that she had resigned from Ragar and was moving to the United States so that her son—she had had a sonogram—would be an American citizen like his father, who would be providing full support, either voluntarily or . . . otherwise. She had already hired a lawyer. In a state of shock Peepgass, in true Peepgass fashion, had done nothing but dither about and beg for time, while she got a paternity suit going.

What with the telephone calls and certified letters, Betty Pierce Peepgass got wind of it, pried the whole story out of him—and then threw him out of the house. He had been lucky to find what he was now standing in: a $625-a-month apartment in Collier Hills, which, by micromanaging the definition, you could call Buckhead, as in "Where do you live?" Answer: "Oh, up in Buckhead." Sirja was currently living not in Finland but in an apartment in some old woman's house in Decatur, over in DeKalb County. She had given birth to her son at the Emory University Hospital, to make him a citizen not only of the United States but of the state of Georgia, and had named him Pietari Päivärinta Peepgass, after some revered Finnish writer or other, and was demanding $15,000 a month in child support. Was she kidding? Was this some kind of morbid joke? Couldn't she get it through her head that his gross pay was only $10,833 per month? Didn't she have a calculator? Couldn't she divide 12 into $130,000?

His counteroffer was $300 a month . . . and he couldn't afford that! What with this miserable hovel in Collier Hills to pay for, plus the house and household in Snellville, plus Brian's and Aubrey's orthodontic makeovers and many and varied extracurricular activities, plus Betty's interminable chronic-sinus treatments and God knew what else, plus the legal fees, which were eating him alive, his yearly nut was now more than his gross salary! Squalid, all too squalid, the whole thing . . . Master Pietari Päivärinta Peepgass was out there somewhere in DeKalb County, eating, gurgling, eating, goo-gooing, eating, growing, eating, growing . . . growing . . . growing . . . and crying for more . . . She would feed him well, the Finnish *femme natale* would . . . That little bugger, Pietari Päivärinta Peepgass, that little bundle of ludicrous Scandinavian alliteration, that budding little butter-bottomed Georgia boy, was her meal ticket . . . and he was eating and growing, someday to rise up on his two hind legs—

"REAL SMART, PUS BRAIN! YOU'RE JUST GONNA LET YOUR SON SLIDE OFF THE ROOF OF A WORTHLESS BEAT-UP 1986 TOYOTA AND CRACK HIS SKULL ON THE ASPHALT, ALL BECAUSE YOU'RE TOO MUCH OF A DICK-HEAD TO LOAD A CAR AND LOOK AFTER YOUR OWN FLESH AND BLOOD AT THE SAME TIME!"

The wife again . . . It was gross and horrible—but a human voice!

Oh, how desperately he wanted the husband to answer. Anything. Anything at all. Any human voice would do. Hello out there . . .

CONRAD HENSLEY'S AFFLICTION, unemployment, cast a shadow upon everything around him, and nothing around him at this moment had ever been much to start with. The chair he sat in, a $9.95 folding aluminum chair from the Price Club, had a plaid nylon webbing that was already beginning to fray. The rug beneath him, from Pier One Imports, was made of sisal, and left waffle designs on the children's feet when they walked across it barefoot. The coffee table was made of a flush door from the Home Depot, with dowels screwed on for legs, and had a depressed crack in the middle where Carl, his five-year-old son, had bludgeoned it this morning with a foot-and-a-half-long plastic figure of Cyber Rex, the robot dinosaur.

A stab of self-loathing. He, Conrad, didn't look any better himself. His T-shirt was worn-out, as well as being too skimpy and too tight thanks to the way his shoulders, his chest, and his back had thickened up during his six months as a beast of burden in the Suicidal Freezer Unit. His jeans were too tight in the thighs for the same reason and had a tear in one knee. His feet were bare except for a pair of zori with Styrofoam soles and rubber thongs . . . *No!* was pouring into his heart . . . at the very time when he should be concentrating on the manual he held in his hands, his huge freezer unit hands (he stared at his massive fingers with wonder and admiration), a paperback entitled *SympaTechnics: The Omni-Brand Word-Processing Home Tutor.*

His latest spark of hope—so many had already died—was the notion of signing on with ContempoTime, an Oakland agency that was always running WORD PROCESSORS WANTED ads in the *Oakland Tribune* and the *Walnut Creek Observer*. "Word Processors" referred to people, not the machines, to the clerical help who *operated* word processors. ContempoTime hired them out as "office temps" for companies in the East Bay. He couldn't even *begin* to buy a PC or any other form of word processor, but he had always been good at using computers when he was at Mount Diablo. His gaze kept returning to his miserable cracked table and his miserable torn jeans, which taunted him, saying, "You miserable failure! You jobless statistic! You pathetic excuse for a father!"

The truth was, how could anyone, or anything, look good in this place? They were living in a duet, a form of cheap housing Conrad had never heard of before he and Jill moved in a year ago. Duets didn't seem to exist outside the East Bay, but here in Pittsburg, thirty miles east of Oakland, everybody knew about duets. They had been built fifty years ago, after the Second World War, and now they were falling to pieces. Duets were rows of small one-story houses about twelve feet apart, with patchy little strips of yard between them. In each house a wall ran right down the middle, the long way, dividing it into two narrow apartments. The apartment on this side of the wall was the flip-flop of the one on the other; and there you had your duet. In the kitchen on your side you could hear bacon frying on the stove next door. This was the dump he had worked like a dog in the freezer unit at Croker Global to escape from, and now the $4,700 he had saved up was melting away, and they were still stuck in it.

All at once: "Leela sluhhhhh! Leela sluhhhhh!"

He could hear it through the wall. He had been hearing it steadily for two days. By now it was a refrain. *Leela sluhhhhh.* He couldn't imagine what the woman was actually saying. She was Asian, judging by her voice and the voices that sometimes tried to answer her. In the two days since the family moved in, Conrad had never laid eyes on any of them, and there seemed to be an absolute mob in there, too. Asians—Cambodians, Laotians, Thais, Vietnamese, Koreans, Sikhs—were moving in all over the duets. Eight or ten would pile into a single tiny apartment.

"*Leela sluhhhhhhhh!*"

This time it was a regular scream, followed by a high-pitched rejoinder from a girl: "You don'—" He couldn't make out the rest of it, just the *You don'*.

Then came a terrific crash, as if a heavy piece of furniture had fallen over. Conrad jumped up. What were they doing to each other? More commotion, more yelling. The action seemed to be moving into the kitchen. He went into the kitchen on his side of the duet wall.

"Leela sluhhhhh!"

"You don'—"

A tremendous slam. Now the two combatants, the woman and the girl, seemed to be heading from the kitchen into the garage, which probably meant they were leaving the apartment. Most tenants came and went through the garages, which opened directly onto the street. To Conrad's sense of alarm was now added an overwhelming curiosity. He went through the screen door from his kitchen into his half of the little twin garages.

The garage's roll-up door was opened wide upon one of those dazzling, cloudless, sky-blue days that follow one another in such an endless procession in the Bay Area in the spring. Yawning at him from across the street were the mouths of more duet garages, revealing every sort of hopeless, pathetic piece of rubbish imaginable. The tenants parked their cars on the street and used the garages as attics . . . or as God knew what. Straight across from his half-garage was the half-garage of an Okie named Boo Tuttle. Down the concrete slope in front of the garage ran a tongue of black sludge. Boo Tuttle himself, Conrad now realized, was underneath an Isuzu pickup parked in the garage. In the recesses of the garage he could make out the inevitable drum of oil. Boo Tuttle did cut-rate oil changes and lubrications. Conrad had used him himself . . . but that didn't improve the view any. Three duets away were the Sikhs. He could see half a dozen of them right now, sitting in who knows what kind of chairs, using the garage as a veranda. The men were wearing turbans and beards and the sort of Indian jodhpur-style pants that were full in the thighs and tight in the lower leg. Conrad had to hand it to the Sikhs. They kept nothing in the garage except the chairs.

Here they came—the woman and the girl. He could hear them as clearly as you please. They were going at it on the other side of the garage wall.

"You don' keh," the girl was saying.

"Boolashih," said the woman. "I keh you dress like you a sluhhh!"

"You don' keh nothin' a—"

"I you mother, an' I care you hair"—it came out *keh you heh*—"look like a nest a rat!"

"You don' keh nothin' 'bout my se'f-esteem!"

"*I* don' keh nothin' 'bout you se'f-esteem? *You* don' keh nothin' 'bout you se'f-esteem! You look like a sluh, like a bim-bim!"

"A bim-bim?" The girl gave a little snort. "What's a *bim*-bim? You don' even know what you say."

"Shuh up! You don' give me you smah mouth, leela sluhhhhh!"

And now they stepped out of the garage, the pair of them, stopping on the concrete apron and glaring at one another, two furious little figures lit up by the sun. Conrad was no more than seven or eight feet away, in the shadows of his garage. The woman, who wore a long, tight skirt wrapped in the Laotian style, was a stumpy creature with a face that looked as if it had been crushed top to bottom. The girl appeared at first to be much taller. She was seventeen or eighteen, slim, delicate, with black hair swept up into an incredible beehive on top of her head. She wore lurid purplish eye makeup, big hoop-style gold earrings, a black T-shirt, jeans cut off almost to the hips so that they revealed the entire length of her legs, which teetered atop a pair of black open-back sandal-style shoes with precipitously high, thick heels. Conrad was all eyes. Not that there was anything unusual about the getup itself. She was dressed like half the girls he had gone to school with just a few years before at Galileo High School in San Francisco. The girls referred to it without a trace of irony as the Hooker Look—and in that moment it occurred to him: "leela sluhhh" meant little slut. But this girl's Midnight Disco eyes were Asian and so exotic, and her legs were so young and slim—

Suddenly the girl's head turned, and she was staring straight at Conrad. Then the mother turned and saw him. There wasn't time for him to pretend he was doing anything other than what he was, which was standing there listening. The mother narrowed her eyes and gave him a poisonous stare. The daughter lowered her head, as if from modesty, but then turned her eyes up toward him. How big and white they were!—there in the shadows beneath the overhang of her false eyelashes. She looked him up and down and gave him the most suggestive smile he had ever seen on a girl's lips. He turned away in embarrassment. Yet he couldn't resist stealing another look as mother and daughter headed off toward an old Ford Escort parked at the curb. And *he* knew *she* knew he would look again . . . from the way her hips went this way and that way as she clicked along on her ridiculous shoes . . . and the way she extended her bare right leg as she slid into the front seat . . . She gave him an eyeful of her leg all the way up to the hollow over the hip joint.

Back inside the duet, he couldn't return to his manual and his sober thoughts of employment. He felt disturbed and aroused. He paced from the living room into the kitchen and then back into the living room. Then he went into the bathroom and looked at himself in the mirror over the sink. He wanted to see himself as *she* had seen him, the leela sluh . . . He studied his lean face, his dark eyes, his mustache . . . Not bad at all! . . . He liked the way the T-shirt stretched across his chest and his shoulders, which were highly defined . . . He pulled the T-shirt out of his pants and slid it up over his ribs so as to bare his midsection, and he tensed his abdominal muscles until they popped out like a six-pack. He was . . . *cut, ripped,* as the bodybuilders liked to put it, from wrestling with all those tons of frozen product at Croker Global . . . Then he lifted his forearms and hands and made two fists . . . His forearms were positively gorged with muscle, and for a brief moment he admired himself enormously.

He could have been an athlete—

He could have finished college by now—at Berkeley—

He might have met all sorts of people—girls—

A familiar stirring took over his loins. He was only twenty-three! Still in the season of the rising sap!—and what an anachronism he was!

That very word, *anachronism,* one of Mr. Wildrotsky's favorites, popped into his head. Conrad had been a virgin when he met Jill, and she had been a virgin, and he had gotten her pregnant, and then he had married her, and he had never even fooled around with another woman. In this day and age who would even believe it? He could hardly believe it himself. He had the same feelings, the same stirrings, as any other young man, and in fact he had those stirrings at this very moment. If the leela sluh were to walk in here, alone, right now, batting those big eyes at him, he would be sorely tempted to go with the flow, and he knew that. But why had *go with the flow* popped into his head? Why one of the favorite expressions of his dad, that past master of euphemisms and other ways of hiding from yourself what you were really doing? His mom was good at that, too, although not nearly so expert as his dad. When his dad decamped from the University of Wisconsin in his junior year and went off to San Francisco, he didn't say he had dashed the hopes and broken the hearts of his parents, who had made great sacrifices to send him to the university. He characterized it as "moving off of dead center." When he and Conrad's mom-to-be started living together in a fly-by-night commune on Haight Street, they didn't call themselves hippies. That was a word they detested and resented. They referred to themselves as Beautiful People, a term they used in the singular also, as in: "Shag? Shag's Beautiful People, man." The fact that his dad had never held a job in his life, other than a temporary one as night desk clerk at the Sailors' Home, didn't mean he was lazy and shiftless. No, it meant he was avoiding that "bummer" known as "the whole bourgeois trip." Conrad, like most little boys, had tried to work out in his own mind that somehow his father was an admirable person. His father did seem to be a big hit among other Beautiful People. When he told his marvelous yarns, they absolutely dissolved with laughter, to Conrad's delight. His dad was a high-spirited, good-looking man, handsome the way a storybook pirate is handsome, and he had a certain foolish daring. When high, he wasn't afraid of sassing figures of authority: policemen, bureaucrats (at the Welfare Office), restaurant managers, and the like. Out of such elements Conrad tried to construct a picture of a man who might be a bit lazy and disorganized but who was an adventurer, a freebooter, a free spirit, a buccaneer—with his mustache, his beard, his ponytail, his single gold earring, and his wild eyes, he really did look like a pirate—who was ready to take on the world. Alas, the picture never held together very long. One night, during a dispute over money, their hashish connection—*connection*, since they never used the word *dealer*—slapped his mom across the face, and his dad didn't even lift a finger. Conrad could never forget that.

His mom was a very pretty, sweet, sentimental, but terribly lax soul who would smother him with affection one moment and neglect the most elementary duties the next. He always remembered sitting with his fourth-grade teacher in a tiny school office for thirty minutes . . . while his mom forgot to show up for the conference. The teacher, believing Conrad showed unusual musical aptitude, had hoped to encourage her to provide him with piano lessons. Home was a mess. Dishes piled up in the sink until the top ones began to slide off onto the floor. They actually slid off and crashed. Another thing Conrad always remembered was the time a dirty, used Band-Aid, mashed by footsteps, had lain on a door saddle for a month. He was seven when he first asked his mom and dad when and where they got married. He wanted to hear about the wedding. They gave him foolish grins and vague, conflicting answers. Soon enough he stopped asking, because even a child could figure out the truth. By and by he came to realize that the imprecation "bourgeois" was supposed to explain all such matters. Only bourgeois people got "hung up" on things like marriage, school, appointments, tidy homes, and hygiene. He was not even eleven when he first began to entertain the subversive notion that "bourgeois" might in fact be something he just might want to become when he grew up. By the time Conrad was twelve, his dad had given up heavy drugs in favor of being pretty much an ordinary North Beach drunk who also smoked pot. He would disappear for days at a time, and his mom would accuse him of staying with a girlfriend. Then came dreadful mornings when Conrad would find some strange man or other in the apartment, some specimen of Beautiful People who had obviously spent the night with his mom. The worst morning of all, however, came one day when he got up to go to school and found his mom and dad asleep in bed—bed being a mattress on the floor and a blanket—no sheets—with another man and a woman he had never laid eyes on before, all four of them naked. He was never able to forget the flaccid areolae of the two women. He felt worse than wounded and betrayed; he felt shamed and dishonored. His father had awakened while he was standing there and had put a sickly grin on his face and said, "Well, Conrad, sometimes you just gotta go with the flow." It didn't take a genius to figure out that this phrase, *go with the flow*, was supposed to put a mystical aura around being a weak sloven and giving in to your lowest animal appetites. His dad said "go with the flow" a lot. Forever after, when Conrad heard people speak blithely of the "sexual revolution," it made him despair about how little supposedly intelligent people understood concerning the world around them.

In high school, at Galileo, he had few friends and almost no social life. He was ashamed and, in fact, afraid to bring anyone home. What on earth would they make of the squalid hole he lived in? What would they make of the unmistakable sweetish but rotten odor of marijuana that clung to the place? Above all, what would they make of his parents, these two aging, rumpled, irresponsible, ruined Beautiful People? When he was fifteen, his father left for good, and Conrad moved to Berkeley with his mom, who now decided she was a radical feminist. They lived in a commune in the Berkeley Flats with five California Granola women, as Conrad thought of them. One thing he never would forget was the way big gruff women kept marching through the living room in logging boots. After high school he left home, enrolled in Mount Diablo Community College in nearby Contra Costa County, and managed to squeeze by on odd jobs. It was in his second and last year at Mount Diablo, in Mr. Wildrotsky's class, that he first learned what "bourgeois" meant in its full historical context. Mr. Wildrotsky, a contemporary of his mom and dad, was sardonic about the concept, but that didn't diminish it for a moment in Conrad's eyes. To live the bourgeois life was to be obsessed with order, moral rectitude, courtesy, cooperation, education, financial success, comfort, respectability, pride in one's offspring, and, above all, domestic tranquillity. To Conrad it sounded like heaven. Even Mr. Wildrotsky was bourgeois enough to take him aside and urge him to fulfill his promise as a student by applying to Berkeley, the crown jewel of the California university system, and getting a bachelor's degree. He had caught Mr. Wildrotsky's attention one day in class when Mr. Wildrotsky had brought up the subject of—ironically, looking back on it, since he hadn't yet moved there—the nearby town of Pittsburg. It seemed that Pittsburg had been founded before the Civil War by land speculators who figured the location, where the Sacramento River emptied into East Bay, would be perfect for a great new Western city, which they laid out on paper and called New York West. But after a decade New York West consisted of two stores and a dozen houses. So when a huge coal deposit was discovered nearby, the name was changed to Black Diamond. But the ore proved to be low-grade, and in 1912, after U.S. Steel built a steel mill on the bay, the name was changed to Pittsburg, without the *h*. But it had never become the Pittsburgh of the West, either, said Mr. Wildrotsky, and now here we were, near the end of the twentieth century, and perhaps it was time to change the name again. Any suggestions? His heart thumping over his temerity, Conrad had raised his hand and said, "How about 7-Eleven?" 7-Eleven? Yes, said Conrad. He had driven through that whole area, from Vine Hill, where he lived, on east to Pittsburg and beyond, and it was now one vast goulash of condominiums and other new, cheap housing. The only way you could tell you were leaving one community and entering another was when the franchises started repeating and you spotted another 7-Eleven, another Wendy's, another Costco, another Home Depot. The new landmarks were not office towers or monuments or city halls or libraries or museums but 7-Eleven stores. In giving directions, people would say, "You take the service road down past the 7-Eleven, and then . . ." Mr. Wildrotsky loved it. It was right up his alley. 7-Eleven! He devoted an entire two weeks of the class to the study of this new urban phenomenon, 7-Eleven Land. Never before or since had Conrad ever felt so important.

As he stood there in a wretched little duet bathroom in Pittsburg, looking at himself in the mirror, he remembered the way Mr. Wildrotsky had finally done everything but get down on his knees and beg him to apply to Berkeley. But by this time he was married, with a son, and another child was on the way—and all over again, as he surveyed his fabulous *cut, ripped, six-pack* build in the mirror, he ached over What Might Have Been.

Just then he heard the Hyundai drive up and stop outside. The engine had a rattling sound you couldn't miss. Little feet were running on the hard ground of the strip of yard beside the duet. He left the bathroom and went out into the living room.

Jill's voice: "Carl! You come back here! Right now! Don't you run away from me! You come back here right now and apologize to your sister!"

More running, plus the sound of a child crying and gasping for breath at the same time.

"Carl! Come here!"

The door to the living room burst open, and here came Carl, five years old and furious. He was a beautiful little boy, blond and fair like his mother. His hair came down over his forehead in thick straight bangs, but his face was now red and contorted, and his eyes were full of tears.

"Hey, Mr. C.!" said Conrad, smiling. "What's the matter?"

The smile only infuriated the boy more, and he began throwing punches that hit his father on the thighs. Conrad sank down onto his haunches and put his palms up in front of him to catch the punches, and Carl began punching him on the arms.

"Come on, me boy," said Conrad, "tell me what's the matter."

"Mommy's what's the matter. Mommy hates me. All she cares about is her little *bay-bee*."

"That's not true, Carl. Mommy loves you."

"Yeah . . . *right*!" said the boy, and he started punching his father's arms again.

Conrad was startled. *Yeah . . . right.* It was the first time he had ever heard his son use sarcasm. Was that normal? Were five-year-olds sarcastic? Or was that something he had picked up from living in a run-down duet development in Pittsburg, California? He hesitated to imagine what he would pick up next. Whatever it was, sarcasm would be the least of it.

"Carl! Did you hear me!" Jill was now standing in the doorway, glowering at the two of them.

Jill always looked about sixteen instead of twenty-three. She wore her blond hair parted in the middle and flowing down her back, in what was known locally as the Surfer Look; but now two long strands, matted with sweat, hung down over her right eye. Her sweet babyish face had two lines that ran from the middle of her forehead down between her eyebrows and almost to her nose. She was red with heat and fury and too much makeup around the eyes and on the cheeks. She wore a man's-style blue-and-white-striped shirt with three buttons undone down the front and a pair of jeans that squeezed her hips and the declivity of her lower abdomen within an inch of her life—and it occurred to Conrad, sadly, as he looked at her, how hard it must be to try to keep on being a California Girl when you were a mother with two small children. Still down on his haunches, he smiled up at her with warmth and sympathy.

That was a big mistake. Jill looked as angry as he had ever seen her.

"That's right!" she said. "Turn it into a little game! Play pattycake with him! For goodness' sake don't ever be *firm* with him! Nooooooo! Leave *that* to *me*! Let *me* be the disciplinarian in the family! Let *me* be the heavy!"

"Wait a second—"

"It isn't funny! Carl just hit Christy as hard as he could, right in the stomach."

"Well—how was *I* supposed to know?"

"You're not deaf! You heard me yelling at him! You knew he was disobeying me. So whatta *you* do? You get down on the floor and *play* with him."

Conrad was speechless. He could feel his face reddening. In a way that he couldn't yet sort out logically, he was being terribly humiliated. For what? He stood up, and as he did so, Carl ran down the little hall toward the bedrooms.

"For God's sake, Jill," said Conrad, "let's all calm down."

"*All . . . calm . . . down?* Thank you very much! I lost my temper—that's all that's happened? That's what you're telling me? Your son, who's a year older than Christy and twice as big and twice as strong, your son just hit your daughter in the stomach with all his might *and* disobeyed me, and you don't want to do anything about it? You just want everybody to be quiet? Is that what you're telling me?"

The victim of the assault, Christy, came walking through the door behind her mother, all eyes and ears. Far from appearing done in, she had the solemn, confident look of a little girl who has just won a big round in the sibling rivalry game.

In the doorway behind Christy, bringing up the rear, appeared another figure. It was Jill's mother, a plump, round-faced woman in her late forties wearing a pair of flowered culottes and a white polo shirt.

"Hello, Conrad," she said with a certain smile. It was the weary, tolerant smile of Patience on a monument, smiling at Grief.

"Oh, hi," said Conrad.

He knew he should call her by name, but he couldn't bring himself to do it. Her name was Arda Ella Otey, and she had indicated he should call her Della, which had been her nickname since childhood. He would have preferred "Mrs. Otey," but that would have sounded distant. At the same time he couldn't bring himself to call her anything so familiar as Della. As to why, he couldn't have said in so many words, but it boiled down to this: Mrs. Otey had never forgiven him for being the Low Rent boy who had gotten her daughter pregnant and then married her. He was the son of a "hippie slob and God knows what for a father"—a verbatim quote Jill had passed along to him in the early rapturous Us Against the World phase of Being in Love—whereas Jill was the daughter of Dr. Arnold Otey, the eminent gastroenterologist. The eminent gastroenterologist had left Mrs. Otey for his twenty-four-year-old receptionist. This was back in Rosemont, Pennsylvania, a high-toned town, apparently, outside Philadelphia, when Jill was fifteen. Doing her best to cope, Mrs. Otey had become intoxicated by a faddish notion spread by books, women's magazines, and television shows: namely, that such a divorce was not a defeat but a rebirth, an exit ramp from the Rut, a chance for a new and wonderful life. Suddenly, with Jill in tow, Mrs. Otey had moved to California, to the East Bay, to the brown hills of Walnut Creek, fifteen miles east of Oakland. Reborn!—free of the ogre Arnold Otey!—until one day she woke up to the fact that she was now an obscure woman in her forties, in a strange place, on her own, hunched over a word processor in the circulation department of *The Harvester*, a Contra Costa County shopping newspaper. At this point she began to work into any and all conversations the information that she was, in fact, the former wife of the eminent Philadelphia Main Line gastroenterologist Dr. Arnold Otey. In due course Jill had enrolled at Mount Diablo Community College and met a boy as lonely, shy, uprooted, and good-looking as she was. His name was Conrad Hensley. When the two of them got married at the age of eighteen, Dr. Otey's ex-wife was appalled.

A pattern had developed. Whenever Jill went to visit her mother, she returned to the duet with a large earful of the shortcomings of Conrad Hensley, which oozed out in conversation over the next few hours, however unconsciously. How long did he intend to work as a manual laborer in a warehouse freezer? There had been many variations on that lament. And, of course, now that he had no job at all, not even one as a product humper at Croker Global, the range was unlimited.

Conrad looked at Mrs. Otey's patient, pitying smile and decided to smile back, just to promote peace.

"GO AHEAD, MAKE MY LAY!"

Lay? It was a boisterous teenage voice. All four of them, Conrad, Jill, her mother, and Christy, were startled for the microsecond it took the burst of robot laughter to kick in, whereupon they realized it was television. The minor villain, Carl, had slipped away during the attack on the major villain, Conrad, and turned on the set in Conrad and Jill's bedroom.

Jill glared at Conrad and lifted her palms upward, as if to say, "Don't you even have what it takes to keep him from turning on the TV set in the middle of the morning?"

Beaten in a way he didn't yet understand, Conrad hurried into the bedroom. Carl was reclining belly-down on the bed, propped up on his elbows, the toes of his sneakers drumming up and down on the bedspread, watching television. On the screen three girls dressed as high-school cheerleaders were confronting a grossly fat teenage male clad in a pair of Speedo racing swim trunks, a pair of wraparound dark glasses, and a frizzy apricot-red woman's wig. Over the nipples of his bare fatty chest he sported two tasseled striptease pasties. With exaggerated huffing and puffing he was trying to curl a big silver dumbbell upward with his right arm.

One of the cheerleaders said, "Whattaya think it is, Kimberly?"

"I don't know," said the second one. "You suppose there's such a thing as an alien transvestite?"

Another great burst of unseen robot laughter. Conrad walked over and pressed the Off button.

"No!" shrieked Carl. He burst into tears all over again and began kicking the bed with his sneakers for all he was worth.

"Come on, Carl," said Conrad, trying to put a sharp tone in his voice for the benefit of his accusers in the living room. "You know better than that! We don't watch junk TV in the middle of the morning!"

"Who says so!" A real outburst.

"I say so."

"Who cares?" This piece of impudence was muffled, because Carl had buried his face in the bedspread. Conrad wondered if Jill and her mother could hear it. They probably could. He felt compelled to press on as the stern father.

"What did you say?"

Softly, tearfully, deeply muffled: "You heard me." It was a decidedly halfhearted form of defiance—but what would *they* think?

So he said, "That's right, I heard you, and I didn't like what I heard, Carl. I don't like smart talk." *Smart talk* came off as a pretty weak reprimand, and so he added, "And I'm not gonna have it. You understand?"

Even more softly, even more halfheartedly, sunk even deeper in the bedspread: "Shut up."

Shut up? Conrad felt helpless. To what level of anger was he supposed to ascend now?

Suddenly Jill was in the room, her face full of fury and righteousness. She ignored Conrad, grabbed Carl by his upper arm, rolled him over on his back, shook her forefinger in his face, and yelled:

"All right! That's it! You hit your sister, you disobeyed me, you don't listen to your father—now you're gonna get punished!"

It was a real screech. Conrad prayed, hopelessly, that the Laotians next door couldn't hear it.

"Get up!" shrieked Jill. She gave the boy's arm a jerk. He went limp. So she dragged him off the bed by one arm in a furious series of jerks. Carl began crying and screaming and grabbed a handful of bedspread with his other hand. The bedspread came off the bed with him. Jill had pulled him almost as far as the door of the tiny room, but the child still clung with a terrier's determination to the bedspread, which had caught on the metal frame that supported the box springs. His little body was now stretched out like the weak link in a chain about to be pulled to pieces by an overwhelming force.

Conrad gasped, "Jill!" He didn't know which was more appalling, the possibility Carl might get hurt or the vulgarity of the scene. The Laotians next door were hearing it all! What was a mere shout of *Leela sluhhhhh* compared to this exhibition?

He moved toward Carl with the idea of gathering him up, but in that moment the boy lost his grip on the bedspread and went sliding across the floor toward his mother. She grabbed him by both arms and turned toward Conrad with as hateful a look as he had ever seen on her face.

"Don't you . . . *Jill!* . . . *me!*" she said. "*Some*body's gotta teach him he can't be disrespectful."

Carl struggled to get his breath, then let out a wail, went limp again, tried to fall to the floor, and, failing that, started writhing and kicking.

Jill screamed, "Don't you—! Cut that out! You can walk or you can get dragged, but you're going to your room! Now march!"

Still holding on to his arms, she propelled him, half-stumbling, half-sliding, toward the other bedroom, which he and Christy shared. She slammed the door shut behind her but there was no problem, inside or outside the duet, no doubt, hearing the tirade that followed.

Conrad stood staring pointlessly at the snagged bedspread. His face was burning.

From down the hall: "Do you hear me? Do—you—hear—me?"

Not knowing what else to do, he returned to the living room. Mrs. Otey sat on the folding chair holding Christy in her lap, enclosing her protectively with her arms. From the look on Christy's face it was clear that her triumph was now complete. The music of her mother's excoriation of her brother continued to pour down the hall.

Mrs. Otey looked up at Conrad with a certain smile of forbearance that he always found condescending; and never more so than at this moment.

"Jill tells me you're applying for a job in Oakland." She said it in a way—or so it seemed to Conrad—calculated to show that she was only making conversation to divert attention from the general embarrassment over his failure as a disciplinarian.

"That's right," said Conrad.

"Some sort of office job, I think she said?"

"Well—it's an agency called ContempoTime." He tried to explain what ContempoTime did.

All at once Mrs. Otey stopped looking at his face and stared at his left hand. "My goodness. I never noticed that before. Are you able to get your ring off?"

Conrad turned his palm upward and looked at his wedding ring, although he knew the answer perfectly well.

"I've never tried," he said.

"Conrad, you've got the . . . *biggest hands* and the . . . *biggest forearms* I've ever seen, for someone your size."

Male vanity is such that he took it as a compliment. Now he turned up both palms and spread his fingers out, which made his hands seem even bigger. For an instant he thought perhaps his four-year-old daughter might be impressed, too. He proceeded to explain what a demanding test of strength work in the freezer unit at Croker Global had been.

"Well," said Mrs. Otey, "I just hope—do you have a long-sleeved shirt or maybe a jacket with nice long sleeves?"

"Long sleeves?"

"If you're being interviewed for an office job, you might want to wear long sleeves and try to keep your hands in your lap. That's all I mean."

Now came the scalding realization. Far from being favorably impressed by his pride and joy, his powerful hands and arms, she saw them as the seal of his fate, which was to work with his hands forever, at least during the periods when he wasn't part of America's chronically unemployed.

Speechless, Conrad lowered the offending extremities to his side and stared at Mrs. Otey and the little girl in her lap. Christy was still looking at his arms and hands, having just learned that they were monstrous. He had a terrible vision of three generations of Otey women, Della, Jill, and Christy, arrayed against him at this low point in his life.

"I'll try to remember that." He had trouble raising his voice above a hiss.

Down the hall his wife, efficiently shouldering the man's role in disciplining their five-year-old son, had no such problem.

Chapter VIII

The Lay of the Land

"WELL, WES, OLD BOY," SAID ROGER WHITE UNDER HIS BREATH, "this one better be good."

Sullenly, sulkily, surlily, Roger sank back into the white tweed couch in the Mayor's City Hall salon, wondering how much damage his sudden exit had done to his relationship with Gerthland Fuller. Fuller was president of the Citizens Mutual Assurance Society, one of the largest insurance companies in the South—which was to say, the *white* president of a *huge* white company—and he was prepared to pay Wringer Fleasom & Tick $1.4 million to have Roger White II handle the company's conversion from one owned by policyholders to one that issued stock and was owned by shareholders. To call him Roger's number-one client was putting it mildly; number two didn't even qualify for the game. Moreover, the Citizens Mutual account proved to one and all at Wringer Fleasom how easily he could clear the race barrier. Gerthland Fuller had been in Roger's office when Wes called, summoning him to City Hall. Why had he done what he did? Why had he hopped to it, made up some gibbering "emergency" for Fuller's benefit, and left him there? Now, as he sank into the Wes Jordan white couch and surveyed the Wes Jordan ebony walls, he was beginning to hate himself for giving in and skipping out on Fuller—and Wes for having the power and charisma to make him do it.

True, he hadn't had to wait in the reception room with Miss Beasley and the big white cop for a second. Gladys Caesar had been standing out there expressly to receive him and usher him straight in to the Mayor's suite.

"Big deal," he said to himself, reflecting upon this evidence of VIP status.

Idly he let his eyes wander about the room. On the far wall there seemed to be twice as many Yoruban ivory ceremonial swords as before.

"What's this supposed to be," he said, "a Yoruban war room?"

His lips must have moved as he muttered, because the next thing he heard was: "Say what?"

It was Wes Jordan emerging from his inner sanctum. Big grin. No jacket. Pizza Grenade necktie. "Say *what*?"

Roger now realized it was a parody of a street voice. So he started to say, "I was just asking, What's this supposed to—"

Wes cut him off before he could utter another word. "Roger, I got things to tell you, things to tell you, things to tell you, things to tell you, things to tell you." He pulled up an armchair, sat down, leaned forward until his forearms rested on his thighs, and said, "Do you want to take a guess as to who was sitting on that couch, exactly where you are right now, not even an hour ago?"

"No, because I have a feeling you're going to tell me anyway."

The Mayor stared at him and waited a couple of seconds before saying, "Inman Armholster."

Roger leaned forward himself and said, "You're—" He caught himself before saying "kidding." "Well, I'll be damned. What'd he have to say?"

"Started to say 'kidding,' didn't you. You've got to steel yourself against that particular response to life's little surprises. He was startled and upset by the fact that I knew about his daughter's predicament."

"What'd you say to that?"

"I said things just have a way of reaching the Mayor's office. I told him it's a good thing they do, because this situation with his daughter and Fareek Fanon, given his prominence in the corporate world of Atlanta and Fareek's prominence as a sports star—I told him this situation could blow the city apart. I said if we didn't work together in a statesmanlike manner, this thing could lead to a race riot."

"Race riot?" said Roger. "You said 'race riot'?"

Wes Jordan smiled faintly and said, "That's exactly what I said. In Atlanta I can't think of any two words that panic people more. It's the fear that's always just beneath the surface. The last real race riot in Atlanta—started by white people, by the way—was in 1906. It was horrible, and if we had one now it would be a lot worse."

"So what did Armholster say to that?"

"I don't think he heard 'race riot.' I don't think he heard a thing after 'statesmanlike.' 'Statesmanlike?' he kept saying. 'Statesmanlike like who? Like Bismarck, like Chou En-lai, like John Foster Dulles, like Dean Rusk?' " The Mayor smiled. "I was surprised he remembered Chou En-lai and John Foster Dulles. 'I'll be damned if I'll be statesmanlike,' he says. 'My daughter's been raped, and that sonofabitch is gonna pay.' I'd say the word that was right below the surface on that one was 'lynch.' "

"He said 'lynch'?"

"No, no, no, I'm just interpreting his mood. He didn't say 'lynch,' although if that were any longer a practical choice, I'm sure he'd be considering it. That's how angry he is."

Roger said, "But when you get right down to it, he really hasn't done anything so far. He hasn't gone to the police, he hasn't gone to the press, I don't know what he's doing with people at Tech. I hear things, but I don't really know."

"Have you ever seen Inman Armholster, seen him in action?"

"Mmmmm—no."

"He's fat," said the Mayor. "He is one fat man. He's fat from top to bottom. I'll bet you the soles of his feet are fat. But he's a sort of fat white man who exists only in Georgia. All the fat is pure orneriness, and he's ready to chew your head off. The fat doesn't slow him down. He feeds off it. No, the only thing holding him back is that he doesn't want his daughter's name to be made public. The press never does identify the girl in a rape case. But this case is different. I can think of rape cases in which the man was as well known as Fanon, but I can't think of a single one in which the man was as well known as Fanon and the girl was the daughter of anyone as prominent as Inman Armholster. The combination of Fareek 'the Cannon' Fanon and Inman Armholster's daughter might be more of a temptation than the press can resist. That's the way Armholster looks at it."

"So what did he want from you?"

"Nothing," said the Mayor. "He only came to see me because I asked him to. At the suggestion of my friend Roger White II, although I didn't get into that. Anyway, Armholster is literally and figuratively a loudmouth. But he's also ornery and angry, and I don't see him as being all bluff, by any means. Sooner or later he'll do something. So I suggested a way out.

"I said to him, 'Why not turn the case over to the student government Sexual Harassment Committee, or whatever it's called at Tech? They'd have a much better chance of ascertaining the facts and coming to a decision quietly, without any publicity, than anything involving the police or the court system.' "

"What did he say to that?"

"He laughed in my face. He says, 'A bunch of students? They'll cave in to the Administration or the Athletic Department or some "activist" group or anybody else who puts a little pressure on them.' To tell the truth, he may be right about that."

"Well, what should *I* do?"

"I don't know, other than keep your client out of sight. Or as out of sight as an all-American football player with diamonds in his ears and a couple of pounds of gold around his neck can be. You're supposed to be very persuasive, Counselor. Can't you get your client to take all that junk off his head and his neck?"

Roger said, "I'm afraid Fareek and I aren't—"

"I suppose it would be asking too much to hope he might also grow some hair on his head while he's at it, so he doesn't look like some predatory gladiator."

"Fareek and I aren't on the same page," said Roger. "He thinks of me as part of an alien world of suits and ties."

"I feel the same way," said Wes Jordan. "Your clothes always make me want to get to a mirror and find out what's wrong with mine."

"Might be a good idea," said Roger, looking Wes Jordan up and down. "Anyway, he feels more at home with Don Pickett."

"Well then, get Don to do it. But I didn't really bring you over here to give you advice. I just want to warn you of something that's inevitable, something that's bound to happen."

"What's that?"

The Mayor said, "Roger, this thing is going to spread all over town, with or without the press. Too many people already know about it. So you might as well face facts. This story is . . . *coming out*. The question is not . . . *Is* it coming out? The question is . . . And *then* what?"

"Well . . . I don't know, Wes. I don't have any clear idea of what would happen then. What do you think?"

"Oh, I don't know exactly," said the Mayor, "but I have a general idea."

"Which is what?"

"Which is that—let me think of just how to put it . . . Okay, not to belabor the obvious, there are two Atlantas, one black and the other white, but that only begins to say it." The Mayor paused, as if he was having difficulty putting his thoughts together. "You see all the towers in Downtown and Midtown—that's all white money, even though the city is 70 percent black, perhaps 75 percent black by now." He paused again, and then he said, "Our brothers and sisters in this city are not blind." He paused once more, and Roger wondered what his descent into the conventional political rhetoric of the times, "our brothers and sisters," signified. It wasn't Wes Jordan. "They see," resumed the Mayor—but then he stopped and gave Roger a searching look. "It's hard to put it into words."

Roger smiled. "You? Having a hard time putting it into words? What's today's date? Jot it down."

The Mayor finessed the remark and said, "It's going to be a whole lot easier if I *show* you."

"Show me?"

"I'd like to take you on a little ride, a little tour."

"What kind of tour?" Involuntarily Roger looked at his watch.

"It won't take long."

"Gee, I don't know," said Roger. "I've got some appointments, Wes. I had to interrupt a meeting with my biggest client, biggest client I've ever had, as a matter of fact, to come here. Please don't get me wrong, it's not that—"

"You *are* wrong," said the Mayor. "You may not know it yet, but Fareek Fanon is the biggest client you ever had. I'm not just going to take you sightseeing, Roger. I have something very specific to tell you, but I want to put it in the right context. Okay?"

Wes looked dead serious, and Roger felt powerless to say no, even though his hopes for the value of any "little tour" were negligible. "Well . . . okay," he said, "but I've got to call my secretary first."

"Go ahead," said Wes Jordan. "I'll ask Gladys to get hold of my driver and have the car ready. You look dubious, Roger . . . I promise you, you won't be bored."

"It's not that—"

"And don't worry about Wringer Fleasom & Tick. They may not realize it yet, either, but this is the biggest case *they've* got."

So Roger called up Roberta Huffers, and the Mayor had a talk with Gladys Caesar, and soon they were heading down a small stairway that led to an underground parking garage. A big chocolate-colored man, probably in his early fifties, stood beside a pearl-gray Buick sedan. The man was a tank. His shirt-collar size must have been twenty at least. He had a narrow mustache that ran along his upper lip. He already had the back door open for them. For a chauffeur, he was dapper; no two ways about it. He was wearing a double-breasted bluish-gray twist-weave suit and a navy necktie. Twist-weave! Roger wished he'd thought of that.

"Roger," said the Mayor, "this is Dexter Johnson. Dexter, this is my old fraternity brother, Counselor Roger White."

They shook hands; Mr. Dexter Johnson's hands were so big, each finger so gigantic, that somehow Roger's hand got caught up in the man's forefinger, middle finger, and thumb. He couldn't get his fingers around the entire hand.

Roger and the Mayor got in the back seat of the Buick, which was upholstered in burgundy leather, and Dexter Johnson got behind the wheel. He was so massive through the back and shoulders, the front seat seemed incapable of containing him.

The Mayor said, "Let's go up to Tuxedo Park, Dexter, but take Piedmont instead of Peachtree." Then to Roger: "I want to show you Inman Armholster's house."

Roger looked at Wes Jordan and, with a questioning arch of the eyebrows, motioned his head toward the driver.

"Nothing to worry about," said the Mayor, "nothing to worry about at all. Besides, anybody might swing by for a look at Inman Armholster's house. You know the expression *showplace*? Inman Armholster's house is a showplace."

In no time they were heading north through the old Black Downtown, the onetime center of Black Society, black shopping, black professional life, black restaurants, black nightlife . . . Edgewood Avenue, Auburn, Ellis Street, Houston . . . above all, Auburn. Back in the day, as the old folks said, the black leader for whom Wesley Dobbs Jordan had been named, John Wesley Dobbs, had dubbed it "Sweet Auburn." Nothing sweet about it now, thought Roger. Black Society had pulled out a long time ago in favor of the West End, Cascade Heights, and other neighborhoods to the west. An enormous elevated highway had been built through the heart of Sweet Auburn. The house where Martin Luther King's parents lived when he was born was right over there on Auburn, and in the next block was a big memorial to King, the Center for Nonviolent Social Change. King's remains reposed in a marble bier out in the middle of a reflecting pool within the center's walls. Those two blocks were among the most popular destinations in the country for tourists . . . but they didn't stick around to spend money in Sweet Auburn.

The driver, Dexter, went under the Highway 75 overpass and then past the old Atlanta Convention Center, which meant they were already on Piedmont. Then the Mayor said, "You know what street we just crossed?"

"I didn't notice," said Roger.

"Ponce de Leon."

This required no amplification, since practically everybody in Atlanta old enough to care about such things knew that Ponce de Leon was the avenue that divided black from white on the east side of town. On the west side it was the Norfolk Southern Railroad tracks. They might as well have painted a double line in the middle of Ponce de Leon and made it official, a white line on the north side and a black line on the south.

"Incidentally," said Wes Jordan, "just to put things in perspective, two-thirds of the land in Atlanta is now behind us, back there." He motioned with his thumb. "And 70 percent of the population. But to the rest of the world it's invisible. Did you happen to see any of those 'guides to Atlanta' they published for the Olympics? Big, thick things, some of them, regular books, and I couldn't believe it at first. It was as if nothing existed below Ponce de Leon other than City Hall and CNN and Martin Luther King memorabilia. The maps—the *maps*!—were all bobtailed—cut off at the bottom—so no white tourist would even *think* about wandering down into South Atlanta. They didn't even mention Niskey Lake or Cascade Heights."

"I'm not too sorry about that," said Roger.

"I'm not, either," said Wes, "but you get the picture, don't you? How do you segregate white tourists from black people in a city that's 70 percent black? You render the black folks invisible! Okay, now you'll notice we're on Piedmont Avenue, and we're heading uphill. Now, why do I mention that?"

Wes had on one of his smiles.

"I couldn't begin to tell you," said Roger.

"Right this moment," said Wes, "we're driving up a paved-over foothill of the southernmost range of the Blue Ridge Mountains. This whole city is in the foothills of the Blue Ridge Mountains. That's why there are so many hills in Cascade Heights and, as far as that goes, so many neighborhoods named Something Heights or Something Hills. Atlanta's elevation—Atlanta is up higher than any other large city in the country, with the exception of Denver. Most of the rest are at sea level. They're ports. Even Chicago's a port. Atlanta's elevation is a thousand feet. That's the average elevation, the one printed in the atlases. But some people in Atlanta are more elevated than others, and you know what they say always flows downhill. You and I live in the best parts of South Atlanta, but don't kid yourself. We still live downhill."

When they stopped for a light at Piedmont and Tenth, it dawned on Roger that it was just a few blocks up the slope that he had been stuck in Freaknic traffic on the Saturday night that great rocking hulk, Fareek Fanon, had come, contemptuously, into his life.

The Mayor gestured off to the right. "There's Piedmont Park. But do you know what that is up there on the right, the first building you come to? The one I'm pointing to?"

Roger realized that Wes wished to enjoy the minor status thrill of endowing the ignorant with knowledge, but this was his, Roger's, territory. So he immediately replied, "The Piedmont Driving Club."

Disappointed: "Ah. You already knew that."

"I didn't tell you about the night I met our boy Fareek?" He proceeded to recount the whole incident, with a special emphasis on the young Kentucky board-chairman-to-be's mooning of the black-tie party of white people up on the terrace.

This provoked no reaction from the Mayor, and so Roger turned to look squarely at him. His face seemed to be sagging with disappointment. He was waiting for Roger's lips to stop moving.

"Well, I'll tell you something," said the Mayor. "Last year I was invited—all very quietly, you understand—I was invited to *join* the Piedmont Driving Club."

"You were? So was I!"

Now Wes Jordan looked squarely at Roger. He seemed more disappointed than ever.

"I'm not convinced that's a good sign," said Roger.

"Take my word for it," said Wes, "it's not. And that gets down to a problem I have, which I'll tell you about in a minute."

Now they were driving up the hill past the white fence with the stone pillars that led up toward the Driving Club's entrance. Because of the hill it was difficult to see the building itself.

"I don't want to be *in* that club," said Wes Jordan, "but I do have my eyes on someone who *is* in there."

"You have your *eyes* on someone?"

"I'll tell you about that, too. This all has to do with your client. This entire excursion of ours has to do with your client. I just want to give you a little background first, the lay of the land, you might say, the lay of the land."

Well, Wes knew his topology, in any event. Roger never had noticed just how steep a climb it was from Downtown up Piedmont Avenue and up into the North side and Buckhead. Near the top of the foothill, if this really was a Blue Ridge Mountain foothill, Piedmont had been voraciously developed: all concrete and asphalt, not a tree in sight.

By now they were in the commercial district of Buckhead. A conglomeration of shopping malls, hotels, faceted-glass office buildings, showrooms, and restaurants was spread out before them. This was the shopping heart of Atlanta. Downtown and Midtown were all office and hotel towers; shopping scarcely existed. At the very top of the Piedmont Avenue hill was Peachtree Street, where they turned left.

"Peachtree's built on top of a ridge," said the Mayor. "That's the reason it curves the way it does, all the way into Downtown."

"I always heard it was built on top of an old Indian trail," said Roger.

"The two statements are not mutually exclusive," said the Mayor. "I don't know how smart the Indians were, but I bet they were smart enough to walk on top of the ridge and not on the slope."

At an office tower called Buckhead Plaza they turned right onto West Paces Ferry Road, and in two or three blinks they were beneath a lush canopy of trees. The branches and leaves arched over the road until they created an ethereal green tunnel aglow with the sun. Down below, in fabulous planes that began only three or four feet above the ground, were the dogwood blossoms, the heavenly white ones, that had so impressed Roger that Saturday night, the Saturday night of Freaknic, the heavenly Buckhead blossoms through which he had first laid eyes on Buck McNutter's house.

Bango!—they were crossing Habersham Road.

"Habersham Road," said Roger. "Buck McNutter lives up there." He motioned toward the right. "That's where I met my . . . star client."

"You don't believe me yet, do you," said the Mayor. Then he motioned ahead. "The Governor's Mansion."

The Governor's Mansion was right there, set back from West Paces Ferry Road, a long, low structure with a great many columns, a sort of low-slung Mount Vernon, not particularly grand at first glance. Much more impressive, somehow, was the expanse of brick and wrought-iron fencing that ran the length of the huge piece of property. Soon they were beside a high, blank wall. The wall was so high and the vegetation so thick, you couldn't begin to see what was behind it. It was almost noon on a sunny day in Georgia, but West Paces Ferry Road's glowing green arboreal tunnel kept Buckhead's prime residential artery in the softest, gentlest, richest of shades. Where the wall ended, they turned right.

"This is Tuxedo Road," said Wes Jordan. "We're entering Tuxedo Park. It doesn't get much better than this. Not here, not anywhere."

Again! The same great swollen green-breasted lawns he had seen the evening he went to McNutter's! And perched atop each one . . . a mansion, visible through the low-lying clouds of dogwood blossoms. Up above, reaching astonishing heights . . . the trees, with their canopy of green and gold at the top.

"I want you to notice something, Roger," said Wes Jordan. "These trees? There's pine up here, but there's also lots of hardwood, maple, oak, locust, sycamore, beech, chestnut—whereas we've got practically all pine in South Atlanta, even on that Niskey Lake you're so proud of. Hardwood trees need two or three weeks a year in which they're dormant, and because of Atlanta's elevation we get just enough cold weather for that to happen. But up here in Buckhead, up this high, it's cooler than it is down in South Atlanta, and so they've got more hardwood trees . . . Flows downhill, Roger, right into Niskey Lake."

The road, Tuxedo, wound along at the base of the big-breasted mansions for a while and then made a gentle curve to the east. The mansions and the grounds became bigger and bigger, and the canopy of trees became ever more green and golden.

Wes Jordan motioned out the window. "That's the old Courtney Danforth place. I forget what it was called, Windmere . . . Wood Thrush . . . something like that. That was what having the biggest fortune south of Delaware got you. Stop here for a second, Dexter."

Roger lowered his head so he could see out the window better. There, on a rise, stood an enormous structure of brick with four immense columns before the front entrance. There were quoins and groins and pilasters. Ten windows ran across the front on the second story; nine windows and a doorway on the ground floor. God knew how many rooms there were. The ever-present dogwood blossoms frolicked across the lawn in the foreground.

"Know what they used to call Danforth at the American Chocolate Company?" asked the Mayor.

"No, what?"

" 'Boss.' 'Boss, may I speak to you for a second?' He loved it. 'Boss.' He had a huge plantation near Thomasville called Throno. If it wasn't the biggest plantation in the state of Georgia, then it was second, and he had about a hundred black folks down there calling him 'Boss.' Music to his ears. An old lawyer, John Fogg—Fogg Nackers Rendering & Lean?—was telling me about it. He'd been there. The black folks used to sing spirituals for the Boss and his guests after dinner." The Mayor widened his eyes in a mocking way and broke into song: " 'Jussssst a closer walk with Theeeeeee . . .' All very touching, as you can imagine. I'm sure there wasn't a dry blue eye in the house."

"You've got a good voice, Wes!" said Roger.

"Don't act so surprised," said the Mayor. "Like you, I'm interested in music. It's just that our tastes are different. Mahler, Stravinsky—come on! I'll bet you not even Booker T. dug what those cats were blowing. Okay, Dexter, let's head on a little farther."

So they headed on a little farther, and the Mayor said, "Let's stop about where that mailbox is." Which they did. "This is what I want you to see." Roger looked where he pointed. "With all that vegetation it's hard to make it out at first, but you'll see it."

There were so many trees, bushes, flowers, and billows of dogwood blossoms, it took some doing. But soon Roger got his bearings. There, beneath the glorious green-and-gold canopy of Buckhead, atop a great fat green knoll, was an Italian Baroque palazzo such as you might see in Venice or Florence. It was a huge thing whose stucco façade was painted a soft reddish pink. From above, each of the windows projected a high baroque curved cornice, painted white, that matched the curves and counter-curves of a broken pediment, also painted white, that reached up into the roofline. Under each window on the second story of the façade was some sort of crest in high relief—also painted white.

Everywhere you looked there were flamboyant white curves popping out from the reddish-pink stucco. At one end of the house was an old-fashioned porte cochere with a great barrel-vaulted roof and a great curved wooden cornice, painted white, and at the other end was a wing with a matching vaulted roof and cornice and grand Venetian windows. A white string course ran all the way across the façade and intersected with the truly extravagant curved cornice above the main doorway.

Engrossed, Roger kept staring at this amazing house, whose curves created a curious sense of motion, and he said softly, as much to himself as to Wes Jordan, "Philip Shutze."

"Who?" said the Mayor. "That's Inman Armholster's house."

"Armholster's?"

"That's it, and there's a huge wing in the back you can't even see from here. Check out the driveway."

The driveway was sheer homage to conspicuous consumption. It went up to the crest of the hill, where the house was, in two grand and blithely unnecessary curves. It was lined, all the way up, on both sides, with dogwood, boxwood, and beds bursting with blue-and-yellow pansies.

"According to the tax assessor," said the Mayor, "that's the most valuable single-family house in Atlanta. It's 324 feet across the front. That's longer than a football field. It's got thirty-two rooms, a squash court and a gymnasium, which I don't think Inman Armholster has been using very much, a screening room, a library, a sunroom and porch, a built-in greenhouse, and nineteen bathrooms. Nineteen."

"How do you know all that?" asked Roger.

"It's available to one and all down at the assessor's."

"How many people in the family? I mean, that live here?"

"Three," said the Mayor with his sardonic smile, "a grand total of three: Armholster, his wife, and their daughter. Thirty-two rooms. This is how Elizabeth Armholster grew up. Incidentally, in the rear wing there are eight servants' rooms, a servants' kitchen, and a 'servants' hall,' whatever that may be. Oh, and somewhere out back there's a swimming pool, a pool house, two tennis courts, and a potting shed."

"And it's a Philip Shutze house," said Roger, "or I'll bet it is."

"A what?"

"Philip Shutze was the most famous architect, or residential architect, Atlanta ever had, him and his partner, Neel Reid. This place has the classic Shutze look, Italian Baroque it's called, or Venetian Baroque. This is the kind of palazzo the Venetian merchants used to build back in the sixteenth century, I guess it was. You know *The Merchant of Venice*? They were the richest people in the world. All that fabulous art you see in Venice? That's the merchants competing with each other to commission a bigger, grander, more beautiful ceiling mural, or whatever."

The Mayor looked at Roger quizzically for a few moments, then said, "You really get off on this grayboy art and architecture, don't you?"

Roger felt a hot red tide rush into his face. *Get off? Grayboy?* Why, you bastard! "You don't have to *get off* on it to appreciate it, Wes! For Christ's sake, art and architecture aren't black or white, they're just art and architecture! I'm surprised at you! From your friend André Fleet maybe that's what I'd expect, blacker-than-thou and all that old bullshit! But you?"

Roger didn't realize how angry he had become until he saw Dexter Johnson eyeing him in the rearview mirror to see if by any chance the Mayor of Atlanta was in any imminent danger.

Wes backed off as fast as he could. "Okay, okay, okay, you're right, you're right. Logic is a hundred percent on your side, but sometimes I don't react logically, which is my fault, I'll grant you. I just feel like so-called Western art's got nothing to do with me, much less with the rest of the population of South Atlanta."

"Oh, so now you're part and parcel of South Atlanta! Congratulations! Or is it that Western art doesn't go over with the voters? Is that what you're trying to say?"

Wes looked at Roger crossly for a moment, then relaxed and said, "Perhaps. Perhaps. But I think it runs deeper than that. Sometimes my friends up here on the north side of town—and we're talking about people with money now—contributors—sometimes they try to get me mobilized for some big art exhibition or the opening of the symphony season, or whatever it is, and it just doesn't feel right. It's got absolutely nothing to do with me, all this stuff. That's just the way I feel. I'm totally unmoved by any of it, except maybe by the amount of money they put into it."

"Are you moved by Yoruban art? You've got enough of it in your office."

"Well, at least I—aw, hell, Roger, I didn't bring you all the way up here to argue about aesthetics. We're on the same side."

"I'm not so sure the argument is about aesthetics," said Roger.

"Well—whatever. I'm trying to forge an alliance. You'll see. Your colleagues at Wringer Fleasom will be very proud of you. Dexter, let's head on over to Blackland Road."

"What's on Blackland Road?" asked Roger.

"I'll tell you, but first I just want to show it to you."

Blackland Road was scarcely a quarter of a mile from Armholster's house. The homes were even grander.

"Stop right there, Dexter," said the Mayor.

Roger found himself looking up at an extraordinary house of stone, or extraordinary for Atlanta. It looked like a medieval manor in the west of England, an observation he decided not to unburden himself of. The big central front doorway was surmounted by a segmental pediment, and the façade featured an array of grand windows with cruciform mullions and more small panes than you could count from this distance with the naked eye. Roger decided to keep all that to himself also. Wes Jordan obviously didn't want to hear about grayboy segmental pediments, let alone cruciform honky mullions. In front of the house was a low stone wall with a pair of magnificent ornamental stone piers. A large ungated opening in the wall gave access to a turnaround paved with Belgian cobblestone. The whole thing was very European, not a hint of which did Roger intend to transmit to the Mayor of Atlanta. The only thing he couldn't figure out was the two sculpted birds that were perched, wings spread, as if taking off, on the pediments atop the ornamental piers. Ordinarily you would expect to see eagles or falcons or some other predatory beast. These two birds looked curiously benign, even slightly frightened.

"Not as big as Armholster's," said Wes Jordan, "but quite a pile all the same, hunh?"

"That's true," said Roger.

"I don't get those birds, though," said Wes. "What the hell are they? What do you figure they are?"

Christalmighty. He *would* pick out the one detail he, Roger, knew nothing about. "I don't have the faintest idea," he said a bit petulantly.

From the front seat Dexter went "Heh heh hegggghhhhhh! I can tell y'all never lived in the country. Anybody in Dougherty County could tell you what they are. We weren't supposed to shoot 'em—they were the plantation owner's bird. We were supposed to stick to squirrels and rabbits. But we got our share." He nodded toward the stone wall. "They're quail. They're 'bout ten times as big as a real quail, but they're quail."

"That's great, Dexter!" said Wes Jordan with genuine relish. "A stone mansion, a stone wall, and the plantation owner's bird! I love it!"

"Whose house is it?" asked Roger.

"I'll tell you in due course," said the Mayor, "in due course. I'm not playing games. I'm just trying to construct a narrative, you might say, and I'm just hoping it'll unfold naturally."

"Okay," said Roger, "construct and unfold." He realized his voice had taken on a peevish edge.

"Dexter," said the Mayor, "let's head on over to Vine City and English Avenue. This time go down Peachtree."

"Vine City?" said Roger.

The Mayor nodded. "I'll take you by your old house."

"As I remember," said Roger, "your folks and mine—we both left there about the same time, when we were in—what was it?—the fourth or fifth grade?"

"More like the sixth," said Wes. "Remember how we'd head out in the morning to play, and your momma'd say, 'Now, I want you back here by lunchtime,' and we'd roam all over the neighborhood? We'd go on up to the Bluff and down in the ravines, and we'd finally straggle back for lunch? Nobody thought anything of it."

"God," said Roger, "I'd forgotten about all that. But that's the truth. That's exactly the way it was."

"Today, Counselor," said Wes, "your momma and my momma—they'd have a fit. You can see for yourself when we get there."

On the drive downtown Roger was aware as he had never been before that Peachtree Street was one long hill, and a pretty steep one. Soon they were down in Midtown. On the right was the High Museum of Art, a modern building with all sorts of white geometric shapes going this way and that.

"Look at that damned museum," said the Mayor. "Looks like an insecticide refinery."

A guffaw from Dexter in the front seat.

The museum had been designed by a famous (white) architect named Richard Meier, but Roger Too White kept that to himself. Instead, he said, "I was reading that a big show's going to be opening there before too long, hundreds of paintings by Wilson Lapeth. He'd hidden them someplace before he died? Have I got that right?"

"Unh-hunh. Hundreds of paintings on what they seem to like to call 'homoerotic themes.' "

"Are you going to the opening?"

Wes laughed a cynical little laugh deep in his throat. "No, the Lapeth show will not have the ceremonial blessing of Atlanta's Mayor. I've been invited, invited, and reinvited. The charming ladies who run the museum—and now we are talking about Buckhead ladies, who are *loaded*—they came to see me at City Hall as a delegation to assure me that this was going to be one of those *milestones* in the history of the city that *demand* the presence of the Mayor."

"So what did you do?"

"I smiled and thanked them and told them I'd have to see about my schedule."

"So what will you tell them?"

"That I'm busy." Wes looked straight ahead, through the front windshield, as if toward the row of towers that comprised the Midtown and Downtown skyline. Then he looked back at Roger. "It's sort of interesting. This is one case in which my political instincts line up a hundred percent with my personal instincts." He smiled his *charming* smile. "I'm afraid I've already made myself clear about how I feel about 'Western art.' "

"That you have," said Roger. He couldn't avoid a certain tone.

"And I *think* I told you what I think about the gay-rights movement and its 'struggle.' "

"That you did."

"Well, the opening of the Lapeth show is going to be, among other things, a solemn homage to gay rights. I'd have to sit there at the head table all night with a straight face giving my implied blessing to the 'struggle' and to this poor old departed lulu, Lapeth. I'd not only spend three or four unpleasant hours inside that insecticide refinery, I would *lose* ground with my core constituency."

"How so?" said Roger.

"I don't think the Buckhead ladies or white folks generally have any idea how little interest black folks have in these art shows of theirs. And that's because they don't understand *their own* motivation for making such a big to-do over 'Western art.' When they put on these shows, they're celebrating *their people's* cultural accomplishments and saying, 'We're great! Creativity and talent are all ours! History is on our side!' Oh, every now and then they'll have a show by some black artist, but that's only out of a feeling of guilt . . . or enlightenment . . . or of: 'See? We include everybody—but notice how few are up to our standards!'

They're cultural chauvinists, but that thought has never so much as crossed their minds. Our people have no interest in seeing their black Mayor at one of these celebrations of white cultural chauvinism, and this black Mayor has even less interest, especially in a show that's also celebrating the 'struggle' for gay rights."

By now the towers of Midtown were streaming past on either side of Peachtree, which was *the* place to have a tower. In fact, if it wasn't within a block or so of Peachtree, it wasn't worth having. That seemed to be the thinking. Each one outdid the one before. . . a 38-story ziggurat of rose-colored glass called Promenade Two . . . then a mid-rise building split in two called Promenade One . . . then the 52-story PlannersBanc Tower, a glass skyscraper that appeared bigger at the top than the bottom . . . One Atlantic Center . . . Phoenix Center . . . the GLG Grande . . . the Mayfair . . . Colony Square, the 1100 Peachtree Street Building, the Campanile, the MossCo Tower, First Union Plaza . . . and in no time they were in the heart of Downtown, in the Peachtree Street canyon created by the skyscrapers that rose on either side . . . One Peachtree Center, the even taller Armaxco Coliseum—Wes pointed at it and said, "Inman Armholster's monument to Inman Armholster"—the Hyatt Regency, the Merchandise Mart, the Westin Peachtree Plaza Hotel, 191 Peachtree . . . Quite a parade it was . . .

Wes said, "I wanted to come down here this way, down Peachtree, because Peachtree Street was our friends the business interests' dream for the twentieth century. All these towers were supposed to show you that Atlanta wasn't just a regional center, it was a national center. And you have to give them credit." He gestured vaguely toward the towers that reached up far above them. "They did it! Atlanta favors people who are hypomanic—I think that's the term—people like Inman Armholster who are so manic they refuse to pay attention to the odds against them, but not so manic that they're irrational."

Dexter made a right turn, and the Mayor said to Roger, "Check out the street sign." It said INTERNATIONAL BOULEVARD. "That's a new name. 'International Boulevard.' What we're going to see now is the business interests' dream for the twenty-first century. You know what they want to do now? They want to make Atlanta a *world* center, the way Rome, Paris, and London have been world centers in the past, and the way New York is today. They never say so out loud, but I'm sure they figure it's only a matter of time before New York is only number two. After all, our airport already makes their three airports look like little country strips. And don't bet against them! They're just aggressive enough, just hypomanic enough, to pull it off."

By now they were nearing an immense angular limestone building that rose up on their left, the CNN Center. "Check it out," said the Mayor. "If you're thinking 'world center,' CNN is the biggest thing to hit Atlanta since the railroad and the airplane, and the Gulf War was the luckiest break the business interests ever got. All of a sudden the whole world was watching two CNN correspondents on television, Bernard Shaw and Peter Arnett. Suddenly it made all these people realize that Atlanta's own CNN was the only international television network on earth."

Coming up on the right was a building only four or five stories high but enormous in the amount of ground it covered.

"That thing's half a mile long on the diagonal," said Wes. "And note the terminology. It's not called the Atlanta Convention Center or anything else indicating such a modest view of its place in the scheme of things. It's called the Georgia World Congress Center. And you probably know what *this* is called."

They were passing through a brand-new park, with the Georgia World Congress Center on the right and the Georgia Dome, built in 1991 as a domed football stadium and exhibition hall, on the left. The park was a meticulously mown greensward from which rose a sculpture of two gymnasts in mid-flight and a pair of towering derricks bearing lamps that could illuminate the entire park at night.

"International Plaza," said Wes. "And you want to know why they chose gymnasts?"

"Why?"

"Because gymnastics is a sport Americans utterly ignore except for three days every four years, and that's when the Olympics are shown on television. When you see gymnastics, you think Olympics—and when you think Olympics, you're supposed to think of Atlanta's greatest international coup: the 1996 Olympics. *There* was hypomania, ignoring the unbelievable odds against it and getting the Olympics brought to Atlanta. Not just any Olympics, either—the hundredth anniversary of the Olympics, 1996. The business interests don't intend to let anybody forget that. Have you been to the Centennial Olympic Park?"

"Ummmmmmm no, I don't think I have," said Roger.

"Well," said Wes, "it's right over there. There's a fountain you ought to take a look at. You know the symbol of the Olympics, the five rings?"

"Unh-hunh."

"This fountain spouts up the five rings—five rings of water—every five seconds, or whatever it is. Oh, I wouldn't put it past them. They may just pull it off, turn this town into *the world center*, the center of the world. They know how to generate money, and they know how to give money leverage. You wouldn't believe the interlocking directorates of the corporations in this town unless I showed them to you on a diagram. It's incredible! But there's one thing they don't have, and it's right here in this car."

Wes smiled and pointed his right forefinger at his own chest. "Black power. Did I ever tell you about Isaac Blakey's great line?"

"You mean Reverend Blakey, the pastor? No, I don't think so."

"A whole bunch of white developers, contractors, union people, they approached Isaac about a meeting with 'the neighborhood leaders,' to see if they couldn't do something about all the opposition to Highway 600, which they wanted to run through South Atlanta. So they've got this lawyer who's their spokesman, the white people do, and he starts his pitch, *and* he's talking about Atlanta's place in the regional economy and the global village and the cosmos and one thing and another and Isaac interrupts him and says, ' 'Scuse me, brother, but you mind if I speed things up and get right to the checkered flag? You got the money, and we got the power. We want some money.' "

"You mean he just flat out solicited bribes?" asked Roger.

"Not bribes," said the Mayor. "Atlanta doesn't have a culture of bribery. It's not like New York. It's more like: 'You build us day-care centers, youth centers, health clinics, parks, swimming pools—so we can say to our constituents, "Look what we brought you"—and we'll see about doing something for you.' That's the way it works out."

No sooner had they driven past the Georgia Dome and through International Plaza than Dexter bore left, made another turn, then crossed Northside Drive, and—*pop!*—all the glossy pomposity of the center of the world vanished, just like that.

Now they were right on the edge of the University Center, the campuses of Morehouse, Spelman, and Clark, which had always been the bedrock of Vine City as a neighborhood. The old brick buildings, the greenswards, the landscaping—they had all been brought to perfection for the Olympics back in 1996, and they still looked great.

Soon the Buick was on Sunset, and the Mayor said, "Dexter, stop right there at the foot of University Place-I-think-it's-called." Dexter stopped, and the Mayor pointed up a rise in the ground at the crest of which stood a brick mansion with six two-story Corinthian columns and a pair of matching two-story pilasters giving drama and grandeur to the front entrance. All along the roofline was a white balustrade like Monticello's. "You recognize that, don't you?"

"Oh sure," said Roger. "Alonzo Herndon."

Alonzo Herndon had been born a slave but went on to create the second-largest black-owned insurance company in the country. His showplace up there had been the grand example that had lured middle-class black people to Vine City after the fire of 1917 that destroyed so much of Sweet Auburn.

"You'd have to go pretty far to beat that house," said Wes. "There's some houses bigger than that in Buckhead, but I don't know of any that handsome, if you want my opinion."

"You're probably right," said Roger, who was not going to waste his breath on any more aesthetic debates with Wes Jordan.

They headed on up Sunset, and Wes said, "Slow down along here, Dexter." To Roger: "Recognize that house?"

"Yes . . . Martin Luther King." It was a good-sized but architecturally plain, suburban-style brick house, well kept, next to other houses of the same sort. It was King's home at the time of his assassination. His widow, Coretta King, still lived there.

They moved on. "Isn't that where Floppy Bowles used to live," said Roger, "that house over there?"

"I think so," said Wes.

They kept on going, and the houses looked smaller than Roger remembered them, but they weren't all that bad . . . Julian Bond used to live somewhere around here . . . So did Maynard Jackson . . . Some of the houses were missing . . . gone . . . Made it hard to get your bearings . . . But once they'd driven eight or ten blocks north, dim recollection gave way to astonishment . . . Three vacant lots in a row . . . overgrown with weeds and saplings—and what are those puddles, those ponds? . . . In the middle lot, all but hidden by the wild growth, was a short flight of wooden stairs leading to . . . nothing . . . All that remained of an entire house was the front stairs and a few slabs of a broken cinder-block foundation. Through the weeds on one side of the house he could see a pool of collected water, out of which protruded . . . . *junk* . . . of every sort, a pedal-driven sewing machine, a rusted-out medicine cabinet, what looked like an old fusebox, a bicycle frame with no wheels, a refrigerator with one side staved in . . . how? . . . by whom? . . . why? . . . a coil of plastered wire lathing, automobile tires, an old scorched bile-green quilt whose synthetic stuffing was coming out. A white plastic Clorox bottle floated on the surface. The very sight of this rotting sump made Roger uneasy. His eyes kept going back to the stairs.

"Stop here a second, Dexter," said the Mayor. Once they had stopped, the Mayor said to Roger, "Recognize them?"

"Recognize what?"

"Those stairs. Those were the stairs to the front door of your house."

"My God . . ." said Roger. "That's what they *are*! I remember that funny little diamond design halfway down the balusters." The little lot looked like a wilderness that was returning to drag all man-made creations back into the primordial muck.

"Tug at your heartstrings?" asked Wes.

"Not really. I've always thought of West End as where I grew up. Still . . . it's—this was a nice neighborhood."

"Well"—the Mayor gestured—"here it is, South Atlanta. Families like ours moved west, and the folks that took our place weren't owners, they were renters. By and by, the landlord gives up on making any money on the property and walks away from it, and now the city takes it over in lieu of taxes, and after that it's the same as if nobody owns it."

Roger said, "I'm going to get out and take a look." He started to pull the door handle.

"Not a good idea," said the Mayor.

"Why? There's nobody around."

"These neighborhoods are never as empty as they look."

Wes's tone made Roger apprehensive. He sank back into his seat.

"Go on ahead," Wes said to Dexter, "and stop at the corner."

At the corner the Mayor said to Roger, "What street is this?"

Roger looked up at the street sign, but it was impossible to read. It was covered with graffiti. So was the stop sign. There was only the hexagonal shape to remind you that it was a stop sign.

"Another couple of blocks, Dexter," said Wes, "and take it slow."

The overhead power lines in Vine City drooped as wearily as the houses that remained. They rolled past houses that seemed to be sinking under their own weight. Some were defaced by graffiti along the base . . . There were more vacant lots . . . more pools of collected water filled with half-sunken debris . . . more weeds and tangles and thickets . . . and cannibalized cars. Along the curb there was an old goldtone Mercury Grand Marquis resting flat on the street on its axles and wheel rims. The hood was gone, and the engine and much of the interior had been gutted. Most of the pavement on the street was gone, the sidewalk had been reduced to rubble, and the street itself, not just the vacant lots, had become a dump.

"Stop up there by that house, Dexter."

It was a small two-story frame house notable chiefly for the metal grillwork that covered every window on the ground floor and the front door and the window above the house's little front porch roof. On one side of the house was a vacant lot with not only a pool of collected water but also an enormous and inexplicable mound of sludge. On the other side was the charred husk of a house whose roof had been half burned away. Even the window frames had burned, and the face of the house had been blackened.

"Know whose house that is?" asked Wes, pointing to the house with the barred windows. "Or was?"

"Whose?"

"Mine."

"God . . . I wouldn't even recognize it now, Wes. Look at all that grillwork. Looks like a cage."

"I can tell you who lives there. Or I can tell you what kind of person."

"What kind?"

"Old people. They're too poor to get out, and they can't get anything for their house. So they have to sit here in their cage waiting to be preyed upon by the predators."

"What predators? I don't even see anyone around here."

"Oh, I'll find you some," said West. "Dexter, head on up toward the Bluff."

Don't *find* me any, thought Roger, just *tell* me. But Dexter was already heading up one of Vine City's slopes. Roger could see one of the ravines. It was a real dumping ground, filled with weeds, rusted metal, burnt mattresses. Up ahead, near the corner, in front of the four little houses that remained, was a pack of boys. Actually only five; but to Roger, whose heart bolted at the sight, it looked like a pack, obviously primed for trouble here in the middle of a school day. Three of them were tall, gawky but menacing (as Roger Too White saw it), wearing baggy jeans whose crotches hung down to their knees. The huge pants legs crumpled down in great denim puddles on top of their black sneakers, which had evil rubbery white tongues lapping up from the sole onto the uppers. The arms of their T-shirts hung down to their elbows and the tails hung down to their hips. Two of them had green rags wrapped about their heads, like pirates. The other two boys were no more than twelve, but were dressed like the older boys. They were hanging out up near the corner in front of a burned-out house.

The hostility!—the wariness!—that beamed out of those dark faces as they eyed the Mayor's pearl-gray Buick. Around the corner sidled an emaciated woman—it was impossible to tell how old she was—in a T-shirt, short-shorts, and bedroom slippers.

"Stop here for a minute," the Mayor said to Dexter. *Don't* stop here, Roger said to himself. Dexter stopped. They were about forty yards from the boys and the decaying houses.

"See that last house, Roger, the one that's burned out?"

"Yes."

"That's a crack house."

"But about a third of the roof's gone. What do they do when it rains?"

"Smokeheads are not sticklers for amenities," said Wes. "I want you to notice the curtains, too."

Roger noticed. They were a slippery brown color. "What is that? Plastic?"

"Garbage bags," said the Mayor. "Just to keep prying eyes from looking in. Now look at the one nearest us."

The one nearest them was a one-story house that seemed to be collapsing from the pull of gravity. The roof of the front porch sagged down from either side toward the middle.

"That's the house Fareek Fanon grew up in. He lived there until he entered Tech three years ago. I just want you to soak in the atmosphere a little bit, Roger," said Wes Jordan, "and look at what we have here." He made a sweeping gesture with his right hand toward the tableau of urban living before them.

Roger looked and soaked in the atmosphere and kept his eyes on the five youths, who continued to stare balefully at the Buick.

"See those two young kids?" said the Mayor. "They're runners for the dealers. If they're arrested, it's no big deal, because they're so young. And see that lovely seductress with her hands on her hips? She's an addict and a prostitute who's willing to do anything you can think of for another chunk of crack. "Just think of it," said Wes. "Here we have a kid who grew up right there"—he pointed toward Fareek Fanon's house—"three doors from a crack house in the worst slum in Atlanta, and somehow he keeps his nose clean, or clean enough to go to Georgia Tech, and he becomes an all-American football player known all over the country as Fareek 'the Cannon' Fanon. Six months from now he'll be in a position to sign contracts worth literally *millions* of dollars. Fareek Fanon, a kid from that disintegrating dump—Fareek's got the world at his feet. He could've just as easily ended up in that crack house, but he didn't. Rightly or wrongly, Fareek's an example for every kid in Atlanta, or every black kid anyway, every black kid who ever felt trapped in some shithook inner city neighborhood. He's got one little problem, however. He's been accused of rape by Miss Elizabeth Armholster. So we've been to Miss Armholster's house up in the heights of Buckhead. She's grown up in the most expensive—what was that word you used? —palazzo?—the most expensive palazzo in Atlanta. Her father is president of Armaxco. She made her debut at the Piedmont Driving Club. Just take a look around! That was the top! This is the bottom! Can you imagine this story after the press gets hold of it? And don't kid yourself. They will. They'll show the two houses, too. They wouldn't pass up anything that rich."

"What about that other house you showed me up in Buckhead?" said Roger.

Wes Jordan smiled. "I'm getting to that. I'm getting to that." He smiled some more. "Roger, I've made a decision about this case. It's kind of a dicey one, because at this point we don't really know what happened. A sex case can blow up in your hands. Most politicians won't touch them. But I want to do something for Fareek Fanon. I'm not going to say he's innocent—I mean, at this point how could I possibly know one way or the other? But I *can* stand up for the protection of his rights. I *can* remind the public of his long journey from the Bluff"—he made another sweeping gesture—"to national sports stardom. I *can* make the point that men have rights, too, even athletes, even superstar athletes, even superstar black athletes, even superstar black athletes from the Bluff. I think I can lay to rest once and for all the whispering campaign André Fleet is so busy spreading around, the one that says I duck the 'black issues.' Ordinarily any man, especially any black man, is under a cloud the moment some woman cries rape. I think I can take care of that cloud in short order."

"That would be great," said Roger, "if it comes to that. I'm still hoping that somehow this will all get laid to rest, but if it does break open we'll need you in a big way."

"Now there's just one other thing, Roger, but it's important. I'll go out on a limb for your client, but I don't intend to go out there alone. Once this thing breaks, you're going to see racial tension such as hasn't existed since the late 1960s. I need some prominent white person to get up and say the same thing I'm going to say: 'Fareek's a fine young man who's come a long way after a terrible journey, and there must be no rush to judgment, et cetera et cetera.' I can't afford to make it seem like I'm polarizing the city. And if I may be totally candid, I can't afford to flat-out alienate my friends at the higher elevations." He rolled his eyes in the general direction of Buckhead.

Roger thought a moment. "What about somebody like Herbert Richman?"

"Nahhhhhh," said the Mayor. "He's Jewish. He's a push-button liberal. He's for the minority in *any* situation. His impact would be zero. I need somebody from the real establishment, somebody from the Piedmont Driving Club kind of establishment."

Roger shook his head. "Well, it's a good idea, but as to who—" He turned his palms up in the universal gesture of helplessness.

"I have a candidate," said the Mayor, "but lining him up will take some doing, and I'm going to need your help."

"Who is it?" asked Roger.

"Charlie Croker," said the Mayor.

Incredulous: "The developer?"

"The very one."

"Well, maybe you know something about him I don't know, but he strikes me as a . . . Cracker through and through."

"So much the better," said the Mayor, "if we can get him to come around. You know, he was a big star for Georgia Tech, too, just like Fareek, a running back. They called him 'the Sixty-Minute Man,' because he played both defense and offense. Maybe we'll find out he has a profound . . . empathy . . . for athletes under the dreadful pressures of stardom." The Mayor smiled his ironic smile.

"Well, Wes," said Roger, "I don't want to sound pessimistic, but that'll be the day, if you ask me."

"Stranger things have happened," said Wes Jordan, "stranger things have happened. Oh, by the way, that other house we looked at in Buckhead, the one with the stone wall and the quail statues out front? That's Croker's. Just up the way from Armholster's . . . Can't you see it? He's perfect. And before I forget, he's also a member of the Piedmont Driving Club."

Roger shook his head some more. "Well, good luck."

"We can't leave it to luck," said Wes. "You've got to help me make it happen."

From here in the back seat of the Buick, Roger looked round about the Bluff. So many wretched little huts, falling down, burned out, with pools of collected water in the vacant lots and rusting, rotting junk sticking up out of the scum. And in his mind's eye he could see Armholster's Venetian palazzo and Croker's pile . . . A Georgia Cracker in a medieval manse. Wes was right. This thing was going to erupt. What the hell had he let himself get involved in—he who had leaped so clear of the race barrier? He had a sudden yearning to stick to Peachtree Street and the eminently respectable Gerthland Fullers of the Wringer Fleasom & Tick universe.

"Dexter," said the Mayor, "give us a little cop magic for Mr. White's benefit."

Roger looked at Wes quizzically. Meantime, Dexter, up in the driver's seat, was opening the door and swinging his massive self out of the car and standing up on the street beside the Buick. The five boys were huddling and staring lasers at these intruders. Dexter put a walkie-talkie radio to his mouth, and Roger could hear his rumbling voice but couldn't make out what he was saying.

"Who's he talking to?" asked Roger, all the while keeping his eyes pinned on the boys. (Why stir up the hornets like this?)

"He's not talking to anybody," said Wes. "The thing doesn't work much more than 500 yards from City Hall."

"Then why is he doing it?"

"Cop magic," said Wes. "See what happens."

The five boys, in the coolest possible manner, as if it made no difference to them one way or another, turned around and began beating a retreat with the coolest gait known to the human animal, the Frankenstein Rock.

"They see Dexter," said the Mayor, "they see cop."

But when the boys reached the burned-out house, they stopped. Now they were alternately talking to three older, derelict figures, two men and the prostitute, who seemed to be sliding, like something melting, down the building's front wall—and staring back at Dexter and the Buick.

"Oh, look!" said Wes. "Now they're being good citizens!"

"Good citizens?"

"They're alerting the crack house to our presence. You see what those boys are wearing, the baggy pants with the crotches they're practically stepping on? And those do-rags they've got around their heads? Those are jailhouse fashions. Jailhouse. In jail they don't provide belts, and so if your pants are too big you just let them ride low. And the do-rags? In jail, if you want a headgear, you have to make it yourself, by ripping up a sheet. Just imagine what it really means to be a fifteen-or-sixteen-year-old boy—and to *want* to wear jailhouse fashions. It means you don't think of jail as anything foreign to your life. You don't even fear going to jail. You know you'll have friends there when you arrive! Imagine that—thinking of jail as an extension of the 'hood, as the great André Fleet would put it. In this part of English Avenue the boy who grows up with no police record is regarded, ipso facto, as a model citizen. Just think about that for a minute. Just think about that when you think about Fareek Fanon. Mr. Warmth & Discretion he ain't—but he came from out of here without a blemish on his record and turned himself into one of the greatest athletes in America. Think about it."

By now the five boys, the five Jailhouse Fashion plates, were Frankensteining it, rocking like Druids, away from the crack house and around the corner. The smokeheads on the porch, with only the thinnest veneer of Cool, were fleeing, too, scurrying behind them. Now came an exodus from the innards of the house. Dark faces, men and women of every sort, from teenagers to bent-over old folk, some of them glancing at the Buick but most of them hopelessly glassy-eyed. The sheer numbers—departing that burned-out hulk of a house! No end to them! Must've had them stacked against the walls! After a while one last figure came out on the porch, a big tall man, perhaps forty, barefoot, wearing a filthy grayish T-shirt and khaki pants . . . Can't get his balance . . . His huge frame keeps staggering to starboard . . . He rubs his right hand across his face . . . goes sprawling on the porch . . . manages to get up on all fours, crawls down the porch stairs, crawls along the sidewalk, manages to get to a standing position, lurches forward, lands on all fours, starts crawling again . . . disappears, crawling, all 200-plus pounds of him, around the corner.

"What runs away on all fours like that at the approach of man?" asked Wes.

"I don't know," said Roger. "What does?"

"A rodent," said Wes, "or else a man reduced to a rodent. Fareek Fanon could've very easily ended up like that. Armholster couldn't've. Neither could Charlie Croker. Think about it."

Chapter IX

The Superfluous Woman

R*AM YO' BOOOOOOOOTY!*

"Lof, torque!" *Clap!*

Ram yo' booooooooty!

"Right, torque!" *Clap!*

Ram yo' booooooooty!—

—and the hateful meaning of *booty*, which she had just learned was synonymous with the vulgarism *ass*, and the hateful name of the singer whose voice came over the audio system, which was Doctor Rammer Doc Doc, clicked in and out of Martha Croker's mind as she struggled to keep up with Mustafa Gunt's beat—

"Right, torque!" *Clap!*

—and spring her left foot forward and her right foot backward and torque her body to the right—

Mustafa Gunt was a former Turkish wrestling champion of some sort who kept his head shaved bald. His neck fanned out wider than his ears and merged with a pair of trapezius muscles that sloped like his native Balkar Dagh Mountains down to his shoulders. He wore an Olympic-style wrestler's unitard, and when he clapped his hands to the beat, more muscles popped out in his glistening shoulders, arms, and chest than Martha could possibly remember the names of, despite all the anatomy she had once studied so hard at Emory. Behind the mighty Mustafa was a wall of plate glass looking out on a busy street in the commercial part of Buckhead, off Piedmont Road. Anybody passing by could have looked right in—there was no modesty about group exercise in Atlanta—except that the heat from the bodies of the thirty struggling women kept the glass fogged up. Mustafa's face scowled at the whole bunch of them, as if in some unanswerable accusation.

"Lof, torque!" *Clap!* went Mustafa Gunt.

Ram yo' boooooooty! went the voice of Doctor Rammer Doc Doc.

The exercise was called a straddle-torque, and the springs and thrusts and twists were so fast and so violent, Martha was already gasping for breath. Sprays of sweat hit her in the face and in the back. Every woman who came to Mustafa Gunt's class here at DefinitionAmerica was assigned a rectangle, 3 by 7 feet, painted on the floor, with a number in the middle of it. The young woman in the rectangle in front of hers and the one in the rectangle in back of hers and the ones in the rectangles on either side—all four of them had long, intentionally tangled hair that looked as if a hurricane had just blown through, unimpeded by any sort of bands or barrettes. The very signature of Rake-a-Cheek Youth at the turn of the century, this hairstyle was, and when the Rake-a-Cheek Youth spun their heads in the torques, the sweat flew from their manes and sprayed Martha on all sides. Oh, they could spin, they could, they could, they could. They had nice wide shoulders and nice narrow hips and nice lean legs and fine definition in the muscles of their arms and backs. They were built like boys, boys with breasts and hurricane manes.

Ram yo' booooooooty! went Doctor Rammer Doc Doc.

"Right, torque!" *Clap!* went Mustafa Gunt, urging them on.

Martha wanted nothing more than to just drop, right there in her rectangle. Only the fear of humiliation kept her from it. At fifty-three, she was the oldest woman in the class, perhaps the oldest customer in all of DefinitionAmerica, and already the young woman on her right, a perfect boy with breasts who wore a thin white leotard to make sure you saw it all, was giving her a certain look, as if wondering how she could have had the bad taste to turn up here in their midst at her age . . .

Nevertheless, Martha persevered. Every woman (in *tout le monde*) now knew there was no possible detour around exercise. Only vigorous exercise could help you even remotely approach the feminine ideal of today—*a Boy with Breasts!*—and practically every woman Martha knew in Atlanta, other than those who were irretrievably ancient, joined classes like Mustafa Gunt's. The exercise salons were proliferating like cellular telephones and CD-ROMs. *Boys with breasts!* My God, whatever happened to *voluptuous*? Thirty-two years ago, when she had married Charlie, *the voluptuous woman* had been the ideal of sexual attractiveness. *Voluptuous* denoted fullness and flesh, soft female flesh. She had been a voluptuous woman, or a boarding school and debs' cotillion version of same; enough to drive Charlie Croker wild, in any event. She had had nice broad shoulders, a nice full bosom, and nice full smooth hips and thighs that Charlie had grown rhapsodic over, or as rhapsodic as Charlie, who was no poet, was ever likely to get. She was a woman with a full layer of adipose tissue! That was the way she was made! She had never been *born* to have the shrink-wrapped look these young women wanted, all this *definition* they talked about! O Definition-America!

But that was what Charlie had run off with, a boy with breasts named Serena. That simple, plain truth had obsessed her mind ever since *Atlanta* magazine had arrived in the mail yesterday, but she was determined not to think about the damnable picture—

Ram yo' boooooooooty! Ram yo' boooooooooty!

"Right, torque!" *Clap!* "Lof, torque!" *Clap!*

As Martha spun this way and that in the torques, beginning to gulp for air, her eyes kept alighting—little as she wanted them to—on the perfect bodies in the first two rows of the class. There they were, with their little sculpted buttocks encased in tights and bisected by leotard thongs, straddle-torquing within an inch of their young lives. They were shameless. They *wanted* the world to look in through the plate glass and see them. They wanted Mustafa to get an eyeful, too. She hated them all, except for Joyce, who was right up there in the first row with the youngest of them. Joyce Newman was the one friend Martha had made at DefinitionAmerica. Although tiny, scarcely five foot one, Joyce was an all-too-perfect boy with breasts herself; but she was forty-two years old and, like Martha, divorced after many years and given to making amusing observations about their common fate.

Ram yo' booooooooooooty!—Doctor Rammer Doc Doc continued to rap out his rape threat to some unnamed victim, but Mustafa Gunt was no longer clapping out the beat and barking out his "lof, torque, right, torque." Instead, the mighty Turk rose up, preening, on his toes and threw back his shoulders and drew in his midsection. His waist became tiny, his chest and shoulders became huge, his rib cage inflated. Scowling furiously, he extended his left arm and pointed toward the back doorway, where the EXIT sign was. Martha couldn't believe he was actually going to do this, not after the brutal round of straddle-torques they had just been through. But sure enough, that guttural Turkish take-no-prisoners voice commanded:

"Steers! Steers! Op! Op! Op!"

Immediately the thirty women bolted from their rectangles and scampered toward the doorway. Martha thought she couldn't take another step, but she had no choice. She was swept up in a stampede of leotards, tights, and exercise briefs. Onward the herd took her. They went funneling through the metal frame of the doorway and out onto the fire stairs, shank to flank, elbow to rib. The stairwell was freshly painted (Computer Casing beige) and well lit, but too narrow for a herd of thirty endorphin-crazed women charging full tilt.

"Steers! Steers! Op! Op! Op!"

Op they ran, op five flights of steers. The younger ones were like mountain goats. They fairly leaped *op*ward, their sneakers squealing on the metal risers. *Bump—bump*—two little jolts Martha felt in rapid succession. It was two of the perfect ones from the first row jostling her adipose shoulders and hips as they passed her on the narrow stairway and bounded *op*ward. She could see their perfect little bounding bottoms with the thongs cutting smartly into the ravines of their buttocks. They didn't have the faintest idea that they had just jolted Martha Starling Croker. They had merely passed some . . . old woman . . . on the stairs. And then—*ow!*—a sharp jab in the ribs. A bony elbow, an outrageous head of red hurricane hair, and a pair of skinny hips sprang past her, shot *op*ward. Then Joyce scampered past, making sure not to crowd her, and gave her a smile and a shrug and an arch of the eyebrows, as if to say, "What can you do? We're in the same boat!"

It was all so dizzying. The shaft was quickly filled with the funk of sweat and too much expensive perfume. Desperately Martha tried to gulp in air. By the time she had gone three flights, she was at the tail end of the herd. By the time she had gone four flights, the lead goats, the perfect boys with breasts, were already bounding downward. A laggard such as herself had no choice but to squeeze up against the railing and let Youth have its way.

By the time she chugged all the way up the five flights and back down to the room and her rectangle, she was drenched with sweat and breathing with loud, rapid heaves. Gradually she became aware of . . . eyes . . . She lifted her head. The young woman in front of her and the one to her right were cutting glances at her and then at each other. The two of them were glistening with sweat, but they were scarcely even breathing hard. They were in perfect condition. Oh yes, they were perfect. (Once again the offending page in *Atlanta* magazine popped up into her brain. She could *see* the picture! But she fought it back and cast it out, she did, she did, she did.) The areolae of the perfect breasts of the paragon on her right, plainly visible through the nylon of her white leotard, rose and fell at a perfectly normal rate. She looked at Martha and frowned and said in the sort of Atlanta Little Girl voice she had come to despise:

"Yew awrighhhht?"

The words were not spoken unkindly. They were even filled with concern and graced with a certain sugary, solicitous smile. But the sweetness left an iron-like aftertaste that said: "What's the idea of an old lag like you coming in here and depressing us all with your mortal snorts?"

Martha nodded to indicate she was not dying. She tried to shrink. If her rectangle had had a drain in it, she would have gladly swirled down it and disappeared. Lacking that, she wanted to call out to Joyce Newman to come back here and show these people she was not old and friendless. All she could do, in fact, was to avert her eyes and stay stooped over and give her cardiovascular system a break and try to keep from collapsing on the spot, which would be the ultimate ignominy.

Already Mustafa Gunt was announcing the next exercise, which he called "the seagulls" and pronounced "da zeegols."

Over the audio system Doctor Rammer Doc Doc was singing, if you could call it singing, a new song, if you could call it a song. "How'm I spose a love her," he chanted, or rapped, "catch her mackin' wit da brothers?"

The moron had actually used the word *love*. It was apparently only in the context of some woman's infidelity, some woman whose booty he had no doubt been rutting and grunting over; nevertheless, for Doctor Rammer Doc Doc this verged on the sentimental. The lame half-rhyme, *love her/brothers*, so typical of these illiterate troubadours of dog-like sex, irritated Martha no end. What was Martha Croker, née Martha Starling, from Richmond, Virginia, from the very best part of Richmond, Cary Street Road, daughter of the former president of the

Commonwealth Club—what was she doing here in an exercise hive in Buckhead in Atlanta, listening to a lot of mindless, obscene, totally vulgar "Negro music," as her father had always called it, letting herself be jostled, jabbed, and belittled by a bunch of vain, brainless, narcissistic, body-snobbish girls, dutifully obeying a bald-headed martinet from Turkey named Mustafa Gunt who liked to send her running up a set of fire stairs to within a c.c. or so of her cardiac capacity? She was past menopause. She was no longer too young to have a heart attack—

Why was she in this ridiculous position?

Charlie.

That was it, pure and simple: Charlie.

In that moment all the cumbersome psychological baggage a woman loads herself up with during a divorce fell away. She was fifty-three years old, for God's sake! She had been married to Charlie Croker for twenty-nine years, and she had borne him three children, and she had helped him get started in this glorious career of which he was so obscenely proud! She had every right to be what her own mother had been at the age of fifty-three . . . a *matron* . . . yes, a *matron*! . . . a queen! . . . immovably secure in her family and in society . . . If a matron wanted to help herself to a nice comfortable coating of adipose tissue, she had nothing to worry about, nothing at all. It had merely lent her mother . . . gravity . . .

What was all that nonsense about *relationships* and *role modulation* and *emotional accretion* she had tormented herself with in all those totally useless trips to the therapists and the counselors? You, Charlie, you alone, through an act of capriciousness and utter selfishness, have done this to me! You eviscerated my perfectly good life, Charlie! Here I am at fifty-three, trying to *start over* as a woman—in this ludicrous factory for boys with breasts!

The purity of her hatred got her adrenaline flowing, and the adrenaline gave her body a lift, and her head began to clear.

Mustafa Gunt was saying, "Some of you don' wahnt to be zeegols, ay?—ay? You don' wahnt to fly? I'm diz-abointed."

The Turk was always diplomatic enough not to reprimand any woman directly, personally. After all, these were paying customers. He used only terms that could be taken as applying to the entire class. Nevertheless, Martha knew very well the remark was aimed at her. She raised her head. Sure enough, he was looking her way. Everyone else, every boy with breasts, was already in a half-deep-knee bend with arms stretched out to the sides, lifting them up and down in "the seagull." Dutifully she bent her knees and got down into the crouch and started flapping.

Mustafa Gunt said, "Don' geef op! Flop! Flop! Flop! Flop! Wahn more zet! Geef me twonty! Flop . . . on . . . flop . . . on . . . flop . . . on . . . flop!"

Martha flapped. Her shoulders ached. Her thighs burned from staying so long in one position with her knees bent. But she persevered. Why? Why had she so dutifully obeyed? Was there something in her makeup that made her want to cave in to the wills of big, strong, blustering, manly men? Did she unconsciously *enjoy* being dominated by these iron-lunged Alley Oops? Was she suffering from a repetitive compulsion?

Oh, cut it out, Martha . . . Her daddy had been right thirty years ago, hadn't he, when he told her that, confidentially, psychoanalysis was rubbish from top to bottom . . . She wasn't suffering from any sickness or neurosis. She was suffering from the perfidy of a man named Charlie Croker. She set her jaw, girded her loins, and buckled down to the seagulls. She flapped her arms. She imagined the burning in her thighs was melting away untold ounces of adipose tissue.

". . . on . . . flop . . . on . . . flop . . . on . . . flop . . ."

Obsessively she followed every instruction of the big Turk, Atlanta's hottest new creator of boys with breasts. I'm fifty-three years old, she thought, flapping away like a seagull, and I need a man.

AFTER CLASS, AS they often did, Martha and her friend Joyce Newman drove to a restaurant on Piedmont Road known as the Bread Basket. The Bread Basket was casual enough so that two women who had been exercising vigorously for an hour and had not showered could put hip-length warm-up jackets on over their tights and leotards and go in and sit down and not feel out of place. At the same time the Bread Basket had a certain flashy 1990s California Granola cachet. As you walked in, you found yourself facing an amazing wall of bread, covered with every kind of loaf imaginable, round ones, oblong ones, rectangular ones, freshly baked and arranged up-ended on shelves, like bone-china dishes in a breakfront. In the foreground was a pastry counter beneath a huge globe of light with strips of gold-anodized aluminum orbiting it. Off to the side were several dozen slick black coffee-shop-style tables set upon a flagstone floor beneath a ceiling of etched mirrored glass with streams of free-form Hot Pastel neon tubing running across it. And everywhere . . . a profusion of greenery, hanging plants, plants in tubs, containers of mother-in-law's tongues, those rubbery green fronds that stick up like swords, stretching on at shoulder height atop the room dividers.

Martha and Joyce always sat at a small table by a mirrored room divider beneath a stupendous crop of mother-in-law's tongues, and they always talked about the same thing, although it would have embarrassed them to say what it was in so many words. They were part of that unnamed sorority who met every day, all over Atlanta, all over America, to talk about their common affliction, which was divorce.

Joyce stared at herself in the mirrored wall and said, "Look at my hair."

Martha looked. Joyce's long dark brown hair was now damp, flat, pressed down against her head, thanks to the hour at DefinitionAmerica.

"Every day I drive home from here looking like that," said Joyce, still inspecting herself in the mirror. "I can't stand it anymore. I don't even feel like having the cleaning woman see me like this."

"Well," said Martha, "why don't you bring a hat?"

"I can't wear hats. I've tried every kind of hat in the world. They all make my face look too small. You know what my father used to call me? 'Penny Face.' "

Fleetingly Martha wondered who, or what, Joyce's father was. She was never very specific about her background. Martha's impression was that she was a little girl from a decent but quite ordinary family in Massilon, Ohio, who went to public schools—girls who went to private schools always managed to work that into the conversation within fifteen minutes of meeting you—and came to Atlanta and captivated some sort of software marketing whiz (Mr. Donald Newman of Lodestar Systems) and who, until her divorce last year, had been leading a very good life on Marne Drive in Buckhead.

Her problem, Joyce was saying, expanding on her theme, was that she had nice big eyes—

Martha nodded. Joyce did in fact have lovely big brown eyes, which she carefully called attention to by applying eyeliner and mascara before she came to exercise in Mustafa Gunt's class each morning.

—but her face was too small, so that she needed a lot of hair, full hair, to enhance it.

Martha glanced into the mirror. Her jawline, which had once been a lovely strong smooth oval running from ear to ear, was now in three parts. Her cheeks were like a pair of big parentheses; her chin was a U that dropped down between them. That once-smooth flesh looked terribly . . . mealy. The pale facial hair that came down past her ears to her jaws, hair once so fine and downy and virginal that Charlie used to love to stroke it, now looked . . . coarse.

"You're lucky," said Joyce. "You have *good* hair. It's so *thick*."

Martha paused. One of the conventional courtesies of the sorority was that you matched your sisters woe for woe, to show them that you understood and sympathized and that they were not alone. So Martha started to say that she now had to backcomb her hair, tease it, to make it look as full as it used to be—but that might lead into a discussion of how, after menopause, a woman began to lose hair, and she didn't . . . well, she didn't feel like talking to Joyce as a . . . post-menopausal woman . . . So then she started to tell her how she had to dye it—but that might force an embarrassing disclosure that Joyce didn't want to make . . . So . . . just then she noticed a magazine sticking up in one corner of the open tote bag Joyce had beside her on the seat. Even though the cover was rolled almost into a tube and was upside down, she knew the . . . gestalt . . . of that cover. It was the new issue of *Atlanta*. That cover she knew by heart. And so she found herself responding to Joyce—whether out of conventional courtesy of the sorority or a genuine desire to bare her own stranded-woman's agony she couldn't have said—she found herself responding:

"Thank you, but I've got other problems." She motioned toward the tote bag. "Let me have your *Atlanta* magazine a second."

Joyce handed it to her. Laying it out on top of the table, so that Joyce could see it, Martha turned straight to the offending page. She knew precisely where it was.

"Read that and tell me what you think. Just the little introduction here and that caption there. And that picture. That's all you have to look at."

Joyce pored over it. The article was a picture feature entitled "The Prams What Am," with full-page color photographs of the latest fashions in perambulators among Atlanta women with social or celebrity wattage. There, in the very first picture, opposite the title page, was a glorious portrait of Serena Croker. One hand rested lightly on the bar of a navy-blue British Silver Cross pram gleaming with extravagantly curved chromium parts and great chromium-spoked wheels with fine white tires.

The vehicle was stuffed with about four thousand dollars' worth of pillows, sheets, blankets, throws, quilts, and coverlets from Pierre Pan, plus the pinky-winky face of an infant with wisps of blond hair, all but lost in the bed-linen riches—the latest product of the loins of that fabulous developer, Mr. Charlie Croker. The new Mrs. Croker, Mom Triumphant, wore a tweed jacket, a ribbed cream cashmere turtleneck sweater that went perfectly with her luxurious mane of black hurricane hair, and a little afterthought of a wool skirt that showed how perfectly narrow her hips were and how long, lean, and lithe her perfect legs were. In short, as anyone could plainly see, a boy with breasts *non pareil*. The caption began: "When Charlie and Serena Croker and their eleven-month-old daughter, Kingsley, head off on a family outing . . ."

Joyce studied it for a long time, then looked up at Martha with wide eyes. What was that expression? Puzzlement? Embarrassment? Her eyes seemed to be saying, "Just give me a clue. I'll respond any way you want me to."

"See what it says in the caption?" said Martha. " 'When Charlie and Serena Croker and their eleven-month-old daughter, Kingsley, head off on a family outing.' A *family outing*."

Joyce drew a blank.

"When Charlie Croker heads off on a *family outing*," said Martha, looking at her and adding a sardonic twist to her lips. "Charlie Croker already *has* a family. He's got two grown daughters and a sixteen-year-old son. But they've become invisible. They no longer exist. There's Charlie's family." She motioned toward the magazine. "I can't believe he named that little girl Kingsley. Kingsley Croker. It's like a joke."

Joyce said, "Well . . . I think you're overinterpreting."

"I don't think so. What are Mattie and Caddie and Wallace supposed to think when they read that?"

"Well . . ."

"I won't even get into the question of where it leaves *me*. I mean, I disappeared a long time ago. The ex-wives of these . . . hotshots . . . become invisible immediately."

"Oh, that's not true, not if they've got money."

"It's not? Whatever happened to the first Mrs. Nelson Rockefeller? Whatever happened to the first Mrs. Aristotle Onassis? It occurred to her that this might be ancient history to Joyce, and so she tried to bring the evidence up-to-date. "Whatever happened to the first Mrs. Ronald

Reagan—and she was once a movie star! They're all invisible. They're superfluous."

Joyce just looked at her.

"I wasn't prepared for that," said Martha. "We had a lot of friends, and I really thought a lot of them were much more *my* friends than Charlie's. Like the parents of the children in Wallace's class at Lovett. Those were friends that *I* made. Those were people who liked *me*, or that's what I thought. Half of them didn't know what to make of Charlie and all his Baker County stuff, all that 'down below the gnat line' business he goes on about. When Charlie and I broke up, they were all on *my side*, and they wanted all the gory details, and they gave me all this *advice*. All day long I was talking and talking and talking, to the therapist, to the marriage counselors, to the lawyers, to all my *friends*, and they were all telling me how absolutely right I was . . ."

Joyce smiled and started nodding. "I know that part. It's exciting, isn't it. You're in a state of shock, but it's exciting. You're like the heroine of a big soap opera. And then you start reading all the feminist literature."

"You did that, too?"

"Oh sure," said Joyce, "and it really helped! It gave me a lift. It bucked me up."

"Well, I did more than that," said Martha. "I actually went to four or five meetings of Woman's Fist. You remember them?"

"Oh, come on! You? Martha Starling Croker? I don't believe it."

"It's the truth! The meetings were in an art gallery called Minor Injuries on Euclid Avenue down in Little Five Points. Men weren't even allowed inside. I used to come out of there feeling like an Amazon! How could I have ever put my fate in the hands of a man? Who needed men? It was exhilarating."

"But weren't they a little . . . over the top?"

"Of course! That was all part of it. There was every type you could imagine, lunatics, lesbians wearing paratrooper boots, the whole shooting match. But I swear, it made you feel eight feet tall! You were part of an irresistible movement of the oppressed, rising up from the lower depths, throwing off your chains."

"I wish I could have seen that. Martha Starling Croker . . . But you stopped going."

"Well," said Martha, "one day you wake up and the soap opera is over. All of a sudden it's stopped being exciting, what's happening to you. And all those *supportive* friends—I can't tell you how I've come to loathe that word *supportive*. All those supportive friends, the ones who loved to talk to you and lap up all the gory details, they start receding, like a tide, except for the therapists and the counselors and the lawyers, of course, who will stick by you as long as you're willing to pay them, and what you finally realize you are is, you're a beached whale. You're high and dry."

"Well—up to a point," said Joyce, frowning.

Martha realized she had gone too far. Another of the conventions of the sorority was that you never admitted or even hinted at *utter* defeat. So she hastily added, "Or at least some very obvious things finally dawn on you."

"Such as what?"

"Such as—well, let's be realistic. If you're giving a dinner party, and you might have invited the Crokers, but now they're divorced, which one are you going to invite? The former Mrs. Croker, who really was such a nice person, or Mr. Croker, who still owns Croker Global and gets written about all the time?"

Joyce didn't try to dispute the point.

"One day it has to dawn on you that you're completely . . . out of context."

"Out of context?"

"Or maybe *context* isn't the word. Maybe it's *pattern*. The whole pattern of your life has vanished, including your daily routine. For twenty-nine years I was *Mrs. Charlie Croker*. We had a house on Valley Road, and five people worked for me there every day. We had a plantation near Albany, and there were a dozen people who worked in the house and forty or fifty who worked in the stables and the kennels and the fields. I never particularly liked the place. Turpmtine was a place where Charlie and the boys came to cuss and drink and put on their old khakis and shoot birds and tell war stories, while the girls made sure the food was served on time. Some women are comfortable with that life. I never was, but the plantation and all those people—I was the one who had to keep the place organized, and it was a big undertaking, which took a lot of time, and that was all part of the routine, the pattern, the context, whatever the word is. When Charlie and I broke up—"

Even as she uttered the words—*When Charlie and I broke up*—it occurred to her she couldn't bear the humiliation of the plain truth, which was: *When Charlie abandoned me for a boy with breasts.* And in that instant she saw Serena the way she had seen her the first time she ever laid eyes on her. Four years ago it was now, or almost . . . seven-thirty in the morning . . . in a restaurant not unlike this one . . . Supposedly Charlie was in Charlotte and wouldn't be back until that evening, and she had gotten up early and driven over to a little restaurant on North Highland, Café Rufus, the one she and Charlie used to go to years before because they served waffles with real maple syrup, and there, to her astonishment, was Charlie, in a booth, and he happened to look up. He looked right into her face, and his eyes became big as half-dollars—and the head of black hurricane hair and periwinkle eyes sitting across the table from him turned to see what he was looking at—

"—when Charlie and I broke up, there was no earthly reason for me to try to hang on to Turpmtine. It was bad enough to be rattling around in a house in Buckhead with five servants. That house is a . . . a . . . a . . . you want to know what it really is? It's an aquarium . . . for a beached fish." She couldn't bring herself to say *whale* again, because she was already feeling too fat. "I'm completely cut off from everything my life used to be. I am invisible. I am superfluous. And now I have to pick up this . . . *magazine* . . . and see a picture of *the Charlie Croker family.*"

"You can look at it that way if you want to," said Joyce, "but I think it's self-defeating."

Martha sighed and paused. Joyce was getting tired of her lament. She should stop. But she couldn't leave it at that. Hers was not the usual case of a woman who had let herself become completely the satellite of a man. Her case was different! Charlie had been dependent on *her* when they started out! She had practically lifted him up out of the swamps! She had *created* Charlie Croker and given up a lot to do it!

So she said, "I was a medical student at Emory when I married Charlie."

"You mentioned that once," said Joyce.

She was repeating herself . . . Well . . . "My father, Bunting, was a doctor, and I wanted to be a doctor. But I gave all that up to help Charlie get started. Charlie was a real country boy, Joyce. He was a real South Georgia Cracker. He used to call lightbulbs 'latbubs.' "

"What was he doing for a living?"

"He was a real estate broker. In Atlanta that's what Georgia Tech graduates who aren't equipped to do anything but play football do. They become real estate brokers. You should have seen Charlie's father at our wedding."

She stopped. She couldn't bring herself to tell her friend how she had really felt back then . . . How noble she had imagined herself! How enlightened! How big in spirit! How romantic! Miss Martha Starling had reached down and found a beautiful diamond in the rough, Charlie Croker, and she had lifted him up to her level, and she didn't care what Richmond, Virginia, thought, which wasn't much. If he said *Ah caint* for *I can't* and *latbubs* for the things you put in lamps to create light, she would be Pygmalion and change all that! Which she had! She was the princess in the story who brushes aside all base snobberies to find beauty in the commoner and give him a new life and happiness ever after. She had—had—had—well—*created!*—the Charlie Croker the world had come to know—and now, after three decades, he had the audacity—the *audacity*!—to shuck her, cast her off like any old piece of worn-out baggage, as if she had been merely lucky enough to come along for the great ride, as if *he* had introduced *her* to all the wonders of the Buckhead life rather than the other way around!

That was the fact of the matter, but how could you get the point across without sounding completely vain and foolish?

So instead she said, "I really *worked* with Charlie. When we put up our first building—it was a twelve-story office building on Peachtree Road—Charlie found the location and figured out how to assemble the parcels, but he was totally disorganized. To this day I bet I can tell you more about the steps you have to take to develop a commercial building than Charlie can. I can also tell you about the schemes and the tricks, as far as that goes. If it ever got out, the way Charlie assembled the property for this Croker Concourse of his—I mean, the way Charlie—"

She stopped again. She realized her voice was becoming much too heated. But how could she help it? There was more to the whole thing than just her career as a business partner, co-developer, and indispensable counselor of the man now known as that rugged individualist Charlie Croker. There was so much more! But she couldn't very well tell Joyce about that, either. There was *love*—but how could she possibly find the words to describe it? Success, euphoria, ecstasy, *love*! She and Charlie had been a pair of young, beautiful, bright, strong creatures! The night after Charlie had closed the deal with Harris, Bledsoe & Phee to come into the Peachtree building as anchor tenants—which meant that the project would become a reality, the building would at last be built—and it was she, Martha, personally, who had introduced Charlie to the law firm's general partner, Harry Bledsoe—she and Amanda Bledsoe, his daughter, had gone to Sweet Briar together—that night, in the little house they had in Virginia Highlands, just the two of them, Charlie and herself—they opened a bottle of iced champagne, Dom Pérignon—somehow Dom Pérignon became the national drink of real estate developers—they were in that long, low, dreadful 1950s-style living room, and Charlie reached inside her little linen jacket and put his arms around her waist, and then he slipped the jacket off her shoulders and unzipped her little dress in the back—and just sitting here in the Bread Basket, thinking about it, she could *feel* that moment all over again—they had *dissolved* into one another, utterly, and Charlie's pride and happiness flowed into her until she experienced it as hers, and it became something far beyond anything that could go by the name of ambition—it was *love absolute!*—and for a time there were no two happier people on the face of the earth.

But how could she tell this to anybody?—to Joyce?

She lowered her voice and said disconsolately, "I don't mean to go on about it. It's just that it wasn't an ordinary relationship." *Relationship.* Why had she let herself use that word? She hated *relationship* almost as much as *supportive.* "We were so close, Joyce, in every way you can possibly imagine."

Joyce was silent for a moment. Then she said, "Did you ever consider going back into medicine?"

"Oh, I went over to Emory last year and talked to them about reentering medical school!"

"And?"

"They were very nice, but these days medical training takes eight to ten years, depending on your field, and there's no way they're going to let somebody my age come back and start over."

"Well, what about just moving back to Richmond? You must have a lot of friends there."

"I do, or I did. A lot more than here. But frankly, I just can't go trudging back as Charlie Croker's cast-off wife. I just can't . . . People have very long memories in Richmond, and you know what they'll say? They'll say, 'You marry common as pig tracks, you get treated common as pig tracks.' That's the way they think, and maybe they're—"

Suddenly she stopped and grasped Joyce's forearm. "Don't look up yet, but there's a couple headed our way."

Here came a woman in her fifties with a carapace of lemon-blond hair. Beside her was a dignified-looking man in his sixties.

After a tactful interval Joyce gave them a glance and then turned to Martha. "Who are they?"

"She's Ellen Armholster. You've heard of Inman Armholster." Joyce nodded. "And he's John Fogg of Fogg Nackers Rendering & Lean. Now watch this. I'm gonna look straight at her." Martha sat up straight and did so.

The woman, Ellen Armholster, headed toward them, seemingly deep in conversation with Lawyer Fogg—and swept right on by without giving Martha so much as a flicker of recognition.

"Did you see that?" said Martha with a loopy smile. "I'm invisible! She looked right through me! I still take up space, but I don't exist!"

"Well, she looked pretty preoccupied with Mr.—what's his name again?"

"John Fogg. I've only met *him* on about thirty different occasions, but him cutting me I don't count. He's the sort who doesn't know who wives are even when they're with the husbands he's busy fawning over. But Ellen Armholster! I mean, dear God in heaven! We were—*close friends*! Or at least *I* thought so. Her daughter was going out with some hoody character, some drummer with some group called Overdose, and she called me every day for two weeks, sobbing, asking for advice. I was her . . . *therapist*, for God's sake. She was telling me things about her daughter that you just don't tell to a casual acquaintance. But you saw that! She breezed right on by me, with me looking her square in the face!"

Joyce said, "She *was* pretty wrapped up in your Mr. Fogg."

"John Fogg—I mean, *please*," said Martha. "John Fogg may be the most boring man in Atlanta. No, it's precisely what I was telling you. Without Charlie I'm incorporeal, I'm the superfluous woman, the invisible ex-wife."

Joyce put her elbows on the tabletop. She opened her big mascara'd eyes wide and looked into Martha's and gave her a broad, flat smile of sympathy. "Do you mind if I make a suggestion?"

"Go ahead."

Softly, significantly: "Let it go."

"Let what go?"

"Let 'Me'n'Charlie' go. I thought you were over all that."

Sheepishly: "I am. I was. Something hit me during class just now. Why *should* I let Charlie off the hook? Why shouldn't I resent what he's done?"

"Because you haven't got time," said Joyce. "You haven't got the energy, either, not to waste on 'Me'n'Charlie.' You're not telling me about anything I haven't experienced myself. But I'm not gonna waste any more of myself on Mr. Donald Newman. You said your whole 'context' is gone. Well, you just gotta create a new one! And you can do it. You've got the wherewithal."

"How?"

"*Do* something! Start *living* again! Me, I give dinners. I organize evenings. I get involved in things, and I don't even have the money. You gotta create a—a—a *current* and draw people in. You can't just sit there in—what did you call it?—your aquarium?—and resent Charlie." She gave Martha the sort of smile you use to try to jolly up a pouting child.

"Well, but—"

"You said *context*. But why don't you use a grander word."

"Such as?"

"Such as *destiny*. Why don't you think big? Why don't you treat yourself to a new destiny? You've got the resources."

"It's a nice *word* . . ."

"Oh, for Christ's sake, Martha, give me that magazine." She picked up the *Atlanta* magazine and shook it in front of Martha until the pages rustled. "We're not gonna look at 'The Prams What Am' anymore. Okay? We're not gonna look at Serena Croker. We're not gonna worry about Charlie Croker's family outings. We're gonna create our own outings. We're gonna stop moping. We're gonna get out of the house and start doing things and get involved with new people."

She started rummaging through the back pages of the magazine, where performances and coming events were listed.

"What are you looking for?" asked Martha.

"Something for you to do." She rummaged some more, now moving toward the front of the magazine. "Ahhh . . . how about this? Did you see this? I bet you didn't even look at it, you were so fixated on 'The Prams What Am.' "

She spread the magazine open in front of Martha, just the way Martha had spread it open in front of her. On the left-hand page a splashy title in big thick letters with vertical prison-uniform stripes running through them said: GENIUS ESCAPES FROM SOLITARY. On the right-hand page was a painting of a group of young men in a prison dormitory, some fully clothed in striped uniforms, some half-clothed, some naked, some naked and lying down on cots. The atmosphere was charged with sexuality. The arrangement of the bodies was powerful and striking, but also circumspect, in that no genitalia were visible to the viewer.

Puzzled, Martha looked up at Joyce.

"Have you ever heard of an artist named Wilson Lapeth?" asked Joyce.

"I've *heard* of him. He was from Atlanta, right? He was gay or something?"

"Right."

"And there was a big article about him in the Sunday paper? I only glanced at it."

"That's the one," said Joyce. It seemed that Lapeth was a painter from the early 1900s who had always been regarded as a laudable but minor figure, one of those early Modernists who served as signposts pointing to the later, greater achievements of others. In Atlanta, which was a bit short on big names in art, he had always been a major figure, however; and over the past six months he had become one of the most-talked-about names in art circles nationally. Some nine hundred paintings, watercolors, and drawings of his had been found inside a bricked-over cold-storage chamber of his mother's house in Avondale, a neighborhood near Agnes Scott College, in Decatur, where he had spent the last few years of his life before dying of complications of diabetes in 1935. Practically all of them were on homosexual themes, many of them depicting prison life, some of them highly explicit. So far, a select few critics, including Hudson Braun of *The New York Times*, had been allowed to view these buried treasures, and they had all been swept away. Now, Joyce explained, the High Museum was mounting an exhibition, with a grand opening, showing the Lapeth trove to the public for the first time. That was what the piece in *Atlanta* and the one in the *Journal-Constitution* on Sunday were all about.

Martha chuckled. "The High Museum? Atlanta, Georgia? Homosexual art?"

"You don't know the half of it," said Joyce. "They had a roaring fight on the board, but finally they *had* to have the show. We had the Olympics and everything, and so we're supposed to be this big, sophisticated international city and Lapeth is our only claim to fame in art. All the board has to do is veto this show, and then the Museum of Modern Art or the Whitney puts it on in New York, and the whole town will look like a bunch of Baptist yokels. And that's what everybody in Atlanta dreads, being thought of as a hick. So they didn't have any choice."

Martha stared at Joyce as if to say, "And therefore?"

"That opening's gonna be the biggest event in Atlanta since . . . since . . . since I don't know what."

"You think so?"

"I know so. Of that you can be sure. Take a look at this article. And you're going."

"I am?"

"Yes," said Joyce, "and you're gonna take an entire table and invite a whole bunch of people."

"Oh, *really*?"

"Yes, really."

"And how do I take an entire table?"

"You pay for it. You buy it."

"And how much does that cost?"

"Twenty thousand dollars."

"Oh, is that all?"

"Martha," said Joyce, fixing her earnestly with her eyes, "you've been moaning about your 'context.' This dinner, this opening, is gonna be *so big . . . The world* will be there. If you have an entire table at the Lapeth opening—well, I can tell you one thing that'll happen right away. The High—all these museums, they have people on the staff whose only job is to keep big donors happy and get them involved in social events that have to do with the museum. You'll start meeting people."

"But *twenty thousand dollars*!"

"You can afford it! It's an investment in your future. We're gonna get you out into *the world*."

"Isn't that an awful lot of money to pay for a new context?"

"Forget context, Martha. Think destiny. Think of it as an initiation fee. For a new destiny it's not a bad price."

The two women stared at each other. Martha was conscious of the shining young waitress chirping away over two customers at the next table. Looking into the mirror she could see a whole tableau of white faces across the way, eating, drinking, smiling, burbling, beneath a riot of mother-in-law's tongues, all so happy to be a part of the scene—Young

Atlanta!—at the Bread Basket. She was also aware of the face in the mirror that stared right back at her, a fifty-three-year-old face with a U that dropped down between two big parentheses and a corona of still thick-looking, still blond-looking hair.

"Look at me, Martha," said Joyce. Martha did so. "You're going to that dinner, even if I have to drag you there myself. Think *destiny*."

THAT NIGHT CHARLIE sat in the dressing room clad in a voluminous nightshirt and a bathrobe with his book, *The Paper Millionaire*, on his lap and a pair of half-glasses riding low on his nose. He stared at the words . . . "I tried desperately hard to live with the system. I made it, lost it, made it again, lost it, made it, and stopped. It is the rising damp creeping unseen in your own house which is a danger to the environment . . ."

Rising damp, all right. He was awash in debt, and it had begun to take soaking, spattering, humiliating, everyday forms. There was no end to them. A delegation of dark blue suits arrives from his anchor tenant in the tower at Croker Concourse, Consolidated Surety, and announces to him they want a 30 percent reduction in rent, from $32 a square foot to $21.80, and some thirty-year-old blue-suit lawyer informs him, with maximum impudence: "You have no choice"—meaning, "We can afford to vacate, walk out on a five-year lease, but you, in your precarious position, can't afford to have us leave, which would make your disaster of a tower look worse than ever."

Charlie attempted to concentrate on the book in his lap again. "I tried desperately hard to live with the system. I made it, lost it, made it again, lost it . . ." Christalmighty, his eyes were skimming over the very same words he was just looking at. Panic . . . and he knew it. Out of the corner of his eye—*something moving*. He looked up with a start. It was Serena. He hadn't even heard her come into the room.

"Jesus Christ, I didn't know you were in here. You must be part Indian." He didn't say it with a smile, however, and she could have taken it as a complaint or as just something to say. He didn't know which it was himself.

"She is coming, my own, my sweet," said Serena. "Were it ever so airy a tread, my heart would hear her and beat, were it earth in an earthy bed; my dust would hear her and beat."

"My dust would hear her, hunh?" What was she suddenly being so cute and sweet about? "What's that from?"

"Tennyson," said Serena.

"Tennyson?" The name rang only a far-off bell for Charlie. What was he, a writer or a cavalry officer? If he had to guess, he would have guessed cavalry officer.

"It's from 'Maud.' 'Come into the garden, Maud, for the black bat, night, has flown; come into the garden, Maud, I am here at the gate alone.' At St. Maud's we had to memorize whole sections of it. I bet we were the only school in the country that still studied Tennyson."

Literary references, which he never got, annoyed Charlie, and he gave his wife a wary once-over. She was wearing her little salmon-colored silk robe and not much else, judging by how much of her he could see. For a moment he was afraid she had come in to coax him into bed to have a go at it—something that had not occurred over the past several weeks.

He was afraid. That was the word. Since he believed that his performance as a developer, as an entrepreneur, as a plunger, as a creative person, was bound up with his sexual vitality, then he also believed that if he ever lost that, he would lose his . . . power . . . in business and everything else. And now he was afraid that the pressure had rendered him exactly that: impotent. He could sense it; he could feel it; somehow he *knew* it. But he didn't want to have to take the test and find out for sure. Not tonight.

Serena took a seat in the easy chair near his, and he got an eyeful of the inside of her thigh as she crossed her legs. The slow, voluptuous way she had of crossing her legs and letting a half-slipper dangle on her toes had been enough to set him off all by itself . . . once upon a time. Now he stared and waited for the tingle, which never came.

Godalmighty . . . That was one of the ways he had worked it out in his mind that he was right to break up with Martha and marry Serena. He had *had* to. It had been *necessary*, in order to maintain his vitality. He had been fifty-five when he first started fooling around with Serena, and she had made him feel like twenty-five. She had him doing things you should get out of your system by age thirty at the latest. Serena loved sex mixed with danger. She loved it on the edge of exposure. She pulled him right into this crazy stuff of hers. It was breathtaking! He lost his senses. One night in Piedmont Park, under a full moon—now, that had been truly insane. The founder, president, and chairman of the Croker Global Corporation! The fabled Sixty-Minute Man! Mr. Charles E. Croker of Valley Drive, Buckhead! The police were always patrolling Piedmont Park at night, not to mention malefactors of various sorts. One afternoon they were driving by that sleazy motel on the Buford Highway, The Swallows—"The Swallows!" she started shrieking, as if it were the funniest name in the world—and she insisted that they stop then and there and take a room, on the spot, and they did, and once they got in the room, she produced that little cup from her handbag, and they did that thing with the cup, something he had never heard of in all his life—my God, suppose anybody had seen him, Charlie Croker, master builder—Croker Concourse!—checking into a motel on the Buford Highway with a twenty-three-year-old girl—but he had lost his mind to her demented form of lust. Danger! Imminent exposure! That thing with the cup!

She had made him feel as if he were still young. In a way . . . looking back on it . . . a man is still connected to his youth at fifty-five—but why kid himself? Now he was sixty years old, and the connection was nil, and he was sitting here in a nightshirt with his belly sagging all the way down to the book in his lap.

Still smiling sweetly, Serena asked, "What are you reading?"

Charlie lifted the book up and looked at the cover as if he had never bothered to notice the title before. "It's called *The Paper Millionaire*."

"What's it about?"

"Awww, it's about an Arab, an Iraqi. He lives in London. He makes a lot of money . . . He loses it . . ." He shrugged, as if it wasn't worth going into.

Serena said, "It's non-fiction?"

"I reckon. Supposed to be."

The two of them sat there in silence for a few moments, and Charlie began to wonder just what *was* the purpose of this wifely visit.

Then Serena said, "Did you read the paper this morning?"

"I looked at it."

"Did you read the article about Wilson Lapeth?"

"Who?"

"Wilson Lapeth. An Atlanta artist? Died in the 1930s? He was pretty well known. You must have heard of him."

The name did ring a bell, sort of; another of those far-off bells. "Mmmmmm . . . I'm not sure."

Serena proceeded to give him a quick rundown on Lapeth, treading as lightly as possible upon the fact that the theme of these masterworks was homosexual. Instead, she stressed the excitement the name Wilson Lapeth was creating in Atlanta.

"The High Museum's gonna show them," she said, "and it's gonna be—well, it'll be the biggest art show in the history of Atlanta, I guess."

"Bigger than the Cyclorama?" said Charlie.

He could see Serena studying his face to figure out whether or not he was having his little joke. The Cyclorama was a tourist attraction created back in the 1880s, a temple-like building in Grant Park containing an immense circular mural, a full 360 degrees, illustrating the Battle of Atlanta during the Civil War. Yes, he was having his little joke, although he managed to keep a straight face. Serena couldn't possibly imagine how uninterested he was in some dead homosexual artist named Wilson Lapeth.

She may have divined that much, but she didn't let it stop her. "Well, I'm talking about—you know what I mean. You should see what *The New York Times* wrote about it."

Before he could say no, she had hopped up and gone into the bedroom. In no time she was back with a page from *The Atlanta Journal-Constitution*, folded in two, which she deposited in his lap. The headline said, GENIUS AND TREASURE IN THE CLOSET.

Serena pointed to a boxed inset containing a quotation from a *New York Times* critic named Hudson Braun. "Just read that part."

Charlie was annoyed. He was tired. He didn't feel like reading something by somebody from *The New York Times*. Why was it that when the subject of art came up, everybody in Atlanta immediately had to start talking about what people said in New York? But to humor his wife he read that part.

Annoyance now rose to the level of irritation. "Gay artist" . . . "unabashedly phallic thrust" . . . "zenith of the homoerotic imagination" . . . "Today, at last, we know what Wilson Lapeth really was: quite simply a genius" . . . *Give me a break* . . . The word *gay*, all by itself, was galling enough, especially since he realized that contemporary etiquette demanded that you solemnly accept it as the proper designation. He could think of four or five other words that got the point across in plainer English.

He looked up at Serena and said, "So that's Mr. Lapeth. That's quite a write-up."

"Isn't it?" She smiled brightly.

Charlie looked down at the article again and then said, as if reading aloud from it: "Today, at last, we know what Wilson Lapeth really was: queer as Dick's hatband."

"*What?*" In the next instant she realized her husband was having his fun, which she found completely stupid and gauche. She compressed her lips and gave him a withering stare.

Her anger amused Charlie. He grinned and looked down at the newspaper clipping again and said, "It says right here! 'Today, at last, we know what Wilson Lapeth really was: queer as Dick's hatband.' "

"Hah hah," said Serena. "You know, I hope you don't make cracks like that in front of other people. Not even your cronies. You might get a laugh, but they're not going to respect you. I hope you understand that."

"All right, all right," said Charlie, chuckling. He was pleased over having gotten a rise out of her. "I take it back. Mr. Lapeth wasn't queer as Dick's hatband."

"It's like saying 'nigger,' " said Serena. "I'm sure you have your cronies you can get a laugh out of by saying 'nigger,' too, but you can imagine what they'd actually think of you."

That stung a bit. "You've never heard me say that, and nobody else has. My momma and daddy never used that word, and I'm talking about South Georgia fifty years ago."

That wasn't exactly true, but his folks had been far from the worst offenders in Baker County, and Charlie regarded himself as a great friend and protector of colored people, thanks to his role as the patron of Turpmtine Plantation . . . The nerve of Serena . . . and then he realized he had broken one of his own cardinal rules, which was: In dealing with subordinates and women, never justify, never explain, never back off.

Serena said, "Well, I wish you could say the same for some of your friends."

"Such as who?"

"Billy Bass. The last time we were down at Turpmtine, he was going around saying, 'The niggers this' and 'The niggers that,' especially to the Roths. I don't know what marvelous effect he thought he was creating. I don't know whether they were supposed to think he was some colorful macho good ol' boy who was man enough to flout good taste anytime he felt like it or whether he just felt like shocking them because he knew they were Jewish and from New York. But you want to know what they really thought of him? They thought he was a Neanderthal . . . and a creep."

Charlie wanted to take up for Billy, who was one of his oldest friends, but he was too tired to let this turn into a full-blown spat. So he said, "Well—Billy's Billy."

"I know." Serena offered a philosophical smile. Evidently she didn't care to get into a fight, either. She kept on smiling, and then she said, "Anyway, I'd like to go to the opening. I think we *should* go."

"The opening?"

"The High's gonna open the Lapeth exhibition with a dinner in the museum. Charlie—it's gonna be a *huge* event. We really do have to go. I think we should take a table."

"What does that mean, 'take a table'?"

"Subscribe—take a table for ten, and we'd invite eight people."

"Unh-hunh. How much would that cost?"

"Well—the tables are twenty thousand dollars each."

"Twenty thousand dollars?"

She leaned forward until he could look straight down her robe. It was true; she had nothing on underneath. "*Come* on, Charlie . . ." She was smiling. Then she stood up and came around behind his chair and put her hands on his shoulders. She let her hands run down his chest and leaned over him until her chin was pressing on the top of his head. "We really do have to go to this, Charlie."

"Let me explain something to you, Serena . . . This id'n a great time for me to be spending twenty thousand dollars for dinner at a museum."

Serena's response to this was to settle in even more cozily, until her bosom was up against the back of his head and her arms were around his neck. "You're talking about your—what do you call it?—situation? —with PlannersBanc?"

Charlie sighed and let his eyes wander around the room . . . Ronald Vine's tribute to vanity . . . Closet after closet after closet . . . full-length mirror after full-length mirror after full-length mirror . . . all framed in mahogany . . . In the mirror straight ahead he could see an old man slouched back in an Omohundro easy chair, an old man who was bald, rumpled, weary, beaten. Nestled in on top of his head was the face of a girl, a flawless young thing with long black hair that now streamed down over the old man's shoulders. She had a frolicsome smile on her face. But of course; she was young. Life was still a long, adventuresome climb up a hill. She had no clear idea of what she would see at the top, let alone of the grim slide that awaited on the other side. Foreclosure, default, repossession, bankruptcy, phantom gains—all of it extending down into the gloom of a crevice, which was old age. Even if she understood their meaning, they'd be nothing but words to her. All of a sudden he resented her youth. No, he feared it. He feared its inevitable callousness.

"I'm talking about cash flow, Serena," he said in an old man's voice. "Twenty thousand dollars is twenty thousand dollars."

Her smile didn't waver for a moment. The young face in the mirror looked straight into his eyes. "So is that the signal you want to send?"

"Whattaya mean, 'signal'?"

"If we don't go, don't think nobody'll notice. You've been a major benefactor of the museum, and this'll be the biggest event in the museum's history. If you're not there, everybody'll wonder why."

In the mirror Charlie could see himself slump down still farther. His young wife, with her lineless face, enveloped him still more lovingly as he sank. She was right . . . Back in the days when they were raising money for the High Museum's new building, he—or Croker Global—had kicked in $100,000. Mr. Big-Timer! But that was the way it was. If you wanted to do business in Atlanta, you were expected to step up to the plate and hit that ball for the charities, the museums, the schools, the foundations, the lot. That was what you did. Christ, he had given $5 million to his alma mater, Georgia Tech—$5 *million!* He suddenly had an inspiration. He'd go back to them. He'd say, "Look, when you needed money, I gave you $5 million without batting an eye. Well, now I need money, and so I'd like a million back. You'll still be $4 million ahead." But immediately he lost heart. They'd never go for it. He'd only end up looking like a desperate fool. And the tone of pious regret with which they would turn him down would make him sick to his stomach . . . No, he had no choice but to keep up appearances and brazen it out until he could think of a solution to all this. Fortunately in Atlanta you didn't have to worry about something like your humiliation in a workout session popping up in print the next day. Whatever circulated, circulated on the grapevine. Serena was right. They'd better go to that show . . . of some dead faggot—

"Okay," he said, noticing in the mirror how bleary he looked as he said it, "we'll go. But why can't we just *go*? Why do we have to buy a whole table?"

"Ohhhhh—two reasons," said the young woman who cradled his old head. "One, all the tables could get bought up. That could easily happen. And two, if you just buy tickets, you'll be assigned to a table with —who knows who, and I'm not sure if you want that, either."

Christ; no way out. "All right . . . we'll get a table." Even as the words came out, he was calculating how to manage it. The museum wouldn't dare demand cash up front. So he'd get the table . . . and after that the High Museum could stand in line with everybody else who was yammering at the Croker Global Corporation.

Serena lowered her head so that she could press her cheek against his and began to massage his chest with her hands.

"All right!" said the old man in the mirror, "I give up. You win, you got your dinner." He said it so brusquely it sounded as if he were put out over having been talked into it. But that was not the case. In fact, he was afraid the nuzzling and the massaging might go further and she might try to get him into the next room, where the bed was. He already knew the truth in his loins. He was in no mood to have it demonstrated in an unmistakable fashion.

Chapter

The Red Dog

In Harry Zale's office on the forty-ninth floor at PlanNersbanc the boys had their jackets off and their tie knots at half-mast. Harry himself sat back in his leather swivel chair behind his desk with his elbows winged up in the air and his fingers interlaced behind his neck. The skulls and crossbones on his suspenders were parading up and down his big chest. Everybody else, including Raymond Peepgass, even though he outranked him, faced in toward Harry from chairs or the couch or the marble window seat. They were like the pilots of a fighter squadron in the presence of the Old Man. With the exception of himself, it occurred to Peepgass, none of them actually sat *in* a chair or *on* the couch. They perched on an arm or a back or on the edge of a cushion or the marble ledge with their thighs ajar in an athletic sprawl, as if they were bulging with so much testosterone they couldn't have closed their legs if they tried. Businessmen all over America sat around like this, Peepgass reckoned, but none were more thoroughly convinced of their manliness than these Southern boys were. The subject was Charlie Croker and what to do with that shithead, and they were the ones who had saddlebagged him in the now-legendary workout session. Since then they had been closing in for the kill, which would consist of making Croker sit, lift his paws and say please, roll over, and play dead.

Jack Shellnutt, Harry's rangy number-one sidekick, who thought he looked like Clint Eastwood, was straddling one arm of the couch. "I just got off the telephone with Croker half an hour ago." He gave a short snorting laugh. "That guy's too good to waste on one person. Next time I'm gonna hook up a conference call. You gotta hear him go on about his fucking airplanes. You'd think he couldn't draw another breath without his Gulfstream Five."

"What's breathing got to do with it?" said Harry. "You know all 'at Croker uses that airplane for, don't you?"

"Yeah," said Shellnutt, holding his fist up to his mouth as if it were a microphone. "Ladies and gentlemen, in preparation for landing please return all seatbacks, tray tables, and stewardesses to their original upright positions."

They all cracked up for about the fortieth time in the past ten minutes. Oh yeah, we are men, and we brook no whining by the shit-heads. Even Peepgass started chuckling . . . until the word *stewardesses*, which reminded him of flights to Finland. He had a deposition coming up with Sirja that was going to cost him $400 an hour in legal fees plus maximum humiliation and mortification.

He looked away from Harry and the rest of Team Saddlebags and out the window. This office was part of the main executive floor, PlannersBanc's Olympus. From his desk, through the plate-glass window wall, Harry Zale could gaze south upon the pride of the Atlanta skyline, a whole strutting parade of towers that ran from One Peachtree Center in the foreground to the twin crowns of the 191 Peachtree building in the background. Peepgass outranked Harry on the organizational chart, but his office was down on the sixth floor, where he gazed west upon the Highway 85 expressway and the railroad yards. At this moment in the economic cycle Harry Zale and his Real Estate Asset Management Department were riding very high.

Harry's office was so swell, on one wall he had a huge glass and stainless-steel étagère. The shelves were glass an inch thick, with beveled edges that caught the light, and on the shelves Harry had his trophies: his scalps, so to speak, from victorious workout sessions of the past. There was an elaborate two-foot-long model, exquisitely made, of a yellow manure spreader, from the Heartland Farm Equipment workout. Manure spreader: more irresistible banker's scatology, of course. There was an artificial heart from the Cybermax workout; a molded rubber impression of the size-19 left foot of You Gene Jones, the basketball star, from the Offum Sports (mostly sneakers) workout; and so forth and so on. But Harry's pride and joy was a gold Patek Philippe wristwatch—a fake one, actually—which sat in the center of the étagère on a miniature velvet easel. In the Clockett, Paddet, Skynnham & Glote workout, the law firm's senior partner, Herbert Skynnham, had been so desperate, he had listed a $40,000 Patek Philippe watch as collateral. At a breakfast session Harry had asked if by any chance he had it with him. Yes, said Skynnham. Harry asked if he could inspect it. Skynnham took it off his wrist and handed it to him. Harry weighed this dazzling golden wafer with its gleaming band tenderly in his palm, then smiled, slipped it into the left-hand side pocket of his jacket, and said, "Thank youuuuu." With that, Harry Zale became a legend in his own time. PlannersBanc's chief executive officer, Arthur Lomprey, lord of the forty-ninth floor, was so impressed, he bought a fake Patek Philippe watch from a Senegalese street vendor out in front of Underground Atlanta with $65 of his own money and had it engraved *To Harry. Thank youuuuu! Arthur.*

Dan Friedman, the new Mr. Wonderful from Marketing, sitting on the other arm of the couch, was looking straight at Harry, and beaming, as he said, "But you gotta admit Croker's a playoffs-caliber talker. You have to hand him that much. As long as he's talking, you sort of halfway believe that unbelievable dog's breakfast he's trying to pass off as a business plan. He'll talk to you about Baker County, huntin' dawgs, the ballin' sun, the wale-fare system, his faithful Turpmtine folk, and his two dicks, and blow fairy dust in your face, all at the same time."

Team Saddlebag cracked up again.

"He's a good bullshitter," said Shellnutt, "but when he gets around to the part about spreading out the interest payments, he's straining so hard you can see daylight underneath his shoes."

They all cracked up again.

"Talk about trying too hard," said one of the fellows from Legal, Tigner Shanks, who was perched on the back of a club chair. "Remember the workout session? Remember when he started talking about that fucking plantation of his? I thought he was gonna start crying."

"He wasn't crying," said Shellnutt. "He had such a hard-on for that boffable bimbo sitting next to him, Miss Peaches, it was stretching the skin on his face."

Cracked up again, they did, they did, these victorious warriors. Why do they turn everything into sex? wondered Peepgass. Dicks, hard-ons, boffable bimbos, horizontal stewardesses, fucking this and fucking that . . . They were educated people talking about loans, buildings, and food warehouses, but they had to reduce it all to sex, or sex and shit . . . Well, he was a fine one to feel superior, wasn't he . . . His life was coming apart because some ditzy little horizontal Scandinavian notions buyer was filing a paternity suit . . .

"One thing I gotta ask you, Harry," said Tigner Shanks. "How did you have the—what made you decide to put Croker through the lender's cactus? Remember that? I mean, you already had the saddlebags, you'd already given the guy the unidigital salute"—Shanks extended the middle finger of his right hand, and Harry's Squadron cracked up again—"the guy was about to explode, he was already getting ready to leave the room, and you pulled the lender's cactus on him! I mean, Harry, if you wanna know the truth, I couldn't believe it! *I* just about shit!"

Harry rocked back a little farther in his swivel chair and smiled and shrugged. "I don't know . . . I guess I figured, with a guy like that, who thinks the whole world sways to his big swinging dick, you gotta be absolutely sure you get your point across. You know, one time Curtis LeMay—the general?—one time Curtis LeMay appeared before a Senate committee asking for ten thousand nuclear warheads for the Air Force, and one of the senators, Everett Dirksen, says, 'I thought you told us that with six thousand warheads you could reduce the entire Soviet Union to cinders. Why should we give you *ten* thousand?' And LeMay says, 'Senator, I wanna see the cinders *dance*.' "

Team Saddlebags exploded, blasted off, orbited, experienced a hundred dawns and sunsets in ten seconds as the boys spun around their peerless leader.

Yeah, well, it was great stuff, all right, and he, Peepgass, had enjoyed the demolition of Charlie Croker along with all the rest; but for him the triumph had already grown cold. Maybe he was an accepted member of the mighty Team Saddlebags, and maybe he wasn't, but it wasn't his triumph, in any event. It was Harry's. It was the Workout Department's . . . and as Harry's Squadron yahooed, exulted, cracked wise, and cracked up, Peepgass grew steadily more depressed . . . It wasn't that he envied Harry, or not exactly. The workout people were riding high right now because the bank needed them so badly, what with so many big loans having tanked. But that didn't mean Harry was going anywhere. Elsewhere on this floor, in the CEO's office, the workout artistes were looked upon as special cases, like a special unit in football. No, Harry had a big salary and a big office, but it was important to Peepgass to believe he wasn't going anywhere, because neither was he, Peepgass. Only forty-six years old, and already he'd reached a dead end in the banking maze! And at forty-six there was no retracing your steps!

Through the glass inner wall of Harry's office he could look through other glass walls, into other offices, in toward the very core of the forty-ninth floor. And everywhere he looked, he could see the eerie luminous rectangles of computer screens, and across those screens blipped the two hundred to three hundred *billion* dollars that moved through PlannersBanc every day. They were sailing, Harry, Tigner Shanks, Jack Shellnutt, Friedman, himself, the whole crew, on an unimaginably huge sea of money. But all that any of them could take out of that huge sea for themselves was a little jiggerful. He was a senior officer of one of the biggest banks in the country, and his salary was only $130,000 a year. Oh, he knew he could never say that word *only* out loud, certainly not back in San Jose to his father and mother or any of their friends. But the fact was, he was strapped! Federal and state taxes took almost $46,000. Mortgage payments on the house in Snellville took almost $34,000, and he couldn't even live there since Betty had thrown him out. The apartment in Normandy Lea was costing him $7,920 a year, once he figured in telephone and utilities. The car payments, for Betty's Buick Le Sabre and the Honda Excel wagon he was stuck with, came to $5,400. So there you had more than $93,000, leaving $37,000 for *everything* else, such as food, fuel, clothes—and the children, Brian and Aubrey, were outgrowing clothes every time you looked around—repairs, insurance, the orthodontist, not to mention (was it too much to ask!) going out to restaurants, having a little vacation in the summer, or whatever else senior corporate officers making $130,000 a year might reasonably expect to do. The hell of it was, without the roughly $55,000 a year Betty got from the securities her mother left her, they would have had to drastically lower their standard of living, which wasn't all that great to start with. As for how he was going to pay for the $45,000 in legal fees he had already run up trying to fend off Sirja, he had no idea whatsoever, and there was a $400-an-hour deposition coming up—

The computer screens beyond all the glass walls of the forty-ninth floor glowed and flared and popped out into CD-ROM patterns, and the little phosphorescent lines were skittering from left to right, when a burst of he-man gullet laughter brought him back into this room, Commander Harry's command post.

Harry and Shellnutt and Shanks and the boys were shaking with the mirth of their hearty wit and slapping their gaping manly thighs, and Peepgass wondered how on earth it had ever turned out this way. He was smarter than all the talent in this room put together. Then why had he taken such an unadventurous route at the bank? There was only one organizational chart at PlannersBanc, but there were two kinds of officers. There were line officers, and there were staff officers. The line officers were those who generated new business or otherwise created income for the bank. They were involved in marketing (such as originating big loans to entrepreneurs like Charlie Croker) or in investment banking or novel retail strategies, or workouts, like Harry. They were the officers Arthur Lomprey and the rest of them here on the forty-ninth floor were referring to when they used that grand-sounding term *bankers*. Only a line officer was a real banker. A staff officer wasn't; a staff officer was something else; and there you had Raymond Peepgass. What was he actually? What was any senior loan officer? He was a referee, a monitor. He was supposed to monitor big loans to make sure they stayed within prudent boundaries.

Prudent? It had been a struggle even to be prudent. In the 1980s Prudent hadn't stood a chance; nor in the late 1990s. The boom was on, and the banking business had caught fire, and a wonderful giddy madness was in the air. The line officers from Marketing were pushing through loans, their "big sales," with a pell-mell abandon. If you were a referee who insisted on detecting the madness and blowing your whistle, they just ran right over you, laughed at you, made you feel timid and old-fashioned. Like every other senior credit officer, Peepgass had signed off on tens of millions of dollars' worth of loans with *self-destruct* written all over them . . . including Charlie Croker's, rather than try to stand in the way of the stampede . . . But to tell the truth, that explanation, sad as it was, wasn't the whole story. In fact, he had been swept up in the madness himself. Like many another bank officer, he had started getting a euphoric lift out of being part of the grand schemes and imperial visions of the Charlie Crokers of the world. John Sycamore may have been the high-flying line officer who had brought Croker to the bank and made the big sales, but Sycamore had had to come to him, Peepgass, for approval; and he, too, had become an advocate of this infinitely vital and charming back-country boy, this risk taker with a grand vision and an infallible touch. It had reached the point where he had became convinced that Croker had more than talent, know-how, and drive; that Croker also had a certain magical power that enabled him to pull off the impossible. And he, Peepgass, was somehow his partner. Croker and Peepgass, riding before the wind on the great sea of money!

Instinctively, gloomily, he shook his head at the very thought. There was no denying it. Back then, in the palmy days, he had loved being around Charlie Croker. He was the one who had introduced Croker to Serena; or indirectly he had. In PlannersBanc's Private Banking Department there had been a line officer named Frances Geistman, known *sotto voce* among the boys as the Ice Princess, of whom Shanks had once said, "She's the only banker in Atlanta who can cut your nuts off and give you a hard-on at the same time." The Ice Princess had dreamed up a new marketing strategy called the Art Investment Seminars. The art market in New York had picked itself up off the floor and was surging again, and Frances Geistman got the bright idea of luring big clients into the bank by offering to instruct them in the arcana of this hot and glamorous New York–style form of investment. Businessmen in Atlanta liked to affect indifference to New York and its fashions, but they also liked to show the world that they moved on just as fast a track as anybody else. And the lure? Here the Ice Princess, who was from New York, had demonstrated her sexual genius. As instructors she hired recent graduates of the New York University Institute of Fine Arts. The Institute seemed to graduate nothing but young, gorgeous, socially connected girls with boarding-school accents and tender loamy loins and legs that drove rich men wild. They matriculated in the Art Investment Seminars in droves. The girls cooed to them about Bruegel the Elder and Fischl the Younger and about short- and long-term auction variables. The courses were conducted, covertly, in conjunction with Gillray's, the New York auction house. The bank lent money to its smitten seminarians and steered them to Gillray's to buy art and sell it (and took commissions from Gillray's going and coming) and set them up with deluxe VIP art tours of New York, while they were at it, and then moved in on them to get all their banking business, personal and corporate.

There were so many stories floating around about the Ice Princess and her Art Geishas, Peepgass had dropped in on a few classes—and become as besotted as the worsted-suited marks themselves. Art! He tried to come on to one of the instructors, a little brunette named Jenny; and then another, a willowy redhead named Amy (Amy Phipps-Phelps!). Insofar as he could afford it, he became an habitué of the art world, going to the big gallery and museum openings in Atlanta, including fund-raising dinners at the High Museum, which he couldn't afford. He wangled introductions to collectors and museum trustees—anything to get into the merry swim of Art's sex, money, and glamour. He didn't get very far with Jenny and Amy. The Geishas, if they wanted to fraternize, didn't have to settle for a PlannersBanc staff officer making a pitiable $130,000 a year. There were far, far bigger fish right there in front of them at the bank, at the art seminars: Charlie Croker, for a start.

It was Peepgass who had persuaded Croker to take a class and get the feel of this hot new investment opportunity. Croker had found the class a bore and a joke. He was interested in narrative art of men in action, by N. C. Wyeth, Howard Pyle, Frederic Remington, and Winslow Homer, and that was about it. But he found the instructor, Miss Serena Sharp, all he could ask for. Serena was bright and provocatively sarcastic. She had such a perfect young body, such loosely sprung hips, that even in a simple black minidress (her professional costume) she managed to look naked. Croker never went near the Art Investment Seminars again, but he went after Serena Sharp and divorced his wife of twenty-nine years and married her.

Peepgass was amazed—mostly by the fact that the big tycoon had the nerve to shuck his old wife after all that time, *just like that*. He couldn't have imagined summoning up the fortitude to leave Betty. Nevertheless, the great sexual itch of the 1980s had been spread to Raymond Peepgass. And then he had met Sirja.

"What'll he do *next*?"

It was Shanks's voice, in such a high-pitched whine that it cut right through the morose shell of his thoughts. Evidently he was talking to Harry, because Harry said, "Oh, that's easy. He'll try to hide the airplanes."

"That's a safe fucking bet," said Shellnutt.

"An ordinary human being can't imagine how tightly a shithead bonds with his airplanes," said Harry.

"Yeah," said Shellnutt, "a shithead like Croker never heard of frequent-flier miles or standing still beside an X-ray box while some rent-a-guard making $7.50 an hour runs a Geiger counter up your in-seam. Remember that shithead from Cybermax, Harry? Duber was his name, or something like that?"

"Yeah."

"Fucking hoople sells his King Air, he claims. Turns out he sold it to his sister-in-law for a piece a paper."

"What's a *hoople*?" asked Shanks.

"Ten pounds a shit in a five-pound bag," said Shellnutt. "So now every time he has to fly in here to see us, he has his fucking pilot fly the plane to PDK. He has a limo waiting to drive him in on the Buford Highway to Downtown, and then he gets a taxi to bring him here, so if anybody sees him arrive, he's getting out of a jellybean driven by some guy named Jahmeed."

"What's a jellybean?" asked Friedman.

"Oh, you know, a Chevrolet Caprice. All the taxis are Chevrolet Caprices, and they all look like jellybeans."

"It was worse than that," said Harry. "Fucking guy, while he's flying here from Cincinnati, he calls his secretary and tells her to look up the airline schedules and inform him as to what flight he's supposed to be on right now and which one he's going back on, in case anybody asks. The dickbrain, if he spent half as much time tending to business as he did worrying about his phantom itineraries, we might've gotten outta that one alive." He gestured toward the Cybermax artificial heart up on the magnificent étagère. "What that shithead needed was a left-hemispherectomy."

"And a Vibram scrotum," said Shellnutt.

"Well, whattaya figure our chances are of coming outta Croker Global alive?" asked Friedman. He didn't ask it of Peepgass, however, as Peepgass was quick to note, but of Harry.

"In the current market?" said Harry. "You want my honest opinion? . . . Terrible. I'd love to foreclose on that big shithead, *love* to. They call up here two months ago and say they've 'run into a situation.' That's such pure shithead stuff—'We've run into a situation.' That always means the same thing: they can't make the next interest payment, let alone pay back principal. *We've run into a situation . . .*" Disgust dripped from the words. "Well, we don't have a situation. We got a problem, a real nut-masher. We got a pile a commercial real estate here that's leaking money all over the place, and we got seventeen wholesale food warehouses operating at a loss. The trouble is, you can't just turn these places off and put locks on 'em and wait for a change in the economic cycle and then sell 'em. The buildings have tenants with leases. Lousy leases and not enough of them, but leases. And you close down a wholesale food operation, and it just dies on you. But if you try to keep it open when it's losing money, it's like opening a vein and hemorrhaging. The idea of taking over and running a bunch of buildings and a chain of food warehouses is not gonna put any stars on your shoulder boards on *this* floor." Harry twirled his left forefinger in the air to take in the entire forty-ninth floor, meaning Arthur Lomprey and the rest of the top brass. "And there's another thing. If we commence foreclosure proceedings against Croker, then suddenly we got a $500 million loss on the books. Right now those loans are posted as a $500 million asset. A half-a-billion-dollar loss would make a lotta people— It would not look good." He paused, pursed his lips, and looked around the room significantly. "A half a billion," he said, and then began nodding his head, as if to say, "You get the picture."

"The hell of it is," said Shellnutt, "some of these properties are basically sound, or they would be if you could—"

"Jesus Christ, Jack," said Shanks, "you sound just like Croker."

"Well, I never said he was wrong, did I? All I said was, he's a worthless, useless, lying conniving ball a shit who boffs stewardesses on his G-5 with our money."

"Oh," said Shanks. "I don't know how I ever got the idea you thought he was wrong."

"No, I mean you look at some a those early projects he did, like Buckingham Square, Wimberley Mall, Phoenix Center—there's nothing wrong with the cost basis. They're just overburdened with debt. But this last fiasco, Croker Concourse, that fucking building must a come out to a thousand dollars a foot! There's no way you could make that back, period, much less make a profit and service your debt. If it cost exactly half of what it actually cost, fine. You'd be in good shape. But this way, you could keep it leased to capacity for thirty years and still never get your money back. How the hell these goddamned loans ever went through, I don't know." Then he added hurriedly, as if to spare Peepgass any embarrassment, "Johnny Sycamore was out of control there toward the end."

Shanks said, "Well, as Lenin once said—"

Harry broke in: "Lenin had it easy. He didn't have to clean up after a shithead like Charlie Croker."

Shanks, persevering: "As Lenin once said—"

Friedman broke in and said to Harry, "I say we unload the shit as fast as we can and take the loss. There's bankrupt property beginning to flood the market, and that's gonna drive all the prices down. The longer we dick around with this property, the less we're gonna get for it."

Shanks said, "As Lenin once said—"

Harry broke in: "Like I said, I'd *love* to foreclose on that shithead, but we'd look so goddamned bad."

Raymond Peepgass was only halfway paying attention or, rather, he was thinking about the half-a-billion-dollar shithead from an entirely different perspective. The bank might end up ruining Croker, wiping him out utterly, or it might not. The game had not yet been played out. But one thing the bank couldn't change. The bank couldn't change history. There was no rewriting the fact that Charlie Croker was a man who had come from out of nowhere and built up an empire. The empire might crumble and disappear. But so what? So did Napoleon's. Who does the world remember and respect, Napoleon or Joseph Dominique Louis, his treasury minister (Peepgass had looked it up), who kept his nose clean and retired in 1815 on a pension? He, Peepgass, had gone to the Harvard Business School, whereas Croker couldn't have gotten into Harvard on a bet. But Croker had something that Monsieur Raymond Peepgass did not possess—or, rather, something he had never been willing to let off the leash . . . A certain *red dog* . . . That was the way he suddenly thought of it; as a red dog you had to be willing to let off the leash . . . He could *see* that wild red dog . . . It had a chain around its neck, but the chain was broken . . . It was a red bull terrier with its forehead in a dreadful frown and its lower incisors bared and thrust forward . . . Every man had that red dog inside him, but only real men dared let him loose—

Shanks said, "As Trotsky once said—"

Shellnutt broke in: "Trotsky? What happened to Lenin?"

"Nobody wanted to hear about Lenin, you buncha anti-intellectual fucks."

"Okay," said Shellnutt, "what did Trotsky say?"

"He said you don't have to believe in the trolley company to let it take you where you want to go."

"Trotsky said that? That's pretty funny. I don't know what the fuck it has to do with anything, but I like it. And incidentally, you need a very long vacation, Shanks."

Harry's Squadron cracked up with another macho burst from the gullet, a deep red laugh—

That did it somehow. *You don't have to believe in the trolley company to let it take you where you want to go.* The trolley company . . . Peepgass could feel, actually *feel,* some terribly significant synaptic experience in his brain, and he could see, actually *see,* as if it were some grainy diagram, the outlines of a . . . a . . . a theory, a concept, a strategy . . . It would be illegal. He did not yet know exactly why, but that much he could sense with the sort of visceral rush that precedes logic in the case of dreadfully exciting prospects. It would require secrecy, an intimate knowledge of banking procedures, resourceful confederates, the stealth of a cat, the heart of a thief . . . Strangely, and he was well aware of the strangeness of it, in that moment of revelation he felt that he, Raymond Peepgass, the star Harvard MBA who had been so cautious that he had chosen banking as a career—he suddenly felt that he had all it took, even the stealth, even . . . the *heart* . . . And in that moment his heart began to pound, bang away beneath his breastbone, so frightened and exhilarated was he by what he could see taking shape in his thoughts.

If Croker could be forced to hand over Croker Concourse to the bank, hand over the deed—*deed in lieu of foreclosure* was the term—so that there would be no foreclosure process and therefore no auction . . . and if the bank could be persuaded to unload the building quietly, for a fraction of its cost, as Friedman was already urging Harry to do . . . and if a syndicate could be formed to take it off their hands . . . and if he, Peepgass, were the one who put the syndicate together . . . without anyone at PlannersBanc knowing—

He would crush Charlie Croker! Mash his nuts for him! . . . to use Harry's oh-so-graphic way of putting things . . . and come away from it with untold millions. That was the phrase that actually popped into his head: *untold millions. Untold* was the word, all right! Couldn't tell a soul about it—

Christalmighty, was it really possible?

"Hey, Ray. *You* look like a happy fella." It was Harry himself. Until he heard that grating, rasping voice, he hadn't realized that a smile had crept across his face. Now he was back in this room. The whole squadron, Team Saddlebags, was staring at him. Beyond the glass wall, behind many layers of glass walls, the endless rivulets of a world awash with money streamed across the computer screens with their sickly diode glares.

"Oh," he said, "I was just thinking of something Croker once said, in that fucking interview in *Atlanta* magazine. '*Ex*ercise regimen?' he said. 'I'm fum daown in southwest Georgia, daown below the gnat line, an' if you come daown'eh'n'ask anybody 'bout a *ex*ercise regimen, they won't know what the hale you're talkin' abaout. On the other hand, when I need some farwood, I start with a *tree.*' Jesus Christ. That sonofabitch is so fulla shit, and he has dicked around with us *so* badly . . . I say we go after every piece a collateral he's got on that list, starting with the airplanes and that ridiculous goddamned plantation of his, which he thinks is fucking Tara, and that house he's living in in Buckhead, which he no doubt bought with our money, too. If he's such a Down Home hero, if he's such a son of the South Georgia sod, then just let him start over where his mouth is. Let's just let him start over . . . with his bare ass and an ax and a *tree.*"

Nobody else in the room said a word. They just kept staring. They couldn't believe the evidence of their own senses. None of them had ever heard Ray Peepgass use the word *fucking* before, much less any such terms as *bare ass* and *fulla shit.* None had ever heard him mimic the mighty Charlie Croker or, for that matter, anyone else. None had ever heard him suggest going after some shithead with fangs bared, like the saber-toothed tiger he was not. And certainly none had ever seen him with the sort of malevolent grin he was sporting at this moment. What the hell had gotten into old Ray?

Oh, he knew very well what they were thinking. But, then, there was no way any of them could have possibly known that Raymond Peepgass had just slipped his red dog off the leash and let him out for the first romp of his life.

TO A MAN of sixty, like Charlie Croker, one of the grimmest reminders of the Reaper's approach comes when his doctors, the people who have attended to his body for decades, begin retiring on him . . . or dying on him . . . or both. The orthopedist who had looked after Charlie's right knee since he first injured it in a game against Auburn, Archibald Turner, had retired two years ago and died of a heart attack one year ago. Arch Turner's practice had included many of the best bones in Buckhead. Now his two young associates, Emory Nuchols (rhymed with "buckles") and Douglas Ray, had inherited all those excellent, golden bones, and Emmo Nuchols became the new tender of Charlie's aching knee joint.

At this moment Charlie was sitting on the edge of an examination table, minus his pants and shoes, watching Emmo Nuchols's peculiar mouth as it said, "Look, Charlie, a knee replacement is not a medical decision, not in the sense of your general health. It's a question of how much pain you can stand *without* having it replaced. There's only one person who can answer that question." He waited several portentous heartbeats before adding, "And that's you."

Oh brother. Charlie hated the condescension that inevitably found its way into the young man's voice. Emmo was about forty, a full generation younger than Charlie, and yet he had called him Charlie right from day one. He insisted on being called Emmo, a nickname that reminded Charlie of a motor oil or a laxative. He would have preferred to have called him a curt, formal "Dr. Nuchols," but Emmo was a member of the Driving Club, and at the club he couldn't very well be saying hello to him and introducing him as "Dr. Nuchols." Emmo Nuchols had fast-receding curly black hair and a crinkly black beard that was carefully trimmed so that it created an oval that ran from his nose to his chin and was at no place more than half an inch wider than his lips. The explanation that this small grizzly oval had been designed to fit beneath the standard face mask during surgery was one Charlie had not sought and could have done without. Worst of all were his lips and his curiously tiny teeth. The lips were incredibly red. They curved like a woman's. It was somehow disgusting to watch him speak with this woman's mouth of his set in the middle of such a finickly shaped oval of black shag.

"Okay," said Charlie, "how long are you laid up if you have a knee replaced?"

"That varies," said the red lips, "but usually you're in the hospital five days to a week. But now, I don't want to mislead you. Full recovery can take as long as six weeks. The most difficult part of the whole thing is post-op. You have to undergo therapy immediately, to keep the muscles, tendons, and ligaments from stiffening up, and there's a fair amount of pain involved. I've never seen an operation that was a failure in and of itself. The only failures I've seen have been cases where the patient couldn't take the pain of keeping the joint flexible, and even that's been very seldom, certainly in my experience."

In my experience. And how much is that, in God's name? You're a kid, a calf, a baby! *In my experience*, indeed . . . And in that moment a flash of revelation hit Charlie. It wasn't just Arch Turner's departure from this globe that made Charlie feel old. It was the realization that there were all these kids out there, these children, ready and more than willing to do the job. It got harder and harder to feel indispensable at age sixty.

"Well, I'll think it over," said Charlie.

He never said anything like *I'll think it over, Emmo*. He was damned if he'd use this red-lipped mooncalf's oily nickname if he didn't have to.

Chapter XI

This Is—Not Right!

AN ACCIDENT IN THE CALDECOTT TUNNEL ON ROUTE 24 HAD caused a terrific backup, so that Conrad arrived in downtown Oakland barely five minutes before his 10 a.m. appointment. Where could he park the Hyundai? Where could he park it? Where? He was frantic. Just as his mom and dad had never thought twice about letting appointments go with the flow, he was obsessive about keeping them. Where could he park? *There!* There, a block and a half from the East Bay Insurance Building, where the ContempoTime offices were located, he spotted a space just this side of a strip of curbing painted red, with a fire hydrant in the middle of it. Only a car as small as the Hyundai could have squeezed into the legal space remaining, and even then only by backing up against the bumper of a big Chevrolet Suburban.

As soon as he walked into the premises of ContempoTime, he realized that this "appointment" of his was in fact only some sort of vague traffic slot. Twenty or thirty people, a couple of them middle-aged white men in coats and ties, sat in rows of school-style desk chairs in a bare, spare reception area filling out forms and waiting to be assigned to an interviewer. The room was lit by banks of fluorescent tubes, which kept blinking, so that the entire place seemed to be suffering from a colossal tic. Conrad picked up the forms from a receptionist and sat down in one of the rows of desk chairs and joined the herd.

Acceding, however bitterly, to Mrs. Otey's urgings, he had worn a long-sleeved white shirt, a necktie, his only jacket, which was a single-breasted navy blazer he had bought at Roos-Atkins in Walnut Creek two years before, and a pair of gray worsted pants, which were the only wool pants he possessed. The jacket was now too tight, and he could no longer button the shirt at the neck, causing the tie to look unkempt, and his hands, his laborer's hands, the subject of Mrs. Otey's insulting admonition, extended too far beyond the shirt cuff and the jacket sleeves. Nevertheless, he was glad he had worn this, his only dress-up outfit.

Long after he had completed the forms, he sat there in the dismal, blinking, tic-afflicted ranks of school chairs listening to the hum and clatter of electric typewriters in a maze of cubicles that stretched on beyond the reception area, idly wondering, *Why typewriters?*, since ContempoTime's advertisements stressed word-processor skills.

By and by he was summoned back to the reception desk and introduced to a girl named Carol, who was no older than he was, a sunny creature with milky white skin and bouncy reddish-blond hair, a bit plump but with a perfect dimple in her chin and absolutely marvelous dimples in her cheeks when she smiled, which was constantly.

She showed him into a cubicle with four-foot-high particle-board walls, a so-called work station. There was barely room for the furniture, which consisted of two low-backed gray fiberglass chairs and a desk, upon which rested a big IBM Selectric typewriter. The chattering *rat-tat-tat* of other electric typewriters poured in from cubicles all around. When the girl twisted her body to sit down, her little skirt gripped the full curve of her thigh. She had such a . . . libidinous presence! Confused, a-tingle, blushing, Conrad smiled at her. She smiled back—so frankly! She looked straight into his eyes—so warmly! Then she began studying the forms he had filled out. After a bit she said, "Have you ever done any office work before, any word processing?"

"No, but I studied it in college. I took a course in it. Two semesters."

She went over the forms some more. "Well, that's the main thing, being able to use the computer. That and being able to spell."

A rogue notion ran through his mind. What if he asked her out for coffee or something? Or for lunch! It would soon be lunchtime, and he had brought a little over a hundred dollars with him. He shouldn't spend so much as a nickel on lunch in downtown Oakland, but if he caught on with ContempoTime, or it looked like it was a sure thing at least . . . Not a big lunch, just something quick . . . He deserved—after everything he—it would do him good—and besides . . .

The girl got down to the matter of the test. It was in two parts: a written test concerning the use of a word processor and a typing test. She handed him a clipboard with the written test on it, produced a little white plastic kitchen timer, set it for fifteen minutes, and placed it on the desk.

"Good luck," she said as she left the cubicle. "I'll be back. There isn't much to it."

And, in fact, there wasn't much to it, especially since the answers were multiple-choice. "How do you delete two lines within a paragraph?" . . . "How do you create a second copy?" . . . "To save material, what do you do?" . . . He had finished long before the bell on the timer went off. He scored 100. To set up the typing test, the girl had to lean over him and place some written material on the little stenographic easel beside the IBM Selectric. The warmth of her body set loose the most delicious perfume. Conrad was a-tingle all over again.

She remained bent over, supporting herself with her hands on her knees. Her face was right beside his. "Now this time," she said, "when I say go, you start typing—starting right here." She pointed to the beginning of the paragraph at the top of the page on the easel. "Just keep on typing until I tell you to stop. You'll have five minutes. Okay? It's not a big deal. Thirty words a minute qualifies. I'm sure you can do that."

"I was up to eighty-five words a minute when I took the course at Mount Diablo," said Conrad. "But I haven't done this for a while, so don't expect any world records."

"Eighty-*five*? I don't think I ever tested anybody who could do eighty-five."

She made a little laughing sound deep in her throat as she said it, and Conrad thought he could feel the warmth of her cheek, although in fact her cheek was six or eight inches away. He had a new rogue urge: to hold her face in his hands and kiss her.

Instead, he turned his face toward hers and said, "Do you mind if I ask you something?"

Now she turned toward him. Her face was so close to his, he saw three eyes . . . and many dimples . . . So sunny! So frisky! So full of rude pink animal health! He felt intoxicated. "Go ahead," she said.

His cheeks were turning crimson. Did he dare—could he possibly—don't be crazy! So he stuck to his question: "Why is the typing test—why do you give it on a typewriter? Won't we be using computers?"

"Oh sure," she said. She didn't pull her head back at all. She seemed to be beaming at him. He could detect a faint, sweet aroma of spearmint on her breath. He loved it. He loved everything about her. "But for the test all we want to see is how well you type, how fast you are and how accurate you are. On a computer you can go back and delete your mistakes, and that way we can't tell how accurate you really are."

She pushed a little ribbed wheel on the keyboard, and the big Selectric came humming to life in a delicious cloud of perfume and spearmint.

Then she stood up and turned the chunky hand on the timer once more. "You have five minutes," she said. "Just type as much as you can, as accurately as you can, before I come back. Okay? Ready? . . . Go." She set the timer down on the little desk. "Good luck." A wonderful smile! The most wonderful smile in the world! Then she withdrew from the cubicle.

Conrad took a deep breath and placed his fingers on the keyboard in the standard touch-typing position. The timer was already ticking away. At the top of the page was a paragraph that began: "This ratio can be easily derived by comparing the real (inflation-adjusted) capital fueling the two most recent retail electronics booms: 1971–75 and 1983–87 (Fig. 4-6). The amount of real capital in the most recent period was $736.1 billion, as compared with . . ."

He concentrated on the first words . . . *This ratio can* . . . and started typing. The Selectric's little letter ball jumped about madly and spat out a terrific *rat-tat-tat* upon the paper.

He knew immediately that something had gone wrong. He stared . . . Instead of *This* he had somehow typed *Rhhhodd*. Instead of the *T*, the *i*, and the *s*, he had hit the letters next to them, the *R*, the *o*, and the *d*. He had managed to hit the *h*, but he had pressed it down too heavily and too long, causing it to repeat. He was baffled and appalled. How could that have happened? He would have to start over. He looked about for another sheet of typing paper, but there was none. Then her words came back to him: they wanted a true record of how accurate—or inaccurate—you were.

He scrolled the paper up a few lines and started over. Another clattering *rat-tat-tat*. He inspected his handiwork . . . *This ratip* instead of *This ratio*. He had overlapped the *p* when he tried to strike the *o*. Should he start over again? No time. So he backspaced and typed an *o* over the *p*. Didn't help much; looked like an *o* with a tail.

Then he realized what the problem was. *His hands!* His fingers were now so much wider and heavier and stronger, from working in the warehouse, he was constantly overlapping adjoining keys or else striking them too hard, causing the letters to repeat. He had lost the touch in his own fingers! Two grotesque musclebound strangers, his hands were! *My own hands!* He stared at them as if he had never seen them before.

The ticking of the timer seemed dreadfully loud. A minute had gone by, and he had produced a grand total of a dozen words, most of them mangled. Gingerly he placed his fingertips back on the keyboard, hoping against hope that it would all come back to him. It had to. He stared at the text: "most recent retail" . . . *Rat-tat-tat-tat-tat* . . . and he had written *,pst recemt rwtsil* . . . A burning panic . . . These hands of which he had been so proud just a few hours ago as he stared into the bathroom mirror—they were the paws of a dumb animal, of a beast of burden—*he couldn't believe it!*—and all the while the humming of the IBM Selectric grew louder and louder . . . *Okay, big boy, produce! I'm ready, I'm humming, I'm waiting—what about you?* . . . and the timer went *ticktickticktickticktick*.

He plunged on, trying to batter his way through the text, since nothing else seemed to work, typing right on top of misstruck letters, x'ing out the totally hopeless mistakes and the repeats, letting the hair-trigger keys *rat-tat-tat-tat-tat* amok. Just get through it, that was the main thing.

In no time—*ding!*—the timer bell went off, and the girl, Carol, was in the entryway to the cubicle. Conrad stared at the piece of paper. Far from having produced the minimum of 150 words in five minutes, he wasn't sure he had produced 90. With all the x's, typeovers, repeats, and false starts, the tight little single-spaced patch of words looked like something small and black that had been run over on a highway.

"Well," said the girl brightly, "how'd it go?"

Conrad was speechless. All he could do was shake his head. Her eyes shifted to the page.

"What happened?"

"I don't know," said Conrad. He lifted his hands—and was suddenly mortified that she might notice their size. He hid them in his lap. "I just couldn't—I guess it's been so long—I don't know."

In a low, confidential tone she said, "Well, do you want to try it again? I'm not supposed to, but I can give you another sheet of paper, and we'll do it over."

"Thanks, but it's no use. I don't know what's wrong."

"Why don't you go home and practice some and then come back. You want to? If you call ahead and let me know when you're coming, I can get the desk to assign you to me. We're not supposed to do that, either, but I'll do it." She gave him a sympathetic smile.

"It's just—" He couldn't complete the sentence. "I'll try," he said in a hopeless tone.

He thanked her and left without another word. On the elevator he held his hands up before his face. What had he turned into? The longer he stared at them, the bigger they seemed to become. *My own hands!* And she had tried to give him . . . everything! . . . on a platter . . . He could still see her smile, her dimples (the swell of her breasts, the curve of her thighs) . . . The most shaming part of it was that the ever-smirking Arda Otey had been right, more so than she could have ever even guessed.

THOUGHTS OF JILL and her mother possessed him as he walked down the sidewalk heading for his car. It was a bright sparkling noontime, a fact that couldn't have interested him less. What would they say when he told them? What would they think? Or did he have to tell them? Why couldn't he just say he had had the interview and was waiting to hear back?

Scuffling along the sidewalk, his head down, he scarcely even noticed the knot of idlers and gawkers who had gathered near a truck until he was almost upon them. It was a high-riding flatbed truck painted a hot yellow-green and embellished with swash lettering and pinstriping and gleaming chrome. A sunburnt man wearing a cowboy hat and a leather vest appeared, a regular giant, 250 pounds if he was an ounce. The sleeves of his shirt had been cut off at the shoulders, revealing his huge fleshy arms. He walked to the front of the truck, stepped up on a chrome running board, opened the door, leaned inside the cab, emerged with a metal rod of some kind, and returned to the rear.

It occurred to Conrad, with a start, that whatever was going on, it was in the red zone in front of where he had parked the Hyundai. The gawkers blocked his view. He hurried forward and joined them. He found himself staring at the broad beam of the giant in the cowboy hat, who was leaning over, attaching a tow chain to a car that had both front wheels up on the curb, right in the middle of the red zone, barely a foot from the fire hydrant—

—and in that instant Conrad realized it was *his* car, his little Hyundai Excel. In the middle of the red zone! Up on the curb! Impossible!—and yet there it was. There was a ticket under the windshield wiper.

Standing on the sidewalk, right beside the car, following the tow truck operator's progress, was a meter maid, easily identifiable by her uniform, a short-sleeved powder-blue shirt and navy-blue pants. She was probably in early middle age, so stout that the flesh of her upper arms stretched the hems of her sleeves. She held a walkie-talkie radio up to her mouth. She had a terrific set of Chinese-red press-on nails on her fingers.

Conrad approached from the side. He was scarcely eighteen inches from her, but she didn't give him so much as a flicker of an eye.

"Excuse me!" he said. No response. Much louder: "Ex*cuse* me!"

The walkie-talkie still at her ear, she cut him a glance that said *Don't bother me*.

"Miss!" said Conrad.

She gave him a withering look and said, "Can't you see I'm *transmitting*?"

The terribly official-sounding word, *transmitting*, brought him up short, and he turned toward the tow truck driver. By now the big man had secured the tow chain beneath the Hyundai and was standing up, and you could see just how enormous he really was. He was a mountain of flesh with the sun-beaten, lard-grilled look of a roustabout, clear down to the immense ring of keys hanging from a belt loop beneath the bulge of his belly on one side of his jeans and the cluster of novelty key fobs on the other: a tiny wrench, a disposable butane lighter, a pair of dice, a plastic figurine of Mickey Mouse and Minnie Mouse doing the tango, a miniature dueling pistol, and a little silvery skull with fangs instead of eyeteeth.

Conrad jumped between the fire hydrant and the fender of the Hyundai and over the tow chain and rushed up to him. "Hey!—sir!—this is *my car!* Whattaya *doing?*"

Scarcely looking at him, not even pausing, the giant said, "Towin' it outta the red zone."

He said it in a bored way that made it clear he had said the same thing, or something very close to it, a thousand times before, to a thousand other frantic, befuddled, and, above all, helpless automobile owners. He was now heading for the driver's-side front door with the shaft of metal he had taken from the truck. It was a length of spring steel. Conrad recognized it immediately. It was a device known as a Slim Jim, used to slip through the window seals of locked cars to release the lock mechanisms from the inside.

"Wait a minute! Please!" But the giant was already inserting the Slim Jim between the glass and the frame.

"You're gonna break the glass! I've got the keys right here! I can open the door!"

"Nobody's breakin' any glass," said the giant in the same bored voice, without looking at him. In no time he had sprung the lock, opened the door, and was reaching inside, doing something with the steering wheel.

"Please!" said Conrad. "It's my car! I've got the keys! I can move it!"

The giant didn't even look at him. Utterly nonplussed, Conrad swung back toward the sidewalk to appeal to the meter maid. She wasn't looking at him, either. She was writing something in her summons book. By now the knot of gawkers had grown into a real crowd. They were revved up, ready for some action, eager for the beano, now that the hapless owner of the automobile had materialized and was acting suitably dismayed, frightened, anguished, and frustrated.

This time Conrad yelled at the meter maid: "*Hey! Miss!*"

She looked up, and he jumped back over the tow chain and went straight to her. "Please—you gotta tell me what's going on! This is *my car!*"

She begun studying the summons pad and gestured toward the Hyundai without looking at Conrad. "Car's in the red zone—*and* up on the sidewalk."

Conrad raised his hands in frustration. "But I didn't *park* in the red zone! I swear! Look, miss, listen—I was all the way back there, on the other side of the line!"

"Well, exactly the way it's sittin' right now, that's exactly the way it was sittin' when I called the dispatcher." She said this in a reasonable-enough tone, but it inspired a couple of *unh-hunnnhs* and *hegh-heggghhs* among the gawkers, and she became aware she had an audience. So she added, "And I never seen a car drive it*self* into a red zone yet."

"Woooo-eeee," said one of the gawkers, and another said, "Ohhhhhh yeah," all in the eternal spirit of Let's You and Him Fight.

"Look, miss," said Conrad. He struggled to find the right words, the compelling logic. "I'm telling you, I didn't park in the red zone. Honest. And even if I did, would I put my front wheels up on the curb? Would that make any sense?"

The woman delivered a contralto chuckle deep in her throat and said, "They don't pay me to make sense outta what the drivers do in this town. Couldn't pay me *enough* to do that." This brought such an appreciative round of *unhh-hunnnhhhs, heh-heggghhhhhs*, and *woooo-eeeeees*, the big woman felt uplifted, emboldened. Usually street crowds were against the meter maid, but she had won this bunch over with rhetorical brilliance, and so she headed for new heights: "My job is keeping cars from parking in the wrong place and getting them outta there when they do, and that car right there is parked in about as wrong a place as you can get. That's a *red* zone, and that's a *fire* hydrant, and that's a *side*walk—and that's a *tow* truck."

Woooo-eeeeeee! Hegh-heggghhhhhh! Unhh-hunnnnhhhhhh! Oh yeah! That's a tow *truck!*

Conrad was dumbstruck. In the next moment he realized what had happened. To squeeze into the small space on the legal side of the red zone, he had backed his car up against the bumper of the Chevrolet Suburban behind him. The driver of the Suburban had returned and, finding himself hemmed in, had bulldozed his way out by pushing the little Hyundai forward along the pavement. Conrad must have left his wheels turned toward the curb, so that the sheer brute force of the Suburban had shoved the Hyundai all the way up onto the sidewalk.

"But this isn't *right*!" said Conrad. "The car behind me must've pushed my car where it is! Why else would it be up on the curb?"

His vehemence caused the meter maid to withdraw a little. She sighed, cast her eyes down, and shook her head. "I don't know nothing about another car. Anyway, can't do nothing about it now."

"But why not?" said Conrad. "Please! I'm right here! It's my car! I've got the keys! *I'll* take the car out of the red zone!"

To indicate how compellingly logical his solution was, as compared to the official one now in progress, he threw his hands up in front of his shoulders in the gesture that says, "It's so obvious, only a fool could fail to see it." This did not help his case.

With a bit of a growl the meter maid pinned her eyes on her summons book and said, "It's too late. Already wrote it up and called the dispatcher. Once it's written up, that's it."

"Well—go ahead and give me the ticket. But let me take my car. I've *got* to have my car!"

"I told you it's too late. Once the summons is made out and the dispatcher's notified and the tow's hooked up, then it's a *tow*, and ain't nothing nobody can do about it once it's a tow."

"But this is—*not right*!" said Conrad.

"*Woooo-eeeeeee! Unh-unhhhh-unhhhhh! A tow is a tow!*"

Conrad looked at the gawkers, whose merry eyes seemed to be saying, "*Now* what are you going to do?" He looked at the meter maid, who seemed to be reveling in her new role as street entertainer. He looked toward the tow truck driver—but he had disappeared into the cab of the truck and was getting ready to pull the Hyundai up onto the slant of the flatbed.

But this was—*not right*! On top of everything else—he couldn't lose his car this way!

At that moment the tow truck started up with a great throaty roar, followed by the hideously loud and harsh grinding sound of the winching gear. The gawkers were suddenly quiet, thrilled to see that the drama was approaching its climax. The power! The authority! The mighty truck! Its yellow-green paint job shone from many coats of lacquer in which glittery particles were somehow suspended. Streams of pinstriping swept back from the hood and across the door of the cab. On the door a rollicking silvery script with a shiny black undershadow proclaimed: *Three C Towing, Salvage & Repair*. Conrad stared with his mouth open. Somehow the truck was the mechanical embodiment of the arrogance and imperiousness of the meter maid and the driver themselves.

The little Hyundai began to slide up the slant of the flatbed. In no time it was secured, trapped, in the piggyback position, and the truck was lumbering off. All the while the gawkers were watching him—him!—this helpless nonentity who could do nothing more than stand there with his keys in his hand as they, those with the power, took his car away from him before his very eyes.

My car!

He had not merely been wronged, he had suffered a dreadful, shameful, humiliating defeat, with this bunch of trifling idlers as his audience.

He could barely control his voice when he asked the meter maid how much the fine was for parking in a red zone and what he had to do to get his car back. She answered him in a reasonable and even courteous way, which somehow made it all worse. Her roughshod victory, her humiliation of this young man with his protestations and his this-is-not-right's, her subjugation of Conrad Hensley, was so complete, she could now throw him a morsel of civility.

All the while he knew he had a still more humiliating audience to deal with. In a broken-down little duet in Pittsburg his wife and her mother, they who had already indicted him for worthlessness, hopelessness, joblessness, and the wrong parents—they were now waiting for him and his car. Jill's mother's car was in the shop for repairs, and he was supposed to pick her up when he returned, to fetch it. Surely even he, the otherwise hopeless one, could manage a simple thing like returning from Oakland in a timely fashion and taking Mother over to the garage—

He dreaded the telephone call he would now have to make.

THE ORDEAL BEGAN before he actually made it. A telephone . . . He looked all around on this busy street in downtown Oakland, and there wasn't a telephone to be found. He started walking . . . Three blocks he walked before he finally found one. It was the type that required a quarter to initiate a long-distance call—but he didn't have a quarter. In his pocket he had five twenty-dollar bills, a five, and three ones. The bills, thank God, would be just enough to retrieve the car. According to the meter maid, the fine for parking in a red zone was $30, and the towing fee was another $77. But right now he needed to change one of the dollar bills and get a quarter. But where? He looked all around . . .Nothing but office buildings and the kind of shops you didn't just walk into and ask for change . . . He walked some more . . . Finally he spotted a candy stand in the lobby of an office building on Broadway. The proprietor, a swarthy man, apparently Asian, didn't even deign to answer his question. He just gave him a dour look and kept pointing to a crudely lettered sign on the candy counter: NO CHANGE WITHOUT PURCHASE. In his way he was as humiliating as the tow truck driver . . . dealing in a bored, contemptuous manner with a question he had already heard from a thousand other urban vermin.

The cheapest item was a newspaper, the *Oakland Tribune*, for fifty cents. But by now Conrad was starving, and so instead he bought a Schotter's HDL (for High Density Lipids) Chocolate Health Nut bar for sixty cents, yielding him the quarter he needed, plus a dime and a nickel in change. This decision he would soon regret, even aside from the fact that the candy bar sliced a thin blade of hypersweetness into his stomach and quelled his hunger for all of ten minutes.

He walked the three blocks back to the pay telephone and placed his call to Pittsburg, collect. The telephone was supposed to return his quarter but ate it instead. Jill accepted the call. She repeated everything he said, slowly, loudly, so slowly and loudly she seemed to be mocking him. After a few moments he realized it must be for the benefit of her mother. When he reached the part about finding the car up on the sidewalk in a red zone, Jill started saying:

"You left it in a *red* zone? Up on the *side*walk? You—left—it—in—a—*red*—zone? Up—on—the—*side*walk?"

No! No! No! he protested. He had *found* it that way, upon his *return*!

"In—a—*red*—zone? On—the—*side*walk?"

Not even the meter maid had been quite so contemptuous. Suddenly she asked him how the job interview had gone. Conrad stammered out a few words to the effect that he might have to take the test again. Might—have—to—take—the—test—*again*? At this, he dropped all defenses and circumlocutions and just started telling her what had happened. She cut him off in the middle—as you would anyone who was so predictably hopeless and pathetic that the details of his latest failure simply didn't matter.

"Conrad, I want you back here with that car right away. My mother's stranded, I'm stranded, the children are stranded, everybody's stranded until you—get—in—the—car—and—come—back—here."

When he hung up, he felt feverish, as if suffering from some insidious infection (called inevitable failure). It was a good little hike down Broadway to reach the Parking Violations office at 150 Frank Ogawa Plaza, where you had to go to pay your fines before retrieving a towed vehicle. The meter maid, the giant with the cowboy hat, the gawkers, and now the swarthy man at the candy counter—he felt feverish.

In the Parking Violations office, there was a whole row of windows, but only one was open, and Conrad found himself at the end of a long, ponderous line in another grim gray-beige room with fluorescent lights. It took him forty minutes to reach the window, where a gaunt woman, the very embodiment of Tried Patience, informed him that he owed an additional thirty dollars. He was stunned. Stunned! He didn't *have* an additional thirty dollars! Thirty dollars for what? For parking on a sidewalk. That was in addition to the thirty for parking in a red zone, making a total of $60 in fines he would have to pay in order to get a slip releasing the car from the towing pound. At the pound he would still have to pay a $77 towing charge, assuming he got there by 7 p.m. Any sort of charge for picking it up? The clerk looked at his ticket . . . The tow was at 11 a.m. exactly. Then she looked at her watch . . . If he got there by 7 p.m., he should be all right. He shouldn't have to pay the $50-a-day storage fee. That was a total of $137 he would have to pay out, and all he had was $107.15. Nor was that the end of it. The pound . . . All along he had assumed that the pound was some municipal facility downtown, near this building. Now he was informed that his car would be at the towing company's own lot. Two companies did the towing for the city. His car had been towed by a new one, Three C Towing, Salvage & Repair—which was where? On Keeler Avenue, over in East Oakland. Conrad knew only one thing about East Oakland: it was the slums. A cloud rose up his brain stem and filled his head. His car would be deep in the slums . . . in the domain of a giant roustabout with a cowboy hat.

He paid the $60 and left the Parking Violations office with the release slip, $47.15 in his pocket, a racing heart, and a big problem. How could he get another $29.85? No, he had two problems, three problems, four problems—the tide seemed to rise with every passing second. The only possible way to get the money would be to call Jill again, an appalling prospect in itself. If she had it, she could get it to him—how? Wire it? How was it done? He had never telegraphed anything in his life. Many times, when he was a boy, he had gone with his parents to the Western Union office in San Francisco after they had pleaded desperately, and wholly mendaciously, with their parents or old friends for pity, which meant money in the form of a Western Union money order. He had so botched things, he couldn't even make the call. He had only fifteen cents in change. If only he *had* bought a newspaper instead of the Schotter's HDL Chocolate Health Nut bar, he would have had twenty-five cents. Had to have his candy bar, didn't he!

He tugged absentmindedly at his mustache, then set off at a brisk walk, once more looking for some place to break a dollar bill. Two blocks, three blocks, four blocks—he could feel, or thought he could feel, his blood pressure rising. His extremities seemed to be gorged with blood. At last, a hole in the wall that sold glassine envelopes, little glass pipes, so-called roach clips, sunglasses, candy, cigarettes, and newspapers. Tenderized, he didn't dare ask for change. He bought an *Oakland Tribune* for fifty cents. To his consternation the proprietor, a dour little olive-skinned man with a drooping lip, gave him a fifty-cent piece in change. A fifty-cent piece—you couldn't put that in a pay telephone! A fifty-cent piece—hadn't seen one in years! Why now? Only after repeated entreaties did the man agree to exchange it for two quarters.

Outside, Conrad threw the newspaper away in a receptacle on the corner. He now had two twenty-dollar bills, a five, a one, two quarters, a dime, and a nickel. He started walking again. Over there—a telephone. He deposited a quarter. Nothing; dead; it was out of order; he couldn't get the quarter back; he jiggled the lever; he pounded the machine with the heel of his hand. A panic rose up in him, and now his extremities seemed to shrink and grow cold. He walked all the way back to the first telephone he had found. His heart was beating much too fast. Gingerly he deposited his last quarter—and placed another collect call to Jill—and told her the whole sad story.

This time her long, deadly silence was worse than anything she could have said. She left the telephone. She returned after what seemed like an eternity. Tonelessly she delivered the information that, between them, she and her mother had only twenty-three dollars in cash. Tonelessly she told him she would now have to spend most of that, probably, to take a taxi all the way out to the bank and then all the way to Western Union, wherever on earth that was. Tonelessly, with a seething restraint, she asked him if he realized how utterly . . . utterly . . . and then words failed her. By the time he hung up, his throat felt so constricted, he could barely speak.

The only good thing that came out of it was that this time the machine at least returned the quarter he had used to initiate the call. So he stood on the street in downtown Oakland with $46.40 in his pocket waiting for his wife to chase down $35 in a taxi and call him back. He couldn't budge. He had to stand here and wait by this telephone. Her voice had dripped with insinuation. He had descended to the level of life's hopeless losers. He had lost his job, couldn't pass the simplest employment test imaginable, and now he had gone and lost his car. *No!*

poured into his heart. Forlorn, he looked up at the sky. It was a bright, cloudless day—but something had happened. That dazzling light was becoming steadily lower. It had been 2:35 when he hung up with Jill. Now it was 2:55, and the sun was definitely no longer overhead. The day was sinking, sinking, sinking, and if he didn't reach the pound by 7 p.m, he would have to pay a day's storage, which would be still more money he didn't possess. A current of anxiety ran through his solar plexus.

It was almost 3:30 when she finally called back. Many crabbed details of the ordeal by taxi, which had cost $22.50; finally, the address of the Western Union office where he could go to claim the $35—1400 Broadway. Thank God. At least he knew where that was. But when he reached 1400 Broadway, it turned out to be not a Western Union office but a drugstore . . . Baffled, he started approaching people on the sidewalk. "Excuse me . . ." The first two ignored him, as if he were a beggar. But why? He was wearing a coat and tie! Was there now something people could see in his eyes? Had this feverish anxiety he was feeling done something to his face? The next three said they didn't know where it was. He looked at his watch: 3:32. Finally an old woman walking along Broadway in a royal-blue jogging suit and gleaming white sneakers gave him directions. Western Union was six blocks away, on Franklin Street. He hurried down Broadway, but where she said it was on Franklin Street—a grocery store! Back onto Broadway he went, frantically querying passersby, who now began to look at him as if he had room to let upstairs. Finally a young Asian woman—Korean?—Japanese?—told him it was inside a check-cashing facility . . . up *that* way. So Conrad ran up *that* way. Sure enough, there was a Western Union window inside the place. It seemed that Western Union was now devoted almost entirely to money orders, and its branches were often located inside of drugstores, grocery stores, all sorts of retail outlets, served by a single computer network. Now: 3:35.

By the time he reached Western Union, it was 3:55. Quite a little line of woebegone souls . . . seeking the services of a lone clerk, a courtly Asian behind a teller's window. One and all seemed to be picking up, sending out, or feverishly waiting for money orders.

It was 4:25 by the time he worked his way up to the window and was face-to-face with the clerk. The final all-too-perfect note came when the man asked him the Test Question, designed to make sure the right person collected the money order. Jill had contrived it, and the question, as it came out in the clerk's curious chirping accent, was: "Wot ees Jeel's *fah*ta's *name*? and *ti*-tle?" Conrad heard himself intoning the very syllables that signified All That Distinguishes the Higher Orders of Humanity from Conrad Hensley: "Dr. Arnold Otey."

No sooner did the man slip him the $35 through the slot at the base of the window than Conrad realized he should have asked Jill to get him more money, so that he could take a taxi to the car pound. It was now 4:30. He had two and a half hours to get there—but how? He had only $4.40 to spare. He would have to take a bus. But what bus? From where? Suppose there was no bus that went near the place? So he asked the clerk. The man gave him a funny little smile. "Oh! I don't *know*! East *Oak*land! Hah hah. Dere I don't *tra*vel, 'owever I can a*void* it!"

Out on the street again . . . The light was beginning to fade . . . It seemed to take forever before he found someone (the manager of a Mail Box, Inc., service) who knew where the nearest bus stop was. Just the nearest bus stop; no one knew where one went to catch a bus to Keeler Avenue in East Oakland. In fact, it had taken only nine minutes, but it was now almost 4:40, and every minute was beginning to assume a swollen importance. Only 140 minutes until seven o'clock! Four blocks he had to walk to reach the bus stop. His watch said: 4:45. Only three people at the bus stop; none even knew where Keeler Avenue was, much less how to get there. Finally, at 4:53, a bus arrived. The driver informed him: buses did go out to Keeler, but not from this stop. The nearest stop was six blocks *that* way. Conrad took off, running. He arrived panting, his shirt soaked with sweat under the arms, terribly conscious of the odor, of fear as well as exertion, that rose from his body. It was 4:58. Three minutes later—5:01—a bus arrived. It was the wrong bus; he had to wait for a Number 58. Ten minutes later—5:11—a Number 58 arrived, and Conrad boarded and presented the driver with a dollar bill. The man just shook his head. Either a token or $1.50 in change. *Well . . . take the whole five-dollar bill!* No can do. Conrad pleaded. The man just shook his head. Conrad could hear a sawing sound coming from his own chest. He was hyperventilating. He left the bus dumbfounded. 5:13.

In the first two stores he entered, looking for change of a five-dollar bill, a luggage shop and an office-supply store, the clerks gave him a fishy look and insisted they had no change. Now it dawned on him that he was red-faced, frantic, disheveled, sweating, and breathing too hard. He tried to pull himself together. Finally a lank young thing clerking in a L'eggs store listened to his woeful tale and gave him change out of her own purse. 5:24.

He ran back to the bus stop. It was twenty-two minutes before another Number 58 arrived. 5:46. He boarded and presented his six quarters. He now had a grand total of $79.90, $77 for Three C Towing, Salvage & Repair and $2.90 for himself. The bus lumbered off toward East Oakland.

The slums of East Oakland were slums California-style. There were none of the narrow, squalid tenement buildings Conrad was used to seeing in movies about New York. Instead, block after block of small drab buildings, many of them old wood-frame houses, worn-out, faded, neglected, sagging . . . This grim landscape was highlighted here and there by the lurid contemporary symbols of the Low Rent life: over here, a stucco structure on a corner painted a violent mustard yellow with CHECK CASHING on the sides in black letters a foot high and outlined in red . . . over there, a billboard featuring an eight-foot-high picture of a single High Five sneaker with a cutout showing the inner construction of the sole and the heel . . . and two blocks farther on, a decrepit moss-green building with a rickety old porch just above ground level and a smartly painted sign with blue letters vibrating against a yellow background stretching across the length of the roof: MEDWORLD PLASMA CENTER . . . A line of derelicts with faces so grimy and weathered you couldn't tell if they were black or white or something else were in a line on the porch, looking for all the world as if they had been spat upon the wall and were oozing down it. They were waiting to sell their blood. Deeper and deeper, ever so slowly—6:11 now—the bus made its way deeper and deeper into the Oakland slums. The blocks of shabby little buildings began to thin out. The area was so far gone, half the lots were heaps of slag and dirt. Finally—6:32!—he could see it up ahead . . . Behind a high chain-metal fence, topped all the way around with coils of razor wire, was a sea of automobile hoods and roofs exploding with reflections of the late-afternoon sun. The Three C Towing lot occupied most of a city block, or what was left of it. Even before the bus came to a stop, Conrad could make out people in silhouette against the light of the low-slung sun—walking across the surface of this blinding sea of metal. Across the surface—but was such a thing possible?

He got off the bus and dashed across the avenue and up to the fence. He squinted into the sun. His eyes had not deceived him. There were three or four workmen walking across the hoods of cars, one after the other, and not merely walking, either, but striding, their boots making a *thwop thwop thwop* sound as the hoods torqued under their weight. The cars were jammed in so close together, it was easier to walk across them than to try to squeeze between them. Suddenly, with a whining, grinding sound, an entire car rose up in silhouette against that punishing light, straight up into the air, until you could see burning sunlight beneath its wheels. Conrad knew that sound very well: a forklift. They were moving cars around with forklifts.

Up ahead, along the fence line, a pair of metal stanchions supported a rusting sign with part of the paint peeled away: THREE C TOWING, SALVAGE & REPAIR. Beneath it was a wide opening to an enclosure with a big chain-link gate, the entryway to the lot itself, and two port-a-rooms, trailer-like structures set end to end up on jacks. A crude wooden staircase led to a door. The offices of Three C Towing. 6:40! He had made it, with just twenty minutes to spare.

Inside the port-a-room, a Formica-top counter ran the length of the narrow space. Half a dozen people were in line. Behind the counter was a short, stocky man, deeply suntanned, probably in his mid-thirties. His receding black hair was combed straight back over the top and around the sides to the base of his skull, where it erupted into a cascade of little curls down the back of his neck. He wore a polo shirt with the sleeves rolled up, the better to display his upper arms, which were huge, obviously pumped up through weightlifting. He was grinning—and Conrad now saw that he was deep in conversation with the person at the head of the line, a young woman with an astonishing mane of blond hair. Conrad stared at her, stared at the grinning man, stared at the sign on the wall above his head:

CASH OR POSTAL MONEY ORDERS ONLY
(NO CHECKS, NO CREDIT CARDS)
AFTER 24 HOURS STORAGE FEE $50 PER DAY CHARGED ON ALL CARS
(NO EXCEPTIONS)
TOWING $77 FIRST HALF HOUR, $77 EACH ADDITIONAL HALF HOUR

—and then at the large round clock beside it: 6:46.

"So you're from Pleasanton," said the man.

"That's right," said the blonde.

"You know a girl named Scarlett Antonucci, by any chance? From Pleasanton?"

"I don't think so."

"I used to go out with her. I was in Pleasanton all the time. I like Pleasanton. It's a nice town. Why'd you ever drive into *Oak*land today?" Big smile.

"I was shopping."

"In *Oak*land? You got some terrific malls in Pleasanton. Stoneridge —iddn'at one a them?"

Flirting with her!—and all these people at the counter waiting—6:47—to get their cars before 7 p.m.!

Conrad studied the line for the first time, looking for the likely candidate who would speak up and get things moving . . . But the whole bunch of them, the three men and the two women, merely fidgeted, looked this way and that, craned their necks—and none of them said a word.

Well—should *he*? Dared he? He was the youngest person at the counter. He had the least natural authority. *Could* he? . . . Finally he leaned forward over the counter and stared, hoping this would show the man that everybody was growing impatient. He leaned over so far, he could see under the counter. There was a billy club there, held by a wall clip, the sort of device ordinarily used to hold a broom handle. Beyond the man, through a doorway to the adjoining port-a-room, he could now see two figures. At a metal desk sat an old woman, in her sixties at least, her hair combed flat against her head and dyed blond, wearing a pair of glasses with a chain hanging from the ends of the temples and looped behind her neck. She was looking up at a heavyset man who had a T-shirt stretched over his great wrestler's gut. He was holding a coffee mug in one hand and gesturing with the other, grinning and talking up a storm. Then Conrad noticed the man's dark blue twill trousers and the handcuffs hooked onto his belt . . . an Oakland PD cop with his uniform blouse and his gunbelt off, making himself at home at Three C Towing, Salvage & Repair.

Conrad straightened up and looked at the others in the line. Surely at least the proper-looking man in the suit—but not a peep out of any of them. All at once he heard himself saying:

"Sir—excuse me!"

He was frightened by his own temerity and began sputtering. "I was wondering if—the thing is—I really need—" He broke off, blushing terribly.

The man turned and stared at him with his eyes narrowed. He remained that way, one beat, two beats, three beats. Then he extended his arm toward the girl with the mane, managing to make both his biceps and his triceps pop out as he did so, and he said, "You see this young lady? She'd like to get her car, too, and she's first in line. You got any problem with that?"

"No—"

"Good. You're gonna get your turn." Then he turned back toward the girl, twisting his lips and arching his eyebrows and shaking his head in the way that says, "Some people . . ."

Nevertheless he quickly completed the transaction. The girl paid in cash and left the port-a-room. The man, he who adored Pleasanton, followed her all the way out with his eyes. Her blond mane bobbed and tumbled about with every step. She didn't look back, however.

There were now five people ahead of Conrad—but only four transactions, assuming the couple in the short pants counted as one. The clock said: 6:48. His heart was beating too fast. His stomach was cramped with hunger heightened by despair and fear.

When the couple reached the head of the line, it was 6:56. Conrad was beside himself. His entire body, every synapse in his central nervous system, tried to hurry them along. The woman had a strapped-on belly pouch rather than a handbag. Conrad's feverish eyes tried to unzip it for her, reach inside, remove her receipt from the Records Division, hand it across the counter to the swarthy man with the swollen arms.

It was 6:58 and about 50 seconds, practically 6:59, when the couple departed and Conrad moved into place at the head of the line. His heart was racing.

To his great relief the man scarcely looked at him as he took his Records Division receipt. Perhaps he didn't hold it against him the way he had interrupted him as he was coming on to the girl from Pleasanton . . . Without a word he opened up the binder and riffled through and came up with a carbon copy of a summons. Then he went through the door into the adjoining port-a-room, said something to the old woman, leaned down and made some entries on a sheet of paper, and returned, studying the piece of paper as he walked.

Now he looked at Conrad and said, "Okay, that'll be a hundred and fifty-four dollars."

"A hundred and fifty-four dollars!" exclaimed Conrad. "What *for*! I was *here* by seven! I don't *owe* any storage!"

"Who's saying you owe storage?" said the man in a matter-of-fact voice. "You owe a hundred and fifty-four dollars *towing*."

"A hundred and fifty-four dollars *towing*? How can that be?"

"Took an hour and ten minutes to tow it. Read the sign."

"An hour and ten minutes? How *could* it? This is—not right! I've got—I have seventy-seven dollars! I've got it right here!" By now he had his money in his left hand, which had closed into a fist. Slowly he opened his fingers, revealing a clump of crumpled bills that looked as if they had been gassed.

The man studied his copy of the summons for a moment, as if he was willing to review the case and listen to reason. Then he looked up. "You come on back with a hundred and fifty-four dollars before 11 a.m. tomorrow, you can have your car. After eleven it's $204."

"But this isn't fair! This is—not right!"

The man gave Conrad a look of glorious indifference and motioned his head toward the sign. "There's a line in here," he said. "There's people waiting."

Conrad looked around. Two white men with suits and neckties were watching him with pinched stares. They were not his allies. They were interested in only one thing: seeing him vanish or disintegrate so that they could retrieve their own cars. He turned back toward the man behind the counter and got nothing but the same contemptuously patient and implacable stare. Aflame with anger and humiliation, he wheeled about and hurried out of the port-a-room.

Outside, in the fenced-in enclosure, he became aware of how heavily he was sweating. His mouth and throat were terribly dry. He was breathing too fast. A feeling of panic swept over him. What was to be done? Call Jill again and have her get more money to him? But call her *how*? There wasn't even any *telephone* here!—and he would rather die than go back inside that port-a-room and plead to be allowed to use one of theirs. Head back into downtown Oakland and try to catch a BART train and a bus back to Pittsburg? But *how*? He had only 90 cents in change! They wouldn't even let him on the bus! What was happening was impossible—and yet it was happening. He was stranded out on Keeler Avenue in East Oakland, in the worst slum in the East Bay, and the sun was going down!

The sun was now so low in the sky, it created a terrific glare as it bounced off the metal sea of the Three C Towing lot. It made you close your eyelids down to slits. The sound of truck, automobile, and forklift motors rose from all over. Right in front of him was a tall woman who had been in the line. Her pink scalp showed through her hair. The chain-link gate to the lot began to open. A gaunt, bony roustabout with a baseball cap pulled way down over his eyes was pushing the gate outward. His ears stuck out so far, they took on a translucent orangey glow from the way the sun shone through them from behind. An Oldsmobile Cutlass Ciera came through and stopped. Another roustabout was at the wheel. He got out and turned the car over to the tall woman, then headed back through the open gate, which the roustabout with the glowing ears proceeded to close. The two men began walking back into the lot and, as Conrad watched, soon became two silhouettes against the low, dazzling light of the sun.

Just then, a third silhouette—

Even squinting into the ferocious glare he couldn't mistake that figure. Barely thirty feet away, on the other side of the gate, inside the lot, there was the giant, the tow truck driver, his cowboy hat still on his head.

Conrad ran over to the gate and peered between the chain links. Now he could see him more clearly. The man was climbing down from a heavy-duty forklift, bigger than the ones they had used at Croker Global. No two ways about it, it was him . . . the vest, the huge bare flaccid arms, the enormous ruff of keys protruding from his belt, the novelty key fobs . . .

The forklift was in a big irregular cinder path that was maintained amid the mass of vehicles so they could be moved in and out. The giant began walking between two rows of cars. Every two or three cars he had to turn sideways to squeeze through, and his enormous ring of keys would scrape against the side of a car. The metallic bite of the keys cut through the general ruckus of the lot. Such utterly insouciant destructiveness! Nine or ten cars deep into the metal sea the giant stopped, leaned into a sedan, withdrew something, and put it into his pocket. Over and over, car after car, he removed things. Why? But of course! He was foraging, looting the cars for whatever their owners had been so unfortunate as to have left inside.

Finally he made his way back to the dirt clearing and the forklift, and it was at that moment that Conrad spotted—even with the hellish glare in his eyes—*it!*—his own car!—the Hyundai! It was parked at an odd angle on the outer edge of the mass of vehicles. Now the giant was back up on the forklift. With a great whine it lumbered back to life. The giant shoved the gear stick and pressed the throttle levers. The machine rumbled forward. It was headed straight for the side of the Hyundai. The forks of the forklift slid straight in under the chassis, and the nose of the machine stopped just short of the door. The giant thrust the control levers this way and that, and the forks rose up under the Hyundai, and there was a sickening metal crunch, and the unmistakable groan of metal joints bending, and the nose of the forklift went down, and the Hyundai rose up, up, up, completely off the ground, until Conrad could see a flare of sunlight between the bottom of his car and the hoods of the cars behind it. As the little car rose up, the driver's-side door fell open helplessly, with a sad torquing sound, and hung at a stricken angle.

Conrad yelled out, "Hey!—hey!—hey!—heyyyy! You can't do that!"

The roustabout who had just closed the gate was no more than ten feet away. He looked back at Conrad for a moment, then, without a word, turned his head and continued on in toward the recesses of the lot.

Conrad tried to pull the gate open, but it was locked in some fashion. He dug the tips of his shoes into the gate's metal fencing in order to gain some height and managed to get his arm up over the top and down the other side. But he couldn't reach the locking mechanism. His little Hyundai was now being borne aloft, way up on the forklift's metal elevator, a silhouette against the waning sun, its door flapping, the very picture of defeat and humiliation.

Only one thing to do! Nothing else left! He swung his leg over the top of the gate and got a toehold with his shoe in the gate's chain-link mesh. Then he swung the other leg over and dropped to the ground. He was staring straight into an exploding sun. The roar of the truck and car engines and the whine of the forklifts engulfed him. For an instant the light was blinding, but then he could make out the car and the forklift and the immense back of the giant. The machine was thirty or forty yards away now. The giant was beginning to lower the little car down into the metal sea. Conrad ran toward it. The ground was so hard, he could feel the grit slipping beneath his shoes.

The roustabout who had closed the gate still had his back turned. Conrad raced past him, and he yelled out, "Hey! Yo! Come here!" Conrad kept running. The man called out, "Yo! Morrie! Yo!"

As he ran, Conrad's field of vision was a blur of bouncing sunlight and crude silhouettes. The Hyundai was descending. With a crunching smash it dropped to the ground on all four wheels.

"Stop it! STOP IT!"

The giant turned in his seat on the forklift. His huge chest gave a great heave, and he stared at Conrad, who came skidding to a halt barely three feet away.

"STOP IT! GIVE ME MY CAR! YOU'RE RUINING IT!" Conrad realized he was shrieking, but the words wouldn't come out any other way. "THIS IS—NOT RIGHT!"

Slowly, warily, staring into Conrad's eyes the whole time, the giant slid his great bulk from the forklift seat and stepped down off the floorboard.

Conrad pointed toward the Hyundai. "LOOK AT WHAT YOU DID! YOU BENT THE CHASSIS! THIS IS NOT RIGHT!"

The giant's chest was beginning to heave up and down. His deep voice rumbled to life. "I remember you." He took a half step forward.

With a guttural hiss Conrad said, "I'm taking my car."

He said it so fiercely, the giant stopped. Conrad started toward the Hyundai. The forklift's blades were on the ground beneath the chassis.

"Pal," said the giant, "all you're taking—all you're taking—you're taking shit." He said it calmly, but he was breathing in gasps. His face was turning red.

Conrad tried to walk around him to get to the car, and the giant grabbed him by the elbow. "All you're taking"—wheezing—"is a walk back"—wheezing—"the way you came."

Conrad thrashed his arm backward and broke the man's grip and headed once more toward the Hyundai. The giant grabbed for his arm again but succeeded only in getting a grip on his jacket sleeve, and once more Conrad broke free. He stood his ground and screamed straight into the giant's face:

"STOP IT! IT'S MY CAR! THIS IS NOT RIGHT!"

To his astonishment the giant suddenly grabbed him by the necktie and jerked him toward him, until their faces were no more than six inches apart. "One way or the other, pal"—wheezing—"you're getting the fuck"—gasping—"outta this lot"—gasping—"Which way's"—gasping—"it gonna be?"

Conrad tried to pull his head back, but the giant's strength was too much for him. He was pulling him relentlessly downward. The necktie was cutting into his neck and pressing against his windpipe. Reflexively, he seized the giant's wrist with both hands and twisted it backward with all his might to try to break his hold. The giant cried out—

"Ahhhhhhh!"—and let go, and Conrad sprang back, crouching. The giant was staring at him, his mouth open, his face now a purplish red, cradling his wrist with his other hand, astonished at the power of this slender young man.

"All I"—Conrad was breathing so hard, he could barely get the words out—"all I want—is my—own car."

The giant lunged. Conrad ducked to one side, and the giant's immense bulk came crashing into his hip. The world turned upside down in a swirl of dirt and blinding sunlight. The next thing Conrad knew, he was picking himself up out of the cinders. The giant was three or four feet away, on his back, propped up on one elbow, staring at him out of a blood-red face, with his mouth open, sighing deeply and going, "Aw . . . awww . . . awwwww," as if in profound disappointment.

Conrad made a dash for the Hyundai, figuring that now he could get into it before the giant could climb to his feet. He jumped behind the wheel and closed the door, straightened his body out like a board, and pulled the keys out of his pants pocket. His hands were shaking terribly. *Hanh . . . hanh . . . hanh . . . hanh . . . hanh . . .* It was the sound of his own breathing . . . He managed to get the key into the ignition—and it started.

He looked through the windshield, terrified that the giant would already be up and lumbering toward him. But he was still on his back, still propped up on one elbow, still staring at him with that strange look on his florid face. *Too fat! Out of breath! Exhausted!*

Mustn't try to jackrabbit out of here . . . Clear the forklift blades first . . . Take it slow, take it slow, take it slow, take it slow . . . He could feel the wheels roll over the blades . . . one by one . . . and he was clear. Now gun it! The wheels spun on the cinders, and he took off toward the gate. Two figures were running toward him from the sides . . . roustabouts . . . but they weren't close enough . . . Up ahead, another one, out in the middle, waving both arms over his head, back and forth, signaling him to stop . . . Conrad sped up . . . The roustabout jumped to the side . . .

A clear run to the gate up ahead . . . He could see the backs of the two port-a-rooms . . . He glanced in the rearview mirror . . . couldn't make out a thing . . . geysers of dust roiling up behind . . . The gate . . . He braked and came skidding to a stop four feet away . . . He jumped out . . . Open the gate! . . . a tremendous haze of dust in the late-afternoon sunlight . . . Out of the corner of his eye he saw a figure slip between two cars to the rear of the port-a-rooms and come charging toward him . . . It was the man from behind the counter, the one with the huge arms . . . He was brandishing a billy club . . . He stopped in a crouch, thrusting the club out in front of him like a sword . . .

"Hold it! Hold it! Hold it!" He kept saying. "Hold it."

"This is *my car*!" yelled Conrad . . . He pointed in the general direction of the forklift and the giant . . . "He was destroying it! I have a right to get my car!"

"Just hold it right there!"

Conrad stared at him for an instant . . . The man's chest and upper arms looked huge, but the billy club was shaking . . . Conrad moved toward the gate . . .

"Get away from that fucking gate!" The man advanced on him.

The gate was locked with a spring hasp, and it required both hands to open it . . . The man was right on top of him . . .

"You heard what I said! Don't be a jerk!" With that the man tried to herd him away from the gate by jabbing him in the ribs with the billy club . . .

Conrad spun about and grabbed the head of the club . . . The man pulled it back, but Conrad tightened his grip . . . With a sudden twist he wrenched the club from him . . . The man recoiled . . . He eyed Conrad for a moment, then darted toward the Hyundai . . . *The keys!* . . . Conrad sprang toward the car to try to beat him to the door . . . They collided . . . The man spun backward . . . The edge of the open door caught him in the back . . . He fell to the ground . . . His face was contorted . . . His legs were twisted beneath him . . . He started screaming, "Cliff! Cliff! Cliff!" . . . Conrad was standing over him, fighting to get his breath, still holding the billy club . . .

Such was the scene—Conrad Hensley, a club in his hand, standing over the crumpled, stricken, screaming form of the proprietor of these premises—when a third figure arrived. It was the policeman, an Oakland policeman in half a uniform, his pants and shoes, with nothing but a T-shirt on top. He held a revolver in both hands braced in front of him.

"Freeze!" he yelled. "Drop it! Drop it! Now!"

Conrad was dumbfounded. He had to look down at his own hand to realize that in fact he was standing there holding a club. He opened his hand, staring at his own fingers, and let the club roll off them. It hit the ground with a curiously musical little clink. The implications of what was now taking place swept over him in a sickening wave.

"Now—lie down! Over here! Face down! Arms out to the side! Now!"

Conrad stared at that furious face and at that incredible machine, the revolver, which he held out in front of him. Why? *I can explain!*

"I—"

"I SAID LIE DOWN! NOW!"

Baffled, aghast, Conrad did as he was told. He dropped to his knees, then to his hands. Then he stretched flat out on his chest and abdomen and thighs.

"HANDS OUT TO THE SIDES! NOW!" The policeman was somewhere behind him.

When Conrad stretched his hands out to the sides, he had no choice but to lower his head to the ground. He lay on one side of his face. His body was drenched with sweat. He could feel the dirt caking to his face. His cheek was pressed against some sort of cinders or rubble. Through the dust and haze he could make out figures running toward him. *If only he'll let me explain!*

"Officer—"

"SHUT UP! I TOLD YOU, FACE DOWN!"

Somebody shoved a rod under his head and up against the rim of his ear where it lay pressed against the earth . . . *the billy club* . . . He turned his head until he was completely face down and his chin and nose dug into the dirt. A filthy congestion of dust filled his nostrils. He could hear the gritty sound of shoes coming toward him. He could hear someone panting.

"Corky! You okay?"

"Shit!" A deep groan from the little man with the big arms. "Uggghhhhhhhhhh." Someone seemed to be helping him up. "My baaaaack . . . The cocksucker *blind*sided me."

Running footsteps . . . someone gasping, struggling to get enough air to get the words out: "Hey, Corky . . . Cliff . . . Jesus Christ . . . Somebody's gotta go help Morrie . . . He's lyin' back'eh by the forklift . . . He don't *move*! He don't even *breathe*!"

Prostrate, face down in the dirt of the Oakland slums, a sodden little speck of humanity, Conrad Hensley could feel the very flesh on his head grow hot. His nostrils were caked, choked with dust. His eyes were stinging. So he closed them. All at once, behind his eyelids, he could see two people looking down at him. One was Arda Otey . . . No more than she expected . . . The other was his little boy, Carl, Carl with his perfect blond bangs. He was looking at his father the way Conrad had looked at his own father so many times.

Chapter XII

The Breeding Barn

IT WAS FRIDAY EVENING, AND THE MASTER OF TURPMTINE, CHARlie Croker, was presiding over dinner at the burled tupelo maple table Ronald Vine had devised for the Gun Room, which was the showpiece of the plantation's new Gun House. Logs blazed in a vast hearth, fashioned by Ronald out of Georgia limestone, casting Charlie and his thirteen guests—fifteen, if you counted Serena and Wally—into a pattern of firelit glows and deep shadows. The flames sent highlights flickering up the long barrels and ornate chase-worked clasps of a parade of shotguns, many of them classics from the so-called Golden Age of Shotgunning, Dicksons, Bosses, Purdys, Berrettas, L. C. Smiths, the lot, priceless pieces that lined the entire room, all four walls, rank after rank, encased in burled tupelo gun racks.

Up above the gun racks, between two rows of heavy tupelo cornice moldings, ran an array of stuffed boars' heads with fantastic curving tusks and stuffed coiled diamondback rattlesnakes with their jaws agape, their fangs erect. A boar's head, a coiled diamondback rattlesnake, a boar's head, a coiled diamondback rattlesnake—they alternated, creating, in Ronald's phrase, "The Frieze of the Unfriendly Beasts." Each boar, each snake, was a masterpiece of taxidermy, and they were Charlie's beasts. He had killed or captured them all with his own hands out in the fields and swamps of Turpmtine, a fact he fully intended to impart to his guests, given a halfway natural opening.

Four black maids in black uniforms with white aprons had just finished serving the first course, turtle soup, under the supervision of the butler, Mason, an old black man who stood, erect and watchful, near the kitchen door. The turtle soup gave Charlie an idea.

"Hey, y'all!" he boomed out over the hubbub of conversation around the table. "I want'chall know sump'm!"

He said it so loudly that even Lettie Withers, the Atlanta *grande dame* who was seated on his left, stopped talking to Ted Nashford, the surgeon and chairman of the board of the Emory University School of Medicine, in whom she seemed to be taking such a coquettish interest. Even old Billy Bass stopped telling the bawdy story with which he obviously hoped to shock Lenore Knox, the wife of the former governor of Georgia, Beauchamp Knox, who was just across the table.

"I want'chall to know," said Charlie, "that this turtle soup comes from turtles rat'cheer at Turpmtine. Uncle Bud caught every one *uv*'em. You know how he does it? He ties a line to a bough hanging out over the water and baits the hook with chicken. When the bough bends, he knows the turtle's struck. Turtle don't come any better'n Uncle Bud's." Then he surveyed the table and beamed.

Putting it into words would have been beyond Charlie, but he knew that the magic of Turpmtine depended on thrusting his guests back into a manly world where people still lived close to the earth, a luxurious bygone world in which there were masters and servants and everybody knew his place. He didn't have to explain who Uncle Bud was. He merely had to say his name in a certain way, and one and all would realize that he was some sort of faithful old retainer, probably black.

He had hoped that Uncle Bud's catching the turtles might somehow serve as a transition to just who had caught the boars and the rattlesnakes. But that wasn't happening, and so he leaned across the woman on his right, Howell Hendricks's second wife, Francine, and said to the man next to her, "Well, Herb, whattaya think a yer turtle soup?"

"Oh, it's delicious, Charlie," said the man, with a somewhat embarrassed smile.

Charlie beamed, hoping to coax a little more conversation out of him. But it wasn't forthcoming. Herb Richman was going to be a tough pigeon to bag, a hard one to mesmerize with the magic of Turpmtine. For a start, he was Jewish, which in Georgia meant that your paths weren't going to cross socially all that much. And he was so damned mild-mannered and polite. It wasn't going to be easy to put him under the Turpmtine Spell with the usual hearty, jolly, manly chatter. Nevertheless, Herb Richman was the pigeon he needed. This whole weekend had been created for the sole purpose of casting the Spell over Mr. Herbert Richman, who was known in the Atlanta newspapers as "the fitness center tycoon." Herb Richman was the founder of DefinitionAmerica, a network of 1,100 health-and-fitness centers, which he had started in Atlanta and then reproduced thick as shad throughout the country. He was looking for 360,000 square feet of prime office space to create a new corporate headquarters. With luck and the Turpmtine Spell, that might mean seven floors and more than $10 million a year in lease income at Croker Concourse, a financial and public relations coup that would impress even the workout people at PlannersBanc with their "niche focus" and all the rest of it. Practically every big weekend at Turpmtine had its pigeon, a term Charlie had said out loud only once, to his first wife, Martha, who had found it distasteful. So he had never dared utter it at all to Serena, although he had told her exactly why he had invited Herb Richman and why he would be paying so much attention to him. Turpmtine might not be, strictly speaking, an experimental farm, but it had paid for itself many times over in terms of bagged pigeons, a point he didn't quite know how to get across to those small-brained niche-focused motherfuckers at PlannersBanc.

Charlie continued to beam at his pigeon. Herb Richman wasn't much of an advertisement for DefinitionAmerica, which promised its thousands of members sculpted, high-toned, sharply defined bodies. He was only forty-four but already running to fat. His head popped up out of his blazer and polo shirt like a bubble. His skin was pallid and pasty. A few strands of hair the color of orange-juice stains skimmed back across his otherwise bald pate. His extremely pale hazel eyes gave him a look that was at once eerie and washed out. He looked sleepy. It occurred to Charlie that he himself would have presented a better picture for such a firm, even at the age of sixty. Charlie was wearing an open-necked khaki shirt that brought out the girth of his neck, the width of his shoulders, and the massiveness of his chest. Casual dress was very much the fashion at the grand plantations these days, even at dinner, except for a few spreads in South Carolina owned by Northerners who were infected with British customs.

"I want to make sure you meet Uncle Bud tomorrow," said Charlie.

"Uncle Bud's a walking history of Georgia plantations. He's been here at Turpmtine since a long time fo' I ever was. His folks were all Turpmtine Ni—Turpmtine People from way back, when all you did here was, you harvested resin from the pine trees for naval stores and that sorta thing. I couldn't even begin to tell you how old he is. I don't think he could, either." Charlie shook his head with a salt-of-the-earth significance. "Uncle Bud."

"Sounds like an interesting man," said Herb Richman with a weak smile, great politeness, and utter lack of conviction.

The table's conversational buzz had now dropped badly, even though Charlie had managed to stock the weekend with enough loquacious, colorful, prestigious characters to impress Herb Richman, no matter what his personal tastes were. Down at the other end of the table, on one side of Herb Richman's wife, Marsha, he had put Howell Hendricks, the big, hearty, melon-headed CEO of Serry & Belloc, the second or third biggest advertising firm in the South. On the other side he had put Slim Tucker, the country singer who was one of the first music-business figures to buy a South Georgia quail plantation. They had both been paying a lot of attention to Marsha Richman—who was such a pretty brunette that Charlie figured she *had* to be a second wife—but now all three of them were silently exploring their turtle soup with their spoons. The old ex-governor, Beauchamp (pronounced *Beacham*) Knox, who was sitting next to Serena, was doing the same. Even Opey McCorkle, the Baker County judge who could talk a raccoon out of a tree, had stopped talking to Ted Nashford's young live-in girlfriend, Lydia Something-or-other. In true Opey McCorkle fashion he had turned up for dinner wearing a plaid shirt, a plaid necktie, red felt suspenders, *and* a big old leather belt that went around his potbelly like something you could hitch up a mule with, but for now he had cut off his usual torrent of orotund rhetoric mixed with Baker Countyisms. So it was up to Charlie himself to put some life back into the proceedings. This he felt well primed to do. Before dinner he had downed a couple of glasses of bourbon and water—"brown whiskey," as opposed to the Yuppie Lite stuff that was in vogue in Atlanta these days, the white wine and vodka and so on—although he hadn't made an issue of the point, since Herb Richman had asked for white wine—and then he had brought out some of Uncle Bud's homemade corn liquor. The ladies had turned it down with appropriately terrified ladylike protestations. But naturally Charlie had to knock back a glass of it, despite the fact that it practically took the top of your head off. It stopped his right knee from aching, in any event, and left him feeling . . . *loud*.

"Hey, Mason!" he boomed out to his butler, who was still standing by the kitchen door. "Don't we have any honest-to-God *logs* around here? All's I see in'eh's lightwood and kindling."

Mason, wearing an old-fashioned white cotton mess jacket and a black bow tie, came forward with a worried, slightly wounded look on his face.

"There's logs on'eh, Cap'm Charlie. '*Put* logs on'eh, just a while ago."

"I don't see nothing but *light*wood, Mason," said Charlie. "Go get me some *logs*."

The butler hesitated, then averted his eyes and shook his head. He was a tall man with broad shoulders, now turning bony with age, who wore his hair parted in the middle and combed straight back in little marcelled wavelets.

In a whispery voice, as if they were getting into a subject that didn't bear discussing in front of the guests, he said, "Put too much *wood* on'eh, Cap'm Charlie, gon' th'ow out too much *heat*."

Charlie understood. The problem was that it was warm outside, up in the high sixties even now. But Ronald had given the Gun Room a fireplace big enough to walk into, a fireplace so stupendous it clearly demanded a fire. The only way you could stand the fire on a day like this was to turn the central air conditioning on to the maximum, which Mason had done. Every now and then a frigid draft would sink from a vent overhead and make you feel as if your gums were congealing and your teeth were coming loose. If Mason put a full load of hardwood on the fire, enough to look appropriate for the hearth's colossal andirons, the fire might overwhelm the cooling system completely. But hell . . . you just had to have a roaring fire in a hearth that big.

In a now somewhat softer voice Charlie said to Mason, "Go on. Go ahead and get me some real logs."

"Yessir, Cap'm Charlie . . . but I 'on know . . ." Mason shook his head.

Serena spoke up from down at the other end of the table. "Please, Charlie." Then she looked at Mason. "We don't need any more logs on there."

Mason stared at her for a moment, then stared at Charlie with a pained expression. Charlie was also aware of the expression on his son Wally's face. Wally was sitting three seats away from Serena, between

Doris Bass and Ted Nashford's little Live-in Lydia, and his eyes were going from Serena to Charlie to Mason, and he seemed to be shrinking in his chair.

Now Charlie glowered at his wife with resentment, three kinds of it. She was coming perilously close to countermanding his instructions to his butler. Not only that, if he knew Serena, she was capable of describing to the entire table the battle between the fire and the air conditioning, thereby making him look vain and foolish. And to top it all off, she was making Mason uncomfortable. Mason disliked taking orders from her or having her intervene in household matters in any fashion. Mason remained loyal to Martha even now, three years after the divorce. Charlie could feel it every minute Mason and Serena were in the same room.

Now Mason was standing there awaiting further instructions and a resolution of the conflicting opinions of Cap'm Charlie and his hot new cookie on the subject of the magnitude of the logs in the fireplace. Charlie was afraid to tell him to just do what he said and get the big logs, for fear Serena would jump in and bring up the matter of the air conditioning. Clearly a change of subject was called for.

So all of a sudden he gave Mason a big smile, and then he gave Lettie Withers a big smile, and he said, "You met Mason, didn't you, Lettie? You met Mason when you were here last time."

"I certainly did," said Lettie in the sort of smoker's baritone many older Southern women had from a lifetime of cigarettes. "It's nice to see you again, Mason."

"Fine, Miz Withers." Mason had the habit of saying "Fine" when he met people, regardless of whether or not they asked him how he was. At the same time, Charlie was impressed that he had remembered Lettie's last name.

"Mason's had a lotta good news since you were here, Lettie."

Mason looked perplexed.

"Tell Miz Withers about your son and your daughter, Mason."

Mason hesitated. So Charlie said, "Where's your boy now?"

"Georgia Tech," said Mason.

"Tell Miz Withers what he's studying."

"Electrical engineering," said Mason. His eyes were now jumping from Charlie's face to Lettie's face and back again. This recitation was making him uncomfortable, which Charlie realized, but he was determined to establish a point—and not for Lettie's benefit, either. Charlie's own eyes were beginning to jump from Mason to Herbert Richman.

"Electrical engineering *where*?" said Charlie. "Which school?"

"Which school?" The old butler looked at Charlie quizzically. "Georgia Tech?" It came out like a question.

"Naw, I mean the *graduate* school," said Charlie. "Mason's boy is in the *graduate* school, Lettie. He's already got his BS from Tech. He got that last year. In'at right, Mason?"

"Yessir."

"And now he's in the *graduate* school in the best engineering program in the South, if not the country," Charlie said. "In'at right?"

"Yessir."

"I graduated from Tech, too," said Charlie, "but they wouldna *had . . . me* in the graduate school! I bet you don't doubt that, do you, Mason?" Yet another glance at Herbert Richman.

"No, sir." Mason's face was now twisted into a terribly embarrassed, tortured smile. "I mean, yessir, I speck they'd a had you if that's what you wanted."

"Naw, Mason," Charlie said, laughing, "unh-unnh. They're too smart for that at Tech! Now tell Miz Withers about your daughter. Tell her about Verna. Where's Verna now?"

"She's in Atlanta."

"What's she doing in Atlanta? She's a nurse, in'she? Where's she a nurse?"

"In the trauma center at Emory." Mason was now standing with his shoulders pulled forward and his hands twisted together at hip level, like a dutiful student.

"The trauma center at Emory," said Charlie. "That's a pretty important job, in'it, Ted?" He looked at Ted Nashford, the surgeon, on Lettie's left, then swiveled another quick glance at Herbert Richman, to make sure he was paying attention, then looked back at Ted.

"Oh, yes," said Dr. Nashford, "that's a very important job."

Charlie smiled. He beamed triumphantly. "I think that's great, Mason. You oughta feel very proud."

"Yessir," said Mason.

"And I don' just mean proud a your children. You oughta feel proud a yourself." He gave Mason a long, penetrating stare.

Mason comprehended what his employer now wanted him to say. "Yessir, but I speck—I couldna—couldna done it 'thout you, Cap'm Charlie. You been mighty gen'rous."

"Aw, nonsense, Mason," Charlie said grandly. "All I did was knock on a couple a doors. You've got two fine children there."

Charlie turned again to glance at Herbert Richman, but in that same moment he noticed that Wally, all sixteen years' worth of him, was now slumped way down in his chair as if recoiling from something distasteful and looking anxiously toward Serena. For her part, Serena was giving him, Charlie, a look that expressed anything but pride in his benevolence toward his faithful black servant. In fact, the look was accusatory. About *what*, for godsake? All he was doing was making sure that Herb Richman understood how warm and tolerant and—and—and *enlightened* things were nowadays down here at Turpmtine. What was so bad about that?

An immense, cackling laugh broke out halfway down the table. Unmistakably . . . Billy Bass. Billy's gangling form was thrust back in his chair, and his head was thrown back and his chin was pointing almost straight up in the air. He had the sort of laugh that was so profound, he would lose his breath. He was a big, tall, untidy man with a paunch and drooping eyelids and wattles like a hound and thinning gray hair that always stuck out this way and that. Seeing him now, reared back in his khakis and looking like a big old aging Cracker, which he was, you would never know what a superb physical specimen he had been forty years ago when he was a senior playing end for Tech just as Charlie was starting off as a sophomore in the backfield. This particular old Cracker roosted atop a fortune. He was one of the few real estate developers who had been smart enough to sell his holdings in 1987, near the peak of the 1980s boom in Atlanta. Although Charlie hadn't known him when he was a boy, Billy had grown up practically next door, in Dougherty County, and he had grown up the same way Charlie had, dirt poor and common as pig tracks, and for years now he had been Charlie's great huntin'n'shootin'pal and a fixture, an endless source of good comic low humor, at these big weekends at Turpmtine. The entire table was watching by the time he finally got his breath back and rocked forward, tears of laughter streaming down his cheeks, and looked at Lenore Knox and roared:

"Did you say . . . a *ball* for AIDS? A . . . BALL FOR AIDS?"

As the former First Lady of Georgia, Lenore was an old hand at dinner table conversation who had dealt with practically every peculiarity known to that endeavor, but she seemed genuinely nonplussed by this one. She cocked her head defensively.

"I've *heard* a balls for AIDS," cried Billy, "but this is the fust time I ever knowed anybody that actually *went* to one!" *One* came out *wuh-uhn*; two syllables; in South Georgia, Billy's speech became even more Down Home than Charlie's. The key to his low humor was that he started laughing even before the first words left his mouth, and his laughter swept you along like a wave, no matter what he was actually saying. "I was born at the wrong damn time, Lenore! Hell"—*Hale*—"when I was growing up, if you got a venereal"—*vernerl*—"disease, it was a *stigma*!" Already he was looking away from Lenore Knox and toward the men at the table, as if rallying his troops for a salvo of male laughter. "If you got syphilis or the clap, it was a *dis*-grace!" His eyes sought out Governor Knox's—the old Governor didn't know what to do, since his wife seemed to be the butt of the joke—and then they sought out Howell Hendricks's and Judge Opey McCorkle's and Herb Richman's and Charlie's and Ted Nashford's and Slim Tucker's. Charlie and Judge McCorkle were already laughing, because they were pushovers for Billy's brand of humor when he went on these dinner table jags of his. "I can remember plenty a fellows with vernerl diseases, but I don't remember anybody throwin' *parties* for'm!" exclaimed Billy, bursting with mirth. "I don't remember any DANCES! I don't remember any LET'S RAP FOR CLAP nights! Or LET'S RIFF FOR SYPH!"

"Or LET'S HOP FOR HERPES!" volunteered Judge Opey McCorkle, who was laughing so hard he could hardly get the words out.

"Or LET'S GO GREET THE SPIROCHETES!" contributed Charlie, who was now in the same paroxysmal condition.

"Or LET'S GO ROAR FOR THE CHANCRE SORES!" exclaimed Billy Bass.

"Or LET'S PAY OUR DUES TO THE PUSTULAR OOZE!" exclaimed the judge.

"Or LET'S GO HUG A DYIN' BUGGER!" cried Billy, who was gasping for breath and weeping with laughter at the same time. "Now—now if you get AIDS, you're some kinda saint!—and they give banquets for you! Everbuddy goes dancin'!"

"Glory ME—I got da HIV!" sang out the judge, who had his mouth open, his eyes wide, and both hands flopping in the air up by his ears, as if he were a minstrel performer. This started Billy and Charlie laughing even harder.

"They never used to give lepers banquets for being LEPERS!" shouted Billy. "They put BELLS around their necks so people could hear'em coming and stay OUTTA THEIR WAY! Maybe they could do that with all these characters with AIDS!"

"Yeah," said Charlie, " 'cep when you went to New York or San Francisco or one a those places, Christalmighty, you wouldn't be able to hear yourself THINK! It's bad enough in Atlanta!"

Billy and the judge redoubled their laughter, which pleased Charlie, who was afraid that up until then he had fallen behind in the rounds of wisecracks. Oh, this was the real thing! This was vintage manly humor deep in the huntin'n'shootin' atmosphere of Turpmtine! This was the sort of good times among men that the Gun House and this Gun Room had been built for! "Let's Rap for Clap!" "Let's Riff for Syph!" "Let's go hug a dyin' bugger!" Jesus, Billy was one funny old sonofabitch! This was letting it all hang out down here below the gnat line!

Charlie surveyed the table, to enjoy the sight of the rest of the party caught up in the rich manly humor of Turpmtine. In fact, what he saw surprised him. Howell Hendricks had a grin, or the beginning of one, on his big face, but his eyes were not laughing. They were jumping anxiously from Serena to Dr. Ted Nashford's young Live-in Lydia to Veronica Tucker, who was sitting on the other side of Herb Richman. Billy's wife, Doris, was laughing heartily, but Serena was once more staring accusingly at him, Charlie, and Wally had slumped so far down in his chair and rolled his eyes so far back in his head—he had embarrassment written all over him. Live-in Lydia was staring across at Ted Nashford with her lips parted, as if waiting for a cue as to which way to turn them, up or down. Ted's expression was like Howell Hendricks's: a smile topped by a pair of small, anxious eyes. Charlie had heard Lettie Withers's smoke-cured laugh braying when it had all started, but now she had settled back into her chair with an apprehensive look. Slim Tucker, who wanted to prove he was a natural-born plantation-owning type, had on a big grin, but it was frozen. Marsha Richman, sitting between Slim and Howell, was staring morosely across the table at her husband. And as for Herb Richman—

Herb Richman's fat face looked numb. He was returning his wife's stare with a look that seemed to say, "Well, here we are, and there's nothing I can do about it right now."

What the hell was going on? This was Turpmtine! Not only that, this was the Gun Room at Turpmtine, the very bastion of male camaraderie! What was wrong with these people?

Suddenly a reedy voice piped up from down at the far end of the table: "Why don't you just nuke 'em all, Dad?"

It was Wally. Charlie was stunned. He had no idea what he was talking about, but he sensed revolt. It was in the boy's very tone, which began with a lilt of levity and then swooned into a quaver. The table went stone quiet. The sound of a log burning through and collapsing with a crunch on the hearth seemed like an avalanche.

"Nuke who?" said Charlie. There was his son, shrunken back in his chair, staring like a raccoon transfixed by headlights, his mouth slightly open.

"All the people with AIDS." Not even the pretense of lightheartedness now. Nothing but a sixteen-year-old boy thoroughly frightened by his own audacity.

"Nuke 'em?" asked Charlie. "Why nuke 'em?"

More tremulous than ever: "Because that way the ones that don't die, you can see 'em coming, because they'll glow in the dark."

By the time he reached *glow*, his young voice was close to a sob of panic. Every dinner party's worst nemesis, stricken silence, seized the table.

Then Judge Opey McCorkle forced a country laugh and turned to Charlie and said, "Charlie, damn if your boy ain't bad as you! 'Nuke 'em!' *Heh heh heh heh heggggggghhhhhh!*"

The judge's intervention gave everybody the opportunity to release the tension by joining in the laughter. Everybody but Charlie; he couldn't even feign a smile. Finally he pulled himself together and looked toward the kitchen door and roared out:

"Mason! Bring these folks some more turtle soup!"

BETWEEN COURSES, AS the black women in the black dresses with the white aprons cleared away the turtle soup, Serena got up from her seat and came around to Charlie and motioned toward the doorway and said, "I need you for a minute," as if it were some household matter.

Charlie stood up, discovered his knee had stiffened again, and gimped on out into the hall with her. He could hear the burble of conversation from the table as Serena stopped, looked him in the eye, and said, "Charlie . . . you can't encourage Billy like that. You can't let him go into these good ol' boy *numbers* of his."

Confused and irritated: "Why not?"

"*Herb Richman!*" said Serena in a low, sibilant voice. "You should have seen the look on his face. His wife, too."

"Whattaya mean?"

"They're *Jewish*, Charlie."

"*I* know that," said Charlie defensively.

"Well, then you ought to know that Jewish people tend to be liberals. To them—well, you and Billy and Judge McCorkle carrying on like that—they took it as gay-bashing."

"*Gay*-bashing? Jesus Christ, Serena! Billy didn't say a word about faggots. All he said was—"

"And for God's sake, don't introduce the word *faggots* into the conversation."

"I *didn't*! *Nobody* did!"

"Nobody *had* to, Charlie. Herb and Marsha Richman knew exactly what Billy really meant. So did your own son. You heard what he said."

"That I did," said Charlie. He shook his head. "And I couldn't believe what I was hearing."

"The poor kid," said Serena, "he meant to keep it light. But you could see what he really felt."

"That I could, and I'd like to know where he gets off—" He decided not to finish the sentence. He shook his head some more.

"It wasn't just the Richmans and Wally, either," said Serena. "I'm not sure how it all went over with Howell. He's in advertising, and you know how sensitive they get to—"

"Sensitive to *what*, inna name a Christ!" It was all he could do to keep his voice down.

"I'm not reprimanding you, Charlie," said Serena, whispering. "All I'm saying is, if you're interested in Herb Richman, don't let Billy and the judge—and don't you, either—well, you know what I mean. Just remember that Herb Richman is Jewish and liberal and he's on the board of half the rights organizations in Atlanta."

"Okay," said Charlie, "you've made your point. Jesus H. Christ." He shook his head, but he recognized the practicality of the advice.

The two of them headed back to the table. Charlie's knee hurt worse than ever, and he was limping badly. What the hell were things coming to? What Billy had said was genuinely funny! The judge, too! *Let's pay our dues to the pustular ooze!* That was a hell of a line to come up with on the spur of the moment. Opey McCorkle's courtroom had always been a hoot and a howl when it came to the use of the English language from the bench. *Pay our dues to the pustular ooze . . .* But then he thought of Wally . . . What the hell had gotten into *him*? It was that damned New England boarding school Martha had packed him off to, Trinian. They drilled all this liberal, politically correct stuff into them up there . . . This was *Turpmtine*, for God's sake! This was a *gun house*, maybe the greatest gun house ever built! If a man couldn't speak his mind and be a man here, where the hell could he?

THE MAIN COURSE, as was so often the case at Turpmtine, was quail, served with Auntie Bella's own secret gravy, plus the thinnest imaginable slices of Uncle Bud's smoked ham, mashed potatoes, okra, collard greens, snap beans boiled with ham fat and served with sliced onions and vinegar, and Auntie Bella's own biscuits and cornbread and a rich bread called Sally Lunn, all three. To their own surprise, citified folks always loved Auntie Bella's vegetables, the collard greens and snap beans and all, even young people who these days went through the better part of life eating no vegetables but French fries and lettuce. Even the citified dude Charlie was most worried about, Herbert Richman, was digging into the main course with gusto.

Traditionally, South Georgia plantation country had not been an area where folks went in for anything so effete as European wine, but Charlie had discovered a heavy, slightly spicy German white wine called Gewürztraminer that was fabulous with Auntie Bella's quail and vegetables, and he was now knocking it back at a pretty good clip. So, too, he noticed, was Billy Bass. Feeling ebullient once more, Charlie leaned across Francine Hendricks, to whom he had not paid nearly enough attention—but the hell with it—and said, "Hey, Herb! Whattaya think a that quail there?" *'At quail'eh.*

"It's great, Charlie," said Herb Richman, with far more enthusiasm than anything else he had said all night. "These are great, too." He motioned toward the okra and the greens and the snap beans with his fork. "But the quail is really something."

"Oughta be!" exclaimed Charlie. "Each bird cost FO' THOUSAND, SEVEN HUNNERT'N EIGHTY-FO' DOLLARS!"

Such silence all of a sudden, you could once again hear the logs spluttering in the fireplace.

Herb Richman said, "Four thousand, seven hundred and eighty-four dollars?"

"Well," said Charlie, quite satisfied with himself, "if you figure out how much it costs to run this place every year, and you divide it by the number of birds you shoot, that's what you get!"

"That's amazing," said Herb Richman.

Charlie sensed consternation all around the table. Too late it dawned on him that it was not over the amount but the fact that he had been so . . . so . . . so *vulgar* as to divulge it at all. He could see Serena slowly shaking her head down at the other end of the table.

So Charlie shut up, and the logs spluttered and popped, and the hot glows and deep shadows played across everybody's face, and the boars' tusks curved out into the room more ferociously than ever before, and the rattlesnake fangs did everything but spit venom, and the general conversation rose, and Charlie felt confused and thick-headed, which was a better way of putting it to himself than *drunk*.

The next eruption came when Judge Opey McCorkle, who had drunk plenty of brown whiskey and Gewürztraminer himself, plus a couple of shots of corn liquor, started orating straight across little Live-in Lydia, Wally, and Doris Bass in order to get across a point to Beauchamp Knox.

"Naw, naw, naw, Beauchamp!" cried the judge in stentorian Baker County tones, "this year we gon' have to plead *nolo contendere* when it comes to Tech! Or to say it correctly, *no-li-mus contendere*. Irregular in the first-person plural, present tense. Ain'eben gon' be whatcha call a football game!"

"What makes you say that, Opey?" asked the old Governor.

" 'Cause now we got us a new coach, and he's a prima donna with a halo over his head. Thinks he's the Archangel Ahura of Academia. Any player who don' complete all his course work this year with a 2.5 average or better in'gon' play for *his* Bulldogs this fall, and he means it, for some *ab*-struse, *i*-dealistic, *pig*headed, totally *un*fathomable reason. Ain'eben made the papers yet, but the alumni are already screaming and I'm one *uv*'em! I believe in education, and I believe in high standards at the university, but if you're a football coach and you actually believe football and education's got anythang to do with each other, you gotta be a flat-out imbecile! Never *have* had anythang to do with each other!"

The judge was a University of Georgia alumnus, both undergraduate and law, and as rabid a Yew-Gee-A football fan as existed in the whole huge humming swarm of them in the state of Georgia. He was a learned man and a great reader, but his favorite book on this earth was one entitled *Clean Old-fashioned Hate,* which was devoted entirely to accounts of the Georgia–Georgia Tech football rivalry, dating back to the first game, in 1893, when each team accused the other of using nonstudent ringers, and the university students, whose team lost 28–10, began chanting, "WELL, WELL, WELL! WHO CAN TELL! TECH'S UMPIRE IS CHEATING LIKE HELL!" Opey McCorkle kept *Clean Old-fashioned Hate* on his bedside table. As an old alum of the university and a politician with considerable clout in the southwestern part of the state, the judge had a lock on blocs of seats on the fifty-yard line, no matter whether the Bulldogs and Yellow Jackets played at Sanford Stadium in Athens or Bobby Dodd Stadium at Tech in Atlanta.

For the first time as a conscious thought Charlie became aware of . . . *Football* . . . in Georgia. Here was Opey McCorkle, a distinguished white-haired old judge, a Latin scholar, no less, and there was Beauchamp Knox, an illustrious white-haired former governor of the State of Georgia, and here it was, April, and here they were in the gun house of a 29,000-acre quail plantation—and suddenly Football rises up in the room . . . Football!—an obsession no one can resist. This was so common in Georgia that folks never even noticed it as anything remarkable. At this moment all over the state, in the unlikeliest corners, other folks were no doubt invoking Football, too, in the form of the Bulldogs, the Yellow Jackets, or the Falcons, or whatever ferocious zoological hide the Game put on at the local high school, the Wildcats, the Pit Bulls, the Jaguars, the Copperheads. He, Charlie—the Sixty-Minute Man—was one of the great beneficiaries of this curious mental condition. But *what was it?* How did get *such a grip,* even on wise old men like Opey and Beauchamp? What on earth *was* it? It made Charlie's already cornliquored, Gewürztraminered head hurt.

From across the table Billy Bass, who had just finished off another big glass of the Gewürztraminer, yelled out: "If I was you, I wud'n give up yet, Opey! We got our own problems at Tech!"

"I warrant they ain't as bad as that chubby little cherub a ours, Coach *Mathias Spong!*" As in *spineless worm.*

"Worse," said Billy Bass.

"How you mean?" yelled the judge. The two of them were so loud, the rest of the table had quieted down.

"You know our boy Fareek Fanon?"

"Oh yeah," said the judge, "yowza yowza, Fareek 'the Cannon' Fanon. What about him?"

Billy Bass opened his mouth again, but no words came out. Finally he said, "Let's just say . . . uh . . . it seems our boy has trouble keeping his cannon from going off where it ain't spose go off."

That got a big laugh, and Billy started to go on, but then once more stopped with his mouth open.

"Meaning what?" asked Opey McCorkle.

"I caint tell you," said Billy. "I shouldna told you as much as I just did."

"Aw, come on, Billy," said the judge, "you caint throw out a teaser like that and then say you caint talk about it."

"Don't be coy now, Billy," said Lettie Withers.

"Naw," said Billy, "I shouldna opened my mouth. It's all just a buncha rumors anyhow."

"I can't believe this, Billy," said Dr. Ted Nashford. "What a lame performance!"

Similar protests from all around the table, with Lettie Withers repeating her line over and over again, like a refrain: "Boys can't be coy, Billy!"

A bemused smile formed on one side of Billy's lips, and his eyes looked upward into an unfathomable distance. Obviously the compunction to keep a secret, on the one hand, and natural-born loquaciousness and the desire to star at dinner table conversation, on the other, were locked in mortal combat inside his big head.

To everyone's surprise, compunction triumphed. "I just caint," he said, with his eyes cast down and his head oscillating. "I shoulda kept my mouth shut, and it ain't nothing more'n a rumor in the first place."

Lettie, Opey, and Ted Nashford continued to rag him, while Doris fixed him with a reproving stare.

DESSERT CONSISTED OF three kinds of pies—pecan, lemon meringue, and apple—and three kinds of ice cream—vanilla, peach, and peppermint. All of it was homemade; the ice cream had been hand-churned right out there on the screen porch beyond the kitchen by Auntie Bella and her helpers, as Charlie heartily informed everybody. Afterward . . . a great chorus of praise of what a great dinner it had been. Even Herb and Marsha Richman joined in.

So Charlie said, "Mason, ask Auntie Bella come on out here a second."

Auntie Bella was a fleshy woman with dark skin and gray hair, which she had pulled straight back into a tight little bun. The light from the hearth shimmered on her face and her bare arms, which were already glistening from the heat of the kitchen. She was wiping her hands on a big workmanlike apron. Obviously accustomed to these curtain calls of approbation, she beamed at Charlie and his guests.

"Your ears prob'ly been buzzing in'eh, Auntie Bella," said Charlie. "You been getting an awful lotta compliments!"

In truth, the compliments now poured forth, not only from the regulars, such as Billy and Doris Bass and the judge, but also from Francine Hendricks, Lenore Knox, Live-in Lydia, and, Charlie was pleased to see, Herb Richman, although his soft voice was lost in the general happy clamor.

Then Marsha Richman, turning in her seat so that she could smile directly at Auntie Bella, spoke up in a very ladylike Southern voice: "I don't know how you do it! To tell you the truth, I'm usually not crazy about okra, collard greens, and snaps, but yours just melted in my mouth. You've got to tell me your secret."

Auntie Bella pulled her head back and smiled broadly at Marsha Richman, and shook with a couple of silent chuckles, and then let loose a laugh from deep in her throat, and said:

"Welcome to . . . Grease."

Tremendous laughter from all around the table. *Welcome to Grease!* Oh, it was priceless. Auntie Bella was a card, all right! Not even Charlie himself had ever heard that line before! Everyone was in convulsions! Well, not everyone. Charlie noticed that Marsha Richman was still smiling, but her face had fallen. She looked as if she had just been shot through the heart.

AFTER DINNER CHARLIE led the party out to the stone terrace at the rear of the Gun House. He had instructed Mason to make sure the terrace lights were kept off. He didn't want anything to dilute the effect of the nocturnal landscape he had prepared for his guests. He stuck close to the Richmans, hoping for maximum astonishment.

They didn't disappoint him. "Huhhhhhhhhh!" It was Marsha Richman; a sharp intake of breath.

Flames!

In the middle distance a stupendous arc of fire cut through the blackness of the plantation at night. The silhouettes of the pine trees in the foreground rose like enormous bars. The pungent odor of burning sedge and scrub pine was thick in the air.

Charlie made a point of inhaling and then letting his breath out with a satisfied "Ahhhhhhhhh. Nothing else on earth like it." In truth, the aroma made his heart thump with an emotion he couldn't have begun to describe.

"Wow! What's going on, Charlie?"

It was Herb Richman. Charlie felt he was getting somewhere at last. For the first time the man had broken out of his lethargic mode.

"We're burning over the fields, Herb."

"What for?"

"If you don't burn 'em over in the spring, they'll be so overgrown with saplings, vines, thorns—it'd be like Br'er Rabbit's briar patch. You remember Br'er Rabbit's briar patch?"

"Not really," said Herb Richman.

"Well, they'd get so overgrown, you'd have to forget about hunting. Not even a dog'd be able to get through."

He was pleased to observe that Herb Richman was staring slack-jawed at the sight. "But how do you keep it from . . . from . . ."

"From getting out of control?"

"Yes."

"I got twenty a my boys out there steering it." A fleeting thought told him he shouldn't have called his black help "boys," since, as Serena kept drumming into him, the Richmans were Jewish and liberal. But it was only that, a fleeting thought. "And 'at's why we do it at night, too —when the dew falls and it's damp and there's no wind." He sighed. "You know, Herb, I love that smell. I really do. Far's I'm concerned, nobody ever made a perfume that can touch it."

Still gazing into the distance, Herb Richman said, "It's amazing" . . . but in the irritatingly indifferent way he had of making such observations. Then he said, "What happens to the wildlife in a big fire like that?"

Charlie gave an amused snort. "*Happens* to 'em? They *run*, or else they fly, that's what happens. You can see 'em. I've been out there in the field for a lotta burnovers, and you can see animals you didn't even know was there running ahead a the flames. I'll tell you what's really sump'm. That's the snakes, 'specially the rattlers. People will tell you how fast a snake can move, but they really can't, not in miles per hour or anything like that. They can't outrun the flames, so what they do is, they burrow down into the *ground*? They get under the *earth*? And as soon's the fire's passed over them, they come outta their holes and they get the hell outta there. You can *see* 'em! Of course, you got to watch yourself, because they're not in a good mood at that point. The ground is still hot, and here are all these snakes slithering along like there's no tomorrow. It's just one hell of a sight. No, the wildlife know what to do about fire, because it'll occur spontaneously out in the woods. The only ones that don't make out so well are the turtles. The next day you'll find all these burnt-out turtle shells in the woods."

Herb Richman turned his head to look at Charlie. In the darkness Charlie couldn't tell exactly what the man's expression was, but he said to himself, "Oh shit. Why did I have to mention the dead turtles? Anybody who uses the expression *wildlife* is going to be sensitive about the dead turtles."

Aloud he said, "But you don't have to worry about the turtles. They survive, they survive. There's no older animal in the woods than the turtle."

"You actually burn over the whole plantation?" asked Herb Richman.

"Yep."

"Well then—where do the animals go? Where do the *quail* go?"

"Aw, before you start the burnover, you go out there and you create feedin' patches everywhere. You take your bulldozers and you dig firebreaks in a big circle. Inside the circles they're like islands, the feeding patches are. They got trees, grass, beggarweed, corn, all the things the quail like. The other animals, too, for that matter. By fall the burned-over fields, they got a nice stand a sedge again, but most of the undergrowth is gone, and it's good hunting out there."

"Well, don't the pine trees burn, too?"

"Not if your boy—your people know what they're doing. A good healthy stand a pine, the trunks might get scorched, but the whole tree's not gonna go up in flames. Oh, the scrubs might burn up. But that's nature's way a culling the stock, too. Fire in the woods is a natural thing."

Now Charlie and his guests grew quiet, transfixed by the flaming tableau before them. If you stared long enough, the flames began to play tricks on your eyes. It was an overcast night, and the sky was black, and the ground between the terrace and the arc of flames was black, and the fire seemed to be floating in space somewhere beyond the perpendicular silhouettes of the pine trees, which in turn seemed to draw closer and then recede, draw closer and then recede once more. And now, way out there somewhere, you could hear the boys shouting to one another: not the words, just the music of their voices.

So far as Charlie was concerned, what he was now treating his guests to was one of the greatest pageants, one of the greatest symphonies, in all the world. He noticed with satisfaction that, here in the darkness, Herb Richman had slipped his arm around his wife Marsha's waist and drawn her close to him. Perhaps the man was at last responding to the Turpmtine Spell.

By and by, they all came back inside the Gun House, and Charlie offered everybody something to drink, but the Richmans said they were ready to turn in for the evening, and so did the Knoxes, and so did Dr. Ted Nashford and his Live-in Lydia. Then Wally left, without saying anything, and then Slim and Veronica Tucker pulled out, and then Serena told him she was heading back to the Big House, where the Richmans were staying, to make sure they had everything they needed. Charlie got the picture. Pretty soon there would be just him and Opey McCorkle and Billy, and maybe Doris.

So while there were a few souls still left, Charlie beckoned Billy into a little office he had off the entry gallery in the Gun House and closed the door and said, "Billy, what the hell was that you were getting ready to say about Fareek Fanon?"

Billy, who was already working on another bourbon and water, gave Charlie a funny smile and didn't say a thing.

"Hey, Billy, it's me, Charlie."

Billy knocked back a little more of his drink, and then he said, "I shouldna said the first thing about it, Charlie. I told 'im I wouldn't."

"Told who? Fareek Fanon?"

"Naw . . . Inman."

"Inman Armholster? What's he got to do with it?"

Billy grew silent again, and once more stared at Charlie, but rather vacantly. Then he said, "Well . . . I think Inman's gonna want to talk to you anyway, but in the meantime, this stays in this room. I don't even want you telling Serena. Will you promise me that?"

"Yeah."

"Inman claims Fanon raped his daughter."

"*What?*"

"That's what he says."

"*Elizabeth*? You're *kid*ding!"

"Naw, I'm not kidding."

"Jesus—H.—Christ. How'd he say—they were my guests here just a couple months ago! Elizabeth and Inman and Ellen! Next-to-last weekend of the quail season!—well, hell, you remember that. You were here, too. How'd this happen?"

"Well, according to Inman, Elizabeth was up in Fanon's room at some kinda party on the first night a Freaknik, on 'at Friday."

"Fanon's *room*? The first night a *Freaknik*? What the hell was she doing up in Fanon's room on the first night a Freaknik?"

"Inman says there were two other white students there, two girls, and one *uv*'em saw what happened, but she's scared to death, and now she claims she didn't see anything."

"Christalmighty." Charlie lowered his eyes and shook his head and then looked up at Billy again. "I don't *believe* this! What's Fanon like? Any idea?"

"Aw, man," said Billy, "don't ask. You missed that meeting a the Stingers where McNutter brought him out and introduced him to everybody. He won't do *that* again. It was a disaster. You've heard this term *attitude*? Well, this guy is 225 pounds of attitude. He comes out wearing a diamond in each earlobe and a gold necklace about yea thick. He don't even smile. Unh-unhh, no ingratiating himself with a bunch of old broken-down white has-been athletes from long ago. McNutter gives him the microphone and all he does is mutter a few words that sound like he's taking the Fifth Amendment. He looks at everybody like we're dirt underneath his feet. The worst picture you ever had in your mind about a pampered athlete? There you got our boy Fareek."

"What's Elizabeth Armholster like?" asked Charlie.

"I don' really know," said Billy. "I saw her when she came out at the Driving Club last year. She probably looked fabulous. Most *uv*'m do."

"She's a sexy-*looking* little lamb chop," said Charlie. "She came along with my party, with Inman and Ellen, that weekend. She made sure everybody knew she had a body."

"Well, hell, Charlie, rape's rape, no matter what kind of body the girl has."

"I'm not saying it iddn'! I mean, Jesus Christ. I was just making an observation. What's Inman gon' do?"

"Inman don' know *what* to do. But you know Inman. He's a hotheaded son of a gun, and you can count on it, he's gon' do sump'm. What's got him stumped right now is that he don' want Elizabeth's name to get out, and with her being the daughter of someone as prominent as he is, he don' know how he can keep it *from* getting out. And he says Elizabeth is so traumatized by the whole thing, she don't wanna talk to the police about it or the people at Tech or anybody else. So for now what he's doing is, he's going to the board."

"Tech's board?"

"He's a great buddy of the new chairman, Holland Jasper."

"Aw, yeah, I know him."

"There's been a lotta changes on the board, Charlie, and guess what they're coming out strong on."

"What?"

"The football program. They think Tech's lost too much ground over the past ten years. Everything slumps when the football team slumps. The legislature comes through with less money. Alumni contributions fall off. The SAT scores of the applicants drop. Everything comes down."

"The *SAT* scores come down?"

"That's what Inman told me," said Billy.

"What's he care about the SAT scores?"

"He don't care, but when he talked to Holland Jasper, he got kind of a rude awakening, seems to me. He thought Jasper'd drop everything and call out the cavalry when he told him what'd happened to his daughter. Instead, Jasper starts double talking him and telling Inman how we have to take everything into consideration and how the student government has its own mechanism for dealing with sexual harassment, and he's double talking him some more, and Inman's yelling at him and saying, 'I'm not talking about sexual harassment, you imbecile, I'm talking about flat-out rape!' "

"I'da like to seen that."

"Well, you know what the bottom line is, Charlie. The board's number-one priority is to build the football program. They've hired Buck McNutter away from Alabama for $875,000 a year and given him a big house in Buckhead, and they got an all-American running back named Fareek Fanon. Every magazine, every capital-contributors brochure, every Admissions Office flyer—they got a picture of Fareek Fanon shaking off tacklers and heading for open country. Suddenly Inman finds himself up against some a the harsh realities a modern life."

"Is he angry?"

"*Angry?* He's hopping, Inman is. He's fit to be tied. He's gonna do *sump'm*. Right now, seems like he's trying to line up some Tech people against Holland Jasper. That's why he came to see me and told me all this. And I'll betcha anything he gets in touch with you—only you gotta make out like you ain't heard the first word about the whole thing. He made me swear up and down I wouldn't tell a living soul."

"Well, hell, like I said, Billy, it's me, Charlie."

"I know, but you gotta swear on a Bible."

"Okay," said Charlie, "I swear."

IN THE MORNING, after breakfast, Charlie led them all, all the guests plus Serena and Wally, out to a small but smart-looking barn, made of old brick, with a slate roof, not far from the stables. It was a fine spring day.

Inside the barn, it took a moment to adjust your eyes to the contrasts of light and dark, since there were no windows in the walls, only a row of clerestory windows under the eaves. All at once, as if on cue, a great shaft of sunlight, vibrating with dust particles, streamed down from one of the little windows and lit up the dirt floor like a stage. There, spotlit by the sunbeam, was a narrow wooden enclosure with low walls, a type of stall known as a stock; and in the stock stood a large pale-bay mare. The warm, heavy, gumbo smell of horseflesh filled the place, suffused every rhinal cavity, permeated your very gizzard.

Two stable hands, both of them black, were busy buckling straps that ran from the mare's neck to her hind legs. A short but chesty little white man stood by, giving instructions. He was barely five feet tall and had a close-cropped ginger-red beard that took on a curious sheen in the sunlight. He was Charlie's stud manager, the Australian Johnny Groyner.

Charlie's guests stood off to the side in the shadows. Billy Bass and Opey McCorkle were rocked back on their heels, chatting with Slim Tucker and Howell Hendricks. Lettie Withers had Francine Hendricks, Ted Nashford, Veronica Tucker, and Lenore Knox for an audience. Herb and Marsha Richman were huddled together over near Serena, Wally, Live-in Lydia, and Beauchamp Knox. From time to time everyone glanced at the mare. Herb and Marsha Richman glanced at each other, too. They looked tired and apprehensive. Or was he, Charlie, just imagining it?

Herb Richman turned toward him and said, "What do you call this, Charlie?"

"The breeding barn," said Charlie.

"And you use it for . . ."

"Breeding."

"You mean . . ."

"This is where they mate," said Charlie. "This is where it takes place."

"You need a special building for it?"

"Yep," said Charlie. "You'll see why."

The next thing he knew, Serena had come over and was taking him aside, deeper into the shadows.

"You sure you want to do this?" she said. "The Richmans don't look very happy."

"Well, don't tell me they're Jewish and liberal," said Charlie. "This's got nothing to do with Jewish or not Jewish or liberal or not liberal. This's got to do with the way life is."

"They're—they're not country people, Charlie. They're sensitive."

"Aw hell, they'll be fascinated. Weren't you? You know you were, and you're not a country person, either."

"Well—" She shook her head and grimaced slightly.

"Whattaya want me to do, take them all outta here and say, 'Well, that's it folks'?"

The truth was, since the quail season was over and they couldn't go hunting, Charlie had planned this as one of the weekend's big events. The thought that Herb Richman might not be impressed by what he was about to see had never even crossed Charlie's mind. Richman was about to see one of the greatest horses in the country in a role people always read about—but the true nature of which they couldn't begin to guess. Besides . . . this was the only big event on the schedule today . . . So without another word to Serena, he returned to the guests.

By now the other little Australian, Melvin Bonnetbox, or Bonnie, as everyone called him, had joined Johnny Groyner over near the mare. Bonnie was Johnny's steerer, as this peculiar breed of specialist was known. The two of them, Johnny and Bonnie, looked like a pair of middle-aged elves standing next to the stable hands, all of them black, who conferred with them. And now the mare's attendants, having finished putting the straps on her hind legs, were buckling a leather mantle over her lower neck and her withers and furling her tail up until it looked bobbed.

"What are the straps for?" asked Herb Richman.

"Keep her from kicking," said Charlie. "One kick in the testicles, and you've lost a three-million-dollar stud."

He noticed with satisfaction that the entire entourage was listening. He sucked in his breath and put his shoulders back. The drag of insomnia was finally fading away. He had been having trouble sleeping ever since the workout session at PlannersBanc, and last night had only made it worse. Before they went to bed, Serena had continued her lecture about the Richmans and told him what a disaster the dinner had been . . . Billy Bass and Judge McCorkle and all their broad humor about AIDS . . . Herb and Marsha Richman were Jewish and liberal, and you could read the distress in their faces, and so forth and so on . . . Only Wally had come close to saying what was probably on *their* minds . . .

Charlie had on his khakis and a pair of low Wellington boots. He was wearing a .45-caliber revolver, a huge thing, on his right hip. Herb and Marsha Richman kept checking it out, and so did Wally, even though he had seen it many times before. Good . . . let them check it out . . . For the first time all day he felt like himself, like Cap'm Charlie, the Boss, the Master of Turpmtine.

He called out, "When y'all gon' be ready, Johnny?"

"Ready now, Cap'm," said the little man with the bright red beard.

"Then let's bring him on in."

Johnny Groyner motioned toward one of the black workmen, who left the barn. Presently he returned, leading a light chestnut horse in through the doorway, a stallion, as was obvious from the fact that the animal's penis was already half-distended beneath his belly. The stallion was snorting and pawing the ground and throwing his head and neck this way and that, and lurching into a nervous sidewise gait as the handler struggled to pull his head down and keep him under control. The beast forced his head up and cut loose with a tremendous whinny before the handler jerked it back down again. Charlie's guests were silent, all eyes. By the time the stallion moved out into the shaft of sunlight, it was obvious that he was neither very big nor very young; in fact, he was slightly smaller than the mare. The handler led him to the rear of the stock, where another black workman lifted the wooden bar over the entryway and two more held the mare by her halter. Snorting, highly agitated, the stallion walked into the stock and right up to the rear end of the mare. The mare began twitching and rolling her head and switching her furled-up tail. The stallion's penis was now a tremendous black shaft. Suddenly he extended his head and his long neck and pushed his nose into the mare's rear end, into her vulva. She tried to kick with her rear legs, but the hobble straps prevented it. She tried to bolt forward, but the walls of the stock hemmed her in, and the stable hands held her halter. The stallion kept twisting his head, rooting around in her vulva.

Charlie noticed that most of his guests lowered their chins and pulled them inward, as if shrinking, all the while staring, transfixed.

The deep voice of Lettie Withers: "Good Lord, Charlie, I thought this was the Bible Belt. That looks suspiciously like oral sex."

But no one laughed, and no one else said anything. The truth was, they were . . . shocked.

All at once a gusher of yellowish liquid shot out the rear of the mare. The stallion pulled back. His lower jaw, throatlatch, and breast were dripping with it. It was urine, which continued to spew out. The stallion shook his head and whinnied and started back toward the mare, his penis fully erect, but two black handlers had him by the halter and were forcing him back, away from the stock. He snorted, whinnied, pawed the ground, and started slapping his penis against his underbelly. The handlers kept forcing him to back up. Once he was clear of the wall of the stock, they yanked him away from it altogether and began leading him toward the doorway, while he tried to jerk free of the halter and slapped his penis against his belly some more.

"What's going on?" asked Howell Hendricks. "Why are they taking him away?" The other guests closed ranks in order to hear the answer.

"He's not the stud," said Charlie, "he's the teaser."

"The teaser?"

"Yep. You just use the teaser to get her aroused."

"And she urinates in his face?" said Howell.

"Yep. Always happens."

"And that's all he gets out of it?"

"That's about the size of it."

"Terrific," said Howell. "Reminds me of when I was in high school."

Ted Nashford and his little Lydia, Slim and Veronica Tucker, Francine Hendricks, Lettie, and Lenore Knox laughed. Even Herb and Marsha Richman smiled. Charlie felt superior to the whole bunch of them. City people always felt compelled to make jokes about what went on in the breeding barn, which was in fact the most serious thing in the world.

The mare stood there in the stock with her shanks spread slightly apart. Beneath her bound tail was an astonishingly large, soft, moist, dark liverish crevice of flesh, and the flesh was writhing. It opened up and then contracted, opened up and contracted, opened up and contracted. It was the beast's vulva. She was now fully aroused, writhing uncontrollably.

"My God," said Lettie, "what's *that*?"

"It's called winking," said Charlie.

"Really?" said Lettie with one of her contralto chuckles. "Winking?"

"That's what it's called," said Charlie matter-of-factly, to show he was not making a joke.

By now one of the black handlers was busy swabbing the convulsing crevice with a sponge, which he kept dipping into the bucket at his feet. In the bucket was a PhisoHex solution. To ensure a successful conception, Charlie explained, the mare's genitals had to be kept antiseptic, and there was no telling what kind of dirt was on the teaser's nose. Lettie and the others watched with undisguised fascination.

The stud manager, Johnny Groyner, walked over to Charlie. "I'd say it's about that time, Cap'm. Time for Sy to have his go."

Herb Richman looked from Johnny to Charlie.

"Sy's the stud," said Charlie. "First Draw's his real name. Sy's his barn name."

"First Draw," said Herb Richman. "Why does that ring a bell?"

"Used to race him," said Charlie. "Six years ago he won the Breeders' Cup." Then to the stud manager: "Okay, Johnny, I'm gonna go get him."

With that, Charlie walked out of the barn, leaving Herb Richman and one and all, he assumed, impressed.

As soon as he got outside, he could feel the heat of the sun. It was so bright it took a moment for his eyes to adjust. His knee began to ache terribly, and he wondered if it was because of anxiety over what he now had to do.

Just to the rear of the barn—there he was, the black stallion. He was huge, a behemoth. A stable hand named Clint held him close to the halter by a lead line. The stallion shifted his weight and tried to crane his neck, and his hide rippled in the sunlight. Clint's dark face was already glistening with sweat from the exertion of leading him from the stable to this point. Now the stallion began to snort and jerk his head about. Clint, who was a big man and at least twenty-five years younger than Charlie, had his hands full. The mighty First Draw had made this trip to the breeding barn many times and knew exactly what was coming.

"Unnnnh! He's randy, Cap'm Charlie!"

"He's always randy, Clint. Many time's he's done this, think he'd calm down after'while."

"I know, Cap'm, but this time he is *some kinda* randy. You best be watching out for him when he sets foot in'at barn in'eh."

Charlie surveyed the horse from front to back. "Well, Clint, here goes."

As soon as he took the lead line, he knew he was in for a battle. The stallion began lifting his head and straightening his neck. It was all Charlie could do to yank his head down.

"Hah! Ho! Sy! Ho! Ho! Cut it out!"—this last in as deep and rough a voice as possible, as much to impress Clint as the animal. He slid his hand up the lead line, closer to the beast's mouth. Racing thoroughbreds were so high-strung, they were fully capable of biting if there was enough slack in the line. Jesus Christ, why hadn't he told them to put a breeding bridle on him, which would have meant there was a bit in his mouth to keep him in check? Well—couldn't ask for one now. Cap'm Charlie would lose too much face.

Even before he had led him as far as the doorway, the stallion began breathing heavily through the nostrils in what seemed almost a groan and prancing in an eccentric sideways gait. Charlie could feel the muscles in his forearm tighten as he fought to maintain control. A terrible realization bubbled up into his brain. If this beast knew his own strength and had the willpower, no man on earth could have kept him from doing whatever he wanted. Suppose he, Cap'm Charlie, lost control of him in there—in front of that audience! Suppose—but what was this? He had never before even allowed such doubts to enter his skull.

"Sy! Ho! Ho! Hah! Ho!"

As they entered the doorway, the stallion breathed in the full overpowering smell of the mare in heat and launched into a ferocious show of machismo. He snorted, he rolled his massive shoulders, he flexed his neck up and down and yawed it back and forth, he did a little dance with his hindquarters, and he whinnied. He whinnied in anger, in agony, in desperation and anticipation. Had he possessed bigger vocal cords, he would have sounded like ten trumpets. He bared his teeth, rolled his eyes, whinnied some more. He looked like an immense equine lunatic. Charlie set his jaws and tried to look totally in command and held on for dear life. His eyes were slow in readjusting to the gloom. Over here—a dazzling cone of light—the mare in the stock—the stable hands. Over there—slowly taking shape in the shadows—Lettie, Wally, Serena, Herb and Marsha Richman, and the rest of them—they were huddled together. Their eyes were like saucers. As he fought to keep the beast's head down, Charlie could feel its huge body shuddering—with lust!—the rawest, purest lust imaginable! He could feel his own arm shaking, trying so desperately to keep the stud's head down. Could they tell? The final twenty feet, out into the shaft of light, where the mare waited—the mare and, thank God, Johnny Groyner and his helpers—Charlie had to fight every inch of the way. The brilliance of the sunlight and the heavy, humid smell of flesh made him feel dizzy.

"Johnny," he said, "he's a . . . he's a . . . randy"—he fought to get his breath—"he's a randy sonofabitch!"

"Ain't he always, Cap'm," said the little stud manager. Then he turned toward two of the black stable hands. "Okay, boys."

One of them took the lead line, and the other held on to a halter strap. Charlie hoped that Herb Richman and Wally and the rest of them took note of the fact that it required two men to hold the snorting beast he had just brought in by himself. He walked toward his guests. He was suddenly aware of how hard he was breathing, and he had led the big animal no more than forty or fifty yards. He took a deep breath and displayed the fullness of his chest. He had made it. He had brought the beast in without looking like an old fool. He felt as if somehow he shared in the stud's power.

Both the stud and the mare were now out in the cone of light, along with Johnny and his little Australian sidekick, Bonnie, and six stable hands. All of them, not just the two Australians, looked tiny next to the two great beasts. The stud, snorting, rolling his huge muscles, was fast building up to a full erection. Inside its sheath, his penis looked like a huge, long, dark, evil leather knout hanging down from beneath his legs. All the while the beast trumpeted, whinnied, snorted, proclaimed his power.

Now Johnny was out in the middle of the floor gesturing like a symphony conductor toward the stud and then toward the mare and barking out instructions to his men.

"Okay, Alonzo, bring her on out!"

The three handlers at the breeding stock began backing the mare out of the little enclosure. The beast's vulva continued to writhe. The hobbles on her rear legs made the going slow. Now she was out of the stock, and the stable hands turned her away from the stallion, so that her rear end faced him, while she twitched, lashed her bobbed tail, and shook her neck. The stud was beside himself. His nostrils flared, his eyes looked maniacal, his huge black body shook with waves of lust. The stable hands could barely hold him back. Charlie's guests had dropped all pretense of aloofness or detachment. Even such unlikely mates as Beauchamp Knox and Veronica Tucker were huddled together, wayfarers suddenly marooned in a fast-rising storm. Sex! Lust! Each of the great beasts weighed close to a ton, almost ten times the size of a big man like Billy Bass and fifteen or sixteen times the size of any woman in the little group of well-heeled human beings who now stood bunched together on the dirt floor of the breeding barn.

The mare was beginning to act up. She knew what was coming, too. By now her handlers, holding on to her halter, were having to dance in the dirt just to keep their balance.

Johnny Groyner, his beard flaming in the sunlight, stood between the two animals, both hands up in the air. He pointed toward the mare. "Alonzo! Put the twitch on her!"

The tallest of the mare's handlers, Alonzo, wrapped a length of leather around the flesh above her upper teeth and twisted it tight. The pain would distract her from her concern over what was about to happen to her backside.

"Wilson! Lift her foot! Lift her bloody foot!"

Another handler reached down and grasped the pastern of the mare's right foreleg and lifted the hoof off the ground so that she couldn't bolt forward.

Now Johnny Groyner pointed toward the stud. "Awright, boys, bring 'im up! Bring 'im up!"

A regular platoon was gathered around the big black stallion. Two stable hands held the animal's head by the lead line and the halter. Two more were posted back by his haunches, one on each side. Bonnie stood beside one flank in a slight crouch, his hands up in front of him, as if ready to spring into action. As they led him forward, the stud began snorting and whinnying and prancing more wildly than ever. He was within ten feet of the mare when Johnny Groyner held up his right palm and yelled, "Whoa! Whoa! Montrose! Lewis! Get her some hay!"

The two men hustled off to a bin along the wall and returned with bales of hay, which they proceeded to stack under the mare's belly.

Herb Richman turned toward Charlie and said in a low voice, "What are they doing?"

"He's so wound up, they're afraid she's gonna collapse when he mounts her."

Now the hay was in place, and all the handlers were back in position. Johnny Groyner looked toward the mare's crew and extended one arm, palm up, and said, "She ready?" Alonzo nodded yes. Then he looked toward the stallion and extended his other arm, palm upward, and said, "He ready?" Bonnie nodded yes.

The little stud manager had both arms lifted upward and outward, as if he were spreading his wings. To Bonnie: "Okay, bring 'im up! Bring 'im up! Bring 'im up!"

The stallion's handlers were now struggling for all they were worth, as they let the animal move closer to the mare's cavernous vulva, which was now winking madly.

To Alonzo: "Be alive! Be alive! Don't let her stagger when she breaks down!"

To Bonnie and the stallion's crew: "Awright, boys—awright, boys—awright, boys—"

All at once the mare spread her haunches, opened her vulva wide, and seemed almost to squat. She was breaking down, abandoning her struggle, opening up unconditionally, surrendering utterly. At that moment the stud manager, his beard a brilliant red in the sunlight, his arms stretched out like wings, brought his hands together, slamming the heel of his right hand into the palm of his left with a tremendous *smack!* The stallion's handlers released their hold. The mare's handlers gave her back her foreleg. The stallion reared. His head, his wild eyes, his flared nostrils, his bared teeth, his huge neck, his forelegs, his massive chest rose up until the great beast appeared to be towering on tiptoe above the world. The little Australian, Bonnie, jumped forward, almost beneath the animal's belly. *Smash!*—the stallion came crashing down on the mare's back and drove his enormous penis toward her yawning vulva. The very ground shook beneath Charlie and his band of guests. The quake rattled their innards. The planets collided. The earth wobbled. Sex! Lust! Desperate! Irresistible!

The force was so great, it drove the mare forward. She struggled to keep her feet. Her belly was pressed down on the bales of hay, which slid forward with her. For an instant it appeared that Bonnie must have been crushed between the two of them or else spavined when the stallion's hooves came crashing down. Johnny Groyner was skittering along beside the mare's hindquarters shouting, "Bonnie! Bonnie!"

Now you could see Bonnie again. He had both hands wrapped around the stallion's huge penis, which furiously sought the mare's vagina. This was Bonnie's moment. He was the steerer, he whose task it was to steer the stallion's erect penis squarely into the proper channel of the mare's vagina. His feet danced along crazily, and his head seemed to have disappeared between the groins of the two beasts as the stallion's mighty haunches and two thousand pounds of thrust drove them all, man and beast, across the floor of the barn.

Johnny Groyner kept shouting, "Lower, Bonnie! Lower, Bonnie! Lower and—*up*! Lower and—*up*!"

Bonnie struggled to make sure the penis entered the vulva at the proper downward angle, then thrust up into the vagina.

"Push!" screamed Johnny Groyner. "Push, goddamn it! This way! This way! This way! Steady! This way!"

The three stable hands leaned in at a fierce angle, shoving the mare's flank and skittering across the dirt, three frantic little tugboats attending a stupendous, thundering act of coitus beneath the very belly, beside the very rutting rod, of the stallion.

The stallion was no longer the magnificent thoroughbred who just moments before had reared up on his hind legs, trumpeting as if he were the reigning king of all the animal kingdom. His forelegs, those visions of the graceful racing stride when he had won the Breeders' Cup just a few years before, now hung awkwardly, ridiculously, uselessly, like a pair of vestigial appendages, down either side of the mare's back. His great neck and head and, above all, his eyes, now looked like those of a demented creature as he tried, over and over, to bite the mare's neck. His teeth sunk, instead, into the leather mantle that had been placed over her neck and withers for that very reason. Otherwise, in his uncontrollable sexual fury, he would have chewed her raw. All the while, his haunches, his thighs, his buttocks, the seat of the stupendous power that had propelled him, the great First Draw, this great poem in motion, this embodiment of power and coordination, to glorious victories on the track—this magnificent engine was reduced to a single jerky, spastic, convulsive, compulsive motion: rut rut rut rut rut rut rut rut rut rut rut.

His entire musculature, rippling beneath his hot black hide in the shaft of sunlight, indeed, his very hide itself, every ounce of his one ton, his three million dollars' worth, of horseflesh, was now a hopeless, helpless slave to that single synaptic impulse: rut rut rut rut rut rut rut rut rut rut rut rut—while a sexual valet, an Australian elf, with his bare hands steered the rut-mad penis into a yawning vaginal canal, and an army of human beings, mere Lilliputians, pushed and shoved, and a little red-bearded conductor waved his arms about, and the lot of them, man and beast, careened twenty, thirty, forty feet across the barn's dirt floor with thousands of pounds of rut-lust momentum.

Suddenly the slide ended, the paroxysmal jerks ceased, and the stallion gave a sigh and a noisy groan, a cross between a snort and a whinny. A pathetic whine was what it was, compared to the mighty overture he had sung just seconds before. Then he slid back off the mare. His forelegs looked more ridiculous than ever, as they slithered back over her hide. He was finished, utterly spent. Despite his enormous size, he suddenly looked powerless. One of the handlers took him by the halter—but was it even necessary? He wasn't going anywhere. He certainly wasn't running. His penis—that once-almighty rod—was still distended, but it was now an ugly distorted black mess, slimy, oozing semen and dripping with the mare's lubricant. It looked more like a wet shillelagh than a penis, a lumpy, knotty, misshapen length of stick. Then, before the astonished eyes of Charlie's guests, the tip of it began to swell up. It swelled, swelled, swelled, swelled until it looked like a mushroom, an enormous and exceptionally noxious black mushroom with a long, black, gristly stem. The mushroom and its shillelagh shaft hung down in a weary fashion. The great beast looked dead, out on his feet. His head drooped. His gait was that of an old mule. As the stable hand led him away, he didn't so much as glance back at the mare. Not once. Not a nod, not a twitch, not so much as a sigh or a sentimental snort for the creature who just moments before had obsessed every neuron of his central nervous system.

"Yes, but will he call her in the morning?"

It was the throaty baritone of Lettie Withers. They all looked at Lettie and at one another—Herb Richman, Marsha Richman, Ted Nashford, Lenore Knox, the whole lot of them. They were stunned by what they had just witnessed, and Lettie's joke wasn't enough to snap them out of it.

So Doris Bass tried: "Now watch him light up a cigarette."

Slim Tucker said, "Is this what they mean by date rape?"

Howell Hendricks said, "Don't knock it if you haven't tried it."

Veronica Tucker said, "That was a real meat-and-potatoes kind of guy."

Francine Hendricks said, "Oh, you guys are all the same."

Billy Bass said, "Charlie maybe. Not me."

They all tried, and nobody could manage to laugh. They had been jolted. They had just witnessed something so unexpected, so powerful, so elemental, they were all overwhelmed, however inchoately, by the same question: *What–does–it–mean?*

Charlie knew that much, because he felt it himself. He felt it all over again every time he watched one of these sessions in the breeding barn. And this time, as he had led the stallion into the barn, he had felt the great beast's urge to procreate in his very bones. It had traveled down his arms, the beast's uncontrollable desire had, and into his shoulders, down into his solar plexus. Oh, he *knew* what it meant, but where could he find the words?

He stepped in front of the group, in front of Serena and Wally and his guests, and as he spoke, his eyes locked onto Herb Richman's. Herb and his wife, Marsha, had numb expressions, and their shoulders were up and their heads were lowered, as if they were retreating into shells.

"Well, that's it," said Charlie. He found, to his surprise, that he was breathing heavily and his shirt was wet beneath his armpits. "There you have it. People can say whatever they want. They can talk about gay rights"—*gay rats*—"or anything else they want." He stopped to take a couple of deep breaths. "They can talk about gay rats till they're blue in the face." He was so *out of breath*. "They can worship gay rats as if Moses brought 'em down from the mountaintop. They can close their eyes and dream of whatever'll make 'em feel better. But there"—he gestured toward the stallion and the mare—"there's the heart of it." He took another deep breath. "That's what it all boils down to at the end, the male and the female, and that's it."

He studied Herb Richman's face for a reaction. All he could make out was pain and paralysis. Why? Why? What did that strange look mean? Could Serena possibly be right? Had he been shocked and affronted by what he had just seen? Was he that sensitive? That liberal? That Jewish?

Just then Johnny Groyner came bouncing over. He was obviously elated. He was grinning. His ginger-red beard fairly blazed with high spirits.

"Well, Cap'm," he said, "went perfect!" He was breathing hard and sweating, too. "Couldna been better!"

"Looked great, Johnny," said Charlie. "You guys did a great job." But his mind was still spinning with Herb Richman, Herb Richman, Herb Richman. Then he got an idea. Liberal, liberal. He wouldn't treat Johnny, the conductor of the show, like a hired hand. He'd introduce him. Equality, equality. Liberal, Jewish.

"Johnny," he said, "I want you to meet one of our guests . . . Hebe Richman."

What had he just said! A scalding feeling swept over his brain.

"I mean *Herb* Richman! Godalmighty, Herb, I must be losing my grip. I guess—" He lifted his hands helplessly. "*Herb* Richman, Johnny!" He looked about. *Everyone* had heard him. "Jesus, Herb, that must be my Alzheimer's flaring up!" And why had he said "Jesus"?

Herb Richman's pale face turned scarlet, and then a soft, embarrassed smile spread over his features, and he turned toward Johnny Groyner and put out his hand and said, "It's nice to meet you, Johnny. That was quite something."

What have I just said!

Then Herb Richman turned back toward Charlie and, with the same soft smile on his face, patted him twice on the arm, as if to say, "There, there."

Charlie opened his mouth, but at first no words came out. Then he said, hoarsely, "Herb—I think I'm losing my marbles."

Herb Richman continued to smile, but his eyes were about 33 degrees Fahrenheit. Then he made a grunting noise deep in his chest, approximating a chuckle . . . or a punch in the solar plexus.

Charlie didn't dare look at Marsha Richman or Serena or Wally or anyone else who might have heard. A wave swept through his central nervous system and told him he had just blown seven floors of the Croker Concourse tower and $10 million a year in income.

Chapter XIII

The Arrest

All the way back to Atlanta, on this sunny Sunday afternoon, the gaffe wafted in the G-5's recirculating air like a smell. Charlie sat in the forward cabin upon his leather throne, at his tupelo maple desk, with Lenore Knox opposite him and old Governor Knox and Lettie Withers sitting just across the aisle. Herb not Hebe Richman and his wife, Marsha, and Howell and Francine Hendricks and Ted Nashford and his Live-in Lydia and Serena and Wally sat in the rear cabin. Billy and Doris Bass, who had flown back on Billy's own Learjet, and Slim and Veronica Tucker and Judge Opey McCorkle, who stayed on in Baker County, were not on the flight—but the gaffe was, and it would remain on board as long as Charlie and Herb not Hebe Richman did.

Charlie still couldn't believe he had said what he had said. Couldn't *believe* it. Maybe, upon reflection, everybody would take it as a simple slip of the lip and not as anything racial in origin . . .

Oh *sure*, Charlie.

"What's Beauchamp Jr. got to say about Chicago these days?" Charlie asked Lenore Knox—that and other questions of comparable gravity—but nothing could dispel the smell of the gaffe. Charlie wondered if everybody on board was thinking about the gaffe, the gaffe, and nothing but the gaffe, the way he was.

He had Gwenette ask everybody every three seconds if he or she would like something to drink or some ham biscuits or Sally Lunn with damson preserves, and he had Lud Harnsbarger come out of the cockpit and pay attention to the guests and let them have an eyeful of the spun-gold furze on his big forearms, but nothing was antiseptic enough to remove the stench of *Johnny, I want you to meet one of our guests, Hebe Richman.*

As the great G-5 touched down at PDK, Charlie was so caught up in the subject of how best to say farewell to Herb Richman, he didn't even look out the window to see what might be awaiting him on that hot, sunny tarmac. Let's see . . . he'd make a point of being the first off the plane, and he'd stand at the foot of the stairs and press one last effusion of hospitality upon his guests, and especially Herb and Marsha, as if nothing embarrassing had ever occurred.

The ship came to a halt, and Charlie's right knee began throbbing as soon as he stood up. In due course the G-5's stairs were lowered, and he looked down diligently before putting weight on his aching knee, and so he failed to notice the ten men who were emerging from the arrivals building and hustling across the asphalt apron. Charlie had already assumed his stance of maximum bonhomie at the foot of the stairs, squinting in the bright sunlight, and Lenore Knox, Lettie Withers, Ted Nashford, and Live-in Lydia were heading down the stairs when a sharp voice said:

"Mr. Charles E. Croker?"

Charlie looked about. There, behind him, was a short, balding, squarely built little bulldog of a man, about forty probably, with a prognathous jaw. He wore a gray suit and some sort of go-to-hell necktie and held a sheaf of papers in his hairy paws. At first Charlie didn't make out the composition of the crew of nine he had brought with him.

"Mr. Croker," the little bulldog continued, "my name is Martin Thorgen, counsel representing PlannersBanc, and I have here an order"—he thrust some papers at Charlie—"executed by the Superior Court, DeKalb County, Judge Oma Lee Listlass presiding, calling for the arrest and removal of this aircraft, N-number 741FS, model Gulfstream Five, a chattel against which a lien exists, as partial satisfaction of defalcatory loans owed said bank by the Croker Global Corporation."

Charlie stared at this jut-jawed little man, from whom such a stream of legalistic block phrases poured, and then he began to take in the men who accompanied him. Near him, a step behind, was a tall, rangy, athletic-looking young man with a long neck, a head of thick black hair, and a wild stare, who looked as if he had been wrestled into the lawyer-like gray suit he wore. Behind the two lawyers were three policemen wearing Smokey Bear hats and the navy shirts and gray trousers, with black stripes down the legs, of the DeKalb County Sheriff's Office. All three were tall, and two of them were real country boys, the raw-boned kind who liked to get drunk on Saturday night and go down to the railroad grade crossing and have a rock fight. Behind the cops were three young men wearing navy-blue windbreakers—Charlie couldn't read the lettering on them at first—and two men in suits Charlie realized he knew all too well: Ray Peepgass and that guy Zell or Zale, the one with the rasping voice and the big chin.

The bastards! They wait until the G-5 is full of guests, so they can pull this! Lettie, Lenore, and Ted Nashford and Live-in Lydia had already heard the whole thing and were bound to realize what was in progress.

Charlie looked Lawyer Martin Thorgen up and down and said, "Lemme see that 'order.' "

Lawyer Martin Thorgen handed a sheet of paper to Charlie, and without giving it so much as a glance, Charlie took it and tore it in two and then in four and then in eight, and then he threw the pieces at the feet of the lawyer. Several pieces stuck to his pants legs electrostatically.

"That's what said order amounts to," said Charlie. He looked past Lawyer Thorgen, searching out Peepgass's face. "You dream this stunt up, Ray? Or did your sidekick?"

"Didn't take much dreaming up," said Peepgass. "We talked to you weeks ago about the need to sell this airplane. You never seriously put it on the market. We found you a broker, and you just gave him the runaround."

Charlie was amazed that Peepgass could respond so firmly and with such conviction. What had gotten into old Ray?

Meantime, Lawyer Thorgen was saying, "Whatever you choose to do with the order in its printed form doesn't alter a thing, Mr. Croker. The order has been executed, and the Croker Global Corporation is no longer the owner of this aircraft. It is now the property of PlannersBanc. These gentlemen here"—he gestured toward the three policemen—"and myself are here solely to carry out the dictates of the court."

Charlie stepped closer to the little canine lawyer until he towered over him, and said in a low and, he hoped, menacing voice, "You're gonna carry out dick, that's what you're gonna carry out. Now kindly get all your stooges out of the way, so I can tend to my guests." Then he looked at Peepgass: "Kindly round up all your clowns and goons and get out of my way. I got guests on this airplane, Ray. Either you do the right thing or what happens next iddn' *PlannersBanc* versus *the Croker Global Corporation*, it's me versus you. You understand what I'm saying?"

"You can say whatever you want, Charlie," said Peepgass, "but nothing can change the fact that that G-5 is now ours."

Charlie couldn't *believe* this. Somewhere Peepgass had found the strength to *talk back* to him. He stepped toward his guests, his knee buckling as he did. Lettie and Lenore were already on the tarmac, and Ted Nashford and Live-in Lydia were almost there, and Howell Hendricks and his wife were on the stairway behind them. It was obvious from the wary looks on their faces that one and all had had an earful of what was going on.

Charlie tried to beam confidently at all six of them. With as cheery a voice as possible he said, "Y'all go ahead. G'on into the waiting room. I'll be right there." He *could not believe* what was happening. His mind spun, frantically seeking some workable strategy.

He'd ignore the bastards, that's what he'd do. He'd get his guests off the ship, and then he'd deal with the situation. He beamed broadly at Beauchamp Knox and Marsha Richman, who were now heading down the stairs, and at Howell and Francine Hendricks, Ted Nashford, Lettie Withers, and Lenore Knox, all of whom had held back—probably in the interest of gossip. It was pretty hard to stand there, as Charlie now was, beaming at everyone and trying to act oblivious of an enemy platoon of ten men, especially when three of them were policemen.

Lawyer Thorgen made it worse by announcing in a loud voice: "As soon as your guests and crew have disembarked, Mr. Croker, the aircraft will be arrested and removed."

Now Wally was on the G-5's stairs, followed by Herb Richman and Serena. "Dad," said Wally, "what's going on?"

"Nothing," said Charlie, "a whole lotta nothing." But he could tell from Wally's expression that that wasn't what it looked like.

Lawyer Thorgen's voice: "How many people remain onboard?"

"That's not your concern," said Charlie.

"I'm afraid it is. That's PlannersBanc's aircraft."

Damn, thought Charlie. I need a lawyer, and my lawyer's giving me nothing but grief because he wants his $354,000. I'll—I'll—I'll contest jurisdiction.

"The county court has no jurisdiction," he said. "This aircraft is engaged in interstate commerce."

"This aircraft," said Martin Thorgen in a tone of exaggerated boredom, "is a chattel encumbered by a chattel mortgage and subject to foreclosure *in situ* in DeKalb County."

"What the hell's a chattel?"

"A chattel's a movable possession, and a Gulfstream Five aircraft is eminently movable."

"Oh yeah?" said Charlie. "And just how do you think you're gonna move it?"

"The usual way. Fly it." He gestured toward the three men in the warm-up jackets. "We have a mechanic and two licensed pilots checked out in every model of Gulfstream and, for that matter, most jet airliners."

The three men stared blankly at Charlie. He engaged each one of them eye to eye, then said, "You enjoy slimy assignments like this one?"

The youngest of the three, a tall, lanky fellow with a mouth much too small for his big head, responded insouciantly: "I'd rather be flying the Concorde, if you want to know the truth. Or an F-16. But this is the job that's open."

The young man's impudent nonchalance threw Charlie off. Finally he said, "Anything as long as it pays money, right? You must feel great about yourself."

The young man shrugged. "Like to fly. This iddn' the first time I've worked on one of these chattel-mortgage foreclosures here at PDK, either. G-5's a nice ship."

Now Charlie was aware that Serena and Herb Richman had descended the stairs and were standing near him. Charlie wasn't worrying anymore about how to bid goodbye to Herb Richman. Now he had to figure out how to keep from looking like a hapless bankrupt fool.

Serena said, "What's going on, Charlie?"

"Nothing," growled Charlie. "Just a little misunderstanding."

Herb Richman stood just slightly behind Serena. A soft smile played upon his lips, and he looked sleepier than ever.

At the top of the stairs Lud Harnsbarger had just emerged from the G-5 with the navy overnight bag he carried, and behind him Charlie could just make out Jimmy Kite and Gwenette.

Charlie held up his hand and motioned for them all to stop. "Hold it, Lud! I'm gonna need you and Jimmy and Gwenette." Then he turned to Serena. "Sweetheart, you take Herb"—not Hebe!—"and everybody into the waiting room. The drivers should be there already. Figure out who goes in which cars, and you all head on home. I'm gon' be tied up here for a spell." *Spale*. "Gotta take a short trip."

He turned to head back to the stairway to the plane, and his knee rocked unsteadily. The pain like to kill him. Then, faster than he could have imagined such big men could move, the three county cops outflanked him and set up a line at the foot of the stairs.

The one in the middle, the one whose belly bulged out over his big leather belt, said, "We can't let you back on the plane, Mr. Croker. We're here to arrest it, pursuant to a court order." *Coat awda.*

"Yeah, and pursuant to what kinda awda'd you let yourself be talked into picking out a Sunday afternoon when I'm arriving with a dozen guests?"

"We're just carrying out instructions, Mr. Croker."

"You just work here, right?" said Charlie.

All the while his sense of humiliation was rising alarmingly. This ignominious farce was being played out before his wife, his son, his employees (Lud, Jimmy, and Gwenette), Herb Richman, and some of the biggest and most widely listened-to mouths in Atlanta, namely, garrulous souls like Howell Hendricks and Lettie Withers. How could he get around these three monkeys in the sheriff's deputy uniforms, this beef trust, and take command of the G-5 and get the hell out of here? If he thought he could have done it, physically, the way he could have done it when he was thirty years old, not sixty, he would have muscled the three men aside and stormed up the stairway and into the G-5's cabin and ordered Lud and Jimmy to take off. They would have been astonished by how little never-mind he paid their uniforms, the stupid monkeys. But he wasn't at all sure he could get by them. His right knee was buckling with pain every time he took a step. And these three wouldn't be pushovers. The one with the belly was probably in his mid-thirties, and he struck Charlie as a younger version of Durwood. He looked like the kind who'd love to roll in the dirt with you or whack you upside the ear with his nightstick so that you could no longer hear and were in the grip of a mortal pain from your mastoid process to your occipital rim.

One of the rules Charlie knew all leaders should follow was: Never engage in a fight in the presence of your followers that you can't possibly win. And this was a fight he couldn't possibly win, at least not physically. He sighed and looked about. Over in the doorway of the hangar, all but obscured by the shadows that plunged its immense space into gloom, was a mechanic named Lunnie (for Lunsford), an employee of PDK but one who had been working on Charlie's planes for six years at least. Charlie looked at Lunnie—and got an idea. *Just like that* his entire mood changed.

He broke into a sage smile and said to the beefy policeman before him, "Well, Officer, I can see that—by the way, what's your name?"

The policeman hesitated, not sure whether standing here and dutifully revealing his name would compromise him or not. But Charlie's evidently sincere smile loosened him up, and he finally said, "Hunnicutt, Officer Arra Hunnicutt." Or it came out "Arra." After a couple of seconds Charlie realized the man was a Georgia country boy whose name was Ira, which out in the sticks, including Baker County, would come out "Arra," just the way "fire" came out "far," and "He got hired by the Fire Department" came out "He got hard by the Far Department."

"Well, Officer Hunnicutt, I can see you're a man who means what he says. But I have to give you fair warning: it's unwise for anyone but me to attempt to move this airplane from where it is right now."

"That ain't for me to say," said Officer Hunnicutt. "That's for whoever's acquarrin't."

"Well," said Charlie, smiling again, "I can only pass along my advice."

With that, he turned toward Lud and Jimmy and beckoned them on down the stairs. "Come on, boys, and you, too, Gwenette. I'll treat you to a beer."

He headed toward the waiting room, but suddenly stopped when he came abreast of Peepgass and Zale. Peepgass seemed to shrink, as if trying to pull himself back into a shell, but Zale looked at Charlie down his nose, with his big melon-shaped chin thrust up.

"By the way," said Charlie cheerily, looking at Zale, "you oughta know that a lien on the starboard engine of this airplane is held by MagTrust. We had to go to MagTrust when PlannersBanc wouldn't extend us any more credit. Whether you want to be taking off with

MagTrust's collateral is something y'all oughta be thinking about. I wouldn't, if I were you."

"We'll bear that in mind," said Zale in his high, grating voice. "We'll keep everybody informed."

The young pilot who had bandied words with Charlie stepped forward and called out not to Charlie but to Lud Harnsbarger, " 'Scuse me, I need to ask you something."

Now Charlie could see what was on the back of his windbreaker. In fluorescent Day-Glo yellow letters seven inches high it said REPO. Above that, in smaller letters, about the size of the names printed on the backs of the jerseys of professional football players, it said PLANNERSBANC. That was what all his guests in the waiting room got an eyeful of when they looked out the big plate-glass window: PLANNERSBANC REPO.

Lud looked at Charlie, silently asking if he should talk to the PlannersBanc pilot, and Charlie boomed out, "Sure, go ahead!"

Lud and Jimmy and Gwenette were by now down on the tarmac, and Charlie walked, gimping badly, over to the three of them and said in a hushed voice, "Tell him anything he wants to know. You, too, Jimmy. Just keep him talking. The longer, the better."

Whereupon Charlie went gimping on into the waiting room. Serena and Herb Richman were just ahead of him. They had been hanging back, taking it all in.

Serena said, "What are you going to do, Charlie?"

"I'm gonna relax, take it easy," said Charlie.

"What are they doing?"

A cheery grin. "Nothing. They just enjoy spinning their wheels."

The painting! It came to him—*just like that!*

"One other thing," Charlie said, turning back toward Peepgass and the big-jawed Zale. "I got personal effects on that airplane."

Zale, in a bored fashion: "Don't worry, all personal effects will be returned."

"One *uv*'em I want right now," said Charlie. "It's a painting by N. C. Wyeth on the bulkhead of the forward cabin."

"No can do," said Zale. He had his chest and wrestler's gut thrust forward and his suit jacket wide open, revealing the skulls and crossbones that ran up and down his suspenders. "That painting is listed as collateral, a hundred and ninety thousand dollars' worth, and title was held by the Croker Global Corporation."

Charlie was furious—and anguished. More than anything else he possessed, including Turpmtine itself, the painting symbolized the triumphs of Cap'm Charlie Croker. But he mustn't let them see how he felt. He would just have to get his hands on it tonight or tomorrow—after the surprise this impudent, melon-jawed monkey had coming.

He forced himself to smile in a knowing way. "Well, I'm putting you on notice. Anything happens to this aircraft or its contents, and especially that painting—you're in it up to your armpits."

"I'll try to remember that," said Zale, sticking his chest out still farther.

Charlie felt the urge to kill. He'd like to throttle Peepgass, too. Now that they were barely six feet apart, Peepgass wasn't saying a word. He had his head down and his shoulders pressed practically up against his neck, as if he were trying to get ready to drop through a crack in the earth. But Charlie had presence of mind enough to know that anything he tried to do physically would only make things worse. The three cops . . . his bad knee . . . his guests' greedy eyes . . . which would be treated to the spectacle of Cap'm Charlie Croker rolling around on the asphalt at PDK with three DeKalb County peace officers . . . at his age . . . sixty years . . . The sixty years were what he truly didn't want to have to think about. So he concentrated on the cops, the knee, and the guests. He was determined to make his guests feel that whatever it was that was going on, it was part of the fun of a rollicking weekend with Cap'm Charlie.

The others—Beauchamp and Lenore Knox, Howell and Francine Hendricks, Lettie Withers, Ted Nashford, Live-in Lydia, Marsha Richman, and Wally—were already in the waiting room. The room featured a great horseshoe arrangement of couches that looked out upon the field through a floor-to-ceiling plate-glass window. None of his guests was seated, however, not even old Governor Knox. They were all standing near the window, so as not to miss a trick. And when Charlie entered the room, their eyes were on him. (How complete had his humiliation been?)

In fact, Charlie was all smiles. "Hey, Serena," he said, loud enough for everybody to hear, "figure out who oughta go in which car, and get everybody a Coke or sump'm. I'll be right back." *Rat back.*

With that, Charlie, bad knee and all, hurried toward a door marked EMPLOYEES ONLY that opened out into the hangar. He looked about in the gloom for the round-shouldered form of Lunnie, the mechanic. And there he was, about twenty feet from the hangar's enormous mouth. He looked startled when Charlie came gimping up to him, startled and embarrassed.

"Cap'm," he said, "I'm sorry about what's going on out there. I wish I could help."

Charlie smiled. "Maybe you can, Lunnie. Maybe you can. I want you to tell me sump'm. What's the easiest way a keeping a ship like a G-5 from taking off?"

"Keep'er from taking off? You mean mechanically?"

"Yeah, mechanically. Exactly."

"Hell"—*hale*—"the easiest way is, slide a wrench down the intake of an engine."

"What'll'at do?"

"Soon's it starts up, the wrench'll break all the fan blades. Each engine's got five sets a fan blades. It'll ruin the whole damn engine."

"That'll do it, hunh?"

"Sure will. I seen it happen."

"Lunnie," said Charlie, "how long you been working for me?"

"Six or seven years, I reckon."

"I treated you okay?"

"You the best, Cap'm."

"Lunnie, I want you to do something for me. This is very important, and only you can do it slick enough. I want you to slide a wrench down the intake of the starboard engine of my G-5, that ship right there. How 'bout it?"

Immediately Lunnie's placid features began to contort. You could see loyalty and obedience on the one hand at war with loss of job and possible criminal prosecution on the other.

"I'm not asking you for a favor, Lunnie," said Charlie. "I'm ready to pay for it. It'd be worth a lot to me. Four thousand dollars cash, Lunnie—no, make it five. Five thousand dollars for five seconds of work. Just let it slide down the gullet."

Lunnie's head was oscillating like an electric fan in the summertime and he was massaging his knuckles, first one hand and then the other. "I don' know, Cap'm, destroying a piece of equipment like that . . . That engine's worth about half a million dollars, I reckon."

"Well, shit, Lunnie, it's *my* piece of equipment, and that's what I want."

Faster oscillation and massaging. "I know, Cap'm, but I'd be the one—I can't take the chance."

Charlie put on a furious visage. "Chance, hell, Lunnie! I'm *ordering* you to do it! This is a *direct order*! *Do* it!"

By now Lunnie had begun making imaginary snowballs with his two cupped hands. "I know, Cap'm"—imaginary snowball—"I *unnerstan*"—imaginary snowball—"what you're *saying*"—imaginary snowball—"but it could cost me my job"—imaginary snowball—"the onliest way I got a making a *living*"—imaginary snowball.

Cap'm Charlie Croker, forgiver of children: "Okay, Lunnie, okay. It's all right. Can you do *this* much for me, which ain't much—can you tell me where I can find a wrench and a pair of coveralls?"

The relieved child, off the hook: "I can give you a wrench." He produced one from somewhere in his coveralls. "And there's a whole bunch a coveralls on the hooks ov'air by 'at door you come in."

"And just remember one thing, Lunnie. Me'n'you never had this conversation. That way nobody can drag you into nothing. We never said a word to each other."

"Okay, Cap'm."

Charlie retreated into the gloom of the hangar and found, over by the door, at least a dozen pairs of coveralls hanging on hooks, just as Lunnie had said.

He finally found one big enough to accommodate his 235-pound bulk and pulled it on right over his clothes. In the pocket of another pair was a bandanna. This gave him an idea. He took it out. It had a strange camouflage pattern of white, gray, and black. For what? Hiking over a rocky terrain with melting snow? Didn't matter. Charlie draped it over his bare skull and tied it in back, the way a pirate might have. He put the wrench in one of the coveralls' capacious pockets and headed through the greasy twilight of the hangar and out onto the tarmac.

The G-5 was parked so that the left side, which was outfitted with the main passenger door and the door to the luggage bay, faced the waiting room. The right side was visible only from the hangar or the hangar side of the tarmac, and there was nobody on that side; or, rather, no one but Charlie Croker.

Beneath the belly of the G-5 he could see the feet and lower legs of a whole clump of men who were apparently discussing the G-5. Every now and then he could hear the grating, high-pitched voice of the one called Zale. A whole lot of talk. Good boy, Lud!

Charlie walked slowly and casually toward the starboard engine. He kept the wrench concealed in the coveralls. The G-5's two mighty engines hung down beneath the wings. He began stooping over and looking at the underside of the wing, as if making an inspection. Now he was right next to the engine. He steeled himself, forced himself not to look this way or that—and withdrew the wrench and reached up, and let it slide down the mouth of the engine. Then, stooping as he went, he inspected the underside of the wing from the engine to the fuselage, in the interest of appearing diligent, then sauntered back into the hangar. Once he was safely within its deep penumbra, he removed the coveralls and the bandanna, and put them back where he had got them. Lunnie was nowhere to be seen. He had vanished. Charlie hurried back through the EMPLOYEES ONLY door into the waiting room.

Serena had succeeded in shepherding Howell and Francine Hendricks and Beauchamp and Lenore Knox into one of the BMWs, but the rest, including Herb Richman and his wife, seemed to want to stay on and follow the little drama on the tarmac. When Charlie came back into the room, all eyes turned toward him. They were wondering how he would take this shaming turn of events.

Gesturing toward the aircraft, Ted Nashford said, "That bunch—they're boarding your aircraft, Charlie."

Sure enough, there were Zale and Peepgass making their way up the stairs to the G-5's cabin.

"Where are"—*whirr*—"the pilots?" asked Charlie. Big smile.

The smile was so genuine, Ted Nashford was taken aback at first. "They're both on board, them and the other one, the—the—the—"

"The mechanic," said Charlie, who seemed terribly merry about it all. "Well, I advised them against it, but they were in no mood to listen."

"Why?"

"Why wouldn't they listen or why'd I advise them not to?"

"Why'd you advise them not to."

"The G-5's a temperamental airplane, Ted. A wonderful airplane, but you gotta know each one by heart. They don't know that ship from their left elbow. I wonder if they'll make it as far as the runway."

So now they all watched, Ted, Live-in Lydia, Herb and Marsha Richman, Lettie Withers, Wally, Serena, and Charlie himself, as the stairway folded up into the fuselage of the G-5. If you looked closely enough, you could see Zale sitting in Charlie's seat—at the great tupelo desk facing N. C. Wyeth's *Jim Bowie on His Deathbed*—and sitting opposite him was Peepgass. Both had grand smiles. Then Zale must have said something terribly funny, because you could see Peepgass laughing to beat the band.

"*They* look happy!" volunteered Live-in Lydia.

Ordinarily Charlie would have wanted to throttle her skinny live-in neck. Instead, he chuckled and said, "Just remember, I told every one of them"—*tol' evver one* uv'*em*—"they didn't know what they're doing."

Then the engines started up. One moment you could see a puff of smoke rise from the left engine, the one visible in the waiting room, and in the next you could hear a sound like gunfire, fast stuttering gunfire, as if from an exceptionally loud automatic weapon. *Pang! Pang! Pang! Pang!* The sound penetrated the half-inch-thick glass of the waiting-room window as if it weren't there.

The engines shut down, and now a plume of black smoke rose from the other side of the G-5. The faces at the windows, Zale's and Peepgass's, were etched with the consternation of two men who thought they had just settled in for a swell little ride somewhere with their $38 million booty. Pretty soon the ship's stairway was unfurled again, and here came Zale clomping down, with Peepgass right behind him. They stood on the tarmac at the bottom of the stairs, staring helplessly at the ship. Then down the stairs came the two pilots in their PLANNERSBANC REPO jackets, both of them barking at the mechanic, who was behind them on the stairs, tossing one hand up in the air and then the other. Then all five of them, Zale, Peepgass, the two pilots, and the mechanic, headed around the nose of the ship toward the starboard side.

Charlie chuckled. "Well, you can give people fair warning, but you can't nail 'em to the ground and say, 'Don't move.' "

Hugely pleased, he gave all his retinue a come-on gesture and headed toward the glass door that led to the building's parking lot. "Got cars out here waiting for y'all."

Ted Nashford, who was close behind him, said, "What do you suppose happened to the airplane?"

"I can only guess," said Charlie, "but it sounded like the pilot?—he tried to feed too much power to the engines before they were warmed up?—and it did something to the fan blades in the compressors?—that's what it sounded like to me, but what do I know about jet engines."

By the time they got outside, where Croker Global drivers were waiting with two BMWs, Charlie was laughing as if the havoc wreaked upon the G-5 was one of the funniest things that had happened in years.

Chapter XIV

God's Cosmic Joke

"SO IT'S YOUR TESTIMONY, MR. PEEPGASS, THAT YOU INVITED Sirja to have dinner with you at the Hotel Grand Tatar out of a sudden interest in Finnish art?"

"I didn't know anything about Finnish art at that time," said Peepgass, who was dying to wipe his forehead, "but we had an art program at PlannersBanc and I was interested in exploring the possibilities. She seemed very knowledgeable about Finnish art."

"Nobody disputes the fact that you were 'exploring the possibilities,' Mr. Peepgass, and just what those 'possibilities' were is what we're gonna get to."

Oh God, the tawdriness! The tawdriness!

Peepgass stared helplessly into the smirking mug of Morton Tennenbaum, Esq., who was seated directly across the table from him, and wondered how Sirja had ever found this odious specimen of the DeKalb County bar . . . here in an office in a shopping mall off Decatur Road between a gift shop and a sporting-goods store that seemed to sell nothing but sneakers and violently patterned outfits for non-athletes to exercise in . . . The front half of the dome of Lawyer Tennenbaum's skull was completely bald, but halfway back there rose up a stand of blackish-gray hair so thick, so wiry, so unruly, it looked like incoming surf. The man seemed to have only two expressions: Indignation and Contempt. This one was Contempt.

Next to him sat the Finnish *femme natale* herself, although Peepgass tried his best not to look at her. He could no longer associate the individual across from him, this woman, with the raging lust that had impelled him to invite her to the Grand Tatar Hotel in Helsinki that night and engage in a fervent round of footsie under the tablecloth. Her astonishingly full head of blond hair, which had once swept him away in veritable typhoons of lust, now just made him wonder how she managed to frizz it up like that. Her big blue eyes, which he had once looked into to explore the very depths of Nordic love, now struck him as bugged-out, possibly from a thyroid condition. And those breasts . . . those obscenely enormous jugs . . . Even now, even at this lawyers' deposition in which she was trying to portray herself as an innocent working girl from up near the Arctic Circle seduced, impregnated, and abandoned by a rich American banker, she couldn't resist displaying her huge hooters under a satiny white blouse open almost down to *there* . . . How could he have ever buried his very head in those two pillows? They were grotesque, as if God, careless at the end of a busy day, had hung Isolde's headlights on some scrawny little 105-pound bag of bird bones. Oh, the tawdriness . . . the tawdriness . . . Peepgass's own lawyer, Alexander (Sandy) Dickens, seated right next to him, didn't elevate the level of these proceedings, either, despite the fact that he came from an old Downtown law firm, Tripp, Snayer & Billings, and charged $400 an hour. Too late it had dawned on Peepgass that Tripp, Snayer didn't regard paternity suits as a very classy business and had fobbed off one of the firm's dim bulbs on him. Dickens was an obese, florid, rumpled, fortyish redhead who sat hunched over with the heel of his hand dug into the side of his fat face. He made a noise when he breathed. At the head of the table sat a solemn, apoplectic-faced, middle-aged man with a carefully combed-back head of grayish-brown hair. He was a so-called court reporter, a stenographer who was recording the deposition on a spindly stenotype machine. His expression was a florid blank, but the fact that he was going to hear and preserve all this stuff verbatim . . . Oh, the tawdriness, the tawdriness, the tawdriness, the tawdriness . . . Completing the picture was the room itself, a windowless box in the back with a flush door, covered in a lurid imitation-wood grain, that hung a half-inch short of the floor, so that Peepgass and everybody else at the table could hear the whimperings and fitful cries of Master Pietari

Päivärinta Peepgass, whom the plaintiff in this suit had parked outside with some secretary or other while she laid siege to the assets of Raymond Peepgass.

Morton Tennenbaum's incoming surf kept rolling in. "So as a representative of PlannersBanc, one of the largest banks in the Southeast, you decided to invite to your hotel a twenty-seven-year-old Finnish notions buyer as an art consultant. Is that your testimony?"

"No," said Peepgass, "what I said was—"

"That wasn't his testimony," said Sandy Dickens. It came out bored and slurred, since he didn't bother removing his face from the heel of his hand.

"Never mind," said Tennenbaum, "I withdraw the question. Is it true, Mr. Peepgass, that you asked Sirja to bring along some slides of her own work?"

"Yes."

"Did you think PlannersBanc might want to promote Miz Sirja Tiramaki, someone you had never heard of before, someone who painted at home—you thought PlannersBanc might want to select the work of this young woman for its 'art program'?"

"No—"

"Or did you just want her to come on up and show you her etchings?"

"I'm gonna object to that," said Lawyer Dickens, still talking into the heel of his hand.

"You don't have to," said Morton Tennenbaum, looking at Peepgass with a sneer. "The question answers itself. All right. The two of you are having dinner at the Grand Tatar. Did you have anything to drink?"

"Yes."

"And what did you have?"

"We had a drink called a bamboo cocktail."

Sirja scrunched up the tiny Finnish features of her face and began scribbling furiously on a pad and passed a note to Morton Tennenbaum. She and Peepgass had reached the stage, well known to divorce lawyers, in which the principals no longer speak to each other but only to the lawyers, to whom they pass notes, notes, and more notes, endless notes, exposing the mendacity and evasions of their erstwhile loved ones.

The Incoming Surf read the note and said, "*Both* of you had bamboo cocktails?"

"Yes"—although after he said it, Peepgass wasn't absolutely sure that was true.

Morton Tennenbaum arched his eyebrows in an ironic way. "All right. And what made you think you might like to have that particular drink, a bamboo cocktail?"

Peepgass paused. He could see where it was all headed, and he didn't want to go there. The red-faced court reporter had his fingers poised over his little machine, ready to record and write out every last sordid detail. Peepgass didn't want to get into any of this, but Sandy Dickens had said he had no choice. Peepgass looked at Dickens anyway, halfway hoping he might change his mind and come to life and say, "I object."

"You don't have to look at your attorney," said Tennenbaum. "He can't tell you why you wanted that drink."

Finally Peepgass said, "Miss Tiramaki recommended it." Tennenbaum, in his tawdry way, insisted on calling his client Sirja. Peepgass was damned if he would.

Miss Tiramaki went into a real fury of note writing.

"Isn't it a fact, Mr. Peepgass, that you asked Sirja what this drink on the menu was, this 'bamboo cocktail,' and that she merely described to you a local rural superstition, in response to your question?"

"No, as I recall—"

"All right, let's stick with your recollection. According to your recollection, what was it that this bamboo cocktail had to recommend it?"

Defeated, Peepgass said tonelessly, "It was made with a fertilized egg yolk in it instead of a maraschino cherry, and it was supposed to . . . enhance sexual energy."

"It was supposed to enhance sexual energy. And why did you like that idea so much at that point?"

"I didn't like it or dislike it," said Peepgass. "It was just a . . . a . . . a novelty, as far as I was concerned."

"It was just a novelty as far as you were concerned." Witheringly.

Peepgass felt completely whipped. This was only a deposition, not yet a trial, and already he couldn't take it. What did it matter whether she had started it or he had started it? It was all utterly cheap, sordid, and tawdry, either way. A paternity suit! Forty-six years old, he was, and drowning in a smelly little sexual cesspool, while the clock ticked and the worst lawyer at Tripp, Snayer leeched $400 an hour out of the pathetic remains of his resources.

The Incoming Surf wouldn't let up. He forced him to relive that entire meal at the Grand Tatar. Was he, Peepgass, really testifying, under oath, that it was *she* who had rubbed *his* leg under the table with her foot? That it was *she* who had told *him* it was too noisy in the dining room and that they needed to go someplace quieter to talk about Finnish art and look at her slides? That it was *she* who had suggested *his suite*? Peepgass barely bothered defending himself. He was too demoralized. He braced for the knockout punches he now knew were inevitable.

"All right," said Lawyer Tennenbaum, "and so then you led Sirja over to your king-size bed and you made love. Is that correct?"

"I didn't *lead* her—" But then he gave up. "Yes," he said with an air of infinite resignation and an empty stare. *Made love.* What an absurd and sleazy concoction of words! Made *what* love? He had had an overwhelming, fiery, juvenile itch in his groin, and she had been only too happy to offer the big American banker her pelvic saddle to relieve it, that was all . . . Oh God, the tawdriness, the tawdriness . . . Then the Incoming Surf asked, "Did you use a condom?"

Did I use a condom? Aghast, utterly humiliated by the very asking of the question, Peepgass turned to Lawyer Dickens for protection. Shield me! Help me! It can't go this far! But Lawyer Dickens sat there with his fat red head lolling on the heel of his hand and rolled his eyes toward him with a look that said, "I already told you you'd have to answer such questions."

"Yes," said Peepgass with a doomed tone.

"Where'd you get it, Mr. Peepgass?"

"Get it?"

"The condom."

"The condom? I—I don't remember." Although of course he did. Every single nervous moment he had spent in the pharmacy of the Grand Tatar, before Sirja had arrived, purchasing the condoms and praying that the clerk, with her boyishly short blond hair, wouldn't recognize him as a guest in the hotel—every single red-faced microsecond of it was stored away in his memory bank.

"You don't remember? Well, let's think about it a moment . . . and *try*. Do you carry condoms with you wherever you go, in case these . . . 'possibilities' present themselves? Or does the Grand Tatar Hotel leave them on the bedside tables? Or what? It shouldn't be very hard to remember."

Peepgass was speechless. His mind churned. The Sandy Dickens scenario . . . When the subject of the condom had come up, Lawyer Dickens had never asked him where he got the condom. No, instead he opened up a certain . . . avenue . . . He never suggested, in so many words, that he make up a little fib . . . but if in fact Sirja had happened to have arrived at the hotel with her own supply of condoms—and many young women apparently went about these days so equipped—then it would put the affair in a light advantageous to the defense . . . Peepgass's brain churned and churned and churned—but he couldn't bring himself to do it. Exactly why, he couldn't have explained to himself. God knew, Sirja had undertaken that romp on the bed with a lasciviousness that any hooker would have to go some to top. So what difference would it make if he insisted that she had brought the condoms? *Psychologically* it was true, wasn't it? Nevertheless, he couldn't bring himself to head down that avenue.

The doomed man: "I just don't remember."

Furious scribbling by Sirja; but Lawyer Tennenbaum didn't look at her note. Instead, he made a little motion with his hand that said, "Relax."

"All right, Mr. Peepgass, we'll leave it at that. A condom . . . materialized. We don't know how, but there it is. We have a condom, and the two of you are on your king-size bed in your hotel suite . . ."

Oh, the tawdriness! The tawdriness! On and on it went, until finally Lawyer Tennenbaum had finished with Peepgass and it was time for Lawyer Dickens to depose Sirja. Dickens straightened up and came alive at this point and proceeded to prove that he could be as odious as his counterpart. Tennenbaum at least had two expressions: Indignation and Contempt. Dickens had but one: Scorn. He stared out of a pair of puffy slits for eyes in a way that made clear his scorn for the selective memory of the plaintiff. He breathed audibly from beneath his layers of fat. He sighed with disgust. He asked her whether or not she had ever before met a strange man on an airplane and then joined him for dinner at his hotel.

"No," said Sirja, her thyrotic eyes flashing, "I was *never* doing that. Why you are asking me such things?"

That dry, high-pitched Scandinavian chirp of hers . . . Her English, which was never really *wrong* and yet always *off* . . . Back then, on that first night at the Grand Tatar and in the months that followed, he had found her accent and her eccentric syntax so exotic, so alluring . . . Just hearing it over the telephone had made him think of . . . white nights! Northern Lights! Hot little Finnish bodies popping out of the Arctic snows! . . . He could remember feeling all that, but he could no longer imagine why . . . Christ, there was nothing even remotely alluring about that voice. Quite the opposite; it was brittle, it was bird-like, it was supremely annoying . . . Imagine having to spend a lifetime in a house listening to that voice torturing proper English usage in tiny, maddening ways minute after minute, hour after hour, month after month . . .

Now Dickens was leading *her* through that dinner at the Grand Tatar. *She* was the one who had suggested to Mr. Peepgass that she come see him in his hotel to brief him on Finnish art, wasn't she . . . *She* was the one who had initiated the footsie under the table with Mr. Peepgass. Was that not the case? . . . *She* was the one who had suggested going to Mr. Peepgass's suite, wasn't that the simple truth of the matter?

No, no, and no. "I was speaking very much at dinner concerning Finnish art, but Raymond was speaking always concerning where am I living and am I having a boyfriend and these very much personal things." Chirp, chirp, chirp, chirp. She didn't look at him, not even once.

And then Dickens steered *her* up to that accursed suite in the Grand Tatar. And then to the matter of . . . the condom.

"Now, Miss Tiramaki, who provided the condom?"

Startled: "Who?" Hotly: "Raymond!" Peepgass hated the way she insisted on still referring to him as Raymond. Under the circumstances, wouldn't Mr. Peepgass suffice? "Certainly *I* was not providing a condom!"

"We're only trying to establish the facts here, Miss Tiramaki. That's the purpose of a deposition. I realize these are personal matters, but the nature of your suit makes them germane. Do you understand what I'm saying? Now I want you to tell me—we have this condom. Right?—I want you to tell me who put it on Mr. Peepgass."

"*What?*" Sirja's face turned crimson. Her eyes bugged out alarmingly. Peepgass cringed. He wanted to evaporate, escape into the fourth dimension. How could Dickens bring this up? Why had he, Peepgass, ever been so gauche and gross as to even tell him about it? How could he have been so pointlessly graphic as to mention, by way of showing that Sirja had been the lust commando, the sexual predator that evening—how could he have gone so far as to tell his lawyer how she had insisted on putting the condom on him herself, rolling it down with much stroking and kneading and squeezing and kissing—yes! kissing!—until he thought he was going to *burst*—

Just then, from the other side of the door with the fake veneer, a series of convulsive little sobs. A baby was beginning to cry. Peepgass glanced at Sirja. She sat bolt upright. The sobs suddenly cut off, but you could tell it was merely the prolonged, heart-stopping gasp in which the child struggles desperately to catch its breath in order to explode with an all-out bawl. The moment was rigid with suspense. Even Tennenbaum and Dickens looked toward the door. Would the kid ever get his breath or not? Sirja rose from her chair, her mouth open, her eyes wide.

"Pavvy! Pavvy!" she cried. Her face was contorted. She rushed toward the door. "Pavvy!"

By the time she reached the door, the child had managed to fill his lungs with air, and the full-fledged explosion had begun, and the crisis was over. That didn't stop Sirja, of course. Just like that, she was through the door, and you could hear her clearly:

"Oh, Pavvy, Pavvy, Pavvy, Pavvy!" Followed by something in Finnish that sounded like "Ah dotey dotey dotey ahda hiya dotey."

No longer the Finnish phallus condomizer; now the Eternal Mother.

Oh yes, the crisis was over, but from that moment on Peepgass realized his goose was cooked. He didn't stand a chance. The satyr, the rut boar, was up against the Eternal Mother, and the satyr would never win that contest, not in any DeKalb County court, not in any court anywhere. Not only that, he would lose even if he won. If this pathetic little drama, oozing with cheap lechery, was ever played out in an open courtroom . . . Suppose somehow his children got a snootful of these details? Suppose Betty did? Suppose anybody did? The very thought made him want to shrivel up and die.

The door was open, and the baby's bawling filled the premises of Morton Tennenbaum, shopping-mall attorney-at-law. Every time Master Pietari Päivärinta Peepgass turned off the squall long enough to take a breath, you could hear Sirja cooing away. *Pavvy Pavvy Pavvy.* Pavvy, she called him. Well, that was better than Peepsy or Little Peepgass . . . She was cooing to him in Finnish, but this boy was going to be a Georgia boy, Pavvy Peepgass of DeKalb County, with a hell of a pair of lungs and, Fate being as perverse as she was, a Cracker accent, in which he would tell the world:

"I exist! I'm real! I'm not just a bad joke on a foolish middle-aged man! I eat—every day! I grow—and just try to stop me! I occupy space on this earth—and I will be heard from! And you will know my name!"

How could this have come about out of white nights and Northern

Lights, on PlannersBanc's cuff, in Helsinki, Finland? He wouldn't have a cent left after it was all over. He'd be lucky if he had a job. As it was, he'd had to tell the most pathetic lie to account for his absence from the bank this morning . . .

The thought of impending poverty caused him to look at his watch: 10:50 a.m. They'd been in here almost an hour. Four hundred dollars' worth of Lawyer Dickens that meant, with the clock still ticking, ticking, ticking, even while the Eternal Mother coos over the FinnoCracker-in-Embryo, and they hadn't even reached the end of night one in Helsinki . . .

He needed a new life. He needed a ton of money. That, in turn, made him think of Charlie Croker—which gave him his first spark of hope this entire morning. He had somehow mustered up the courage yesterday to go out to PDK with Zale and the rest of them to confront Croker and "arrest" the G-5, to use Lawyer Thorgen's term for it. Right in front of his guests, too! People the likes of Herbert Richman, Beauchamp Knox, and Lettie Withers! Oh, it was outrageous, but he had stood his ground—or at least he hadn't fled, as an urgent little voice inside him had advised him to do. And it had worked. True, one of the engines had "blown," rather mysteriously, as soon as they tried to move the ship. Nevertheless, the G-5 and Croker's beloved N. C. Wyeth painting were now PlannersBanc's. They had the big boffster's attention. If the G-5 could go—then so could his beloved plantation. By the time they made their offer to spare him utter ruin and humiliation in return for his handing over his deeds in lieu of foreclosure, tough old Charlie Croker would be . . . tenderized.

He had to be . . . *had* to be . . . From just beyond the door came the demanding wails of Master Pietari Päivärinta Peepgass, Master Pavvy Peepgass, Master P. P. Peepgass, Master Pietari P. Peepgass, Master Pete Peepgass—however it came out, it wouldn't be your everyday name . . . Not but so many Peepgasses on the face of the earth . . . The whole situation was ludicrous. Truly, sex was God's cosmic joke.

AT THAT MOMENT Charlie Croker was sitting at his desk on the thirty-ninth floor of his dead elephant, the Croker Concourse tower, conferring with the Wiz. As always, the Wiz looked like an expensive digital appliance with all its diode lights waiting for the cue to wink.

As far as he himself was concerned, Charlie hoped to God he didn't look as bad as he felt. He couldn't remember ever feeling more miserable. Last night his insomnia had been total. He hadn't gone to sleep for so much as thirty seconds. Every time he told himself he was going to refuse to think about the bank's seizing the G-5 and the Wyeth painting—in front of Lettie Withers—Ted Nashford—Howell Hendricks—his own son—and Herb Richman—and how could he have called the man *Hebe* in the first place!—and how many people in Atlanta had they already shot their mouths off to!—and was he a walking dead man—it was no use. There was no way he was going to shut those thoughts out of his skull.

Charlie looked away from the Wiz and out the office's big plate-glass windows toward the towers of Midtown and Downtown Atlanta, which you could see in the distance. They looked like tiny scale models, but you could see them. Southern exposures like this were not so great this time of year. By mid-afternoon the sun would be frying you alive, to the point where the central air conditioning could barely deal with it. But one of Croker Concourse's selling points was that it had the best of both worlds, the sylvan spaciousness of Cherokee County and proximity to the city proper. So he had put the executive suites on the south side of the tower to persuade the tenants that they were not paying top dollar for some remote country outpost. They were . . . in the game. They could see Midtown and Downtown. Well . . . good luck, one and all. The one who was no longer in the game was himself . . . roosting up here atop a tower he had put his own name on . . . behind a desk big enough for a dictator, resting upon a carpet custom made with raised, interlocking C's and G's, in tan, on a slate-blue field . . . Such a riot of egomania!

The G-5 had been merely the beginning. How long would it be before PlannersBanc came after the building itself? And Turpmtine . . . He'd been trying to get hold of his lawyer ever since yesterday afternoon, old John Fogg of Fogg Nackers Rendering & Lean. Maybe he was *too* old—

"You're outside the bandwidth, Charlie!" said the Wiz. Hurriedly he went into a dry chuckle to show that he was only making a pleasantry.

"Bandwidth?" Charlie looked at the Wiz with a puzzled expression, and the Wiz did some more earnest, dry chuckling.

"Just a figure of speech, Charlie. You looked like you were a thousand miles away."

"I did?" said Charlie. "Maybe I did. I was thinking about John Fogg. Might as well be a thousand miles away. It's not just that I want to know how this thing with the G-5 slipped by them, it's that I couldn't get ahold a anybody when I needed them. Ordinarily, if it's a weekend, I call John at home, and even if I have to leave a message I get a call back from *some*body, Justin Nackers, *some*body. This time nothing from nobody, and it's almost nine o'clock Monday morning, and *still* nothing from nobody, and we're giving them tens of thousands of dollars' worth of business."

"Up to a point, Charlie," said the Wiz, "up to a point. They may not see it that way. As I'm pretty sure I've told you, as our creditors go they have one of the biggest footprints. Lately, when I've talked to them, all they've done is growl."

"You're not saying that therefore they're giving this thing less than their best shot, are you? I mean, Jesus Christ. You're not saying they're dogging it on purpose."

"Not consciously," said the Wiz. "On the other hand, they may not be as . . . *incentivized* as we might like to see them."

"Well, I've already got Marguerite putting in calls to Fogg. If I don't hear from them within the hour, I'm going ov'eh and lay waste that damn place with a baseball bat. They gotta do something fast, while that plane and my painting are still at PDK."

Charlie and the Wiz were still talking about the G-5 and *Jim Bowie on His Deathbed* when the telephone on the credenza by Charlie's desk emitted a soft burble. That would be Marguerite.

"Cap," she said, "I've got John Fogg on the line."

"Where's he calling from?" He looked at the Wiz and mouthed the name for him.

"I don't know," said Marguerite. "Shall I put him through?"

"*Aw* yeah."

The voice in Charlie's ear said, "Good morning, Charlie." *Good mawnin, Chollie*; a soft Old Southern voice it was. "What brings you to the office so early?"

"I wouldn't call it early, John. I been trying to reach you or somebody in your firm for seventeen, eighteen hours now." He said it sharply. "We got a critical situation facing us here, and we need a lotta help in a hurry, and I ain't been able to get a*hold* a anybody."

"Well, I'm very sorry about that." Charlie was not aware at first that the voice was becoming considerably less soft, courtly, and Old Southern. "Why don't you tell me about your problem."

Charlie launched into a description of the scene at PDK, the court papers, the policemen, the repo pilots, and the blown engine, which he treated as a piece of mysterious good luck in an otherwise disastrous Sunday afternoon. He ended with: "Now, John, I thought you told me there was no way they could just go around attaching things. Well, they've just attached a pretty big thing, plus a valuable painting. I thought you and your firm were supposed to be on top of things like that."

"Sounds to me as if they've done some motion-jumping," said John Fogg. "That loophole does exist from time to time, but I've never heard of anyone being so devious as to take advantage of it."

"The whole legal profession is devious, John," said Charlie. "That's what we pay you to do: stay one jump ahead of devious lawyers."

"Pay you" turned out be an unfortunate choice of words.

"Sorry if you find us less than diligent, Charlie," said John Fogg with no warmth whatsoever. "But as long as we're on the subject of the relations between our two firms, there's something I should probably mention, little as I've wanted to have to mention it to you directly. The fact is that on numerous occasions I have had to instruct people in my firm to get in touch with people in your firm about this, but they seem to have gotten nowhere. We've had a long relationship, and in the past Croker Global has met its obligations in a timely fashion, and so over the past six months or so we've been willing to accommodate you—but your unmet balance now stands at $354,000. I'm at a loss to see how I can insist that the firm continue to represent you unless the account becomes substantially more current."

Charlie was astonished. "Do you mean—"

"I will pursue the matter of the arrest of the airplane and the painting, Charlie, and I will see what can be done and offer you my best advice. As things now stand, I don't think we can go beyond that."

After they said their goodbyes, Charlie was in a dazed state as he put the telephone back in its cradle on the credenza.

"What did he say?" asked the Wiz.

"He said he'll look into the court order PlannersBanc got for the G-5, and then . . ." He started to let it go at that. He didn't want the word to get out. He didn't want to start a wave of people jumping ship around here, least of all the Wiz. But the Wiz would have to know. Charlie depended on him too completely in matters financial. ". . . and after that they're not gonna represent us unless we pay them a big chunk of our 'unmet balance.' That was what he called it, our 'unmet balance.' I don't know where he gets these airs he likes to put on. His daddy was a clerk in a stationery and art-supply store on Houston Street. Wore a gray smock. Barely scraped by . . . *Unmet balance* . . . well—anyway—is there some way we can shift a couple of hundred thousand from someplace into Fogg Nackers Rendering & Lean?"

"I don't see how," said the Wiz. "We don't have $200,000 just sitting around parked someplace. Every dime of our cash flow is pre-dedicated."

"Well then, let's start pre-dedicating it to Fogg Nackers," said Charlie. "We can't afford to have them shut down on us. Not at this point. He says we owe them $354,000."

"That's true," said the Wiz. "That's the figure. But who do we divert it from to pay Fogg Nackers? We got noise all across the bandwidth as it is."

Just then a door opened and Marguerite came rushing in. A pale, slender woman in her late forties, she was dressed in a tweed jacket and skirt with a lush weave. Her dyed-dark-brown hair was done just so, in a pageboy bob. Charlie was so dependent on her, he was now paying her $90,000 a year. Marguerite had never married, and every penny went into her clothes, her hair, and her Mercedes. As usual, when she was perturbed about something, she pressed her lips together, distorting her even features. She came straight to Charlie.

"Cap, your first visitor has arrived."

"My first visitor? Whattaya mean, my first visitor?" Charlie looked at his watch.

"It's that fat man, Colonel Popover. Sal—what's his real name?"

"Gigliotti?" said Charlie.

"Right!" said Marguerite. "I never can remember it."

"What the hell's he doing here?"

"He says he wants his $17,000. Says we've owed it to him since last November."

Charlie looked at the Wiz and arched his eyebrows, as if to ask, "What's the story?"

The Wiz nodded. "He catered the Croker Concourse Caramba last year, last November. We owe him $17,000. Colonel Popover, Inc."

Marguerite said, "You probably don't remember it, Charlie, but he showed up here late in the afternoon on Thursday."

"He didn't have any appointment, did he?"

"No, he just hung around. Says he hasn't gotten anywhere by calling. He came back here Friday afternoon, but you'd already left for Turpmtine. So here he is, out in the waiting room again, and I wish you could take a look at him."

"Whattaya mean?"

"Well, this time he's not dressed in a suit. This time he's dressed like Colonel Popover. He's got on white shoes, white pants, one of these white—tunics do they call 'em?—the kind that chefs in the magazines wear—and a *toque blanche,* and he's *very* fat."

"*Toque blanche?*"

"You know," said Marguerite, "one of those sort of white chimneys they put on their heads with a sort of puff of cloth on top—and he's a very fat man. He's already perspiring, and the day hasn't even begun."

"So what did you tell him?"

"I told him you have appointments all day."

"And what did he say?"

"He said he'd wait."

"Well, let him wait. He'll get tired of it."

"I hope so—but he's a little bit repulsive, Charlie. He's *very* fat and *very* sweaty, and he's got on this outfit."

She didn't need to say any more. Charlie could see it vividly enough. He himself had insisted on having Colonel Popover for the Croker Concourse Caramba, which had been a party with so-called heavy hors d'oeuvres for the entire real estate community and every likely prospect in the business community. The idea was to stir up interest in the tower and the rest of the complex. The heaviest of the heavy hors d'oeuvres were Colonel Popover's specialty, swans sculpted of ice with shelled lobster tails for feathers. The lobster tails were set in ridges in the ice. Cost a fortune; but in Atlanta real estate circles a party just wasn't a party without Colonel Popover's ice swans—and the Colonel himself. The presence of this very round, very fat, and, as luck would have it, very sweaty man in his chef's rig and—what had Marguerite called it? —*toke blonsh?*—was the necessary trademark, telling one and all that this event had been done up as royally as an event could be done up in Metro Atlanta.

And now the fat man—he must have weighed close to 300 pounds

—was sitting out in the waiting room of the Croker Global floor in the same outfit, angry and sweaty. Now he was the trademark of the beginning of the end. God knew what he was likely to say to other visitors in the waiting room. Ought to throw him out, but who was going to do it? Guy was a blob of suet, but he weighed a ton. Not only that, he was altogether right in his complaint. Croker Global had stiffed him.

Charlie looked at the Wiz. "Can't we find $17,000 for this guy? He's not a bad guy."

The Wiz said, "This is what I'm talking about, trying to shift money from one place to the other. Colonel Popover's been on the PC's list."

"PC's?"

"Stands for 'patsies'—'pat-*sies*'—the ones who are in no position to give us a lot of trouble. We hate to give up anybody on that list. But if Colonel Popover has found a way to be truly obnoxious, then we may have to take him off the list." The Wiz looked at Marguerite. "Just let me know."

Charlie said, "Jesus Christ—is Sue Ellen in?" Sue Ellen was the receptionist.

"Yes," said Marguerite.

"Well," said Charlie, "turn the fat man over to her. You got other things to think about. Who's my first appointment?"

"Jerry Lovejoy and some of his people, from VectorCom, at nine."

Jerry Lovejoy and his people did, indeed, arrive at nine. His three people were, like Jerry Lovejoy himself, a bit on the flaccid side. Their jowls rose out of their shirt collars absolutely smoothly and, as is often the case with men not much over forty, in a way that doesn't strike you as fat so much as young and swollen with rich food. Charlie had had Marguerite set things up at a round table in one of his office's conference alcoves, with windows looking out toward Atlanta. He had her make a pot of New Orleans coffee with chicory and warm up some of Uncle Bud's ham biscuits. It was time to do whatever he could to please Jerry Lovejoy, his sidekicks, and VectorCom. It was well known that this aircraft navigation giant was looking for new corporate headquarters, which could mean anywhere from four to eight floors of the Croker Concourse tower.

At first, Jerry and his colleagues had turned down the coffee and the ham biscuits, but pretty soon the warm aromas got them, just as Charlie knew they would. Most men didn't eat enough breakfast. In the case of hungry men like these porkers, the miraculous offer of Uncle Bud's ham biscuits was irresistible.

Jerry Lovejoy had popped a ham biscuit into his cheeks, and hadn't even finished chewing, when he said, "This is great ham, Charlie! Speaking of good food, guess who we ran into out in your waiting room?"

Oh shit, thought Charlie, but all he said was "Who?" The circuits began racing.

"Colonel Popover, the caterer." He flicked a glance that Charlie didn't much like toward one of his people.

Charlie made a big point of looking at his watch. "He's early, sure-'nough. Appointment's not until the middle a the morning."

"Well, he's there, all right, big as life, and he's wearing his outfit—you know, that hat they wear?"

"Aw, that's his trademark," said Charlie.

"I know him—slightly," said Jerry Lovejoy. "We've used him for a couple events—and so I said, 'What brings you to Croker Concourse?' and he says, 'Seventeen thousand dollars.' " He beamed at Charlie.

That fat buttery blob! Charlie had the urge to go out there to the waiting room and throttle—but he made himself focus on the here and now. He put on a big smile and reared back in his chair and said, "Godalmighty. I hope that's not what he's planning to charge us for our open house! We're planning an open house." He made himself chortle. "He's a character, Sal is!"

"That he is," said Jerry Lovejoy, "that he is."

Charlie took a deep breath and tried to swell his chest with confidence, enthusiasm, energy, warmth, and manly charm. "Jerry, how about another ham biscuit?"

"Uhhhmmmmm," said Jerry, who already had a mouthful.

"That ham's cured in a smokehouse on a place a mine down in Baker County. Nothing quite like home-cured ham."

"Uhhhmmmmmm!" Jerry Lovejoy added a smile and arched eyebrows to his picture of cheek-popping gluttony.

Charlie said, "Then I want to show you some space I think will interest you, just three floors below here. Has the same view." He gestured with a sweeping grandeur toward the towers of Atlanta, which from this distance looked like a miniature Oz.

Suddenly he had an overpowering urge to yawn. He had to fight his jaw muscles to keep them from flexing. The effort made his lips expand laterally. He hoped to God the porkers from VectorCom hadn't noticed it.

It wasn't just the insomnia. Every day in this office—events propelled him in *this* direction and then whiplashed him back in *that* direction. One minute he's in a sweat lying to creditors, double-talking creditors, hiding from creditors, and yes, even he, Cap'm Charlie Croker, *beseeching* creditors, beseeching like a drowning dog—and the very next he's got to shift gears, recircuit his whole central nervous system, put on a whole new face, become a big, happy, hearty personification of confidence, omnipotence, charm, and trust, and talk people into leasing millions of dollars' worth of space in a tower that had no business standing up forty stories high out in Cherokee County in the first place.

Charlie rose from his seat. The effort made him slightly light-headed, and his knee hurt. He stood still for a moment to get everything back in focus.

"Let's take the scenic route," he said to Jerry Lovejoy and his jowly sidekicks with a big manly smile. "We'll take the stairs. It's just three stories down, and that way you can get a look at the whole fire system. I'm real proud a how . . . how we built the fire-stair envelope. State a the art."

Not only that, the fire stairs were not in the line of sight of that 300-pound sack fulla suet known as Colonel Popover, the way the elevators were. All Charlie needed was that clown waddling over to expound upon what he had meant by his cryptic "seventeen thousand dollars," and he could once again say goodbye to all prospects for $10 million a year in Uncle Bud–ham-biscuit-buttered-up porky boys' leasing space in Croker Concourse.

Chapter XV

The Rubber Room

IN ALAMEDA COUNTY, CALIFORNIA, AN EAST–WEST FREEWAY, Route 580, separated the town of Pleasanton from the Santa Rita Rehabilitation Center, which sprawled over two square miles of dusty rangeland just to the north. The freeway created such a good barrier that most people in Pleasanton never even thought about Santa Rita, as it was called, except when they saw some young black male walking through town, carrying a clear plastic garbage bag full of personal belongings he had kept in his cell and looking for a bus to the BART station, where he could catch a train back home to Oakland. Why a county jail had to give released convicts clear plastic bags, revealing all their miserable junk, as opposed to bags you couldn't see through, and why they didn't give them a lift to the bus and eliminate all this walking along the streets of Pleasanton, nobody knew. The townspeople seldom complained, however. They reckoned they ought to be thankful that Santa Rita at least gave these ominous hombres tickets out of town.

The freeway cut right through what until not all that long ago, the 1860s, had been a magnificent Spanish finca known as Rancho Santa Rita. The southern part was the richest farmland imaginable, perfect for grapes, plums, apricots, and avocados. The northern part, where the jail now was, ran up into the hills and had been used for grazing horses and cattle. That was the part the U.S. Army had acquired during the Second World War for Camp Parks, a training ground for soldiers heading off to the Pacific. They had slapped together a bunch of clapboard buildings to house the troops.

Today, more than half a century later, on a cloudless, dazzling, sky-blue Sunday in May, drivers speeding by on Route 580 could see that very same huddle of big gray-brown wooden structures squatting on the ground. Anybody might have guessed that here were a bunch of moldering military barracks from a long time ago. What they were not so likely to figure out was that the old barracks had been converted into the Alameda County jail.

Being Sunday, this was visiting day at Santa Rita, and, as usual, in the visitors' area of the jail's West Greystone Building a row of prisoners sat behind some Lexan windows on one side of a concrete wall, and their visitors sat on the other. Lexan was a sandwich of two stout layers of glass with a thick sheet of clear plastic in between. Nothing short of a sledgehammer could break through it. The metal stools the prisoners sat on were bolted to the floor. That way none of them could pick up a stool and assault the Lexan, the deputy at the end of the row, or each other. They all wore short-sleeved pajama-style uniforms, with V-neck tops, made of a coarse cotton twill dyed yellow, and P-ALAMEDA COUNTY JAIL stamped on them. The yellow indicated that the wearer had been convicted of a felony. On their feet were rubber flip-flop sandals with nothing but bands over the insteps to hold them on. The sandals were suitable for walking but not for running or kicking people in the abdomen, groin, knees, or ankles.

Through that concrete wall, through those Lexan windows, you couldn't have heard a sound, not even a scream. The prisoners and the visitors had to converse by telephone. So there they were, inches apart —holding telephones to their ears. They could see each other and they could hear, although the telephones' poor acoustics smothered the high and low tones, but they couldn't touch. It was like being sealed in a tomb with a porthole through which to glimpse some fragment of the living world that existed beyond the grave, or so it seemed to Conrad, who was hunched forward, his nose almost up against the Lexan, petrified, waiting for Jill to come in through the door from outside, afraid that if he missed so much as one second of her visit he could not possibly survive another week in Santa Rita.

The door, a huge wooden thing that slid back like a barn's, was wide-open, creating a rectangle of daylight. He could see the cinders on the ground outside cooking in the sun. He drank in the sight, even though they were nothing but cinders on bare gray dirt in a jail yard. In ten days in Santa Rita this was the first time he had seen any of the world outside at all.

Seated at the window to his right was a young Mexican, perhaps even younger than himself, a big but flaccid boy who was talking to his mother. Conrad couldn't see the mother and couldn't hear her, but he could hear the boy's words gushing out through sobs and his continual chorus of "Oh, Mama . . . Mama . . . Mama." He glanced toward him. The boy's body was convulsing with despair. Tears were rolling down his cheeks and accumulating in beads on the wisps of the pathetic little mustache he was trying to grow. Reflexively, Conrad touched his own mustache—and had his doubts about its making him look the least bit older or tougher.

He didn't dare glance at the inmate to his left. He knew who he was, because everybody in the pod, his section of the jail, knew who he was. He was the most prominent figure you saw in the pod room, or recreation room, the only place inmates congregated at Santa Rita, since there was no outdoor prisoners' yard. His real name was Otto, but he was known as Rotto, after the so-called dude with attitude in the television show *Smoke 'at Mother*. Rotto was white, about thirty, with prodigious upper arms, chest, and shoulders, obviously buffed up, to use the current phrase, by lifting weights during long stays at state penitentiaries, and a wrestler's gut. He had three ugly welted scars on the left side of his face. The bridge of his nose was abnormally thick, as if it had been broken many times. He was almost bald on the top of his head but had grown his hair long on the sides and pulled it back into a greasy, scraggly, sublimely Low Rent ponytail. Three-quarters of the inmates were black. In Conrad's pod Rotto was the shot caller, or faction leader, for an inner core of white toughs known as the Nordic Bund. Rotto was one of the last inmates any new fish would want to make eye contact with, especially a young, slim, good-looking, white new fish (he had learned this demoralizing jailhouse term immediately) like Conrad; for no matter how much you might want to deny it, suppress it, or forget it, the same fear burned day and night in the brain of every white first-time inmate at Santa Rita: *homosexual rape*. Rotto's visitor, whom Conrad couldn't see from where he sat, was apparently a girlfriend, because he kept saying, "Aw, come awn, sugar, you ain' no toss-up. You my bottom lady—my bottom lady!"

This refrain, like the sobs and moans of the Mexican boy, kept bursting through the shell Conrad hoped to create around himself during this precious interval. He wanted to shut out everything else. His very soul depended on what he could see through this window and that barnlike door beyond . . . the sunlight . . . and Jill, who would appear at any moment. The fact that he had been led to this window meant that she was already waiting outside.

His very soul! To Conrad, all twenty-three years of him, *soul* had never been anything more than a word. He had never heard his father or his mother even mention the soul. They had taken one stab at religion, just as they had taken a stab at Oriental diets. Once, for about a week and a half, they had pronounced themselves Buddhists. There had been a lot of talk about karma and kiriya and the dharma and the ten bonds and the five hindrances and the four something-or-others. Above all, there had been a lot of chanting—"Ohmmmmmmmmm, ohmmmmmmmmm, ohmmmmmmmmm, ohmmmmmmmmm"—until, as with so many of their enthusiasms, they wearied of the discipline it required. He had grown up associating religion with the self-delusion and aimlessness of adults. But now he thought about the soul, *his* soul. Or he tried to. But it was only a word! He didn't know how to give it any meaning! He had lost everything, every cent, his freedom, his good name, every shred of the respectability he had struggled toward, even his dreams. What was there left to dream of? And yet there was *something* left, something that caused him to care whether he lived or died and to worry about Jill and Carl and Christy. Perhaps that was his soul. Whatever it was, it was not confined within his body and his mind. It could not exist without . . . *other people* . . . without the only people he had left, his wife and his two children. Other inmates had their children come in on Sundays for visits, but the thought of Carl and Christy seeing him like this, even as small and uncomprehending as they were, was more than Conrad could bear. That left Jill, and he stared at the big door as if the rectangle of sunlight it framed were all that remained of the world.

In the next instant there she was. At first, coming in through the door with the sunlight behind her, she was just a silhouette, but then the overhead fluorescent lighting of the visiting area picked her up as she walked the fifteen or twenty feet to his window. The fluorescence gave everything a washed-out dead-of-the-night look, but Conrad saw a perfect . . . Jill! Her fair white skin! Her long blond hair! Her full lips! Her flowered blouse! Her tiny waist! Her tight jeans over her perfect lithe loins! He drank in every detail as if there had never been anything so perfect as the deity in blue jeans who approached him.

As she sat down opposite him, his heart burst forth. He smiled with a smile that released everything that had been pent up inside him. He started to reach to touch the Lexan, if only to show her how desperately he wanted to embrace her. She smiled back—and he felt a jolt. His mind would have to interpret it later, but his eyes caught it immediately. Her smile was a smile of patience and tolerance. It was her mother's smile.

He picked up his telephone, and she picked up hers. All at once he realized he had no idea what to say. How could he possibly tell her everything? He'd end up like the poor sobbing boy next to him. So what he said was "Did you—did you have any trouble getting here?"

"Not *getting* here." She said it with an exasperated look, which she quickly changed into a smile. This smile was another one whose origins he knew: Patience on a monument, smiling at Grief.

"You had some trouble *here*?"

Jill opened her mouth, then paused, with her lips apart, and changed her mind. "Not really." She sighed. She smiled patiently again. "So how are you, Conrad?"

"I'm okay." His voice sounded so hoarse, it surprised him. His throat felt constricted. "I guess I haven't been sleeping very well. That's the worst thing." He stopped. That wasn't the worst thing, but suddenly, for reasons he couldn't yet comprehend, he felt wary, as if it would be a tactical mistake to come right out and tell her just how desperate, hopeless, and frightened he felt.

Jill stared at him intently, abnormally so, it seemed to Conrad, and then said in a shaky, far-off voice, "You're not sleeping well?"

Conrad shook his head.

Jill tried another smile, but her lower lip began trembling, and tears came into her eyes. She glanced to either side and put her mouth close to the telephone and leaned in toward the Lexan window.

"Conrad," she said in a voice just above a whisper, "what's a 'hubba ho'?"

What's a hubba ho? He was startled. He couldn't have imagined a more unlikely question. "A *hubba ho?*"

"Yes."

"Why? Where'd you hear about a hubba ho?"

Jill put her forefinger to her lips, as if it were important that he keep his voice down, and whispered, "What *is* a hubba ho?"

Baffling! *Hubba ho* was a piece of black street argot, peculiar to Oakland, which he had heard for the first time three nights ago, while in his cell.

"Who'd you hear say that?"

Jill's whisper was so low, he could barely make it out over this crude telephone. "What's it *mean*, Conrad?"

He studied her face. She seemed frightened. "Well," he said, "a ho is a whore, and a hubba ho—you ever see a piece of Hubba Bubba gum?"

She shook her head.

"I bet you have. You just don't remember the name. You know those little pieces of gum? Well, they look like a chunk of crack. The drug."

She nodded. Puzzled, he watched her face. *One visit per week, thirty minutes, and we're talking about hubba ho's!* Nevertheless, he went on. "A hubba ho is a whore who hangs around crack houses—and like, they're addicts. They trade sex for a chunk of crack or a smoke on a crack pipe. Or at least that's what *I* was told." He motioned back over his shoulder to indicate the innards of the jail. "Who told you about a hubba ho?"

Now Jill lifted her shoulders, as if to shield her voice from prying ears. She lowered her head so far, she had to turn her eyes up to look at him. Her irises peeked out from beneath her upper lids.

"I was standing in line out there, Conrad." A quavering whisper. "You've never seen such people. All these—" She broke off and closed her eyes tightly and seemed to be about to cry. "All these—women."

It seemed that just now, while she was standing in line in the jail yard, waiting to enter the building, the woman in front of her had a four-or-five-year-old girl in tow who kept running off to explore the yard. The woman kept yelling at her, to no avail. Finally she ran after her and pulled her back to the line, jerking her arm and shrieking and threatening to hit her. Then she seized her by both shoulders and began shaking her. She shook her so hard, the woman standing behind Jill began screaming at the first woman to stop before she hurt the child.

The first woman turned on her accuser. "You mind your own damn business, you old hubba ho!" She kept repeating this imprecation, *hubba ho*, until the second woman began firing back. "Who you calling a hubba ho, you old fucked-over toss-up!" In no time the slanging match swelled up into a frenzy: *Hubba ho—fucked-over toss-up—hubba ho—fucked-over toss-up!* Jill was shocked, appalled—and caught between the two of them. She wanted to flee, and yet she didn't want to lose her place in line. Finally, the first woman was drowning out her challenger. The furious cry *Hubba ho!* filled the yard, the sky, the cosmos. *Hubba ho! Hubba ho! Hubba ho! Hubba ho!* The two women were about to come to blows when a man in uniform stepped in and told them to quiet down. Jill had been terrified. She was still shaken. With an elaborate dumb show, much motioning of her head and rolling of her eyes, she indicated that the first woman, she who had kept screaming "Hubba ho," was seated to her immediate right. She was the one who had come to visit Rotto.

"Conrad," she said, "who *are* these people!" Her face was twisted with anguish.

Conrad looked at her helplessly. He was stupefied by the turn their conversation had taken. *The minutes were rolling by!*

Finally he said, "I don't know. They're the same people as the ones in here, I guess, except that they're women. Be thankful they weren't the men, that's all I can tell you." Immediately it occurred to him that might sound like a bid for sympathy. And then he wondered why he was so wary of seeking sympathy from his own wife—and he wasn't sure he wanted to know the answer. So he said, "Tell me about Carl and Christy."

"*Carl and Christy?*" She looked at him as if this were an astonishing change of subject.

"Are they okay?"

Long pause. "Yes, they're okay."

He stared at her imploringly, desperate to hear that the children asked about him, talked about him, missed him, loved him, longed for him, even though he also wanted to hear that they were at peace and happy and believed the story they had decided upon, which was that he was off on a trip.

"You might have called," she said.

"Jill—there's two telephones. I can't get near them." He started to tell her about the pod room and the black faction and the Nordic Bund and how they controlled the two public telephones, but he decided not to, on the chance that Rotto might possibly overhear. He pulled the telephone's mouthpiece close to his lips and said, "There may be a few white inmates who can use them, but I'm a—" He started to say "new fish" but thought better of that, too. "—I'm new here, and I can't get near them."

"Well," said Jill, "if you want to know the truth about your children—we're gonna have to move in with my mother, Conrad. You know how wonderful that's gonna be? You know how big her place is? You know how happy—" She broke off. She lowered her eyes. She heaved a big sigh. When she looked up, there were tears in her eyes. "I have no money, Conrad! What am I supposed to do? Live in a duet in Pittsburg next to a bunch of—those people?—and go on welfare? Or you want me to park the children in that *day-care center*?—where all the kids have *strep throat* and impetigo and head lice—and try to get some job that's not gonna pay enough in the first place? You tell me which!"

Conrad was speechless. Tears were rolling down her cheeks, when all at once she glanced to one side in alarm. At that moment Conrad heard a baritone voice rising in volume:

Yeah . . . yeah . . . oh yeah, baby . . . you got it, you got it, you do it, you do it . . . oh, how you do it, sugar . . .

It was Rotto. Conrad risked a glance. The big man held his telephone to his ear with one hand and had the other hand cupped over his groin, while he thrust and swiveled his pelvis as he sat on the stool.

"Conrad!" said Jill. "What is this woman doing!" Her eyes were darting back and forth from Rotto's girlfriend to Conrad's face.

"I don't know," said Conrad, even though he had a pretty good idea.

"She has her legs spread!" whispered Jill, who now ducked her head down very low and leaned forward until her nose was almost up against the window. "And she's . . . *touching* herself and *moaning*!"

Conrad shook his head, as if in consternation. In fact, he now knew for sure. He had already heard about it more than once. It was called beavering. The inmates' girlfriends arrived for the visit wearing miniskirts and no underpants. Then they hiked up the skirts, spread their legs, bared their crotches, and went through the motions of sexual ecstasy.

Jill put her hand over her eyes and shook her head. When she took her hand away, her face was contorted and streaked with tears. She said softly, "I can't stand this."

"Please don't cry. I'm sorry. I don't know what to say."

Bewildered: "What are you *doing* here?"

At first he couldn't figure out what she meant. "*Doing* here?"

Accusingly: "They offered you *probation*!"

"I—we've already been over this a hundred times," said Conrad. All the while he could hear Rotto going *Tuh-unnhh, tuh-unnhhh, tuh-unhhhh . . . Honey pie . . . You the one, you the one, don't stop, don't stop* . . . "How could I plead guilty? I wasn't guilty of anything. They wanted me to plead guilty."

"Yes," said Jill, her eyes wide with dismay and exasperation, "to a misdemeanor!"

"To assault," said Conrad, "but I didn't assault anybody. *They* assaulted *me*. I only kept them from hurting me and destroying our property."

"But you jumped over their fence, Conrad! That was trespassing! After that, anything—" She lowered her eyes and shook her head over the uselessness of rehashing it. When she looked up, she was crying once more. "All right, Conrad, you were totally innocent. So what have you gained by insisting on that? What did you gain by going through a trial? They were willing to give you probation! They were willing to give you a break! I don't understand you!"

Rotto was going, *Do it, sugar, do it, sugar, do it, sugar, do it, sugar, do it, sugar.* Jill's eyes kept darting to one side and back again.

Chastened by her tears, Conrad said softly, "You're right. I didn't gain anything. I didn't think any jury would ever convict me, because I knew, and I still know, I was innocent. But they did, and I lost. I lost a lot. But I kept something, Jill. I kept my honor, and I didn't bargain away my soul."

Incredulous: "Your . . . *soul*? Well, hats off to your soul. We're all very proud of your soul. Did your soul by any chance stop to think about your son and your daughter and your wife?"

"That's all I was thinking about, Jill! When the time comes, I wanna be able to look Carl and Christy in the eye and say, 'I was innocent. I was falsely accused. I refused to compromise with a lie. I went into prison, but I went into prison a man, and I came out of prison a man.' "

A mirthless smile took over Jill's face. She began shaking her head, and then the tears began again.

Rotto was going, *Keep on—keep on—keep on—keep on—keep on, baby, keep on, baby, keep on, baby, keep on, baby, keep on, baby—*

"Please—don't cry," Conrad pleaded over the telephone.

Pleaded; rare, indeed, is the male soul so staunch that it can withstand a woman's tears.

"This is better for them?" Jill said in a pathetic, broken voice. "It's better for their *souls*? It's better that they know you're in jail for felonious assault? Their father's a *convict*? What kind of big favor have you done them, for God's sake?"

Rotto was going *awnnnh—awnnnh—awnhhhh—awnnnnnh—awnnnhhhhh—awnnnnnhhhhhhh—AWNNNNHHHHHHHHHHHHH!*

Conrad lowered his eyes and then hung his head. He felt as if the ground had been cut out from under him. All at once his rationalizations, his principles—his soul—seemed like the emptiest propositions imaginable. His soul—the very idea began to seem like a foolish delusion. His soul, if there was such a thing, was losing its last tie to all that was good and sane. He looked up again at Jill. She was sobbing silently, the telephone still at her ear.

His peripheral vision detected the huge form of Rotto rising up from his stool. Thank God, the man was leaving. He let out a sigh of relief. Then he felt a tap on his shoulder. He looked up. Rotto was looking down at him, smiling. He seemed immense, staring down that way.

"Hi, Conrad," he said. "How you doin', bro?"

A red alert burst forth from somewhere inside Conrad's skull and surged out to the surface of his skin until the very pores of his scalp felt like little fiery craters. He said nothing. He looked away and tried to concentrate on Jill's face. *Hi, Conrad. How you doin', bro?* This man, this brute Rotto, knew his name! How? Why?—or was it all too obvious why! In Santa Rita for only ten days—but long enough to know that the last thing any young inmate in the pod wanted to do was to attract the attention of someone like Rotto!

Conrad kept his gaze fixed on Jill. She was crying, her lips were moving, the sound of her voice was running through the receiver at his ear, but he had completely lost track of what she was saying.

"At least *ask* him, Conrad!" The look on her face was begging him, but begging him to do what? Ask *who*? Something about the lawyer, Mynet, but he had lost the thread. *Hi, Conrad. How you doin', bro?* His heart was racing. He felt feverish. What was it Jill was talking about? Mynet? The lawyer Mynet? Mynet, the lawyer, had gone through his pitiful savings, his last $2,900, like *that,* in a snap of the fingers, and that was all that lawyer Jack Mynet wanted to know about Conrad Hensley.

"*Will* you?" Jill beseeched him.

"I will," said Conrad.

"You don't mean it. You're just saying that."

It was true. He was just saying that. He was so rattled by what the brute Rotto had said, he could barely think of anything else. Finally he said, "Did you get a chance to send the book?"

Jill gave him a puzzled look, an exaggerated expression that seemed to ask, "What's that got to do with what we're talking about?"

"*The Stoics' Game,*" said Conrad. "Did you have any luck?" *The Stoics' Game* was a new novel by a writer of spy thrillers, an Englishman named Lucius Tombs whose work Conrad particularly enjoyed.

Jill sighed. "Yes, I sent it. Or *they* sent it, the bookstore sent it, a *week* ago. *Thirty dollars*, by the way, plus the postage." Jail regulations forbade inmates from receiving books unless bookstores or publishers did the packaging and mailing.

Conrad sensed her exasperation but plowed on: "We just sit in the cell for hours at a time, and then we go to this place, this sort of recreation room, the pod room, and then we just sit *there*. I'm going crazy. You can get books from a sort of bookmobile, but it's all trash." He was conscious of how nervous he had become. *Hi, Conrad. How you doin', bro?*

Jill said, "I sent the book. And you *have* something to do, Conrad. You've *got* to—*talk* to—*Mis*ter Mynet."

Conrad opened his mouth and, instead of speaking, breathed very deeply and nodded yes.

"Please don't just yes me," said Jill. "I don't understand you. I don't know what's happening to us. I talk to my mother about it—and she thinks I shouldn't even wait. I'm gonna *wait,* Conrad, but can't I have some little shred of hope?"

Wait? As opposed to what? he wondered. And then the drift of it dawned on him. In California a felony conviction was automatic grounds for divorce. A sickening feeling came over him.

He tried to smile. "To tell you the honest truth, I don't know. I don't know what hope there is at this point. I made a decision, and it may have been the wrong decision, but I made a decision, and here I am. I honestly don't know what can change that. I love you, I love Carl, I love Christy, and I did what I thought was the honorable thing. There's either some hope in that, or there isn't."

Jill's eyes filled with tears, and her lips and chin began trembling, and then the tears began flowing down her cheeks.

"I'm not trying to get sympathy, Jill. That's all—that's exactly what I feel, and I don't know what else to tell you." He lifted his hand helplessly and then let it fall into his lap.

Jill was still sobbing, soundlessly, when a deputy cut in on the line to tell them time was up. Conrad couldn't believe it. He felt as if two minutes had gone by. All that time spent talking about . . . *hubba ho's!*

Holding the telephone close to his lips, he said to Jill, "Tell Carl and Christy you talked to me, will you?" She nodded. "Tell them I love them very much. Tell them I think about them all the time." She nodded again. He paused and gazed at her not so much longingly as helplessly. "I'll see you next week." He knew the expression on his face had turned it into a question.

She nodded again. She didn't say anything.

Conrad said, "I love you, darling."

Ever so softly Jill said into the telephone, "I love you." Then she hung up the receiver and, still sitting there, stared at him with her lips tightly compressed.

What did they mean, those compressed and despairing lips? What was he to conclude? He brought his fingertips to his lips and threw her a kiss and lifted both hands, still holding the telephone, to show her he would embrace her if he could. She brought her fingertips to her lips, too, but her lips remained compressed. As she turned to go, he had the terrible feeling that he would not see her next Sunday or any Sunday. What future was there but the pod?—where the world shrank until there was no room for speculations about the law, let alone the soul. *Hi, Conrad. How you doin', bro?*

THE OLD BARRACKS at Santa Rita were built like barns, with big, gloomy, dark wooden bays two stories high. The cells were unlike any jail cells Conrad had ever heard of. They were stalls; or perhaps the word was *sties*, since, as on many pig farms, they were made of a dirty beige concrete and plaster. Each cell was about 5 by 9 feet, barely big enough for a double-decker metal bunk, bolted to the floor, and a unit-welded metal toilet-and-basin ensemble. There were no windows, and the door was a solid slab of wood, like a ship's hatch, painted black, with a slot for passing in food. Instead of a ceiling, each cell had a heavy wire screen for a cover. The inmates were like lizards in those boxes or the terrariums children get from pet shops, the ones with the screens over the top. When you looked up through the screen, you saw the underside of a wooden catwalk, where the deputies patrolled, peering down at the creatures below. Somewhere above the catwalks were clerestory windows, for light and air. A few ancient belt-driven attic fans were always grinding and screeching away, but the heat kept pressing down. It never lifted, not even at night.

At this particular moment the screeches of the fans were cutting through the soft, warm soup of a solo by a jazz saxophonist named Grover Washington, piped in over the PA system from an Oakland radio station, KBLX, devoted to classical music and jazz. Whether this was the deputies' idea of soothing the inmates or annoying them, Conrad couldn't figure out. The deputies were all local boys, from the Sheriff's Office, out here in the country, in the Livermore Valley, Okies mostly, but also a few Latinos, whereas the inmates were mainly black youths from the streets of O-town or Bump City, as they referred to Oakland. O-town music the deputies detested and resented; and if they were trying to annoy the homeboys by piping in Grover Washington, they were succeeding.

"Motherfuckin' com*mute* music!"

"Motherfuckin' *weath*er station!"

"What they think this is, a motherfuckin' *el*evator?"

"Ain't these motherfuckers ever heard a the year two motherfuckin' thousand?"

Conrad sure was getting tired of this motherfuckin' word *motherfuckin'*. After ten days it had begun to beat him down. You couldn't get it out of your head. It rained down from everywhere, from that cell—and that cell—and that cell—and that cell—and that cell way over there. Wherever it came from, you were going to hear it, because there was nothing over anybody's cell but a wire screen. In Santa Rita you heard everything. *Motherfuckin'* battered every skull and finally penetrated every brain, and then came out of every mouth, or almost every mouth, the whites', the Latinos', the Asians', even the deputies'. All this O-town talk got to the deputies, too. You'd hear some Okie up on the catwalk sound out to another one: "Yo! Armentrout! Where you at? Wa's up? What's the motherfuckin' matter *now?*"

Conrad sat on the concrete floor of his cell with his back against the wall, his knees drawn up, his arms around his knees, his head down, his eyes closed, letting the whole absurd symphony run through his head, trying to keep out every thought . . . *Buh buh buh buh bubba boooooo uh-oooooooooooooo,* the long soft ripe soupy notes of Grover Washington's saxophone . . . *Scrack scrack scrack scrack scraaaaaaaaccccckkkkkkkk,* the grinding screech of the attic fans . . . *Motherfuckin' motherfuckin' motherfuckin' motherfuckin',* the motherfuckin' chorus of one and all . . . *Thragooooooom thragoooooooom,* the roar of the toilets flushing . . . *Glug glug glug glug glug glug glug,* the sucking noise they made when they finished flushing . . . and then *motherfuckin' motherfuckin' motherfuckin' motherfuckin'* all over again . . .

He kept his eyes closed, because if he opened them, things would only get worse. If he opened them, he would see this tiny, filthy sty, this lizard's cage he was trapped in, and he would see his two cellmates, and he would start thinking again; and if he started thinking again, he would have to face again the horrible possibility that Jill was right, that all his posturing about principles had been nothing but that, posturing . . . that he had ruined his life and hurt those he loved for no other reason than to indulge his obstinate ego . . . in a world in which principles were dead . . . and that his descent into this hole, this Hell on Earth, had been in the name of nothing but vanity and foolishness. *No!* He had done it for his children! It was an example he would hold up to them, proudly, when they were old enough to appreciate what he had done and why he had made such a sacrifice. His eyes closed, he tried to bring Carl's and Christy's faces into his mind, every detail, with utmost vividness, and—he couldn't! All that would appear behind his eyelids were a pair of small, vague, pale, ghostly images. Even Jill, whom he had just laid eyes on, was fading fast. He was losing all three of them, even in his own memory. If Jill failed to visit him next Sunday—and the next Sunday—and the next Sunday—if she divorced him . . . His heart was thrumming. He was abloom with heat and anxiety. The sweat underneath his arms had turned into an oily slick. Gas pains were moving around like a lot of little knives in his bowels. He was aware of the funk of his own body, which was now part of the inescapable odor of Santa Rita—the smell of human beings!—the stench of defeat, frustration, anger, aggression, sexual madness, and, above all, fear. *Hi, Conrad. How you doin', bro?* Thanks to Santa Rita's chronic overcrowding, he was the third and latest inmate stuffed into a cell that, like all the rest, was only barely big enough for two. His cellmates were an Okie called Mutt and a Hawaiian called Five-O. Both seemed to know their way around jails, and both seemed to wish he would disintegrate. He was a useless new fish who understood nothing about anything and who, moreover, as the third man in, was to blame for the overcrowding. The Okie, Mutt, had the bottom bunk, and the Hawaiian, Five-O, had the top bunk, and Conrad slept on a mattress on the floor. His cellmates resented the mattress, too. At night it took up all the space between the bunk and the door and, even then, had to be folded up against one wall, forcing Conrad to sleep with his legs bent. During the day it went under the bottom bunk, leaving him no place to sit but on the floor. Mutt and Five-O didn't want to see the mattress and they didn't want to see him. So he sat on the floor with his eyes closed, hoping against hope that the gas pains didn't cause him to have to get up and have some sort of appalling bowel movement twenty-four inches or so away from these two men, who already resented the mere fact that he existed.

"MOTHERFUCKER, FIVE-O! WHAT THE FUCK'D YOU JES DO?"

The outburst was so sudden and loud, Conrad opened his eyes. Mutt and Five-O were sitting cross-legged on Mutt's lower bunk. Mutt had removed the shirt of his yellow jail uniform, and Five-O was tattooing a three-inch-long picture of an AK-47 assault rifle on his chest, just beneath the hollow where the two halves of his collarbone joined, with a sharpened piece of guitar wire.

"Motherfucker hurt like a *mother*fucker!" said Mutt.

"Bummahs, man," said Five-O. "I only tryeen fo' make da bullet clip, li'dat, ass why."

"Well then, shit, don't make it li'dat!"

" 'Ev, bummahs, man, yeah, but you ever wen spahk da AK-47, da bullet clip, get s'koshi *da* kines?" He described a little curve in the air with his hand.

"Li'dat?" As Conrad had finally figured out, in Five-O's Hawaiian dialect, which was called Pidgin, *spahk* meant *inspect* or *check out, s'koshi* meant *a little bit*, and *da kines* meant *that kind, like that,* or *like you know*.

Mutt was a wiry little man, no more than 140 pounds, if that, with networks of veins protruding on his forearms. He reminded Conrad of Light Bulb, who worked in the freezer unit at Croker Global, except that Mutt had a nervous habit of lowering his eyebrows, over and over, which made him look perpetually angry. On one shoulder he had a tattoo with the legend LIVE TO RIDE, RIDE TO LIVE. Beneath that was a small but extravagantly detailed tattoo of a winged motorcycle ridden by a phantom. On the other shoulder was a tattoo of a death's-head wearing a Nazi officer's cap. These were jailhouse tattoos, artfully done, or artfully enough, but all black and marred by welts of colloidal tissue, where they had become infected and healed over. Tattooing was tolerated at the state penitentiaries but was forbidden at Santa Rita. Mutt and Five-O had solved that problem by sitting on the lower bunk where the deputies couldn't see them from up above on the catwalk.

Conrad judged Mutt to be in his late thirties. Five-O was probably ten years younger. He was heavyset, fleshy rather than muscular, with smooth putty-colored skin, a shock of jet-black hair, and a broad flat nose. His full lips had a stretch of skimpy mustache running above them, but his wide jaws and well-developed chin pulled all the elements of his face together and gave him a strong, rather handsome look. Conrad had watched him draw the AK-47 with a ballpoint pen on a slip of paper. It was a surprisingly sophisticated piece of work. He had applied a waxy film of roll-on deodorant, from the commissary, on Mutt's chest and pressed the drawing onto it. When he peeled the paper away, the drawing of the rifle was transferred to Mutt's skin, and he went to work on it, holding the guitar wire like a lancet and pricking out the design in the little Okie's flesh. His concentration was so intense, his eyebrows seemed to wrap around his nose. Conrad was fascinated. He stared at him.

Five-O stopped, froze, with his hands poised above Mutt's chest, and turned toward Conrad and glowered with the look that says, "What do you think *you're* looking at?" Then he growled, "Boddah you? I owe you money, or wot?"

Mutt turned toward him, too, lowered his eyebrows, squinted accusingly, then turned back and said under his breath, "Shit. Motherfucker."

Conrad shrugged and looked away and closed his eyes again. Despite all their jailhouse bluster, he didn't fear these two men. Mutt, from all he could gather, was a far-gone petty criminal who had been in jails more than he had been out of them and was currently awaiting trial on a charge of dealing in a drug called crank, a form of methedrine. He claimed to be a member of the Nordic Bund, and perhaps he really was, since he was one of the few white inmates able to penetrate the blacks' control of the two telephones in the pod room. But his tough-guy pose had failed to cover up the fact that he was a nervous wreck, plagued by twitches and tics and given to stretches of gloomy silence interrupted by bursts of anger. Five-O was in jail on a charge of forgery, involving credit cards, and not for the first time, apparently. Having a sound instinct for self-preservation, he, like most knowledgeable Asian inmates who could manage it, had hooked up with a Latino gang known as Nuestra Familia.

All such matters of jailhouse manners, mores, and vocabulary Conrad had come to know through Mutt and Five-O's interminable conversations. Cooped up in the cell for hours at a time, they sometimes read books from the bookmobile cart that came around to the pod every two weeks. Mutt was reading a novel called *Berkut*, about the last days of the Third Reich and Hitler's escape and capture by Stalin, which he devoutly believed to be based on fact. Five-O was reading a novel called *Dr. Snow*, about pimps and "their bitches," by a writer named Donald Goines. He kept slapping it down on his bunk and saying, "Wow, bummahs. Wot a junk book." Then he would pick up a tablet of writing paper and a ballpoint pen from the commissary and start drawing stupendously muscular men and women, after the fashion of comic-book superheroes. They were grotesque in their extreme muscularity, and yet the big Hawaiian knew his human anatomy. The gods and goddesses kept pouring out of his fingertips, often in attitudes of violent action, involving complex foreshortening. Mutt would pester him for pornographic creations, and occasionally Five-O would oblige, sending Mutt off into wild cackles of pleasure. And now Five-O was tattooing an AK-47 for him, on his chest, while the two of them continued their verbal chronicle of jailhouse days.

Five-O struck Conrad as a *moke*, which, he had deduced, was Pidgin for an ordinary Low Rent knockabout fellow. He had gotten in trouble here on the mainland and was scuffling to survive in a bad fix known as Santa Rita.

At the moment, as Conrad sat on the floor with his eyes closed, Five-O and Mutt were discussing jailhouse bodybuilding and the problems it was causing currently in the pod room. The only bathing facility in the pod—Five-O said *bafe-ing*—was a lineup of showers on one side of the pod room separated from the rest of the room by a waist-high concrete wall with a narrow opening midway. There was no weight lifting equipment at Santa Rita, and so "buffed-up cons" had taken to standing in the opening and placing one hand on each section of the wall and doing dips, an exercise that pumped up the shoulders, the chest, and the triceps muscles of the arms. The black inmates in the pool outnumbered the white inmates by better than three to one; and their shot caller, a brute named Vastly, who wore his hair in cornrows with tiny yellow ribbons like a jailhouse crown, was even bigger than Rotto. When "the popolos"—black people—were busy doing dips, Five-O observed, no one else could take a shower.

"You try go eenside," he said, "you ass-out."

Ass-out was not Pidgin; it was the universal Santa Rita term for *out of luck.* Conrad was curious as to what Mutt's reaction to this declaration of the jailhouse facts of life would be, and so he parted his eyelids slightly, just enough to see without his cellmates realizing he was looking at them.

"Shit," said Mutt, "any motherfucker tries to keep me out the motherfuckin' shower, I'll show you who's ass-out."

"Yeah, den I hope you get plenny lakas, bruddah." *Get* meant *have; lakas* meant *balls*. "You know dat buggah, Riffraff? Dat buggah wen fo' try cockaroach"—*slip*—"on by one dem beeg popolos fo' go eenside, and chee!—Vastly-dem broke his face fo'im! Dey bus'up dat buggah!" He made a gesture with one hand over the biceps of his other arm to indicate how big the muscles of Vastly'n'them were.

"Fuck doing dips 'n'all'at shit," Mutt said, with infinite disgust. "You wanna know what'll pop all 'ose motherfuckin' *in*flated muscles real fast?"

"Wot?"

"A length a metal, Five-O. Gimme a shank, and I'll go up against any pumped-up ugga-bugga in this whole motherfuckin' jail." He closed his fingers and gave his hand a sudden twisting thrust, as if shoving a knife into someone's solar plexus.

Just then there was a *clack* at the door, the sound of a deputy sliding open the slat that covered the food slot.

"Hensley!"

Conrad looked up. He could see part of the deputy's face peering in. "You got a package." Conrad got up and with a single step was at the door. Through the slot he could see the deputy, a pale, stout Okie with big arms bulging out of his short-sleeved gray uniform blouse. The man was pulling open the zip-strip on a padded manila envelope. He withdrew a book. Conrad barely had time to make out the word *Stoics* on the jacket before the deputy removed the jacket and tucked it under his arm, along with the padded envelope. Then he seized the book's hard front cover with his right hand and, without another word, began shaking it for all he was worth. The pages and the back cover flapped about violently.

Conrad was appalled. The binding would be torn to bits!

The deputy suddenly stopped flailing the thing and looked at Conrad through the slot. "You can have the book, but you can't have this." He nodded toward the hard cover, which he still gripped, holding it up at eye level.

So saying, he seized the pages of the book with his other hand and hunched over and, with a furious grunt, ripped the front cover off and then the spine and then the back cover. When it was all over, his face was red, and he was breathing hard. He held up the remains, a pathetic stack of folios that were coming apart, with clots of glue sprouting all over the place.

"Okay, this is yours." He passed the stricken clump through the slot, and Conrad took it. "Next time, whoever sent you this, you tell 'em you want *paper*backs." Then he walked away.

Conrad stood there for a moment, holding what was left of this grossly violated object. He was shocked. Somehow he had been terribly degraded and humiliated. Such a gratuitous, utterly pointless exercise of power! *My book!*

Still holding the sheaf of paper chest-high, he turned and looked at his two cellmates, halfway expecting some expression of sympathy, despite their obvious resentment of his very existence. Both were watching him from the lower bunk.

"Mother*fuck*er!" said Mutt, but not to Conrad. He was now looking at Five-O. "I'd like to get *my* hands on 'at motherfuckin' book cover. Talk about *shanks*, man . . . It don't have to be metal, long's it'll go in. I learned that the first day I ever spent in jail. I was—" He stopped. He looked off, as if he were gazing into the distance instead of at a filthy beige wall two feet away. Then he glanced at Conrad. Conrad averted his eyes and stepped back toward the wall and sat down on the floor again and looked at the remains of the book, as if he was about to start reading it. Holding the folios together with his left hand, he turned the first page with his right. It was the blank sheet that began the book.

Next came a page with the title; only that, the title: THE STOICS . . . How strange . . . It didn't say THE STOICS' GAME, and STOICS didn't have an apostrophe—

Mutt resumed. "I was just a kid," he told Five-O. "I was seventeen, but I musta looked twelve. I don't reckon I weighted a hunnert'n ten pounds, and they th'ew me in a cell with three a these big buffed-up motherfuckers." He made the same motion over his biceps that Five-O had made in describing Vastly and his retinue.

"T'ree popolos?"

"Naw, they was three white motherfuckers. First thing I know, they jump me, and two a those buffed-up motherfuckers, they hold me down, and the third one—he tries to rape me." He stopped again. Another long pause. "Shit . . . he *did* rape me, Five-O, he *did* rape me. The other two uv'em, they had my arms and legs pinned down, and there wasn't one goddamned thing I could do about it. I was seventeen years old. And then they took a nap, all three uv'em, just like they'd all had 'emselves a nice big meal. Well, one a those motherfuckers had a book just like'*at* motherfucking book *he* got, with the stiff cover, and the front uv'it was prackly tore off the rest uv'it. So I tore it off the rest a the way, quiet as you please, and I started bending that cardboard while they was sleeping, like this here." He pantomimed bending the cardboard back and forth with his hands. "I worked me loose a piece of it about like this here." He made a wedge shape with his forefingers. "Then I started bending 'at piece a cardboard the long way until I had me a double-thick piece like this here." With his fingers he described a long, narrow triangle, the shape of a dagger. "Then I took it around the big end like this here"—he clenched his fingers in the air, as if holding a knife—"and I leaned over that big motherfucker, the one 'at'd had me—and I—so help me, Christ, Five-O—I DROVE 'AT CARDBOARD SHANK RIGHT IN HIS MOTHERFUCKIN' EYE!"

With that he brought his clenched hand down with such ferocity that Five-O drew back on the bunk. Mutt's outcry was so loud, it was no doubt heard in every cell in the pod.

"Chee!" said Five-O. "Wot happen den, bruddah?"

Mutt was now leaning forward on the bunk, his arms and his bare torso rigid. His eyes were blazing with the recollection of that incident long ago. "That motherfucker, he wakes up screamin', and there's blood spoutin' th'oo his fuckin' fingers where he puts 'em over his eye, and he looks up at me with the other eye, and I was glad he could look up and see it was me who done it, because that was the last thing that motherfucker ever got to use his eyes for except to cry his fuckin' guts out, because, Five-O—THEN I DROVE 'AT CARDBOARD SHANK TH'OO 'AT MOTHERFUCKER'S OTHER EYE!"

He brought his hand down again, and Five-O flinched again, and a chorus started up from the cells all around:

"Who's 'at talkin' all 'at eyeball shit?"

"Where's at cardboard J-cat at?"

"Yo! Motherfucker! Shut up or I'm gon' shove 'at cardboard a yo's up Mr. Brown!"

These messages "over the wire," as it was known, riled Mutt up still further, until he was leaning toward Five-O like an animal about to pounce.

"It wasn't nothing but a piece a cardboard off a book, Five-O, but it was the sweetest shank I ever had! Ain't no metalworker in the world ever made a sweeter one! It was sweeter than if I'd *killed* the motherfucker! That motherfucker, if he's still livin', then all he is is one miserable goddamned shufflin' gimp-along gork with poached eggs for eyes—AND FUCK HIM! AIN'T NO MOTHERFUCKER IN NO MOTHERFUCKIN' JAIL EVER TRIED TO FUCK WITH ME AGAIN!"

The chorus swelled up anew:

"Yo! Superman! Kiss my sweet ass!"

"Who's 'at J-cat? Cat got cardboard fo' brains!"

" 'At cat's got a reservation in the Rubber Room, 'at's what *he's* got!" *Heh-heh-hegggggghhhhhhhhhhh!*

The mere memory of the rape had already roused Mutt to a manic intensity. The mockery and laughter of the chorus of black voices now pushed him to the edge. You had only to look at him to see that. He jumped off the bunk and looked up through the screen, his lips parted and his teeth showing, breathing rapidly. You could tell he was about to deliver a message to the world. Which he now did:

"SO DON'T TRY TO TELL ME SOME BUNCHA BUFFED-UP NIGGAS GON' KEEP ME OUT THE SHOWER!"

That did it.

"Hey! Who used the N-word?"

"Who's the motherfucker said that?"

" 'At J-cat motherfucker just used the N-word!"

"Yo! Deputy! Better pack 'at motherfucker off to Wackyville or he's dead meat!"

The cries rose from cells all over the pod. A regular ruckus it was. Conrad no longer pretended to look at the book. He sat upright in a state of alarm. The N-word was the most taboo word at Santa Rita, if you were white.

"Where's 'at J-cat at? What's his motherfuckin' cell number?"

J-cat was the jailhouse lingo for a crazy person. Many Santa Rita inmates were first sent to the state prison facility at Vacaville, up in the Napa Valley, for psychiatric evaluation. The Vacaville designation for psychotics was category "J"; homosexuals were category "B"; and inmates referred to Vacaville as Wackyville and Faggotville. Well—maybe Mutt *was* a candidate for Wackyville. Conrad, sitting tensely on the floor, chanced a look at Five-O. Five-O was sitting on the edge of the bunk, not so close to Mutt any longer. He had put the piece of guitar string down. He looked at Conrad—for the first time with something other than the aloofness of the jailhouse veteran lording it over the new fish. What did Conrad now see?—perhaps even a glimmer of the comradeship of two poor devils thrown together, for they were both thinking the same thing: this wound-up little Okie with half an AK-47 freshly tattooed on his chest had just snapped.

Sure enough, Mutt began raging at his detractors. He threw his head back and screamed up through the screen: "WHO THE FUCK YOU TALKIN' TO, YOU BUNCH A MOTHERFUCKIN' UGGAH-BUGGAHS!" Then he started hopping about like a monkey and scratching his ribs with his fingers and screaming, "UGGAH-BUGGAH! UGGAH-BUGGAH! UGGAH-BUGGAH! UGGAH-BUGGAH!"

The roar of the pod was now deafening.

"Hey! Knock it off down 'eh!" It was one of the deputies leaning over the railing of the catwalk.

From somewhere one inmate's voice rose above all the others: "Tell 'at racist J-cat motherfucker knock it off or he gon' get his cap peeled!"

"Gon' peel yo' cap, motherfucker!"

"Peel yo' cap!"

"Peel yo' cap!"

"Peel yo' cap!"

Kenny! It all came back! On the night Conrad had gotten laid off at Croker Global Foods, Kenny had come barreling into the parking lot with his brand-new red boom-box car thundering out some Country Metal song called "Brain Dead," in which a group called the Pus Casserole kept bawling, "Peel yo' cap, I said—peel yo' cap, I said—peel yo' cap, I said," and Kenny, from his eminence as a man of the world talking to a poor square kid named Conrad Hensley, had informed him this was jailhouse talk. How ironic! How little Kenny actually knew! If Kenny had thought and thought for a thousand years, he couldn't have imagined being penned up like a lizard at Santa Rita, where people threatened to peel each other's caps—with the utmost sincerity!

Mutt stood beside the bunk, looking up through the screen, his teeth clenched, his arms out to the side as if he were ready for a movie cowboy gunfight. He was bare from the waist up. His slim torso was all gristle, nodes, and veins. His eyebrows were flexing up and down at a furious rate. The phantom motorcyclist and the death's-head Nazi on his shoulders took on a crazed reality. The AK-47 emblazoned on his chest looked as demented as he did. Half of it was still in the dull black of Five-O's ballpoint rendering. The other half, the half Five-O had already incised into his skin, stood out in an inflamed red relief. Sweat poured down his face. His half-naked body glistened. He began screaming again:

"SHUT THE FUCK UP! SHUT THE FUCK UP!"

"Easy, brah!" said Five-O. "Cool head main t'ing!" But it was no use.

"SHUT THE FUCK UP!" screamed Mutt. "OR I'M GON' PUTCHOO BACK ON THE SIDE A THE MINUTE RICE BOX, YOU BUNCHA UNCLE BENS!"

The ruckus increased. Someone yelled out, "Motherfucker's dead meat! Dead meat!"

Then it became a chant: "DEAD MEAT! DEAD MEAT! DEAD MEAT! DEAD MEAT!"

Splaaatttt—

—something hit the floor of the cell just inches from where Conrad was sitting. Right there—a runny yellowish gooey mess. The smell of urine rose up, that and a high sweet smell besides. He jumped up before the pool could spread. Above him a long viscous string of goo hung from the screen, gradually lengthening, thanks to its own weight. Bombardment! From an adjoining cell! The pizzooka! The pizzooka was part of the perverse weaponry of Santa Rita. Inmates urinated into plastic shampoo tubes from the commissary, poured in syrup saved up from the morning servings of pancakes, shook it all up, screwed the tops back on, got on the top bunks, and squeezed the tubes to propel the noxious mixture up over the cell walls.

Mutt stared at the mess on the floor for a moment, then leaped past Conrad. When he reached the door, he gave it a terrific kick, like a karate kick, with the heel and the sole of his foot. This was a way inmates commonly expressed dissatisfaction. He stopped, stared at the lower part of the door, then began kicking it repeatedly: BANG BANG BANG BANG BANG BANG.

"Yo! Simms! Was a matter wit chew?" It was one of the Okie deputies, yelling down from the catwalk. "What the hell you think you're doing?"

Without looking up, still facing the door, Mutt said, "I want some crank!"

The deputy said, "You want some *crank*?"

"Gimme some crank, goddamn it!"

"Guess what, Simms—you're ass-out!"

A chorus of catcalls and laughter from the other cells. Mutt's face became contorted with rage.

"I SAID I WANT SOME CRANK!"

Someone yelled, "You can crank my johnson, Dead Meat!" Raucous laughter.

The deputy yelled, "Yo! Simms! Look at me!"

Mutt looked up through the screen, and so did Conrad and Five-O, who had now gotten up off the bunk. They could make out the deputy leaning way over the catwalk railing and looking down at them. "Chill down, Simms," he said. Then he lowered his arm over the railing until his hand was at the level of his groin. He curled his fingers and extended his thumb and began jiggling his hand in the male semaphore that means "Go masturbate."

Apoplectic with rage, Mutt extended his arm and his middle finger toward the deputy, then wheeled about toward the door and began kicking it even more furiously than before: BANG BANG BANG BANG BANG BANG BANG BANG BANG.

The deputy yelled, "Cut that shit out, Simms! That's an order!"

Mutt didn't cut it out. "FUCK YOU!" He was hammering away at the door with his heel.

Another voice from the catwalk, a deeper voice: "Goddamn it, Simms! Cut it out! You want Michael Jackson come gitchoo?"

Heh-heh-hehhhhggggghhhhhhh! That got a big rise out of the chorus over the wire.

"FUCK YOU!" screamed Mutt to one and all.

" 'Ey, Mutt!" said Five-O. "Easy, brah! Cool head main t'ing. Laydahs fo' da Michael Jackson, da kine."

But Mutt was long past cooling down and taking advice. He was in a frenzy, a rage, which the catcalls from all over the pod only made worse.

Conrad and Five-O had both gravitated toward the other end of the cell, near the toilet and the basin. Presently they could hear the *clack* of wooden slats being slid shut over the slots in the doors. Only the deputies, outside the cell, could open or close the slats. They always closed them when they had to remove an inmate forcibly, so that the other inmates couldn't look out and watch. The *clacks* came closer and closer, and you could hear the sound of a whole group of men speaking in low voices. Mutt stopped kicking the door. Now he just stared at it, but he kept jerking his shoulders and elbows about. Then you could see a pair of eyes at the slot, and a deep Okie voice said, "Okay, Mutt, I'm gonna open this door, and I want you to walk on out like a nice fella."

"Fuck you. You don't call me Mutt. You don't *know me*. You ain't no friend a mine."

"Okay, Mutt, you can be Mutt or you can be Mr. Simms, but I'm gonna open this door, and I want you to come on outta there peaceful, like a good fella. Otherwise, you're Mr. Ass-out."

"Fuck you."

"I don't wanna have to bring Michael Jackson in 'eh, Mutt."

Mutt's response to that was to lunge toward the door and spit through the slot. "*Shit!* Cocksucker," said the deep voice. *Clack!*—someone slammed the slat across, closing the slot. The deep voice now came over the door and through the screen: "Always gotta be the hard way, hunh, Mutt?"

Then silence. All three of them, Mutt, Five-O, and Conrad, stared at the door. The cell doors at Santa Rita opened outward and had no handles on the inside, so that the inmates couldn't prevent the deputies from opening them. The entire pod was abnormally quiet. The inmates, or most of them, were confused as to their allegiance. Ordinarily they were on the side of any other inmate in a set-to with the deputies, and all the more so when the issue finally boiled down to brute force. But

Mutt was the J-cat who had used the N-word. The fans overhead went *scrack scrack scrack scraaaacccckkkkkk.* Grover Washington's saxophone went *buhoooomuhoooooooom.* Conrad's eyes were pinned on the black door.

Suddenly it swung open, revealing a whole gang of deputies in their short-sleeved gray shirts and navy pants. The lead man held a clear plastic riot shield in front of him and had a billy club in his other hand. He was the Okie named Armentrout, and he was the most imposing of the deputies who regularly worked the pod. The short sleeves of his uniform blouse, which had obviously been hemmed still shorter, revealed the sort of massive arms that can come only through weight lifting. His was the deep voice they had already heard, and now that voice said:

"Give it up, Mutt, and come on outta there. Use your head. We won't lay a hand on you, long's you use your fuckin' bean."

Mutt, who was in a crouch, stepped back and then seemed to relax. Nonchalantly he leaned against the wall at the end of the bunk and folded his arms and bent one knee and propped his foot up on the wall as well.

"Good man, Mutt," said the deputy. "Now just stay cool."

Slouching still farther, Mutt lowered his head and eyed the deputy dubiously, but with no great concern, the way you might check out a stray dog that happened to be walking by. For a few seconds it was a Mexican standoff, with the adversaries looking each other in the eye and doing nothing about it. Behind Armentrout and his shield and his club was another deputy, a lean, rangy Okie with a rubber glove on his right hand. It was a great ugly thick black thing that came all the way up to his elbow. And in that instant Conrad got it: that must be the "Michael Jackson," named for the singer whose trademark was a single glove. The rest of the deputies were bunched in the doorway. The cell was too small and crowded for them all to come inside at once.

Armentrout took a step forward, his shield before him—

—and suddenly, more suddenly than Conrad would have thought humanly possible, Mutt sprang off the wall with a kick, the same karate-style kick he had been giving the door. It caught the shield on one edge, spinning the deputy around and knocking him off balance. Mutt was on top of him, in too close for the big man to use either his club or his shield, and he drove his right forearm into the deputy's face and his left forearm into the side of his head, across the ear. Stunned, Armentrout staggered, slipped on the pizzooka mess, and fell. Blood was streaming out of his nose. Mutt was on top of him. The rangy deputy leaped forward on top of Mutt and clamped his huge gloved hand on Mutt's upper left arm. Mutt's body stiffened. There was a smell of burning flesh. His arm and his shoulder began convulsing; and then his entire body. His eyes rolled back into his head, and his mouth opened, and his tongue filled his mouth like a big fish. He looked like someone having an epileptic seizure. He was sprawled on the floor, on his back, shuddering. His head kept clattering against the metal leg of the bunk. The inflamed red half-an-AK-47 on his chest stood out redder, more feverish, more grotesque than ever.

The big deputy, Armentrout, managed to regain his feet. He still had a compulsive grip on his club and his shield. His face was a stream of blood, from the nose down, and his nose was swelling up. It looked as if someone had taken a wide paintbrush and stuck it under his nose and painted a swath of red straight down over his chin. There was blood on his blouse and on his chest and chest hair where the blouse was open at the top.

"Oh, you little cocksucker," he said, and he lifted the club and bent over as if to smash Mutt in the head. But two more deputies squeezed through the door and restrained his arm. "Goddamn it, Armie! Motherfucker's out cold!"

The rangy deputy released his grip with the rubber glove on Mutt's upper arm. Conrad could see now that there were two metal prongs sticking out of the palm. However they managed to store it up in the contraption, it had a tremendous electrical charge. Mutt's body was still convulsing and struggling to take in air. The smell of burnt flesh was sickening.

They hog-tied Mutt's wrists together behind his back with plastic cinches, and then they hog-tied his ankles together the same way, and then they ran a length of plastic from his wrists to his ankles, so that he wasn't going to hit or kick a living soul if and when he came to. By the time they carried him out, he had grown still. He appeared shrunken. He was so limp and fragile, it was hard to imagine the rage and animal strength that had exploded out of that little creature just a few minutes earlier.

The last deputy out of the cell was Armentrout, who now had a handkerchief pressed against his streaming nose. The handkerchief was soaking red, and there was more blood on the back of his right hand and forearm, from where he had first tried to wipe it away from his nose and mouth. Conrad and Five-O couldn't keep their eyes off it. Armentrout must have detected that, because he stopped and stared them down until they looked away.

Then he took the handkerchief from his mouth, and, through that mad-dog crimson orifice, in his deepest voice, soaked through with threat, he said, "Shit removal's free a charge around here. Have a nice day."

Then he slammed the door shut and locked it.

Conrad looked at Five-O. Five-O arched his eyebrows and opened his eyes wide and twisted his lips into a half-smile and began nodding his head slightly, in the way that says, "Wow! Astounding! What is one to make of all that?" To Conrad the man's expression offered hope. Perhaps this big Hawaiian would now stop freezing him out. Perhaps he might even have a cellmate he could talk to. For that reason, not because he had any interest in the answer, he asked, "Where they taking him?" He motioned his head in the general direction of the departed Mutt.

"From now," said Five-O, "Armentrout-dem going broke his face, if I know dem. Den dey goin t'row 'im in da Rubber Room."

"The Rubber Room?"

"Get rubber walls, get rubber floor, li'dat, fo'da crazy people. No mo' blankets, no mo' baferoom, no mo' basin, no mo' notting. Ass why hard, bruddah. Da Rubber Room stay nails."

Conrad could feel a strange wave spreading through his central nervous system, and he could hear a sound like rushing steam inside his skull. It was the rush of madness, the incorrigible madness of this place. He had just witnessed something horrible. Before his very eyes, barely an arm's length away, a tormented little man had lost his mind and turned into a cornered beast. Then they had attacked and reduced him to a grisly, spastic, convulsive length of live meat burning in the throes of neurons gone amok and hauled his shriveled carcass off to some madhouse called the Rubber Room. And yet that was the least of it, wasn't it . . . There was something much worse . . . His mind fought against sorting it all out and letting it up to the surface, but the wave was irresistible, and he already *knew* the source of his terror. Live meat!—to be devoured! And now he stared the terror right in its filthy face. Mutt Simms!—the reduction of that little Okie to such a pitiful state had begun with a homosexual rape in a county jail when he was seventeen years old, not all that much younger than he, Conrad, was now. *Such things did happen!* In an hour they would be turned out of their cells and into the pod room, where all the mad creatures were thrown together and it was every man for himself. *Dead meat! Dead meat! Dead meat! Dead meat! Hi, Conrad. How you doin', bro?*

Chapter XVI

Gotcha Back

AT ABOUT 7:15 P.M., WITH SERENA IN THE PASSENGER SEAT, Charlie drove the Ferrari up the slope of the Piedmont Driving Club's driveway and stopped under the porte cochere, muttering imprecations about Serena and anybody else who might have had anything to do with this useless fucking evening, which was called the Mayflies Ball. Why did he have to put on a tuxedo and leave home and have dinner with the likes of Tilton and Elaine Lundeen and Freddy and Whatthehell'shiswife'sname Birdwell and that kid Perkins Knox, who was old Governor Knox's nephew, and Whathehell's*her*name and Slim and Whateveritis Tucker, who Serena thought were such a great catch—and pay for it? *Pay* for it! He had reached that stage of depression in which going out in public seems fraught with the danger of exposing the sorriness of your sorry fucking self to the entire world.

On top of that, his right knee was aching so much, just putting on the brakes was a killer. He had even thought of having Serena drive, but that meant that when they arrived here under the porte cochere, he would have to come teetering out of the car in full view of the club members going in or out of the main door. Poor old bastard has to have his young wife drive for him . . . How old *is* he, anyhow? . . . This way only the parking attendants would notice the old man with the rusting joint, and what difference did they make?

Actually they did make a difference. The egotism of the male of the species is such that he is embarrassed to let another male get an eyeful of his infirmities, no matter who it is. Charlie's plan for exiting the driver's seat was to plant his left foot on the driveway pavement and then thrust himself upright with his arms, so that when he dragged his right leg out of the car his weight would be fully supported by his left leg and his sound left knee. But when he tried to thrust himself up, he didn't make it and went keeling over backward onto the seat.

"Cap'm Charlie—"

Don't need *anybody's fucking help!*

"Cap'm Charlie—"

Stop fucking hovering *over me!*

This time he pulled himself upright by planting his left foot and then grabbing the door frame with both hands. Took forever . . . plus a lot of trembling of his right arm and shoulder, but he was standing and prepared to go gimping into the Piedmont Driving Club.

"Cap'm Charlie," the parking captain, whose name was Gillette, said once more, "let me give you a hand!"

Two parking attendants, younger black men, were looking on impassively and no doubt thinking, *These old crocks with their Ferraris and their money* . . .

"Thanks anyway, Gillette," said Charlie. "Just don't take up football, Gillette. It always racks you up in the end." It seemed supremely important to let Gillette know that it wasn't age or plain old arthritis that had done this to his knee. It was football, which qualified it as an honorable wound of war.

"I don't speck I will, Cap'm Charlie," said Gillette, shaking his head and smiling and chortling, as if Charlie had delivered one of the funniest lines he had ever heard here at the portals of the Piedmont Driving Club.

Gillette made Charlie feel marginally better. *Cap'm Charlie* . . . Charlie couldn't even figure out how the employees here at the club had ever learned that he was called Cap'm Charlie down at Turpmtine. But they had, and Cap'm Charlie he was. But then his spirits fell all over again. What if . . . *the word* . . . concerning Cap'm Charlie Croker gets out to everybody, to all the world . . . *The bank seized his airplane!* . . . Who would feel like calling him Cap'm Charlie Croker then?

Charlie went limping around the front of the car (not the back, where the lights of the car behind him would illuminate his decrepit old carcass for one and all) and caught up with Serena, who was patiently waiting near the door.

The doorman, Gates—Charlie had never known whether Gates was his first name or his last name—said, "Evening, Cap'm Charlie. Evening, Miz Croker."

"Evening, Gates." And thank you for not offering to fucking carry me over the threshold or otherwise calling attention to my fucking knee.

"Charlie," said Serena, taking his arm as they entered the club, "are you sure you're all right? I've never seen your knee flare up this bad before."

Testily: "I'm fine." And thanks so much for making sure I couldn't fucking set foot inside the club without being reminded of my knee. Which, by the way, is a football injury, not arthritis, for your fucking information.

"Why don't you go see Emmo Nuchols again?"

"I don't *need* to see Emmo Nuchols again. I know exactly what he'll tell me. I need a knee replacement. I don't *want* a plastic knee."

"Well—it's up to you."

Thanks, thanks a lot. And thanks for forcing this stupid evening on me. I really am going to enjoy an evening with some of "the younger crowd," aren't I . . . That was one of Serena's . . . *themes* . . . It was necessary to keep in touch with "the younger crowd" in order to stay current on the ideas that were circulating. Too bad, sister, you knew how old I was when you married me. Besides, Freddy Birdwell and Tilton Lundeen—Christ, they're children! I doubt that either one of them's forty yet. I know their goddamn parents! I know their parents a whole lot better than I know *them*. Ike Birdwell's son and Tilty Lundeen's son . . . saw them when they were still wearing seersucker sunsuits and playing in the sandbox . . . They're going to have to fight the impulse to call me *Mr. Croker* . . . Mutter mutter mutter mutter . . .

As a piece of architecture the Driving Club was one surprise after another. Visually it unfolded like the chambers of a nautilus. Because of its position on a hill, it was impossible to grasp the size of the place as you drove up. Neither the porte cochere nor the main entrance was very imposing. The rough stone of which the porte cochere was made gave it a rustic rather than a grand look. The main entrance opened into a hallway of adequate but by no means elegant proportions. The surprises lay beyond. The original building, back in 1887, had been a farmhouse—with rusticated brick and stone. Since then the club had burned down three times and been rebuilt and enlarged three times and expanded some more in flush times, so that it had rambled on across the hillside in stages. Some of the grandest parts of the interior, such as the lobby and the ballroom, bore the signature of the most hallowed name in Atlanta architecture, Philip Shutze. The members loved the fact that the club and the building had such a rich archaeological history. In Atlanta anything that dated as far back as 1887 was ancient.

Up ahead, in the lobby, in a cackling throng of black tuxedos, white shirts, and party dresses, he could already see Lettie Withers, Ted Nashford, and Live-in Lydia—what the hell was club policy toward Live-in Lydia?—a guest fee anytime she set foot in the place?—and Beauchamp Knox and Lenore—if even *one* of them brought up the subject of the G-5 and its "arrest," he was going to drive his—and maybe her—teeth down her gullet—or else go out and find a rock to crawl under . . . His face was already *scalding* with shame and nobody had even seen him yet, much less said anything.

This was a big night at the club. The ecstatic cries of the crowd in the lobby, the straining voices and constant yawps of laughter, made it seem as if nothing could be more rapturous than being together in this place beneath such a high ceiling and so many of Maestro Shutze's intricate moldings. If he hadn't had eight guests, plus Serena, dependent on his generosity, he'd leave right now. Why did people want to belong to the Driving Club in the first place? Everybody said that the day when the Driving Club had been the center of the most important network in the city was long gone . . . that the Atlanta definition of an aristocrat was someone whose parents knew the doorman at the Driving Club by name, too . . . that the club was filled with old people who didn't mean much one way or the other . . . and yet, much as he might want to, nobody could convince himself that that was actually true . . . You might have the grandest house in all of Buckhead and the summer place on Sea Island and the biggest private jet and the ranch or two in Wyoming, every toy a man could possibly long for—and yet your failure to make the roster of the Piedmont Driving Club would always be hanging over you, like a reproach. The mere fact that it was . . . *there* . . . that it . . . *existed* . . . was a challenge you didn't know how to meet . . .

Charlie knew very well, when he was being honest with himself, that if it hadn't been for Martha, he would have never gotten in. Martha was from Richmond, and in Atlanta things *Richmond* (like things *New York*, when it came to the arts) had *authenticity*. Charlie kept telling himself that he couldn't care less about the Driving Club one way or the other; but had he been excluded, his Hard Cracker resentment would have known no bounds. It was the very fact that it was . . . *there* . . . that mattered so terribly much.

Well, one thing you had to admit, anyway. The Driving Club was the one place you could go in Atlanta and count on hearing real Southern accents. Other places . . . Christ, you never knew. Suddenly the face and the voice of this guy Zale at PlannersBanc popped into his mind—the guy must be from New Jersey or someplace—and he was sorry he'd ever thought about the subject.

Now they were in the lobby, amid all the fancy Shutze plasterwork. Lettie Withers came braying over to him with her cigarette-baritone voice—and was discreet enough to say nothing about the G-5. Serena had veered off to talk to Lydia, who was young enough to wear a short black silk-and-chiffon outfit that invited you to take a long look at her Live-in body. Gibble gabble cackle cackle gibble gabble cackle cackle —there was Arthur Lomprey, the president of PlannersBanc, whom you couldn't miss because he was so tall and his neck and head were bent forward like a dog's, and Charlie wondered if the old bastard was going to give him some grief over his loan situation, but then he realized Lomprey wouldn't have the nerve to do that in the lobby of the Piedmont Driving Club at the Mayflies Ball, which he didn't. They gobble-gobbled for a little while, and then Charlie noticed Serena on the other side of the lobby whispering something in the ear of . . . Elizabeth Armholster! Elizabeth wore the sort of party gown that the young crowd favored currently, a simple black number with spaghetti straps and a plunging neckline. Whatever Serena was saying to her, Elizabeth was beaming. They looked every bit as conspiratorial as they had at Turpmtine. Elizabeth Armholster. There she was, big as life. She didn't look like some traumatized and ravished wreck of a girl to Charlie. If Elizabeth was here, where was . . . and then Charlie saw him, that squat, round figure himself, Inman Armholster. Inman was deep in conversation with Westmoreland (Westy) Voyles, who used to be chairman of the board at Georgia Tech. Charlie kept staring. He stared at the roll of fat that rode up on the back of the stiff collar of Inman's formal shirt. He really didn't want to have to talk to Inman. Should he pretend he didn't know about Elizabeth, which in fact he wasn't supposed to? Should he keep it light—all the while knowing how Inman must feel? He was staring at the roll of fat on Inman's neck and considering these things, when suddenly Inman turned around. Charlie turned away, in hopes that Inman wouldn't notice him. Then he slowly rotated his eyes back toward Inman, to make sure Inman had turned his attention elsewhere, and . . . *caught!* . . . *nailed!* . . . Inman was looking him right in the eye. The collar of his tuxedo shirt was obviously too tight, which made him look even more apoplectic than usual. That round head with its tarmac of black hair combed back over it . . . *had* him . . . There was no turning away a second time. Now that he had him, Inman lifted the fat fingers of his right hand and beckoned him over, all with a morose look on his face, without smiling for so much as an instant. Charlie managed to maneuver his way around several knots of people who were in the way, and by the time he reached Inman, Westy Voyle had departed.

"Hey, Inman," said Charlie, trying out a smile.

Inman didn't bother with a smile or any other preliminary. He glowered and said in his deepest cigarette voice, "You *know*, don't you."

"Know what?" said Charlie, already feeling like a fool.

"About Elizabeth," said the deep rumble of the furious fat man in front of him.

Charlie's mouth opened, but he had no idea what to say. Finally he said, "That's true, Inman. I do."

"Who told you?"

"What made you so sure I knew?"

"The look on your face, Charlie. You're not a hard guy to read, in case you don't know it. You did *not* want to have to talk to me tonight, did you?"

"Well . . . shit," said Charlie. "I knew about it, and yet I wasn't supposed to know about it. I didn't know what to say."

"Okay," said Inman, "so now you know I know you know. That being the case, there's some more I want you to know." He looked about at the crowd here in the lobby. By now there were people on all sides. Over there was Howell Hendricks with his smooth buttered jowls rising smartly out of the stiff, black-tied collar of his shirt. His grinning mouth had more teeth than a perch's. "Let's go to the ballroom, Charlie. There won't be anybody down there yet."

Charlie looked about, trying to spot Serena. There she was, heading into the Bamboo Room with Elizabeth Armholster. Ordinarily, except for a big occasion like the Mayflies Ball, dinner was served in the Bamboo Room, which had been added in 1938 after yet another fire. Why the hell were Serena and Elizabeth Armholster going off by themselves?

Inman and Charlie managed to extricate themselves from the lobby, but only after a lot of handshakes and social grins. Charlie found it all very depressing. The whole time he had his eyes cocked to catch people who were looking at him and thinking . . . or saying . . . "The big sonofabitch, after all his big talk and egotistical plans, he's finished! Belly-up! PlannersBanc just took his G-5 away from him! He's a walking dead man! A ghost—and how pathetic! He dares show his face here!"

Eventually they made their way to the ballroom, where there was no one except for a few black waiters making last-minute fine tunings of the table settings for the dinner. The ballroom was Philip Shutze's crowning touch at the Piedmont Driving Club. It was immense. It had a vaulted ceiling and two majestic colonnades, complete with arches, cornices, and plaster garlands running down either side of the room, the long way. The tables, ablaze with hotel silver and acres of stemware, were arranged in front of and behind the columns on both sides, leaving the center of the great parqueted floor free for dancing.

Inman gestured to show Charlie they should take chairs at a table in the corner. So they sat down. That was a mistake. Sitting down made Charlie feel so damned sleepy. He never slept anymore, but as long as he stayed on his feet, he was all right.

Inman said, "I haven't seen your knee flare up this bad before, Charlie."

"That's the one thing I regret about playing football for Tech," said Charlie. Even though Inman knew it was football, not age, damnit, he felt as if he had to underline the fact.

Inman gazed off into the distance and said, "Football at Tech . . ." Then he looked at Charlie and said in his smoke-cured voice, "I've told myself any number of times to talk to you about what's happened—*especially* because you played football at Tech. In your day you were even more famous than this black sonofabitch."

"Inman, if there's anything I can do for you, all you got to do is name it."

"Thanks, Charlie," said Inman, who suddenly seemed to be on the verge of tears. "I can't tell you what that means to me." Then he took a deep breath and sighed and looked about the ballroom, as if to make sure none of the waiters were close enough to overhear, and said, "I can't figure out what to do, Charlie. Here's the facts—here's what happened, and maybe you can tell me what to do. This was the Friday night of the Freaknik weekend. You remember that weekend?"

"Yeah."

"I had a hysterical girl on my hands, Charlie. She'd just gone through the worst nightmare a girl can imagine."

"What *did* happen? Bi—I didn't get any details."

Inman said, "There's this stuff all the universities try to cram down the throats of their students about 'diversity' and 'equality' and 'multiculturalism'—but don't let me get off on all that. You know what it is, Charlie? It's bullshit. It's—well, anyway, there's this restaurant near the campus called the Wreck Room. It's popular with the students because it's popular with the big-time athletes, which is synonymous with *black* athletes. So it's about eleven o'clock at night, and Elizabeth and two of her friends, two white girls, are in there having a pizza or something, and in comes this sonofabitch Fanon and three or four of his hangers-on, you know? This . . . shitbird . . . is the most famous person at Tech. More kids recognize him than the President, probably. Anyway, he and his friends sat down in a booth right across from Elizabeth and her friends. The first thing Elizabeth knows, this Fanon and his boys are coming on to them. Elizabeth—she and her friends think it's harmless. That's what I mean about all this diversity, multiculturalism, equality bullshit, Charlie. In years gone by, and not all that long ago, either, if three white girls from good families, or even respectable families, never mind 'good,' if three white girls happened to be in a restaurant in Atlanta, Georgia, and a bunch a niggers happened to sit in a booth across from them and start making comments, no matter how harmless they might sound, those girls would refuse to respond and, if it kept up, they'd leave. That's right, that's the word, *niggers*. It's not a word I use, and I got nothing whatsoever against black people. I've known 'em all my life, and there's plenty of black people wouldn't even make me think of the word *nigger*; André Fleet is one, and, for that matter, Wesley Dobbs Jordan is another. They're gentlemen. I never use that word. But there's a certain type of black person who's a nigger, and nothing's gonna change that. But these white students nowadays can't see that. Or if they do, they've got no vocabulary for it." Inman shook his head so hard his sloshing jowls lagged behind his chin. "So they get brainwashed by all the stuff they're hearing from teachers, from visiting lecturers, from the administration, from all the bullshit artists on television—they get brainwashed to the point where it's gross bad manners to not respond to the likes of Fareek Fanon. So when he invites them to come up for a Freaknik party, they're so brain-damaged by all this liberal bullshit, they accept. Yeah! The Friday night of Freaknik, 11 p.m., and they accept the invitation! That's how much brain damage they got!"

"Did you say he invited them to 'come up' for a party?" asked Charlie.

"Yeah. It turns out that in addition to a dorm room this creep has a two-bedroom apartment not even half a block from this place, the Wreck Room. Who pays for it, I don't know, but I'd like to know, that fucking vine-swinger. He's gonna—"

Inman suddenly shut up. A black waiter was approaching the next table to add some silverware. Inman looked at Charlie and gave him a smile that so quickly turned down on one side, it became a grimace.

As soon as the waiter departed, Inman said, "So anyway, Elizabeth and the other two girls go on up there with this bastard, thinking that there's some big Freaknik party in progress, and they're gonna be *enlightened*. It's all in the name of *enlightenment* and *equality* and all that shit, when her instinct shoulda been 'Let's get outta here. This guy has trouble written all over him.' So anyway, they go up to this apartment, and instead of a big party there's nobody. Fanon says, 'Well, now we *do* have a party, don't we.' The girls, they don't hear any warning bells. How could they? They've been addled by *enlightenment* and *diversity*. They even had a couple of drinks. Meantime, this sonofabitch Fanon is paying Elizabeth a lot of attention, and she's flattered, because, A, here's this famous football player, maybe the most famous college player in the country, and B, she's *enlightened*! She thinks she's doing the right thing! So when he says something about another room, she thinks he wants to show her the rest of the apartment. The next thing she knows, she's in the sonofabitch's bedroom. And that's when he—forces himself on her. That's what he was doing when Elizabeth's two friends walked in. They were getting a little edgy, and they were looking for Elizabeth to see about going home."

"So you've got two witnesses!"

"I thought I did. But now they won't say a thing. Those girls are afraid of something. I don't know what. They swear they haven't been threatened—but if you've been threatened and you're scared to death, then what you say is 'I *haven't* been threatened.' So I don't know."

"How's Elizabeth taking it?" asked Charlie.

"Oh my God," said Inman, "at first she was desolate. Desolate! She was afraid to leave the house. She made me promise not to tell anybody about it, least of all the police or anybody at Tech. Just to have her name come out in any sexual connection to that . . . animal . . . the idea makes her feel completely filthy. But at least she's gotten enough of her old self back to go out in public and go through the motions and put on a brave smile. Thank God for that much at least."

"So what are you doing in the meantime?"

"I'm trying to get certain things lined up for the day when she has the courage to go to the police. I've assured her that the press wouldn't print her name anyway. Iddn'at right?"

"Always has been, seems to me," said Charlie.

"I wanna be ready," said Inman. "I've got two investigators, used to be detectives on the Atlanta police force, back before the chief of police was black or a woman or a black woman or whatnot, and they're going through that sonofabitch's background and his financial situation and what the hell he's doing with his own apartment downtown, and everything else. I got nothing against Georgia Tech, Charlie, but I'm gonna blow their big nigger outta the fucking water or die trying. I'll do whatever it takes."

"Charlie! Charlie!"

It was Serena, who had just entered the ballroom. Then she saw him and Inman. "Charlie, I couldn't imagine where you'd gone to."

Inman stood up, to be polite. So Charlie followed suit, even though it hurt his goddamned knee to do so. Before she reached them, Charlie turned toward Inman and said, "I know exactly how you feel." Then he held out his hand and looked Inman in the eye and said, "Inman, you can count on me a hundred percent. Anything I can do for you at Tech or anywhere else, you just tell me." They gave each other the kind of handshake that's just short of a blood oath.

Now here came Serena. For an instant Charlie saw her just the way he had seen her when he first entered the art seminar room at PlannersBanc . . . way back when . . . a simple black dress with a sort of scoop-out in the front and tiny straps over her shoulders . . . the pale skin . . . the wild mane of black hair, only slightly contained . . . the blue eyes so vivid they were startling . . . the playful lips that always seemed to be smiling over a secret . . .

"Inman," she said, "I've just had such a good time talking to your daughter! She's so lovely and so much fun!"

"Thank you," said Inman. "Her daddy kind of feels a little partial to her, too." He looked at Charlie. The two men nodded slightly to one another and thought in unison, Oh, if she only knew.

Serena said, "Charlie, all our guests have arrived now, and I think we ought to say hello to them."

"Guess so," said Charlie, taking a deep breath and beginning the long gimp back to the lobby.

ROGER TOO WHITE—the old nickname was *really* burning up his brainstem tonight—sat in his Lexus, brooding. He could probably make it unscathed to the church, which was just over a block away, but the bad boys would descend upon the Lexus like . . . like . . . like . . . He couldn't even imagine what the bad boys here in this part of Southeast Atlanta would be like. He had a vision of a window bashed in until the remains looked like crushed ice and holes in the steering column and on top of the dashboard where there used to be air bags . . .

Wes Jordan was the one who had dispatched him here, and Roger was beginning to wonder who the hell Wes thought he was working for, him or Fareek Fanon. André "Blaq" Fleet was having a rally, or whatever it should be called, up there in that church, the Church of the Sheltering Arms, Reverend Isaac Blakey, pastor. The Mayor was alarmed that Ike Blakey was implicitly endorsing Fleet by letting him have this meeting in his church. Down here in Southeast Atlanta the ministers were the political leaders, like the party district leaders or ward chairmen in other cities, and Ike Blakey was one of the best. He represented many votes. Wes wanted Roger Too White to record the meeting with a device that had been somehow secured inside a folded newspaper, which was at this moment resting on the passenger seat next to him. When Wes had described it—"This is a *public* meeting, and so it's practically *begging* to be recorded"—it had all seemed natural enough. But now that he was here, with his fancy car and his fancy clothes, Roger wasn't so sure anymore about how *natural* it was, being here with a hidden recording device; or how healthy. When he got dressed for this little escapade, he had thought it would be wise to dress down, be casual and inconspicuous. Hence the suede shoes and the tennis collar and the knit necktie and the twill pants and the tweed hacking jacket. Casual.

Inconspicuous. Sure. What planet had *he* been beamed down from? While he had been sitting there, in the gloaming of dusk, gazing out on the little lots with water standing and chunks of concrete sticking up out of the water and white plastic containers and forty-ounce plastic bottles of King Cobra malt liquor floating in it, and the askew tilts of decaying little houses reflected in it, a few people had walked by, presumably to go to the meeting: older people, not bad boys, and even among them dressing *up* meant wearing a shirt with a collar. Dressing *down* . . . he didn't even want to find out. But if he didn't attend, if he didn't take the hidden recording device with him, he would have the scorn—not the anger but the scorn—of Wes Jordan to contend with. That he knew he couldn't stand, and so with a big sigh he picked up the folded newspaper and the hidden micro-microphone and got out of the Lexus and looked this way and that for bad boys and pressed a button on his key chain, whereupon the doors of the Lexus made a sound like a set of snare drums and locked smartly.

The Church of the Sheltering Arms was so little like the church he and Henrietta went to over in Southwest Atlanta, it made Roger feel guilty. He and Henrietta went to the Beloved Covenant Church in Cascade Heights, a decidedly Uptown church with a pulpit that was situated over on the left side of the stage so as not to impede your view of various sacred tabernacle objects and the fanlights of stained glass and the soaring pipe organ that filled most of the wall at the rear of the stage. Roger's father, Roger I, would have said, "Unh unh unh," and shaken his head, had he been alive when that Beloved Covenant Church went up in Cascade Heights. The Reverend Roger I would have seen all this for what it was: an attempt to look high-class. At the heart of the Beloved Covenant Church was The Word, and The Word was brought to the flock by a pastor standing right in the center of the stage, as was the case here in Reverend Blakey's Church of the Sheltering Arms. Behind the pulpit was a crescent of choir boxes that went from one side of the stage to the other. In the center of the wall behind the choir boxes was the only piece of stained glass in the entire church. Instead of being intricate and rather abstract like the stained glass at the Beloved Covenant Church, this was a slightly primitive but powerful depiction of Jesus looking straight at you, with his arms, his sheltering arms, outstretched, as if he were saying, "Come ye unto me." All along the side walls was something more moving than stained glass: watercolor paintings of Bible scenes by the church's Sunday-school children. On the floor just below the stage, off on the right side, a Curland electric organ, a behemoth, a gleaming piece of high-tech machinery. Roger knew about what such an organ cost: twenty-five thousand dollars. Choir boxes, a Curland organ — no matter what else this might be, it was not your everyday poor little church in the slums.

Now the pews were filling up. It was a good-natured crowd, and many people knew one another. Most of them were middle-aged or close to it, exactly the segment of the population most likely to vote, it occurred to Roger. Suddenly—a tremendous vibrating crash of chords from the Curland organ, followed by a walking bass and a rollicking treble, out of which emerged, as if through a musical miracle, the clear melodic line of the old spiritual "Won't You Stay Here in the Garden Next Time, Eve." Roger Too White craned his neck upward and this way and that, and even pushed himself up from the seat of the pew on his fingertips in order to get a look, over and through the forest of heads in front of him, at the organist. It turned out to be a slender, dark woman in a deep burgundy choir singer's robe who clenched her jaw muscles every time she hit a big chord.

Now from both sides of the stage came a choir, in robes of the same dark burgundy, entering with military precision, so that singers from the two sides met in the center of the choir boxes in perfect synchrony. The organist hit another set of chords in the same key and the singers began swaying in unison. Without Roger's knowing where he came from, a choirmaster had materialized in front of the arc of choir boxes, a small dark man with gray hair and a large bald spot in the crown of his head, like a monk's tonsure. His burgundy robe spread out like wings as he raised his hands and surveyed the choir. Then he brought both hands down sharply, and the choir came alive like one great human chord:

Won't you stay here in the garden next time, Eve?
Won't you give this poor old sinner time to grieve?
Won't you pray to our dear Lord before you leave?
Won't you stay here in the garden next time, Eve . . .

No one could fail to be swept up by this music, thought Roger, not even a Roger Too White who admired Igor Stravinsky. It vibrated in your bones and resonated in your solar plexus and made you feel that, yes, your people did have a spirit that a hostile world outside could never exterminate. It made you feel a whole lot less like a . . . Roger Too White.

The choirmaster turned both hands palm up and then lifted them slowly, bringing the choir to a dangerously high note—or dangerous for the ordinary chorister—then turned his palms over and slowly brought the choir back down to a calmer register, at which point he gestured toward a singer close to where he stood. A slim, dark young woman stepped forward:

"Won't you stay here in the garden next time, Eve?"

It was a soprano voice of great beauty and clarity, drawing out the longest note without even a hint of vibrato, a voice with a purity that couldn't possibly survive past age thirty, a voice so close to perfection it brought a mist to Roger's eyes.

She was still singing when a more mundane matter popped into his head: "What does all this have to do with a political outing for André Fleet?" Which in turn reminded him that he had not yet turned on the recording device hidden in the newspaper on the seat beside him. With great trepidation, looking this way and that way and that way and this, he found the little switch with his fingertips—and his career as a spy for Wes Jordan began.

It wasn't terribly long before the choirmaster with the tonsure led his singers to a soaring finale that ended on a sustained F-sharp. Then silence. After five or six seconds the silence seemed to sizzle, and you wondered what would happen next.

From out of a narrow aisle between two choir boxes came a burly, beaming black man, about fifty, wearing a chocolate-brown suit, a white shirt, and a flowered necktie. He was big as a barrel around the middle, but somehow his heft went with the smile he was beaming at everybody. The way he walked toward the pulpit, with an almost tiptoed gait on his curiously tiny feet somehow doubled and redoubled the jollity of his appearance.

Cries of joy broke out in the audience: *Ike! . . . Ike! . . . Tell it, Reverend! . . . Get it said, Reverend! . . . Daddy Mention! . . . Get it said, Daddy Mention!*

What "Daddy Mention" meant, Roger had no idea. When Reverend Isaac Blakey reached the pulpit and looked out on the audience with his radiant smile, they gradually grew quiet.

The big man said, "The Holy Ghost"—he pronounced it as if it were all one word, accented on the first syllable: *Ho*lyghost—"the *Ho*lyghost is amongst our choir tonight, praise God!" Applause . . . shouts of "Get it said, Reverend Blakey!" . . . *Unnh-hunnnh! Oh yes!* "And the *Holy*-ghost is with Brother Lester Monday, praise God!" He turned and made a grand gesture toward the choirmaster, who had taken a seat in the first row of the middle choir box. Then he turned toward the Curland electric organ with another grand gesture. "And Sister Sally Blankenship! She turns that organ into an *en*-tire orchestra, and that orchestra makes heavenly music, praise God!"

Cries of *Praise God, oh yes! . . . It's gettin' said, Reverend! . . . You right at home, Sister Sally!*

Then the Reverend Isaac Blakey grew slightly more serious and said, rather softly for him, "One of our good brothers just said, 'You right at home, Sister Sally,' and I'm here to tell you *that* . . . was getting it said." *Sister Sally! . . . Praise* God! . . . *Gettin' it said!* . . . "Because when we come together in this place, we're all ho-o-o-o-ome . . . Praise God . . . We're home where none of the evil and meanness of the world outside can touch us, because right here, in the presence of one another, testifying before one another, testifying and *getting it said*, praise God" . . . *Praise God! Tell it, Reverend Isaac* . . . "We're home in the sheltering arms of the Carpenter, the Carpenter who walked on the waters."

The stained-glass figure of Christ, with the sheltering arms, seemed, to Roger Too White, to step forward a couple of feet, so powerful was the Reverend Mr. Blakey's invocation of Jesus the Protector.

"But inevitably," he continued, "comes the time when we have to look outside, too, beyond these walls, and think about the future of our children and of our brothers and sisters all over Atlanta. For as the prophet says in Isaiah, 'Cast thine eyes about and thou shalt see thyself many times over in the eyes of thy people,' praise God." *Praise Him! . . . Thy people, praise God!* . . . "Brothers and sisters, tonight we're going to hear from a good brother of ours who has a new vision for our city. Sometimes we hear Atlanta referred to as the Chocolate Mecca . . . the Chocolate Mecca, yes . . . and that makes us feel good, because it reminds us that our brothers and sisters, they predominate in the city government, they head up many departments of the city government, including the office of mayor. Yes, that makes us feel good, but sometimes we can't help asking ourselves, 'Are they *really* our brothers and sisters? Do we really see ourselves when we look into their eyes? When you get up in the morning and go outside your house and say hello to your neighbor, can you imagine any of those folks, the commissioner of this or the commissioner of that, or any of the others of them walking on your street, looking you in the eye, and saying, 'I'm here to help. I'd like to know about your concerns." Or are they a little too busy tending to business over on . . . the other side of town?" Laughter . . . hoots and howls . . . *Gettin' it said, the gospel truth!* Roger froze. He felt radioactive, as if a sickly blue aura was radiating from his head and body, immediately identifying him to one and all as the very personification of the Westside, of Cascade Heights and the Greenbriar Mall and Niskey Lake.

"So like I was saying," said Isaac Blakey, "tonight we're going to hear from a good brother who rose up from amongst us, or from nearby, in Summerhill, who was an excellent student at the University of North Carolina and a great athlete, a great basketball player who then went on to play in the NBA . . . the NBA . . . for the Philadelphia 76ers and the New York Knicks. Oh yes, he was a star athlete in New York, where all of life's sensual pleasures are laid out for professional athletes like cookies on a plate . . . on a plate, see . . . But this young man never forgot his home folks, he never forgot that he came from the South side of Atlanta—from the *east* side of the South side, if you get my meaning—and he never forgot that his first allegiance is to his wife, Estelle, and the children, who now number three in all. I can see . . . *him* . . . walking up to any of us, in this neighborhood, which, God knows, has its problems, and *saying* . . . 'I'm here to help. I'd like to know about *your* concerns . . . here in Southeast Atlanta . . . where I came up the same way as you." He paused, and his gaze panned across the entire audience, and he leaned forward on the pulpit and smiled and said in what for him was a soft and intimate voice, "Now who you reckon I'm talking about?"

Joyful cries erupted. *Blaq! . . . Blaq! . . . Brother Blaq! . . . Brother André . . . Brother Fleet!*

Now Isaac Blakey switched to his most stentorian voice and boomed out: "You got it! You're right on, brothers and sisters! Brother André Fleet is *with* us—and not for just tonight, either!"

Roger Too White expected to see André Fleet emerge from one of the two wings of the stage, as the choir and Isaac Blakey had. But Blakey gestured toward the very rear of the church, and everybody, including Roger Too White, turned about in his seat. There, in the aisle, level with the very last row of seats in the hall, was André "Blaq" Fleet. In the ranks of the National Basketball Association he had been anything but a tall man. He had played point guard for Philadelphia and the New York Knicks. He was known as a good playmaker and a good but not great outside shooter. Probably his greatest asset was his speed and agility on defense. In any event, he had seemed like one of the smaller players, merely six foot four. In fact, by any standard other than the National Basketball Association's, he was a giant. He seemed to tower over the rest of the hall. He wore a navy blazer and a pale blue turtleneck jersey that hugged the thick, smooth column of his neck. He was built in a V, from the extraordinary width of his shoulders down to his narrow waist. And he was dark. Oh yes; no question about it. He had the good looks of a Sidney Poitier, and his flawless teeth fairly gleamed against the deep chocolate of his skin. The man had good looks and then some.

No sooner had Roger twisted about to take a look than Sister Sally Blankenship had plunged her two amazing hands into the Curland, and the stirring Toreador Song from Bizet's *Carmen,* that rousing refrain, was roaring forth, vibrating in every gizzard in the church and making André "Blaq" Fleet seem like even more of an invincible champion. He was working the crowd, reaching deep into each row, on both sides, to touch the hands that reached out toward him. He wasn't the sort of politician who materialized elevated above you onstage, having just departed some unseen VIP room. Oh no; he was here among you, starting with the very last row, yours to see up close, to touch and hear from. Blaq Fleet had something to say to everybody, although it was doubtful that anybody could hear a word of it. Quite in addition to the organ's triumphal anthem, the cries had begun. At first: *André!* . . . *André!* . . . *Fleet!* . . . *Blaq!* . . . *Blaq! Gotcha back! Blaq!* . . . *Gotcha back!* . . . *Fleet!* . . . *Gotcha back!* . . . Then cries from every quarter of the audience: *Gotcha back!* . . . *Gotcha back!* . . . *Gotcha back!* . . . from here, from there, from way over there and the other side: *Gotcha back!* . . . until it became a single, unified chant springing forth from hundreds of gullets: *Gotcha back, gotcha back, gotcha back!*

It took a few moments, but then it dawned on Roger that *gotcha back*—"got your back"—was an Atlanta street expression meaning "I'm behind you—I am your follower—and I'll protect you against attacks from the rear."

Roger wouldn't have believed it possible, but the chant continued to swell in volume as Blaq Fleet made his way down the aisle: "GOTCHA BACK! GOTCHA BACK! GOTCHA BACK!"

Damn! thought Roger. Why did I take a seat on the aisle? What would he do when Fleet got to where he was sitting? So far, every single soul sitting in an aisle seat had enthusiastically touched the flesh of the great champion. But he, Roger, was not only Wes Jordan's backer but his agent. What should he do? Well, it was obvious what he would do. He'd stay in his seat and keep his hands in his lap and look straight ahead.

Blaq Fleet was now just one row away, and the crowd was roaring GOTCHA BACK! in overwhelming unison. Roger was going to keep looking straight ahead, no matter what—but I already stand out in this place! My clothes give me a radioactive aura that everybody in this hall can see! If I don't stand up and pay homage to this V-shaped savior and touch the hem of his garment—or his hand, in any event—they'll all scrutinize me . . . and notice my newspaper . . . and inspect what's inside and peg me for what I am, a spy, a secret agent!

As if there were two motor systems inside him, one of which existed separate from his free will, Roger felt himself rising to his feet and putting on a grin and extending his hand to the towering presence of Blaq Fleet, who beamed his eyes and his pearly teeth down at him and shook his hand and then leaned way in over him to shake or touch the hands of others in the row. As he was straightening up to continue on, he leaned down very close to Roger's ear and said, "I'll throw you down for that tweed jacket, brother!" Then he beamed some more teeth at him and moved on.

Roger found the whole thing deeply disturbing. What did he mean, "I'll throw you down for that tweed jacket, brother"? Presumably it was said in jest. But at the very least it meant that he, Roger, stood out in this place like . . . like . . . like . . . like a member of the Morehouse elite among hundreds of people who were obviously primed to give elites the boot.

Before he went onstage, Fleet stopped by the electric organ and gave Sister Sally Blankenship a kiss on the cheek while she was still playing the Toreador Song, a gesture that brought tumultuous cries and clapping. Then, instead of going up onstage via the stairs at either end, he went up near the organ—in a single bound! The stage was at least three and a half feet high, so that this feat brought gasps of astonishment. How could anybody's legs be that strong? (Nothing to it if you were the great Blaq Fleet.)

He approched Blakey, who was standing just to the side of the pulpit, and raised his hand in the high-five gesture, and Blakey raised his hand

and gave him five, and it was as if that were the smack heard round the world. People in the audience rose to their feet and whooped and applauded more wildly than ever. Roger couldn't help but think of Wes Jordan's high fives. Like Wes's high fives, Fleet's high five had an element of humor about it. After all, people don't go around greeting preachers of the Gospel with high fives. There was humor—but there was no irony, which, it occurred to Roger, was a big difference.

Blakey gestured toward the pulpit, as if to say, "It's all yours." Fleet first lowered his head and touched his brow with the tips of the fingers of his right hand as a form of salute, appreciation, and homage. Blakey took a seat just behind and off to one side of Fleet in a high-backed leather-upholstered armchair Roger had not even noticed being brought onstage. Fleet now took the pulpit and beamed his fabulous smile at the audience, which renewed its chant of GOTCHA BACK! GOTCHA BACK! GOTCHA BACK!

Once they had quieted down, Fleet leaned forward as if to become closer to one and all. "Thank you, brothers and sisters," he said in a rich baritone, "thank you and God bless you. You know, brothers and sisters, it don't often fall to our lot to get to know and be close to a truly great man. But you and I been among the fortunate ones." While Fleet paused and scanned the audience for what would no doubt be some sort of rhetorical effect, Roger wondered if his mistakes in grammar were genuine or just part of his Blaq Fleet act.

Once the pause was suitably pregnant, Fleet said, "You and me, we know . . . REVEREND ISAAC BLAKEY!"

More wild applause and shouts of *Tell it, brother! . . . You gettin' it said, Blaq! . . . Right on!*

Fleet continued: "A man as . . . *brilliant* . . . as Reverend Blakey can take any fork in the road he wants, but the man we know with reverence as . . . *Ike* . . . he stays with his people! With US! WITH HIS BROTHERS AND SISTERS ON THE SOUTH SIDE! HE AIN'T NOBODY'S OPPORTUNIST!" Or at least Roger thought he said, *He ain't nobody's opportunist*, but he couldn't be sure, because the roar of the audience swallowed it up. The Reverend Mr. Blakey, meanwhile, was attempting to look suitably modest. He gave Blaq Fleet the smile of gratitude, the one that turns down ever so slightly at the corners to show a mixture of happiness and some more profound emotion.

Fleet was saying, "No, I'm grateful just to be in the presence of this great man and in the church to which he has devoted his life." He said this in a lower-pitched, more intimate voice, to indicate that no more applause was required on this subject. "Just a moment ago Reverend Blakey said something as only he could say it." He turned toward Blakey and smiled, and then turned back toward his audience. "He said, 'Right now, in this beautiful church, we're *home* . . . we're home in the sheltering arms . . . see . . . the sheltering arms of the Carpenter. But then Reverend Blakey said, 'Comes the time when we have to look outside, too, beyond these walls, and think about the future of our children and of our brothers and sisters all over Atlanta.' As usual, Reverend Blakey's said it best. So I just want to add a *footnote* . . . to what he's told us. Reverend Blakey said we have our brothers—and a few sisters, a *few* sisters—all over City Hall and the current administration. But like Ike, when I go down to City Hall to the buildings department, when I go by the Mayor's office, I get the feeling I'm dealing with some kind of . . . *beige half brothers* . . . You unnerstan' what I'm sayin' . . ."

That brought out some gasps and laughs and the whinny of people suddenly thrilled by the prospect of the speaker drawing blood.

"I get the feeling they're not *hearing* . . . what I'm saying . . . either that or they're not *listening* to anybody but each other . . . see . . . They're not listening . . . There's certain of our beige half brothers who are used to having things go . . . *their way* . . . They've never seen any *other* way. Just as Reverend Blakey put it so well, right on the money, they're used to the West side way. Over there on the West side is Morehouse College. Now, don't get me wrong. I love Morehouse College, even though I never attended Morehouse College, just as I love Spelman and Clark and Morris Brown. These are great institutions with a great heritage, which have done great things for our people. But there is also something called the Morehouse Man—again, don't get me wrong, I think it's great to aspire to be a Morehouse Man or a Spelman Woman or whatnot. But what you have to guard against is coming to think you're part of an . . . *elite* . . . and living your life as if you're part of an . . . *elite* . . . and running the government of this city as if you're part of an *elite* with an *attitude* . . . a Daddy Knows Best attitude . . . cutting the deals any way you see fit . . . Well, I can tell you this: they need to be reintroduced to their own people!"

Right on! . . . Tell it like it is, Blaq! . . .

"The way I see it," said Fleet, leaning toward his audience, his eyes blazing, "it's high time Atlanta had its first . . . BLACK MAYOR!"

An initial confusion—and then the audience exploded with cackles, guffaws . . . *You gettin' it said, Blaq!* . . . applause and belly laughs that went *Heh heh hegggggggggghhhhhhhh!*

"Just *think* for a minute about how many times our representatives have reached compromises with the business establishment, addressed the *concerns* of the business establishment, courted *money* at election time from the business establishment, even catered to the concerns of *the rhinos*—the rhinos in Grant Park—during Freaknic—and what about the concerns of African-American young people who used to come to Atlanta every spring for Freaknic—*used to*—until our representatives began walling off highway exits and turning entire areas of the city into frozen zones—and why?—because our young brothers and sisters had the . . . *gall* . . . to want to do what white college students do all the time, which is to go off somewhere at spring break and . . . be *young* . . . be *free* . . . *feel their oats*, as they used to say—and why these anti-Freaknic crackdowns? Because our young brothers and sisters upset the nerves of the business establishment—and of course you know who they are, and they do not live in the South side—they never even put one *toe* in the South side . . . except to go to baseball games in a stadium called Turner Field, which *should* have been named for the greatest player in the history of the game, our own Hank Aaron—"

The waves of emotion in the audience were rising and cresting and breaking faster and faster. *Unh-hunnnnhhhh . . . Oh yeah! . . . Hank Aaron! . . . Tell it, Brother Blaq!*

"Oh, they'll tell you six ways from Sunday how you have to tread lightly with the business establishment. They don't want to frazzle the *nerves* . . . of the North side. I say it's time we had . . . democracy in this Atlanta city, I say it's time we heard the voice of the people who make up 75 percent of this city, I say it's time we held our representatives in this city STRICTLY ACCOUNTABLE! . . . see . . ."

Oh yeah! . . . Unh-hunnnnhhhhhh! . . . You testifyin', Blaq! . . . You gettin' it said! . . . GOTCHA BACK! GOTCHA BACK! GOTCHA BACK! They broke into the chant again.

Roger Too White didn't move his head, but he cut his eyes this way and that. He was afraid that everybody in the hall was looking at *him*. If there was any candidate for membership in that beige elite in this hall, it was him, him with his necktie and his hacking jacket and his collar pin. But in fact the audience seemed so absorbed in the royal figure of Blaq Fleet, they weren't wasting their time on a run-of-the-mill sinner like Roger Too White. He couldn't wait to get out of here with his beige hide and Wes Jordan's recording device. But he couldn't do so just yet. To bail out in the middle of Blaq Fleet's sermon from the pulpit truly *would* drew attention.

Blaq Fleet knew what he was doing at that pulpit. Sometimes he was the Preacher. Sometimes he was the Next-Door Neighbor, having a chat with you out by the cedar picnic table in the back yard. Sometimes he was Shorty, crooning to "you women." Sometimes he was Your Fishing Buddy, putting a strong arm across the shoulders of "you men." And often he was the NBA star, telling everybody how life was like a basketball game:

"One time, when I was playing for the 76ers, we were up against the Boston Celtics in the playoffs, and this was back when the Celtics had Larry Bird." White, it occurred to Roger Too White. "We were down three games to one in the series, and it was the fifth game, and we were down by 21 points going into the fourth quarter. *Twenty-one points* . . . So our coach, Buster Grant"—black, thought Roger Too White—"calls us all together in a huddle in front of our bench. Have you ever wondered what coaches say in those huddles in the middle of a basketball game? Well, Buster Grant was like Reverend Blakey. He didn't waste words. He didn't just try to give you a pep talk. He got down to business. 'Boys,' he said, 'we're down 21 points going into the fourth quarter. But guess what? You're not gonna go out there playing like you're desperate. You're gonna play like this game is just beginning. You're not gonna go out there throwing up bombs from row Z, looking for treys. You're gonna play basketball. The only one who shoots is the open man, and that goes for everybody.' Right away you sort of knew what the 'goes for everybody' meant. We had a forward—you may remember him—a forward called Gunner Wycoff"—white, thought Roger Too White—"who was a great shot, but he was gonna keep on shooting no matter what kind of defense they put up against him and whether he was open or not. That's why we called him Gunner. His real name was Eric. Buster Grant didn't single the Gunner out, he just let his eyes rest on him longer than anybody else. 'You're gonna go out there and be a basketball *team*. You're gonna crawl all over them on defense, and slice through them on offense—and you're gonna be prouder of yourselves than you've ever been in your whole life.' Some of you may remember what happened next. We went out there and outscored the Celtics 35 to 13 in the final period and won the game, 84 to 83. Our scoring was spread out among seven players, and none of us scored more than six points. Gunner Wycoff only got four points, and two of those were foul shots, but he got something much bigger that night: the knowledge that he could pass and make plays, as well as gun that ball, and from that moment on, he was a hundred percent better basketball player. We were *all* better basketball players from that moment. We were better not because Buster Grant had given us good advice but because somehow his plain speaking had reached . . . our souls . . . see . . . our souls.

"Well, life is a lot like a basketball game. Maybe that's why so many folks like basketball. The lessons are right there in front of you. It's a *team* sport. There are games where a player—and I've been in'em—games where a player scores 44 or 45 points, and his team still loses badly. It's the same way with life in this city. You can go into politics and be a big star, but if you're a gunner . . . see . . . a gunner who just wants to cover himself in glory, then you're not going to do anything for this city. But if you truly make our people a *team*, make'em brothers and sisters who act with *unity*, then there's nothing we can't accomplish. And do we have a Buster Grant to reach our souls? That we do, brothers and sisters, that we do. We have more than one, but one of them is right up here on this stage." He pivoted and gestured. "And his name is Reverend Isaac Blakey!"

Applause, cheers, cries of *You the one! . . . You shootin' treys every time, brother! . . . You dunkin'em, Blaq!*

Then Fleet leaned forward in his intimate mode once more and said, "That's why I'm running for mayor in November. I want to create the . . . *team* . . . that our people have needed. As Reverend Blakey has said, Atlanta has been called the Black Mecca. Well, as long as Atlanta is in the hands of beige half brothers busy wooing the vanilla people . . . see . . . the vanilla people . . ."

Laughter . . . *whooeee . . . heh hegggghhhhhh . . . Lay it down, Blaq! . . . tuh unnnh! tuh unnnnnh!*

". . . then we don't have a *team*. All we got's *gunners* . . . and we can do better than that." He pulled back and straightened up and raised the volume of his voice: "We *will* do better than that! Brothers and sisters, let us pledge to one another that we will *unite*! We don't *care* 'bout the *e*-lites—of *any* color! We're gon' be a *team*! Oh, face facts. We're way behind, going into the quarter period. But we're gonna make sure our souls . . . *catch fire!* . . . see . . ."

Oh yeah! . . . You gettin' it told, Blaq! . . . Catch fire, the burning bush! . . . Praise God!

" . . . Ain't nobody gon' be telling us the game is over, because when we got the *unity*—ain't nothing can stop us! Ain't nothing *gonna* stop us! We gon' WIN THIS GAME!"

Blaq Fleet thrust his arms out in a fashion curiously similar to that of the Carpenter in the stained-glass window behind him. The audience exploded with applause. People rose to their feet. From out of the confused roar came the chant once more: GOTCHA BACK! GOTCHA BACK! GOTCHA BACK! GOTCHA BACK!

Cravenly, Roger Too White rose to his feet, too. He glanced back up the aisle. Could he leave *now*—at last? People were beginning to step out into the aisle, not to leave, but to somehow magnify their approval of the great strapping young man at the pulpit. Roger Too White stood there, frozen, all too white.

After a long while the applause subsided, and the Reverend Blakey, who by now was standing beside Fleet, stepped to the pulpit.

"Brothers and sisters," he said, "brothers and sisters . . . I've asked Brother Fleet to do one more thing before he goes. He didn't want to do it. He thought it wasn't the right place. But if he's talking about unity, I want to *show* him unity." With this, Reverend Blakey stooped down behind the pulpit and came up with four small buckets, ordinary silvery galvanized buckets, one resting inside the next. "I want Brother Fleet to be passing amongst you—and I'm gonna be with him, and so are two fine ladies from our choir—we're gonna pass amongst you, and I want you to tap those buckets with anything you can spare, to support Brother Fleet's campaign. He's not gon' have the big corporations making contributions, because he hasn't cut any deals . . . with the North side. If you can't tap the bucket, nobody's gon' hold it against you, because not even Brother Fleet himself came here with the idea of raising money. I'm *making* him do it!"

Fleet smiled and lowered his head and shook it. He was the very picture of humility in the face of the good fortune that was about to come his way.

Damn! thought Roger. I can't leave until they finish tapping their damn buckets! If I leave now, it'll look like I'm leaving just to avoid making a contribution.

Soon he could hear the sound of coins tapping the bottoms of the silvery buckets.

Damn! he thought. The bucket for my row is the one Fleet himself is passing!

What should he give? How small an amount would be enough to get him off the hook? Slowly he eased his paper money, which was folded in two and held by a gold clip, out of his left pants pocket. As covertly as possible he surveyed it. He couldn't believe it. What he had were two hundred-dollar bills, one fifty, and a single. Could he get away with a one-dollar contribution? No. That would be almost as bad as stiffing him altogether. Now the great Fleet was right beside him again, waiting for the bucket, which was being passed from the opposite end of the row. When it reached Roger Too White, it was as if, once more, some other being were overriding his free will. He found himself depositing the $50 bill in the bucket.

Blaq Fleet leaned over as if merely to take the bucket, flashed Roger another gleaming grin, and said in a low voice, "Thank you, brother. If you have time, I'd like a word with you backstage after this is over."

Roger Too White nodded yes helplessly. But as soon as the others stepped out into the aisle to depart, he beat a retreat—literally ran—with his mortal hide and the newspaper with the recording device inside.

Outside, it was now dark. The car!

To his immense surprise, the Lexus was in one piece, and there were no bad boys to be seen.

Chapter

XVII

Epictetus Comes to Da House

FOLLOWING MUTT'S DEPARTURE, FIVE-O SET ABOUT REARRANGing "da house." "The house" was what inmates, or veteran inmates, routinely called their cells. Whether this was irony, nostalgia for home and hearth, or just more jailhouse simplemindedness, Conrad had no idea; although given what this reeking lizard cage looked like, it sure struck him as simpleminded.

Five-O took Mutt's bottom bunk, and Conrad took Five-O's top bunk, right under the lizard screen. A deputy appeared and removed the mattress on the floor, the one Conrad had been using, and two tissuey polyethylene bags, which commissary orders had come in, containing Mutt's personal belongings. Five-O emptied his own bag full of . . . stuff . . . out on the lower bunk and took inventory. Conrad saw a plastic commuter mug, a toenail clipper, a package of Ramen noodles, a can of Dr Pepper soda, the Donald Goines novel *Dr. Snow,* another paperback novel called *White Horse,* by Ahu Junghyo, a timeworn little paperback book of silhouettes by an artist named Eric Gill, a stack of postmarked letters, a photograph of a smiling Hawaiian girl sitting in a booth inside a diner with a palm tree visible out the window, a toothbrush, two small tubes of Crest toothpaste, writing paper and envelopes, three disposable Bic ballpoint pens, a Salvation Army address book, a plastic bottle of Fabergé Organic Shampoo for Normal Hair, an ice cream cup filled with instant coffee powder, and another ice cream cup that for some reason had its circular top, which had been heavily blackened, shoved down inside the cup and a piece of clear polyethylene sandwich wrap stretched over the opening. Conrad now had a place to sleep where he could lie down full-length. But the biggest change in da house was that Five-O started talking to him. All the time.

Two things he learned about Five-O very quickly. First, to Five-O talking was as necessary as breathing, so great was his need for human company, any human company. Conrad wondered if the man could have survived half a day in solitary confinement. Second, Five-O believed one hundred percent in what Mr. Wildrotsky used to refer to as *Realpolitik*. Every day, every minute, if need be, he was willing to erase the blackboard of history and make alliances with whoever could serve him best in the battle lines as now drawn. Mutt's poor body had scarcely stopped twitching before Five-O started talking to Conrad as if they were buddies from small-kid time, as they said in Pidgin, and the past week of glowering at him as if he were a parasite sucking away the very air he breathed had never happened.

Now, all of a sudden, Five-O couldn't tell him enough about the things a new fish needed to know in order to survive in jail. Whatever the motivation, Conrad was grateful. *Hi, Conrad. How you doin', bro?* He was dying to ask Five-O what to do about Rotto's alarming overture in the visitors' area, but a sixth sense made him hold back. He didn't know yet how far he could trust Five-O; and besides, Five-O was himself in some way connected with the Latino gang, Nuestra Familia; and Nuestra Familia were likely to strike any young white new fish as only marginally less threatening than Rotto and his gang.

The dinner trolley was due soon, and the pod was relatively quiet, even though the deputies had loaded the PA system with something even more irritating to the O-town homeboys than Grover Washington's saxophone. It was a chorus of white singers, backed up by a lot of bubbly, bouncy clarinets and trombones, rendering a song with a very old-fashioned beat called, apparently, "The Chattanooga Choo-choo." But aside from the occasional comment over the wire—such as "The fuck they singin'? Them lame gray motherfuckers, they the motherfuckers that ought to be *down*"—the inmates didn't get particularly exercised about it. They were more upset because of the Bugler tobacco crisis.

The inmates made out commissary slips and had items charged to their accounts, and a trusty pushed around a cart delivering orders to the cells. The cart had come around, and the inmates discovered there was no Bugler rolling tobacco for roll-your-own cigarettes. One by one, as in a row of falling dominoes, they'd yell up through the wire, "Motherfuck, no Bugler?" And the deputies on the catwalk would answer, "Yeah, I guess you're ass-out." Finally one of the deputies said, "Stop complaining. They're talking about a no-smoking rule around here, and then you're really gonna be ass-out." And one of the inmates yelled back, "Then you better buy some earplugs, Sheriff, 'cause you gonna hear a whole lotta goddamned door-kickin'."

Up on the top bunk, beneath the lizard screen, Conrad sighed and propped his back against the wall and tried once more to read his book, even though it had turned out to be a terrible disappointment. It was not *The Stoics' Game* by the magnificently entertaining Lucius Tombs, after all. The title was simply *The Stoics*. On the title page it said, "The complete extant writings of Epictetus, Marcus Aurelius, C. Musonius Rufus, and Zeno. Edited and with an Introduction by A. Griswold Bemis, Associate Professor of Classics, Yale University." He couldn't believe it! The bookstore had sent the wrong book! How could fate turn this completely against him? As if to rub it in, the deputy had then raped the book's physical integrity, leaving him with the tattered remains, these limp clumps of unbound pages—of *the wrong book!*—in his lap. Still, it was a book, and the only book he had. So he started browsing through the introduction by Professor Bemis . . . *Scrack scrack scraaacccк* went the ceiling fans . . . *Thra-goooooom! Gluglugluglug* went the toilets . . . *Motherfuckermotherfuckermotherfucker* went the inmates . . . It was pretty tedious going, this book, which was all about the Greeks and the Romans and "the origins of philosophy, the speculative spirit of inquiry into the mysteries of life and the universe" . . . These people, Epictetus, Marcus Aurelius, C. Musonius Rufus, and Zeno, were philosophers from nearly two thousand years ago in the days of Imperial Rome . . . Conrad was drifting on the swollen river of words when a detail, a mere detail, caught his attention. The author happened to mention that this Epictetus had spent time in prison as a young man. He had been tortured and crippled, but he had gone on to become one of the greatest Roman philosophers. Conrad began hurrying through the thick, leisurely prose. Very little was known about Epictetus, not even the dates of his birth and death, but it was known that his parents, who were Greeks, had *sold him as a slave,* when he was a boy, to an officer in the Emperor Nero's Imperial Guard. He had begun his life stripped of everything, his family, his possessions, his freedom.

Now Conrad couldn't read fast enough. He leafed through the pages to find this man Epictetus' own words . . . Book I, Chapter 1: "On Things in Our Power and Things Not in Our Power" . . . and he came upon this passage: "To ye prisoners"—*prisoners*—"on the earth and in an earthly body and among earthly companions, what says Zeus? Zeus says, 'If it were possible I would have made your body and your possessions (those trifles that you prize) free and untrammelled. But as things are—never forget this—this body is not yours, it is but a clever mixture of clay. I gave you a portion of our divinity, a spark from our own fire, the power to act and not to act, the will to get and the will to avoid. If you pay heed to this, you will not groan, you will blame no man, you will flatter none.' "

And then Epictetus said: "We must die. But must we die groaning? We must be imprisoned"—*We must be imprisoned!* he said!—"but must we whine as well? What say you, fellow? Chain me? My leg you will chain—yes, but my will—no, not even Zeus can conquer that. You say, 'I will imprison you.' I say, 'My bit of a body, you mean.' You say, 'I will behead you.' I say, 'When did I ever tell you I was the only man in the world that could not be beheaded?' It is circumstances which show what men are. Therefore when a difficulty falls upon you, remember that Zeus, like a trainer of wrestlers, has matched you with a rough young man. 'For what purpose?' you may say. 'Why, that you may become an Olympic conqueror; but it is not accomplished without sweat—' "

"Yo! Conrad!" It was Five-O, who was sitting on the edge of the bunk below. "One noddah t'ing mo', brah. Okay? Da new fish, dey t'ink so if—"

And Five-O was off on another lesson for the first-timer on the ways of jailhouse life. Conrad didn't want another lesson just now. He had a sudden, overwhelming thirst for the words of this man he had never heard of before, this man whose name he couldn't even begin to pronounce, Epictetus. At the same time, he didn't want to risk losing the newly acquired goodwill of his cellie (as the prisoners called their cellmates), and so he figured he had better pay attention.

"Da new fish," Five-O was saying, "dey t'ink so if dey stay real quiet kine, if dey no make ass, if dey ac' like dey jes coasting kine, if dey boddah no mo' nobody—den dey going stay eenveesible." Invisible. "Cannot, brah! You edah dis t'ing or you one noddah t'ing. You no stay eenveesible. You edah one player or one punk, yeah? An' dees buggahs"—he raised his hand high enough for Conrad to see it and made a circle in the air, as if to take in the entire pod—"if dey t'ink you one punk, den you real had-it. Bumbye dey going grind you."

Conrad didn't want to start a conversation. He wanted to get back to Epictetus. But the word *grind* got him. It frightened him. *Hi, Conrad. How you doin', bro?* In Pidgin, as he knew by now, *grind* meant *eat*: bite, chew up, swallow, obliterate.

"But how do you get to be a . . . a player?" he asked Five-O. "What can you do?"

"No *do* no mo' notting, brah. Use da mouth. No make beef wit' da buggahs. Use da mouth."

Conrad pondered this advice, but couldn't imagine what it actually meant.

The white singers and the clarinets and the trombones were now bobbing along in some rickety old song about "jiggers of moonlight." The pod was going *scrack scrack scrack scraaaccccckkkkkk thra-*GOOM *glug glug glug glug motherfucker motherfucker motherfucker* . . . and then you could hear the aluminum clatter of the meal trolley beginning to roll though the pod . . . *Yo! Trus-tee!* . . . *Trus-tee!* . . . Inmates elevated to the status of trusty, thanks to good behavior—at Santa Rita the word was always pronounced *trus-tee*—dispensed the meals off the trolleys on thin paper plates with the cheapest plastic utensils imaginable. If you liked pancakes for breakfast and roast chicken for dinner, you wouldn't starve at Santa Rita. The lunch, which was always a sandwich of processed meat shot through with what looked like blood vessels and tendons, was inedible, as were the powdered eggs at breakfast, which tasted oddly like prunes; but you could get by on the pancakes and the chicken . . . *Yo! Trus-tee!* . . . The meal trolley rattled closer.

Five-O picked up the ice cream cup with the sandwich wrap stretched across the top and went to the door, stuck the cup out the slot, then cocked his head and squinted out at the cup. Then he pulled the cup back in and turned to Conrad and said, " 'Ey, try look."

So Conrad walked over to the door and did as Five-O had done. He stuck the cup out through the slot and squinted at it. The cup's top cap was the one Five-O had blackened with a ballpoint pen. The top, which he had forced down into the cup, plus the stretch wrap, which he had pulled tight over the opening, created a mirror, a rearview mirror, as it were. He could look down the line of cells. He could see the meal trolley, a tall aluminum cart full of shelves, two cells away. He could see the stacks of paper plates with roast chicken legs on them . . . Croker Global! Eighty pounds! Croker Global supplied Santa Rita. He had just finished humping a Santa Rita order the night he was laid off. The cartons of frozen chicken legs weighed eighty pounds apiece. For an instant he was back inside the icy cliffs of the Suicidal Freezer Unit, struggling with those frozen dun-colored cubes. Maybe Kenny or Light Bulb or Herbie had humped the very carton these chicken legs came from. And he was now on the receiving end in this unbelievable place . . . The trusty pushing the meal trolley was a tall but terribly thin and gawky Chinese wearing a pair of big round black-rimmed glasses. He was probably in his late twenties. He looked like an ancient Mandarin scholar in embryo.

Conrad pulled the cup and his arm back inside the cell, and Five-O, standing right beside him, lifted a forefinger straight up, at eye level, as if to say, "Hark!" and said, "Try listen, Conrad. Use da mouth." He winked.

Soon there was a rap on the cell door, and you could see the big black-rimmed eyeglasses of the Chinese trusty at the slot. In a reedy voice he said, "Yo, mealtime."

Five-O walked to the slot, squared his jaws, and stared at the trusty with a steady, deep, malevolent gaze. The trusty passed a paper plate with a chicken leg on it through the slot. Five-O took it, turned back toward Conrad, winked again, picked up the chicken leg, took a huge bite, and put the remains back on the plate. Almost half the meat was gone. Then he turned back to the trusty and pushed the plate and the chewed chicken leg back through the slot, and, his cheeks still crammed with food, managed to say, " 'Ey, bummahs, man. Try look. Some buggah wen grind half da muddahfuggin' cheecken. You going give me one noddah plate, man!"

He beamed such a malevolent look at the gawky Chinese that if looks could kill, the man would have died on the spot.

But he didn't take the plate back. He just stared at Five-O and said, "Say what?"

"Spahk"—check out—"da muddahfuggin' cheecken, bruddah! Some buggah wen grind half da muddahfuggah! You going give me one noddah one!"

"Aw, come on, man," said the trusty wearily. "You ate half 'at leg a chicken yo'ownse'f."

Conrad saw a glimmer of dismay in Five-O's eyes. The trusty's voice had deepened, and he didn't sound like some weak, skinny Chinese. If anything, he sounded black. Five-O narrowed his eyes and clenched his jaws and tried a growl: "Haaaaaahh? Wot? Like beef?" Five-O's face was so furious, you didn't have to know Pidgin to know that he was saying: "You want to fight?"

The skinny Chinese with the big spectacles said, "Look, bruvva, I'm a number in here, and you a number in here . . . see . . . an' I ain't tryin' a disrespectchoo. I'm jes' tryin'a do my time . . . You unnastan' what I'm sayin'? I ain't tryin'a sweatchoo, and I ain't tryin'a play you. So whatchoo doggin' me for? I ain't rollin'is motherfuckin' trolley th'oo here to come sweatchoo, play you, dog you, git over on you, run a game on you, or any other damn thing . . . see . . ."

By now Conrad was as perplexed as Five-O. Pouring out of the larynx of this slight, bespectacled, scholarly-looking Chinese was the voice of an East Oakland homeboy, a righteous one, with heart, a blood among bloods who knew how to get down and tend to business.

"So, bruvva, you kin have half a dis pod and half a Santa Rita and half a Alameda County and half a the whole damn East Bay, for all I care, but don't be doggin' me 'bout no half a damn leg a chicken, 'cause ain't a damn thing in the world I kin do wid the other half of it 'cep'n git myse'f all fucked up wid my shot caller. My shot caller, he say, 'You let yo'sef git dogged, bruvva, you gon' git yo'sef double-dogged—by *me*' . . . see . . . So whyn'tchoo kindly do the right thing, bruvva, and take 'is here paper plate and 'at half a damn leg a chicken and go with God, Shakem Alakem, and you'n'me's fifty-fifty and everything's cool."

His jaw slack, his mouth half open, Five-O pulled the plate back through the slot without a word, in slow motion, all the while staring at this skinny Chinese with the bleary glasses and the baggy yellow felony pajamas. The light went out in Five-O's eyes. He moved slowly away from the door, holding the plate at chest level, looking toward the bunk, as if in a trance. Conrad stepped up to the door and took the second plate, which the trusty now put through the slot. Five-O was sitting on the edge of his bunk, staring at the wall. You could hear the trolley rattling as the trusty pushed it to the next cell.

Conrad didn't know whether to look at Five-O or not. The man had just been humiliated. After all his big talk, he was the one who had backed down. But Five-O himself solved that one for him.

"No laugh, you!" He stared at Conrad angrily, but then his expression changed from angry to doleful. " 'Ey, bummahs, man, yeah? Hear dat buggah? Wow, dat buggah get connections! Dat buggah get connections wit' da popolos from long time. No bulai"—*No bullshit!*—"brah. Maybe da Black Guerrilla Family, yeah? Maybe da Crips. No can affo'd'um, make beef wit' dem buggahs." He shook his head disconsolately.

What ran through Conrad's mind was: Do I dare say the obvious? The tactful thing would be to say nothing and perhaps just nod to note the sagacity of this latest advice. But something told him this might in fact be a moment when he could forge a bond with his cellie. So he dared: "That trus-tee's not a big guy like you, Five-O. He's just a skinny, weak-looking guy with thick glasses."

Irritably: "An' den?"

"And then so maybe he took your advice."

"Yeah? Ass what?"

"Remember what you just told me?" said Conrad. "You said, 'Use the mouth.' You said, 'Don't get into a beef. Use the mouth.' Well, that trusty can really use the mouth. That bugger can *talk*, Five-O."

Sitting there, holding his plate in his lap, Five-O narrowed his eyes and scowled. Then his face relaxed and he looked straight ahead at the wall, as if deep in thought. Then he turned back toward Conrad, and a smile stole over his face. He started nodding.

"Fo' real, brah," he said softly, "fo' real." He chortled ruefully. "Dat buggah wen use da mouth. Dat buggah—dat buggah's mouth mo' big dan mines! Dat Chinaboy, he stay one motormouth—to da max!" He started laughing. "No mo' mind me, Conrad! Try listen dat China buggah!"

EVERY AFTERNOON AT one and every evening at six the deputies turned the inmates out of their cells and led them into the pod room for four hours of communal "pod time," as it was known. Strictly speaking, you didn't have to leave your cell. But if you didn't, you were locked in, and that was that. You couldn't go back and forth from the cell to the pod room. Conrad was so afraid of having to deal with Rotto, he was sorely tempted to stay inside. But on the other hand . . . staying inside that 5-by-9 lizard cage all day long, looking up through the screen at the catwalk, listening to the attic fans struggling, was a grim prospect . . . and sooner or later you *had* to come out, to take a shower . . . and he didn't want his now-friendly cellie to think he was eccentric or, worse, frightened . . . and his body ached for the chance to move around, if only in that grim gray pod room . . . and something within him—his useless, deluded *soul?*—told him he must not surrender to fear. So he trooped on out with Five-O and the others.

The pod room was a large rectangle of concrete with two rows of metal tables and metal stools out in the middle. The tables and the stools, like every other piece of furniture in the pod, were bolted to the floor. Along one side of the room were the open showers with the concrete retaining wall in front of them; and along the opposite side, also separated from the rest of the space by a retaining wall, was a line of open toilets and basins. Down at one end were two public telephones that could be used for outgoing collect calls only. Not too far away was a television set up on a metal stanchion. To change the channels you had to be somebody tall standing on one of the metal tables. Overhead there was no wire screen and no catwalk. The main instrument of surveillance was a video camera high up in one corner that fed a screen the deputies monitored. From the position of the camera you could tell that . . . things . . . could go on in the shower area without the deputies ever knowing.

Of this, at the moment, Conrad was dreadfully aware. His job was to stay as far away from Rotto and his boys as possible without getting anywhere near Vastly and his boys. Every time he so much as glanced toward the telephones and the television set, he could pick out Vastly immediately. The yellow ribbons on his cornrows created a strange floating field of gold above his head. Right now he was seated, along with a half dozen of his followers, at the table that offered the best view of the television screen.

They had found a channel showing a concert, in some huge arena, featuring a black singer named Lorelei Washburn. Lorelei Washburn was a screamer. Given a choice between a high register and a low one, she always went high and screamed in order to reach the note . . .

"tearing out the heart of meeeeEEEEEEEEEEEEEEeee!" . . . Her screams ricocheted off the gray concrete of the pod room. But Vastly and the boys had no interest in Lorelei Washburn, who was wearing a white dress that was sleek, silky, and tight-fitting, but also long and not particularly revealing. No, their entire attention seemed to be pinned on her backup singers, three tan-skinned girls wearing pleated miniskirts that barely covered their bottoms. When they swiveled their hips or whirled—and they swiveled and whirled constantly—the pleated skirts rose up like pinwheels, revealing tiny glittery bikini panties. Little more than *cache-sexes* these panties were, and the sight of so much nearly bare booty drove Vastly's gang wild.

" 'At's the real deal, baby!"

"Right on, bro! No mo'at homosexual-faggot-drag-queen-B-cat-turned-out-punk shit!"

"Yeah, 'at's the *real* shit! It's *live,* man! It ain't Memorex!"

"I'm fulla jook, sugar!"

"Looka the booty on 'at mama!"

"Shake yo' booty!"

"Jook yo' booty!"

Conrad's blood ran cold. *Turned-out punk.* The message he heard in these shouts had nothing to do with the three sexy young performers on the screen. These men—the rulers of the pod at Santa Rita—preferred women, but they regarded homosexuals as a perfectly acceptable substitute while you were in jail. And in jail, in addition to the drag queens and the B-cats, who might be found anywhere, there were also the "turned-out punks," young and slightly built new fish, like the Mutt Simms of long ago, who were forced to commit or submit to homosexual acts.

Conrad now surveyed the pod room with a horrible clarity. It was a foul gray chamber inhabited by grim organisms in yellow felony pajamas who arranged themselves in primitive territorial packs. The prime territory was the end of the room where the two telephones and the television set were located, and the blacks had all of that to themselves. Most of the black inmates kept their heads shaved, or close to it, but some of them wore their hair long and wrapped do-rags around their heads. All the do-rags were green, because the only way they could get the material was to rip it off the green sheets the jail issued. It infuriated the deputies, all these insults to county property, but the practice never died. The most sinister-looking do-rag wearer, as Conrad saw it, was sitting next to Vastly at this moment, a tall, gaunt young man with sunken cheeks and a degenerate slouch, known as Rapmaster EmCee New York. He wrapped his do-rag down so low, it almost covered his eyes. He looked like a black pirate. A few, most notably Vastly, wore their hair in cornrows or dreadlocks. Bunched together the way they were, they looked supremely powerful; and in the pod room, in fact, they were. The possibility of some white or Latin inmate just ambling over and using a telephone or changing the television channel without Vastly's permission was nil.

The Latinos mainly hung around one side of the room over by the open toilets and the basins. Most of them were Mexican. They kept their hair short and liked to wear necklaces with crosses, which they wove out of plastic lace left over from packaged items from the commissary. They seemed to spend half the pod time shadow-boxing. Lefts, rights, hooks, combinations—their brown fists were tearing the air to pieces. What good that would do anybody in a jailhouse fight, Conrad couldn't imagine. You only had to look across the way to where the black inmates had commandeered the entryway to the showers to do their dips . . . to buff up . . . to keep accumulating the brute power that ruled the pod . . . The Latinos gave each other mildly deprecatory nicknames such as Flaco (Skinny), Gordo (Fat Man), Weddo (Blondie), Oso (Grizzly Bear), and, curiously, Wino. Wino was the Nuestra Familia shot caller. He was a short, heavyset, sleepy-looking man, probably in his early thirties, not very prepossessing; and yet everyone, even Vastly & Co., seemed to give him plenty of room. The white inmates, who congregated up here, far away from the telephones, gave each other nicknames that were straight out demeaning: Rotto, Mutt, Riffraff, Slimy, Sleaze Man—and, like Mutt, took offense if any outsider presumed to call them that. The inner core, members of the Nordic Bund, were heavily tattooed and wore their hair in ponytails or else combed it back on the sides and let it run down the backs of their necks in wild mongrel tangles—like Morrie, the giant from the tow-truck company. (His huge figure rose up once more in Conrad's mind.) There were only four Asians in the pod, Five-O and three young Chinese drug dealers from Oakland. Like Five-O, they stuck close to the Latinos during pod time.

Packs! Dens! Utterly primitive animal turfs!

Conrad sat down by himself at a table. He had brought along a writing tablet and a Bic ballpoint pen and his book, *The Stoics*. He set about writing a letter to Jill—and Carl and Christy. Right away he realized it was really the children he wanted to reach. He was so afraid they would forget him altogether. He tried to draw a picture of an elephant, with a comic-strip balloon over its head, saying, "Hi, Carl! Hi, Christy!" But he wasn't much of an artist, and he couldn't figure out where the elephant's mouth went or which way the hind legs were supposed to bend . . . Well, at least it was something that might make them think of their father . . . As for Jill . . . he realized he didn't know what to say to her. Should he pour his heart out? . . . Something told him that would be a tactical mistake. A *tactical* mistake. What a sad thing it was to have to think tactically about your own wife . . .

Every minute or so he lifted his eyes and cut a glance toward the end of the room, where Rotto held court. He could feel his heart strumming along far too fast. If anything happened, he would have no allies, and he couldn't imagine where he would ever find any. His new pal in da house, Five-O, had scarcely looked at him once they reached the pod room, let alone talked to him. Obviously he didn't want to be seen hanging out with some new white fish. Conrad wasn't even surprised. That was Five-O. Five-O spent the pod time with his Latino buddies, although Conrad now saw him chatting with a couple of the hard-looking Okies. Evidently he was giving them the details of Mutt's set-to with the deputies. He made a little kick in the air and then lunged forward a step with his forearm raised, pantomiming Mutt's surprise assault on Armentrout. Conrad couldn't hear what he was saying, but no doubt he was assuring them he had been Mutt's staunch ally, shoulder to shoulder, shank to flank, until the bitter end.

He studied the Okies for a moment. They were white, but there was no way he could approach them. The Nordic Bund—they were all bigger and tougher versions of Mutt. Except for the color of their skin, they were as alien as the Black Guerrilla Family. The only other whites were hopeless cases who could offer no protection at all. There was a pudgy man, in his mid-forties, if Conrad had to guess, with thinning light brown hair, who was referred to only as Pops or Old Man . . . *Yo, Pops! . . . Hey, Old Man!* . . . But that, apparently, was true of all inmates who were over forty. Unless they were brutes with fearsome reputations, they lost not only their real names but also their nicknames. They were written off. They were history. They became just *Pops* or *Old Man.* This particular Pops walked around the pod room with his puffy eyes half-closed and his feet dragging across the floor in a pathetic gait known as the Sinequan Shuffle. Sinequan was a drug, like Thorazine, which was used to tranquilize J-cats. This Pops was pathetic, and he did the Shuffle, but he wasn't so crazy. He kept shuffling around throughout the entire pod time, never standing still, apparently not looking at a thing, but he never shuffled near the Latinos, much less the blacks. He wasn't J-cat enough to do some stupid J-cat thing like let himself stray from the white turf.

Then there was Pocahontas. Pocahontas was a new fish, newer than Conrad, tall, six-three or six-four, skinny, practically anorexic, pale, close to being albino, young, as young as Conrad. He had a Mohawk haircut, no eyebrows, and four tiny sinkholes in the rim of his left ear, where there had no doubt been a row of earrings prior to his arrival at Santa Rita. The Mohawk was a narrow brush of auburn hair bisecting his shaved head. He had shaved off his eyebrows, too, while he was at it. His movements, the way he walked, the way he carried things, were effeminate. He had immediately picked up the nickname Pocahontas. The fact that the real Pocahontas was a Powhatan princess rather than a Mohawk was a historical nicety not likely to trouble anybody in D Pod, West Greystone, Santa Rita Rehabilitation Center. The boy sat with a shell back and a collapsed posture at one of the tables, his pale green eyes blank, looking utterly miserable. Conrad not only felt sorry for him but also felt an obligation to try to help him in some way—but what could he possibly do? And then he felt guilty . . . since he also knew he didn't want to be lumped with him as a pal . . . and fellow B-cat . . .

On the screen atop the metal pole Lorelei Washburn continued to wail and fill the pod with her screams . . . "—at the heartless feet of yoooooooooooooooooooou!" . . . and her three backup singers continued to swivel and whirl and shake their nearly bare booties . . . and Vastly and the boys offered up more prayers to their god, sexual conquest:

"Oooooooooo-weeeee, baby, I been down in Santa Rita too long!"

"This is the lick!"

"This is the *real* lick fo' a change, bro!"

"No mo' B-cat booty, man!"

"Gimme the booty all-roooooty!"
"I'm gon' mack a *sweet* meat crack!"
"No mo' jookin' punks, I want some *booty* in my bunk!"

TO CONRAD'S GREAT relief, the pod time ground by without Rotto even seeming to notice his existence, much less making a move in his direction. By the end, shortly before 10 p.m., he had managed to complete his letter and his clumsy, labored drawing and to read three chapters of "the extant writings" of Epictetus.

The words of this onetime prison inmate from two thousand years ago resonated across the millennia with an electrifying clarity. It seemed that in fact these were not Epictetus' writings but his dialogues, his colloquies, with his disciples, as recorded by one of them, whose name was Arrian. Thanks to the conversational tone, there was an immediacy about everything he said. Conrad had a picture of a crippled old man with wisps of gray hair on his head but a full beard—according to the introduction, all the Roman philosophers wore beards—an old man wearing a beard and a toga, sitting on a chair in a bare room with a small group of young men, also wearing togas, sitting at his feet. (And now they are joined by a young man wearing yellow felony pajamas and flip-flop sandals and a mustache, who takes a seat on the floor, at the rear of the group, ever so quietly and reverently . . .)

In Book I, Chapter 2, the group gets into a discussion of what a man should do when faced with the choice of either submitting to something degrading or else suffering severe punishment or death.

Epictetus says, "To the rational creature, only the irrational is unbearable; the rational he can always bear. Blows are not by nature intolerable."

One of his disciples (no doubt a young man, about Conrad's own age, in a toga) says, "What do you mean?"

Epictetus proceeds to tell how Florus, a Roman historian, was summoned by Nero to act in one of his notorious spectacles. Nero delighted in forcing famous and noble Romans to put on costumes and go onstage and act out degrading roles in so-called tragedies he devised. To refuse was to risk death. Badly shaken, Florus goes to see his friend Agrippinus, the Stoic philosopher.

"What should I do?" says Florus. "If I refuse, I will be beheaded. If I take part, I will be humiliated before all of Rome."

"Nero has summoned me, too," says Agrippinus.

"So what do we do?" says Florus.

"You appear in the tragedy," says Agrippinus.

"And you?"

"I will not," says the Stoic.

"But why should I, and not you, appear in this spectacle?" says Florus.

"Because you have *considered* it," says the Stoic.

Then Epictetus tells them about an Olympic athlete who was threatened with death if he did not allow himself to be castrated so that he might serve as a statuesque eunuch, a human ornament, in Nero's seraglio. His brother, who was a philosopher, came to him and said, "Brother, what will you do? Are we to let the knife do its work?" The athlete refused and was executed.

"How did he die," asks one of the disciples, "as an athlete or as a philosopher?"

"He died as a man," says Epictetus, "and a man who had wrestled at Olympia and been proclaimed victor, one who had passed his days in such a place as that, not one who merely parades about the gymnasium anointing himself with oil so that all can admire him. Another man would have consented to have even his head cut off, if he could have lived without it. That is what I mean about keeping your character: such is its power with those who have acquired the habit of carrying it into every question that arises. You can be the ordinary thread in the tunic, or you can be the purple, that touch of brilliance that gives distinction to the rest."

His final example is from his own life. It seemed that the Emperor Domitian, Nero's successor, had ordered all the philosophers of Rome to go into exile. But if they shaved off their beards—i.e., symbolize for all to see that they were no longer philosophers but ordinary men bowing before the Emperor—they could remain in Rome and live in peace. Epictetus refused.

"They said, 'We must behead you then.'

" 'So be it,' I said. 'Behead me, if it is better for you that way. When did I tell you that I was immortal? You will do your part, and I mine. It is yours to kill, mine to die without quailing: yours to banish, mine to go into exile without groaning.' " He was sent into exile.

One of the disciples says, "How then shall we discover, each of us, what suits his character?"

Epictetus says, "How does the bull, when the lion attacks, discover what powers he is endowed with? It is plain that each of us who has power of this sort will not be unaware of its possession. Like the bull, the man of noble nature does not become noble all of a sudden; he must train through the winter and make ready, and not lightly leap to meet things that concern him not."

Conrad looked up from the pages before him on the metal table. He was aware of all the yellow felony pajamas, eddying and fidgeting about in clumps, in their various turfs . . . The pudgy white man, Pops, still had his head down and his eyes nearly shut, doing his Sinequan Shuffle not far from Rotto and a clutch of his tattooed Okies who were huddled with downcast shit-kickin' looks on their faces . . . Pocahontas was sitting collapsed over a metal table with his head, his ludicrous auburn Mohawk and all, resting on his forearms, which seemed terribly thin, pale, and spidery . . . The Mexicans were still pulverizing their phantom enemies with their hooks, jabs, and straight rights in the air, while Five-O joked about with the one with the light hair, Weddo . . . One of Vastly's boys, a short, very dark man, with prodigious shoulders, neck, and chest, was over by the showers doing his dips in the opening of the retaining wall while two more waited their turn . . . and Vastly himself still held court with most of his retinue at the table in front of the television set . . . The tiny yellow paper ribbons seemed to fairly gleam above his cornrow hairdo . . . He and his boys were watching a television show called *Posse*, about a black gang in Los Angeles, full of gunfire, maudlin laments about "da 'hood," and dialogue that struck Conrad as totally unrealistic, since on television nobody said *motherfuckin'*.

" 'At's da law a da 'hood, man," said a character on the screen, a young man who rocked along in a Frankenstein gait, wearing a pair of bulky black sneakers, voluminous homey jeans whose crotch came down to his knees, a black leather jacket with numerous lethal-looking zippers, a do-rag, and an expression of terminal anger, "an ain'no *po*-lice you can run to to take care da law a da 'hood."

Vastly nodded, and his boys nodded with him. They were engrossed. This was drama. This was the real lick, no doubt.

What would Epictetus have done with this bunch? What *could* he have done? How could you apply his lessons two thousand years later, in this grimy gray pod, this pigsty full of beasts who grunted about motherfuckin' this and motherfuckin' that and turning boys into B-cats and jookin' punks? And yet . . . were they really any worse than Nero and his Imperial Guard? Epictetus *spoke* to him!—from half a world and two thousand years away! The answer was somewhere in these pages! What little bit Conrad had learned about philosophy at Mount Diablo had seemed to concern people who were free and whose main problem was to choose from among life's infinite possibilities. Only Epictetus began with the assumption that life is hard, brutal, punishing, narrow, and confining, a deadly business, and that fairness and unfairness are beside the point. Only Epictetus, so far as Conrad knew, was a philosopher who had been stripped of everything, imprisoned, tortured, enslaved, threatened with death. And only Epictetus had looked his tormenters in the eye and said, "You do what you have to do, and I will do what I have to do, which is live and die like a man." And he had prevailed.

But most important of all, only Epictetus understood. He *understood*! Only he understood why Conrad Hensley had refused to accept a plea bargain! Only Epictetus understood why he had refused to lower himself just a rung or two, demean himself just a little bit, dishonor himself just a touch, confess to a minor crime, a mere misdemeanor, in order to avoid the risk of a jail sentence. "Each of us considers what is in keeping with his character . . ." His lawyer, even his own wife, wanted him to compromise and plead falsely. But he knew himself and at how much he put his worth. He did not count himself as an ordinary thread in the tunic, but as the purple, that touch of brilliance that gives distinction to the rest.

When the deputies announced the end of pod time, Conrad gathered up the folios of *The Stoics*, his letter, his writing tablet, his ballpoint pen, and walked to the cell with his shoulders back and his head high.

LIGHTS-OUT WAS AT 10 p.m. There was no announcement. The lights hanging from the underside of the catwalk went off, and so did the music being broadcast over the PA system. The deputies had lights somewhere up on the catwalk, however; so the pod was never pitch-black. Five-O was lying on the bottom bunk, and Conrad was stretched out on the top bunk, beneath the lizard wire. As usual, it was too hot. He could hear the deputies moving around on the catwalk. The place must have been even hotter for them, since they were up near the ceiling. *Scrack scraaack scraaaaack.* The attic fans were still screeching. *Thra-goooooom thra-gooooooom.* The toilets were still flushing. *Glug-lugluglugluglug.*

Conrad's thoughts kept racing and tumbling in the semidarkness . . . his last glimpse of Jill . . . Carl and Christy—would he ever see them again? . . . Rotto, the Nero of the Pod, and the inevitable showdown . . . Or did it have to be? . . . Epictetus, his only hope . . . He longed for light, so that he could get back into the poor bedraggled pages of that book, which he kept up here on the bunk next to the wall . . . Now he could see Epictetus' beard, his old thin body, his toga . . . What would Epictetus have had to say about Jill and Carl and Christy?—and once more his thoughts spun around. He couldn't begin to relax enough to sleep.

But, in fact, there was no sleep for anyone in the pod. Every night, at lights-out, a session began in the darkness, a therapy session, a jam session, a hoedown, a prayer meeting, a Pentecostal confessional, a tribal rumble, a shriek into the void, a wailing for that which never was and that which never would be, a lamentation concerning Fate. Conrad didn't know what to call it, but every night it took place in the darkness, over the wire.

Someone began moaning: "Meds . . . meds . . . mehhhds . . . mehhhhds . . . mehhhhhds . . ." Medicines were distributed each day, to those on the "meds list," by a nurse named Maggie, who was referred to, sometimes to her face, as Maggot. "Mehhhhhhds . . . mehhhhhhhds . . . mehddddddds . . ." The moans stretched out longer and longer.

From somewhere: "Shut the fuck up, you J-cat motherfucker!"

"Mehhhhhhhhhds . . . mehhhhhhhhhhds . . . mehhhhhhhhhhds . . ."

From somewhere else: "Pill call, Maggot!"

Cries began to rain down, over the wire, from all over the pod.

"Where you at, Maggot? Git on in here and give the motherfucker his Sinequan!"

A new voice: "Fuck the meds! I want a rollie! I want some Bugler!"

The voice that had been moaning for the meds said, "You know Hank Aaron?—the first Negro slave baseball player that owned a yellow wool suit?"

"Mother*fuck!* I gotta listen'at shit all night? 'At motherfucker's gone J-cat again! Where's'at Maggot at?"

"Voice on the TV!" said the J-cat. "Told me I gon' die if I go outside. I DON'T WANT TO DIE!" It was a real shriek.

"You gon' die fo' damn sure, you don't shut the fuck up!"

"I want a rollie! I want some Bugler, goddamn it! Yo! Sheriff! Where the Bugler at?"

A black voice imitating an Okie deputy: "New *pro*-cedure. Gawn stick yo' right leg out yo' porthole so's I kin see you. Then you gitcho Bugler."

"I want a light!"

"How 'bout a Bud Light?"

"Yo! Brothers! Yo!" Conrad's heart jumped. It was a big voice, such a big voice that he thought it must be Vastly's, even though he didn't really know what Vastly's voice was like. "Just come over the wire. 'At gray motherfucker 'at burnt the cross in Hayward?" In O-town street parlance, *gray* meant *white*. "They got that motherfucker over'n B Pod!" There had been an incident, mentioned on television, in which someone had burned a cross on the lawn of a black family. B Pod was the isolation pod, where prisoners were removed from the general population and kept one to a cell.

"The fuck, he's ass-out, that motherfucker!"

"*Ass-out! . . . Ass-out! . . . Ass-out! . . . Ass-out!*" The cry swept the pod.

"Ne'mind'em peckerwoods. Got a ex-*po*-lice rightcheer in D fo'teen!"

A huge voice: "Who the fuck are you, motherfucker, talkin 'bout ex-*po*-lice? The fuck, you sayin' you got some paperwork on me? Man, you outta pocket!"

"I'm sayin'—"

"You motherfucker, you the one'at's trying to put jackets on everybody!" A jacket was a file prison authorities kept on informants. "You trying to fire everybody's ass up! You the one 'at's *under*, motherfucker!" Short for *working undercover*. "You the one 'at's the snitch!"

"Unh-hunh, yeah, well—"

"Fuck yo' *unh-hunh yeah well*. You keep on trying to hang jackets on people, you gon' gitcho cap peeled!"

The huge voice had won the debate, and a chorus of imprecations against the accuser rolled through the pod.

"Motherfucker's running a game!"

". . . messin' with the unity!"

"He the snake his ownself!"

"Mehhhhhhhhhhhds . . . mehhhhhhhhhhhhhds . . . mehhhhhhhhhhhhhhds . . ."

"Yo! One a y'all! Kite me a rollie!" To kite something was to send it from one cell to another hand by hand through the openings in the wire cages overhead.

"Yo! Dinky Man! Where you at, baby brother?"

"K aisle, man, K aisle."

"Call my woman and tell her to take that six G's to my momma's house and get the deed to her house and take it to my bondsman. My momma's got another forty-five hun a ma money. Tell her I'm gon' beat her ass if she don't do it."

"Man, she say she don't have no six G's a yo's."

"What? Just tell the bitch to do what I said!"

"Okay, man."

"Thank you, baby brother. Shit, I got two *hunnert* G's. The fuck do I wanna stay in jail for!"

"Wooooooo-eeeeee!"

"Su-perflyyyyyyyyyyyyyyyy!"

"Yo! Deputy! There's a spider in my house! I don't play that shit! You gotta do something! Call the exterminator!"

The voice of an Okie from up on the catwalk: "Whyn't you both go to sleep? Spider say he's ass-out, too."

"Yo! Heavy! Read me that kite again, from that African bitch over in East Greystone! Need some music to jack off by!"

"Dark in here, man. How you speck me read 'at kite?"

"Then *remember* it, Heavy! Part about gettin' *licked* ten times a day!"

Masturbation was so prevalent at Santa Rita after lights-out, you could actually hear the joints and flat springs of the metal bunks groaning and squeaking. Conrad could hear them now. He could hear undisguised groans . . . *Unnnnh* . . . *Awnnnnnnnnnhhhhhhhhh* . . . He could hear exclamations of satisfaction . . . *God-damn!* . . . *Good jookin'!* . . . And now, amid the whiffs of body funk, urine, bowel movements, and Bugler smoke, there arose, as it did every night, the sickly sweet smell of semen. Geysers of it! Gallons of it! Jook! Jook! Jook! Jook! There had been nights when Mutt and Five-O had both been going at it at the same time, Five-O on the upper bunk and Mutt down below, barely a yard from where Conrad lay jackknifed on the mattress on the floor. In these lizard cages of despair and terror, he couldn't imagine unlocking his nervous system's defenses long enough even to fantasize about sexual joy. But few others seemed to have any such constraint. They were lying back on their bunks, slogging away. They were transported. Testosterone! Brute sexual energy! A herd of young male animals! He had the impression that if some night they managed to masturbate in a harmonic wave, Santa Rita would rise right up out of the ground and flip over.

And then the *tuckatuckatuckatuckatuckatucka* began. It was the sound of scores of tiny makeshift bongo drums starting to beat. Every night the inmates, including many of the white ones, took plastic spoons and began rapping on the bottoms of empty ice cream cups. This was the invitation for the great entertainer, the wraith with the do-rag, Rapmaster EmCee New York, to begin his act. In the light, in the pod room, he looked like someone wasted and ravaged beyond all hope. But at night, in the dark, he seemed as big as all of Santa Rita. His voice filled the old barracks.

The ice cream cup percussion swelled in volume, and a voice sang out: "And now . . . direct from the Apollo Theater . . . in New York City . . ." This was Dinky Man, the Rapmaster's herald and backup singer. ". . . Rapmaster EmCee . . . NEW YORK!"

A burst of cheers, and then the pod grew quiet. All you could hear at first was the thrum of an electric bass, which an inmate called Beat Box was able to create, *a cappella*, deep in his throat, as the O-town boys waited for the opening line they loved. And here it came. The big baritone voice of the Rapmaster chanted:

> *"Yo, sugar!—think 'at's a ruby*
> *You got stuck inside yo' crack?"*

Ummmmmmmmhhhhhhhh. A collective moan of approval swept through the pod.

> *"The fuck, yo' booty turned to gold*
> *While you was lyin' on your back?"*

The chorus began to keep time by slapping their hands on the bunk frames as well as rapping the cups.

> *"Ain' tryin' no mo' sweet talk, baby!*
> *Hubba ho know street talk, maybe!*
> *So you gon' get a homey's dick, 'cause*
> *This homey's got a dicky itch!*
> *An' I ain't gonna play 'at shit!*
> So . . .
> *Give it up, bitch!"*

By the time he reached the *it* in *Give it up, bitch,* the pod was screaming the refrain over the wire, for this was the Rapmaster's theme song. In an instant the pod was resounding with the hymn to its one god, raw masculinity:

GIVE IT UP, BITCH!
GIVE IT UP, BITCH!
GIVE IT UP, BITCH!
GIVE IT UP, BITCH!

Lying there on the top bunk, as the sound rolled over him, Conrad felt his hands grow cold and his torso grow terribly hot, and he broke out into a sweat. He had been hearing "Give It Up, Bitch" every night for ten days, but now its meaning truly sank in. At Santa Rita "Give it up, bitch" was the cry of absolute male conquest. "Whatever you have, your body, your *booty*, your *ass*, your money, your honor, your self-respect, your good name, it's now *mine*, and you'll either give it to me or I'll rip it out of you"—and when would Conrad Hensley's moment come?

The percussion of the ice cream cups and the slaps on the bunk frames continued, but the voices grew silent, as the homeys, the O-town homeboys, waited for the Rapmaster's second stanza. The second stanza was always something new. You could hear Beat Box making his electric bass sound deep in his throat, and then the Rapmaster resumed:

"Shorty's johnson, he go roamin',
Homey jeans a his is packin' heat
Inside that Cracker hack's own home, an'
Bottom lady wants 'at sweet dark *meat."*

Hideous laughter. The O-town homeys picked up every reference right away. *Shorty* was code for the sort of man who goes around making love to other men's *bottom ladies* when the men are out of the house. Shorty's *johnson* was his penis, which was hot as a pistol (*packin' heat*). A *Cracker hack* was an Okie deputy.

"No mo' tiny Cracker dickies, Lordy,
Gimme yo' big jimbo, Shorty!

Fo'at Cracker come back, 'cause I
Caint take'at tiny gray hack's mackin'!"

Howls, cries, ululations—the boys were beside themselves. *Mackin'* was lovemaking. This was a ballad of the O-town boys subjecting the Okie deputies, who were up on the catwalk at this very moment, to the ultimate ignominy: cuckolding them in their own homes.

"*At gray ho's dyin' fo'* Shorty's *pitch!*
So . . ."

This time the chorus didn't even wait for the Rapmaster. With a contemptuous laughing roar they broke into the refrain. The very air of the pod exploded with

GIVE IT UP, BITCH!
GIVE IT UP, BITCH!
GIVE IT UP, BITCH!
GIVE IT UP, BITCH!

Most of the code the deputies couldn't figure out. But *hack* was an old and familiar slang term for jailhouse guards, and *Cracker* was the standard O-town derogation for white people; and so at the very least the deputies knew that this particular stanza of Rapmaster EmCee New York's composition was about them. As soon as the ruckus died down a bit, one of them yelled from the catwalk:

"YO! KNOCK OFF 'AT DAMN JUNGLE MUSIC!"

Laughter, whistles, catcalls, and then the voice of the Rapmaster himself: "What's the problem, man? We just having a little *unity* down here."

The deputy yelled: "Steppin' on your fuckin' knuckles and hollerin' is what *you* doin'!"

More laughter, ruder catcalls. They were so wound up they didn't even take offense. The Rapmaster had just put this bunch of lamebrain Crackers in their place—but good!

On the top bunk Conrad propped himself on one elbow. He looked up through the screen, past the silhouette of the catwalk, until he could make out a corner of one of the clerestory windows. He stared, stared, stared, hoping for some glimpse of the outside world, a star, a fragment of the moon . . . But there was nothing. His world was now this lizard cage in this pod, which was gorged with anger and testosterone. Everything boiled down to the power of the brute, which was constantly expressed in terms of sexual conquest.

He lay down flat on his back and closed his eyes and listened to the testicular squall as it raged over the wire. Sooner or later his time would come. Of that he had no doubt. And what character would he bring to the encounter? How would he act? How does the bull, when the lion attacks, discover what powers he is endowed with? It is plain that each of us who has the power will not be unaware of its possessions. Like the bull, the man of noble nature does not become noble all of a sudden. He must train through the winter and make ready . . . He tried to review his own life . . . He had . . . He had . . . Well, he had refused to accept a plea bargain . . . He had . . . He had . . . His spirits sank all over again. No matter what he had done, how could it help him? He was young, white, and slightly built, and he had no comrades, and he was penned up with the brutes in Pod D, West Greystone, Santa Rita. Lying there in the dark, he ran his right hand down his left arm, from the shoulder to the hand, and then he ran his left hand down his right arm. He still had his big forearms and wrists and hands, the only legacy of six months as a beast of burden in the Suicidal Freezer Unit at Croker Global. But what earthly good would these poor arms be against Rotto and his boys? He was barely half the size of any of them . . .

"I gave you a portion of our divinity," said Zeus, "a spark from our own fire." His eyes tightly shut, Conrad sought to shut out everything, all sounds and all other evidence of his senses, so as to feel the spark of Zeus and open himself to his divine energy. Where it would come from and what it might feel like, he had no idea. All he knew was that it was time to beckon it and surrender himself to it. Zeus . . . Zeus . . . how would he even know it when it came? Having never believed in a god, and having never prayed before, he didn't even know that this was prayer.

Chapter XVIII

The *Aha!* Phenomenon

IT HAD JUST TURNED DARK, AND ATLANTA'S PRIDE AND JOY IN the arts, the High Museum, was ablaze with the light that poured from its windows up on the eminence of a knoll at Peachtree and Sixteenth Streets, right across from the First Presbyterian Church. The museum was fiercely different from the church. The church, built in 1919, was a stately, dark, and stony neo-Gothic pile. The museum, built in 1983, was pure white and modern in the Corbusier mode. It stretched on for half the length of a football field in a parade of white geometric shapes, from cubes to cylinders and everything in between and back again, all of it adorned with white pipe railings. *Le tout Atlanta* was there, for this was the opening of the notorious but glorious Wilson Lapeth exhibition.

A storm of voices, a regular typhoon, raged in the museum's grand atrium, until the very air seemed to exert an unbearable pressure. It made Martha Croker dizzy. So many tuxedos and extravagant dresses! So many grinning white faces! So many boiling teeth! So many cackling laughs! So many white ramps and railings! So many throats screaming with the euphoria of knowing they had arrived in the one place in all Atlanta where anyone of any social wattage whatsoever was supposed to be on this particular evening in May! (Oh, Destiny.)

Martha turned toward her escort, a tall, plump, pleasant, fiftyish man named Herbert Longleaf, whom Joyce had found for her, and he smiled and leaned toward her and said something that was immediately swept away by the deafening screams and cackles of the tuxedos and fancy dresses. Joyce's boyfriend, Glenn Branwaist, a handsome but gloomy-looking forty-two-year-old, rolled his eyes as if to say, "Useless to even try to talk." Joyce's little face was resolutely radiant with makeup and her party smile. She looked at Martha and swung her big brown mascara'd eyes upward, as if to say, "Isn't this something!"

The atrium was an immense space, almost fifty feet high and pure white, like the building's exterior. Up a great curved window wall with white industrial muntins rose a series of curving ramps, one above the other, with white pipe railings and white wire grilles instead of balusters. Spotlights and floodlights beamed down from all over the place in a Factory Work Bay galaxy. On a balcony, an exhibition wall bore two immense Wilson Lapeth paintings, the same two Martha had seen in *Atlanta* magazine. The size was startling; the figures seemed twice as big as life. There was the chain gang—and the two handsome young prisoners, clad in prison stripes, reaching out toward one another with looks of abject romantic yearning on their fair young faces. And there was the prison dormitory and all the fair young flesh . . . prisoners half-clad, prisoners practically naked, prisoners without a stitch on . . . The painting throbbed with pent-up sexuality . . . The boys seemed to be about three seconds from plunging into a homosexual rout . . . And this, a gay delirium, was the aegis underneath which *le tout Atlanta* had assembled in this place . . .

Martha looked about her, half-expecting to see hundreds of amazed faces turned up toward the vast tableau on the balcony . . . but not at all. They were like the crowd at any other Atlanta gala. They had eyes only for one another. The way they grinned and screamed and cackled, it could just as easily have been the Juvenile Diabetes Ball or a Georgia Tech alumni banquet. Perhaps by now everybody, even in Atlanta, just accepted the notion that art was supposed to be perverse, troublesome, and—what was the word?—confrontational? Perhaps they had all glanced at those two paintings and decided that if the late Mr. Lapeth's libidinal kinks hadn't been any more outrageous than this, then Atlanta could take it.

The happy bawling mob was packed in all around Herbert, Joyce,

Glenn, and Martha, but somehow a young man wearing a tuxedo and a mint-green bow tie appeared with a tray full of flutes of champagne, and they each took one. The mint-green bow tie was the familiar insignia of the caterer, Colonel Popover, and for an instant Martha flashed back to all the parties and ribbon cuttings Croker Global had staged with Colonel Popover, an enormously fat man, whatever his real name was, as the caterer—but she hadn't come here to think about Charlie. Quite the opposite. (A new Destiny.) She took a sip of the champagne. Not bad. She smiled at Joyce and Herbert and Glenn. Smiles all around; another sip of champagne; and another.

The crowd surged and heaved and roared. Before she knew it, a very tall man was standing barely an arm's length away, talking to someone she couldn't see. His back was almost completely to her, but she had no trouble recognizing him. He was so hunched over that his neck jutted forward and his nose looked like a pointer's. Arthur Lomprey it had to be, the president of PlannersBanc. She had sat next to him at dinner on at least three different occasions back when Charlie was trying to get the financing for Croker Concourse. There was something patronizing about the way Arthur Lomprey always cocked his canted-over head and squinted and smiled as he talked, as if he were letting you in on secrets from on high that you probably couldn't comprehend anyway. But she did know him, and something was gnawing at her: the urge to show that she was part of the social swim. After all, this was her return to . . . Society. She had paid $20,000 for a table and invited nine guests. She had bought this dress—a black silk taffeta embroidered with tiny red dots, bare-shouldered and scarcely even knee-length—she was proud of her wide shoulders and well-turned calves—for $3,500. She had anointed her shoulders with baby oil to make them glisten. She had spent $4,200 for this necklace—watch-chain gold with small rubies—$225 for hair coloring (pineapple blond) and a hairdo at Philippe Brudnoy's, $150 for makeup at LaCrosse, $850 for these black lizard-and-patent-leather high-heeled shoes, plus she couldn't remember how much on Mustafa Gunt's class at DefinitionAmerica in hopes of giving herself a body more like a boy with breasts'.

On top of that, she had just downed a glass of champagne. So she inched closer to the tall, stooped figure and exclaimed: "Arthur!"

Arthur Lomprey turned and looked at her, and his smile spread so far she could have counted his teeth. But his eyes were pure panic.

They contracted into little frozen balls. "May Day!" they said. "Code Blue! I've met this woman somewhere before, but who in the name of God is she?"

"Heyyyyy!" he exclaimed. "Howya doin'!"—all the while grinning foolishly as his eyes began a frantic search for a clue. They bounced all over her hairdo, her tinctured locks, her made-up face, the necklace, the dress, the glistening shoulders, and whatever else he could see of her rigorously exercised body.

"How're the children!" he exclaimed finally, taking a desperate chance.

How're the children? This was the deepest wound of all. The man had just scanned the best she could possibly present to the world after spending $8,925 plus untold hours of cardiovascular agony at the hands of a Turkish martinet—and that fully analogue, non-digital, chemically activated computer, his brain, had arrived in milliseconds at the answer: matronly. So . . . *How're the children?*

Martha wanted to scream, but in her stunned condition the best she could do was say lamely and mechanically, "Fine."

"That's terrific!" exclaimed Arthur Lomprey, who probably hadn't even heard her. "That's terrific!"

He kept bobbing his head to show just how terrific it was and looking straight through her, trying to devise some way to remove himself from her presence before he was compelled to introduce her to the people he was with. Who *was* this superfluous woman? Who *was* this invisible ex-wife? Who *was* this social ghost (without a husband at her side to give her an identity)? She didn't wait for the situation to become any more painful. She pivoted and turned back to Joyce, Joyce's Glenn, and Herbert Longleaf.

AT LAST, IN that roaring sea, Peepgass spotted another of those lads with the mint-green bow ties and the trays of champagne. This one looked like a blond prep school boy on the precipice of his first plunge into debauchery. But that was merely a mental blip, the fleetest of passing thoughts. The main thing was to get to him and lay hands on another glass of champagne.

All the grinning faces shrieked to be heard. The noise choked the air. The crowd was packed so close together in this part of the atrium, he would have to wriggle like a fish to get through. The path to the champagne lay between a man and a woman who had their backs to each other. The woman had on a black dress with an extravagant flounce of material, a gigantic bow, just below the waist, surmounting her buttocks. The man was a real porker with a bottom so big it forced apart the vent in the back of his dinner jacket. Peepgass took a deep breath. He tried to flatten himself. He made his move, turned sideways, tried to slip through. He got stuck. Both of them, the man and the woman, turned their heads and glowered at him.

"Excuse me!" he exclaimed. "I'm very sorry!" A smile of social shame slithered across his face—but with a supreme, ungainly, much-resented effort he forced his way through. Thank God, the boy with the mint-green bow tie hadn't been able to budge. Peepgass took a glass of champagne from the tray. A quick look about: he was hemmed in on all sides by people he didn't know. A quick look above: on the balcony Wilson Lapeth's pale and handsome young prisoners, *très gay*, reigned over Atlanta's big money . . . All very odd . . . He lifted the champagne to his lips and took a sip. He loved it. He was torn between the desire to dawdle over the glass, so as to have something to do, some bit of party business to perform, even if it was only to drink a glass of champagne, so that he wouldn't appear to be an utter social cipher—and an urge to . . . *knock back another glass of champagne*. The animal urge overcame the social insecurity. He downed the champagne in four rapid gulps, put the empty flute back on the tray, and grabbed another one. The boy with the bow tie gave him a startled, reproving look. Peepgass offered a smile of apology. A delicious warmth rose from his stomach and filled his head like a cloud. He had an overwhelming urge to find somebody to grin at and talk to. But whom did he know, other than Marsha? And so far, in this mob, he had been unable to find her. He had met Marsha four years ago when she was Marsha Bernstein and had opened a gallery of contemporary art called the Alma (for Alma Mahler, whom she thought she resembled) down on Ponce de Leon. Opening a gallery of contemporary art in Atlanta, Georgia, was not a sound business decision, and the venture began foundering immediately. Peepgass, eager to demonstrate his clout in the world of banking to this pretty and very likable young woman, had engineered a $100,000 loan from PlannersBanc. This would have inevitably earned him shit-head status, except for the fact that it was in her role as proprietress of the Alma Gallery that Marsha had met Herbert Richman and married him, after which paying back a mere $100,000 loan was no problem.

Marsha was not one to forget a friend; so she had invited Peepgass to join her table at the Wilson Lapeth opening.

Peepgass stood on tiptoe to see if he could spot her . . . Marsha . . . He craned about . . . No Marsha . . . but there, almost directly behind him, a towering and yet oddly stooped-over man—no question about it! Lomprey, lord of the forty-ninth floor at PlannersBanc! Lomprey was grinning at a matronly woman with pineapple-blond hair and big bare shoulders that glistened as if they were oiled. Peepgass had seen her somewhere before, but who on earth was she? The woman suddenly turned away, and Lomprey was left standing there with a foolish grin on his face.

Like many another man with sweet clouds of champagne in his head, Peepgass did not stop to think. He could only feel the tremendous relief of spotting someone he knew.

He was no longer timid. He forced his way through the crowd without so much as a diffident wrinkling of the brow.

"Arthur!"

Lomprey turned, stared at him, then squinted, did a double-take, cocked his head, and smiled. It was a smile that did not in any way involve the eyes, however.

"Well, well, well . . . Peepgass," he said.

The hesitation and the dead smile were bad enough, but it was the *Peepgass* that did it. At the bank Lomprey always called him Ray. But his instinctive reaction at this breathtaking social altitude, a $2,000-a-plate opening at the High Museum, was to call him by his last name, as if he were no more than a petty functionary in his employ. Peepgass felt the insult before he could sort it out logically. But he sorted it out fast enough. Lomprey, no doubt feeling like a great lion of finance, had bought an entire table—with the bank's money, of course—and filled it with people appropriate to his eminence in the world. The unexpected and inappropriate presence of a mere underling, a mere staff officer from the bank, a mere cog, a mere loan monitor, a mere Peepgass, diminished the magnitude of his social triumph. And now Lomprey just stared at him with that dead smile, as if to say, "Okay, you got in here somehow—and what of it?" He made no attempt to introduce him to the two men and the woman in his little conversational knot.

Suddenly feeling embarrassed and ransacking his brain for something to say, Peepgass shouted above the roar of the crowd, "I can't remember, Arthur! Did we sell Lapeth futures?"

Immediately he regretted the crack. He was alluding to a scheme Lomprey himself had dreamed up during the heady days of the late 1980s, back when art prices were skyrocketing. In connection with the Art Investment Seminars the bank had begun selling what were, in effect, futures on certain fashionable artists. The scheme had failed miserably. It may have been innovative, it may have been cosmopolitan, but it wasn't about to fly in Atlanta, Georgia.

"I don't think so," said Lomprey's lips. But his eyes said, "Kindly disintegrate."

The moment stretched out, stretched out, stretched out—until Peepgass had no choice but to leave.

"Well, Arthur," he said, "happy landing!"

Then he wheeled about and headed back into the shrieking sea of humanity.

Happy landing? Why had he said that? How could he be so flippant? But that worry was soon replaced by a champagne surge of anger and resentment. Why, that stiff neck! That party whore! That petty snob! That great social-climbing hunchback! Wouldn't even introduce me to the people he was talking to!

Just ahead, no more than six feet away in a roaring swell of tuxedos and pouffed dresses, was another young man with a mint-green bow tie and a tray full of champagne. This time Peepgass was neither diffident nor even remotely subtle about it. He practically bowled over two women as he bulled his way to the tray and seized a lovely fluteful. Bottoms up!

CHARLIE CROKER STEADIED himself with both hands on the white pipe railing of the balcony and leaned over and surveyed the scene below. A confused cackling gabble swelled up from the atrium floor. The fools! Reminded him of a flock of turkeys.

He leaned over a little farther and stared straight down at the tables, which were set for dinner. The tablecloths were white, and they gleamed with stemware and hotel silver, and in the center of each table was a dense cluster of reddish-orange flowers with black spots in their centers. Two thousand dollars a plate—and he had bought an entire table—$20,000—and oh, how he'd love to go home to Buckhead—*right now . . .*

Charlie felt more depressed than ever by the thought of doing what he was now doing, *going out among them*, among friends, admirers, rivals, *the world*. He had the feeling that his big body and his square jaws and his bald head now gave off an aura and that this aura flashed BANKRUPT! BANKRUPT! FRAUD! FRAUD! FRAUD!

So badly had he wanted to avoid the crowd that it was he, Charlie, who had suggested that Serena and he and Billy and Doris Bass walk up the ramp to the balcony and see the rest of the exhibition. So now he led them from the balcony into the labyrinth of exhibition panels here in the recesses of the second floor.

Even before he saw anything different, he could sense the change. There were scores of people in tuxedos and party dresses up ahead of them, but all the sound now came from behind them, from the shrieking voices on the floor below. Up here things were oddly quiet. A large white exhibition panel faced them head-on. A cluster of partygoers stood before it, looking terribly pensive. Charlie moved closer. On the panel was a single painting, perhaps five feet high and six feet wide. Another chain gang . . . The point of view was from down inside a deep ditch. Far back in the ditch and in the middle ground you could see prisoners wielding picks and shovels. Above the ditch, in the background, you could see the torsos of two meaty sheriff's deputies wearing short-sleeve gray shirts and sun helmets and brandishing shotguns. Up above them was a sky filled with brutal sunlight. In the immediate foreground, down in the ditch, bathed in the cool colors of the ditch's shadows, were two young white men, both prisoners. One was sitting back against the red clay wall of the ditch, naked from the waist down, his thighs akimbo, revealing a tumescent, although not erect, penis. The other one was standing over him, bent at the waist, lowering his pants over his buttocks. A caption on the panel said, *Arrangement in Red Clay. 1923*.

Charlie was . . . shocked, speechless, stupefied. He averted his eyes . . . and they lit upon another exhibition panel just beyond. On this one, another huge painting . . . a dozen young white prisoners marching in a circle in a jail yard. Each wore a striped prison shirt and nothing else . . . Around and around they went, a circus of penises and bare bottoms . . . He averted his eyes once more . . . He couldn't believe what he was seeing. Everywhere, all the way into the deep recesses of the exhibition space, he could see white exhibition panels, clusters of silent onlookers, and images of prison garb, bare flesh, and an endless stand of penises.

Like anyone who sees his most basic assumptions about propriety being flouted, he looked to the people around him for confirmation of the righteousness of his objections. He glanced at Serena. She didn't glance back. She was studying the painting as if she had found something profound in the red clay ditch before them. Then he looked at Billy and Doris, who were at that moment looking at each other without saying a word. They were probably as shocked as he was, but it remained silent as a church up here. Just beyond Billy and Doris he noticed the stately, portly presence of Abner Lockhart and his beanpole of a wife, Katie. Abner was not only a partner in one of Atlanta's oldest law firms, Wringer Fleasom & Tick, but he was also a deacon of the Tabernacle Baptist Church. He was cradling his chin with the thumb and forefinger of his right hand, studying the painting as devoutly as Serena. A Baptist deacon! True, Tabernacle Baptist was an In-Town Baptist church, a bit sophisticated, at least, as compared to a good old Footwashing Baptist church out in the countryside, but Godalmighty, *nevertheless*—he was a *Baptist deacon*!—and he was looking at these pictures of . . . of . . . of . . . prison-pent *faggots* . . . as if they were Madonnas with halos . . . What made it still more unbelievable was the setting. This part of the museum was what was ordinarily the Decorative Arts section, which mainly meant furniture. That had always been the High Museum's strong suit, antique furniture. For decades the true passion of the matrons who ran the establishment had been interior decoration, and the High was heavy with furniture from the nineteenth century, immense pieces, many of them, startling contrivances of carved and inlaid wood, beds, sideboards, armoires, breakfronts, the sort of stupendous hulks that cow you into silence the moment you enter a room. The smaller pieces had been moved out for the Lapeth show. But some of the major pieces, the real monsters, were too big or too precious to be moved about, such as the famous Herter Bed, which was . . . right over there . . . a fabulous creation in ebonized cherry inlaid with light woods, rosewood, brass, and Japanese marquetry, a veritable monument to Victorian dignity, solidity, respectability, and grandeur—the Herter Bed had now been overrun by this . . . this . . . this homosexual orgy—

A sudden stab of doubt . . . Was it he, Charlie, who was out of step? Had his eyes been closed when some irresistible shift took place on the moral terrain? Or were all these people, even Abner Lockhart, just plain intimidated, afraid to let it be known that they weren't sophisticated enough to be cosmopolites of the new Atlanta, the international city?

Whichever, Charlie experienced his first surge of spirit of the entire evening. He was damned if he was just going to stand here piously like the rest of them. He brushed past Abner Lockhart and went up close to the panel and looked at the caption: *Arrangement in Red Clay. 1923.* Pretending to read, he said in a full voice, "Two cocksuckers down in a ditch. 1923."

Billy Bass let out a loud guffaw, but Doris didn't seem to know what to do, and Serena said with an exterminating hiss:

"Don't be stupid!"

Charlie was aware of people cutting glances at him from all sides, except for Abner and Katie Lockhart, who acted as if they hadn't heard a thing. Gradually all the faces turned away, and the solemn perusal of the treasures of Wilson Lapeth continued. The great Charlie Croker was being treated like a child who has done something infantile in church.

AT DINNER THE crowd, drunk on champagne and the thought of being at *the* place in Atlanta *where things are happening* this evening, shrieked and cackled until their bawling seemed to bounce off the walls and the ceiling fifty feet above and roll back over them in waves. Martha's table was out in the middle of that sea of round white tables on the atrium floor. At the center of each table was a startling *cachepot* of fully opened poppies, made all the more startling by the implacable whiteness of the atrium itself.

At Joyce's urging, Martha had seated herself between the two best-looking and most eligible bachelors in their entourage—finding such men was Joyce's specialty, her mission, at this stage of her life—Oskar von Eyrik, who had been born in Germany but had only a trace of an accent now and was vice president of ProCor, an HMO with headquarters in Atlanta, and Sonny Beamer, who had his own public relations firm, called HiBeam. Both were in their late forties, a bit fleshy, but handsome, hearty, gregarious, and great talkers. Oskar von Eyrik, leaning toward his hostess in order to make himself heard, was off on a long discourse about the security precautions that various major business executives were taking. Martha kept a smile fixed on her face while she racked her brain for something she might possibly contribute to the subject. Suddenly it came to her, that much-sought-after social resource—a nugget!—a conversational nugget! The architect Charlie had chosen for Croker Concourse, Peter Prance, had once told her how

Jimmy Good, the young Silicon Valley microchip billionaire, had instructed him to build a secret room in his 30,000-square-foot house in Los Altos, a room that not even his wife and children would know about. The idea was that when *predators* broke into his house in the night—he was quite paranoid on that score—he could slip into the secret room and no one, not even his own flesh and blood with guns at their temples, would be able to divulge his whereabouts. As soon as Oskar von Eyrik's lips stopped moving, she attempted to drop this nugget into the conversation in a brief, condensed form—since, being a veteran of dinners like this, thanks to her twenty-nine years with Charlie, she knew that a woman can ask questions, introduce topics, interject the occasional bon mot, even deliver a punch line now and again, but she is not to launch into anecdotes or in any other fashion actually *tell long stories* herself.

But no sooner had she enunciated the phrase "Jimmy Good's house" than Oskar von Eyrik broke in and exclaimed, "Jimmy Good's house! Oh my God!"—whereupon he was off on a long anecdote about the time he was actually *in* Jimmy Good's house, and Jimmy—he referred to him as Jimmy, as if they were pals of long standing—Jimmy had taken up skateboarding at the age of thirty-three and had built an enormous half-pipe on his back lawn, and—

Martha didn't so much mind the fact that he had expropriated *her* conversational nugget as the fact that when Sonny Beamer, who was on her other side, turned their way to listen in, Oskar von Eyrik began to look right past *her* and direct the entire story into *the man's* face. Not only that; when Sonny Beamer was distracted for a moment by Joyce, who was on his other side, Oskar von Eyrik stopped talking. He stopped in mid-sentence with his mouth open and his eyes pinned on Sonny Beamer. He remained frozen that way, as if his pause button had been pushed, as he waited for Sonny Beamer to finish with Joyce. He didn't so much as flick a glance toward Martha.

After all, why waste a terrific yarn on a superfluous woman, even if she happens to be your hostess?

BARELY EIGHT FEET away, in this boiling social sea, Peepgass was struggling to keep up a conversation with the woman on his left, Cordelia Honeyshuck, the widow of Georgia's Senator Ulrich B. (Eubie) Honeyshuck. It was not that she was difficult to talk to, for she was adept at prattling on about almost any subject. It was that she was too old and too much of a has-been, and Peepgass was too highly primed with champagne and too eager for the joys of *le monde* at this table where Herbert and Marsha Richman, the fitness-center tycoon and his scintillating wife, reigned. Marsha was too many seats away for Peepgass to talk to her, but Herbert Richman was only two seats away, just on the other side of Cordelia Honeyshuck, and Peepgass was busy trying to overhear what Herbert Richman was saying to Julius Licht, a wealthy lawyer known as Mr. Class Action, who was two seats to *his* left. They were talking right across the face of a young thing Peepgass didn't recognize, a bony but pretty blonde, whose head oscillated like an old-fashioned electric fan as the two men conversed back and forth. In fact, Peepgass was all ears, since the subject at this moment was Charlie Croker.

His voice raised to surmount the din of the banquet, Herbert Richman was regaling Julius Licht with an account of a weekend he had recently spent at Croker's plantation, Turpmtine, and of how he had gotten an earful and an eyeful of the Good Ol' Boy taking on the world . . . on race . . . on gay rights . . .

Licht, a trim, silver-haired man whose face was all sharp angles, shook his head and said, "That guy—he's such a throwback. He's here somewhere." He craned his head about. "I saw him earlier. He's bought a table. I'd love to eavesdrop and hear what he thinks of *this* show."

"This show?" said Richman.

"Wilson Lapeth's coming-out show," said Licht.

Richman laughed in his soft way. "Me, too."

A wave of fear shot through Peepgass, who was busy not listening to old Mrs. Honeyshuck on the subject of horticulture. Croker—somewhere in this room! Reflexively he glanced about at the swarm. Wouldn't want to run into that big tank without a few DeKalb County peace officers running interference! At the same time, the subject was perfect. Now! thought Peepgass. Now's the moment!

There was no way he could hear this old woman out on the subject of aerated camellias—*and*—jump into Richman and Licht's conversation about Charlie before they changed the subject, after which it would be too late. Must move now!

So without any preamble or apology whatsoever, he looked past old Mrs. Honeyshuck toward Julius Licht, put on a 300-watt grin, and shouted, "Did I just hear you say Charlie Croker's bought a table at this dinner!"

He caught no more than a peripheral glimpse of Mrs. Honeyshuck's shocked face—utterly rude, of course, to abruptly end one conversation in order to join a better one—but there was no time to worry about that! He was leaning so far toward Licht and Richman that his shoulder was practically on top of Mrs. Honeyshuck's clavicle.

"That's right," said Julius Licht, a bit tentatively, since he had no idea who this grinning man was.

"Then he's being a naughty fellow!" said Peepgass. "He's bought it with *our* money!"

"Your money?" said Herbert Richman.

"Ours—PlannersBanc's," said Peepgass, rolling his eyes in the way that says, "Discretion keeps me from going into the details." Aloud: "You know Croker Concourse?"

Richman and Licht nodded yes. They were both leaning toward him, avid for the gossip. Peepgass rolled his eyes again.

"What's wrong with Croker Concourse?" said Herbert Richman.

"As a building? Nothing," said Peepgass. "It's a fabulous building. As a *situation*—" He rolled his eyes once more.

"Whattaya mean?" asked Herbert Richman.

"Let's just say that if Charlie Croker still owns Turpmtine Plantation six months from now, it'll be a miracle," said Peepgass. Still more rolling of the eyes.

"No kidding," said Herbert Richman.

Peepgass gave his lips a terse pursing and shook his head.

By now the three men, Herbert Richman, Julius Licht, and Peepgass, were leaning so far toward one another that the two women, old Mrs. Honeyshuck and the pretty, bony young thing, were flattened against the backs of their chairs.

Peepgass loved the way he himself sounded. He had spoken with the authority and omniscience of a Lomprey at the very least. He loved the new Ray Peepgass. He felt that he now existed on the same social plateau as any of the most exalted creatures in this vast room.

"Speaking of Charlie Croker," said Julius Licht, "do you know who that woman is?"

"What woman?" asked Peepgass.

To be discreet about it, Licht kept his hand close to his chest and pointed toward a woman at the next table. Peepgass had to turn in his seat to see her. It was the same matronly, middle-aged woman with glistening shoulders whom he had noticed earlier in the evening. She was leaning disconsolately back in her chair while the men on either side of her leaned toward one another and talked.

"Who *is* that?" said Peepgass. "I noticed her earlier. I've seen her somewhere or other."

"That's Croker's first wife," said Julius Licht. "I haven't seen her for a long time. To tell you the truth, I'd totally forgotten about her. Nice woman."

Peepgass stared at the woman and tried to size her up. Croker's first wife . . . Her eyes appeared to be focused on some point far beyond the walls of the High Museum . . .

All at once the *Aha!* phenomenon swept Peepgass's central nervous system.

"What's her first name?" he asked Julius Licht.

"Martha."

"Martha," said Peepgass, nodding up and down and echoing this information. "Now it all comes back. She *is* a nice woman. Martha Croker, Martha Croker . . ."

He made it sound as if he was indulging in pleasant recollections of days gone by . . . In fact, he was trying to nail her first name down in his mind.

Martha Croker, Martha Croker, Martha Croker, Herbert Richman, and Julius Licht . . . Martha, Herbert, and Julius . . . Unless he was wildly wide of the mark, he had just found his nucleus, his center of gravity . . . Julius, Herbert, and Martha . . .

A smile stole onto his face while the atrium of the High shrieked and boomed and roared.

CHARLIE DIDN'T FEEL the slightest urge to project the hearty Croker personality upon his "guests" at the table. Billy and Doris were the only ones he cared about. The rest had been chosen by Serena, and he didn't have the slightest interest in knowing why. He just wanted the evening to be over. He just wanted to escape from the gaze of all the people in this ridiculous room. Serena was sitting across the table from him. Some Atlanta hostesses always sat husbands next to their wives, but Serena favored the New York (and therefore cosmopolitan) way. She was having such a grand time, she would have to be dragged away. That much was obvious, not just from her constant, hemorrhaging laughter, but also from the way her vivid blue eyes danced about.

Meantime, the woman on his right, a sharp-nosed fortyish creature named Myra Somethingorother, kept pestering him with inane conversational gambits. In fact, at this very moment she was asking him: "Tell me, Mr. Croker, how did you come to be interested in art?"

The presumption made him angry. "Good Lord," he said, "who on earth told you I was interested in art?"

Startled, the woman lifted her hand and gestured vaguely toward the table, the atrium, the museum . . .

He felt almost as if somehow his manhood had been called into question. "I'm not interested in art, and I'm sure as hell not interested in this show or this museum. But if you want to do business in Atlanta, you come to these things." He shrugged, as if to add, "It's as simple as that."

The woman was left speechless, which suited him fine.

JULIUS LICHT SAID to Herbert Richman and Peepgass, "Look at Colonel Popover over there! I never saw that great tub of lard move so fast in my life!"

Herbert Richman said to Licht, "Oh, one way or the other, that guy's pretty speedy. He's got the banquet business in this town locked up." Then to Peepgass he said, "Whattaya suppose he clears on a dinner like this?"

Peepgass hadn't a clue—but he was elated! Satisfaction swept through him like a neural wave! Richman had asked *him* and not his pal Licht! He regarded him as an equal—a man on his plane in the grand scheme of things! A man who would know about such things—a man who could, after all, provide such broad hints about the stunningly cataclysmic fate of the likes of that boorish throwback Charlie Croker! One's very presence at a social event like this was a permission slip to deal knowingly with such nabobs as Herbert Richman and Julius Licht! He felt like a Cinderella liberated, if only for this divine interlude, from the squalor of Normandy Lea and the staff side of the PlannersBanc hierarchy.

"Well, let's see . . ." he said to Herbert Richman. He had no idea what he might say next, since the hiring of a caterer was so far beyond the scope of his world that he couldn't even make an intelligent guess.

Fortunately, Julius Licht intervened: "I've used him, so I can give you a pretty good idea. He's charging the museum about one hundred dollars a head. So what's 100 times 400?—forty thousand? Yeah. So let's say his overhead is half that—although it's probably not even that. He's got a lot of kitchen help to pay, but these waiters, they're all students and actors and artists and so forth. They don't cost him much. So he's clearing twenty to twenty-five thousand dollars here. Not bad."

Peepgass nodded sagely, as did Richman. Me'n'Herb'n'Julius . . . *Not bad!* In no time Ray, as he insisted they call him, had their addresses and telephone numbers. They, in turn, had his assurances that he would "be in touch" about something he was "sure will interest you."

By and by, dessert was served, lovely deep slices of lemon meringue pie, that and more champagne. Ray held his flute of champagne up to the light and grinned, intoxicated by Fortune, at Herb and Julius.

By now the two women, Cordelia Honeyshuck and the young blond thing, were driven ever more deeply back into their chairs, almost as deeply, in fact, as Martha Croker at the next table.

THE LIGHTS DIMMED, and some sort of theatrical illumination beamed down upon a podium at the far end of the atrium. The ceremonial part of the evening was about to begin. That was okay by Charlie. He didn't want to be seen, and he certainly didn't want to have to talk to the two women anymore. He didn't even know the name, first or last, of the woman to his left, a reasonably young woman with her hair done in a so-called Palm Beach Crash Helmet. She not only dropped names, she dropped places and conveyances. If she let Charlie know once that her husband had a ranch in Wyoming—and that the only practical way to reach it from Atlanta was to have your own jet—she must have let him know fifty times. By now Charlie had tuned out.

He remained tuned out as the president of the museum's board of trustees, Ingebaugh Blanchard, the widow of Baker Blanchard, a hefty, boisterous woman known to her friends as Inky, came to the podium and said all the usual things, and then introduced the museum's new director, Jonathan Myrer. Charlie would have tuned him out, too, except that his appearance was so remarkable. He was no more than forty-two or -three, very tall and very narrow through the shoulders. His body seemed to tilt to one side, as if he suffered from scoliosis. He had a long neck and a small head with a wild overgrowth of dark curly hair that stuck out on the sides like horns.

"As you know," said this strange-looking man, in rat-tat-tat bursts of words, "this museum was originally founded by Caroline High—in her house—which was situated precisely where we are tonight. What may not be so well known—is the fact that she was acquainted with Wilson Lapeth. In the catalogue of this exhibition—you will find a photograph of Lapeth and several long-since-forgotten Atlanta artists at a picnic on her lawn. We don't know whether she knew Lapeth's secret or not. His secret, of course, was not that he was gay. In her day—in his day—such things were often silently understood—and never talked about. No, Wilson Lapeth's secret was that his sexual orientation was the engine—the driving force—the font, if you will—of a genius he felt compelled to hide from the world. This did not demonstrate a lack of courage on his part. It merely demonstrated that he was a realist. The lack of courage was society's—a society that was quick—and remains all too quick today—to repress and disempower those who—like Walt Whitman, another gay genius—have the temerity to proclaim their 'barbaric yawp' over the rooftops of the world. How fitting it is"—

Charlie looked about to see if everybody else heard what he was hearing. But even Billy's and Doris's heads were turned in a polite blankness toward the podium.

—"that Lapeth chose the prison as the subject matter of the art treasures we see around us tonight. As Michel Foucault has demonstrated so conclusively in our own time—the prison—the actual *carcerel*, in his terminology—the actual center of confinement and torture—is but the end point"—

Who? thought Charlie. Michelle Fookoe? He looked at Serena, who was turned about in her chair drinking in every word as if it were ambrosia.

—"the unmistakable terminus—of a process that presses in upon us all. The torture begins soon after the moment of birth, but we choose to call it 'education,' 'religion,' 'government,' 'custom,' 'convention,' 'tradition,' and 'Western civilization.' The result is"—

Am I hearing what I think I'm hearing or am I crazy? thought Charlie. Why wasn't somebody at one of these many tables *hissing*?—or something—

—"a relentless confinement within 'the norm,' 'the standard,' a process so"—

Oh, how he twisted those words *norm* and *standard*! Such passionate contempt!

—"so gradual that it requires a genius on the order of a Foucault—or a Lapeth—to awaken us"—

Fookoe again.

—"from the torpor of our long imprisonment. Lapeth chose to join the *out*laws—those who want *out*—those who refuse to be confined by convention—*in* prison. Even within prison walls, of course, our society does not relent. Even incarceration, as Foucault has pointed out, is called 'correction' in our enlightened time. The *out*laws are supposedly 'corrected'—bent back toward the norm—when, in fact, in so many cases it is *they* who are in a better position to correct *us* in the ways of independence and"—

Charlie looked about again. This table, the next table, the table next to that—people with absolutely untroubled countenances, as if the man were making the usual, entirely appropriate remarks that one makes on an important civic occasion.

—"and fulfillment. So while we have every reason to celebrate the discovery of a treasure of inestimable value—which this exhibition represents—we also have every reason to mourn—mourn not only the loss of Lapeth's genius to his own time—but also to mourn the loss of all the Wilson Lapeths we will never know about. We must find the courage, as a society, to invite—not allow but *invite*—genius into our lives, no matter what troubling, upsetting, turbulent, defiant, rude, and unconventional forms it may take, for such, more often than not, is the face of greatness. You who have come to this exhibition—you who have shown such generosity to this museum tonight—you have proven that you have that courage—the courage to consider the ultimate 'jailbreak,' if you will, that our society must accomplish if any of us—in any profound sense—is to become free. Such will be the true legacy of this historic moment—even more than the very real contribution you have made to our stability, our health, our future as an institution. For this, above all, I salute you."

General, unquestioning, routine, ceremonial applause. How could the man go on that way, that long, without mentioning what this exhibition was actually about!

Charlie began hissing, but nobody even noticed, except for the woman with the Palm Beach Crash Helmet, who looked at him not only as if he were repulsive but also as if he had a room to let upstairs.

EVEN AFTER THE lights came up and Inky Blanchard bade the crowd farewell and they headed away from the white tables and poppy *cache-pots,* Martha remained in a daze. Twenty thousand dollars she had poured into this evening—and for what? Herbert Longleaf was suddenly at her side, all smiles and patter, as if he had actually paid her some attention from the moment they first arrived until now . . . and within thirty seconds, although he walked beside her, he had turned his head to Joyce's Glenn Branwaist. Joyce was all smiles, too, clearly ecstatic about being in the thick of such a fabulous event. She had a strange piping laugh that went *eye eye eye eye eye eye eye eye* as she listened to something rich that Oskar von Eyrik was saying to Sonny Beamer.

One and all were heading for the front entrance, which was far too cramped for a crowd this size. Scores of tuxedos and party dresses were converging. A blur of fancy-dressed humanity slowing down to a shuffle—

Suddenly right beside her—Charlie. Charlie and Serena—so close there was no avoiding them.

They were as startled as she was. Charlie's huge chest swelled up inside his white shirt, and for an instant his big square face looked as helpless as it had that fateful morning when she had surprised him with Serena. Serena stood stock-still, her lips parted, her eyes wide, motionless, as if holding her breath.

Martha knew exactly what was coming. It was as if she could hear the synapses firing in Charlie's skull. He had a look she had seen so often before. He broke into a smile. Then his eyes lit up. She didn't know what he was going to say, but she already knew how to characterize it: *a real hambone performance.*

"Heyyyyyyy, Martha!" he said in the heartiest voice imaginable. "As I live and breathe! How you doin', gal? I didn't know you were here!"

The *How you doin', gal?* was the worst of it. *How you doin'* was pronounced in a certain tiny, intimate, mincing way—"Heh yew dewin'?" —that was pure South Georgia. And the *gal* was just short of obscene. Martha stared at him, paralyzed, speechless. So Charlie turned to Herbert Longleaf and gave him the sort of intense Friendly Bear grin and thrust of the head that he used to charm people he was meeting for the first time and put out his hand, and Martha could see she had no choice but to croak out:

"Charlie, this is Herbert Longleaf."

"Herbert?" said Charlie with the sort of pseudo-rapt Southern manly stare she had seen him use so often during their twenty-nine years of marriage. It was terribly tiresome to see him use it yet once more, in this place, at this time. "Charlie *Croker*, Herbert! It's real nice to meet you. I want you to meet my wife, Serena."

He steered Serena—Serena and her tiny black dress with the deep cleavage that was so fashionable among *young* women this year—toward Herbert Longleaf. Martha instinctively withdrew. She didn't want to have to force a smile onto her face and say hello to Charlie's perfect boy with breasts.

To make matters worse, Herbert Longleaf, her supposed escort, *was* charmed, immediately. A big submissive grin came over his face, and he began blurting out pleasantries. The next thing Martha knew, Glenn and Oskar von Eyrik and Sonny Beamer began moving closer to the great man as well. Immediately mesmerized, the whole bunch of them! The fabled tycoon—and his perfect boy with breasts! No quick hello, so long, not for Mr. Herbert Longleaf. Oh no. Now he and Charlie were deep in conversation, and Serena, listening in, laughed sociably, and so did Glenn and Oskar and Sonny Beamer. Their grins became more and more worshipful, helpless, grateful, and ingratiating. The great man stoops to converse with us! Oh, bless our lucky stars! They were paying more attention to Charlie than they had paid to her the entire evening. Joyce was loyal and stayed by her side, although who could say? Maybe in her heart of hearts she wanted to meet the great man and bask in the radiance of his manly grandeur like the rest of them.

"So that's Charlie," said Joyce.

Martha made no reply. Involuntarily she pulled back still farther, until now the stream of people trying to get to the door had made its way between her and the worshipful knot of people around her ex-husband. Except for Joyce, her eighteen thousand dollars' worth of guests were no longer aware of her existence. She was afraid to say anything to Joyce. She was afraid she might start crying.

"Martha! Martha!"

She turned her head. It was a pleasant-looking man, late thirties, early forties, with a nearly lineless face and thick sandy-colored hair. He was in a crouch, as if hiding from something. He also looked a bit drunk.

She had no idea who he was—but at the very least he was that rare creature in this teeming place: a man who actually remembered her name.

"Ray Peepgass, Martha! From PlannersBanc!"

She still had no recollection of him, but she did remember the many hours she spent in the company of people from the bank while Charlie was romancing them for stupendous loans.

He came forward, still in his crouch, and shook her hand. "I saw you earlier but I couldn't get over to you, there was such a mob!" He kept smiling but also looking this way and that. "This is so funny, because I was thinking about you just yesterday and wondering how to get in touch with you!"

"With me?"

"Yes! There's something I need to run by you! Could I give you a ring?"

He grinned and grinned, and his eyes darted this way and that. No question about it, the man was drunk.

On the other hand, during this entire night of her great re-debut, of her new Destiny, he was the one human being who had shown the slightest spontaneous interest in her existence.

"Well—of course, Mr. . . ."

"Peepgass!" he said. "Ray! Make it Ray!"

He produced a ballpoint pen from an inside jacket pocket and then began ransacking his tuxedo for a piece of paper. Finding none, he thrust out the cuff of the left sleeve of his shirt and positioned the pen above it and grinned and said, "What's the number?"

"Not on your *shirt*! It'll never come out."

"You're right! Here—I'll put it here!" He positioned the pen over the back of his left hand and grinned some more. Drunk; no question about it. But she gave him the telephone number and he wrote it on the back of his hand.

"That I won't misplace!" he said with a merry gleam in his eyes. "The shirt—you never know!"

Still crouched, Mr. Ray Peepgass said goodbye and departed, and Martha didn't give him a second thought. She was staring morosely at Herbert Longleaf and the rest of them and wondering how long it would take them to relinquish their eye-to-eye adoration of the great Charlie Croker.

"Who was that?" said Joyce.

"To be perfectly honest with you," said Martha, "I have no idea. Somebody I must have met back when Charlie was busy borrowing money from PlannersBanc."

She resumed her bitter observation of the manly Mr. Croker and his new admirers. More scalps taken by the Croker charm.

Some Destiny.

Chapter XIX

The Trial

THE NEXT TWO DAYS, MONDAY AND TUESDAY, WERE SO UNeventful, Conrad began to believe that things were settling down into a routine: a dreary one, but bearable. There were the boring times in the cell, in which he listened to the Pidgin chatter of Five-O and the motherfuckin' laments over the wire, and there were the long, anxious interludes in the pod room, in which he kept one eye on Rotto and his retinue while trying to act as if he were paying attention to nothing at all. Either way, he was able to write letters to Jill, Carl, and Christy and to read the words of Zeus' messenger, Epictetus. He kept the poor bedraggled pages of *The Stoics* with him at all times.

There wasn't a truly tense moment until the next day. During the evening pod time Rotto left the white turf and approached Vastly. He walked right into the heart of the black turf, to where Vastly, surrounded by his boys, sat on the edge of a metal table watching television. Even a blind inmate would have known something was up, because the whole pod grew quiet, except for the television set, which was tuned to a show called *Planet Retro*, about a morbid, dysfunctional world of the future in which only the explosives, automatic weapons, and combat vehicles seemed to work with any regularity. So now there was dead silence in the pod, punctuated by tinny explosions, fusillades, rpm surges, and tire screeches from up on the stanchion where the TV set was.

Rotto wasn't as big as Vastly, but with his welted scars and brawler's nose he was the meanest-looking man in the pod, Vastly included.

"Yo, Vastly," he said. "I got people here needs to use the telephone, man."

"Yeah," said Vastly, who didn't budge from the edge of the table and kept one eye on *Planet Retro*, to demonstrate the coolness with which he took Rotto's big excursion, " 'know how it is. But hey, bro, check it on out." He gestured sadly toward the two telephones. Two black inmates were using them, and six more were waiting. "Heavy night, bro. Next pod time, you got it."

"Come on, man," said Rotto. "I got people here needs to get holt their lawyers and their old ladies. How 'bout showing a little respect? We show you guys respect."

"That's cool, bro," said Vastly, "that's cool. Next pod time, no problem. Tonight's just one a those nights." He shook his head with an air of exaggerated regret.

It went on like that for a while. In terms of sheer numbers, physical power, and toughness, there was no reason why Vastly and his faction ever had to let the Nordic Bund or anybody else use the telephones. But with the Nordic Bund, as Five-O had explained it to Conrad, one never knew. They were crazy enough to cut, bite, kick, or gang-stomp Vastly or anybody else if pushed too hard, no matter what the consequences might be. Having seen the very smallest of the breed, Mutt, in action, Conrad believed it.

The standoff dragged on until Rotto finally walked on back to the other end of the room with more assurances of "next pod time," which meant exactly nothing, since next time all prior negotiations were always forgotten. Rotto returned to the white turf with a dark cloud across his face. He didn't look at anybody, not even Riffraff and Sleaze Man. He had just been totally disrespected, and everybody knew it. In any case, everybody let his breath out, and the usual ambient noise of the pod room rose back up, and a commercial came on the TV screen. A slender blonde appeared, and her face suddenly filled the screen. "Super-smoooooooooth," she said, closing her eyes and giving her lips an exaggerated O-shape and then opening her mouth and sticking the tip of her curiously blood-red tongue out between her teeth.

"You kin smooth this out for me, baby," said Rapmaster EmCee New York, looking to Vastly for approval.

After pod time, back in the cell, Five-O said to Conrad, "Bummahs, brah! Vastly wen diss Rotto to the max! Dat moke going make somebody pay." He pulled a face and rolled his eyes up into his head.

THE NEXT AFTERNOON, at pod time, all seemed tranquil.

Conrad sat down at a table and returned to Epictetus. By now he had learned how to sit on a bolted metal stool at a bolted metal table and place the forlorn pages of *The Stoics* before him and shut out the rest of the pod. What Epictetus had to say was supremely simple, and he said it over and over again in different ways. All human beings are the children of Zeus, who has given them a spark of his divine fire. Once you have that spark, no one, not even Zeus, can take it from you. This spark gives you the faculty of reasoning and the will to act or not to act and the will to get and the will to avoid. But the will to get and avoid what? "To get what is good," says Epictetus, "and to avoid what is evil." There is no use spending your life agonizing over the things that are not dependent upon your will, such as money, possessions, fame, and political power. Likewise, there is no use spending your life trying to avoid the things that are not dependent upon your will, such as the tyranny of a Nero, imprisonment, and physical danger. (Conrad nodded as he read it.) Epictetus had a special scorn for those who "merely tremble and mourn and seek to escape misfortune." "Zeus!" he cries out at one point, "send me what trial thou wilt! For I have endowments and resources, given me by thee, to bring myself honor through what befalls!" Then he says to his disciples, "What do you think would have become of Hercules if there had not been a lion and a hydra and a stag and a boar and unjust and brutal men, whom he drove forth and cleansed the world of? What would he have done if there had been nothing of this sort? Is it not plain that he would have wrapped himself up and slept and slumbered all his life in ease and luxury? He would never have been a Hercules at all! What use would he have made of his arms and his might and his endurance and noble heart, had he not been stimulated and trained by such perils and opportunities?"

Another sudden drop in the noise level of the pod room . . . Conrad looked up. His heart bolted in his chest. Rotto! Rotto had left his circle of Nordic Bundsmen and was sauntering toward the metal tables with a rocking gait, the Frankenstein, which he had apparently picked up from the O-town brothers. His nose and scars looked unusually hideous, set off as they were by the smile he had decided to paste on his mug. His upper arms looked freshly pumped up to a prodigious girth. His greasy ponytail bobbed at the base of his mostly bald skull as he rocked Conrad's way. Conrad stared, too startled to even pretend he wasn't riveted, paralyzed, by the sight.

But Rotto wasn't looking at him. He went right past him and headed straight for Pocahontas, who, as usual, sat slumped over a metal table. Nobody was moving a muscle, except for the old man (all of forty-five), Pops, who now Sinequan Shuffled as far away from Rotto as it was possible to get without leaving the white turf altogether. Rotto sat down on the metal stool next to Pocahontas's. Pocahontas raised his pallid face off his forearms just far enough to look at his visitor and then remained in that position as if frozen. He looked like an animal mesmerized by a snake. (Conrad's entire knowledge of snakes mesmerizing animals came from a Disney animated movie, *The Jungle Book*.) Rotto gave the poor boy a hideously warm smile and leaned toward him and said something Conrad couldn't make out. Pocahontas's lips wavered spastically between a polite smile and an incoherent mumble. But his eyes never varied. They stared with a look of stark transfixed fear. His head remained at a cockeyed angle near the tabletop. He was breathing so hard the auburn Mohawk brush down the middle of his skull bobbed up and down. Rotto laughed as if the boy had said something terribly amusing, then talked to him some more. This dreadful parley seemed to go on interminably, although in fact it was only for three or four minutes. Then Rotto gave Pocahontas a few comradely claps on the shoulder, smiled, got up, and went walking back to his mates with his Frankenstein rock.

Conrad was shaken. (What if it had been me!) As to what had just transpired, he could only make a horrifying guess. Everyone else seemed to be doing the same. Everyone took one last look at Pocahontas—who straightened up on the stool for a moment, breathed a prodigious, helpless sigh, and then laid his eyebrowless face and arms supinely down upon the table again. After that everyone avoided looking at him, as if the very sight might spread some terrible contagion.

Conrad tried to return to Epictetus. At first the words just ran together in a goulash, so turbulent were the thoughts and fears that had taken possession of his mind. But fifteen minutes went by, half an hour, an hour . . . and the pod eased back into its usual precarious equilibrium, and he was finally able to calm down . . . Still, he couldn't stop thinking about this poor boy, Pocahontas. What was his duty toward this sad, strange, friendless soul, if worse came to worst? What would Epictetus have done? He remembered something he had read—where? Book III, it was . . . Book III . . . Book III . . . He began riffling through the pages of the folios before him . . . Book III . . . and finally he found . . . Chapter 29 . . . The chapter was entitled "That We Ought Not to Spend Our Feelings on Things Beyond Our Power." It began: "If a thing goes against another's nature, you must not take it as evil for you. For you are not born to share humiliation or evil fortune but to share good fortune. And if a man is unfortunate, remember that his misfortune is his own fault; for Zeus created all men for happiness and peace of mind."

One of his disciples asks, "How then am I to prove myself affectionate?"

"In a noble and not a miserable spirit," says Epictetus. "Prove yourself affectionate, but see that you observe this rule: If this affection of yours, or whatever you call it, is going to make you a miserable slave, it is not for your good to be affectionate. We abound in every kind of excuse for people with degenerate spirits; with some of us it is a child, with others our mother or our brothers. We ought not to let anyone make us miserable, but let everyone make us happy, and Zeus above all, he who created us for this."

Conrad looked up and stared at Pocahontas, who seemed to have abandoned himself utterly to his fate, so forlornly and helplessly was he now draped over the table. How very sad he looked—and how hard-hearted Epictetus was! Was this the other side of the sternness with which he bade him face adversity? He wasn't sure he could be that hard-hearted . . . He studied Pocahontas some more . . . Look at what he had done to himself, to his head, all of which screamed, "Look at me! I'm here to shock you!" Judging by the puncture holes in his earlobe, you could tell he had worn a whole array of earrings, to make the scream even louder. He had shaved off his eyebrows, which made his eye sockets and his pallid eyes look ghastly. He walked with a mincing gait and held his elbows in and let his forearms waggle out like a girl's. "If a man is unfortunate, remember that his misfortune is his own fault

. . . We abound in every kind of excuse for people with degenerate spirits . . ."

The words ran through Conrad's mind, and he tried to make them fit the sad case he beheld . . . We could *make* them fit, and yet—what *was* the obligation of the Stoic, the man of noble spirit, to the people around him?

It dawned on him that he didn't even know Pocahontas's real name.

BACK IN THE cell, as they waited for the dinner trolley, all that Five-O could talk about was Rotto's pod call on Pocahontas. He sat on the edge of his bunk, holding the sides of his head with his hands and shaking it at the same time.

"Dat beeg haole mahu"—*that big white faggot*—"he wen make ass to the max." *He blundered totally.* "He mockay-die-dead." *He's deader than dead.*

Conrad stood with his back propped against the wall and his arms crossed over his chest. "But what could he do, Five-O?"

"*Any*t'ing! Anyt'ing . . . You remember wot I tell? You either one player or one punk. You no stay eenveesible. Cannot! An' dese buggahs, dey t'ink you one punk, you real had-it. Bumbye dey going grind you. Dat Pocahontas—dat mahu—wow, bummahs, man. He wen get one chance: bus' up da guy, broke his face."

"Are you kidding?" said Conrad. "He's just a weak, skinny kid. He's like a noodle. Rotto would kill him."

"Yeah?" said Five-O. "Better dat mahu going get his face broke den wot Rotto'dem going do to da buggah. Garans, brah." He began shaking his head some more. "Rotto wen get disrespected by Vastly. Now he going prove he beeg, tough moke all'a same. Make li'dat to da max. Pocahontas real had-it."

During the evening pod time, after dinner, Conrad felt agitated. He sat at a table, as usual, with the pages of *The Stoics* open before him. But he kept raising his eyes to keep tabs on Pocahontas . . . and Rotto. Pocahontas was no longer sitting at a table. He was on his feet, slowly walking around the edges of the white turf, as far as he could get from Rotto without straying into the Nuestra Familia or black turfs. His posture was dreadful. His gangling body was humped over at the shoulders, and his head, bearing its auburn brush, hung forward like a dog's. His long, dead-white, hairless arms stuck out of the armholes of his yellow felony pajamas like lengths of bone barely covered in flesh. He didn't seem to have a single muscle. Conrad was possessed with the urge to do something for him, to talk to him, give him some encouragement (but how?) . . . or something . . . Everyone else was treating him like a disease. Five-O was over on the Nuestra Familia turf huddled with one of his Mexican pals, Flaco. The two of them glanced at Pocahontas, and then Five-O did some more of his exaggerated head-shaking, all the while smiling sardonically. Not even Pops was having any truck with that piece of dead meat. Whenever his shuffle took him anywhere near the perambulating Pocahontas, he would turn on the heels of his flip-flops and go shuffling back the other way.

So that left Conrad . . . But hadn't Epictetus said, "We ought not to spend our feelings on things beyond our power"? Hadn't he said, "You are not born to share humiliation or evil fortune . . . and if a man is unfortunate, remember that his misfortune is his own fault"? Hadn't he said, "We abound in every kind of excuse for people with degenerate spirits . . . we ought not to let anyone make us miserable"? Yes, he had said that, and Epictetus was now his only compass . . . And so he would stay out of it . . . But suppose he was misinterpreting the long-dead master . . . or using him to shirk his clear duty, to absolve himself of guilt? . . . But hadn't Epictetus said, "If this affection of yours, or whatever you call it, is going to make you a miserable slave, it is not for your good"? . . . Yes, he had said that . . . Around and around it went in his head . . .

Vastly was over at the entryway to the showers, doing his dips. He had taken off the shirt of his felony pajamas, and his neck, trapezii, shoulders, and chest, as well as his upper arms, seemed to swell out to a prodigious size as he lowered and lifted his body. Five or six of his buddies hung about, fawning. Not even Rotto and his crew were paying any attention to Pocahontas—or himself—or not as far as he could detect.

The hours went by, slowly at first but then faster, as he relaxed and became absorbed once more in a letter to Jill, Carl, and Christy and Book II of Epictetus. Before he knew it, it was time for lights-out and cries into the void and O-town ballads by Rapmaster EmCee New York.

IT WAS POD time the following evening. When Conrad had last looked at them, Pocahontas was pacing quietly and dejectedly around the outskirts of the white turf, and Rotto and his boys were out in the middle, as usual. The television set was tuned to a sports channel on which some sort of bobsledding event was in progress. The hushed, modulated voice of a commentator was interspersed with the whooshing, scraping sound of the bobsleds going down their chutes. This was such a relief from the explosions, tire shrieks, Lorelei Washburn screams, and Hollywood wannabe street talk that ordinarily poured out of the TV set on the pole, there was something lulling about it. Conrad had sunk back into Book III of Epictetus . . .

> Will you realize once and for all that it is not death that is the source of a mean and cowardly spirit but rather the fear of death? Against this fear then I would have you discipline yourself—

Without knowing why, he looked up. Then he was aware that the noise level had dropped once more. He cut a glance toward Rotto and his boys—or where they usually were. Not there, not any of them . . . Then he looked for Pocahontas. No tall, sickly, languid figure with a degenerate plume walking near the wall . . . Neither was he draped over the metal table. At the table where Pocahontas usually sat was a group of Nuestra Familia Latinos plus Five-O, who was deep in conversation with Flaco. Five-O shot a glance toward the shower area. So did Flaco. So Conrad looked that way, too. To his astonishment, a half dozen of Rotto's boys, including Riffraff and Sleaze Man, stood in a line in front of the entrance to the shower area, as if they were sentinels, blocking not only anyone who might want to go inside but also anyone who wanted to look inside. Obviously they had made some kind of arrangement with Vastly and his crew. No sign of Rotto himself. The bobsleds whooshed and scraped away . . . The hushed voice murmured and droned . . . Occasional applause . . . Pops was doing his Sinequan Shuffle as far away from the showers as he could get . . .

Whatever was happening, it was happening in the shower area at this moment. Conrad felt an impulse to get up and go over there, but he didn't. He didn't budge. He sat on the metal stool, staring. The air seemed to be crackling.

After what seemed to be an eternity but may have been only a minute or two, the line of Rotto's Nordic Bundsmen stirred a bit at the entryway. Two of them moved apart, and from behind them appeared the tall, rangy, degeneratedly slouched figure of the one they called Slimy. Behind him came the fat, bearded Okie they called Gut. He was hitching up the pants of his yellow felony pajamas. As if on a military command, Rotto's boys moved away from the showers and began walking toward their end of the pod room, single file, hugging the wall. And then Conrad realized why. That way they remained just out of range of the surveillance camera up in the corner near the ceiling. Wino and the rest of Nuestra Familia, including Five-O, made a point of not looking at them. The Sinequan Shuffler put the maximum distance between himself and their march. But from the black turf Vastly and his boys looked on with what appeared to be amusement and curiosity. Conrad stared unabashedly. He couldn't help himself. He was too appalled by the thought of what must have just happened to do anything else. And then he saw what he somehow knew he was foreordained to see. He saw the bald head and the greasy ponytail behind the retaining wall of the showers. Then the brute rose to his full height and looked all about. Rotto was bare from the waist up. His buffed-up body was glossy with sweat. He leaned over and, as nearly as Conrad could tell, went through the motions of putting on his pants. Then he stood up again and nonchalantly walked out of the shower room with his Frankenstein rock, hooking his thumbs inside the elastic waistband of his felony pajamas to adjust them over the crests of his hips. With his shoulders moving this way and that from the stiff-legged gait of the Frankenstein, he looked all around, as if anxious for the entire pod to know what he had just done. Consciously, Conrad wanted to avert his eyes, but some autonomous impulse wouldn't let him. For an instant their gazes locked, Rotto's as he rocked along the wall, Conrad's as he sat at the metal table before the words of Epictetus. Rotto's lips moved ever so slightly, but what that expression was, Conrad couldn't decipher. And then the brute looked away and continued his triumphal stroll back toward his domain.

The pod remained quiet, except for the television set. A commercial must have been on, because Conrad could hear the laughter of what sounded like a group of overstimulated small children, while a saxophone played.

Then another figure rose from behind the retaining wall of the shower room . . . The auburn Mohawk on the pale, pale skull was the first thing Conrad saw . . . Pocahontas came staggering toward the opening in the wall. When he reached it, you could see that he was still trying to pull the pants of his yellow felony pajamas up over his hips. His midsection, emaciated and dead white, was bare. His face, more ghastly-looking than ever, bore a strange expression. The flesh of his eyebrowless brow was contorted and his mouth hung open, as if he were trying to remember something very important. Then he closed his eyes and hung his head, and he twisted up his mouth and began bobbing his chin. He took a single step out into the pod room, sobbing without making a sound. Then he opened his eyes and looked all around. The entire pod seemed to shrink from the sight. The Nordic Bund, Nuestra Familia, Five-O, even Vastly and his boys, and Pops, who did another of his spins and began shuffling in the opposite direction, away from the stricken youth—one and all averted their eyes, with the single exception of Conrad. Pocahontas straightened up slightly and put his hands on his hips, with the thumbs forward, as if he was trying to pull himself together and regain his dignity. And then, *just like that*, he collapsed. He crumpled, he swooned, he fell to the concrete floor in a sprawl. Rotto, Sleaze Man, Five-O, Flaco, Weddo, Wino—none of them was more than twelve feet from the boy, and none made a move. The bobsleds were whooshing and scraping again, and you could hear a ruffle of applause out in some cold open country, God knew where. Conrad got up from his metal stool, impelled by something he could no longer reason with, not even with the help of Epictetus. A rushing sound rose inside his skull until he couldn't hear the television set or anything else. The faces of the Nordic Bund and Nuestra Familia stared at him as he walked between their two turfs. Five-O gave him such an uncomprehending, wide-eyed look, he knew what was going through his mind: "My cellie, he going crazy." When Conrad reached Pocahontas's side, he thought at first the boy was dead. He was sprawled chest-down, but his head and neck were twisted at an odd angle. He appeared to be trying to look at the ceiling, but his eyes were focusing on nothing at all, and his mouth was wide-open, as if he had just taken his last breath. *A mold!—a fungus!—spreading over his skin!*—but in fact it was only a faint reddish-white stubble that had begun to grow not only on his face but also on his skull, where he had shaved it.

Conrad knelt down and started to speak to him. Didn't even know his name! Couldn't very well call him Pocahontas—

He touched the boy's shoulder and said, "Can you hear me?"

No reply. Conrad put his fingertips on the boy's neck and could feel a pulse in his throat. Now he became aware of the stench that arose from his body. Terrified of the shower room, Pocahontas probably hadn't bathed since he arrived at Santa Rita. His legs were twisted and spread out in such a way that it looked as if he must have been running when he fell. Between his legs, in the folds of the yellow felony pajamas, barely visible because of the grotesque sprocketing of his legs, you could see a long red stain, about two inches wide.

Conrad put his hand back on the boy's shoulder and said, "Don't try to move! We're gonna get you some help!"

Still on one knee, he looked about beseechingly at his fellow inmates . . . these yellow figures frozen in their zones . . . He picked out Five-O with his eyes.

"Get a deputy! This guy's bleeding!"

Five-O tucked his chin down and arched his eyebrows, as if he had just been presented with a completely irrational proposition. Conrad looked all around the pod, craning his head wildly—*the videocamera*. He spotted the surveillance camera up near the ceiling line at Vastly's end of the pod room. He stood up and stepped farther out toward the center of the floor, directly in the line of the camera lens. He stared right into it and raised both hands in supplication and yelled out:

"Yo! Deputy!" In the very instant it left his lips it occurred to him that he had never uttered the cry *Yo!* before. But this was Santa Rita. "We got a man injured in here!" He started pointing toward Pocahontas, all the while keeping his eyes pinned on the camera. "He's bleeding! Yo! Deputy! We got a man here's bleeding!"

In no time two deputies, Armentrout and the younger, leaner one who had clamped the Michael Jackson love glove on Mutt, materialized.

"What the hell happened to *him*?" said Armentrout, leaning over and peering down at Pocahontas.

Conrad paused. He was keenly aware that the entire pod was hanging on every word. "I don't know," he said finally. "He was standing here —and then he—he collapsed." To himself he said, "I've gone this far. Why don't I tell them the whole story?" But he didn't.

And now the nurse, Maggie, was kneeling beside Pocahontas. This much-mocked Maggot was in fact a rather sweet, plump woman, about forty. Conrad had never seen her up close before, and he was surprised. Not even her mannish uniform, the white blouse, pants, and flat white shoes, could detract from her complexion, which was so smooth and milky white, or her hair, which was a reddish gold and pulled back into an elaborate plaited bun. She leaned down close to Pocahontas's face and began talking to him softly. Presently the boy's eyes focused on hers, and he murmured something. Armentrout stepped over Pocahontas's body, so that he had one foot planted on either side of his waist, and he bent down and hooked his hands under his shoulders and picked him up. In Armentrout's powerful grip his frail form came up off the floor like a plastic doll's. His fungoid head, with its auburn plume flopping to one side, lolled forward on his neck, a long, pale stem that seemed ready to snap off from the weight of the grotesque noggin it supported. Pocahontas's legs did a helpless half-shuffle as the two deputies led him off with his arms hooked over their shoulders. The bloodstain was now plainly visible. It extended from the seat four or five inches down the inside of one leg of his pants. Before the nurse, Maggot, left, walking behind them, she turned and gave Conrad a look. It wasn't exactly a smile. It was a look of such warmth . . . He couldn't think of her as Maggot . . . He wanted to embrace her. He wanted to hold her and put his cheek next to hers. No woman had given him a look like that since . . . since . . . since . . . He couldn't even bring himself to think about it, and precisely why he wanted to hold this woman he couldn't have explained in a thousand years.

He was now standing by himself in the spot where Pocahontas had fallen—aware that he was now what he had certainly never wanted to be, the center of attention of the entire pod. He could hear the television set once more as it droned away up on top of the metal stanchion in the black zone. The commentator with the TV sports voice was speaking, but no longer in hushed tones:

"Al Westerfield! Captain of the U.S. bobsledding team—the champions!—winners in the finals of the European winter games here in Vogelsbein, Austria. Congratulations, Al."

Out of breath: "Thank you, Sam."

"Al, that was a stupendous victory, the first championship for a U.S. bobsledding team in these games in—what is it now?—almost two decades. But it was terribly close."

Still out of breath but obviously elated: "Too close for comfort, Sam."

"Frankly, for a second there I thought you'd lost it on that third turn."

Taking a big gulp of air: "I did, too, Sam. It was my fault. I overcompensated, and we almost came up over the lip." Panting. "But then when I snapped back, it gave us like a little kick in the butt, and I think maybe we even picked up a fraction of a second."

"Sounds like a mighty *big* kick in the butt, Al, maybe the biggest kick in the butt in these games so far. Al Westerfield!—captain of the victorious American bobsledders!"

As Conrad walked back toward his table, he perceived—*perceived*—it registered first as a sensory perception rather than a thought—that no one was looking at him. Both the Nordic Bund and Nuestra Familia seemed to pull back rather than risk contact with this pariah. He caught just a glimpse of Five-O's wide, putty-colored face. For an instant Five-O shrugged his eyebrows upward in the look that asks, "What can I tell you?" before turning away and leaning toward Flaco, as if he had something important to tell him.

Back at the metal table, sitting on the metal stool, Conrad couldn't even make himself pretend to look at the pages of *The Stoics*. He sat bolt upright, looking straight ahead at . . . nothing . . . at the shadow of the recesses of the shower room behind the retaining wall. His heart was pounding. His armpits were abloom with heat. He was churning with fear, anger, and guilt. He was now the lone white new fish in the pod, young, slightly built, and all at once highly visible—and scorned and held in contempt. Not only had he come to the aid of an untouchable, a poor, ravaged, humiliated, turned-out, freakish homosexual—a punk—he had also come close to being a snitch. Rotto and his crew had barely departed the shower area when he was out in the middle of the pod room screaming "Yo! Deputy!" and calling the hacks to the scene of the crime—yes!—and which one of these paragons of manhood, who on the black turf, who on the Latin turf, who on the white turf, with their tattoos and crosses and gorged muscles, had the courage or the simple human decency to help a poor, pathetic kid like Pocahontas? None of them! Not one! What kind of manhood was it to look the other way and not snitch when a brute decides to have his way with the hide of another human being? Yes . . . and what about himself? He had come to Pocahontas's aid, all right—when it was altogether too late. Why had he never offered him the hand of, if not friendship, comradeship? Why had he let him flounder in this gray concrete hole, totally isolated, totally without the simplest word of encouragement or counsel? . . . Why had he—or was he being too hard on himself? What chance had the boy ever had, from the very beginning? Pocahontas had turned himself into a freak. He had shaved his own head, shaved his own eyebrows, grown his own Mohawk plume, punctured his own earlobes and rims and studded them with earrings, slumped him*self* over with a slacker's posture, screamed to the world with his own sick, perverse defiance: "Look at me! I'm a freak and I'm glad of it!" Epictetus' words resounded in his mind: "You are not born to share humiliation or evil fortune . . . If a man is unfortunate, remember that his misfortune is his own fault

. . . We ought not to spend our feelings on things beyond our power."

So agitated was he that now all of it—his fear, his anger, and his guilt—was suddenly directed toward Epictetus. What would the great master have him do, simply turn away, avert his eyes, like the others, like the Mexicans, like Five-O, like Pops in his shuffle, like Vastly, for that matter, and do nothing? Was this newly found god of his, Zeus, a false god? And Epictetus a false teacher? If that was so, then he had nothing, no one left and nothing to draw upon, not even that little spark of divinity upon which only this morning he had based every last tiny hope that still existed for his miserable life . . . Suddenly—a wave of the purest guilt. What was he doing? Under the pressure of the very first test sent by Zeus, he was buckling!—abandoning his faith! "It is for you then," Epictetus had written, "to say, 'Zeus, send me what trial thou wilt! For I have endowments and resources, given me by Thee, to bring myself honor through what befalls.' " But no, he then scolded, "Instead of that, you sit trembling for fear of what may happen, or lamenting, mourning, and groaning for what does happen, and then you reproach the gods. What else but impiety indeed can attend upon so ignoble a spirit as yours?" *Impiety*. His very first test—and already he was doubting the power of Zeus. He felt ashamed. He was denying not only Zeus but the existence of his own soul. "What are you, slave," Epictetus had demanded, "but a soul carrying a corpse and a quart of blood?" What was this body of his, which he was so worried about, but a corpse and a quart of blood? The living part of him was his soul, and his soul was nothing other than the spark of Zeus.

Still sitting bolt upright, he put both hands, palms down, on the pages of *The Stoics* and closed his eyes. He knew they would all be looking at him, the entire pod, but so what? He rejected the pod's code of false manliness. He kept his eyes closed and banished them, all of them, from his central nervous system, them and all their yammering and motherfuckin' and inane TV shows . . . He opened up his mind, his heart, his connective tissue, the pores of his skin, the coupling of his joints, the very marrow of his bones . . . He emptied his body, that corpse with its quart of blood, of all sensations. He became a vessel, yearning only to receive the divine . . .

So profound was this state, this trance, that he had no idea how long he had been in it when something—he had no idea what—caused him to open his eyes. The ambient sounds of the pod room, the burble of voices, had dropped off all over again. But in the corner of his eye he saw him. Rotto was coming straight toward him. Consciously he wanted to look away, but something made him stare right into the brute's face. *Zeus! Send me what trial thou wilt!* Rotto looked enormous. There were deep shadows in his yellow felony pajama top shirt beneath the slabs of muscle on his chest. The hair on the sides of his head was so greasy, it reflected the overhead light. The shot caller. Conrad looked about for Five-O, not because he thought his cellie would ever step in and help him in some way, but because he was his last comrade, his last tie to the earthly beings from whom men are used to deriving their courage and support. And there he was, Five-O, with his smooth flat face and his shock of black hair, about thirty feet away, standing there with his Latino buddies, looking on, waiting for the confrontation, for the beano, like everybody else.

And now the brute was standing over him, looking down. His eyebrows were lifted, and he had a small, indecipherable smile on his face. Conrad fastened on the most insignificant thing, the milky, slightly yellowish cast of the whites of Rotto's eyes.

A deep voice with a soft and obscenely friendly lilt: "Hey, dude. Mind if I sit down?"

Conrad had no idea what to do. The entire pod was watching this little set-to. He could not afford to be like Pocahontas and do nothing. But do—*what?* The next thing he knew, Rotto was sitting on the metal stool next to his and leaning over with his elbows on the table and cocking his head and looking directly into Conrad's eyes—just as he had with Pocahontas.

"So how you doin', Conrad?" The same soft, deep, insinuatingly friendly tone.

Conrad's mind spun, desperately searching for a strategy. *Epictetus!* What had he said? The trial had begun—what was he supposed to *do*?

A soft, almost sugary voice: "So this your first time bein' down, Conrad? Unnh-unnhhh-*unnnhhhh!*" groaned Rotto in an unctuously sympathetic way. "I know that trip. I know that trip." He looked away and shook his head as if tormented by the memory of it. Then he turned back and leaned even closer to Conrad, until his face and his milky eyes and his hideously benign smile were barely a foot away, and he said, "Any a these motherfuckers tryin' a sweatchoo?"

Conrad kept staring at him, his mind racing. *Treating me just like he did Pocahontas! And I'm transfixed just like Pocahontas—by the snake! Act!—do something—now! But what?* Five-O had said: *Use da mouth.*

"Tell ya what," said Rotto with an exaggerated croon, "you wanna make a phone call outta here? You wanna call home? You wanna make a phone call *right now*? I made an arrangement with those motherfuckers"—he motioned toward the black turf with his head. "They opening up those phones for me and my buddies."

Just what he did with Pocahontas!

"Ain' no damn shuck, dude. Take you ov'eh right now. Talk long's you want. Tell you one thing: take care a one thing real fast. Show all'ese motherfuckers you got somebody on your side. Ain't one uv'um gon' run no damn game on you after—"

Suddenly, before he was even conscious of his own will, Conrad sprang to his feet and looked down at Rotto with a furious expression on his face. Startled, Rotto recoiled and slid back on the stool and half-staggered to his feet. His insinuating smile had vanished.

"Hey, brother, look!" Conrad said with a rasp deep in his throat. "You a number in here, and I'm a number in here . . . see . . ." He was only halfway aware of what was happening to his accent. "And I ain't tryin'a disrespectchoo none . . . see . . . All's I wants is to do my time. I ain't tryin'a sweatchoo none, play you none, dog you none, or git over on you none. I ain' doin' nothing but settin' here tryin'a read my book and write a letter to my wife and my chil'run. You unnerstan' what I'm sayin'? So ain' no cause for nobody be playin' me or doggin' me or runnin' a game on me, neither."

Rotto's expression was one of blank incomprehension. The man was baffled. This gave Conrad courage—and at the same time the word *fox* popped into his mind. The fox, the craven, godforsaken beast of mischievousness and deceit, said Epictetus—that was what he was trying to be, the fox. But it was too late to turn back. The borrowed soul of the Chinese trusty, who had learned to talk blacker than the homeyest East Oakland homeboy, swelled up in his voice box:

"I ain' askin' you for no favors . . . see . . . I don' want no damn telephone. I don' want no damn TV. All's I wants is what I already got. You know what I'm sayin'? I mean, brother, you can have yo' telephone, and you can have yo' TV, and you can have this whole damn pod and this whole damn jailhouse and this whole damn Alameda County and this whole damn East Bay, an'at's cool . . . 'at's cool . . . 'cause all I'm askin' is, lemme serve my own damn time, lemme eat my own damn clock . . . see . . . So whyn't you kindly do the right thing, brother, and

I'll go my way and you go with God, and you'n'me's hello, so long, goodbye, nice knowin' you, an' evvythang's cool."

Rotto's baffled expression now changed to a puzzled scowl. A ditch ran down his forehead, between his eyebrows, making him look extremely angry. But then he forced a smile onto his face and laughed with a snort that shook his whole torso. The laugh ceased abruptly, although he kept the smile on.

"That's nice," he said in a low baritone. "Fac', 'at's real *good* . . . unh-hunh . . . yeahhh . . . Fac', 'at's real *cute*." He forced out another snorting laugh. "You're a cute little dude . . . Conrad."

With that he brought his right hand up and seized Conrad's left cheek between his thumb and forefinger and shook it, as if in a playful tweak.

Conrad felt a dreadful fear and then a terrible rage. *We cannot be free from fear, we cannot be free from anxiety. Yet we say, "O Lord Zeus, how am I to be rid of anxiety?" Fool, have you no hands? Did not Zeus make them for you? Has he not given you greatness of mind, has he not given you manliness? When you have these strong hands to help you— My hands!* In that instant—a fiery energy. With his left hand he seized Rotto's right hand and wrenched it off his cheek. Immediately he sensed that his grip enclosed all four of Rotto's knuckles. For all his massive shoulders, arms, and chest, the brute's hands were not big. Conrad's, product of the Suicidal Freezer Unit—*and of Zeus!*—were bigger and more powerful. *When you have these strong hands to help you!* He brought up his other hand—and now both his hands had the brute's knuckles in a crushing vise. He felt himself possessed of a superhuman strength. *Hercules—he who cleansed the world of unjust and brutal men!* Rotto's face quivered from the pain. He groped for Conrad's throat with his other hand, but the pain was too much. His right hand was being crushed. He lowered his left to try to pry Conrad's fingers off. Too late! Conrad was now an engine devoted solely to closing the vise. The muscles of his chest, his back, his abdominals were contracted to their very limits at the service of his hands. Rotto's knuckles and metacarpal bones—he willed their destruction—willed it—*willed* it—

An audible *snap*.

"Awwwwwwwhhhhhhhhhh!" A groan, very nearly a howl, rose from deep inside the brute. His eyes closed, and his face became terribly contorted. He kept clawing at Conrad's hand, but now Conrad forced his wrist over backward. The brute had no choice but to try to shift his weight to get out from under the fierce torque.

"Awwwhhhhh!—awwwhhhhh!—awwwhhhhh!—awwwhhhhh!" The moans were coming out in spurts. Rotto couldn't get his breath. For Conrad—life, existence, consciousness had but one purpose. *Cleanse the world of an unjust and brutal man.* The very words themselves—*from Zeus!*—fastened upon his mind. He could see his own forearms swelling with the stupendous exertion. He could feel the brute's bony processes collapsing inside his grip. He forced the forearm backward, against the natural rotation of the elbow. All at once Rotto lost his footing. He went down on one knee. His head went back. His eyes were closed. A hideous grimace was on his face.

Snap.

"AHHHHHHHHHHHHHHHHHHHHHH!" A scream, a full-fledged scream, the sort of scream that breaks loose once all defenses are gone. Rotto collapsed. He fell over on one side, then flopped on his back. Conrad was on top of him, a terrier who won't let go. He could feel the fight going out of Rotto's wrist. So he forced it backward—backward—backward—backward—

Snap.

"AHHHHHHHHHHHHHHHHHHHHHHH!" Another scream, followed by a huge tearful sigh. Rotto was staring at him in a cockeyed way, breathing rapidly, with little heaves, but his eyes weren't focusing. His ponytail stuck out on one side, on the floor. It looked filthy. His face had the stricken slackness of defeat.

Only then did Conrad hear the ruckus, the shouts.

Git'im, Rotto! . . . Whack 'at sucker! . . . Off 'at little motherfucker! . . . Git up, man!

They were all around him, the entire pod, Vastly's gang, the Latinos, the Chinese druggies, Rotto's Nordic Bund, the whole bunch. Out of the corner of his eye Conrad was aware of the wraith-like Rapmaster EmCee New York with his green do-rag . . . Vastly with his cornrows and paper ribbons, . . . and Five-O, who stared in wonderment, his eyes big as quarters . . . They wanted more! More thrashing! Looser teeth! Blood! Bone fragments!

Rotto's boys obviously thought their champion, their shot caller, was going to rise up off the floor and teach this insignificant fish the most terrible lesson of his life. They weren't jumping in, because why would Rotto ever need help against anyone so puny? They didn't know he was already out of it, finished, shut down for the night.

Conrad lifted himself to a sitting position, straddling Rotto's midsection. He relaxed his grip on the brute's hand. Slowly, staring at him in a strangely distracted way, going *ahhhhhhhhhhhhhhhh ahhhhhhhhh-hhhhh ahhhhhhhhhhhhhh*, Rotto lifted his huge left arm. For an instant Conrad thought he was going after his throat again. But then the arm collapsed, fell, and flopped down on the other arm, as if to protect it from further damage. Conrad let go of the brute's hand and rocked back on his heels. He looked up at Rotto's boys, fearing the worst. But they were stunned. Slack-jawed, they, too, stared, but not at Conrad. They stared at Rotto's right hand. The wrist was twisted about like a rope. The knuckles were no longer in a straight line. The flesh of the back of the hand was hideously swollen. His face bore a look of such agony, the crowd grew quiet. An unbelievable truth was dawning: the champion, the mighty shot caller, had just been vanquished . . . by a new fish half his size.

A ripple ran through the crowd. Heads began turning toward the entry to the pod room. Conrad felt a grip on his shoulder. He swung his head about. It was Five-O, leaning down toward him.

" 'Ey, bruddah! Get up! Bag it!" He nodded toward the entrance. "Deputies, man!"

To his amazement—he didn't think Five-O would dare help him in front of Rotto's boys—Five-O hooked his hands under his shoulders and gave him a hoist up and steered him back into a cluster of Nuestra Familia Latinos. Otherwise, the yellow felony pajamas were moving this way and that, heading for their racial turfs, as if it were the beginning of pod time.

"Yo! You yo-yos!" Armentrout bellowed. "What's *this* cluster fuck all about?"

Breathing rapidly, dazed by what had just happened, Conrad stood with Five-O and a group of Latinos in the white section of the pod room. Armentrout led four gray-shirted deputies wielding batons, looking this way and that. There, in the middle of the white section, on the concrete floor, lay a single white figure in yellow felony pajamas, rolled over on his side and moaning. That there was a wounded inmate, even a grievously wounded inmate, lying on the floor would not have surprised the deputies. But when they realized who it was, they were dumbstruck: Rotto, the white shot caller.

For a moment Armentrout stared at Vastly, who was facing the other way, the usual simpleminded look of jailhouse insouciance on his mug. He stared at Rotto's boys in the center of the white turf. You could hear a low rumble of mutterings and grousing. They were glowering at Conrad, a fact that did not even register on the deputies, since he would have been one of the last inmates they would have suspected of having done in the mighty Rotto.

Then Armentrout looked down at Rotto. "Jesus Christ, what's going on in this shithole tonight?"

"Ahhhhhhhhhhh ahhhhhhhhhhhh ahhhhhhhhhhh . . ." The brute was still gasping for breath and moaning. His eyes were shut, and his face was twisted.

"Can you get up?"

"Ahhhhhhhhhh ahhhhhhhhhh ahhhhhhhhhh . . ."

"Shit." Armentrout looked about at his men. "Hey, Reese, better go get Jerry's Kid." Jerry's Kid was the prison doctor, who had a withered left arm and leg and reminded them of the afflicted children on the annual Jerry Lewis television program in behalf of muscular dystrophy sufferers.

Then he announced to the inmates in his huge voice: "Awright! Pod time's over! Line up! You're going back to the cells! You guys wanna clusterfuck, you can clusterfuck over the wire." He looked at Riffraff. "Awright, you guys line up first!" He looked at Wino. "And then you guys." He looked at Vastly and Rapmaster EmCee New York. "And then you guys! Anybody starts any more bullshit gets a vacation in the Rubber Room!"

BACK IN THE cell, as they waited for lights-out, Five-O was beside himself. He was acting as if he had been in Conrad's corner the whole time during the fight with Rotto, urging him on to victory.

" 'Ey, brah! You wen bus' up dat buggah, yeah? Bus' him up!" He said it in a hoarse whisper. "Da whole pod, brah—da whole pod, dey wen spahk"—*they watched*—"dat beeg moke"—*that big tough guy*—"sit down wi' one new fish, you, brah"—*sit down with a new fish, you, brother*—"an' den he wen make eyes da kine, an' den he wen say, 'Get chance, baby, get chance?' Da kine!"—*and then he kind of made eyes at you and as much as said, "You want to get it on, baby?"*—"an'all dem buggahs, dey wen t'ink so you going make ass, an' Rotto, he going treat you like one mahu"—*and everybody thought you were going to screw up and he was going to treat you like a faggot*—"but den, onreal, brah! No mo' polite little haole! You wen use da mouth—an' den you wen use da heart—an' den you wen broke up dat buggah!"—*but then, unreal, brother! You stopped being the polite little white boy! You used the mouth—and then you used the heart—and then you beat up that bugger!*

Five-O was trembling, quivering with joy at the triumph of his cellie, like a fan whose idol has just won the fight for the championship, and yet his voice never rose above that excited whisper. Ever the realist, he was looking ahead. Sound carried over the wire in the pod at Santa Rita, and he didn't want it known that he was the cheering partisan of the new fish who had humiliated Rotto.

"Oh, bruddah," he said, shaking his head and looking at the wall. His whisper was lower than ever. "Dis one beef to da max, Conrad. Dat beeg moke, he da shot caller."

"Don't worry," said Conrad. "Everybody saw what happened. He started it. He grabbed me by the cheek. I *had* to do something."

"Dey wen spahk, yeah." *Yeah, they saw it.* "But den you wen broke up dat buggah!" Five-O put his head down. When he finally lifted it, he looked Conrad in the eye and said softly, "Dey try fo' kill you."

Conrad just looked at him. Five-O shook his head yes. "Mockay-die-dead, Conrad."

Conrad smiled slightly. Exactly why, he couldn't have begun to say. *Dey try fo' kill you.* It seemed like an oddly abstract concept.

"I can't believe any of this is happening, Five-O. I keep thinking I'm gonna wake up and be somewhere else."

"I know, brah," said Five-O. "From long time I want one timeout. 'Yo! Deputy! timeout!' kine. Pull da plug and t'ink about no mo' notting and do da time, li'dat. Dis place stay funny kine"—*this place would be kind of funny*—"if only dey let you take a break every now'den."

When lights-out came, Conrad climbed up to the top bunk and stretched out on his back. It was much too hot in here, and his heart was beating much too fast, and he knew he would never go to sleep. But he would need to rest before . . . He couldn't even imagine what might happen tomorrow in the pod room. He stared up through the lizard screen and listened to the ceiling fans struggling and the catwalk creaking as a deputy walked along overhead. Soon, over the wire, the nocturnal yammering had begun. The J-cat, the one who was obsessed with Hank Aaron in a yellow wool suit, began moaning for his medication: "Meds . . . meds . . . mehhhds . . . mehhhhds . . ."

A voice from somewhere. "Oh shit. Heh we go again. The fuck, give the man his shuffle pills."

"Where's'at Maggot at?"

"Yo! Maggot!"

"Emergency med call, Maggot! Code blue! Name of Hensley!"

It was an Okie voice, a high-pitched playacting voice. Conrad felt a burning sensation inside his skull. So now it began.

"Motherfucker don't need no pills," said another voice, "motherfucker needs a motherfuckin' *shower*, is what the fuck he needs. Motherfucker, he be too *funky*! Smell like the motherfucker's *dying*! You a *dis*grace to the brothers, motherfucker!"

"But they *told* me!" said the J-cat. "Told me I gon' die if I go outside my house!"

"Hensley! Hensley!" said the Okie voice. "Do you copy? Do you copy?"

From the bunk below, Five-O whispered, "Ey, brah, you wen hear'um?"

"Yeah, I heard 'em, Five-O."

"Hensley! Stick yo' ass out yo' porthole so's we kin see you. Then you ass-out."

The next thing Conrad knew, Five-O was off his bunk and standing up and looking at him and pointing in the gloom toward the catwalk. "Maybe dey put you in da Rubber Room, Conrad. Maybe dey put you in da B Pod."

"Whattaya mean?"

"Ac' crazy kine, man. Like Mutt. Yell crazy t'ings, keeck da do', go J-cat, li'dat. An' den da deputies, dey going take you outta here."

"I wouldn't even consider it," said Conrad. "I—" But he stopped. He wanted to say, "I want to keep my character. Why did I fight Rotto? Because I refused to be dishonored. Outside this hole, this pigsty, no one will ever know that I lived as a man and fought like a man and refused to sell myself at any price. But in this grim little universe, the pod, the only world that is left, they will know, and Zeus will know, and I, a son of Zeus, will know."

"But dey going *kill* you, brah! Mockay-die-dead!"

"This bit of clay you mean, Five-O? They'll do what they have to do, and I'll do what I have to do. Besides, when did I ever say I was immortal?"

For several seconds Five-O didn't say anything. Then he sighed and said, "Edah you get plenty lakas"—*Either you have big balls*—"or you going crazy like Mutt. 'Dis bit a clay,' yeah? Don' go crazy on me, Conrad. Every cellie going crazy—bummahs, man."

Tuckatuckatuckatuckatuckatucka the ice cream cup bongo percussion had begun . . . and then the slaps against the sides of the bunks . . . and then the voice of Dinky Man: "And now . . . direct from the Apollo Theater . . . in New York City . . . Rapmaster EmCee . . . NEW YORK!" Conrad didn't know if it was his imagination or what, but the cheers that followed seemed like brutal cries, and a strange mad ululation spread throughout the pod as Beat Box thrummed his *a cappella* electric bass. Rapmaster EmCee New York—Conrad could *see* his bony ravaged visage and his pirate's do-rag—began as he always did—

"Yo, sugar!—think 'at's a ruby
You got stuck inside yo' crack?"

—but this time the great moan over the wire rose immediately to something just short of a scream in a cry for blood, and throughout the first stanza it never let up, and the chorus—"GIVE IT UP, BITCH! GIVE IT UP, BITCH"—burst forth with a fury, then quickly died down and was supplanted by a whinnying sound, as if the inmates just *knew* what was coming next and could barely restrain themselves long enough to actually hear it.

Some more *a cappella* strumming by Beat Boy, and then Rapmaster EmCee New York resumed:

"Little punk, he gon' get turned out,
He gon' learn 'bout comin' through
For the real funk, he be ass-out!
Ram 'at sucker, he gon' pass out!
Fucker, he gon' switch from him to her,
'At jissum-sucker won' know which,
An' ain't that rich!"

The inmates didn't even wait for the Rapmaster. With a laughing roar they broke into the refrain. The very air of the pod exploded with

GIVE IT UP, BITCH!
GIVE IT UP, BITCH!

GIVE IT UP, BITCH!
GIVE IT UP, BITCH!

Conrad lay there with his heart racing. Then he closed his eyes and tried to visualize Carl and Christy and Jill, all that remained to him outside this doomed universe of men who had reduced themselves to the level of the bodies they shared with the animals. Carl . . . Christy . . . He could no longer see them at all . . . couldn't bring their features into focus . . . just a couple of tiny ghosts with little coronas of blond hair . . . Jill . . . He couldn't see the beautiful Jill he had fallen in love with. He couldn't see that face. Instead, he saw a knit brow, an angry brow. He saw her body and tried to *feel* his love for her . . . and instead he merely saw the flesh. Nevertheless, he reckoned, as his heart banged away and the ceiling fans *scracccked scraaaaccccked* and *scraaaaccccked* overhead, and the bloody ululations resounded over the wire, it was through that flesh that he had transmitted the spark of Zeus to Carl and Christy. He tried once more to visualize Carl, and he couldn't, and tears came to his eyes. One day Carl would be a man, and long before that time he would need someone to tell him what a man was.

He rolled over and lowered his head below the edge of his bunk and said, "Five-O!"

"Yeah, bruddah?"

"Promise me one thing."

"Wot's dat, bruddah?"

"Whatever happens tomorrow, you'll write it all down and send it to my wife."

"Write it down?"

"Yeah, write down everything. Will you promise me that? Start with what happened tonight, with Rotto coming over and everything. I want my son to know, Five-O. I want him to know I didn't lie here trembling and moaning and groaning and whining and— It's important, Five-O. Will you promise me that much?"

"Yeah, I promise, bruddah. But remember, cool head main t'ing. Don't go crazy on me. You promise *me* dat."

"Don't worry, I'm not going crazy. I've never been clearer about anything in my life."

He rolled over once more onto his back. His heart continued to race, but he could feel the tension begin to recede from his knees, his thighs, his abdomen, his arms, his shoulders, his neck. And then even his heart began to calm down. Breathing deeply and rhythmically, he tried to imagine his very . . . *self* . . . opening, opening, opening up . . . his pores, the very fibers of his muscles, his nerve endings, the chambers of his heart and lungs, his solar plexus . . . An energy seemed to spread out in a single wave from his heart to the tender flesh beneath the nails of his fingers and toes and to the rims of his ears and the flesh on his scalp, and he was sure that he saw a bright light behind his eyelids.

"Zeus! Send me what trial thou wilt!" He hadn't meant for it to be audible, but it came out as a hoarse whisper.

From below, Five-O whispered back, " 'Ey, bruddah, you don' go crazy on me. You *promise* me dat."

Chapter XX

Mai's Army

S*CRACK SCRACK SCRACK SCRACCCKKK SCRACCCCKKK,* THE BELT-driven turbines were struggling away up in the roof, to no avail. The pod remained hot and airless, despite the fact that it was now—what?—1 a.m.?—2 a.m.? As Conrad lay there on his bunk, staring up through the lizard screen above his head, the ambient light from the catwalk created huge silhouettes that gave the darkness a delirious quality. *Roarrrrrrrrrrr,* somebody flushed a toilet *glug glug glug glugluglug.* "Aw, mannnnnnnn," somebody protested. Half a dozen inmates were snoring so loudly, with such helpless surrender, you could *feel* their exhaustion. Every mindless rattle of it came croaking in over the wire.

But they were fortunate, weren't they . . . They could sleep. Rotto's crew could sleep. Rotto, wherever he was, could sleep. They could store up energy for the assault, however it might come. They were not lying here with their hearts played out, ratcheting, drained by the constant alert alert alert alert alert alert alert alert . . .

Conrad was so hot, he had a slick of oily sweat where the underside of his upper arm lay against his rib cage and another where the underside of his chin met his neck. He had finally taken off his felony pajamas and was wearing only his shorts, like Five-O, down below, and practically every other inmate, even though he didn't want to be that naked if the onslaught began. Not that there was any way they could *break into* a cell in the middle of the night—or was there? The ingenuity of the brutes, who made mirrors out of ice cream cups and daggers out of book covers—their perverse power of invention knew no bounds.

He had never felt so utterly depleted. He was dying to sink into the oblivion of sleep. He would start to sink, sink, sink, sink, and then the sentinel, somewhere deep in his brain, would jerk him back into consciousness. Sweat was collecting in his eyebrows, his mustache, and the stubble of his beard, which had an irritable feel to it, like a rash. Absentmindedly he pressed his mustache on either side with his thumb and forefinger, as if to wring the moisture out . . . It made him think of the freezer unit . . . the way his mustache used to freeze and sparkle . . . zero degrees Fahrenheit . . . He closed his eyes . . . immersed himself in that frigid zinc-gray box . . . an upper slot, L-17, trying to rock a huge carton of frozen pork loins loose, and the breath fog was coming out in spurts, and Dom was looking at Kenny and saying, "I got good news and bad news," and—*whuh?* He jerked himself alert. His heart was hammering away. He was sweating profusely. Yet the pod was as quiet as before.

He tried to think of Carl and Christy . . . and Jill . . . She *would* care, she *wouldn't* disappear, she *would* come back to him . . . He closed his eyes . . . The duet . . . He was in the sad little living room. No, he was out in the garage . . . The door was up. A slim young figure . . . but it was not Jill. It was the leela sluh . . . wild teased hair, heavy eye makeup, almost like a burglar's mask . . . a sleeveless black T-shirt with such big loose armholes he could see the sides of her little breasts . . . She came toward him, smiling . . . She pressed her little breasts against his bare chest—

Thomp! Thomp! Thomp! Thomp! Thomp!

He came to with a start. He rolled over on his abdomen and stared down at the floor of the cell. Someone was battering the floor from underneath with the upright end of a broom!—a mop!—a pole!

Thomp! Thomp! Thomp! Thomp! Thomp!

But there was no room, no cellar space, no foundation under the floor, which was a slab built flat upon the ground. Rotto's crew! They had tunneled under the ground! Coming up through the floor!

Thomp! Thomp! Thomp! Thomp! Thomp!

The entire bunk began to rock, end to end, the long way. The battering beneath the cell grew louder. All at once—no more light from the catwalk. Instead, the flash of a bright moon through a clerestory window, which was swaying. The screeching of the ceiling turbines ceased at the same instant, and a colossal creaking, groaning sound commenced, as if some prodigious force were trying to jimmy the catwalk off the wall, pry the metal bunks apart, pull the nails out of the timbers, wrench the water pipes out of the toilets. And then the cries began:

"The fuck, motherfucker!"

"Dinky Man, where you at!"

"Yo! Deputy! I don' play this shit!"

"Yo! Armentrout! The lights!"

"The fuck, you feel that?"

"Mira! Terramoto!"

"Motherfucker!"

"Motherfucker!"

"Motherfucker!"

The bunk was bucking back and forth and groaning at the joints. Conrad grabbed the end of the bunk ladder that stuck up by his head and held on, to keep from falling off. He heard a thud on the floor. He looked down. It was Five-O, who had been thrown out of his bunk.

" 'Ey, Conrad! Wha's da haps!"

"I don't know!" But then he could feel the bunk pitching and rolling in S-waves. "Earthquake!"

"Bummahs, man!" Five-O tried to stand up and was immediately thrown down to the floor again.

Afraid of being thrown from the upper bunk, Conrad gripped the ladder uprights and swung himself down the side and dropped to the floor. He lost his footing and almost hit his head on the rim of the toilet. The very concrete of the floor seemed to be rolling. Conrad and Five-O were on all fours. The sweaty sheen of Five-O's back reflected a pale phosphorescent light from the clerestory window above. Conrad looked up. The lizard wire itself appeared to be dipping and swaying.

Five-O shouted, " 'Ey! Deputy! Open da do', you!"

Similar cries were coming from all over the pod. Rats trapped in their cages, the inmates were desperate to flee to open ground.

Amid all the lurching, bucking, pitching, rolling, yawing, groaning, and swaying, there arose a tremendous cracking sound overhead. Something had blotted out the moonlight in the clerestory window. It was the catwalk, which had come loose from the wall. A beam of light shot out at a crazy angle—a deputy with a flashlight.

"Yo! Fry! Where you at?"

Conrad struggled to his feet, lurched toward the bunk ladder, held on, turned to Five-O, and held out his hand. "Get up! Grab hold! The catwalk's coming loose! We gotta get under here!" With his head he indicated the space between the upper and lower bunks.

Five-O grabbed his arm, and the two of them piled onto the lower bunk. The bunk's metal frame was swaying. It sounded as if the wall was cracking in the corner. A pungent smell filled the atmosphere, oddly sweet and yet rotten. *Dust!*—as the hulk of Santa Rita began coming apart and the accumulated filth of half a century burst forth and filled the mouths, the noses, the lungs of the trapped rats, who gulped for air.

Suddenly—a force so great, both men were thrown against the wall, Five-O on top of Conrad. The lower bunk rose beneath them and pitched them head-first. A tremendous roar. Huge masses gave way. The sound of wood, metal, glass, concrete falling and smashing the bunk frame. The floor heaved up at an angle and Conrad felt himself drop head down into—*what?* Utter blackness. *Buried! Suffocating!* His hips were somewhere above his head. His torso was wedged between—*what?* He could see—*nothing!* His left arm was free. He groped wildly. He tried to reach up. Impossible! A mass of incalculable weight pressed down on him. He reached back. *Flesh!*

"Five-O!" The effort of calling out made him cough. *The dust!* He was choking on it.

"Conrad . . . bruddah . . ." A feeble voice, and then he felt a grip on his leg. "Bruddah . . . bruddah . . . bruddah . . ." Five-O's voice had become a high, frantic peep.

The terrified voice and desperate grip sent a new wave of claustrophobia through Conrad. *Buried in utter darkness! A tomb!* He was hyperventilating, and the harder his lungs worked, the more dust they drew in. Choking! Dying! And yet he was getting air from somewhere. He could hear moans, shrieks, piteous cries from all over the pod. He reached down. An empty space. What? A pit? He prayed, although he couldn't have called it prayer, in the words of Epictetus. "Lead me, O Zeus, and Thou my destiny."

"Bruddah . . . bruddah . . . bruddah . . ." Five-O was whimpering, crying, clinging desperately to his leg.

"Shut up, Five-O! Save your breath!" The primal urge . . . *to protect* . . . gave him strength.

He wriggled his head, shoulders, and chest down into the hole, the pit, the space, whatever it was. The earth had stopped moving. Screams from all over: *Yo! Help me! . . . The fuck, help me . . . Aggghhhh! Motherfucker! Aggghhhh!* He could hear someone bleating, "Mehhhhhhds . . . mehhhhhhhhhds . . . mehhhhhhhhds . . ." It was the voice of the J-cat.

"No leave me, bruddah!"

"I'm not leaving you. Let go my leg and follow me." Obediently, Five-O let go.

Conrad slithered all the way down into the space below. Five-O scrambled behind him. They were on their bellies, struggling for breath. Pitch-black. Conrad tried to lift his head, but an immense jagged mass weighed down from above. Choking, he slithered forward. *Lace!* He could see it! Faint pinpoints of light. He slithered forward some more. It was a pale light coming through a tangle of debris up ahead. They were inside some sort of crevice no more than a foot high and barely the width of their shoulders.

Conrad felt a terrific grip on his leg. Five-O was gasping and moaning, "Help me, bruddah . . . help me . . . real had-it . . ."

"Let go!" said Conrad. "Start crawling!" But the grip only grew tighter. Five-O was whimpering like a baby.

Like a baby . . . Conrad managed to snake his arm behind him until he found Five-O's face, which was mashed against his legs. He stroked his cheek, just as if he were his child, and said softly, "Five-O . . . I'm *with* you, and you're with *me*, and we're gonna get out of here now. You hear me? We're gonna get out, Five-O, and I'm gonna be with you. You're gonna be right behind me, and I won't leave you. We're gonna crawl, and so you gotta let go of me and put your hands on the ground. I won't leave you." He kept stroking his cheek.

Big sighs, moans, coughs, sobs, and the ferocious grip slackened.

"Okay, Five-O, here we go." It was even harder to snake his hand back from behind him and bring his arm forward again. His shoulder kept wedging against the jagged mass that threatened to entomb them. He began slithering on his belly. There was no way he could lift his back high enough to get to his knees and crawl. The space was terribly narrow. All he could see was the faint lacework of light ahead. Five-O was right behind him, struggling for breath.

Suddenly the earth was wet beneath his hands and forearms . . . Muck . . . Water streaming in from somewhere. The earth they crawled through was mud. Now he was near enough to the ghostly light to see a small irregular opening, where a floor had heaved up beneath a wall and torn away from it. He could see the silhouette of an old-fashioned plaster lathing in the breach. An ungodly mass of earth, concrete, and debris above him. He kept inching forward.

A section of wire lathing hung straight down. He put the heel of his right hand against it and pushed with all his might. It bent outward. He was looking up through a fissure . . . into some sort of room . . . In a phosphorescent gloaming he could see a row of windows in a wall, but the wall had keeled over at an extraordinary angle, almost 45 degrees. It had torn away from the ceiling, which was itself ruptured and pitched downward in a precarious way. The wall seemed to be suspended by the electrical cables buried in it. Then he realized what it was . . . the pod's visiting area . . . The windows were the Lexan windows through which he had talked to Jill on the telephone. The ghostly light was moonlight from the doorway that led out to the dusty yard where the visitors lined up. Somewhere outside an unmuffled motor was throbbing away, creating a terrific racket. He could hear shouts, screams, cries for help. His lungs and his throat were burning. Could he possibly squeeze through the opening? Was it even six inches top to bottom? By shoving his elbows back against the sides of the crevice he was in, he managed to get his head up and through. By twisting sideways he got his shoulders through. Every time he took a breath, the expansion of his rib cage pinned his arms against his sides. The wire lathing was digging into his back. It was the visitors' area, all right. In the silvery light he could make out the stainless-steel stools, still bolted to the concrete floor, which had pitched up at a bizarre angle. The telephones, jolted out of their cradles, hung down by their cords from the windows.

He dug his bare feet into the earth and thrust his body upward with all the power of his legs. A sharp pain—but his right elbow was through the opening, and from that point he was able to wriggle the rest of his body through. He remained on all fours, trying to regain his breath. The floor was tilted at a disorienting angle. Mud all over his body . . . his belly, his face, his nostrils, his eyelashes . . . Gobs of it fell from his nose and his forehead . . . There was a raw, burning sensation high up in the small of his back. He contorted his left arm behind him and reached up . . . *blood* . . . blood and muscle . . . Wildly he looked about . . . a strange moonlit gloaming . . . This place, the visitors' area, looked as if a gigantic pair of hands had picked it up, buckled it, wrenched it, and then slammed it down on the earth. No two planes were any longer at right angles. The floor had heaved up, pulling away from the rear wall and leaving the opening he had just come through. The barn-like entrance door had been sprung clean out of its tracks and lay cracked almost in two on the ground outside, allowing the moonlight in. The wall with the Lexan windows had not only torn loose from the ceiling above but also from the far wall, creating a big V-shaped opening. *An opening—*

An opening! A rage to . . . *flee!* . . . surged through his nervous system. His every synapse, from head to toe, now transmitted the horrible news, understood only by those creatures who have floundered atop a major tremor of the earth. The one constant, the one dependable fundamental of life, namely, the solidity of the earth under your feet—just an illusion! A sham! *Terra firma*—what a terrible joke! It moves! It writhes! It bucks! It rises up in thunder! It swallows you!—buries you alive. And it *will* move again—*soon!*

Flee!

Then, almost at once, a revelation: *Zeus!*

"Conrad! . . . bruddah . . . No leave me!"

Conrad spun about. Five-O's eyes were at the opening, pleading. But the big Hawaiian could never make it through that little opening—*and if I stay here and try to help him—*

"Five-O," said Conrad. He paused. He wrestled with the implacable giant claustrophobia. *Zeus!* "I'm—I'm not leaving you. I've just gotta . . . get you . . . get you something . . ."

"Bruddah . . ."

Conrad looked about the wreckage of the space. Up there . . . he could make out a length of broken riser pipe. He had to climb up the slope of the concrete floor to get it. *It sloped!* The entire room, the entire structure—*could collapse at any moment! Flee!* He was hyperventilating again, just as if he were still trapped underground. He fought himself, fought himself, fought himself—*No leave me, bruddah*—and finally retrieved the pipe and came back down the slope in a wary crouch and brought it to the opening.

"You got to pull back, Five-O, so I can stick this thing in there! I gotta make the opening bigger!"

"No, bruddah . . ."

The eyes looked up at him hopelessly, from out of a dark hole, but then he pulled back. Conrad jammed the pipe into the opening and tried to use it as a lever. He couldn't budge the wall, but little by little he was able to make the concrete of the floor crumble, until the opening was a few inches deeper.

"Okay, Five-O, we're gonna try it now! Put your head through!"

At first, nothing . . . Then the stricken face appeared. Five-O was covered in mud. His skin, his hair, his mustache—streaks, gobs, smears of mud. His eyes looked like two frantic little white organisms trapped in the muck. He was breathing with rapid, shallow gasps. He worked his head through the opening.

"Okay, Five-O, now push!"

Panting with a rumble that came from deep in his chest, Five-O managed to force his shoulders through. But now he was stuck, just as Conrad had been.

"Bruddah . . . bruddah . . ." He was breathing with desperate heaves, and his eyes were fastened upon Conrad, begging, begging, begging.

"You gotta use your legs, Five-O! You gotta push! You gotta kick! *I* did it! *You* can do it!"

More desperate heaves, and Five-O managed to get enough of his body through to free his arms.

"Push! Push!"

The lathing dug into his broad back, but Five-O finally made it through, whereupon he flopped facedown on the sloping concrete floor, desperately trying to regain his breath. There were long cuts on his back . . . smears of blood . . .

The loud motor, whatever it was, was still grinding away. Agonized cries rose from the interior of West Greystone and beyond. All at once —a shuddering thunder. Tons of . . . *structure* . . . collapsed right behind them, down onto the crevice they had just crawled through. The wall buckled. The ceiling canted with a tremendous groan. The opening Five-O had just struggled through no longer existed.

"Come on, Five-O! Get up! We gotta get outta here!"

At that instant he understood with the sharpest clarity: *This was Zeus' handiwork.*

Five-O rolled over on his side. His mouth was wide-open, and his body was glossy with sweat and blood in the moonlight that came through the doorway. He looked up at Conrad, but he was breathing so hard he couldn't speak. Conrad took his hand and pulled him to a seated position and finally managed to get him to his feet.

"Put your arm around my shoulders!"

He did so, and Conrad steadied him and led him down the slope of the floor. His arm around Five-O's waist, he helped him through the V-shaped opening. His arm was covered with blood, the blood that was streaming down Five-O's back. Both of them were smeared in mud, naked except for their shorts, which the mud had plastered to their bodies. Five-O's mouth remained wide-open. He was fighting for breath.

They emerged through the big doorway, into the jail yard. Conrad was staggering under Five-O's weight, and finally Five-O sank helplessly to the ground. *No! It will move again!* But Conrad managed to say nothing. Five-O was slumped over in a heap, neither sitting nor lying, breathing with a deep rasping sound.

A three-quarter moon was high in the south, over Pleasanton. The sky was bursting with stars. Stars! This was the first time he had seen the open sky since he had been in Santa Rita. *Zeus' stars!* It suddenly became so sharply clear.

The grinding motor was louder than ever. Barely thirty yards away, on the stomped earth of the jail yard, was a shed-like building. A weak light shone from the windows. The noise came from a gasoline-powered emergency generator. Two beams of light emerged from the shed and came bouncing across the yard. Deputies with flashlights. In the distance, from Pleasanton, most likely, came the *woooo-woooo-woooo-woooo* of police car sirens and the Klaxon horn of a fire engine. Conrad looked back toward the doorway they had just emerged from. The entire West Greystone building had been thrust upward on one side. Its big tar-and-gravel clerestory roof had cracked down the middle and was canted up at a bizarre angle. And now, for the first time, in the moonlight, Conrad saw the little cliff, the escarpment. A low but sheer cliff, three or four feet high, had heaved up out of the earth. It ran under the building, under D Pod, and straight through the grounds of the jail on a north-south axis. Conrad gazed beyond. The vast plain of the Livermore Valley—suddenly so clear and peaceful. He looked to the south, toward Highway 580. No sign of it—no lights. Electricity was knocked out everywhere. In the jail yard more beams—flashlights—danced this way and that. Men were shouting. Without looking up, Five-O said, "I real had-it . . . ass-out, bruddah . . ."

"Just hang on," said Conrad.

A beam of light came lurching and bouncing toward them. Then it hit them head-on. The light was so powerful, Conrad covered his eyes with his hand. He couldn't even make out the shape of the person holding it.

"Where'd you come from? What's your unit?" It was an Okie voice, a Livermore Valley farmboy voice.

"In there," said Conrad, motioning toward the caved-in building. "D Pod."

"Well . . . get moving," said the voice behind the flashlight. "You guys are all going in the repair shed."

Five-O didn't budge. In the harsh glare of the flashlight, sitting on the ground, slumped over the way he was, almost naked, smeared from head to toe in mud and blood, he looked as if he was about to die. His head hung over on his chest and rose and fell with his labored breathing.

"Get up," said the man with the flashlight, but not very forcefully.

"He needs a doctor," said Conrad.

"Yeah, well—"

Just then a voice from nearby began yelling, "Yo! Leon! Where you at?"

"Over here!" said the man with the flashlight. "Got two inmates!"

"Ne'mind 'at! Come back here! Need you at East Greystone!"

The flashlight beam lingered on Five-O and then hit Conrad in the face. "You're gonna stay right here, you understand? I'm coming right back, and you guys ain't gonna move one fucking inch. Anybody caught heading for the perimeter is gonna get shot. Anybody goes near the fence is ass . . . *out*!"

Whereupon he hurried off at a jog.

Five-O, still sitting, turned and supported himself on his right arm and looked at Conrad. "Conrad . . . bruddah . . ." He continued to struggle for breath. "Bag it . . . bag it . . ."

"Bag it?"

"Run, brah! Split!"

"Split?"

"Dey going put all da inmates in da shed—in da dark—all-dem to-gedda. Rotto-dem, dey going kill you, brah! Mockay-die-dead!"

Conrad could hear the generator throbbing away. There were cries and shouts. Rods of light, from flashlights, bounced around in the dark.

Conrad got down on his haunches, so that his head was level with Five-O's.

"I'm gonna bag it, Five-O, but not because I'm afraid of Rotto and them. Look . . ." He made a sweeping gesture with his hand, to indicate the devastation. "You know who did all this?" He caught himself. He remained there on his haunches, his mouth half open, staring at Five-O, not uttering a sound. He knew it would be pointless to bring up the name of Zeus. Five-O believed only in the moment-to-moment strategies of the realist.

Five-O said, "You mean dat buggah you wen tell about before?" *You mean that bugger you were talking about before?*

"Yes."

"Garans?" *Guarantee it?* "Den tell dat buggah fo' bring me one hamburger weet' mustard and one beer. Me, I no can move. I real had it."

Dat buggah—a scalding realization rolled through Conrad's skull. *The book! The Stoics!* His very lifeblood—*gone*! For an instant he looked back at the remains of West Greystone to see if there might not be some way to retrieve it—although of course there wasn't. But this was more than a book! This was . . . living tissue—this was . . . the word of Zeus! He looked forlornly across the infinite nightscape of the Livermore Valley.

"Huhu, brah?" said Five-O. *What's wrong, brother?*

"My book's gone, Five-O."

"Da book all about dat buggah?"

Gloomily: "Yeah."

"I wen spahk"—*I've seen*—"you read dat book to da max. By now you get'um memorized."

Conrad shook his head despondently, then looked at Five-O and said, "I'm gonna take your advice. I'm gonna bag it, Five-O. But where can I go? What can I do? Look at me. I don't have any clothes. I don't have any shoes. I'm covered in mud."

"Try use da head, bruddah." Five-O said it wearily, as if talking to someone who was proving to be dense.

"Use my head?"

"How you like fo' leave here, bruddah—in Santa Rita baggies and zoris, li'dat?" *How do you want to leave here, brother—in Santa Rita pajamas and rubber sandals?* "Cannot! Dees da one night in yo' whole life you can run t'roo da shtreets weet' no clothes on, covered in mud, and no mo' nobody going t'ink you one crazy person. Oh no! Da Okies-dem, dey going tell, 'Poor little haole! Eardquake victim! We going help him!' Garans. Garans ballbaranz. Use da head. Bag it, brah. Hitchhike. Da Okies-dem, dey help you."

"But he said they're gonna shoot anybody who goes near the fence!"

"Bulai. Dey no get dat many deputies. Dey try fo' scare you, man. Dey jes' sucking wind. Bag it."

Still down on his haunches, Conrad stared at the Hawaiian for a few seconds, then said, "What are you gonna do?"

Five-O smiled faintly. "I going handle 'em. I always handle 'em."

Conrad stood up. He extended his hand toward Five-O and said, "Wish me luck."

Five-O grasped his hand with both of his and held on tightly and looked up. The moonlight played over his mud-smeared face. He blinked, and his eyes misted over. "You my bruddah, Conrad. You wen save my life. Now—bag it! Split! Laydahs for dees muddahfuggin' Rotto-dem an' dees muddahfuggin' junk place!"

Conrad straightened up and looked all about in the darkness. The generator continued to throb away, flashlight beams and dim silhouettes were milling about over toward the parking lot, sirens and horns could be heard in the distance to the south, in Pleasanton—and yet a heavy stillness had settled over the Livermore Valley and the hills that rose to the north. At one stroke the earthquake had obliterated the electrical galaxies that had always lit up the night. It had brought back the stupendous presence of the moon, the stars, and the earth itself. The very floor of the world had *moved* . . . with a power that still resonated in the bones of everyone who had been through the upheaval. A cliff now ran straight through Santa Rita where none had existed before. A new wave of fear and hopelessness swept Conrad's nervous system. He felt as if the very last roots of his past had been ripped out. Zeus had done all this and he was in Zeus' hands. He gave Five-O one last smile and a little wave and then began running alongside the escarpment, away from the remains of West Greystone.

What could he do? *Hitchhike* . . . This vague notion was the only plan he had. Try to reach Route 580 or Pleasanton . . . and hitchhike . . . Where? It didn't matter . . . Wasn't actually escaping from jail . . . just staying out of harm's way until . . . until what, he didn't know . . . The ground hurt his feet as he ran. He hadn't run barefoot for a long time. He hadn't run at all for a long time. His lungs were already beginning to burn. The flesh of his back was beginning to hurt from where the lathing had cut into it. But fear and his pumping adrenaline overrode everything else.

He kept running toward the highway. Up ahead, in the moonlight—looked like huge filthy marshmallows floating in the air. What were they? Now he could make it out. The earthquake had uprooted the razor-wire-topped Cyclone fence when it created its new cliff. The "marshmallows" were the enormous concrete blocks with which the metal posts had been anchored in the ground. Beyond the fence was the steep embankment upon which Highway 580 had been built. But it was no longer level. There was an astonishing jagged silhouette. The earthquake had thrust an entire section of the highway upward, until it was eight or ten feet above the other. He could see the beams of car lights. They were going nowhere. Then came the flashing lights and the wailing of a police cruiser approaching the stranded cars. So much for hitchhiking on Route 580.

Conrad ducked under the upthrust fence and started running west, away from Santa Rita. A phrase popped up in his mind: *escaped convict.* And yet it wasn't accurate. He was merely exercising his will to avoid. Rotto and the Nordic Bund would no doubt kill him, or try to. Zeus had given him this way out. Zeus had demolished Santa Rita and lifted up the very fence for his benefit. Of that he didn't have the slightest doubt. *Lead me, O Zeus!*

He ran, leaping over ruts, hillocks, drainpipes, rocks, bottles, roots, shags of tulare grass, whatever rose up before him in the moonlight. Ahead—how far?—a mile? half a mile?—he could see a galaxy of automobile lights that seemed to be moving about aimlessly. As he drew closer he could hear car and truck engines accelerating. Shouts bawled out in the midst of it all, shouts and frantic exhortations over a bullhorn. Conrad's first instinct was to avoid the place. Then he remembered Five-O's words: "This the one night in your whole life you can run through the streets with no clothes on, covered in mud, and no more nobody going think you one crazy person."

He was approaching some sort of parking area. Headlights came on and shot this way and that in the darkness, accompanied by great roars and squeals. People were yelling. Whatever this place was, all was uproar and confusion. The headlights hit long shapes and cast prodigious shadows . . . A barracks, tilted precariously and about to collapse . . .

Barracks! . . . *a prison!* . . . like Santa Rita! . . . But in the next instant he realized that couldn't be . . . No fence, no wall . . . He didn't know whether he was seeing things or not, but as the headlight beams swung this way and that, he seemed to keep getting glimpses of young men in underwear, men no older than himself, scampering about in the dizziest fashion . . . And here in the parking lot, he could now tell, were rows of Jeeps painted in camouflage patterns.

A figure came running toward him . . . It was a man about thirty-five with close-cropped blond hair, a long face, and a big nose, a real beak, hurriedly buttoning up a camouflage jumpsuit. Conrad ducked behind a Jeep. The man bounded up into a Jeep nearby. It roared to life. The headlight beams shot forth, revealing an ancient barracks building, now keeled over sidewise. Two young men were trying to climb into a window. One had on a T-shirt and boxer shorts; the other, only the shorts; both were barefoot. The man with the big nose jumped out of the Jeep, leaving the motor running and the lights on, and ran toward them. The lights of the Jeep cast a long, crazy shadow ahead of him.

"Whatta you idiots think you're doing?" he shouted.

"We gotta get back inside, sir!" said the young man with no T-shirt. "Our uniforms are in there!"

"Forget about it!" yelled the man in the camouflage suit. "That goddamned thing's about to fall down! We got enough casualties already. There's uniforms in J-23, Jay for Jonathan!"

"Yes, sir!" The young men hurried off in the darkness. Shouts from all sides, over here, over there . . . engines roaring to life, wheels churning, headlights shooting this way and that . . . Beams suddenly hit Conrad as he crouched behind the Jeep. He stood up. He froze in his tracks. The man with the big nose, returning to his Jeep, spotted him and barked out: "What's the matter with you, soldier? Whattaya doing?"

Conrad's mind spun. "I—I fell, sir! I fell in a ditch!"

"You *fell in a ditch*?" The man made it sound as if it were the most absurd thing he'd ever heard of. "Well—Jesus Christ, are you *hurt*?"

"No, sir!"

"Then snap out of it! Get your uniform! What's your barracks?"

Desperate, not knowing what else to do, Conrad pointed in the direction the two young men had gone and said, "Right over there, sir!"

"Then get over there! And pull yourself together!"

Conrad started running out of the parking lot. Set back from the lot was a low wooden sign, now illuminated by headlights: CAMP PARKS U.S. ARMY RESERVE CENTER. There were letters and numbers, apparently designating buildings. Soon he was amid long rows of barracks, flimsy wooden structures, many of which had been damaged by the earthquake and were tilted at precarious angles. Confusion and uproar reigned. Young men were running about, some in camouflage uniforms, but many in the underwear they had been sleeping in. Someone had got hold of a bullhorn and was bellowing out instructions that, thanks to screels of feedback, were utterly incomprehensible. Conrad could see two buildings lit up by generators, but most of the light now came from vehicles moving about on the edge. Raw glares and long, baffling shadows slid over the camp, over the skittering Reservists, over the teetering barracks.

A beam of light moved across a shed-like building . . . *J-23!* . . . Conrad ran toward it. Inside was bedlam. Young men were rooting through boxes of camouflage fatigues. Nobody challenged Conrad for a moment. Half of them were barefoot and clad in nothing but boxer shorts, too. Although he couldn't find any socks or boots, he emerged from the building wearing a set of camouflage fatigues and even a camouflage cap.

More incomprehensible bullhorns were bellowing away. Straight ahead was another parking area. Two young men jumped into Jeeps and went screeling off, their headlights beaming deliriously through the rows of stricken barracks. Two Jeeps had their headlights beamed in toward the center of the camp, apparently to provide some semblance of general illumination. Conrad drew closer and could hear the two Jeeps idling. There were no drivers; the Jeeps were just sitting there, running. He walked up beside the closer one and looked inside. No keys! Nothing but a lever on the steering column! But of course! This was a military vehicle, and in the military you couldn't afford to have keys floating around and getting lost or misplaced.

But he wouldn't take this one. It was providing illumination, and its departure might be noticed right away. So he walked two rows back and picked out one. He tried the ignition lever, and just as he had deduced, that was all it took. The engine sprang to life. Slowly he pulled out of the row, turned on the headlights, and headed down the corridor between the rows of vehicles. Heading . . . *where?* . . . His mind churned . . . To Pittsburg?—back home to the duet? Didn't dare. First place they would look. To Jill's mother's? She'd turn him in *just like that*. He knew that as well as he knew anything in the world. Mynet the lawyer? Had no idea where he lived—and he'd turn him in, too. Suddenly, as he neared the end of the row of Jeeps, a pair of headlights beamed on, and a Jeep pulled out, right in his path. *Cutting me off! Coming after me!* But instead of blocking his way, the Jeep accelerated with a terrific roar and turned down the corridor, going away, spinning its wheels madly, sending up a tremendous geyser of dust, so that Conrad's headlights illuminated nothing but the roiling yellow cloud immediately in front of him. *You lunatic—*

And in that instant he thought of Kenny.

—the parking lot at Croker Global Foods . . . a beat pounding across the hardpan . . . a funnel of dust . . . a crazy skirl of electric guitars and a chorus of raw-throated young male voices screaming *Brain* DEAD *Brain* DEAD *Brain* DEAD . . . a veritable tornado of dust lit up a feverish yellow by the floodlights . . . Kenny's outrageous boom box of a car fishtailing in the dirt and rocketing in right beside his . . . *Ayyyyyyy, Conrad—*

Kenny!—the freezer unit came to work at 9 p.m. on Sunday nights. Kenny would be there at this moment! The warehouse was only thirty or thirty-five miles north of here! Kenny would think of something! Kenny would get word to Jill! Kenny would—Kenny would—the truth was, he didn't know what Kenny would do. He didn't even know if he was still working at the warehouse. Suppose they had changed his schedule? Suppose they dismissed the entire crew as soon as the earthquake hit? No, they wouldn't do that. They had emergency generators to protect the racks full of frozen product. Dom would have them working like dogs. On the other hand, suppose—

The possibilities whirled about in his head. But there *was* no other possibility, was there . . . There was no one else he, Conrad Hensley, a fugitive from the Santa Rita jail, could turn to in the middle of the night in the aftermath of an earthquake.

The yellow cloud began to clear as the Jeep ahead of him reached the paved road out of the lot. It was tearing along at a terrific clip, apparently heading south toward the highway. Conrad sped along behind it.

He glanced off to the side. Camp Parks appeared to be dancing in a madhouse of light beams and shadows. All in shock, the whole lot of them! The earth had risen up and shown them how helpless they actually were! Life was anchored by—nothing at all!

NEAR THE BAY there was far less destruction, although electricity was out everywhere. The Croker Global warehouse's immense hulk lay there in the darkness inert, dead, barely discernible, seemingly deserted. *They had shut down—sent everybody home!*

But in the parking lot the lights of Conrad's Jeep hit rows of cars, although not nearly so many as were usually there at this time of night. Now he could see a glow from one end of the vast black silhouette of the warehouse. The freezer unit; the backup generators; the light from the freezer spilled out onto the loading platform. Truck headlights came on at the other end. He could make out the ghostly shapes of several big white Croker Global trucks and hear the sighs of the air brakes.

He cruised slowly up and down the rows of cars. He rounded the last row, and his headlights hit the Cyclone fence, the razor wire, and cars and cars and cars and cars and—

—*there*. Thank God!

He stopped the Jeep and just let the lights stream over Kenny's ridiculous little low-slung boom box of a car.

Then he nosed in beside it and turned off the engine and the lights and sank back into the seat. A terrible weariness came over him. His head seemed to drain. He was sweating profusely. His heart was beating so hard beneath his sternum, he could hear it when he opened his mouth . . . *tchhhhhhh tchhhhhhh tchhhhhhh tchhhhhhh* . . . The veins on the backs of his hands were gorged with blood. His bare feet, which rested on the floorboards, were so sore and swollen . . .

He closed his eyes and tried to think it all through. How could he get to Kenny? He couldn't very well just go walking into the unit. Everybody would recognize him, Dom, Light Bulb, Herbie, whoever was there. So he would wait for Kenny here, wait for him to come back to his car. But suppose he stayed inside? Suppose Dom kept him in there overtime because of the emergency? Suppose Kenny didn't come out until the sun was up and the new shift started? How long did he dare stay out here in a U.S. Army vehicle done up in battle camouflage?

He was thirsty . . . Had to get something to drink . . . But how? . . . So thirsty . . . above all, thirsty . . . Had to think . . . He slid down and tried to stretch out . . . and collect his thoughts . . . But his knees were sticking up, and suppose somebody saw them? . . . So he rolled over on his side and jackknifed his knees . . . He pulled the cap down over his eyes for good measure. Let's see . . . Kenny and the freezer unit and what could he get to drink . . . How could he call Jill and let her know what had happened? How could he find out about her and Carl and Christy? . . . Strange movies were sliding by behind his eyelids . . . If Kenny was inside and Dom was giving him instructions . . . Dom, grunting with great bursts of mouth fog . . . complaining about the tailgate parties over at Bolka . . . Kenny going, "Crash'n'burn!" . . . and Light Bulb and the rest of them answering him in falsetto . . . Herbie brooding . . . Nick the bald man with the necktie . . . inside the cold, cold, cold, cold icy cliffs . . .

"EAT SHIT! EAT SHIT! EAT SHIT! EAT SHIT!"—right beside the bunk—they'd broken into the cell, crying out, "EAT SHIT! EAT SHIT! EAT SHIT! EAT SHIT!"

Conrad rolled to slide down off the bunk. His knee hit the gearshift. He came to with a start—

"EAT SHIT! EAT SHIT! EAT SHIT! EAT SHIT!"—from right outside the door of the Jeep—

He propped himself up on one elbow and tried to make sense out of it—

"EAT SHIT! EAT SHIT! EAT SHIT! EAT SHIT!"—the car right beside him roared in neutral, ready to shift into gear—

Kenny!

Conrad lifted himself high enough to look out the window. In the darkness a silhouette . . . Kenny with his baseball cap and his bony Adam's apple . . . hunched forward in the driver's seat . . . his twenty-inch boom box speakers yowling, battering the air with the anthem that had so infuriated Dom: "EAT SHIT! EAT SHIT! EAT SHIT! EAT SHIT!"

Conrad yelled out: "Kenny!"

"EAT SHIT! EAT SHIT! EAT SHIT! EAT SHIT!"

No way Kenny could hear him—and now he was gunning the engine, ready to leave.

Conrad scrambled toward the door.

Kenny's car was backing up. "KENNY! KENNY! STOP!"

The crash'n'burner anthem—"EAT SHIT! EAT SHIT!"—filled the world.

Now Conrad was out of the Jeep, screaming, but Kenny had his head turned to the rear as he backed up. In another second he would be gunning his car through the dust of the parking lot, the way he liked to do. Only one way—

Conrad ran toward Kenny's rakish red car and dove. He landed in a sprawl on the hood. The car came to such an abrupt stop that Conrad rolled right up onto the windshield with his face flattened on the glass, staring head-on at Kenny, who was barely a foot away.

Kenny stuck his head out his side window. "The fuck, you crazy? You? In the Army? In the middle of an earthquake? Jumping on the hood of my car? This I don't fucking believe!"

"EAT SHIT! EAT SHIT! EAT SHIT! EAT SHIT!"

TO KENNY THIS was a great crash'n'burner adventure. He had Conrad follow him in the Jeep and abandon it in Northtown, up in Richmond, where its chances of being stolen, Kenny assured him, would be approximately one hundred percent, thereby obliterating the Jeep's recent history. At that point Conrad got into the front seat of Kenny's little red boom box of a car and closed his eyes.

Kenny told him why he was driving him to Oakland, but Conrad was too groggy to comprehend. His nervous system had sunk below the threshold of logic. His eyelids felt immensely heavy. A stupefying weight bore down on his cerebral cortex, driving him lower lower lower lower lower. Get word to Jill . . . but soon he couldn't think even about that . . .

He didn't come to until lights and voices roused the sentinel, fear, deep in his nervous system. He opened his eyes. It was still dark. Kenny was cruising along a street with traffic and lights and voices . . . a wide street . . . four lanes . . . sodium vapor lamps overhead . . . So many people . . . dark faces . . . out on the sidewalks . . . standing about in clusters in a park . . . treating themselves to a neighborhood beano in the aftermath of the greatest event of recent history, the earthquake.

Conrad turned toward Kenny. "Where are we?"

"O-town," said Kenny, cackling. "Bump City, Shattuck Avenue, Oakland, California."

"Where are we going?"

Kenny laughed without explaining why. "Mai's 24-Hour Mini-Mart. You're gonna meet Mai and Mai's army."

Kenny turned onto the asphalt apron of what looked like a service station. Lights beneath a shed-like roof shone down on two islands of self-service gasoline pumps. The sign over the entrance to the small building just beyond them said: MAI'S 24-HOUR MINI-MART. The place was doing a lively business in the middle of the night, post-earthquake. Cars were backing out of the row of parking places on either side, and others were pulling in. With a sharp intake of breath Conrad realized that Kenny was pulling into a spot right next to a police cruiser.

"Ayyyyyy," said Kenny. "This is Shattuck Avenue, not Danville. You're gonna see police cars. Just be cool. You can be sure there's no cops out on Shattuck Avenue in the middle of the fucking night looking for some *white* boy who's escaped from the Santa Rita jail."

Inside, Mai's was a shabby space lit with fluorescent lights so bright they made you wince. The place was crammed with racks of merchandise and glass-faced refrigerators full of every sort of soda, ice cream, milk, beer, and malt liquor imaginable, and stacks of cartons that had never been opened and others that were empty and lying in jumbles on the floor. There were at least two dozen customers in all, loose souls rolling around O-town, Bump City, after an earthquake. Overhead, a battery of surveillance cameras, aimed at the entrance and down the aisles between the racks and toward the checkout counter and the cash register, recorded their jack-legged progress on videotape.

From behind the register came the loud, angry voice of a woman: "Youie faggot, what you are! You look da boys! You be da girl!" A contemptuous laugh. "You don' care dey steal me everyt'ing! Youie faggot!"

"Bu'shit, Mai, I find it like dat."

With a sneer: "You find a lotta dicks you look at, what you find! Now you go home. You *fire*."

"C'mon, Mai! What I do to you?"

"You let dem steal me everyt'ing! And you—you look da pornos!"

Mai, the proprietress of Mai's 24-Hour Mini-Mart, wore black jeans and a sleeveless black cotton blouse. She was a Vietnamese, no more than thirty, with full, smooth Asian features, a glowing complexion, and full, sweetly curved lips. Not even anger could ruin such voluptuous good looks.

The object of her scorn was a Chinese, a thin, almost gaunt boy in his mid-twenties, wearing a knit golf shirt and jungle camouflage pants, like Conrad's, with what appeared to be a lock-blade folding knife in a pouch on one side of his belt and a small shiny flashlight in a holster on the other. Thoroughly cowed, he kept gesturing toward Mai and blurting out excuses. Kenny turned toward Conrad and grinned and winked.

As Mai's harangue continued, the nature of the offense became clearer. The Chinese, whose name was Hong, was supposed to manage the store whenever Mai was away or upstairs sleeping or working back in the office. But, as she now realized, if she was absent for any length of time, Hong liked to unscrew the hinges on the locked wooden cabinet that stored all the video surveillance equipment and watch pornographic tapes from the store's own rack on the monitor screens, thereby shutting down the entire surveillance system. Mai had been upstairs sleeping when the earthquake shook the city and had come downstairs to find a pornographic film rolling on her screens. All the cassettes were made for a heterosexual audience, but Mai was now convinced, or claimed to be, that Hong was homosexual and was interested only in the nude men "wit' big dicks."

"Go *yo'* home and be faggot!" she was screaming at the hapless Chinese.

In the background, enjoying it all immensely, was a group of six young men who had gathered at the far end of the counter. One was a tall Chinese dressed like Hong, in camouflage fatigue pants. Two were Sikhs with pale-blue turbans and upswept beards and mustaches, both of them heavyset and muscular. The other three had very dark skin and thin, fine-boned features.

While Mai and Hong continued their set-to, Kenny sidled over to Conrad and said out of the corner of his mouth: "Mai's army. You see that guy, Hong?" Hong was now insisting that he could *prove* he was not homosexual. "And his buddy?" He motioned toward the tall Chinese by the counter. "They were both a them Chi Coms."

"They were what?"

"Chinese Communists, soldiers. They were born in Cambodia, and they speak Khmer, but they were trained in China, and they fought for China somewhere ov'eh, and then they turned around and immigrated over here as Cambodians. You see that flashlight on his belt?" He nodded toward Hong. "That's aircraft steel. That's a weapon, bro. He could kill you with that thing." Kenny was profoundly impressed—and excited—by lethal capabilities and the men who possessed them. *If only he really knew.* "And you see that Sikh there, the tall one? His name is

Torin, Torin Singh. He was a guerrilla in India, a sapper, is what he told me, fighting the government. And that black guy, the one on the left? His name's Achilles. He was a commando in Ethiopia, and a paratrooper. But then they found out his old man had been a buddy of Haile Selassie, and so he went underground and finally got here. The other two, they're from Eritrea. You ever heard a Eritrea?"

Conrad shook his head.

"It's north a Ethiopia. The both a them, they were college students, and then they joined some revolutionary movement, or whatever it was, and they were blowing up trucks and shit, and then they came here. These guys, they work nights at convenience stores, just like Hong does. They drive taxis at night, like Achilles. They work nights at the Pioneer Chicken, like Torin. I mean, you got to be a commando or something to work nights at that damned Pioneer Chicken where he works. That neighborhood's worse than this one. And they all come here, to Mai's. This is Mai's army. While everybody else sleeps, there's an *army* out here. There's sappers, guerrillas, tunnel rats, commandos, terrorists, volunteers for suicide missions—and I mean they're from Asia and Africa and God knows where else, and nobody knows how they got here or what they want or what they're really doing or where they want to go, except for Mai maybe. This is where they come for fake ID's, fake licenses, fake Social Security cards, cell phone numbers, credit cards, green cards, plane tickets, jobs, whatever they need. These jobs don't pay shit. What does a guy like Hong make? Maybe five dollars an hour. And they're dangerous. Working in these places is a good way to get yourself killed. But they're jobs, all the same, and Mai'll keep you going. Mai's army."

Kenny's eyes were lit with the romance of it all, the idea of a lethal foreign legion of the night, of young men hardened into a brotherhood of violence, a fraternity that Kenny, he who would make "Brain Dead," "Eat Shit," and "Crash'n'burn" his anthems, so innocently admired. Conrad found such a vicarious thrill all too sad and deluded. In Conrad these young men stirred an entirely different emotion. A wave of sadness came over him, and his heart sank. He saw seven pitiable creatures, young men torn up by the roots from all that means home and hearth and reassurance in this life and blown halfway around the world to the bowels of Shattuck Avenue in Oakland, California, seven young men almost as hopelessly lost as himself.

Mai turned away from Hong, shaking her head. Then she saw Kenny. She broke into a smile, and the loveliness of her wide, smooth face burst forth.

"Ken-ny! I t'ink about you!"

"Hey, Mai!" said Kenny. "Get off Hong's case and come here."

She came out from behind the counter, beaming. Kenny put one arm around her shoulders, and she put one arm around his waist, and they gave each other a big squeeze. Three or four customers, lined up at the checkout counter, waiting to pay for purchases, glowered.

Mai looked up into Kenny's eyes and said, "Wha' hoppen up dere? I worry 'bout you." Before he could answer, she turned her head around and gestured brusquely toward Hong with her free hand. "Get back dere. You don't see? Got customers."

Forlornly Hong trooped back around behind the counter to the register.

To Kenny once more: "So wha' hoppen?"

Kenny steered Mai toward the rear of the store. Conrad felt dizzy, nauseated, terribly weary, thoroughly conspicuous, and frightened. He was an escapee from the county jail standing out in the middle of a convenience store at three o'clock in the morning in his bare feet, muddy, swollen, bloody bare feet, at that. The fact that he looked no worse than the rest of the loose souls who were up and around on Shattuck Avenue in Mai's 24-Hour Mini-Mart in the wake of an earthquake seemed like no safeguard whatsoever.

Now Mai and Kenny were heading back toward him. Mai's hips went this way and that way, ever so insouciantly, as she walked.

"Okay," said Kenny, "Mai'n'me just had a talk. Here's what's gonna happen. Mai's gonna take care a you here tonight. Okay? You're gonna be fine. Mai's gonna look after you. After you wake up, I'm gonna come back, and I'm gonna bring you some things. Got it?" He paused. He studied Conrad's face and then his camouflage outfit and then his feet. He looked at his feet a long time. "You wanna know something?"

Conrad stared back dazedly.

"You're a mess. What size shoes you wear?"

He quizzed him about all sorts of sizes: shoes, shirts, jackets, underwear. Then he said to Mai, "You got razors and shaving foam and combs and all that stuff here, right?" Kenny gestured toward the racks where the loose souls grazed in Mai's store, and Mai nodded yes. Kenny said to Conrad, "You're gonna have a shave, old buddy, a big shave. You ain't gonna have a *mus*-tache anymore. That's what you owe Mai for one night's lodging."

"Okay," said Conrad, "I guess that . . . makes sense . . . Look . . . one thing I've got to do is, I've got to get hold of my wife and let her know what's happened. Is there some way I could call her?"

"I been trying to reach Antioch myself," said Kenny. "You can't get through. All the lines are tied up, plus there's a relay station totaled in Concord. Besides, I'd be careful if I was you. They got automatic records of every call that's made."

"They do?"

"Aw, yeah."

Conrad didn't know if this was some fantasy of Kenny's infatuation with soldiers, weaponry, surveillance, and espionage—or a real danger. He closed his eyes, lowered his head, and sighed deeply. It made him feel dizzy.

"You come with me," said Mai. She laughed. "Now you in Mai's army."

She led him back behind the counter to a tiny office. In the far corner were a narrow spiral staircase and the door to a cramped lavatory. Then she led him up the stairs, pausing at the top. A light came on. A few more steps, and the two of them were in a cramped attic space, beneath sloping eaves, that had been turned into a makeshift bedroom. Because of the steep slopes of the eaves, they could only stand in the center, side by side. He became aware of the jasmine perfume she wore.

She pointed out two cramped, flimsy, upright cabinets. One served, somehow, as a shower; the other as a toilet.

"Okay, my friend," said Mai, "you take a shower."

"Thanks," said Conrad with another great sigh, "but I think I'm just gonna lie down a minute."

She laughed. "Not just gonna lie down. You a real mess, my little friend. You in Mai's army." She gestured toward the mattress and the sheets. "And that's Mai's bed. You take a shower, you feel better. Then you lie down."

She nodded a few times, to indicate she meant business, then slipped past him to head back downstairs.

As he took off the camouflage uniform, his shadow swept grotesquely across the ceiling. He was a mess, sure enough. Mud was smeared over his chest, his midsection, his thighs, his knees. Mud had plastered his shorts to his groin. Chunks of dried mud fell to the floor as he took them off. His clothes were so filthy that after he took a shower and dried himself, he crawled into the makeshift bed with nothing on. He reached over and turned off the lamp on the floor. He lay there, on his back. The sheets were redolent of jasmine. Soon his ability to reason began sliding helplessly away, and there was nothing but darkness, the drone of a fan, and a great fluffy cloud of jasmine.

IT WAS ALMOST 11 a.m. by the time Conrad woke up, put on the plaid shirt, chinos, and construction boots that had materialized beside the bed, shaved off his mustache, per Kenny's instructions, and made his way downstairs to look for Mai. Sunlight was flooding in through the plate-glass windows of the mini-mart.

Mai was out at the cash register haranguing Hong, as usual. When she saw Conrad, she led him back into her little office, berating Hong for not taking her place at the register fast enough. She stood still for a moment and stared at Conrad's face.

"You look better!" she said. "No more mustache." She laughed. This struck her as a very funny turn of events.

Then she sat down at her desk, picked up the telephone, and ordered in some food. She had barely hung up when Kenny arrived. Conrad had never seen him look more manic. His pale blue eyes were electric. His grin showed all his teeth. He was carrying a navy-blue duffel bag heavy enough to bring out the huge muscles of his forearm.

He flashed his wildest grin, for Conrad's benefit, stroked his own wispy blond mustache with his thumb and forefinger, and said, "You wanna know something? You did yourself a favor. I never did like your mustache. Damn thing *drooped*. I'm not kidding!"

"Look better!" said Mai.

"You got it, Mai," said Kenny. Then he set the blue duffel bag at Conrad's feet. "Here's all the clothes you'll need, or everything I could think of." He handed Conrad a newspaper and said, "Take a look. You're on the front page!"

Genuinely frightened: "Me?"

A headline stretched all the way across the upper half of the *Oakland Tribune*: QUAKE ROCKS EAST BAY. From smaller headlines you quickly picked up: "Massive Destruction . . . 6.2 on Richter scale . . . Hayward Fault . . ." and there, just below the main headline, a big picture, in color—must have been taken at dawn—of Santa Rita and the ruins of

West Greystone and the escarpment that had risen beneath it and broken it almost in two. Above was a headline reading, JAIL BREAKS. Below was a caption that began, "The quake's irresistible force created this cliff near Pleasanton, destroying an entire cell block at the Alameda County Jail. All the jail's buildings were heavily damaged. Rescue workers search the ruins for survivors."

Kenny said to Mai, "You get the ticket?"

From a drawer in her desk she produced an envelope and handed it to him. Kenny studied the ticket for a moment, then handed it to Conrad. "Hang on to this. This is a ticket from Portland to Atlanta tonight at ten."

"Portland? To Atlanta?"

"Portland'll be safer than Oakland or San Francisco, and Atlanta's where Mai can get things organized for you right away."

Mai handed him another envelope, explaining that it contained the name—Lum Loc—of the Vietnamese who would meet him at the Atlanta airport and drive him to an apartment.

"How will we recognize each other?" asked Conrad.

"You not recognize him," said Mai. "He recognize you. Baggage area."

She reached into another drawer and pulled out one of what appeared to be a dozen apple-green baseball caps with yellow lettering outlined in dark green. The lettering said, "HI-GRO. We feed gardens."

"Lum Loc look for this hat. Social Security card, driver's license, birth certificate, whatever you want, he get it."

"He's gonna want $750 cash," said Kenny.

"I—"

"Don't worry, you got it." With that, Kenny stood up and removed a doubled-over envelope from the back pocket of his jeans. "Here. Count it."

Astonished, Conrad did so. Five hundred-dollar bills, twelve fifties, and twenty twenties: $1,500 in all. He looked at Kenny with a baffled, wondering grin.

"Good," said Kenny, "I'm glad *some*thing makes you smile. You can pay me back when you got a condo in Danville, a Volvo station wagon with side-impact air bags, and a set of Fuzzy Zoeller golf clubs."

Mai left the office to go out into the store, and Conrad went over to Kenny and said, "I hate to ask you to do anything more'n you've already done, but could you try to call my wife? Maybe from a pay phone someplace? Just tell her I'm okay, I'm out of Santa Rita, and I'll be in touch with her as soon as I can? You don't have to be any more specific than that. You don't even have to tell her who you are."

Kenny found a piece of piece of paper and a ballpoint pen on Mai's desk and wrote down Conrad's telephone number in Pittsburg and his own in Antioch and tore off his number and gave it to Conrad.

Thirty or forty minutes later Kenny and Mai introduced Conrad to the big muscular Sikh, the Mai's warrior he had seen the night before, Torin Singh, who was about to make his regular truck run to Portland. They walked him out to the Sikh's huge rig, which he had pulled up to the curb out front on Shattuck Avenue. There were Sikh truck drivers all over California now, but Torin Singh, perched way up in the driver's seat of the silvery cab with his pale blue turban and an upswept beard as magnificent as the King of Diamonds's, looked like a monarch of the breed.

Conrad turned to Kenny and smiled. "Kenny, I can't even begin—"

Kenny cut him off. "*Don't* begin. I ain't even close to catching up. Just promise to send me a postcard when you get there. What the hell *do* they have postcards of in Atlanta?"

Conrad climbed up into the cab, and the Sikh threw the engine into gear, creating the sort of roar Conrad had always disliked when he was working at Croker Global Foods.

Conrad leaned out the window and looked back and waved. The last thing he could see was two figures standing upright on the asphalt out by the gasoline pumps, one of them all bones and knobs and eccentric angles, wild-looking even in the abstract, the other one Mother Earth in black jeans.

Chapter XXI

The Real Buckhead

AS SOON AS THE MAYOR CAME OUT OF HIS LITTLE INNER OFFICE and into the mayoral parlor, Roger Too White knew there was something different about him, but couldn't figure out what. He had on the same sort of nondescript dark gray suit as usual. True, he wasn't wearing a Pizza Grenade necktie this time; he had on a darkish red tie with a faint print design; but it wasn't the necktie. So what was it?

"Brother Roger!" said Wes Jordan, giving him his customary mock–high five and then gesturing for him to sit down on the couch. Wes pulled up an armchair and sat across the coffee table from him. On top of the coffee table was a copy of today's *Atlanta Journal-Constitution* with a color picture of something about yesterday's earthquake in California.

"Brother Wes," said Roger Too White, "you look different today, but I can't put my finger on what it is."

"I know. I'm leaner and harder. Either that or I have a better tailor now."

"You go to a *tailor* for those suits?"

"No, I'm only kidding," said the Mayor. "No politician or lawyer should ever go to a tailor."

"Well, *I'm* a lawyer," said Roger Too White in an exaggerated tone of disappointment, "and *I* go to a tailor."

"I'm not too surprised. All those nipped-in waists and peaked lapels. Who do you go to?"

"A fellow named Gus Carroll. Has a little tailor shop down on Ellis."

"Well," said Wes Jordan, "at least he's south of Ponce de Leon. Besides, you're not a litigator, are you? If you ever start going into the courtrooms, I advise you to buy off the rack like me."

"What difference does it make?" said Roger Too White.

"People can always tell there's something a little too studied, a little too smart, whereas charisma consists of being like everybody else."

"Did you make that up?"

"No, somebody said it. I can't remember who. I just remember it was in Dr. Crawford's sociology class at Morehouse."

"Anyway," said Roger Too White, "there's something different about you. I just haven't quite figured it out."

The Mayor shrugged and gestured toward the newspaper on the table. "Did you read anything about this or see anything on TV?"

"Not really," said Roger Too White, looking down at the big color picture. It was of an escarpment that had risen up out of the earth and torn a large wooden building in two and twisted it every which way. The caption read: "NATURAL BORN JAILBREAK: A California earthquake measuring 6.2 on the Richter scale creates an instant cliff, demolishing the Alameda County Jail southeast of Oakland and leaving a guard and eight inmates dead. Another twenty inmates, as yet unaccounted for, may have escaped."

With one of his familiar wry smiles the Mayor gestured toward the newspaper and said, "Our press office has had about two dozen queries about the risk of an earthquake in Atlanta."

"So what do you say?" asked Roger Too White.

"So far as we can tell, there hasn't been an earthquake in this region in recorded history. The nearest geological fault line is somewhere in Tennessee. But we promise eternal vigilance. Makes me want to say, 'All we've got here is a racial fault line.' But I don't say that."

"And its initials are F.F.?"

"Whose are?"

"The racial fault line's."

"Ahhh," said the Mayor, "that is true, that is true."

"And I presume that's why you asked me over?"

"There are many reasons why I enjoy your company, Roger, but in this instance that is the case, that is the case."

"Well, at least it hasn't hit the press."

"Depends on how you define the press," said the Mayor. "Take a look at this." He handed Roger a piece of paper.

At the top, in exaggerated Oriental-looking letters, it said "Chasing the Dragon." Up in a square in the corner were the call letters of an Internet Web site. Beneath that was the inscription "Opening the Doors of Perception." The rest of the page was presented as a news bulletin . . . Fareek Fanon . . . a Freaknik party . . . rape charges . . . It didn't mention Elizabeth Armholster by name, but the description of her unnamed father's industrial and social might was so detailed, down to the dollar volume of (unnamed) Armaxco, they might as well have supplied a picture of his house on Tuxedo Road and put an arrow over it.

"Godalmighty," said Roger. "Where the hell did this come from?"

"You know my press secretary? Gloria Loxley? Gloria came walking in with this. She'd just downloaded it from the Internet. Then she started making some calls. Roger, people all over Atlanta are downloading this item from the Internet."

Roger looked at it again. "What the hell is 'Chasing the Dragon' supposed to be?"

"It's sort of an . . . Internet gossip column, I guess you'd say. A lot of what they run seems to concern petty drug busts and drug availability on the street. 'Chasing the dragon,' so I'm told, is some new way of taking heroin without using a needle."

"In other words, they're totally irresponsible," said Roger.

"Totally unsavory," said Wes Jordan, "but not necessarily totally irresponsible. Gloria checked out a couple of their drug-arrest items with Elihu Yale at the police department, and they were right on the money. They just weren't big enough stories to make the *Journal-Constitution*. What they're running about Fanon and the Armholsters, you'll notice, is accurate in every detail."

Roger looked at Wes with wide eyes, as if to say, "What does this mean?"

"This doubles, triples the pressure on the 'responsible' media to break the story. They know people all over town are reading what you just read. They're dying to publish it, but they don't have anybody to attribute it to. They don't have anybody to confirm the rumor. Armholster hasn't filed charges because his daughter's begged him not to—because she's traumatized and won't even leave the house—or that's what he told me—and as far as that goes, Armholster himself, he's petrified that his daughter's name will end up in the press. Meantime, he's going around trying to round up support behind the scenes for whatever retaliation he has in mind for your client."

"Which will be what?" asked Roger.

"I don't know, but he knows a lot of influential people. So I want to make sure your client has a fair shake when the time comes." The Mayor smiled again. "I know a lot of influential people myself."

Roger Too White didn't say anything. He just looked at Wes Jordan and waited and tried to figure out what it was that was . . . different . . . about him. He was aware of yet more Yoruba carvings mounted on the ebony walls.

"But that isn't what I wanted to see you about," said the Mayor. "What I wanted to see you about is . . . our man."

"Our man?"

"Our man Charlie Croker."

"Ahhhhhh," said Roger, tilting his head back in an ironic, mock-significant way. "What about him?"

"He's the one. No doubt about it. 'The Sixty-Minute Man.' People used to point him out on the street and say, 'There's the Sixty-Minute Man.' I'm sure he knows precisely what pressures a big-time athlete is under. He knows how jealous and resentful people can be. He knows how fast people are to find fault with a sports star and how they over-interpret every little thing. And the time to approach him is right, because this thing's going to blow wide-open any moment."

Roger knew there was a missing link in the logic of what Wes had just said, but he confined himself to a simple "Unh-hunh."

"Oh, he's our man," said Wes, "but we've got one big problem. The man's practically bankrupt. Yeah! He's about to lose everything he's got. They've already seized his corporate jet, a huge thing called a Gulfstream Five, big as an airliner. It won't have the same effect if he tries to stand up for Fareek Fanon while he's going down in flames as just another megalomaniacal Atlanta real estate developer who didn't know enough to quit while he was ahead."

"*Who* seized his corporate jet?"

"PlannersBanc."

"How do you know that?"

"Oh, I know a lot of what goes on at PlannersBanc. We—I'm talking about the city—we keep a lot of our deposits, the municipal deposits, at PlannersBanc. That's a *huge* asset for them. We're talking about millions of dollars a year they can lend, based on those deposits. That's a *huge* asset. Believe me, they'll do a lot to keep us happy. And it's not just a matter of money. You remember we were talking the other day about the 'Atlanta Way'?"

"Unh-hunh."

"Well, these big firms like PlannersBanc—and the interesting thing is, the bigger they are, the more willing they are—they're willing to do us big favors just for the sake of . . . oh, keeping everything smooth, warm, congenial, and well oiled with the black power structure. It's sort of like 'paying tribute.' Remember old Pomeroy—the historical sense in which he always used that term 'paying tribute'?"

"Unh-hunh."

"That's one of the ways we keep ourselves busy in the city that's too busy to hate," said Wes Jordan with a classic Wes Jordan ironic smile.

"Maybe I'm slow or something, Wes," said Roger, "but I still don't get it."

"Roger—I'm speaking to you as a brother now. Okay?"

"Okay."

"I have a delicate mission for you to perform," said Wes Jordan. Roger searched his face for a twist of the lips, a twinkle of the eyes, that would indicate that the phrase *delicate mission* was yet more Wes Jordan irony. But he looked completely serious and mayor-like. "This is something," he continued, "that you mustn't tell your client about or your colleagues, Mr. Salisbury and Mr. Pickett. Can I have your word on that?"

"I love you, Brother Wes, but I can't see how I could possibly give you my word, since I don't know what you're talking about."

"You can't even do that much for me, hunh?" said Wes Jordan. "All right, then I'll just appeal to your sense of civic concern."

Roger searched his face once more. No smile, no wink, no arching of the eyebrows.

"This case," said the Mayor, "has the potential to do more damage to this city than anything since the murder of Martin Luther King or the Rodney King riots, because it gets right down to the core of the white man's fear. Do you see what I'm saying?"

"Yes," said Roger Too White, "I can see that."

"All right, so what I'm saying is, I'm saying that Charlie Croker, or somebody like Charlie Croker, could be an essential figure to keep the city from getting split apart."

"Along the racial fault line," said Roger Too White.

"Exactly, along the racial fault line. Very well put. Along the racial fault line. So if he's willing to stick his neck out to that extent—and for somebody like him, this'd really be sticking his neck out—this sixty-year-old Cracker with a—did you know he has a 29,000-acre plantation down in Baker County?"

"No."

"Just for shooting quail? All very *antebellum*? Even got African-American servants who sing gospel for the guests after dinner?"

"You're . . . exaggerating." He had started to say "kidding."

"Not at all, not at all. He calls the place Turpmtine. T,u,r,p,*m*,t,i,n,e. Originally the cash crop at this place was not cotton but turpentine, from the pine trees. Apparently slashing the pine trees for resin was the worst work in the world, much worse than picking cotton. Croker seems to enjoy calling them the 'Turpmtine Niggers.' "

"Aw, come on! And you think you're gonna get him to stand up for Fareek Fanon against Inman Armholster?"

"I have my reasons for thinking he might. And if he does, then I think the city would owe him a debt of gratitude, which might take the form of removing some of the other pressures that now bear down on the man."

"Such as?"

"Such as the threat of bankruptcy, to be specific. I would think that PlannersBanc would find it in its long-term interest, as a part of this city, to restructure the man's debt load in some significant fashion, so that in the same moment he speaks up for your client he isn't revealed to be one of the biggest deadbeats in the history of commercial real estate in Atlanta."

Roger Too White pondered all this for a moment. He wasn't sure what he was actually hearing. "All right, Wes, assuming all that makes sense—which I'm not sure it does—I don't see where I would fit in."

"I need someone to outline the facts of the matter to Croker. It can't be me, because that might be misinterpreted. But if it comes from your client, from counsel representing your client, then it's perfectly appropriate. You're not asking him to testify in court. All you're doing is asking him to render a judgment in the arena of public opinion. We're not talking about the law. We're talking about public relations."

"But what kind of opinion, Wes? What kind of opinion could you possibly expect Charlie Croker to have—or express?"

"That Fareek is a fine young man. That young athletes like him have always been setups for all sorts of pressures, schemes, and vilifications. That he can't believe that Fareek is guilty of the sort of thing he's being smeared with now, and so forth and so on."

"Where's he going to do this?" asked Roger. "At a protest demonstration or a rally or what?"

"No, no, no, no," said Wes. "You don't have protests or rallies in a sex case. What I envision is a press conference, a press conference whose ostensible purpose is simply to urge calmness and restraint in the face of a potentially explosive situation. In the course of that I establish the point that men have rights, too, even big black men, even big black sports stars, every bit as many rights as white women half their size. This is all in the context of maintaining public order, you understand. Then Croker gets up and makes the point even stronger. He says that Fareek is a fine young man—"

"Wait a minute, Wes," said Roger. "He's gonna say Fareek is a fine young man—on the basis of *what?* I wonder if he's ever even laid eyes on Fareek, unless it was from a seat in the grandstand."

Wes Jordan smiled. "He has to meet Fareek, Roger, and get to know him. And as you know, to know him is to love him."

Roger let loose a laugh that ended up sounding like a snort. "For God's sake, Wes, *you and I* can't stand the sonofabitch!"

"I think you might be surprised, Roger," said Wes Jordan with a familiar ironic gleam in his eyes. "I think you might be surprised. I think Mr. Croker might see something in Fareek that we don't see."

"Well—where's he supposed to meet him?"

"I'll leave that to your best judgment, Counselor. But it's essential that he meet him and that he come away from that meeting ready to say favorable things about Fareek, for the record. It's also essential that he know that you, as a representative of Fareek and his many supporters, are in a position to see to it that the banking interests in this city restructure his loans on highly favorable terms so as not to damage his credibility at this pivotal moment in Atlanta's history. And if he says, 'Why me?' then you say, 'Because you're the only Atlanta business leader with a sports career like Fareek's. You're the Sixty-Minute Man.' "

Now Roger gave the Mayor an ironic smile of his own. "And he's supposed to believe all that because some black lawyer he's never heard of drops by and tells him his troubles are over?"

"I already thought of that," said the Mayor. "I think what you have to do is offer him a practical demonstration, a sort of field experiment, as it were. I think what you have to tell him is 'Go see Fareek, and then decide if you want to do your part for the city at the press conference, and if you say yes, then all communication from PlannersBanc concerning outstanding loans will immediately cease.' I think Mr. Croker will look upon you as a black prophet he can believe in."

"And you really think you can see to that?" asked Roger.

"If I can't, then the field experiment will be a failure. But I'm not worried." Wes Jordan leaned back in his chair and thrust his chest out in a certain satisfied way, as if he had already won a great battle. The ironic smile that Roger had known for so many years played upon his lips. "Roger, you're about to see the way politics actually works in a city. It would be nice to think that certain laudable positions prevail because they have an irresistible logic all their own. But that is seldom the case . . . seldom the case . . . And I'm sure the Charlie Crokers of this town, dense though they may be in certain respects, already understand that."

Roger sat bolt upright on the couch, opened his eyes wide, and flashed a big grin. "I've figured it out!"

"Figured out what?"

"What's different! About *you*!"

"Really? You gonna let me in on it, too?"

Roger Too White slapped the side of his leg and grinned some more and started laughing. "You're *darker*, Brother Wes, you're *darker*! What'd you do? How'd you do it?"

The Mayor ran his hands over his own cheeks, as if in wonderment. "Darker? Well, I'll be damned. It is true that I've gotten in a lot more golf than usual."

"Golf?"

"Been playing a lot of golf recently, Brother Roger."

"You? Give me a break, Brother Wes!"

"Yeah, I know. I used to make fun of golf. But I figured I ought to get outdoors more, smell the newly mown grass and the newly raked sand traps. Lanny's been playing, too."

"Lanny? Your wife, Lanny? You *must* be joking!"

"No, I'm not joking," said Wes Jordan. "Everybody's entitled to change his or her mind. The good old Georgia sunshine does wonders for a person."

"Well, you sly old dog, you!" exclaimed Roger Too White. "You're getting . . . a *sun*tan—for the election campaign! You're getting . . . *darker*!"

Wes Jordan winked and chuckled deep in his throat. "It just naturally happens to us golf lovers, just naturally happens. And besides, everything is relative. I've always been blacker than thou, Roger Too White."

PEEPGASS TOLD PEOPLE he lived "in Buckhead," but *this* . . . was *Buckhead. This* . . . was the real thing. At the wheel of his little Ford Escort, he had just turned off West Paces Ferry Road onto Valley Road, on which, less than a quarter of a mile from this point, according to Martha Croker, he would come upon her house. Peepgass was all eyes. Rolling lawns, absolutely perfectly cut, watered, landscaped, and ornamented by flowers and deep-green bushes, every leaf of which seemed waxed and polished by hand—rolling lawns swelled up on either side of Valley Road, leading to stupendous piles of Georgian brick with real slate roofs or romantic but equally stupendous villas of Italianate stucco atop the crests. And even though it was nine o'clock in the morning, on a hot day in May that had already turned the asphalt slopes of Collier Hills into an oven, here in the real Buckhead all was serene and green and cool, thanks to the soaring trees, left over from virgin forest, that created a great green canopy for the entire neighborhood.

Peepgass slowed down, as much in awe as in the interest of spotting Martha Croker's house number. The house numbers seemed to be mainly on mailboxes at the foot of the driveways. In a neighborhood like this, if you actually put the number on the house, no one would ever see it; it would be too far away from the road. The street itself, Valley Road, was laid out in suitably wasteful serpentine curves, like the floor of a valley winding its way between the eminences of the castles that rose up on either side. Peepgass drove his little Escort around a big bend, ever so slowly, and—

—there in the middle of the street . . . *women!* . . . six or eight of them . . . walking right in the middle of the road . . . at a leisurely pace . . . laughing, talking . . . black and Latin women of various ages, but none very young, some in dresses, some in blouses and pants and sneakers, walking right in the middle of Valley Road . . . In the next instant it dawned on Peepgass . . . *Maids,* housemaids, for the castles! They arrived by bus, on the line, the Number 40 line, that ran along West Paces Ferry Road, got off at the corner of Valley Road, and walked the rest of the way to the castles, which were their places of employment. There were no sidewalks in this part of Buckhead—who other than servants would be walking anywhere anyway—and they had to walk in the street. But why out in the middle?

Peepgass swung way over to the left and passed them, very slowly . . . Only one or two of the women even bothered to look his way. Just ahead he saw Martha Croker's house number on a mailbox by the driveway. And up the driveway, at the crest of the great swollen green lawn —Peepgass couldn't believe it. The house was a colossal pile of brick with a portico and white columns and windows with white muntins that seemed ten feet tall. It took Peepgass's breath away. He suddenly felt terribly intimidated.

Jesus Christ, he thought. I can't drive up to that place in a five-year-old Ford Escort.

So he continued past the driveway and made a U-turn—plenty of room on Valley Road to make a U-turn in a Ford Escort—and headed back the other way. Now he had to pass the battalion of maids by swinging to the right. More of them gave him the once-over this time, no doubt wondering what he was doing. Once he passed them, he made another U-turn and pulled over to the curb about fifty feet from Martha Croker's driveway. Now plenty of the women had turned their heads around to give him a dubious look. Who *was* this creep who kept driving by them and was now getting out of his car so he could follow them, on foot, out in the middle of the street?

He'd *walk* up her driveway, Escortless, that's what he'd do. He soon discovered why the maids walked out in the middle of the street. On the edges, the street sloped so much to allow for water to run off, walking was uncomfortable. So now, out in the middle of Valley Road, came a battalion of maids . . . with Raymond Peepgass of PlannersBanc bringing up the rear.

Martha Croker's driveway was also laid out in yet more graceful, wasteful Buckhead curves. On either side were banks of green-and-white-striped hostas. So this is what Croker had to give up when he shucked Martha, thought Peepgass. He was beginning to get a bit winded from the long climb. His armpits were already cooking. This in turn made him think of how second-rate his clothes were. This old gray pinstripe suit that had come back just a bit . . . shiny . . . from its last trip to the cleaners . . . the buttonhole in the front that was frayed and needed selvaging . . . this striped shirt that was beginning to get a bit threadbare where the collar met the necktie . . . and the necktie, which suddenly seemed far too loud to be wearing into a house like this . . .

You had to walk up three steps to the portico and pass between two great white Doric columns to reach the front door, which was a colossal thing, painted dark green, with all sorts of raised panels and architraves a foot wide, plus window lights running down either side. Peepgass pressed the doorbell, and everything—the walls, the glass, the door—was so big and heavy, you couldn't hear it ringing inside.

Presently the door opened, and a middle-aged black maid in a white uniform was standing there.

"Ray Peepgass," said Peepgass. "I'm here to see Mrs. Croker."

"She's expecting you," said the woman. "Come on in."

Peepgass found himself in an astonishingly—to him—large hall with a marble floor of white, into which were set, at discrete intervals, black diamond shapes. At the rear of the hall a colossal staircase swung up in a half-spiral to the floor above. The curve of the staircase created a silhouette against the light that flooded in through an enormous arched window behind it.

In no time Martha Croker had emerged from one of the rooms off to the side. She was wearing a long-sleeved navy blouse and a tan gabardine skirt. She struck Peepgass as a little heavy, but her legs weren't bad at all—and this place was lavish beyond anything he had imagined. On the other hand, he also happened to know her age all too well: fifty-three.

"Good morning, Mr. Peepgass."

"Good morning, Martha, and please—make it Ray!"

They shook hands, and Martha Croker said, "I'm sorry I had to make this so early—would you like some coffee?"

"No—actually, to tell you the truth, some coffee would be great!"

So she sent the maid off for some coffee and led Peepgass into some sort of den or library. It wasn't a big room, but every square inch of it looked as if it cost more than the sum total of Peepgass's possessions in Collier Hills. The Oriental rug . . . the antique secretary at which she seemed to have been working . . . the fabric on the walls . . . the bookshelves . . . the chintz-covered easy chairs . . . and, above all, a charming bay that was set off from the rest of the room by a parabolic wooden arch and a sumptuous display of Victorian moldings that surrounded the bay's three big windows . . . In the bay was a round rosewood Regency table with a pair of upholstered Regency dining chairs pulled up to it.

"Let's sit by the window," said Martha Croker. "It's a nice place to have coffee."

And, sure enough, it was. The windows looked out on a small formal garden, bursting with statice, delphinium, and peonies that seemed to have been created especially for the view from this one room. An ancient gardener, a black man, was down on his knees doing something with a trowel. He wore old-fashioned puttees, an article of dress Peepgass had never seen before, except in pictures of the World War I military. At the perimeter of the garden was a dense semicircle of boxwood bushes, mature ones, waist-high and grown together and immaculately clipped until they looked like a single fat green wall. Beyond the boxwood was an immense lawn, partly in open sunlight, partly in the shade of huge old trees, and everywhere bordered by carefully groomed shrubbery and beds of flowers.

Peepgass gazed out the window and, without turning toward her, said, "It's absolutely beautiful, Martha." Something told him to tuck in as many *Martha*s as he could.

"It's a lovely time of year for gardens," said Martha. "I can't take any credit for it." She motioned toward the old gardener. "Franklin does it all."

Mr. Ray Peepgass of PlannersBanc's little *Martha*s were somehow so casual and intimate . . . pleasantly so. She gazed at Mr. Peepgass while he gazed out the window. He was nice-looking, handsome even, but in a rather soft way, with a lineless, boyish face, perhaps a bit too boyish —how old was he, anyway? A full head of sandy hair, but with traces of gray . . . bright blue eyes, but his eyelids drooped at the outer corners . . . the beginnings of a double chin . . . all of which gave her hope that he might be closer to fifty than to forty . . . clothes a bit the worse for wear . . . an appalling necktie with an explosive burst of colors that had nothing to do with his shirt or his suit . . . a small faint patch of beard stubble below the joint of his jaw, which his razor had missed . . . all of which perhaps indicated he didn't have a wife to monitor such things . . . not a strong man, obviously . . . drunk the other night when she first met him . . . but friendly and warm, and he *had* remembered her name . . . and friendly and warm this morning, whatever he had come over for . . . all of which flashed through the Wernicke's and Broca's areas of her brain in a matter of seconds—far faster than it would take to say it out loud . . . She was now happy she had chosen to wear what she had on . . . the dark blouse that minimized her heaviness through the shoulders and back . . . the tight gabardine skirt that brought out her best feature, which was her legs . . . the tan pumps with black caps that more or less matched the skirt and the blouse . . . semi-high heels, just high enough to bring out the excellent contours of her calves . . . and her makeup, almost as carefully done as it had been for the opening at the High, although she had gone far easier on the mascara . . . and her heavy gold chain-link choker, which helped cover up the lines in her neck.

"Did you have to drive far to get here?" she asked Mr. Ray Peepgass, which really meant: "Where do you live, and is there a wife there?"

"Not very far, really," said Peepgass. "I live in Buckhead, too, but there's Buckhead—" He paused and chuckled and made a little gesture out the window. "And there's Buckhead. I have an apartment in Collier Hills. I used to have a house in Snellville before my wife and I separated." He had a vague awareness, which he couldn't have explained, of wanting Martha Croker to be apprised of that fact. "To tell you the truth, it's a lot easier to drive here from Collier Hills at this time of the morning than it is to drive down Peachtree Street to PlannersBanc."

Martha said, "Well, I'm sorry I had to make it so early. This is just one of those days."

Which really meant: one of those days when I have a 10:30 appointment at DefinitionAmerica for Mustafa Gunt's class.

"Not at all!" said Peepgass. "This is actually a perfect time for me."

Except that I'm so damned hungry, he thought. For an instant he wondered if he might possibly suggest that perhaps her maid might be good enough to whip up some pancakes or waffles for him—but only for an instant. Out loud: "I hope I haven't made all this—the purpose of my visit, I mean—sound mysterious or anything. It's just that I'm afraid I'm going a little out-of-bounds with what I want to talk to you about—" He paused, lifted his eyebrows, opened his eyes wide, and gave her a vulnerable smile. "So anytime, if you want me to shut up and forget about it, just say so, and I won't proceed any further."

"Well—now you *do* make it sound mysterious," said Martha.

Peepgass gave a shrug, also of the vulnerable sort. "You remember when I saw you at the museum the other night, I told you I had been thinking about you that day, or I *think* that's what I said. Anyway, that's quite true. The only thing I'm not sure about is how much of all this it's appropriate for me to tell you, since it's the bank's business, but it's even more critically *your* business, it seems to me."

Martha smiled patiently. "*What* is?"

Peepgass put on a dead-serious look. "I'm not sure whether or not you know about the jam Charlie—your . . . former husband—has gotten himself into."

"No, I don't," said Martha.

"The bank would probably take a dim view of my telling you this, but to all intents and purposes, Charlie Croker is bankrupt."

"*Bank*rupt?"

"Yes," said Peepgass. "The only question that remains is how hard a line PlannersBanc wants to take. He owes us approximately half a *billion* dollars and several other banks and two insurance companies another $285 million. Of the total, he's guaranteed $160 million personally. He's already hopelessly in arrears on interest payments, never mind principal."

"What happened to 'non-recourse loans only'?" One of Charlie's cardinal principles, from the very beginning, had been that a developer should never accept a loan for which he was personally responsible. The bank's only recourse should be the assets of the corporation.

"Charlie was determined to build Croker Concourse, no matter what, and now he's paying the price. He spent *eight million dollars*—of *our* money—putting in an astronomical light show at the top of the tower, which nobody wants to look at at lunch in the first place. Now . . . why am I telling *you* all this? Because we've begun workout proceedings in his case—do you remember 'workout proceedings'?"

"I remember Charlie involved in a workout back in the seventies."

"Well, he's in the workout of all workouts right now, believe me. Which means that we're going through his finances with a fine-tooth comb. In the course of it I've seen the terms of his divorce settlement with you. So I've seen the dollar amount he's supposed to give you each month, and I can only assume it's a significant part of your income. Forgive me if I'm way off base or out of line."

Subdued: "No . . ."

"Well—what I see happening is that the approximately seven million dollars a year Charlie takes as a dividend out of the Croker Global

Corporation is no longer gonna be there. We've already seized his Gulfstream Five, and we're probably going to go after Turpmtine next. And there's no way his creditors are going to let him take seven million dollars a year out of this drowning corporation of his."

"Good Lord," said Martha. She seemed genuinely shocked by the whole business. "If he loses Turpmtine, he'll absolutely die."

"If I may be frank about it," said Peepgass, "I don't particularly care what happens to Charlie and Charlie's plantation. My concern is the effect all this might have on you. I thought that at the very least you ought to know about it, even though, as I say, I don't know what my own superiors would think of my coming here and telling you all this. What worries me—or what you might want to think about—is that Charlie is going to be lucky if he takes $300,000 a year out of Croker Global, much less the $600,000 a year he's supposed to give you under the terms of the settlement—and if he keeps on with the hardnose, uncooperative attitude he's been giving us so far, he could wind up with nothing. Every single asset he possesses, right down to his cuff links, if he wears cuff links—I don't recall—everything he's got is on the line. I just thought somebody ought to give you at least the rough outlines of what's been happening."

Martha Croker didn't say anything at first. Peepgass studied her face. She must have been a very pretty woman back when Croker married her. She was a very *handsome* woman even now. But the lines in her face had begun to creep down over her jawline, the better to hook up with the lines in her neck. And yet what a chain of gold there was around that neck! He wondered if it was real gold. Well, why shouldn't it be? The lawn, the gardens, the gardener in puttees were all real.

Just then the black maid, Carmen, arrived with a tray, a silver tray with gadrooned edges, upon which were not only an ornately wrought little silver coffeepot with an eccentric ivory handle (Peepgass had never heard of Georg Jensen silverware) and two sets of outsized bone-china coffee cups and saucers (the saucers had handles designed in flamboyant swoops) and a silver sugar bowl and creamer that matched the coffeepot (viscerally he could sense how much the sugar bowl, a mere sugar bowl, must have cost, which was in fact $1,250) but also a silver bread gondola from which, beneath a covering of damask napkin, came the most delicious aroma of hot bread—or was it possibly cake?—an aroma that proceeded straight from Peepgass's nose to the aching, starving void in his stomach, exciting that organ in a delirious way. He wanted to reach out and pull back the damask napkin and—get at it! But he restrained himself. Meantime, the maid poured the coffee. Another ecstatically rich aroma!

Martha Croker said, "Thank you, Carmen!"—adding the sort of warm smile that, as Peepgass had already observed, Southern women used to show their guests how considerate they were of their *help*.

Then she folded back the damask napkin on the bread gondola—and there they were: thick, rich, cake-like slices of a sort of bread Peepgass had never seen before.

"Please—have some Sally Lunn, Ray."

Ray she had called him! Out loud: "Sally Lunn?"

"It's a Virginia recipe," said Martha. "No one I know has ever made it any better than Carmen"—this loud enough for Carmen, who was heading out of the room, to hear. "I'm not even going to tell you what's in it. I think it's wonderful with damson preserves." She motioned toward the little crock on the table.

Peepgass didn't have to be told twice. He took a thick slice of the bread, which was still warm to the touch, and spread on some margarine and the preserves, which had tart pieces of plum skin that gave it a wonderful tactile quality, and took a big bite. It was . . . wonderful! marvelous! the answer to a forty-six-year-old bachelor's prayer!

"Great coffee, too!" exclaimed Mr. Ray Peepgass.

"I'm so glad you like it," said Martha. "I get it from Louisiana. It's called Café du Monde. It's made with chicory."

"Chicory . . . hmmmmmm. Well, it's great!" The rich warmth of the coffee, the richness of the bread, the ambrosial sweetness of the preserves, the translucence of the bone china, the sheer conspicuous *cost* of the silverware, which, he now realized, featured tiny, exquisitely wrought little bunches of silver grapes, the intricacy of the crocheted place mats, which were obviously handmade, the patterns of sharp angles and ogee curves in the woodwork around the windows, the view beyond, the formal garden created solely for those who sat in this bay, the ancient gardener kneeling in the dirt in his puttees to maintain this perfect little vista—the luxury of it all coursed through Peepgass's central nervous system as a *sensation*, a visceral feeling that played upon a man's sixth sense, his sense of well-being.

"Anyway," said Peepgass, "I just thought somebody should let you know what's going on, since it seems to me your exposure in this mess Charlie has made of things is in a way as great as ours." The old boy also gave you $10 million in cash and securities, thought Peepgass, and why wouldn't you want to roll the dice with a couple million and join the syndicate? But he wouldn't get into all that right now.

"Well, this is all certainly news to me," said Martha. "You know, I ran into Charlie the other night at the museum. He certainly didn't *seem* to be in a bad way. He was the same old Charlie."

"Then all I can tell you is that he's a good actor," said Peepgass. "In fact, he comes under the heading of Too Much. Did you know he bought an entire table for that dinner? Twenty *thousand* dollars? Of *our* money? Believe me, that did not go unnoticed at PlannersBanc. That's so typical of the way he refuses to be impressed by the seriousness of the situation he's in. Even after we arrest his Gulfstream Five, he doesn't seem to get it."

"Arrested?"

"That's the technical term for seizing a piece of collateral like that. We took it right in front of him, out at PDK. He was right there and yelling about the painting on the bulkhead, the one by N. C. Wyeth."

"Oh my God," said Martha Croker, "you mean *Jim Bowie on His Deathbed*?"

"That's it, yeah."

"The two things Charlie loves most in this world are Turpmtine and that painting."

"And he *still* doesn't get it. There he was at the Lapeth show acting as if nothing has changed. The fact is, for *him* . . . *everything* has changed."

Martha's face grew hot and reddened . . . Charlie in the atrium of the High Museum . . . Charlie preening about with his boy with breasts, captivating the very people she had spent $20,000 on to bring to the show . . . To Peepgass she said, "Charlie went through a bad time in the mid-seventies. At one point he was paying back creditors twenty cents on the dollar, and they were happy to get it—and somehow he managed to pull out of the situation. I think he thinks he's immune." In her mind she could hear Charlie saying, "Hey, gal! Heh yew dewin'?"

Peepgass said, "If he thinks he's immune, then he's in for a big shock. We've offered him a very good deal, but I don't think he understands that." He paused and looked straight into Martha Croker's eyes and said, "What I'm about to tell you is strictly *entre nous*. Okay? If Arthur Lomprey"—Martha could see his hateful hunched-over form—"knew I was over here telling you all this, I don't know what he would say, but something tells me it wouldn't be good. But—I've gone this far, so I might as well tell you. We've told Charlie he can keep his house on Blackland Road, Turpmtine, and his beloved N. C. Wyeth painting if he'll hand over the deeds to the Phoenix Center, the MossCo Tower, the TransEx Palladium, and Croker Concourse."

"Hand over the deeds?"

"It's called 'deed in lieu of foreclosure.' In effect, he just gives us the properties. That way he spares himself the humiliation of foreclosure proceedings and all the publicity that would generate, and he keeps his home, the plantation, and the painting."

"What does he say to that?" asked Martha. "I hope you realize that he's almost as fanatical about Croker Concourse as he is about Turpmtine and *Jim Bowie on His Deathbed*."

"Oh, he's got his back up," said Peepgass. "He as much as dared us to try to come after Turpmtine. He's gonna have a *big* surprise coming."

But Martha was still thinking about Croker Concourse. The very name set off a *feeling* in her, for it was when Charlie was in the thick of the Croker Concourse project that he had met Serena. She no longer had to articulate the thought in her mind to feel the pain and humiliation. She merely had to hear the name, and the *feeling*—which was in fact worse than pain and humiliation—which, at bottom, was *shame*—swept over her in a scalding wave.

"What's the big thing about Croker Concourse, the fact that he has his name on it?"

"Partly that," said Martha, "but mainly because he's always thought it was so clever, so shrewd, the way he put the deal together. People don't think of Charlie as clever and shrewd, they think of him more as a force of nature, but in this case he pulled off something very clever. Not very admirable, if you want my opinion, but very clever."

"Oh?" said Peepgass. "What was that?"

"Do you remember the racial protests in Cherokee County, the demonstrations and all that business? It made the national news on television for a couple of nights, do you remember?"

"Ummm . . . yeah."

"That was all Charlie." Martha Croker had a tired smile.

"Whattaya mean, 'all Charlie'?"

"Charlie orchestrated the whole thing!"

"Aw, come on," said Peepgass. "Charlie Croker? Orchestrated a demonstration against Redneck racism? That's a little hard to believe."

"I know," said Martha. "That's one reason it worked so well. What happened was, Charlie had the theory that the next big growth in Atlanta was going to take place in the outer perimeter, the rural counties north of the city, places like Gwinnett County, Forsyth, Bartow, Cherokee. So Charlie goes out to Cherokee County, which was all trees and pastures, and he thinks he's going to buy 150 acres or whatnot for a song, except that he finds out people thought of all this before he did, and the land costs a fortune because it's already investor land."

"What's investor land?" asked Ray.

"That was another one of Charlie's terms. Investor land is land that's too valuable to be devoted to farming or timber but not yet ready for developing. So investors buy it for a song, like Charlie thought he was going to, and then they just sit on it, waiting for the time when they can sell it for a big price for development. Charlie couldn't believe it. Cherokee County, or at least the southern part of it, was all investor land. He's driving around through these back roads up there one day when he sees an old friend of his, or an old acquaintance, a real old Cracker named Darwell Scruggs. They'd gone to school together years ago down in Baker County. So Charlie stops the car and gets out, and he and Darwell Scruggs have a little reunion out by the side of the road. One thing Charlie always remembered about Darwell Scruggs was that he had joined the Ku Klux Klan back when he was seventeen or eighteen years old. So he asks him about the Klan, and sure enough, Darwell has organized a chapter, or a kave, or whatever they call it, of the Klan in Cherokee County. It was really pathetic, Ray—"

Ray!

"—I mean, I wonder if there were a dozen members, and most of them were teenagers of the sort Darwell had been when he first joined. But there they were, and a lightbulb went on over Charlie's head. He takes down Darwell's address and telephone number, and he waits three or four weeks and calls up Darwell and tells him he has it on good authority that a black group called Operation Higher is planning a march through Canton—that's the county seat of Cherokee—protesting racism and de facto segregation in this old rural county that's practically all white."

"How did Charlie know that?"

"He didn't! He had to *find* somebody! Now that he'd started the pot boiling, he had to find somebody to put in it, so to speak."

"Now wait a minute," said Peepgass. "Are you telling me—this I find hard to believe—but go ahead." By now he had his elbows on the table and was leaning forward, an utterly rapt expression on his face.

"This is the truth," said Martha. "I pledge you my word. One day Charlie read in the papers that this fellow André Fleet was organizing a rally for Operation Higher against something or other."

"André Fleet—the guy who's talking about running for Mayor."

"I think so. I think it's the same person. So Charlie goes to the rally. He was the only white person there, and he stood out like . . . like I don't know what . . . this big, fifty-some-year-old white man wearing a coat and tie. At the end of the rally André Fleet came over to Charlie and said, "If you have a moment, brother, I'd like to see you backstage after this is all over.' "

Peepgass, leaning forward even more, said, "Were you *there?* Did you *see* this?"

"No," said Martha Croker, "but I've heard Charlie tell the story a hundred times."

"So what happened next?"

"I'm not sure exactly what happened next, but it wasn't too long before André Fleet was leading a march on poor little Canton. And Darwell Scruggs did his part. He had all ten or twelve of his Klan kave out on the sidewalk." She shook her head. "Those poor pimply little boys—they didn't wear the pointy white hoods and all that, but they did yell a lot of racial epithets, which the television crews were delighted to record, of course, and for about three or four days the whole country was looking at Cherokee County, Georgia, as this vile bastion of . . . of . . . of bigotry, and so forth and so on. You may remember that Frank Farr filmed his talk show right on the main street of Canton. He acted as if he were doing something so courageous, broadcasting a television show inside this benighted backwater. He was talking about poor old Darwell Scruggs and a dozen children. Anyway, land values in Cherokee County suddenly dropped. Investors couldn't unload their investor land fast enough, and Charlie bought a 142-acre parcel for less than $200,000. Before the march it would have brought four million easily."

"So he *paid* Fleet to march on Canton?"

"I don't know," said Martha. "He never said so. All I know is that he pointed the man in the direction of Cherokee County. Maybe Fleet was *looking* for someplace to have a demonstration. He's in that business, after all. I just don't know."

"Godalmighty," said Peepgass, smiling a smile of wonderment and looking into Martha Croker's eyes. He wasn't sure what it meant, but he knew it meant something big and promising. "Does anybody but you know about all this?"

"As I said, there are people who know how he met André Fleet, because I've heard him tell that story to people. But I doubt that many people know about Charlie and Darwell Scruggs."

A big loopy grin spread over Peepgass's face. Martha couldn't figure out why. Peepgass himself wasn't entirely sure. All he knew was that what he had just learned was . . . dynamite.

Martha said, "Have some more coffee, Ray, and some more Sally Lunn."

"I will!" said Peepgass, taking another slice of the fabulous bread from the silver gondola. While he loaded the bread with margarine and damson preserves, Martha Croker poured him another cup of coffee. Peepgass took a big bite of the bread, and as his tongue savored the sharp but sweet taste of the preserves, he looked out the middle window of the bay. The moldings around the window were like a frame, and the view was like a perfect painting by . . . Millais . . . no, Tissot . . . or maybe Millais *and* Tissot . . . or maybe some Pre-Raphaelite . . . in the foreground, old Franklin down on his knees . . . the earth tones of his shoes, his ancient puttees, his old khaki pants, his gray shirt, the faded gray-green Bemberg of the back panel of his vest seemed to blend into the earth into which he was so diligently troweling . . . then came a dazzling band of royal blue, pink, and white flowers, then the dense dark green of the boxwood border . . . and beyond that the big-breasted green lawn, suddenly radiant, almost chartreuse, with the sunlight that had made its way between two tall trees . . .

A fellow could learn to like this.

Chapter XXII

Chambodia

POPOLO LOLO POPOLO GRIND YOU BRUDDA MOCKY DIE-DEAD NO make ass no want beef, pouring, gurgling out of Five-O's mouth as he lay pinned under tons of concrete and the earth shifted and Conrad could feel himself falling off the top bunk—"*Hunnh!*"—which woke him up.

For an instant he couldn't get his bearings. Couldn't be Santa Rita, because he was lying on a floor with a carpet, a filthy carpet, but a carpet all the same. People—Asian faces standing over him and looking down at him, and someone was saying, "Lum loc mung ve nha pao poc, Conrad."

He propped himself up on one elbow and rubbed his face with his hand. High-pitched giggling. Women. The tiny living room was now packed with people, with Vietnamese—must be fifteen or sixteen of them at least. Last night not nearly so many—last night—and with the recollection of last night, things began to sort themselves out in his mind.

He was on the floor of a shabby little modern apartment at ground level in a town called Chamblee, just outside Atlanta, Georgia. It had happened just the way Mai had promised him it would. He was met at the airport, in the baggage claim area, by a Vietnamese named Lum

Loc, who recognized him by his Hi-Gro baseball cap. They got into Lum Loc's pickup truck, and Lum Loc, a voluble little man, chattered in broken English all the way to Chamblee, to a two-story stucco apartment building with a sign out front reading MEADOW LARK TERRACE. Lum Loc pointed it out and laughed and said:

"Better they call Saigon West! Know what they call Chamblee? Chambodia." He convulsed with laughter. "You in Chambodia! And this Saigon West!"

He had led him to the rear of the building, where he opened a sliding plate-glass door that also served as a picture window and swept aside some sort of rubbery plastic curtain—and Conrad had found himself in a room full of Vietnamese, ranging in age from five or six to eighty-something, the octogenarian being a wizened, shrunken woman who sat on the floor with her back propped up against a wall. There was a strong odor of fish cooking. Three middle-aged men were hunkered down and leaning forward with their arms between their knees, holding plastic deli plates up to their mouths and using chopsticks to shovel in some sort of rice dish. Two men and a woman were stretched out on the floor on futons, fast asleep. Another woman lay sleeping on the bare carpet, and yet another was asleep on the room's only piece of furniture, an old-fashioned porch "glider," which was a couch with plastic-covered cushions set into a metal frame with a big rusting yellow metal armrest at either end. Children were scampering about between the bodies of the quick and the dead asleep, playing some form of stoop tag, and suddenly their eyes and the old woman's eyes and the eyes of the three squatting men were wide-open and pinned on Conrad. The place was ripe with the smell of too many human bodies in a small space.

Lum Loc had put on a stern voice and barked out something, the only part of which Conrad could make out was his own name, Conrad. To Conrad he said, "Morning I come back with ID." Then he left via the sliding glass door.

Gingerly Conrad had made his way through the sleeping forms and past the hunkered-down men to investigate the rest of the apartment. All eyes had followed him. No one had said a word. He had had the impression that they didn't speak a word of English and were almost as newly arrived at Meadow Lark Terrace, at Saigon West, in Chambodia, as he was. The rest of the place consisted of nothing more than a kitchenette, where some sort of fish stew was simmering, a tiny bathroom, and a tiny bedroom, no more than 12 by 9 feet, with at least eight or nine Vietnamese crammed into it. In here the carnal heat was even worse. Conrad had returned to the living room, to the only unclaimed stretch of floor in the place, and lain down, clutching his little traveling bag to his abdomen. The Vietnamese had all stared at him, and he had no idea who they were. He had thought he would never fall asleep, but within sixty seconds he had slid down that never-remembered, deep-folded slope of oblivion.

And now it was morning and the room was lit by daylight that came in through the sliding door where the rubbery curtain had been pulled back. The room was jammed with still more people. He struggled to his feet. He was terribly stiff . . . and foggy, almost light-headed. Vietnamese everywhere, standing up, lying down, hunkered down. The old woman had at last gotten access to a futon and was stretched out, snoring. Once more they stared at Conrad, or many did. Half a dozen men were engaged in a loud argument. One of them kept saying what Conrad heard as "Phao co nwha tong!"

Conrad smiled at everyone whose eyes he met, to show that he was a . . . friendly . . . alien . . . in this strange place. He had an overwhelming urge to urinate. He made his way through the crowd, smiling as he went toward the bathroom. There were four Vietnamese already lined up in front of the bathroom door.

He waited his turn. The bathroom was a mess. There were footprints on the toilet seat. He couldn't imagine why. He was just departing the bathroom when he heard his name called out. It sounded like Lum Loc. Smiling as he went, he threaded his way through all the people. Now he could hear Lum Loc shouting something in Vietnamese. The six men suddenly stopped arguing. Lum Loc was berating them. Then he spotted Conrad.

"Conrad, you come here!" Sternly.

Conrad made his way through still more people and followed Lum Loc outside, through the sliding door. He looked this way and that, expecting to find—he didn't know what. "I'm an escaped convict," he said to himself. It was a thought so strange, he said it to himself again: "I'm an escaped convict."

He could tell by the light that it was much earlier than he had thought. "What time is it?"

Lum Loc showed him the face of his wristwatch: 6:40.

Conrad said, "It's early."

"Must deal all these people," said Lum Loc. "Must deal you."

Between the buildings of Meadow Lark Terrace were wide swaths of grass. Six or seven black-haired children were already playing on a little cluster of swings and jungle gyms. Two Vietnamese women, both wearing black pajama outfits, stood by. Lum Loc motioned for him to step around the corner of the building, out of sight of the street.

"Okay, Conrad." Lum Loc twisted his arms out of his backpack straps and unzipped the backpack and withdrew a cluster of small paper bags, the sort a stationery store might put greeting cards in when you buy them. He shuffled through them. Most of them had Vietnamese ideographs drawn on them in felt-tip marker. Then he came to the one marked "Conrad." He opened it and withdrew three items. One was a Social Security card bearing the name Cornelius Alonzo DeCasi. The second was a state of Georgia driver's license bearing a picture, a head shot, of Conrad and the name Cornelius Alonzo DeCasi. The third was a state of Michigan birth certificate, embossed with an official stamp, bearing the name Cornelius Alonzo DeCasi, born December 2, 1977, to Margaret Stuart DeCasi and Demetrio Giovanni de Bari DeCasi.

"My God . . ." said Conrad. "How'd you do this?"

Lum Loc laughed. "You don't need know that. Birth certificate—real." He put the embossed seal between his thumb and forefinger and gave Conrad a look that invited appreciation of this wonder. "Now you Cornelius Alonzo DeCasi." This struck Lum Loc as extremely funny. When he stopped laughing, he said, "Cornelius Alonzo DeCasi died in 1982. Sorry, but you don't get death certificate!" This struck him as even funnier, and he laughed and laughed. Then he turned serious. "Now you get a job." He motioned toward the apartment. "Cannot stay here always."

"Where can I get a job?"

"An American? Young as you? Hey, no problem. Those people"—he motioned toward the apartment again—"they work in the chicken plant."

"Chicken plant?"

"Very big chicken plant in Knowlton. Always they can get jobs in the chicken plant."

"Doing what?"

"They work on the assembly line. Always they have jobs on the assembly line."

"Whattaya *do* on the assembly line?"

With a mixture of words and pantomime Lum Loc described how

some slit chickens' throats all day and some slit their bellies and disemboweled them all day and some took their feathers off all day and some sliced them into parts all day.

"Work hard and very smelly—but I have rule. I help you—then you get work. These people, I tell them they stay inside the building until I give them IDs and they get work. Cannot always walk around doing nothing in Chambodia." The term *Chambodia* made him laugh all over again. "But you American, and you have ID, so you can walk around. But you must get job. That is Lum Loc's way."

Conrad said, "Where can I get something to eat?"

"You got money?"

"I have . . . some."

"Ohhhhh . . . Buford Highway. Doraville. You can walk." Lum Loc went on to explain how he should walk down the street in front of Meadow Lark Terrace and through the underpass beneath the MARTA railroad tracks—MARTA, he gathered, was a commuter railroad—and up New Peachtree Road to the Buford Highway, which apparently was a shopping strip of some sort. "MARTA," he repeated. "This side, America. Other side, Chambodia." He laughed again.

So Conrad headed off on foot, toward Buford Highway, carrying his overnight bag and thrusting his hand into the pocket of his jeans for the reassuring feel of the $700 he had left. The road out front of Meadow Lark Terrace was wide but ran through groves of trees and had the sleepy feel of any rural road in the early morning. Soon he came upon a cluster of apartment buildings up on a little knoll. A wooden sign out front read: HICKORY HEIGHTS. Duplex Apts. Three black-haired men, Latinos—Mexicans, it seemed to Conrad—were leaning on the railing of the outdoor walkway of the second floor of the building nearest the road. They checked out Conrad, and he looked straight ahead and kept on walking. Just around a bend in the road he came upon a little convenience store with a sign above the front entrance that read B-KWIK and, at each end, featured a picture of a bumblebee with a smiling human face. Out front was a pair of decrepit-looking gasoline pumps and a group of six Mexicans, if that's what they were, standing with their hands in the pockets of their jeans. They kept looking up and down the road. A pickup truck driven by a middle-aged white man pulled up, and after a brief conversation, two of the Mexicans climbed in, and the truck took off, and now there were four Mexicans with their hands in their pockets, looking up and down the road. They eyed Conrad suspiciously, and he kept on walking. He figured he must be getting near the center of town—Chamblee?—Doraville?—because of all the small commercial establishments . . . Liza's Restaurant, which had flowers jigsawed out of wood and painted lilac stuck on the sign at the corners . . . a little place called the 24-Hour Play Skool . . . antique shops with names such as Hello Again, the Rust 'n' Dust, and Antique Junction . . . and then a small building housing the City Hall and the police station . . . Chamblee this was . . . Two policemen, big meaty white men, came out the door and walked toward a cruiser . . . Conrad's scalp suddenly seemed to be on fire . . . He was . . . *an escaped convict!* . . . For the first time in his life any policeman he saw anywhere was a threat to his freedom! He was a fugitive! . . . Out of the corner of his eye he could see that the two officers had stopped and were looking him up and down . . . Zeus! Give me coolness! Give me the . . . will to avoid! . . . He kept walking at a steady pace, eyes straight ahead, shoulders back . . . He could hear the cruiser starting off . . . and going the other way . . . What if they had stopped him? He hadn't even figured out what he would say. What would he say his name was? He couldn't say Cornelius Alonzo DeCasi. It was too strange a mouthful. He'd say . . . he'd say . . . Connie . . . Connie DeCasi was believable . . . Looking for work, warehouse work . . . He'd make sure they saw his big hands and forearms . . . They'd believe him . . . He ran his hand over his face . . . He needed a shave . . . Needed to be spic-and-span . . . An underpass up ahead . . . but it wasn't a railway line, it was a highway . . . Once he went through the underpass, he could see the elevated MARTA line, which looked so strange rising up like a massive wall in this little country town. He walked through that underpass, and on the other side . . . another world! Just as Lum Loc said it would be! Ming's Auto Service . . . Kien Ngay Brake Land . . . Minh Ngoc Travel Agency . . . Le Phan Mini-Storage . . . and now he was on New Peachtree Road where it ran into a six-lane strip . . . the Buford Highway . . . Hoang Nhung Jewelry . . . Hong Kong Bakery . . . Chuyen Tien Money Transactions . . . Quoc Hu'ong Chicken World . . . Pho Hoa Insurance Agency . . . Kim's Pharmacy . . . Kien Ngay Music, which featured Vietnamese videos, CD's, and tape recordings . . . Many shops had no English at all in their signs. Instead, ideographs such as Conrad had never laid eyes on before . . . Thai? Cambodian? Laotian? Korean? Vietnamese? A big sign on a metal stanchion said ASIAN SQUARE. The cars pulling in—all driven by black-haired people—Asians. Barely ten feet away, a Pontiac Firebird, customized and painted lavender, nosed into a parking space, and from it emerged three young Asian males with long black hair, combed back but extending all the way down the neck to the shoulder line, dressed entirely in black: black warmup jackets, black T-shirts, baggy black homey pants gathered at the ankles where they met sneakers that were black with tongue-like white stripes. With a pumping gait they walked into a restaurant called the Pho Ca Dao.

Conrad was starving. On a corner of the shopping center, overlooking the highway, was a restaurant with a sign in English: MR. SAIGON NOODLE PARLOR, with Vietnamese characters beneath it. He sat at a table by the window overlooking the highway. As far as he could tell, all of the smattering of customers in the place were Asian. The menu was printed in Vietnamese with English translations in small letters to the right. He ordered Tranh Van Five Different Flavor Seafood Noodle Soup, even though it cost $5.95, an appalling sum to someone with $700 in his pocket that had to last him God knew how long. But he couldn't hold out any longer. He had to eat. As he waited for the noodle soup, he gazed out over the Buford Highway. Except for the Asian signs rising skyward on aluminum stanchions, it was the sort of stone Low Rent American retail strip that could be found on the outskirts of almost every American city . . . six lanes of black hardtop bounded by blasted heaths of concrete and hard-baked dirt studded with low tilt-up concrete buildings and wires strung with fluttering Day-Glo pennants, signs that rose far above the buildings on aluminum stanchions, and every other device that might catch the eye of someone driving along a highway at 60 miles an hour beneath a broiling Georgia sun. Across the road . . . the Pung Mie Chinese Restaurant, but also Collision City and an astonishing array of pawnshops . . . PAWN Car Titles . . . PAWN 50% Off Gold & Diamonds . . . and still more PAWN Car Titles . . . EMISSION TESTS, beneath which was always a quonset hut–shaped tan tent, in which you could have your car's emission system tested in keeping with Georgia motor vehicle laws . . .

All at once he could hear Lum Loc's voice inside his head: "You get a job. That Lum Loc's way." Outside, on the sidewalk in front of Mr. Saigon Noodle Parlor, was a yellow metal box, about waist high, a vending machine for a newspaper, *The Atlanta Journal-Constitution* . . . The classifieds . . . He wanted to go out, buy a newspaper, and go over the want ads at the table. But—mustn't do anything to make them think he was stiffing them for their bill. So he paid the bill, then went outside and dropped 60 cents into the vending machine and took a newspaper and returned to the restaurant, to the same table, and ordered green tea . . . another 75 cents . . . and began going over the want ads. All at once a wave of fear: the earthquake!—Santa Rita!—escaped convicts!—perhaps even my very picture! He started on page 1, devouring the headlines at a furious rate . . . There!—page 11!—a five-paragraph story beneath a headline reading EARTHQUAKE DECLARED WORST IN 20 YEARS . . . He read it ravenously . . . "Long-dormant Hayward fault . . . The Governor asks President to declare Alameda and Livermore Counties disaster areas . . . Santa Rita!"—there were the words! Three blocks of downtown Pleasanton, the Camp Parks Army Reserve training camp, and *Santa Rita*, the Alameda County jail, demolished . . . eight deaths, twenty inmates remain unaccounted for . . . But that was it . . . No names . . . no mention of a manhunt . . . But who knew? This was just an Atlanta newspaper. If only he could call someone . . . didn't dare call Jill . . . Did he dare call Kenny? Or Mai? . . . He was very disturbed . . . How *did* they hunt for escapees? In an age like this—computers, the Internet—sitting here in the Mr. Saigon Noodle Parlor in the Georgia town of Chamblee, now better known as Chambodia, he felt a hollowness that no amount of Tranh Van Five Different Flavor Seafood Noodle Soup could ever fill. He lifted his hands toward the heavens and beckoned Zeus into his solar plexus.

Not even at Santa Rita had loneliness seemed so complete. At least at Santa Rita there had been others who, whether they liked it or not, had to share his life with him . . . Five-O . . . Mutt . . . people who, for better or for worse, he saw every day and dealt with every day . . . And who was there now?—other than Lum Loc, who by now probably could not care less and was off with his latest batch of $750-a-head illegal aliens skulking into Atlanta, Georgia, from half a world away . . . What was this craving for humanity, even, lacking all else, for humanity in its lowest forms?

AS SOON AS Peepgass entered the room, Herb Richman rose from behind a huge trapezoidal desk, beaming, and walked toward him across a carpet of tango orange and aquamarine trapezoids and put out his hand and said, "Ray! It's great to see you!"

Ray! What an immense relief that simple exclamation was to Raymond Peepgass! It spoke volumes! It meant that in Richman's eyes he was still the great banking authority—and social equal—he had been the other night under the aegis of the highly expensive, highly social Lapeth opening of the High Museum. Thank God! He hadn't turned back into a mid-level PlannersBanc functionary at midnight!

Richman gestured toward an easy chair with an odd trapezoidal back, and he himself sat down in another one with an orange sunburst tufted into its back. Then Peepgass noticed the walls. Two of them were curved into waves. Not only that, they were tilted in toward you, as if they were about to fall over. At the bottom they stopped three or four inches short of the floor. How this was achieved, Peepgass couldn't imagine. But he had heard of the style. It was called Deconstructionist. Even Herb Richman's clothes were of the moment, when it came to CEO wardrobes. He wore a turquoise shirt, open at the neck, a white cashmere sweater cut very full in the sleeves, and white flannel pants.

Peepgass sank back into the eccentric chair. "Well, Herb, how's Marsha?"

"Oh, she's terrific," said Herb Richman. "And by the way, we both enjoyed your note, especially the part about the widows of Buckhead who run the High, and the *real* Wilson Lapeth."

"Ahh!" said Peepgass with a confident smile. "I only wish I could've been a fly on the wall when they were debating whether or not to put *that* show on."

"Me, too," said Richman. "You know, things have improved here in Atlanta, but they only make their little forays into the terra incognita of Culture when they're terrified somebody in New York will call them provincial if they don't. That's the one thing they can't stand, the idea that somebody in New York might be calling them Southern hicks."

So then they talked for a while about how provincial it was here in the provinces.

Behind Richman's trapezoidal desk, Peepgass noticed for the first time, was an immense slab of slate, two or three inches thick, framed in walnut. Chiseled in high relief was a map of the United States with orange and aquamarine pegs representing DefinitionAmerica fitness centers all over the country . . .

"I just noticed that," said Peepgass, nodding toward the huge map. "There must be hundreds of them!"

"One thousand one hundred and twelve," said Richman. "We're opening new ones at a rate of a hundred and twenty-five a year."

"Amazing," said Peepgass. "Looks like there's no limit."

"I wish that were true," said Richman. "In this business you're always limited by the threat of a collapse in taste."

"Taste?"

Peepgass mostly just listened as Herb Richman delivered some mildly cynical observations about the current mania for exercise, one that DefinitionAmerica's founder and CEO obviously had never succumbed to.

"But currently," Richman said, "more than 20 percent of adult Americans follow some sort of exercise regimen—or tell themselves they do."

Peepgass saw that as a good opening. So he said, "Well, our friend Charlie Croker has his own ideas when it comes to exercise."

"Oh?"

"Yowza, yowza," said Peepgass. "*Atlanta* magazine did a piece about him, and they asked him what sort of exercise regimen he followed. And so he says"—Peepgass decided to try his Croker mimicry again since it seemed to have gone over well at PlannersBanc—"he says, 'Who the hale's got time fer'n *ex*ercise reg'men? On the other hand, when I need some *far*wood, I start with a *tree*.' "

Richman laughed and said, "That's Croker all right. I'm sure he thinks he leads the natural life."

"I heard you telling Julius the other night"—(our pal Julius)—"you'd spent a weekend at Croker's plantation. How'd you happen to do that?"

"Aw . . . I hardly know the man, but he invited me. I'm pretty sure I know why. He probably knows we need more space, and he's having trouble leasing that Croker Concourse of his."

"*I'll* say he's having trouble," said Peepgass with a knowing grin.

"Anyway, I'm glad I went," said Richman. "He's a certain type of Southerner you hear about but you can't really appreciate unless you see him up close, on native ground, as they say. He has this"—he shook his head—"*thing* about Southern manhood. He hasn't got the first clue that this happens to be the beginning of a new century. He thinks he's a great patron of the African Americans who work on his plantation. You should've heard the way he brought his butler out and made him recite to the whole dinner table all the ways ol' massa's helped him and his children out. He"—he shook his head again—"you had to be there to believe it, it was all so patronizing. You also had to hear him on the subject of gay rights. Gay *rats*, he pronounced it. Him and this old buddy of his, Bass his name was."

"Billy Bass," said Peepgass. "He's a developer, too, and he's also borrowed a lot of money from PlannersBanc, but he's paid *his* back."

"And Croker?"

"Croker's one of those debtors—incidentally, we never use the word *debtor* until a loan has stopped performing—Croker's one of those debtors who are so egotistical, they just can't bring themselves to recognize the obvious. He's hanging off the edge of a cliff, right, and he doesn't seem to know it. We could force him into bankruptcy anytime we wanted to, like *that*"—he snapped his fingers—"but there are a number of reasons why that would not be to our advantage. Anyway, the biggest fiasco of all is this Croker Concourse of his. He spent $175 million of *our money* on the damned thing, and that loan wouldn't perform right even if he were able to lease it up fully at the top dollar in the current market, which he can't."

Herb Richman's mouth opened and remained that way, as if he were struggling to find the right words. Finally he said, "I don't see—how could you lend him that much money? Surely you must have some system of internal controls, some way of going over a developer's plans and estimating construction costs in some fairly accurate way—or am I wrong?"

"You're right," said Peepgass, "but banks get caught up in the boom mentality, too. And that's one of the things I was talking about, one of the reasons why it wouldn't be to our advantage to just foreclose on him. It would become perfectly obvious that we were fools, and that's the last thing in the world any bank wants the shareholders to know."

"So what are you going to do?" said Herbert Richman.

"Ahhhh!" Peepgass raised his forefinger, cocked his head to one side, and opened his eyes wide, as if to say, "Now we're getting down to cases." Then he said, "My plan—and I've got everybody's go-ahead on this—is to force Croker to hand over the deeds to four of his developments, including Croker Concourse. This is a procedure known as 'deed in lieu of foreclosure.' If we went the foreclosure route, it would all become very public, because then you'd have to go to auction, a public auction. This way, if he just hands over the deeds, we can make our own deals very quietly—which we would want to do quickly, because we're in no position to manage a bunch of commercial properties." He paused and stared into Herb Richman's puffy round face in a searching way. "I think I can assure you that PlannersBanc will unload Croker

Concourse for about $50 million." He gazed even more searchingly. "I'm not telling you that as a senior officer of PlannersBanc. My superiors at PlannersBanc would not be happy about my telling you what a low price they're prepared to sell at. I'm telling you that as a private individual, although I'm ready to help any person or syndicate interested in such a deal. In the process, in fact, I think I would be doing PlannersBanc a favor."

Herb Richman gave Peepgass a searching gaze of his own and ran his hand through the scarce red hair of his balding pate.

"I can deliver it," said Peepgass, "if there's a buyer—let's say a syndicate—a syndicate that can make a 20 percent down payment and has a credible likelihood of paying off the balance in a timely fashion. So we're talking about a down payment as low as $10 million for a property which in two or three years is bound to bounce back up to its true valuation, which is about $120 million. Let's say we're talking about a syndicate of four investors, with each investor putting up two and a half million. In two to three years they sell the building for $120 million. Even leased up the way it is now, just 40 percent, there'd be enough cash flow to operate the building and service the debt, because the mortgage would be for only $40 million instead of $175 million. In two or three years you sell the building for $120 million, and each investor gets $27 million, for a long-term gain of $24.5 million. Not bad, hunh?"

"Wait a minute," said Richman. "If we're talking about four investors, then each one would get $30 million if it's sold for $120 million. Or am I missing something?"

Peepgass kept his expression as deadpan as he could. "Well, at sale," he said, "there'd have to be a brokerage fee of 6 percent."

"A brokerage fee?"

"Yes. For the firm that led the syndicate to the property and put the deal together." Peepgass looked Herb Richman straight in the eye and steeled himself against blinking.

Herb Richman eyed Peepgass in the same fashion and said, "And that firm would be . . ." He let the question just dangle in the air.

"Arthur Wyndham & Son Realty," said Peepgass. "Its home base is in the Bahamas."

Neither of them said a word for what seemed like an eternity. The way Richman's eyes remained fixed upon his, Peepgass knew Richman saw through the scheme straight to the bottom.

"A new firm?" asked Herb Richman.

"No, a very old one, at least as far as real estate firms in the Caribbean go. It was founded forty-eight years ago. Very solid, well respected."

Herb Richman was still studying him . . . still studying him . . . Then he broke eye contact and put on his modest smile again. "I've never run into a situation quite like this before, Ray, but you pique my interest . . ."

Then he stared at Peepgass some more and kept the smile on, and then Peepgass put on a smile of his own.

The feeling that swept through him, the feeling that suffused every pore in his skin and made his hands turn cold, was one of fear—and giddy elation.

Well, he had done it now. He had let the red dog out for a romp, and there was no slipping a leash back on him.

ROGER AND FAREEK FANON'S white criminal lawyer, Julian Salisbury, and his black criminal lawyer, Don Pickett, stood in an alcove of the Wringer Fleasom & Tick library watching the shaggy beasts slouch into the library's grand reading room. They were the raggediest, maggotiest collection of men and women that had ever assembled here on the fortieth floor of the Peachtree Olympus. Their name was . . . the Press. Wes Jordan had been right. In no time flat the Fareek Fanon story—the name of the young woman was not mentioned—had been beamed up from the Internet into the newspapers, which, with toothless courage, insisted they were merely reporting on the widespread dissemination of the story via the "Chasing the Dragon" Web site. One ran a pious editorial entitled "Chasing the Internet."

Roger was nervous, never having taken part in a press conference before. But Julian Salisbury was smiling and humming to himself and rubbing his hands, as if to say, "Lemme at 'em." Don Pickett, a lean, graceful man about Roger's age who truly did know how to wear a double-breasted suit, leaned back nonchalantly against a bookcase, watching Julian's mannerisms with amusement. Don was a dark-skinned man who reminded Roger of the Nicholas Brothers, the great acrobatic tap-dance team of the 1930s. He looked lithe and athletic and didn't seem to have a nerve in his body.

"Well, Rodge," said Julian with a big smile and holding up his left wrist, which bore his watch, "looks like it's getting on towards time"—*lack it's gittin' on toads time*—"to go slop the hawgs." With that, he gestured toward the Press, who were still being seated and assigned camera positions by Wringer Fleasom's office manager, Mercedes Prince.

There you had two of the things about Julian that annoyed Roger. He kept calling him "Rodge." No one had *ever* called him Rodge before, but Julian had called him that from the moment they met. Also from the moment they met he had talked about *hawgs* and other barnyard creatures. Three years ago, Julian had become famous locally by winning a murder trial for a defendant named Skeeter Loman with a summation that began: "The district attorney admits that his case against Mr. Loman is based entirely on circumstantial evidence. Now, a case based on circumstantial evidence is like a hog." *Hawg*. "Most folks don't even know a hawg is covered with hair, because every last"—*ever las*—"hair on a hawg is lying down, ever las one *uv*'em. Anytime you see a critter's got some hair standing up, you ain't looking at no hawg. It's the same thing"—*thang*—"with the district attorney and his circumstantial evidence. If even *one piece* a that circumstantial evidence is sticking up and won't lie down, then you ain't looking at no guilty Skeeter Loman." Ever since then he'd been strewin' slop-trough tropes and sententiae thick as hog swill. Julian was no more than five three or four. So he had his white hair set in waves and puffed up into a three-inch-high meringue on top and had one-and-a-half-inch elevators set in his ankle-high boots down below. He had also begun affecting Edwardian dress, with four-button jackets and shirts with high, stiff, round-pointed collars that seemed to be made of plastic or celluloid. Julian was determined to be a Character, and the presence of the Press made him throb with excitement.

Not so, Roger. Shook with trepidation was more like it in his case. Not even his flawless sartorial armor—a new hard-finished worsted navy suit from Gus Carroll, a high-necked tab-collar shirt, and a pale-blue crêpe de chine necktie with a *perfect* dimple—could make him feel secure. He would have to lead off. The three of them had decided that Wringer Fleasom would be the best setting for the press conference, because it had such a grand and sedate decor and precisely because it was *not* a firm that ordinarily handled criminal cases. So Roger would be the host. When Roger had asked the firm's general partner, Zandy Scott, if it would be all right to use the library for a press conference,

Zandy had ruminated for what seemed like four or five minutes—it was probably no more than twenty or thirty seconds—before he said yes. That hadn't made Roger feel any better.

Julian must have detected Roger's shakiness, because he kept sidling up to him and, in a low voice, offering advice, as he was doing at this moment:

"One more thing," he said. "Just remember: speak firmly but slowly and in a low voice, a normal voice. People take a loud, hurried voice to mean you're insecure. No matter what they say to you, don't rise to the bait. Don't argue—or if you have to, make it short. At a press conference, the more you argue, the shakier you sound. Above all, remember: we're not here to *defend* Fareek against *charges*—because nobody's *made* any charges, and so he don't *need* any defending yet. You don't have to shoo flies off a hawg in a shady sty."

Roger nodded to show that he understood, but his eyes had drifted back toward the gathering press. Mercedes Prince was directing a fifth —or was it a sixth?—television camera crew toward a place in the rear of the throng. Ninety percent of this mangy collection of humanity were white. They seemed to range in age from twenty-five to fifty. The older men's taste, if it could be called that, ran to gray beards consisting of out-of-control ten-week stubbles that had spread like crabgrass on the undersides of their jowls and practically down to their Adam's apples. Made you itchy just looking at it. They wore baggy polo shirts, completely unbuttoned at the neck, with short sleeves hanging down to their elbows. There were no neckties; not one. There were two jackets, one on the hunched-over back of a paunchy white man, a newspaper reporter, judging by his notebook. He had on an ordinary cotton button-down shirt—the dignity of which had been subverted by the fact that he had been one button off when he buttoned the shirt, causing the right side of the collar to wind up two and a half inches lower than the left. There were four black members of this herd, two of whom he knew or knew of. One was a woman, the only decently dressed person among the whole bunch of them. Her name was Melanie Wallace, and she lived at Niskey Lake, although he barely knew her to say hello. She was a pretty, light-skinned woman who did on-camera reports for Channel 11. She had relaxed hair that was . . . *done* . . . in expensive-looking waves . . . She wore toffee-colored pants with a matching silk blouse. The other was a heavyset dark man who wore a black chalk-striped suit over a black T-shirt. Just so; a suit and a T-shirt. Roger had seen his picture many times in local black publications. He was part of the seemingly endless ranks of professional protesters and complainers, to Roger Too White's way of thinking. Just looking at the man made Roger Too White's damnable nickname pop back into his head. The man was Cedric Stifell, and he edited a weekly called *Atlanta Alarm*.

There he was, Cedric Stifell, posing insolently against a backdrop of the library reading room at Wringer Fleasom & Tick. Wringer Fleasom was paneled in mahogany from one end of its two floors here in the Peachtree Olympus to the other. The mahogany-paneled hallways were so dark, you had to stand directly under a downlighter in order to read a letterhead. But the reading room of the library was the firm's *pièce de résistance* when it came to mahogany. It was a veritable mahogany theme park. Panels, pilasters, cornices, shelves, tables, chairs, and even light switch wall plates—all of it was mahogany. And down at that end was the mahogany chair Roger Too White would soon have to sit in, before a thicket of microphones already in place on the big mahogany table. Six big television cameras would be aiming at him like lasers. He was consumed by fear. He had memorized what he was going to say, but suppose he became an ignominious casualty of nerves? What made his nervousness worse was the fear of suddenly appearing to white clients like Gerthland Fuller as just another black careerist riding the "activist" train—while in the eyes of the Cedric Stifells of Atlanta he would always be . . . Roger Too White. Wringer Fleasom & Tick, indeed! He had informed Zandy Scott that he had Fareek Fanon as a client as soon as he had been brought into the case, but he had never told him the nature of the case in any detail, and certainly had not told him it was a potential stick of dynamite. Zandy had not looked happy an hour ago when Roger Too White sought him out to introduce him to that sartorial curiosity, Julian Salisbury, and to a black criminal lawyer, Don Pickett, a dark, dapper, smooth-looking figure obviously not from the orbit of Wringer Fleasom or anything close to it. So Christ God!—what must he think of this rabble, the Press!

No sooner had Zandy Scott possessed Roger Too White's thoughts than here he came, walking from the rear of the reading room toward the alcove. Zandy was a tall white man, probably six four or so, in his early fifties, with red hair that was yielding to a rising tide of gray. He had the sort of full, smooth jowls and hefty midsection that used to denote prosperity and position in portraits by Copley. He was capable of ferocious displays of temper. Roger's first thought was: He's going to call off the press conference and throw everybody out! The entire damnable un-Wringer un-Fleasom & un-Ticky rabble!

Instead, when he reached the alcove, he broke into a smile. "Hey, Julian! Hey, Don!" Then he looked at Roger Too White. "Mercedes tells me the telephones are still ringing! People are coming in from all over the place! I hope you guys know what you're going to say!" An ingratiating grin. A beseeching grin! The man was thrilled to be a part of it all. It was through *his* law firm that the thrilling electric current of the microphones and television cameras would soon run! After decades of contracts, briefs, wills, and codicils in this mahogany mausoleum, Wringer Fleasom was for this brief moment part of the hurly-burly of the gaudy world outside.

"Julian and Don know what they're doing, Zandy," said Roger. "I'm the one to worry about. I've never done this before. I want you to sit up front and be my prompter."

"Awwww, you'll be fine," said Zandy.

"That's exactly what I told him, Zandy," said Julian. "I think Roger here's like the fella who tells you, 'Well, you know, I'm jes an ol' country lawyer? That's when you got to keep a good grip on your watch fob!" Then he held his wrist up again, the one with the watch on it. It showed a few minutes past eleven. "Speakin' a timepieces," he said, "I think it's like I said. 'Bout time to go out there and slop the hawgs."

Roger could feel another uptick in the adrenaline as he entered the reading room, followed by Julian and Don. For a moment he was frightened by the glare of the television lights. It was as if he were all at once in an entirely new atmosphere that his eyes and his lungs were not used to. He was aware of small red lights turned his way. They were the red lights that indicate television cameras are on and filming. To Roger they seemed like eyes, and they followed him all the way to the table, where he sat down in a banker's chair, a carved mahogany chair in which the arms and the backs created a great horseshoe curve. Julian took a seat to his right; Don, to his left.

Roger looked down at the surface of the table and then up at the mob of reporters and cameras and then became acutely aware of all the microphones in front of his face. From one side to the other they were pointed directly toward him, as if he generated some sort of magnetic field. At first he could scarcely make out the people standing before him. Because of the lighting, or something, they seemed to exist in a haze. He knew what he wanted to say, but he wondered if the words would come out if he opened his mouth. Television cameras! The thought first occurred to him: Those red-eyed machines will expose me to thousands, millions! I'm not just in this room! I'm streaming through the air in every direction! How can I do this? But in that instant he thought of Wes Jordan. He had called Wes early this morning to let him know what was about to happen. But somehow Wes already knew. In any case, Wes would be watching. It would be dreadful to look like a frightened fool in front of Wes Jordan! So, like many another man before him, Roger White pulled himself together and gulped his fears back down mainly so as not to look like too great a ninny.

He surveyed the tiny red eyes and all the mangy faces looking at him and managed to say:

"Ladies and gentlemen, I'm Roger White"—it was *strange* to hear himself uttering his own name in front of these people. "I'm a partner here at Wringer Fleasom & Tick." Had he just told them more than they needed to know? Did he sound as if he was bragging? These worrisome questions circulated in his skull even as he opened his mouth again and said, "On my right"—he gave a tentative gesture—"is Attorney Julian Salisbury, and on my left"—a more authoritative gesture—"is Attorney Donald Pickett. We're representing Mr. Fareek Fanon. Now, we'd like to say—"

"Is he here?"

It broke in—just like that—a deep gravelly voice. It was the white man who had buttoned up his shirt wrong. It startled Roger Too White and made him angry. The man had thrown him offstride.

"Is *who* here?"

"Fareek Fanon."

Roger remembered Julian Salisbury's advice: "A firm voice, low and slow." For a moment Roger's mouth hung open awkwardly as he stared at the man and his aging grayboy wattles, and then he said, lowly, slowly, firmly: "Given the erroneous and completely irresponsible nature of the rumor that has brought us all here this morning, there isn't the slightest reason why Mr. Fanon should even have to *think* about being at this event." The fact that this went down without any yammering or grumbling made Roger feel immensely stronger. "Now, as I was about to say, we're going to make a statement, and then you can ask questions." He looked from one end of the mangy crescent to the other, into the red eyes of the cameras, into the cynical mug of Cedric Stifell, into the pretty, inscrutable face of Melanie Wallace, and was aware of his heart drumming away. "This morning, as you know, an article was printed in a traditionally responsible organ concerning Fareek Fanon. The basis of this article was the existence over the past week of an item carried by a *Web site*"—pronounced *porn shop*—"on the Internet. Now, the Internet is an uncontrollable medium and, in this case, an out-of-control medium. That anyone could make an item carried by a *Web site* on the *Internet*"—pronounced *porn shop* in a *massage parlor*—"the basis of a printed article is disturbing. The fact of the matter is that there *are* no facts and there is no *matter*. No charges of any sort have been brought against Fareek Fanon in any forum whatsoever, not the courts, not the police department, not Georgia Tech. Mr. Fanon denies involvement in any act such as the one mentioned in this *story*"—rhymes with *fairy tale*—"and no one has stepped forward to assert otherwise. We are here to enlist the help of the press in seeing to it that this talented young man's reputation is not stained in this wholly baseless, irresponsible fashion."

With that, Roger leaned back in his mahogany banker's chair and took a deep breath, as if to say, "That's the statement. That's that."

"Then are you saying," said the big man who had buttoned his shirt wrong, "that there is no 'leading Atlanta businessman' who has been leveling such a charge against Fanon?"

That had Roger stumped, since in fact he did know of such a creature. The moment grew longer and longer.

Julian Salisbury spoke up. " 'At's like asking if there's a brood sow out there somewhere dancing a minuet. Could be, I reckon, 'cause a hawg's smarter'n a hound dawg. But it's what I'd call a moot point! There *ain't* no charges!" By the time he got to *a moot point*, Salisbury was convulsed with laughter, which must have been why the Press started laughing, too; either that or they were amused because the bouncy little lawyer worked his *hawgs* into every conversation.

Melanie Wallace said, "Then Fareek Fanon is denying these charges—"

"There *are* no charges," said Roger. "No one has *made* any charges."

"All right—is he saying that the events . . . uh . . . the matter referred to in the press today did not occur?"

"Absolutely." Firmly, lowly, slowly. Roger was pleased to see that the Press was dancing coyly about the subject. So far no one had used the word *rape*.

"If nothing happened," said the man who had buttoned his shirt wrong, "then why are you here, Julian, and you, too, Don? You're both criminal defense lawyers."

"We're here . . . if needed, Bryce," said Don Pickett, who had a slow, pleasant voice. "So far we haven't had anything to do, and in this case we like it like that."

A deep and indisputably black voice spoke up: "How do you suppose rumors like this one get started, and why does anybody want to circulate them?" It was Cedric Stifell of *Atlanta Alarm*.

"I have no idea," said Roger Too White. His good sense told him to leave it at that. But Cedric Stifell was the *black* press—and he, Roger, was Roger Too White, and contrary to all logic, it was important to him, in this place, the white-as-white-can-be Wringer Fleasom & Tick, to be liked by this man—yes, this man in his ludicrous outfit. Besides, he, Roger White II, just might want to let it be known that he was a *learned* lawyer as well. So he didn't leave it at that. Instead he continued: "You know, Nietzsche once said that resentment is the least explored of the primary human motivations. He said there are certain types of people who can't improve their own place in the world, and so they devote all their energies to tearing down others. He called them 'the tarantulas.' I suppose there's a certain type of person who resents a young man like Fareek Fanon rising up from English Avenue, from the Bluff, and becoming a great sports star."

As soon as the words "up from English Avenue" passed Roger's lips he wished he could pull them back from out of the air, from out of the ether, from out of the electric gullets of all those microphones in front of him. No matter how indirectly, he had now introduced the matter of race into the discussion. There was probably not another neighborhood in Atlanta more completely identified with black folks than English Avenue.

"Who do you have in mind?" It was a white man, about thirty-five, wearing a shirt open almost to the waist, the better to reveal a T-shirt with the face of a grotesque clown on it and the name KRUSTY. The man wore his pale brown hair down over his ears, like the clown.

"I don't have *anybody* in mind," said Roger anxiously. "I was just making a speculation that was probably not worth making. I doubt that the fact that Fareek Fanon is from English Avenue has anything to do with . . . uh . . . uh . . . with anything." He was aware that his voice now sounded terribly anxious, even a bit desperate. But sounding unnerved wasn't the end of the world. At least he had retracted . . . most of it . . . Had to show off your knowledge of late-nineteenth-century philosophy, didn't you! You vain, overreaching fool! You . . . Roger Too White!

The questions continued, but Julian and Don took most of them. Roger sat there in a daze, tuning in and out . . . Nietzsche and the tarantulas . . . Why had he said that? . . . Would anybody print it or broadcast it? . . . Nahhhhhhhhh, who was going to quote Lawyer Roger White on the subject of Friedrich Nietzsche? But suppose they did? How bad would it be? . . . But English Avenue, too! . . . Why in the name of God had he ever mentioned English Avenue? Why had he said "rising up from English Avenue"? Why couldn't he have left it with "becoming a great sports star"? . . . Had to pander to Cedric Stifell and the readers of *Atlanta Alarm*, didn't you! Had to prove you weren't really Too White, isn't that so? But none of that shaggy pack standing before him was talking anymore about English Avenue or the tarantulas, were they . . . They were talking about this, that, and the other thing, aimlessly fishing for something substantial in this titillating situation . . . The tarantulas and English Avenue were not substantial, either . . . Yet he couldn't help but notice that Julian and Don, no matter how many more *hawgs* Julian threw in, and no matter how broad Don Pickett's smile became, stuck strictly to the text: there *are* no charges, and so there's nothing to discuss—and no matter how many times you have to say it, say it firmly, lowly, slowly.

Suddenly a woman's voice: "Mr. White, you mentioned 'tarantulas.' Let's suppose there's a tarantula out there who's the head of a very large corporation with headquarters in Atlanta, and he makes charges openly, through some official public channel. Do you think your client will be at a disadvantage because he comes from English Avenue and is black?"

Roger stared at her for a moment. She was a white woman with short, bobbed blond hair, wearing a black jersey and pants and a black canvas Cargo vest. She had an aggressive, terribly rapid-fire delivery. *Tarantulas! English Avenue! Black!* The woman had hit every single blunder he'd made right on the head!

"Please forget my tarantulas," he said. He tried to add a disarming smile, the way Don Pickett did, but he could tell that his smile had congealed right in the middle of his face, revealing his discomfort. "I never meant to introduce spiders into the discussion." Not a single laugh. They could all tell how nervous he was. "I was making a speculation in answer to a question, and it was a pointless speculation, and I apologize for that, since it was pointless speculation that created the need for this press conference in the first place." The words were coming out right, but the tremor in his voice was sending an entirely different sort of signal.

By the time the press conference was over, his head hung so low he had to roll his eyes upward to see the raggedy pack he feared, the Press.

Afterward, as the reporters were departing and the television crews were packing up, Roger, Julian, and Don stood behind the table, and Julian said to Roger: "See? Wasn't so bad, was it. You did great."

He didn't say it with the slightest bit of exhilaration, however, not the way you would with a rookie athlete who has just performed admirably in the fray. No, he said it mechanically, as if he really meant, "See, that may have been bad, but it wasn't as bad as you were afraid it was going to be."

"Just a couple things," he added. "Stay away from things like tarantulas. We don't want to make Armholster any angrier than he already is. Even a 800-pound hawg's cuddlier than a spider. And there's no need to bring in English Avenue. We want to present Fareek as a nice young man who goes to college at Georgia Tech. But don't worry, you did fine."

Roger stood there massaging his hands and worrying a lot.

THE NAME "NASSAU, the Bahamas" had always conjured up in Peepgass's mind a tropical capital that looked like an enlarged version of some posh resort such as the Pinehurst Inn in North Carolina or the Greenbrier in West Virginia—but with an ocean, palm trees, manicured greenswards, white columns, shady verandas, green-and-white awnings, and trim black policemen clad in white pith helmets, short-sleeved white officer's blouses, pleated white shorts, knee-high white socks, and white shoes, contrasting smartly with their dark skin, standing on white platforms in the middle of the main intersections, crisply directing traffic.

In fact, there was nothing crisp about Nassau at all, so far as Peepgass could tell, and it wasn't an enlarged version of anything, or not anything in the U.S.A. It was a tiny, moldering old colonial capital with a lot of patched-up, painted-over old buildings, cramped and crowded and leaning against one another for support. The whole of downtown wasn't bigger than Normandy Lea, where he lived. Number 23 George Street, the official address of Colonial Real Properties, Ltd., was a laugh and a half. As he walked up the narrow stairs that began scarcely a yard inside the front entrance, he couldn't help but smile. Staggering up the wall in a line parallel, more or less, with the staircase were forty-one brass plaques bearing the names of American and European banks and corporations, including, he couldn't help but be pleased to notice, First Gould Guaranty, one of the biggest banks in New York. The shiniest plaque of all, since it was the newest, was the forty-first: Colonial Real Properties, Ltd. And that was all his.

It was no use walking up any farther, because there was no office of Colonial Real Properties to be found. But there wasn't one for First Gould Guaranty, either. For the biggest—First Gould—as well as the smallest—Colonial Real Properties—this was merely a dummy address that enabled one to carry out so-called overseas financial operations. The banks, for example, could use the Bahamas to set up Eurodollar accounts for their customers. Individuals could hide money here, in Bahamian banks, with a secrecy that was tightly protected by Bahamian banking laws. Not for nothing did Nassau call itself Little Switzerland. Ever since the Civil War, when blockade runners—such as Rhett Butler in *Gone with the Wind*—used the Bahamas as a safe harbor from which to do business with the Confederacy, Americans had been using the Bahamas to get around American laws. Bootleggers used the Bahamas for warehousing during Prohibition. Drug dealers were using it for essentially the same purpose at this moment. Nassau was so close to the U.S. mainland, it was only a thirty-minute flight from Miami and an hour from Atlanta. Peepgass wasn't so deluded as to compare himself with Rhett Butler, Frank Nitti, or . . . or . . . or—he couldn't think of the names of any drug lords—nevertheless, there it was, etched in brass: COLONIAL REAL PROPERTIES, LTD.

Pleased with himself, he walked slowly down the stairs, savoring his forty colleagues in brass all over again, and out onto the street. He glanced at his watch: almost 10 a.m.; only thirty more minutes to kill before his appointment. This was the beginning of the hot season in the Bahamas, but the streets were still jammed with cars, mostly small Japanese cars, or so it seemed to Peepgass, with motorbikes that sounded like chainsaws, with exhausted barouches and horses that went clop, clop, clop, clop, and policemen with no pith helmets who kept blowing whistles. Somewhere a vendor kept crying out, "Doctor Shells! I yem

Doctor Shells!" Tourists, many of them with pinned-on ID tags from some cruise ship that had pulled into Prince George Docks, had poured onto the sidewalks in a hiving mass and were swarming over the shops and arcades and emerging with straw hats, conch shells, and every imaginable knickknack of straw, wood, and glass. For an instant Peepgass looked down his nose at this scene of frantically roiling indolence, but in the next instant he was grateful for it. He was thankful for the protective coloration, having gone to considerable trouble and expense to dress like a tourist himself. He was clad in a number of items he would never have been caught dead in otherwise, a straw hat with a floppy four-inch brim, black sunglasses, a pale blue short-sleeved sport shirt of the sort that is designed for wearing outside the pants and has a pair of big pleated breast pockets and a pair of purely decorative buttons at the base of each side seam, a pair of Old People's checked pants—why was it that old people were so crazy about checked and plaid patterns?—and a pair of putty-colored suede Sperry Top-Sider laced moccasins. The outlay for the clothes alone had come to close to $200; the bill for three days and nights at the Carnival's Crystal Palace Resort and Casino would come to something in the neighborhood of $600, the round-trip airfare, Atlanta/Nassau, was $266 and would have been more if it wasn't for the Saturday-night layover—in other words, awfully close to $1,000, a sum he couldn't begin to afford for a weekend in the Bahamas or anywhere else. But it was necessary. It was an investment, an investment, an investment, he kept telling himself. And if there ever came a day when anyone cared to check out his travels, it would look like a perfectly ordinary long weekend for a lonely, middle-aged man, a perfectly ordinary member of that hive of American worker bees known as middle management, separated from his wife and family, cut off from the familiar, cozy weekend chores associated with owning a middle-class house in Snellville with a basketball backboard and hoop set up on a stanchion near the garage on the edge of the driveway. A tourist he was, a tourist rooting here and there with a whole swarm of tourists; only that and nothing more.

Like any other tourist, he made his way east on Marlborough Street and down Frederic Street and then walked along Shirley Street until he reached the Public Library. He had already heard about this curious place, but it was nothing like what he imagined. Like everything else in Nassau, it was tinier . . . and touched with the taint of . . . seediness. It was a circular building, no more than twenty feet in diameter, best

Peepgass could judge, with seven or eight open cubicles along the circumference. In the cubicles were shelves of books along two sides and a window on the third. In the center of the circle was a small wooden enclosure where a rather bored brown-skinned librarian sat. From her post she could see into every cubicle, although she seemed to have no particular interest in doing so. The building, which was now close to 200 years old, had originally been built as the town jail. What were now library cubicles had originally been cells with barred windows and doors; and where now sat a librarian who could see into every cubicle had been a warden who could see into every cell. All at once it occurred to Peepgass—and probably to no one else in Nassau that day—that 200 years ago, at the turn of the century, the circular prison had been the very latest in modern penology. All at once he froze, staring fixedly at this odd little room, and his spirits plummeted. *Modern penology* . . . he'd learn about modern penology, all right, at *this* turn of the century, if he took a misstep in this little . . . overseas venture . . . But damn it, Peepgass, are you going to remain a wimp, a dork, a staff nerd until it's too late to do anything about it? Are you going to keep your red dog chained up until PlannersBanc gives you a Steuben glass phoenix—which was already known, intramurally, as "getting the bird"—the bank was far too cheap to give retiring drudges something made of precious metal, such as a gold watch, anymore—are you going to wait until Lomprey or some other hunchback gives you the bird and waves bye-bye? That—your own willing self-imprisonment—would be a far worse fate than any actual incarceration, is it not so?

Thus, gradually, Peepgass bucked himself up, took a deep breath, and left the library to keep his appointment with his erstwhile Harvard Business School classmate, Harvey Wyndham, whose real estate office, Arthur Wyndham & Son, was just two blocks away. The "& Son" was Harvey's encoded sign of defeat, just as "staff officer" was Peepgass's. Like almost everyone entering the Harvard Business School, like Peepgass himself, Harvey, with his father's blessing, had indulged in dreams of dazzling entrepreneurship or corporate leadership or, at the very least, getting stunningly rich through investment banking. But Harvey's temperament had been like his own: passive and, by the standards of the late twentieth century, fatally soft. Perhaps, without realizing it, that was why Harvey and he had become such pals in Cambridge. Every month they saved up as much of their modest remittances from home as they could and splurged on a big lobster dinner at Durgin Park, which to them was an absolutely Lucullan dining experience. Harvey's father, Arthur Wyndham, ran a successful real estate business in the Bahamas and had flourished in the 1960s when so many newly rich Americans began to discover the Bahamas' far-flung islands and clear (utterly) blue (truly) water. The "& Son" he had added to his firm's name in the early 1960s, mainly to flatter and perhaps delight his little boy, only six or seven at the time, on whom he absolutely doted, but also to give the firm an aura of venerable long-standing, which it in fact did not yet have. He loved Harvey far too much to have ever pressured him to stay in the Bahamas and take over the business. But Harvey had found out soon enough, on his own, the hard way, that he was not the sort of young man from a tiny oceanic colony with a British accent who was going to set the business world on fire in the United States. Within eight years he had drifted back to the Bahamas, him and his Harvard MBA degree, and become the "& Son" that had been merely his father's fond hope. And—you had to give him credit—Son, with his mild manners and low-keyed charm, had proved to be an able salesman of island real estate to status-hungry Americans and Brits and Germans, and the old man had happily turned Arthur Wyndham & Son over to Son five years before he died.

Peepgass had not actually laid eyes on Harvey Wyndham since they graduated from the Business School, but they had continued to exchange Christmas cards all these years and had talked on the telephone half a dozen times. These calls had been occasioned by Peepgass's becoming aware of property that PlannersBanc needed to liquidate or have appraised in the Bahamas. Whenever he could, he had steered the business Arthur Wyndham & Son's way.

The offices turned out to be on the second floor of a superannuated but rather pretty three-story pink stucco building with white trim and a white tile roof on a corner of two busy little streets not far from the old Jacaranda and East Hill mansions. In the outer office were eight to ten women at computer terminals or on the telephone and, along a wall, a whole lineup of well-dressed men and women at handsome wooden desks, salespeople and property management personnel, presumably. God knew how many more employees there must be on the floor above. This was an impressively large staff for a real-estate firm. A plump woman with a heavy and, to Peepgass's ears, somewhat mannered British accent immediately ushered him into Harvey Wyndham's office, which was on the corner.

The room was not especially large, but the stylishness of it struck Peepgass right away. Walls of darkest aubergine that set off four magnificent old-fashioned triple-hung windows that ran floor to ceiling, framed by spanking white louvered shutters on the sides and ornate white Victorian woodwork in the form of an ornate cornice at the top and an ornate eighteen-inch-high skirting at the bottom. Through the windows you could see the old-fashioned sloped roofs of Nassau, the tops of palms, and an infinite blue sky. Harvey Wyndham stood up. Peepgass could notice the changes immediately. His once-thick brown hair was no longer all that thick or all that brown. On top were a few lonely strands that barely bridged the two remaining crops. He wore a long-sleeved white guayabera shirt, quite an exquisite one, that only halfway successfully hid his much too broad midsection and hips. But the greatest change of all, as he smiled to greet his old MBA compatriot, was in his eyes. They were the tired but amused eyes of a man who had been in on this smuggler's paradise of an island for so long, he had by now seen it all and could no longer be surprised.

As Harvey gestured to indicate he should have a seat in a big old King George armchair, Peepgass said, "Well, Harvey, I don't know how you do it. You haven't changed a bit."

"Oh my God, please," said Harvey, placing both hands on his big belly where it swelled out against the guayabera shirt, "there's an American author I never heard of before I went to Harvard, Washington Irving, and do you know what he said? He said, 'There are three ages of man: youth, middle age, and you-haven't-changed-a-bit.' "

Peepgass laughed as they sat down. "Well, I guess I was talking about the inner you, Harvey."

"The inner me likes to eat, too. Three times a day. Likes rum also. You're the one who hasn't changed, Ray."

"Well . . . only in the Washington Irving sense," said Peepgass, although his honest feeling was that it was true, in his own case. "My problem is that my career hasn't changed, either." He felt comfortable enough with his old friend to say that right off the bat.

So they did a little Business School reminiscing and gossiping about what A had achieved, what B hadn't achieved, and C, who had never been heard from again. Then they briefed each other on their marriages.

Finally it was Harvey who narrowed the focus down to the present moment. "Look, Ray old boy, I have to admit I'm dying of curiosity. You sounded . . . awfully . . . *mysterious* . . . on the telephone."

Peepgass smiled. "I didn't mean to be mysterious. I was just being . . ." —he paused and raised both hands as if trying to seize upon the right word—". . . discreet, I suppose. The thing is . . . I've formed a corporation, Harvey, right here in the Bahamas. It's called Colonial Real Properties."

"Oho!" said Harvey. "Competition!"

"No," said Peepgass, "I could never compete with you, Harvey, even if I were so ungrateful as to want to. No, the word isn't *competition*, it's *cooperation*. A little *synergy*, to use the current Business School patois."

Harvey sat back in his chair, cocked his head, and gave him more of the look he had detected when he first walked in the room, a smile surmounted by a wrinkled and weary amusement about the eyes. He lifted his right hand languidly from his lap, palm up, and said, "How so?"

Peepgass tried to look as relaxed as Harvey obviously was, but he knew he wasn't pulling it off. "*Entre nous*, I've formed my company for a single real estate deal. If I am correct—and I think I *am* correct—PlannersBanc is about to acquire a prime piece of property in suburban Atlanta, a big mixed-use complex, via a deed in lieu of foreclosure. You follow me so far?"

Harvey nodded.

"Now, the bank," said Peepgass, "will be ready to unload this piece of property for something in the neighborhood of $50 million, just to get it off its hands quickly and quietly and with a minimum of embarrassment. I mean, the loans we made to the developer for the construction of the tower were insane—the sort of nutty thing that happens when you let yourself get caught up in the frenzy of a real estate bubble and you start talking about lending as 'marketing' and big loans as 'big sales,' that sort of thing."

"How much *did* you lend him?"

"A hundred and seventy-five million."

Harvey made a whistling noise between his teeth.

"Exactly," said Peepgass, "and nobody at the bank is particularly anxious to advertise this corpse to the shareholders. So I think they're ready to unload it for something in the vicinity of $50 million and bury it and forget about it. Now, I know of a syndicate in Atlanta, made up of people with impeccable financial statements, and I think they'd *love* a little bottom-fishing like this. But they need to be led to the proposition by a real estate broker. I'd be happy to do it myself, but A, I work for the bank, and B, I'm not a real estate broker. Do you know what I'm going to say next?"

"No," said Harvey with a jaded smile and regular crinkles of amusement about the eyes, "but I'm all ears."

"The broker would have three tasks to perform," said Peepgass. "First, he'd have to broker the initial transaction, the purchase of the building for about $50 million. He'd get a 6 percent commission. That's $3 million. Second, the syndicate would want to sell the building within two to three years. And by then, I feel certain, such a building will have regained its true and fair value on the market, which would be about $120 million. The brokerage commission on that sale would be $7.2 million, making a total of $10.2 million in brokerage fees over a two-to-three-year period. And third, the same firm would be the broker of record for new leases. The building is less than half leased up now, and so I figure there's another $300,000 in leasing fees. That gives us a total of $10.5 million in fees altogether. Is all that clear so far?"

Harvey nodded, eyes atwinkle.

"Now . . . I'd like for you to be the broker, Harvey, in cooperation with a modest, retiring . . . in fact, one might say silent . . . partner, Colonial Real Properties, Ltd., of Nassau, the Bahamas."

Harvey leaned back in his chair and interlaced his fingers and rested them atop his capacious paunch and eyed Peepgass intently.

"In the first transaction," said Peepgass, "the bank's sale of the property to the syndicate, you wouldn't have to do a thing other than pick up the telephone occasionally and come to Atlanta for the closing. You could be back home in time for dinner. For that transaction I propose that Wyndham & Son's share of the commission be one-third and Colonial Real Properties' two-thirds. When you get home for dinner, you'll have a cashier's check for $3 million in your pocket. In keeping with a contract that will have been drawn up here in Nassau and executed here in Nassau, $2 million will be transferred to Colonial Real Properties. But I'm not greedy, Harvey. When it comes to the resale of the property by the syndicate—and, as I was saying, that should be in the neighborhood of $120 million—when it comes to that part, and when it comes to the leasing fees, we'll split it right down the middle, fifty-fifty."

Harvey leaned back still farther, gazed off toward a corner of the ceiling, and sighed, expelling such a long jet of air between his lips he looked like the West Wind. Then he eyed Peepgass again. "So all told, you figure, Colonial Real Properties would receive five and three-quarter million dollars and Wyndham & Son would receive four and three-quarter million."

"Harvey, you always were nimble with mental calculations. You're right as rain. How does it all strike you?"

"As the saying goes, like pennies from heaven," said Harvey. "But why would such a syndicate agree to be represented by a real estate company in the Bahamas?"

"Because they're not even going to be able to bottom-fish for the property in the first place, unless an agent of Colonial Real Properties, who shall go unnamed, paves the way for them. There'll be no deal at all unless you're in on it. They won't give me any trouble on that score, because they stand to make six or seven times as much out of this thing as we do."

"Where is this complex, Ray, and what's it called, if you don't mind my asking?"

Peepgass opened his manila envelope and took out the elaborate full-color brochure Croker Global had produced as the calling card for its leasing campaign. He let Harvey take a good look at the picture on the front. It was one of those architectural photographs that are so super-sharp in detail, they make you blink. The paper it was printed on was so thick, rich, and creamy, it made you want to eat it.

Both of them, Harvey and Ray, once again comrades in arms after all these years, had leaned over so far to take a look at Croker's cathedral of Mammon that was going for a song, their heads were almost touching. Each was thinking of the figures and building his own castles in the air.

Chapter XXIII

The Deal

ORDINARILY, FOR ROGER, THE VERY FIRST MOMENTS OF THE day, when he woke up and opened his eyes and glanced down toward the foot of the bed and took a peek at the World of Roger White, as he was now doing—these moments were . . . sublime. Ten or twelve feet from the foot of the bed were a pair of French doors that opened onto a balcony, and the balcony looked out over Niskey Lake, and beyond the lake he could see the lordly pines on the opposite shore. True, no hardwood trees—he wished to hell Wes had never told him about that—but the pines were lordly. Was there a more heavenly vista anywhere in all of Atlanta? Not very likely. Look at his beautiful home! Look at his beautiful wife! Henrietta was next to him, still fast asleep, her head turned the other way. Hadn't he arranged things sublimely—

He sat bolt upright in bed, no longer aware of anything beyond his own head, which was suddenly feverish.

"What's wrong, honey?" said Henrietta. The flexing of the mattress had awakened her.

"Nothing," said Roger. "I . . . must have woken up out of a dream."

In fact, it was no dream—the panic from last evening that now came surging back into his brain.

He had uttered three unfortunate words at the press conference, "tarantulas" and "English Avenue," all of which he had promptly taken back. Nevertheless, *they*, the media, had fastened on them like hyenas and put *his* face, Roger White II's, on television uttering the vile imprecations. They made it sound as if he were referring to some complex racist plot to ruin Fareek Fanon. On the news broadcast he and Henrietta had watched, it was the lead story. From the calls they got from friends later in the evening, he learned that he and his insinuations had been the lead on at least two other channels as well. Oh, they were all very upbeat, their friends were, and they all said the right things, but he knew what they were thinking . . . *Old Roger, he's turned into a rabble-rouser or a paranoiac or both* . . . Him! Roger Too White!—after years of tailoring every detail of his speech and dress to his role as a partner in the immaculately white firm of Wringer Fleasom & Tick!

The dining room, whose French doors opened out upon a deck, offered more smashing views of Niskey Lake, and Roger's seat, the seat of the master of this dream house, offered the best view of all. Absentmindedly he pushed his cereal (Alpen with raspberries and sliced bananas and skimmed milk) this way and that in his bowl with his spoon. His eyes were fastened upon idyllic Niskey Lake, but it didn't take a genius to realize that he was seeing nothing whatsoever.

"Roger," said Henrietta, "what's wrong?"

Without so much as turning his head: "Nothing."

"You're still stewing over the press conference, aren't you."

"I guess . . . I just can't figure out why I said what I said." He wasn't about to tell anybody, not even Henrietta, that he had spouted out all those Nietzschean tarantulas for no more profound reason than that he wanted to sound acceptable to the likes of Cedric Stifell of *Atlanta Alarm*.

Henrietta said softly, "Roger?"

He looked toward her.

"The press conference is over, honey," she said. "That was yesterday. This is today. Besides, what you said was perfectly fine."

What he heard: "No use crying over spilt milk, and you spilled a lot of it."

The truth was, the press conference *wasn't* over. The damned thing wouldn't lie down. Right there on the table before him, on the front page of the morning newspaper—the bottom of the page but the front page nonetheless—was a headline that read:

Lawyer says:
"TARANTULAS"
SEEK FAREEK

Lawyer was . . . *him!* It was him, Roger White, who had dropped the spiders in the soup!

By the time he drove his Lexus out of the driveway, heading for the office, he had worked up a good case of nerves. Suddenly he heard three *beep beep beep*s coming up from behind him and overtaking him. Roger braked to a stop. A gunmetal-gray BMW sedan, a big one, four doors, pulled up on his left. The passenger-side window rolled down, and the driver's smiling face leaned toward him and said, "Hey, neighbor, I saw you on television last night!"

Roger knew that dark, rugged face with its gleaming teeth and its narrow, flawlessly trimmed mustache just above the upper lip. It was Guy Thompson, whose radio station, WBBB, was one of the most successful black-owned stations in the South. Roger knew he lived on Niskey Lake, he knew he was the one with the fabulous gray BMW, he knew how well his athletic frame carried a suit like the gray nailhead worsted he had on this morning, and he wasn't surprised by how much crisp white cuff, fastened by gold cuff links, protruded from his sleeves. But he had never met the man—and he had no idea that Thompson had the vaguest notion who he was.

Guy Thompson's face grew serious. "You said something that's needed saying in this town for a long time. Keep it up!" Then he flashed his wonderful smile again and gave Roger the thumbs-up gesture of approval and support . . . as he cruised off in his steely BMW.

What on earth had he said that needed saying? Roger wondered. Nothing that he could think of. Nevertheless, this encounter with the estimable Mr. Guy Thompson, who now knew who he was and approved of him, left him with a warm feeling.

As usual, once he reached Midtown, Roger drove down into the underground parking garage of the Peachtree Olympus building. Once you reached the STOP HERE sign, there were eight or ten valet attendants available to park your car for you. This morning it was a young, slender, boyish-looking black man named Bo. Roger knew his name only because he had heard other attendants call him that. In the random rotation Bo parked his car once every two or three weeks. Roger had never even spoken to him beyond the most perfunctory *thank yous*.

This morning, as he emerged from the car, he saw the young man do a double take. He broke into a smile of gape-jawed wonderment, and his eyes opened wide, and he brought his forefinger up in front of his face. "You . . . you . . . you—you're Roger White, right?"

Tentatively, not knowing where it was all leading: "Yes . . ."

"Awriiiighhhhhhhht!" said the young man. "I saw you on TV last night!" With that he extended his hand.

Roger shook it, and then this Bo did something with his thumb and his fist. It was like some sort of fraternal grip that, apparently, Roger should know but didn't.

"This is an honor," said young Bo. Then he winked. "You're gettin' it *said*, Mr. White!"

"Thank you," said Roger.

The young man slid into the driver's seat of the Lexus to take it down into the parking bowels of the building—then popped out again and said, "Mr. White!"

Roger turned about.

"Gotcha back!" said young Bo. Then he slipped back into the car and drove down a ramp.

Gotcha back!

At first, of course, he thought of André Fleet. But this had nothing to do with André Fleet. This was about Roger White, who had gotten it said. Did he dare even let himself speculate? Somehow he had reached . . . his own people . . .

The lobby of the Peachtree Olympus was a fifty-foot-high extravaganza of marble carved into the columns, ribs, ogeed curves, raised panels, and interminable architraves and cornices of classical architecture. The whole place glistened manically thanks to innumerable downlighters aimed at the polished marble walls. In the wall opposite the main entrance was an arched niche of heroic proportions. In it was mounted a twelve-foot-high abstract sculpture by Henry Moore. To Roger it looked like a great melting doughnut. Atlanta's major developers, all of whom were white, looked upon Henry Moore as "class" when it came to sculpture. Look at the damned thing . . . absolutely stupid and pointless. To that extent he agreed with Wes Jordan. Everything in this enormous lobby strove for "class." On one wall hung three enormous and almost threadbare Belgian tapestries. Not far from the elevator bank was the pianist at a huge Yamaha concert grand. He was a slender, thirtyish black man wearing a tuxedo—at 8:30 in the morning. At the moment he was playing Ravel's *Bolero*. Management wanted *class*, but nothing unnecessarily . . . *taxing*, especially during the morning rush. Old Maurice's sultry chords and aroused treble were pouring forth and ricocheting off the marble and then ricocheting again and then ricocheting, ricocheting, and ricocheting. Roger had walked within twenty feet of the piano and its black pianist every workday morning for . . . how long now? . . . months . . . and they had never so much as exchanged glances . . . but this morning there was something ironically *lush*, cleverly *hammed up*, about the way he was splashing old Maurice's gouts of sexuality off the *classy* marble walls . . . and so Roger looked at him—and *he* was staring back so intently that Roger couldn't break eye contact. Then the pianist gave him a big wink and a little smile. While his left hand dug deep into *Bolero*'s tropical chords, he lifted his right hand and, still looking Roger in the face, opened the first two fingers into a V, the peace sign.

Him, too!—the pianist in the lobby! What did it mean?

On the elevator his spirits fell. In the mahogany halls of Wringer Fleasom & Tick, all this approval—by the brethren—would mean literally less than nothing. At Wringer Fleasom all these things that have made you feel so warm, dear Roger, will have minus values. You've been a bad lawyer—introducing "tarantulas" and "English Avenue" where there was absolutely no need for them—and you've shown your true color by gratuitously playing the race card.

Roger entered those morose wooden corridors almost on the balls of his feet. The first person he came upon was Bob Partridge, a well-built man, fortyish, one of those white people who are so blond their eyebrows look strange. After Zandy Scott, Bob Partridge ranked highest in the firm.

Roger eyed him warily—but Partridge broke into a grin and said heartily: "Heyyyyy, Roger! How's our in-house celebrity this morning?"

It was the grin, more than what he said, that did it, and Roger relaxed. Bob Partridge wouldn't go around beaming at Roger White II purely on his own, not after the events of yesterday. No, that grin meant that Zandy and one and all had approved. Roger couldn't think of any reason on earth why. But approve they did. He could scarcely believe it. The World of Roger White was intact, despite all.

LIKE MOST PEOPLE suffering from advanced, prolonged, and intractable insomnia, Charlie found morning to be the worst part of the day.

All morning, no matter what he did, his head felt like a burnt-out husk. His mind became a ravenous void, ravenous, that is, for sleep, but sharply, cuttingly, aware that he, this big meaty organism known as Charles Earl Croker, was incapable of going to sleep. Gradually the events of the day, meals, meetings, conversations, problems, righteous anger, began to fill the void . . . somewhat . . . and his energy would build up to about 10 percent of normal. But now, this morning, as he sat at his desk on the thirty-eighth floor of the tower at Croker Concourse, there was only the emptiness and hopelessness of the burnt-out husk.

He had told Marguerite to hold all calls except for those that truly required immediate attention. That way he could continue to do in peace precisely what he was doing at this moment: ignoring his much-vaunted view of half of Atlanta, its golden northern half, and its most sought-after great green tree-shaded suburbs, slumping down in the very cockpit of the Croker Global Corporation . . . with his head keeled over until his chin touched his clavicle, his chest compressed down upon his belly, his eyes shut, eyelid movies forming and dissolving in his optic chiasma, hoping for hypnagogic hallucinations that might pass for a substitute for sleep . . . This far the great Croker had sunk . . . nothing more than a poor beaten self-deluding fool passing for the omnipotent Croker of old . . .

He thought of Inman, whom he had finally reached this morning. Inman was feeling so sorry for himself. He couldn't let this big black animal—he kept using the word "animal"—get away with what he had done to Elizabeth, but Elizabeth, Inman kept saying, was still a frightened creature who had made him swear not to press any formal charges that might force her to confront Fanon again or reveal to the world the monstrous defilement she had suffered . . . Oh yes, Inman felt very sorry for himself—not realizing for a moment what a luxury it was to have your child's honor as your biggest worry, whereas he, Charlie, now stood to lose . . . *everything*.

Just as the eyelid movies inside his drooped head began to take on the contours of a great black and mauve abyss, a low beep-beep sounded on the telephone by his desk. That would be Marguerite, buzzing him. He picked up the receiver and said, "Yeah."

"Charlie," said Marguerite, "a lawyer from Wringer Fleasom, said he's a partner there, a man named Roger White, just called to say he needs to see you on an urgent matter."

"I already told you," said Charlie, "refer all bill collectors to the Wiz."

"He said this had to do with a client of his, but he wouldn't tell me any more than that. He wanted to speak only to you."

"Roger White . . ." said Charlie. "Why does that name sound familiar?"

"I don't know," said Marguerite. "I guess it's a fairly common name."

"Ring up the Wiz for me," said Charlie. "Maybe he'll know."

So Marguerite rang up the Wiz for him, and the Wiz said, "Roger White . . . I don't know. There's a lawyer named Roger White who's representing this football player, Fareek Fanon, in this thing that's been in the news the past two days, this rape case or whatever it is? I'm pretty sure *his* name is Roger White."

"Is he from Wringer Fleasom & Tick?"

"I don't know. I don't think it said. Why?"

"Some lawyer named Roger White from Wringer Fleasom called me this morning."

"Doesn't sound much like a Wringer Fleasom case, does it," said the Wiz. "But this is an age of anomalies."

Whatever that's supposed to mean, thought Charlie. Aloud: "Well, look, do me a favor and see if you can find out who this guy is, Roger White, Wringer Fleasom & Tick—he wants to talk to me on some 'urgent matter.' If this is some cheap bill-collecting dodge, I'll throw the sonofabitch out the window."

"There's no fenestration in this building," said Wismer Stroock, "only glass walls."

As often happened, Charlie didn't know whether this was Wiz biz-school technogeekspeak literal-mindedness or just the Wiz having his sallow, hollow-cheeked fun.

In less than ten minutes the Wiz called back. "He's one and the same lawyer. He's representing Fareek Fanon. And by the way, just so you'll know, he's black."

"And he's a partner at Wringer Fleasom?"

"Affirmative," said the Wiz.

"Well," said Charlie, "it figures"—although if pressed to say in so many words why it figured, he wouldn't have been able to respond very well.

After hanging up, Charlie swiveled in his chair until he was looking due north, away from the city. Another sunny day in May! He resented it. He resented God's or Nature's making it a sunny day. It reminded him too much of the optimism and energy of his youth, when he thought of life as a hill that led up to about age fifty-three or -four, a hill you climbed with gusto and boundless energy, somehow sure that what you would see at the crest would be the full glory of that dazzling Future you were always heading toward. In those days he would have been irresistibly curious about what the likes of Roger White, a black partner at Wringer Fleasom, wanted to see him about. But now he was not curious, not in the least, because he now knew that the golden glow at the top of the hill was merely the twilight at the rim of an abyss.

No, he only decided to go ahead and see the man out of loyalty to Inman. He had promised to do whatever he could to help, and maybe he would learn something Inman might want to know. Gloomily, with no zest left for the city and its great frays, he told Marguerite to go ahead and have the man come over here this afternoon.

EVER SINCE HIS conversation with Wes Jordan about Charlie Croker, Roger had been compiling a file on him, and quite a fat file it had become, a good two inches thick. Wringer Fleasom's research department had retrieved everything available on Nexus and Lexus, which was a lot but went back only as far as 1976. There was even more from before that, starting with Croker's days of football glory as Georgia Tech's "Sixty-Minute Man." You could tell by the endless photographs in the *Constitution* and the *Journal* and, for that matter, in *Time*, *Newsweek*, *Life*, and *Look*, you could tell that back in those days, the 1950s and early 1960s, Charlie Croker had seemed like a giant. At six-foot-two, 215 pounds, he had hit the line "like a runaway Trailways bus," wrote someone in the *Journal* in a typical, childishly exuberant sports-page simile of those days. The great Sixty-Minute Man . . . oh yes . . . It was hard for any black person to review all this adulation from forty years ago without getting into a resentful or at least a rueful state of mind. The great Charlie Croker had been a great *white* athlete of that period . . . which wasn't saying much. In retrospect it was obvious that up against any average Grambling or Morgan State football team of those days, the Georgia Tech Yellow Jackets and their Sixty-Minute Man wouldn't have lasted sixty seconds. No, to realize just how many black lives, how many black talents, had been wasted, doomed to obscurity even a full century after the Civil War, you only had to do what he had been doing: go over the sports pages from forty years ago and review all these inflated grayboy bubble reputations, such as Charlie Croker's. But that wasn't the worst of it. The worst of it had been going over a big article in *Atlanta* magazine that included a description of a visit to Croker's plantation, Turpmtine, down in Baker County, which was real Cracker country. There was a "Big House," as in the days of slavery. There was an "overseer" as in the days of slavery. There was a "master" of Turpmtine, as in the days of slavery. Croker's employees referred to him as "Cap'm Charlie." The writer was not so uncouth as to identify them as black, but it was perfectly clear that they were. No, this two-inch-thick Croker file made Roger's blood boil.

And now that the time had come to confront the man in person, his contempt was commingled with a touch of . . . apprehension. (He avoided using the word *fear*.) In photographs Croker reminded Roger of Coach Buck McNutter . . . the same massive, muscular hulk made even bigger by a thick coating of lard . . . the huge body and the tiny evil eyes . . . like the cruel plantation lords of old.

This . . . apprehension . . . was amplified when Roger got off the elevator on the thirty-ninth floor of the tower at Croker Concourse and looked through a pair of floor-to-ceiling glass doors adorned with great brass handles and saw the slab of granite or marble or whatever it was in front of the receptionist's desk incised with the words CROKER GLOBAL and the corporation's logo: a globe—the world—dominated by the enormous curving forms of a C and a G. When the glass doors, which must have been an inch thick, closed behind him, he felt he was now as deep into the alien country of Atlanta's white establishment as he had ever been in his life. He began to wonder just how much fury Croker would dare unleash when he revealed in all its newborn nakedness the suggestion that he say a few good words about Fareek "the Cannon" Fanon.

Roger was thankful for the clothes he had chosen to wear today, because if there was ever a time when he needed sartorial armor, it was right now. He had on a navy hard-finished worsted single-breasted suit, a shirt with white collar and cuffs and a body of pale blue stripes, a medium blue crêpe de chine necktie with tiny navy pin dots at half-inch intervals, and cap-toed black shoes. From his breast pocket debouched a plain white silk handkerchief. In Atlanta, white or black, north of Ponce de Leon or south of it, sartorial armor didn't get much more bulletproof than this.

The receptionist, a young white woman, checked him out from face to necktie to cap-toes. When he announced his name, the young woman smiled and told him to please take a seat; someone would be out very soon. He had just sat down in a leather armchair and was weighing the woman's promise to decide whether it was sincerity or a faux-polite runaround he had detected in her voice, when an older white woman did, indeed, emerge from somewhere beyond the receptionist's desk and invite him in. She led him through a small, windowless gallery that suddenly opened onto an enormous room. Light poured in, seemingly from all sides. Behind a desk so big it seemed like a satire on the executive life, in a great leather-covered swivel chair, sat the unmistakable Cracker bulk of Charlie Croker. With a heave of his chest, Croker rose and came walking—or, rather, limping—toward him. He seemed so much older than his pictures, and wearier. He gave Roger a smile, but it was a tired smile, and he had circles under his eyes. Yet he radiated physical power. He had on a white shirt and a dark red necktie, but no jacket. His neck, trapezius muscles, shoulders, and chest seemed to be a single unit-welded mass. They were so big, it was as if he were wearing a chest protector beneath his shirt. His hands were so big, Roger braced as they shook hands, for fear he might be another hearty bonecrusher, like Buck McNutter. Roger's hand disappeared inside this huge white man's, just as had been the case when he met McNutter, but in fact there was nothing unusual about the pressure Croker exerted.

Croker indicated that they should go to an alcove that opened off the big room and sit in a pair of low but plush leather swivel chairs. There were floor-to-ceiling windows. Down below in the foreground was a rolling thicket of green treetops that ran together so densely there was no sign whatsoever of the earth below, let alone the houses and roadways. The expanse of greenery was so vast and lush, it made you blink.

"Spectacular view!" said Roger.

Croker turned his head and looked at it himself for a moment, then turned back to Roger and said wearily, "Yeah . . . I reckon it is. The trouble with views is, after the first coupla weeks they don't surprise you anymore." Roger didn't know what to say to that, and so Croker continued: "I'd like to write a history of views, if I could write, which I can't." *Caint.* "If you look at Atlanta real estate long enough, you'll notice there was a time, not all that long ago, when folks didn't care about views one way or the other. Views came cheap as the air and a lot cheaper than dirt. Then along about the 1960s, I reckon it was, folks discovered views, and that gave everybody one more thing to get competitive about."

The man sounded like the Old Philosopher, wiser but wearier, a note Roger found disarming.

Croker sighed and said, "So you and Zandy White are partners—I mean *Scott!*" He shook his head and cast his eyes down, and said, "Nothing wrong with me. Godalmighty. Scott, Scott, Scott."

Roger tried to analyze *that* one. Was it a simple transposition, his name for Zandy's, or was it a Freudian slip that said, "He, Zandy, is white, but you're not"?

By now Croker had started over. "Okay, as I thought I was saying, so you and Zandy Scott are partners."

"Well, yes," said Roger, smiling to show he didn't care about the slip. "We're partners, although some partners are more equal than others. I don't know whether you know Zandy or not. I haven't mentioned to him that I was coming to see you." This was by way of notifying Croker that this was something Zandy Scott didn't know about and didn't have to know about. That, in turn, made him wonder what was on Croker's mind at this moment.

To tell the truth, Charlie was thinking about the fact that this black man—whose name, like an idiot, he had just pinned on a white man—had no black accent at all. He had begun to run across that more and more, especially since the Clarence Thomas Supreme Court hearings on television, when there you had one black person after another, professional people, and if you closed your eyes you couldn't tell if they were black or white.

"Well," Croker said, "what can I do for you?"

He said it with such a tired smile that Roger felt as if he was talking to someone who had come out on the losing end of a very long war.

"Mr. Croker," he said, realizing as soon as the words left his mouth that the little speech he had rehearsed was going to come out sounding stilted, "I represent a young athlete at Georgia Tech, a football player named Fareek Fanon."

"So I gather," said Croker. "I read about it in the paper this morning." He looked at Roger with a level and slightly suspicious gaze. Then he yawned and quickly covered his mouth with his hand. Roger was startled, taken aback, since he didn't realize that this was a sign not of boredom but of advanced insomnia.

"I assure you," Roger said, "that everything I've tried to do for my client thus far has been with an eye toward avoiding this kind of publicity, but that battle I've already lost." He sounded terribly pompous to himself. "So now my main objective is to try to keep this thing from turning into a racial battleground."

Charlie was busy trying to calculate where all this was leading. He decided that this solemn, somewhat stiff, educated black man was now going to ask him to intercede with Inman. The only interesting part would be listening to him trying to articulate the reasons why.

Lawyer White was sitting quite upright in the leather swivel chair. He had begun massaging the knuckles of his left hand with the fingers of his right hand . . . nerves . . . trying to figure out just how to put it, no doubt . . . Bathed in the light that came flooding in through the window wall, he didn't look very dark at all . . . almost pale, in fact . . .

"As you know," said Roger, "Fareek Fanon is an all-American running back, probably the most famous Georgia Tech running back since one named . . . Charles Croker." Just as he had rehearsed it, he paused and smiled warmly. To his dismay, Croker yawned again and covered his mouth. He could think of nothing else to do but plow on:

"So I'm sure you're aware—probably more aware than anyone else I can think of—of the pressures that suddenly converge on a young man when he has achieved fame of that magnitude, pressures of every sort, social pressures, public pressures, personal pressures—so that all at once you're vulnerable to forces you've never even thought about before, forces you were never even aware of."

He paused and looked at Croker, hoping to coax at least a nod of agreement out of him concerning that broad, general principle. All he saw was the big white man's mouth and mandibles twisting and struggling mightily to avoid another yawn. So he put the question squarely:

"Do you agree? Is that true, generally speaking?"

"Awwww, I reckon," said Croker. Then he lifted his hands from his lap and gave them a little ironic toss in the air and said, "And therefore?"

Is he mocking me? Roger wondered. Aloud, somewhat flustered: "Well, the thing is—we'd like for you to *meet* Fareek, spend a little time with him if you can, see what he's like, see if you agree with us—see if you think he's the kind of young man who would do what all these rumors and anonymous reports accuse him of doing."

Croker sighed, leaned back in his chair, and put on a big smile that was without any doubt ironic . . . and disconcerting . . . and then he said, "Who's *we*?"

Roger said, "Well—Fareek and a great many backers of the Tech athletic program and a great many people who look upon Fareek as a role model. This thing could turn into a very ugly situation even if—by the usual standards—the charge is proved to have no basis in fact, which in fact is the case." He was aware of tripping on his own verbal vines and thickets.

Croker gave his smile a twist to one side. Definitely ironic. "So . . . *we* want *me* to spend some time with Fareek Fanon . . ."

Roger's heartbeat quickened. This was going to be the tricky part to put into words. "We realize that . . . uh . . . this would be an imposition on you. It would be an imposition on anybody, but especially you, since we realize that you . . . uh . . . have far more urgent problems right now than the fate of Fareek Fanon. But we think we're in a position to clear the deck of those problems, so to speak, so that you'll have the time to . . . uh . . . devote some time to what we hope you'll be able to do." He paused again, desperately hoping Croker would at least come out and meet him halfway on this misty terrain he had just sketched in.

Croker cocked his head to one side and said, "What 'urgent problems' are you talking about?"

"May I speak frankly?"

"Sure. Go ahead."

"We're very much aware of the fix you're in with PlannersBanc. We're aware of what happened with your Gulfstream Five aircraft and other measures the bank is threatening to take." Croker still had his head cocked to one side. "Well—the fact is—if I can figure out the most exact way to put this—the fact is that Fareek, as an Atlanta celebrity with a big following, if you will, and various backers of Tech's athletic program have enough friends so as to . . . so as to . . . be able to convince PlannersBanc that it's . . . uh"—how the hell did this part go? He'd gone over it a hundred times in his mind—"that it's . . . in their interest—as a big part of the city themselves—in their long-term interest—and possibly their short-term interest, even—since this thing has the potential to rip apart the entire fabric of the Atlanta Way in race relations—it's in their interest to put your financial troubles behind you—and behind *them*—for good—so that you can devote your time and your interests to the role that you can now play in this crisis—or what could easily develop *into* a crisis, for the entire city." He was aware of the sweat that had begun to flow in his armpits, beneath his T-shirt, the striped body of his shirt, and his 12-ounce navy worsted suit with its fashionably high-cut armholes.

"Put them behind me *how?*" said Croker. He still had his head cocked to one side, but he wasn't giving him the ironic smile anymore. Perhaps he had taken a few baby steps out into the mist.

"Completely restructure the loans," said Roger. "And call off the bank's workout department."

Croker said, "All this in return for my spending some time with Fareek Fanon."

"*And* an expression of your sympathy and support for Fareek as someone who's been in precisely the same situation himself, at the same college, someone who was once a young man with the same pressures and vulnerabilities—I mean, *if* you genuinely feel that way after getting to know Fareek. I realize that's a big if."

"And just how would I go about expressing my sympathy and support?"

"A press conference."

"A press conference . . ."

"Yes."

"And then my troubles will disappear . . ."

"Well, obviously, it can't be as simple as that," said Roger, "since what actually hangs in the balance here is the concern of many important players in the civic life of this city—their desire to defuse what could develop into a very ugly situation for them and the Atlanta Way and . . . well, the whole city—but in a word, to answer your question . . . yes."

"So what would I do," said Croker, leaning forward in his seat and lowering his head slightly, "just take your word for it that you can deliver on such a promise?"

"I know what you're saying," said Roger, "and I don't blame you." All the while thinking: *Oh, yes! He's definitely out on that misty terrain now!* "There'll be a very simple test. Once you've met with Fareek, you decide whether or not to go ahead with the press conference. If you say yes, then you let us know, and *immediately* all pressure from PlannersBanc will cease. If you then do your part at the press conference, it will cease for good, and the bank will restructure the loans on the most generous terms imaginable. If you say no"—Roger drew in his chin and pulled a face that as much as said *They'll sic the dogs back on you.*

Croker put his tongue in his cheek and just stared at him for what seemed like an eternity. Then he said, "If I'm hearing what I think I'm hearing, then this is the goddamnedest proposition I ever heard of."

"Well," said Roger, "this is an unusual situation, and it *could* become a critical situation in the life of this city, especially if the identity of the young woman in this situation becomes known, and a lot of people know it already. Do you know who it is?"

Croker hesitated. Then he said, "Yes, I do."

Roger said, "A lot of people—a lot of people in a position to try to head it off—they see this as a situation like the Rodney King case or even the death of Martin Luther King, a situation where the city becomes polarized. Atlanta's claim is, we're the city that has put all that behind us. So if this city lets itself get polarized again, the implications, including the economic implications—there'd be just no end to it. So people are willing to go to great lengths to try to head such a situation off."

"Okay," said Croker, "let's say that's so." No more mocking smile. "How do you—we—they—whoever you're talking about here—how do you expect to put that kind of pressure on PlannersBanc?"

Roger said, "That I'm not at liberty to go into. That's why we're proposing a test. We can either deliver or we can't."

Croker crossed his arms over his chest and put on the sort of ironic smile that says: This is all pretty far-fetched, but since we're playing this little game of make-believe, let's play it out to the end. Aloud he said: "Okay, let's suppose that you manage to call off the dogs and then I go see Fareek Fanon and come away telling everybody what a great human being he is—how am I supposed to be sure PlannersBanc won't turn right around and come after me again?"

"Then you'd disavow your support for Fareek."

"On what ground? That some very nice young man came by one day"—Croker gestured toward Roger—"representing Fareek Fanon, and he told me he'd take care of everything if I said something nice about his client?"

"Whatever," said Roger. "Anything you said at that point would make it look bad for us. We'd have the same sort of recourse. If you reneged on your support for Fareek, the bank would be turned loose on you again. Look, Mr. Croker, even in the most tightly drawn contract there's always the risk of one party committing an act of betrayal that makes the contract meaningless. That's one of the first things we were taught at the UGA law school. All agreements are founded on the proposition that at the end of the day it doesn't pay to be known as someone who is utterly perfidious."

At the end of the day, thought Charlie. Even this black lawyer from UGA was lapsing into Wizspeak. Already his mind was churning. Was it even remotely possible that he could do what he claimed he could do? Who would have that kind of leverage with PlannersBanc? Certainly not him. And not even Wringer Fleasom & Tick, which was nothing but a high-class valet service for corporate Atlanta. His contempt for lawyers, people who made their living speaking out of any side of their mouths you paid them to speak out of, was profound. Assuming it wasn't all bullshit, who *was* he talking about? It had to be Georgia Tech itself. The Institute's leverage in Atlanta, if they really wanted to exert it, was incalulable. But why would they choose a relatively young black lawyer to rally the troops? That would make no sense. Or was there something about racial PR that he, Charlie, didn't comprehend? And was Fanon so important to them that they would just hang Inman and his daughter out to dry? Did it really get back to what Billy Bass had told him that night at Turpmtine—namely, that Fareek Fanon was the cover boy for the Institute's entire capital fund-raising campaign and that money talks and bullshit walks? *Money talks and bullshit walks.* Ruefully he realized that he had picked up that little expression from that character with the big melon chin, Zale, at the PlannersBanc workout session. And what if he *did* endorse Fareek Fanon? How could he ever look Inman in the face again? Twice he had offered Inman his support—*offered* it—once that night at the Driving Club and again yesterday morning. No, he could never turn his back on Inman . . . But . . . *still* . . . think of the *miracle* that was being dangled before him . . . the obliteration of his entire mountain of debt!

As if reading his mind, the black lawyer said, "I can't stress it too strongly, Mr. Croker—the crux of the matter is that this thing involves far more than any one person's reputation—more than Fareek Fanon's, just to start with my client. You would be rendering a public service by expressing sympathy for Fareek even if you didn't mean it, even if it turns out you don't like him, which I hope won't be the way it'll turn out. To have someone like yourself in his corner would defuse the whole situation, keep it from turning into an outright black versus white issue. We're not talking about any legal process here. We're talking about the . . . the . . . the mental atmosphere of an entire city."

"But why me?" said Charlie.

"I'm not gonna try to pussyfoot around the subject, Mr. Croker. You're in a unique position. You're the Fareek Fanon of another period, a star running back for Georgia Tech and in some ways an even bigger star, since you also starred on defense, and you were known as the Sixty-Minute Man and everything." (Even though it was coming from a black mouthpiece, a special pleader, Charlie liked this warm breeze wafting by his ears.) "And you're a member of the white establishment in this city. You're a member of the Piedmont Driving Club and everything else that's worth belonging to. You're not some push-button liberal. You're uniquely qualified to do what has to be done."

In spite of himself, Charlie could feel himself weakening, feel himself *trying to believe* all this arrant flattery pouring out of this slick black lawyer. So he fought back. His sense of loyalty, his sense of honor, his strength of character in the face of temptation—well, not counting *sexual* temptation, which a man really had no rational control over—his personal courage, which had never deserted him, not even in the deadliest moments on the field of battle in Vietnam—all of this would make him do the right thing, and—but of course at the same time it wouldn't *hurt,* would it, as a matter of curiosity, as a sheer experiment, to see if this lawyer dressed up like a British diplomat actually *could* control the workout department at PlannersBanc with a mere snap of his fingers, implausible as that sounded—it wouldn't hurt to *see* if such a stunt could be pulled, would it?—wouldn't *compromise* him in any way, wouldn't *force* him to support Fareek "the Cannon" Fanon if he didn't want to, wouldn't even force him to lay eyes on the man—

—and so before he knew it, he heard himself saying: "All right . . . If you want my honest opinion, not you and not Fareek Fanon and not anybody who *knows* Fareek Fanon and not all of Georgia Tech and all of Georgia Tech's friends, working together, can pull off what you say you can pull off. But maybe I'll give you a chance to prove me wrong." He smiled his biggest, broadest, most insinuating smile, to indicate that this was merely a little game he was interested in. "I'll go see Mr. Fanon, and then I'll let you know what I think. Fair enough?"

"Fair enough, Mr. Croker. I hope you'll like Fareek and give him the benefit of the doubt. For a kid from the Bluff, he's done pretty well. He's not polished, he's not sophisticated, and he's susceptible to temptation, like all of us, but he's been a good kid. Never been in trouble with the law, never been in any kind of disciplinary trouble at Tech—

given the strikes he's had against him, he's done pretty well." To himself he said: "Jesus Christ . . . between now and then we gotta put Fareek in some kinda . . . Courtesy Boot Camp! We gotta get him some new clothes—out of the Ralph Lauren catalogue! We gotta get the diamonds out of his ears!—the sneer off his lips!—the shanks-akimbo spread out of the way he sits in a chair!—the Homeboy Hangin' in Fronta the 24-Hour Mini-Mart slouch out of his posture!—the Rape! Pillage! Loot! leer out of his eyes! But something tells me a cosmetic makeover is all we really need . . . Something tells me the Sixty-Minute Man has already taken the hook."

"Aw, hell, I'll give anybody the benefit of the doubt, far's that goes," said Croker. "I didn't exactly grow up in any palace myself."

He smiled more broadly than ever, as if to show that he regarded all this as nothing more than a game.

ATLANTA WAS NOT one of those older cities, such as New York, Boston, Seattle, or, for that matter, Paris, London, or Munich, in which the smart restaurants were to be found in the middle of town or on the fringes of old residential districts. No, in Atlanta both Downtown and Midtown, as they were called, shut up tight at 6 p.m. Monday through Friday and all day Saturday and Sunday, with their soaring towers standing there like glass ghosts. The only strollers on the streets at night downtown were hotel guests utterly thwarted in their desire to go window-shopping at the big city's glossy restaurants and boutiques—them and the muggers. The Atlanta police had their own name for areas where it wasn't advisable to walk if you looked like you had more than two cents to rub together: "dead zones"; and Downtown was one of them.

No, in Atlanta the smart restaurants, like the smart boutiques, opened in Atlanta's Edge Cities (as the inimitable Joel Garreau had called them), commercial clusters that formed in and around shopping malls and other big mixed-use developments far removed from Downtown and its tired old problems. So it was that Peepgass had decided to take Martha Croker to dinner at a restaurant all the way over at the West Paces Ferry Mall, a place called Mordecai's, which was recommended by all the restaurant guides.

This decision had presented Peepgass with two big problems. For a start, he had to rent a car. At first he thought of having Martha meet him at the restaurant. That way, presumably, she would never have to know which of the cars in this mall full of cars was his. She wouldn't have to learn that he drove a five-year-old Ford Escort with a big dent in the left front fender which he couldn't afford to have fixed because his insurance policy had a $500 deductible. But making her drive solo to a shopping mall at night would not create the effect he needed to create. So he had started calling the car rental companies, Hertz, Avis, Budget, Alamo, the lot. The only vehicles they offered at even halfway humane rates were as dinky as his Ford Escort, even if newer. If you elevated your sights to the plateau of full-size sedans, you were talking about a fortune and still getting nothing more than a Ford Taurus or a Chevrolet Lumina. So he had to go luxury full-size, an appalling $92 a day, for the car he had tonight, a black Volvo 960 with veal-beige leather seats. Then there was the restaurant. Mordecai's had just reopened after a complete renovation, and was the restaurant the social bees (*le tout Atlanta*) were currently "hiving" about—to use a term he had picked up the other day from Jack Shellnutt, his only live source of information about such matters—and so there was no way he was going to get out of there for less than $80 for two. So you had $172 right there. A guy like Shellnutt, of course, would say, *Big deal—$172*, but the plain fact was that to Peepgass it was yet another toehold missing on the face of a cliff that was terrifyingly high and to which he was already clinging for dear life. He now had twenty-two different VISA cards, and nineteen of them he had already run out to the absolute limit of their credit line. His only hope was that yet more unsolicited VISA card applications would arrive in the mail—he seemed to receive at least two a month—and he would have a little more rope to ponzi around with. The problem was that the monthly interest nut *all by itself* was more than he could handle. He was having to kite checks between PlannersBanc, SouthBank, BancCharter, and BancoHijoChico, where he also had accounts, in order to keep halfway current on the interest owed the VISA accounts. One VISA card, he noticed, had been issued by a bank called JoshuaTree Federal, in Tempe, Arizona. He felt far more at ease—irrationally so, he realized—dealing with pueblo desert lunatics like that than with the many Delaware banks whose cards he also had.

And so this outing, ordinary as it might have seemed to a Jack Shellnutt or to so many of his neighbors to the north of Collier Hills in the *real* Buckhead, was to Peepgass a dizzyingly wild leap that only his red dog could have made him do.

Attired in his one new shirt, his new Sincere necktie, and his one halfway decent suit, the gray one he could get by with as long as he never let her view it from the back, where the shiny spots were, Peepgass pulled up to Martha Croker's house on Valley Road in his one-night-stand-$92-a-day Volvo 960. As soon as he escorted her out to the car, he noticed something different about her. She looked great, given what she had to work with, namely, her mileage, fifty-three years, and the heft she had across her back and shoulders . . . When she got out of the Volvo at the West Paces Ferry Mall, he tried to study her a little more . . . There was something so damned gloomy about dinner at these fancy restaurants in the mall. It was so damned dark, since all the shops were closed. The light of the overhead lamps was soaked up by the blacktop of the parking lot, so that nothing more than a pallid gloaming remained. But in this American Mall artificial twilight, once he got used to it, Martha Croker looked . . . not bad at all . . . A white skirt . . . pretty short, that skirt, for a woman her age, but you know what? Great legs . . . If all you saw were her legs, you'd think she was twenty or twenty-five years younger . . . And inside, when they sat down—at a pretty good table, not too far back—she really looked different . . . leaner . . . a long-sleeved navy silk blouse with these sort of flame-like white shapes in it . . . a choker of ivory ovals framed in gold . . . gold earrings . . . her blond hair done *just so* . . .

He was suddenly conscious of the way he was just sitting there staring at her, and so he smiled and said, "Well, what do you make of this Fareek Fanon business?"

Of the fifty-four tables at Mordecai's—and the place was packed—at least forty-five accommodated white Atlantans who right now were, or just had been, or soon would be, talking about Fareek Fanon and what he had or had not done with an anonymous flower of Atlanta's white establishment. Christ, it was noisy in here! All restaurants these days were noisy, but the noise in here was what he imagined (and intended never to find out) it would be like to go white-water rafting in some vicious river like the Columbia. Peepgass had to lean across the table toward Martha to hear what she was saying.

"I don't know what to think," she said, "but I must say it has me curious about who this white 'business and civic leader' might be, the one whose daughter she's supposed to be."

"I'll tell you what I'm curious about," said Peepgass. "I'm curious about why all these black athletes have such a thing for white women."

Martha Croker just lifted her eyebrows and shrugged her shoulders.

So Peepgass figured he ought to get off that street . . . Talking about black people was a delicate business in upper-stratum white Atlanta, particularly if the subject moved onto the terrain of racial . . . *tendencies* . . . Even though everybody (*le tout Atlanta*) was wild about the topic, you had to walk a very narrow, very academic, sociological, disinterested line, or else you were guilty of . . . a breach of etiquette. It was sheer . . . bad manners. It showed poor . . . intellectual upbringing. But how could one *not* talk about the Fareek Fanon case? And how easy it was for one's hunger for every morsel about the case to push one over that narrow line!

Peepgass glanced about. So many animated white faces! The white-water rush of the diners had reached something approaching a roar. In decor, Mordecai's was curiously grand, stiff, gloomy, musty, austere, and ostentatious all at the same time, like one of those doges' palaces in Venice, where everything seems to have been soaked in the gray-green water of the canals five centuries ago and hung out to dry . . . slowly . . . century by century . . .

As for Martha, she wanted to talk about the Fareek Fanon case, too, but Ray's—she already thought of him as "Ray"—Ray's comment had suddenly reminded her of those Saturday nights at Turpmtine when Charlie and Billy Bass and Judge Opie McCorkle and the other good old Baker County boys would belt back a few bourbons and branch water and get on the subject of race and lean forward toward each other and mouth the radioactive words in their discourse in the mistaken belief that what they were saying would not be picked up by the black help who went back and forth from the kitchen and so attentively attended to their every need.

She noticed Ray scanning the room with his eyes, and so she looked about, too. Over near the entrance she noticed Mordecai's owner, a man named Jack Kashi, in a dark double-breasted suit and a very loud tie, hovering over a table for six and bathing it in his famous bonhomie. She, Martha, had walked right past him on the way in, had looked him right in the eye, and his eyes had bounced a couple of times off hers. He knew he knew her, but he didn't know who she was—so he had turned away suddenly as if responding to someone behind him. She couldn't believe it! She had been at Charlie's side at least a dozen times when they dined here, and the man had fawned over the two of them . . . "Mr. Croker! Mrs. Croker—and now he didn't even have a clue who she was! Well, who was he spending all his time paying attention to tonight? A great big man with carefully coiffed blond hair—could it be—that was *exactly* who it was!

"Ray!" she exclaimed. "You'll never guess who's here tonight!"

"Who?"

"Don't turn around all of a sudden, but right behind you, about four tables away, up near the entrance, a table for six—that's Buck McNutter, Buck McNutter and his wife."

Ray slowly turned about, then glanced back at Martha. "Which one is him?"

"The immense one with the cute blond hairdo."

Ray took a good look, then turned back around. "I'll be damned. I wouldn't mind listening in on *that* conversation. You know him?"

"I've never met him, but I met his wife once."

Ray said, "Which one's the wife?"

"The youngest one," said Martha. "With the hair."

Ray turned around again and took another good look. Then he turned back with a grin and said, "I see what you mean. You think if we sent them a bottle of champagne, they'd tell us the name of the girl in the Fanon case?"

A terribly severe-looking waiter, or captain he probably was, arrived and asked if they'd like something to drink. Martha asked for a Kir royale, which Peepgass had never heard of. All he knew was that it sounded expensive. He ordered a glass of red wine, figuring that would be the cheapest thing in the house short of a split of sparkling water. Mordecai's was the sort of restaurant in which, when you sit down, there's an elaborate silver plate sitting right in front of you. As soon as they bring you a drink, they take it away. Peepgass had no idea what that was all about, but to him it, too, spelled expensive.

In due course the dour-looking captain returned—he *had* to be a captain—returned with menus, very formal menus, which arrived inserted into stiff leather bindings. The oppressive atmosphere of expense weighed even more heavily upon Peepgass. With dread he took a glance at the entrees . . . all over $20. He didn't kid himself. In a place like this, when the entrees were more than $20, you knew you were heading up toward . . . not a mere $80 for two, but more like $100.

Martha ordered smoked salmon on rectangles of ciabatta bread to start—Peepgass winced: $8.50—and blackened red snapper on a bed of kale leaves and dilled mashed potatoes—winced again: $26.50—Jesus Christ, no wonder she was hefty through the torso. He ordered the cheapest first course he could get away with, which was tortellini al brodo, some kind of soup, apparently, for $5.50, and a pasta as his main course: risotto with sectioned baby octopus—$18.50—but he knew he couldn't down the goddamned risotto and octopus without a bottle of nice cold wine to take the edge off it, and so he suddenly found himself ordering a bottle of Rushers Quarry California Chardonnay for $36, which blew all his economizing right out of the water—his facile mind, which had scored 780 out of a possible 800 on the math SATs, realized immediately that they had now ordered $95 worth of food and drink plus the Kir royale and the glass of red wine, which would certainly bring it up *over* $100, and they hadn't even gotten to dessert and coffee and the tax—but—but—but . . . what the hell . . . Thank God he had a brand-new VISA card with him, from some bank called FirstButte in Mission Creek, Colorado.

He knocked back two glasses of the Rushers Quarry California Chardonnay, and she knocked back one, all so fast that he could foresee the necessity of ordering a *second* bottle in no time, at which point he decided to give up and maintain an even strain and let FirstButte eat the bill. They talked a little more about the Fareek Fanon case, which in turn got them to talking about how absolutely sports-crazed Atlanta was, and Martha told him about some Neanderthal judge down in Baker County who had sat on the fifty-yard line for every Georgia Tech–University of Georgia football game for the past fifty years, she was sure, and he asked her if Charlie had been hung up on his memories of gridiron greatness. Not really, she said, but other people were. Total strangers, older people mostly, still recognized him on the street and referred to him as the Sixty-Minute Man, and Charlie did enjoy that. Peepgass had to lean farther and farther across the table, to within a foot of her face, just to hear her over the din of the place.

"Speaking of Charlie . . ." said Peepgass. He figured that was a smooth enough transition to what, for him, was the underlying agenda for this back-breakingly expensive evening. "I have some interesting news about Croker Concourse."

"Really?" She didn't seem terribly keen about any protracted discussion of her former husband.

Peepgass leaned forward and said, "Charlie is about to hand over Croker Concourse and the other properties, and we'll let him keep Turpmtine and his house on Blackland Road and the Wyeth painting."

"What's he going to use for money? Do you have any idea what it costs to run Turpmtine?"

"Not exactly."

"Close to two million dollars a year."

"He has it on the books as an 'experimental farm,' " said Peepgass.

"I don't doubt that," said Martha, "but the only experiment I've ever seen at Turpmtine is Charlie trying to see if he can go through a whole day of shooting quail, from dawn to dusk, and shoot only the males."

"How do you tell the male from the female?"

"It's not easy. The male has a little fleck of white on his neck." She touched the front of her own neck.

Peepgass said, "I bet he's rolled every cent he's spent on the place right into his corporate tax deductions."

"Probably," said Martha.

Peepgass experienced the *Aha!* phenomenon. If necessary, he'd confront Croker with an income tax problem. The IRS would no doubt be delighted to learn that he had written off millions—*millions!*—in personal expenses in the form of a nonexistent experimental farm.

"Anyway," said Peepgass, "there's been an interesting development regarding Croker Concourse. This I'm not supposed to be telling anybody, either, but I think you have a legitimate right to know. I guess the word has gotten out that Croker Concouse may be up for sale, because a syndicate is being formed to approach the bank with an offer."

"A syndicate?"

"A group of investors," said Peepgass. "The leading figures—but this really does have to remain confidential." He looked at her inquiringly.

"All right."

"The leading figures, the people putting the whole thing together, are Herbert Richman and Julius Licht."

Both Jews, thought Martha, without even knowing why it occurred to her. She started to say so out loud but caught herself and thought better of it. What she said was "I go to one of his gyms, Herbert Richman's. DefinitionAmerica, on East Paces Ferry Road."

"Do you know Herb Richman?" said Peepgass.

"No, I don't think I've ever met him," said Martha. She started to add, "He's Jewish, isn't he?"—but once again she caught herself. All this took place beneath the threshold of rational thought, in much the same way that Herbert Richman, if someone had mentioned the name Martha

Croker, would have said to himself, "She's not Jewish." Such was the way things still went in Atlanta.

"Well, he's met Charlie," said Peepgass, "just a couple of weeks ago. You know Herb's Jewish, don't you?"

"I suppose—no, I didn't." As if the thought had never crossed her mind.

"Charlie invited him down for a weekend at Turpmtine."

"Is that how Richman found out that Croker Concourse might be for sale, from Charlie?"

"I don't know," said Peepgass, "but I doubt it. I don't think Charlie has fully faced up yet to the fact that he's gonna lose a lot of property. Anyway, here's what Herb Richman and his syndicate would do—and again, I'm really not supposed to be telling anybody about this, but I think it's something you might want to know."

He proceeded to outline the deal—leaving out only the matter of the $6.5 million he stood to make from it. "Now, I don't know anything about your financial situation, beyond Charlie's obligations to you under the terms of the divorce agreement, but you might want to consider getting in on this."

"Me?"

"I think you ought to ask yourself where it leaves you if Charlie is to all intents and purposes dead broke."

Martha didn't say anything. She just looked at him. Suddenly she was acutely aware of the ecstatic hyperburble of all the voices in this week's restaurant of the century. The fact was, she couldn't even imagine her own financial situation if there was no check for $50,000 each month. That had always been the least of her concerns about Charlie. What was that compared to the fact that he had deceived and discarded her? Exactly!—nothing more or less than that—discarded her!—as a superannuated piece of baggage!

"Look at it this way," said Ray. "The reason Charlie's going broke is that he totally lost his head over this building of his, this great monument to himself, Croker Concourse. Do you realize that no other developer in the history of Atlanta has ever named a building after himself before!"

Martha started to tell him exactly why Charlie had suffered such an inflation of himself. He had just started his affair with Serena and wanted to show her that despite his age, he had the confidence and puissance of Youth. But she was loath to let Ray know just how profoundly humiliated she had been. So all she said was:

"Oh, I know . . . When Charlie loses his head over something, he loses it all the way."

Ray said, "What I'm suggesting is—and it may not interest you at all—but what I'm suggesting is that if Charlie has created a situation in which he can't come through with what he owes you, in cash, you have the right to follow his money where it's disappeared to, namely, into that building."

Martha's first reaction had nothing to do with the content of what he had just said. Rather, it was that she . . . liked him more this way. He now seemed . . . more of a man. He was no Charlie, but he had Charlie's passion for *the deal*, which was perhaps where the contemporary male's passion for battle went these days. She studied his face as his lips moved. He was actually a good-looking man, and his passion for the deal put an edge on the softness that you initially detected in a man like this. His clothes were a mixture of the slightly seedy and the slightly gaudy, but this was a period in which men's clothes were pretty dreadful all the way around. Charlie hadn't been much of a dresser, either, but his sheer massive physical presence had made that not matter.

Peepgass could see Martha Croker studying his face, and it made him apprehensive. Was she merely confused or did she fear a trick, some sort of swindle? Maybe she was thinking, If I'm going to be cut off from Charlie's money, why should I throw a lot of what I have left into some speculative real estate deal? So he said:

"Look, I can't engrave anything in stone, but here's a chance to triple or quadruple an investment in two to three years, and it would be taxed as a long-term capital gain. Richman and Licht are ready to invest $2.5 million each, and they're not speculators. As businessmen, they're both conservative. Richman won't even take DefinitionAmerica public, for fear of losing control, and do you have any idea of what that company would be worth as an IPO? *Whahhhhhh*," he added, by way of emphasizing the sheer visceral impact of such an idea.

"Well, I couldn't begin to put up $2.5 million," Martha Croker said.

"No one would expect you to," said Peepgass. "They're putting up approximately half the down payment themselves, and they're looking for other investors to put up the rest. I'm sure it wouldn't make any difference to them how big a share you went in for. And I . . ." He hesitated and turned his eyes downward, then turned them up again, as if this ocular pitch and roll were a product of emotion. "Well, frankly —I don't mean to say anything out of line, but I think it would be poetic justice, and no more than you deserve, if Charlie had to give up the building entirely—and believe me, that he's going to have to do—and you became one of the owners." He looked at her with Sincerity engraved upon his face.

To Martha the scheme—the investment—the odds—the risks—were remote matters she would have to think about later. What she comprehended at this moment was that here was a man who seemed to care about her fate.

"I don't know," she said. "I'd have to think about it. I'd have to think about how much I could possibly commit to something like that."

It struck Peepgass that she said it sort of dreamily. What that could mean, he couldn't imagine. Well, she didn't say *no*! She held it out as a possibility! Suppose she put up one million . . . His facile head for figures ran it through the intracranial chemical analog computer in no time . . . She'd come away with $7 million, not counting the commissions . . . He'd have $6.5 million . . . Add them together, along with Martha's other $9 million, and you've got $22 million . . . invest it conservatively, at 6 percent, and you'd have $1.3 million per year in income . . . plus a house in the very best part of Buckhead already paid for and decorated to the hilt . . . You could live a damned good life in Atlanta . . . A damned good life *any*where! . . . Peepgass! What are you thinking! The woman's fifty-three years old, for Christ's sake! What about Priapus? Doesn't *he* have any say in all this?

Peepgass was suddenly aware that a couple, a man and a woman, who were heading toward the entrance, had stopped by their table. He looked up. Both were beaming down at Martha. Lots of teeth. The woman, close to fifty, a carefully coiffed helmet of pineapple-blond hair, slender, nice angular features, handsome as opposed to beautiful, which she once must have been, expensive-looking cream tweed jacket and skirt, about 500 watts of jewelry—the man, slightly older, a big rectangular face resting upon a set of buttery jowls, good head of silvery hair combed straight back, not one cilium out of place, as if he just emerged from the locker room of the Augusta Country Club, navy cashmere blazer and a striped tie lying as if they lived there on the heft of his sirloin midsection, *lots* of teeth—

"Martha!" said the woman, shrieking to be heard above the roar of the rapids.

"Why—Adele!" said Martha Croker. "And Jock!"

"I *thought* that was you I saw across the room!" said Adele. "I feel like I haven't seen you in ages!" Then she glanced toward Peepgass.

"Adele!" said Martha Croker, "I'd like for you to meet Ray Peepgass! Ray, Adele Gilchrist! . . . and Jock Gilchrist!"

Peepgass struggled to his feet, while Adele Gilchrist made protestations to the effect that he shouldn't get up. He put on a big smile and shook hands with both of them. A hearty, deep-voiced Jock Gilchrist began compressing Peepgass's knuckles in a manly handshake.

Meantime, Adele was shrieking to Martha Croker, "Have you been here before!"

"No! . . . Have you?"

"Once!" said Adele. "It's too noisy! But I love the food! Please, sit down, Ray! I didn't mean for you—"

"Oh, not at all!" said Peepgass.

"Jock, we've got to let these people finish their dinner! But anyway, it's so nice to see you, Martha! You must give me a call! Ray, it's so nice to meet you! Have fun!"

As the pair made their way toward the front, Martha Croker began laughing soundlessly. This made Peepgass smile. "What's funny?"

"Oh, nothing," said Martha Croker. "I was just thinking of the last time I saw Adele Gilchrist. It's not very interesting, and it would take too long to go into."

"That's not Gilchrist of Cary Gilchrist, is it?"

"Yes, it is. That's Jock."

Peepgass whistled to himself. Cary Gilchrist was one of the biggest investment banking firms in the South.

Martha began chuckling to herself again. Peepgass started to ask her why again, but he figured she would tell him if she wanted to. So he just stared at her quizzically.

Martha was tempted to tell him . . . Two weeks ago, at DefinitionAmerica, she and Adele had been in Mustafa Gunt's class, and Adele had cut her dead. No, *cut* indicated an act of volition, and this had not been a cruel and willful act. The truth was that she had *ceased to even see her,* as if socially she, Martha, had disintegrated and no longer existed, all because she was no longer attached to the great Charlie Croker. But now that she had popped up in this week's restaurant of the century with a rather good-looking man, she had become resubstantiated, if there was such a word, was once again corporeal, a woman whose life suddenly stimulated curiosity in the likes of Adele Gilchrist, who no doubt wanted to ascertain just who it was that the long since vanished and long since vanquished Martha Croker was out on the town with. Oh, she was tempted to tell Ray. But if she cared to see more of Mr. Raymond Peepgass—and she realized that indeed she did—it would be far wiser not to reveal the depths of her humiliations.

Still chuckling silently, she said to Ray, "I'm sorry, it's just that Adele's so two-faced. But it's too petty to go into."

Peepgass couldn't have cared less about Adele Gilchrist's two faces. Martha was on a first-name basis with people like Jock Gilchrist. She not only had a mansion on Valley Road, she could take a man immediately, socially, into the upper strata of Atlanta. In an era like this one, the twentieth century's *fin de siècle*, position was everything, and it was the hardest thing to get. Once you had position . . . there were innumerable places to go for . . . life's merely carnal delights.

XXIV

Chapter

Gridiron Heroes

HABERSHAM ROAD . . . HABERSHAM ROAD . . . IT WAS ONLY A stone's throw from his old house on Valley Road, where Martha still lived, but that was only a fleeting thought. Much more on Charlie's mind was the fact that it was less than a quarter of a mile from Inman's house on Tuxedo Road . . . A stab of guilt, one among many he had endured since promising to go to Buck McNutter's house to meet Fareek Fanon . . . He was slowly tooling along Habersham in his Cadillac, not in any hurry for this rendezvous, thankful that it was now almost dark by 8:30 p.m. He didn't want to have to think of any nosy souls peering out the windows of any of the palatial piles in this golden swath of Buckhead, just off West Paces Ferry Road, saying, "There goes Charlie Croker to Buck McNutter's house. I wonder why."

He realized that was paranoid of him, and he was not the paranoid type. But that was what betrayal did to you; it made you run untrue to form. *No!* He kept telling himself, "I'm not betraying Inman by just going to *meet* this clown. I haven't *committed* myself to any particular course of action. I may even find out something that will *help* Inman." But in his heart he knew the plain truth: he was . . . *tempted*.

He flicked on the Cadillac's high beams, the better to see the house numbers, which were always on or near the mailboxes at the foot of the ever-green, ever-groomed lawns . . . There it was . . . Dogwood, magnolias, chestnut trees, and Japanese maples adorned the lawn in such profusion he couldn't see the house at first. But as the Cadillac ascended the steep, curving asphalt driveway and came closer—he could scarcely believe it. Langhorn Epps's old house! Lang Epps, who had inherited a fortune in Southern Railway stock and been president of the Piedmont Driving Club and the chairman of every charity drive you could think of, possessor of the Oldest Money you could find in Atlanta, no two ways about it—that was his old house, built in the French château style—all those casement windows—and now the Georgia Tech football coach had it! He, Charlie, loved the game of football, but Jesus Christ!—the world was changing too fast—

—a wave of self-loathing . . . He himself was changing too fast . . . Inman—but he hadn't been disloyal to Inman in any way. He couldn't control the future, but he could control his own conduct—

He stopped thinking about it, pushed it out of his mind. McNutter had quite a border of liriope around the loop of asphalt in front of the house. Charlie pulled up behind a silver-gray four-door Lexus sedan. A $65,000 car. He wondered whose it was. McNutter's? Lawyer White's? Fareek Fanon's? Given the cockeyed nature of everything these days, it just might be Fanon's.

Laboriously he got out of the car, wincing from the pain of his right knee as he tried to steady it beneath his 235 pounds, and went limping over to the door, wondering how much of the pain was psychological, how much of it shot down to his knee from his guilt-riddled brain. He rang the doorbell, and in less than ten seconds the door opened—and there stood a startling vision: a young woman with a head of blond hair as full and meticulously untamed as Serena's, a long-sleeved chiffon silk blouse with sprays of many colors against a deep purple background, open at the throat and plunging down to a deep cleavage.

"Mr. Croker!" She lowered her head, so that her eyes had to open a mile wide to look into his, and gave him a sly smile that promised the devil knew what. "Come in! I'm Val McNutter!" She put out her hand, and he shook it.

"They're in there," she said, motioning to a doorway off to one side. "But first I just have to tell you something." She paused, and her big insinuating eyes compelled him to ask what.

"What's that?"

"I had lunch at your Cosmos Club the other day—and I absolutely adored it! I could've stayed there all afternoon!"

"Well," said Charlie, "I'm glad to hear that. But I'm afraid that puts you in the minority."

She looked at him as if his very words were an aphrodisiac. If he hadn't been in such a depressed frame of mind, he would have felt a bit of the old tingle.

Then she said, "May I get you something to drink?"

Charlie's throat was terribly dry, which he realized was a sign of nervousness. In his depressed state, alcohol helped at first, but after an hour or so only depressed him more. But he decided he needed help right now. The short-term gain—or the long-term loss? The hell with the long term. He wasn't even sure he would last that long. He wanted help now.

"Well," he said as offhandedly as he could, "wouldn't mind a tall Scotch-and-soda, if'at idd'n too much trouble."

"Not a'tall. Come on in here and I'll go get it for you." She led him to the doorway of a room off the hall, stuck her head inside, and said, "Buck? Mr. Croker's here."

The doorway was suddenly filled with the huge familiar figure of Buck McNutter—familiar not because Charlie had once met him, literally just that, met him, shook hands and exchanged a couple of pleasantries at a Tech reunion, but because he had so often seen the man's smooth bulk and curiously fussy silver-blond hairdo on television and in the newspapers. The big man flashed him a grin and exclaimed, "Hey, Charlie!"—as if that one meeting had made them lifelong but long-time-no-see friends—and thrust out his hand and gave him a handshake that made him think his knuckles were being crushed. Two could play that game. Charlie squeezed back, using all the strength of his muscles. The two men stood there, an exquisitely balanced picture of giants in pain. McNutter unclenched first and said, "Great to see you, Charlie! Come on in here and meet some folks!"

The room was paneled in so much heavy, ornate dark wood it seemed to absorb every lumen of available light. It was a second or two before he fully took in the forms of the other two men. One, on his feet and smiling cordially, was Lawyer Roger White, once again decked out like an ambassador on an official visit. The other was a much younger, much darker black man with a shaved head, who sat sprawled on a tufted leather couch. McNutter turned toward him and glowered, and the young man slowly rose, as if weighed down by the weariness of the ages, and stared at a point beyond Charlie and McNutter as if his only interest in this weary world lay far removed from the walls of Château McNutter and the rolling green lawns of Buckhead.

"Charlie," McNutter was saying, "I believe you know Roger White?"

So Charlie and Lawyer White shook hands and smiled cordially.

"And, Charlie, this is Fareek Fanon. Fareek, Charlie Croker."

As he extended his hand, Charlie gave this now-notorious all-American a once-over. The ears . . . He had been told that the Cannon had pierced ears with a diamond set in each lobe and wore a heavy gold necklace. But there was no jewelry at all. He was slightly taller than Charlie and had very wide shoulders, made even wider by the suit he was wearing, a dark blue double-breasted suit with the lapel rolled down to the bottom button. It looked to Charlie like a felony suit, the sort of dark blue suit defense lawyers put on their clients when they go to trial. He wore a white shirt whose collar looked as if it had never been properly introduced to the big powerful neck it had been buttoned around and a necktie with wavy navy-and-gray stripes running vertically. He was giving Charlie a wary look typical of his generation, white, black, or whatever else: the Felony Hangdog. You tuck your chin down toward your clavicle, turn your head fifteen or twenty degrees to the side, and look warily at the adult confronting you, as if you've just committed a felony. You also offer only your first name during the introduction, as if you might be a drug dealer. Gloriously bored, Fareek Fanon presented Charlie a limp hand.

"Hey, Fareek," said Charlie, "nice to meetcha. Howya doin'?"

His head still in the Hangdog, Fareek "the Cannon" Fanon didn't offer so much as a polite smile. He merely compressed his lips and nodded. He had everything but a sign around his neck reading DON' WANNA.

"Have a seat, Charlie!" said McNutter in a voice about 20 percent cheerier than necessary, indicating an easy chair that had been pulled up near one end of the couch. Roger White sat down in the chair at the other end, and McNutter sat in a chair facing the young athlete.

Still beaming, McNutter looked at Charlie and said, "I was just telling Fareek how they used to call you the Sixty-Minute Man. How *did* that happen?—I mean you playing the whole game, defense and offense."

Fareek broke in: "That's the truth? That's what they called you, 'the Sixty-Minute Man'?" Fareek had a big grin on. At first Roger took this as a sign he was warming to the task.

"Well"—*wale*—"you know how the newspapers dream these things up," said that model of modesty Charlie Croker.

"Hunnnhhhh," said Fareek with a dismissive chortle, while his smile turned into a sneer. "Then you be the one that song's about."

"What song?" said Charlie.

" 'The Sixty-Minute Man,' " said Fareek. He began to hum it. 'Hoo hanh hoo hum hah heyyyyy, Sixty-Minute Man.' "

"What's it about?" said McNutter, who now had a desperate smile on his face.

"It's about this dude can keep a bitch happy for sixty minutes without stopping. 'Hoo hanh hoo hum hah heyyyyy, Sixty-Minute Man.' More sneering and grinning. "Zat what they meant?"

Long silence.

McNutter turned back to Charlie and said, "What *was* it like, playing sixty minutes of Division I football?—or what we'd call Division I today?"

"Hoo hanh hoo hum hah heyyyyy, Sixty-Minute Man," Fareek sang softly, as if to himself.

"Oh, I wasn't the only one," said Charlie, looking toward McNutter. "It was kind of a transition period between the old rules, when if you left the game you couldn't come back in until the next quarter, and the new rules, with platooning." Taking a chance and looking toward Fanon with a Charlie Croker winning smile, he said, "It helped to be a little crazy, I mean wantin' to butt heads for the whole sixty minutes if you didn't have to." His gaze intersected with Fanon's only up to the word *little*. At that point the black youth's eyes strayed off into the distance. No smile at all, not even a sneering one. So Charlie turned back toward McNutter as he said, "For a little while there were even guys in the NFL and the AFL—remember the AFL?—guys who did the same thing. I think the last one was Chuck Bednarik. Used to play for the Philadelphia Eagles."

McNutter gave him a smile that indicated he found that the most fascinating piece of information that had come his way in a long time. But his eyes betrayed a state of panic. He turned toward Fanon, his face seemingly wreathed in merriment, and said, "How'd you like to play defense *and* offense, Fareek?" Then to Charlie: "You played linebacker on defense, idd'n'at right?"

"Hum hah heyyyy," sang Fareek mock-softly.

Charlie nodded yes.

McNutter tried out the question on Fanon once more: "How'd you like that? I could arrange it!" As if this were the merriest conversation in years.

Fanon lowered his head, cast his eyes downward, expelled a big snort of air through his nose, looked up with a gaze that shot halfway between McNutter and Lawyer White, and said, "I 'unno. Never thought about it."

McNutter was speechless for a moment. Then he began twisting a huge ring on his left hand—a college ring, a Super Bowl ring, whatever it was—with his right hand. Then he said to Charlie, "I was trying to explain to Fareek and Roger here about that thing you were famous for in'at game with the Bulldogs, the time you were playing defense and took the ball from their quarterback, but I didn't know any of the details."

"Aw, it was mostly luck," said Charlie. "We were down by six points with about forty seconds in the game, and the Bulldogs had the ball on their own twenty-five. So all they had to do was eat up the clock with runs up the middle and they had the ballgame."

"Y'all'd just kicked off to 'em, right?"

"Yeah."

"Because you'd just broken loose on a 48-yard touchdown run, right?" McNutter looked toward Fanon as he uttered the last part of the sentence, frantically hoping he had ignited at least a *show* of interest in his twenty-year-old all-American. But Fanon remained regally removed from the sphere of conversation.

"Hoo hanh hoo hum hah heyyyyy, Sixty-Minute Man . . ."

Now McNutter looked frantically toward Charlie: "So how'd it happen?"

"Well," said Charlie, "they had a quarterback named Rufus Smiley. He was a smart quarterback, but sometimes he got a little too smart." Charlie looked toward Fareek Fanon to see if this story was as yet engaging him. The Cannon looked as if he had just departed the room via astral projection. So Charlie turned back toward McNutter. "On first down, he handed off to this big fullback they had, Rudy Brauer, and he ran right up the middle. On second down, he did the same thing. By now he's eaten up twenty seconds, and there's only twenty seconds left on the clock. So I figured we got to *make* something happen. That's the only chance we had. So I decided to blitz, right between center and guard—hoping for a fumble? Well, this was when Smiley got a little too cute. This time, on third down, to eat up more time, he fakes a handoff to their wingback, who's in motion between Smiley and Rudy Brauer." Charlie looked at Fanon again. No one there. So then he looked at Lawyer Roger White. The man at least pretended to be engrossed. So Charlie kept looking at him, meantime maintaining a vigil out of the corner of his eye for the attention of Fareek "the Cannon" Fanon. "So I'm blitzing between center and guard, hoping to dislodge the ball from Smiley or Brauer, and I get there—and I can't believe it!" Charlie faked as much animation as he could with this yarn, hoping against hope to draw the mighty Fanon back into the conversational orbit. "Smiley's still holding the ball out like this"—he pantomimed a quarterback holding the ball out for a handoff—"to hand it off to Brauer after the fake to the wingback. So instead of going for Smiley, I went for the ball—and I know this is hard to believe, but I took it just the way I would've if I'da been on offense. It was a handoff—a wrong-way handoff." He was still looking at Fareek's lawyer, Roger White, who was smiling and nodding encouragingly. Fareek Fanon, meantime, had the look on his face that you get when you're in line at a pay telephone kiosk and the fellow on the telephone just won't get off. Charlie plowed on: "A split second later here comes Brauer charging forward to take the handoff, and *bam!*—I smack right into him. Like I say, he was a big sonofabitch, but I had the momentum, because I'd blitzed from all the way behind the line a scrimmage, and he got knocked right on his back. There was nobody between me and the goal line, and so I scored and we got the extra point and won the game 14–13. I'm tellin'ya, I couldn't hardly believe it myself! If Smiley hadn'a fooled around with'at fake to the wingback, we'da lost'at game."

With a big smile Charlie surveyed his audience. Roger White, smiling, shook his head with the shake that says "Wow, that's amazing!" Coach Buck McNutter was smiling and nodding, not at Charlie but at Fareek, as if he thought his big head might create some psychokinetic vibrations and cause his shaved-pate young all-American to smile and nod with him. As for Fanon himself—well, at least he was looking at Charlie for a change. He wasn't smiling, he wasn't nodding, he wasn't showing any particular reaction to this bit of Tech sports lore as related by the hero himself. The look he gave Charlie was a cross between dubious and skeptical, but at least his attention had been engaged.

So Charlie said to him, "Fareek, I saw you make'at seventy-yard run against Tulane"—*Tu*lane—"last year, the one where you shook off six tacklers?"

Fareek kept looking at him, twisting his lips and nodding his head up and down a few times, as if to say, "That's true, that happened, and so what?" Then he sprawled back even farther on the couch, his long shanks akimbo, and said to Charlie: "Tulane, they teach'em to tackle headfirst," and then he shrugged, as if to say, "That explains that," and looked to McNutter for confirmation, which McNutter gave with enthusiastic nods of the head. His big star had at least deigned to speak to the Sixty-Minute Man of yore. Fanon turned back to Charlie. Challenging:

"Who'd you play against?"

"Who'd I *play* against?"

" 'At game you was talkin'bout, where you took the ball from the quarterback."

"Georgia," said Charlie. "University a Georgia."

"But who'd they have?" said Fanon.

"Who'd they *have*?" said Charlie.

"Playin' for'em."

"Who'd they have *playin'* for'em?" Out of the corner of his eye Charlie could see both McNutter and White. Their faces were sagging with concern.

"Yeah," said Fanon, "*who*?"

"Well, hell," said Charlie, "I remember some *uv*'em . . . Smiley, Rudy Brauer . . . they had this end named Goodykoontz, I remember him . . ."

"Unnh-hunnnh," said Fanon, "but what'd they be?"

"Wha'ya mean, what?" said Charlie.

Fanon said, "How many uv'em was African Americans?"

Roger sagged back in his chair and closed his eyes. He knew exactly where this little Socratic dialogue of Fareek's was heading. Why had he, Roger Too White, been so foolish as to tell Fareek that all the records set by Southeastern Conference greats of long ago didn't mean but so much, because all black athletes were shut out of the competition by racial segregation? Why had he told Fareek that at the very least all the records in the record books of that time should have asterisks with a footnote reading "Black athletes"—or, rather, "African-American athletes"—Fareek had already picked up the new nomenclature on his own—"African-American athletes denied access to Conference schools"?

Why had he wanted Fareek to know that the likes of Charlie Croker would have probably been mediocre in contemporary competition? He knew why. Oh yes, he knew why . . . He had been desperate to ingratiate himself with Fareek, so he would seem black as thou, so he would be treated as something other than a bitch in a suit by this egomaniacal all-American with the diamonds in his earlobes. But he never dreamed the kid would be stupid enough to use it against Croker! If he'd told the kid once, he'd told him ten times that Croker was sympathetic to his plight, that even though he hadn't played against black athletes, he was a big star in his day and understood how people always tried to take advantage of stars like him, Fareek. He'd done everything but write the kid a script of how this meeting should go! He'd told him a hundred times that Croker was an old man, a bit of a throwback, part of the old white establishment, but that he could also help him a great deal for that very reason! All he, Fareek, had to do was be polite and act interested! He didn't even have to be nice! All he had to do was be agreeable! And now the kid was throwing all the background information in the man's face and saying the hell with the foreground—which was his chance to get free and clear of the mess he was now in.

How many uv'em was African Americans? The question rocked Charlie. He stared at Fanon for a moment with no expression at all. Then he cast a glance toward McNutter, who opened his eyes wide and pulled his mouth over to one side in the look that says "Don't blame me! I can't control this situation!" Then he cast a glance at Lawyer White, who was leaning back with his eyes closed in the look that says "Aw shit! I give up!" Then Charlie said, in as even a tone as he could manage, "None *uv*'em."

"So all'em records in the record books, they oughta all have axericks and little things saying 'African-American athletes *ex*cluded.' "

God *damn*, thought Roger, he even remembered the asterisks. He's throwing the whole goddamned thing into Croker's face, asterisks and all!

Charlie's consternation gave way to a surge of anger. "Look, my friend, let me tell you something." *Tale you sump'm.* "I was a kid like you back then. It wasn't me who wrote the history of the South, and it wasn't me who ran Tech and the University a Georgia. I played the hand they dealt me, but I can tell you this much: I woulda played against any sonofabitch they put out there on the field. I was twenty-two, twenty-three years old, and I didn't give a shit. I was ready to crawl any asshole they put up in front a me. Right after that I went off to fight in Vietnam."

Roger pressed back as far in his chair as he could go and braced for an explosion from his uncontrollable client—who had just been called, by proxy, a sonofabitch and an asshole. Instead, Fareek was just staring at Croker, frozen, his lips parted. He looked as if the wind had been knocked out of him. And now, all of a sudden, Roger was afraid Croker would try to *crawl* Fareek. So he blurted out:

"That's more or less what I was telling Fareek!"

"*What* was?" said Croker with a cross, puzzled look on his face.

"About how you were decorated during the war," said Roger Too White.

"Decorations ain't the point," said Croker, whose diction was becoming more and more Down Home Baker County, the angrier he became. He shot an accusing look at Fareek. "You ever been in a war? You ever been in a far fat?"

"What's a far fat?" said Fareek.

It took a moment for Roger to figure out that *far fat* meant *firefight*. He said hastily to Fareek: "A firefight. A fight with gunfire, in a war."

"Naw," said Fareek in a surly but at least not hostile way, "I ain't been in a war, and if they tried to make me, I'd do what Muhammad Ali did. He refused to fight for the Devil."

"Yeah," said Croker, still fuming, "Muhammad Ali wunt the fust man to ton yalla inna face a gunfar."

Roger Too White closed his eyes again. He wasn't about to translate that line for the benefit of his client. The situation was degenerating too rapidly already.

Croker bulled on: "Prize fats—and football, too, fars'at's consunned, they's nothin' but *share*-raids fuh far fats."

It took Roger a moment or two to figure out that "*share*-raids" meant "charades." He just prayed that Fareek never *would* figure that out. He shut his eyes tighter.

"Mr. Croker? One Scotch-and-soda!"

At the sound of the woman's voice, Roger opened his eyes. Coming through the doorway was Val McNutter. She had her strange leering smile across her face, as if this were the happiest bunch of Buck's pals who had been in the house in a long time and they were all panting for the arrival of Venus in the flesh. She carried the tall glass of Scotch-and-soda as if it were a gift from the goddess.

One belligerent, Croker, was suddenly neutralized, as if a switch had been flipped. The other belligerent, Fareek, was speechless, all eyes.

"Thank you," said Croker in an oddly faint voice as he took the glass, "thank you veh much."

Then Val McNutter pivoted on her high-heeled pumps, and this and that and them and those went hither, thither, whither, crevice, crevasse.

"Anything I can get for any a you *other* gentlemen?" Such an insinuating leer!

"No," said Roger, almost meekly, "no thanks."

"No thanks, Val," said Buck McNutter in the voice of a whipped male.

Fareek, drinking in this vision as if preparing for a trip across a terrible desert, just shook his head.

The goddess stood motionless for a moment, turned to leave, then turned back with the most suggestive grin yet, and said, "If you change your mind, just . . . let me know."

Say what you want about her, thought Roger, but Madame McNutter's wiggle in her walk had just defused a bad situation.

To Roger's surprise, Mme McNutter's mate, Buck, offered the following soothing opinion as soon as his wife left the room: "You gotta admit one thing, Charlie. Some things never change. I betcha they were the same for you, they sure's hell were the same for me when I was at Ole Miss, and I know for a fact they're the same for Fareek now. I'm talking about the way these little groupies come on to you if you're on a football team. Everybody talks about it as if it's something just happened yesterday." *Sump'm jes happened yest'y.* The mighty McNutter had always been a Cracker, thought Roger, but now he was trying to get right down on the same wavelength with Croker. "But it's just more of the same." *Jes motor same.* "Now, tell"—*tale*—"the truth, Charlie, ain't'at the case?"

Charlie looked away and sighed and took a sip of Scotch-and-soda and said, "I spose . . ." Charlie was still angry, but his more calculating self said, "This kid's an obnoxious arrogant asshole, but you need this deal, Charlie, and McNutter's offering you a way back into it." So he looked at McNutter and nodded, as if to say, "That's true, that's true."

Encouraged, McNutter said, "The only difference today is that the girls *flaunt* it so much. You know what I'm saying? When we're on the road, I prack'ly have to keep these characters"—he smiled slightly and nodded in the direction of Fanon—"under lock and key, because all these little cookies, these little groupies, they'll come right into the hotel lobby or wherever the hell else we're staying. They're not even subtle about it. Right, Fareek?"

Fanon gave a couple of grudging nods, just like Charlie's. Maybe he wanted to get back in the deal, too.

"And at the same time," said McNutter, anxious not to lose the momentum he seemed to have built up, "at the same time'at these little cookies're more aggressive about it than anybody my age or your age could even imagine, there's a lot more *jailbait* out there. You know what I mean? I'm not just talkin'bout under*age* girls—although God knows there's them, too—I'm talking about *sexual harassment* . . . *sexual assault* . . . *date rape* . . . I mean, in my day all those terms, they didn't even *ex*ist . . . You either had *rape* or you *didn't* have rape. There wud'n anything in between, the way they have now. Iddn'at the truth, Charlie?"

Charlie nodded. He nodded dourly but with one more up-and-down of the chin than the last time, and another wavelet of guilt began rolling through his nervous system. Yes, the sad truth was . . . he wanted back in.

"I mean, you get some kid twenty or twenty-one years old," McNutter was saying, "and he's in the season of the rising sap, and he's a football player, and the college has pep rallies, whole stadiums fulla students the day before the game, cheering and carrying on and telling'em how wonderful they are—what's a kid that age supposed to think? It's a goddamned sexual *minefield* out there, Charlie!"

All at once Charlie thought of Serena—and Martha. McNutter had his own Serena, obviously. That little cupcake who was just here didn't come marching out of Ole Miss with Buck McNutter . . . Maybe it was all just an inflammation . . . an epidemic . . . Maybe he shouldn't condemn this big black kid just because . . . Inman . . . Elizabeth Armholster . . . How did he know what Elizabeth Armholster was like? As McNutter said, this was a different world put there today for kids Fareek Fanon's age—

Crrrraaaccckkk—Fanon was leaning back on the couch, his weight resting on the base of his spine and his head hanging down, busy wrapping one massive hand around the other and cracking his knuckles. His legs were spread wide apart. Charlie noticed for the first time that the

Cannon had on a wristwatch with a massive gold band and gold rings on both hands. The hands were so huge, the cracking of the knuckles sounded like vertebrae breaking. He was so big, it was hard to fit him in with any general statement about "kids."

McNutter was leaning forward in his chair, looking at Charlie. The coach's neck was wider than his head, and his head was so big his eyes looked like two tiny peepholes. "Fareek's a great football player, Charlie, the greatest I personally ever had the pleasure a coachin', but he's a babe in the woods as far as bein' a celebrity's concerned." He shot a glance toward the great lad. "I'm just telling it like it is, Fareek." Fanon hung his head down even farther and stared at his mentor through a pair of sinister upturned eyes. McNutter said, "What example's he ever had, Charlie—I mean, to deal with all this stuff? Tell Charlie about your dad, Fareek."

A whispery rumbling voice came out of the great hung shaved head: "Never knowed him."

"Never knew your own father," said McNutter in a solicitous voice.

More whispery rumble: "My mama, she point him out one time, but I never knowed him."

McNutter said, "Tell Charlie where you grew up. You grew up on English Avenue, iddn'at right? In the Bluff?"

"Yeah," said Fareek Fanon. His head still hung low, and he seemed to be staring through the floor.

"And your mama," said McNutter, "she looks to you as the first child she ever had, the first person in her whole life, far as'at's concerned, who ever made something of himself. Iddn'at true?"

Hangdog: "Yeah . . ." Suddenly he lifted his head and, eyes ablaze, said to McNutter: "And now they be messing with my endorsements!"

Roger Too White attempted to head off this particular lament. "I'm sure that's the least—"

"Ironman and Mars and Mishima," said an indignant Fareek Fanon, running right over Roger's words, "they be biddin'gainst each other for three months, and now I don't hear nothing from any *uv'*em ever since this girl run this game on me!"

Roger closed his eyes again. Technically Fareek was still an amateur, even though amateurism in Division I intercollegiate football had become pretty much a joke. Fareek was not only not supposed to be encouraging three sneaker manufacturers like Ironman, Mars, and Mishima to bid for his endorsement when he turned pro, he wasn't even supposed to *know* about such things. Worse, by presenting his plight as a matter of money, he was throwing away his sentimental advantage as the put-upon Boy from the Ghetto Who Made Good.

"Muh'fuh . . ." said Fareek, "all some hubba ho got to do is run a game on you, and these bitches in suits'at run these companies, they don' wanna know your name no more." Fareek shook his great shaved head as if human perfidiousness had never before been pushed to such an extreme.

Roger said, "But that isn't really what bothers you, is it, Fareek."

Bitterly: "Naw, it don't bother me, it just pisses me off totally."

McNutter said, "A lotta girls hit on you, come on to you, iddn'at right? Black girls, white girls, Asian girls, Hispanic girls, every kinda girl, iddn'at the truth?"

Fareek wrapped his eyebrows around his nose and finally said, "I never knowed any Asian groupies."

"But plenty a all kinds a others, right?" said McNutter.

Fanon's eyes blazed at McNutter again. "What's'ese three white hubba ho's doing at a Freaknic party, 'cep'n they wanna hook up and do some jookin'? This girl, I never even *seen* her before'at night. All she's doin's trying to get her ownself off the hook—"

Roger broke in: "We're not here to go into details, Fareek. We're just here to share our experiences in general. Mr. Croker's in a unique position to understand . . . uh . . . uh . . . *your* position." He was fishing for words, anything to keep Fareek from saying something in Croker's presence that could be used against him, especially considering the fact that the hoped-for deal with Croker appeared to be heading straight down the toilet.

Fareek gave his lawyer a petulant look. "All I'm saying is, ain't no way you can call it rape."

"Charlie," said Buck McNutter, "it's very important to Fareek that he not be charged with any crime. He's never been in trouble with the law, and if you grew up in the Bluff, the way he did, that's saying something. Fareek, tell Mr. Croker about the boys you used to run with in the Bluff."

"What about 'em?" said Fareek, genuinely nonplussed.

"Tell him where they are now."

"Aw yeah," said Fareek, as if suddenly remembering the lines of a song. "They's in jail or they's dead, most *uv*'em." He looked not at Charlie but at McNutter, as if waiting for approval.

"I'm sure Mr. Croker can relate to that, Fareek," said McNutter. Then to Charlie: "I know, from sump'm I read, you didn' have any picnic growin' up, either."

I can relate to that . . . What bullshit! Charlie was offended, but all he said was "Relate to that? Let's see . . . From the time I was born to the day I went off to the Army, I knew one boy, Bobby Lee Kite, who got arrested for disturbing the peace after the usual Saturday-night rock fight outside a McCrory's store up at Newton." He gave McNutter an annoyed look and wondered if he got the irony. But then he asked himself, "Why am I bothering to be ironic? Why don't I tell these clowns what I really mean? Am I *that* weak? Am I *that* desperate to keep the deal alive?"

To his surprise, Fanon turned toward him—he hadn't looked squarely at him since he entered this room—and said, "He says"—he motioned toward Lawyer White with his head—and it occurred to Roger that Fareek had never referred to him by name—"he says you own a *plan*tation."

Charlie gave him a dubious look and said, "That's right."

Roger said, "I was showing Fareek the article about you, in *Atlanta* magazine."

"I heard about 'em," said Fareek Fanon, "but I never seen one."

Charlie had no idea what to say to that, and so he said nothing.

Fanon said, "He told me you be having these weekends down'eh where you *in*vite a lotta people."

Charlie shrugged.

"You know what I'd like?" said Fanon. "I'd like to see one. I'd like to come down'eh for one a those weekends."

Charlie studied him for a moment. Fareek Fanon now had his arms stretched out along the ridge of the couch's backrest. He was so big, his fingertips reached almost from one end of the couch to the other. Charlie was taken aback by the proposal, which came from out of nowhere, so far as he was concerned. The moment lengthened . . . lengthened . . . lengthened . . .

Charlie said to himself, "If I'm around this sonofabitch much longer, I'm gonna have to *tangle* with him." But what he said was "You wouldn't like it, my friend. This iddn' a good time to go to Turpmtine, not when it gets hot like this."

Fanon smacked his fist into the palm of his hand, and he said with great animation, " 'At's what he told me! He told me 'at's what it's called—Turpmtine! He told me you go there and shoot quail! Whattaya shoot'em with?"

"Whattaya shoot'em with?" Charlie studied the young black man's face. Was he taunting him—or what? "You shoot'em with shotguns."

"Shotguns . . ." Fanon had a strange, dreamy smile on his face. "I'd like to try that."

"Quail season's over," said Charlie. "Only runs from Thanksgiving to the end a February. Nothing to hunt down'eh now but mosquitoes, gnats, horseflies, yellow flies, and privy flies."

Fanon looked to McNutter instead of Charlie, as if McNutter were the daddy in charge of what was going on here. "I don't care. I wanna go see it anyway." Once more he motioned his head toward Lawyer White. " 'Told me's just like it was a hundred and fifty years ago, before the Civil War, when they still had slaves. I wanna see that."

Jesus Christ, thought Roger, his face turning hot with embarrassment, this kid's got the discretion of a flea!

Jesus Christ! thought Charlie, that's all I need! He tried to imagine it . . . introducing this big black oaf to Durwood as his guest of honor . . . Fareek "the Cannon" Fanon sitting at the great tupelo-wood table in the Gun House, while Auntie Bella, Uncle Bud, and Mason get a load of His Insolence . . . His Insolence slouched back in his chair, shanks akimbo, cracking his knuckles while the help gather after dinner and sing "Just a Closer Walk with Thee" . . . His Insolence on the grand tour, pausing to appreciate the designs in scrip on the face of the plantation store . . . Everybody—Billy Bass, Judge Opey McCorkle—Inman!—finding out—*and they would find out!*—that he had the notorious ravager of Elizabeth Armholster as his guest of honor at Turpmtine . . . No! It was beyond imagining!—a plunge into unfathomable shame! He looked at McNutter, looked at Roger White—maybe they would say something!—get him out of this!—but they just sat there as if it were a perfectly normal thing, Fareek Fanon inviting himself to Turpmtine.

Finally, Charlie heard himself saying, "Sorry. No way. Place is closed for the season. Couldn't open it if the King of England was coming by." Fleetingly it occurred to him that there *was* no King of England. "I'd have to bring a whole lotta people in. Don't know if I could even *find*'em at this late date." All the while he thought to himself, You're weak! You're buckling under! You're implying that if the timing were better, you *would* invite the sonofabitch to Turpmtine! He could see

Buck McNutter and Roger White casting glances at each other. Could they be thinking the same thing? He felt himself plunging helplessly into an icy lake of shame.

He slapped the tops of his knees in the way that says "That wraps it up. It's time to go." Then he stood up, with a feeble lurch, wincing at the pain of one big bone grinding against another in his knee.

"I gotta go," he said.

Fareek Fanon said to McNutter, "What's he saying? I get to go to the place or not?"

McNutter stood up without answering the question. Lawyer White stood up, too, and so, at last, did Fareek Fanon. White said, *sotto voce*, to Fanon, "Come here a minute," and led him out into the hallway.

Charlie started to leave, too, but McNutter held up a forefinger and said, "Oh, Charlie . . ." Then he drew closer and said, "There's just one other thing, Charlie. We can't let this whole business become just an issue where you have a 120-pound white girl from a good family—or whatever she weighs—you can't have her saying one thing and this 225-pound black athlete from the Bluff saying another thing, and that's all it is, just some—you know—isolated sex crime complaint. We have to show there's a whole . . . whole . . . whole community of support for this young man and that this support cuts across the usual lines of race and class, and so forth and so on."

"So you don't think he did it," said Charlie.

"Look, Charlie," said McNutter, "I can't prove anything one way or the other, but Fareek's version of what happened makes sense to me, from everything *I* know about the way things go these days."

"And what's Fareek's version?"

"Between you and me?" asked McNutter, arching his eyebrows and waiting for a reply.

"Okay, between you and me."

"Between you and me, what Fareek says happened is, he says the girl's at this party and she comes on to him and so he takes her into the bedroom, and bam-bam thank you ma'am, that's it, and he don't think anything more about it."

"And you believe that?" said Charlie.

"Like I say, I can't swear to anything, but I can tell you this much: I wasn't kidding when I said there's girls out there coming up to these athletes all day long and shakin' their little booties at'em and sayin' 'Help yourself,' and a kid's being African-American don't make any difference if he's a big enough star, and Fareek's real big-time so far's being a star's concerned."

Charlie studied McNutter all over again. It was the term *African American* that got him. What the hell had happened to McNutter? He had always figured the guy to be a good old boy from Mississippi, and here he was observing this new . . . etiquette . . . or whatever it was.

"Now, here's the thing, Charlie," McNutter was saying, "it's real important for you to be a part of Fareek's defense."

"*Me?*"

"Look, nobody's gonna ask you to say Fareek ain't guilty in this thing, because that you don't know. Just like *I* don't know. And nobody's even gonna ask you to say anything *nice* about Fareek. I know he's not the easiest kid in the world to get along with. Although a lot of it is that nobody ever raised him to *be* polite. Nobody ever taught him about everyday common courtesy. All you'd have to do would be to tell what you *do* know, namely, that you've *been* there before. You know the pressures being a football star for Tech, in a town like this that goes crazy over the sport. You know how people try to exploit you—or whatever—however you want to put it."

Charlie was speechless. His lips were parted.

"And look at it this way," said McNutter. "You wouldn't be speaking out on behalf of Fareek or even on behalf of Tech, although it would mean a lot to Tech, and I'm talking about from Welly Swindell all the way down. No, you'd be doing something for the whole city. You'd be saying, 'Whoa! Slow down! Let's don't rush to any judgments here! Let's don't tear ourselves apart along racial lines! And you know what? The whole town will applaud you. Everybody'll talk about your courage, including the *Journal-Constitution*. You can be sure that they'll be behind you a hundred percent. Your very presence there — a press conference is what we're thinking of — your presence, saying 'Stay cool, let's wait for the facts, let's have open minds, let's be fair'—the press will hail your very presence as an act of leadership and courage."

"Great," said Charlie. "And what other courageous white people you think are gonna show up for this?"

"That's a fair question, Charlie," said McNutter, "and I'm gonna answer it as candidly as I can. So far all I know of is Herb Richman. You know, the guy who owns all the fitness centers, DefinitionAmerica?"

"Yeah, I know," said Charlie. *Jewish and a liberal*; the phrase was by now fixed in his brain.

"But he don't really carry much weight," said McNutter.

"And what about *you*?" said Charlie.

"Me?"

"Yeah. Are you gonna speak out for Fareek?"

"Well, we been thinking about whether I ought to or not. I'd come across as an obviously interested party."

"Unnh-hunnnnh," said Charlie dubiously.

"So how about it?" said Buck McNutter.

Charlie just stood there staring at McNutter's huge head and its fussy silver-blond hairdo here in Langhorn Epps's old mahogany-paneled study. So he was to be the lone white person speaking out on behalf of this lout! *Inman* . . . It was impossible! Who could he look in the face after that? Who of all the people he had entertained at Turpmtine would ever come again? On the other hand, if he refused—then suppose he *lost* Turpmtine, lost everything he had, including his house on Blackland Road—was wiped out! demolished!—the result would be the same, wouldn't it! No one would come visit him then, either! All that which comprised the great Cap'm Charlie—punctured, deflated, humiliated abjectly, pitied . . . and not even that for very long.

Chapter XXV

Starring Darwell Scruggs

LATE THIS PARTICULAR AFTERNOON, AS USUAL, CHARLIE DROVE home from Croker Concourse and went in the house and headed for the library, where Jarmaine Woo always left his mail in a neat, squared-off pile on his desk, right in front of his chair, an old walnut swivel chair upholstered in oxblood-red leather, the most comfortable chair in the house to Charlie's way of thinking. As usual, he took off his jacket, loosened his necktie, and opened his shirt at the collar as soon as he entered the room, sat in the chair, turned on the desk lamp, leaned back, exhaled a contented sigh, and eyed his stack of mail, which was no greater and no smaller than usual. In an age of telephones, faxes, and computers, the mail seldom required any true cogitation. Fund-raising requests, invitations, bills, mail-order catalogues; and there you had it. Charlie had come to look forward to this mindless interlude. Mindlessness meant not thinking about PlannersBanc, Fareek Fanon, Inman Armholster, perfidy, betrayal, or financial ruin.

And then he noticed a package Jarmaine had placed to the left of the stack of mail and slightly behind it. Idly he leaned forward and picked it up and sank back in the swivel chair again. No postage; must have been delivered by a courier service. It was one of those padded manila mailers that books come in, and indeed the contours of what was inside looked like a book's. In the upper-left-hand corner, in a typeface with a lot of bold flourishes that Charlie couldn't have begun to describe, was the legend STONE MOUNTAIN PRODUCTIONS, with an address in Decatur. In the lower-left-hand corner was a large gold seal, almost three inches in diameter, bearing more fancy type, which said: *Croker Concourse: A Vision of the Future*. Then in smaller letters: "A Stone Mountain Production."

Charlie sat upright in the chair. What the hell was this supposed to be? Croker Concourse? A Vision of the Future?

He found the mailer's little opener tab and ripped it open and pulled out . . . a videotape cassette. On one edge was a label in the same typeface, but smaller, saying: "Croker Concourse: A Vision of the Future. A Stone Mountain Production." Various possibilities came churning through his mind. His own publicity people? Had they made a promotional tape without his knowledge? Or was he always so groggy from insomnia he had forgotten?

Wearily he got up from his beloved chair and limped over to the television set, a monster concealed in an old-fashioned cherry-wood cabinet the size of a closet, and inserted the tape in the VCR slot. The set immediately came to life, and Charlie limped back to his desk, withdrew a little remote-control gadget from a drawer, and sank back in his chair once more. At first, no sound: just an FBI warning about unauthorized use of this material—Never saw a promotional tape with an FBI warning, thought Charlie—and then "Croker Concourse: A Vision of the Future" and "A Stone Mountain Production" in bold white lettering against a black background, and then music, just music at first, no picture. The music Charlie recognized. *BOOM boom BOOM boom*—it was the same as the theme song for that movie—what was it called?—*2001*, that was the name of it, *2001: A Space Odyssey*. *BOOM boom BOOM boom DAH dahhhhhh*—but wasn't that a little . . . bombastic for a real estate video? Then came the picture. The camera seemed to be swinging across an infinite sea of green. The tops of trees were what you were looking at, a lush forest stretching on toward the horizon, and then, in the distance, a tower with a dome-like top: the tower at Croker Concourse. The *2001* music continued, and as the camera drew slowly closer to the tower, a voice . . . a solemn baritone voice . . . said: "From out of the tangled trees and thickets of Cherokee County, Georgia, a land formerly devoted to hoed rows, lowing cattle, and country stores with Coca-Cola emblems at either end of the sign out front, rises . . ."

The camera now had the tower in a close-up—"one man's vision of the future . . . for metro Atlanta . . . if not, indeed, metro America." The *BOOM boom DAH dahhhhhhhh* music swelled up into a veritable thunder of grandiloquence. The camera was now above Croker Concourse and showed the roofs of the mall, the hotel, the apartments, the tower, before lingering, for some unfathomable reason, over the immense blacktop of the parking area, which was practically empty. The camera lingered and lingered and lingered over all that empty asphalt. Charlie was going to have to have a few words with whoever approved the editing of this damned thing.

Meantime, the voice was saying: "And that man is . . . Charles Earl Croker." A stock publicity shot of Charlie filled the screen. *Earl?* He never used the *Earl,* and he had told them not to use it in publicity material . . . Take your eye off the ball for a couple of seconds and these people will find some way to screw up on you every time . . . "And that development is . . . Croker Concourse . . ." *BOOM boom BOOM boom BOOM boom BOOM boom* . . . Now the camera lingered lovingly on the tower itself, moving slowly down one side. Floor after floor . . . you could see clear through them . . . Looking through the window on this side you could see through the window wall on the far side . . . floor after floor after floor . . . because there were no tenants in them . . . The damnable term *see-through building*—the name for new developments that were desperately short of tenants—popped unbidden into Charlie's brain. The solemn voice said: "And that future? . . . a future free from leasehold obligations and, for that matter, leases." What the hell was that supposed to mean?

Suddenly—no more Croker Concourse, no more trees, no more music. Instead, a man in a gray suit sitting alone at a long plastic-laminate conference table in a practically bare room. The man was smiling and looking straight into the camera as he said:

"Good morning, Mr. Croker, or good afternoon or good evening, whatever the case may be."

Him! The insolent one with the big chin! Zale or Zell or whatever it is! What the hell was this? Charlie wanted to kill the picture with the clicker, the remote-control gadget, but he was too morbidly hypnotized by what he now saw.

"We've chosen this unconventional way of saying hello because our conventional attempts—I might mention innumerable telephone calls, letters, faxes, E-mail, FedEx envelopes, and in-person requests for audiences—have produced no response. But we feel sure that you will respond to this documentary about the creation of Croker Concourse."

Now Charlie recognized where this bastard was. The conference table he was sitting at was the same one they had used for the workout session. You could see the modular units that made up the table but didn't meet truly. In the background, over there, was that same dying dracaena plant with the drooping yellow fronds. And visible on a side wall: one of the huge rude NO SMOKING signs.

Zale's rasping, grinding voice was saying: "Our story begins seven years ago, when Charlie Croker was looking for land in the southern part of Cherokee County for a grand outer perimeter mixed-use development. To his surprise, he learned that speculators had already decided that the county had a great future and had bought up most of the land and were willing to sit on it until the moment for high-priced development arrived. As things now stood, the land was prohibitively expensive. The acreage Charlie Croker required for Croker Concourse would have cost approximately $4 million."

The sound of this man's grating voice, the cocksureness with which he tilted his great melon of a chin up whenever he wanted to make a particularly salient point, reminded Charlie all too grimly of how much this bastard had already humiliated him. Yet he couldn't turn him off. He was spellbound. What nasty surprise did his nemesis have for him this time?

The nemesis continued: "One day Charlie Croker was driving slowly through a Cherokee County back road, looking for land the speculators might have missed, when he came upon a familiar figure walking along the side of the road. His name was Darwell Scruggs."

Now a picture of Darwell filled the screen, but a picture from way back. It was from the high-school annual! No mistaking Darwell: that thin, hollow-cheeked face coupled with huge ears that stuck way out to *here* and a nose about twice too big for his face. Back then the annual was a homemade job. You got Ping-Pong pictures of yourself for everybody in the class, and you wrote each other's captions, and you pasted it all up in scrapbooks, and you made one extra, which the school kept.

This man Zale was saying: "Charlie Croker and Darwell Scruggs had been classmates in high school in Baker County thirty-five years ago, and so Croker stopped his car, greeted his old friend, and talked a bit. In high school Darwell Scruggs had been memorable mainly because he had joined the Ku Klux Klan as a teenager and bragged about it openly. Darwell was now living in Cherokee County, where he had formed a Klan kave himself. "Aha!" said Charlie Croker.

The wrenching, rasping voice of this man Zale proceeded to tell the whole story of Charlie's oh-so-ingenious and oh-so-insidious scheme. There was André Fleet leading his placard-carrying black protesters from Atlanta through Canton, the county seat. There was Darwell Scruggs, albeit not in white raiment and pointy hood, screaming vile racial imprecations along with a pack of raggedy youths. There were television crews from around the country, and there was Frank Farr's network talk show boldly broadcast from the very main drag of Canton as a fist in the face of racism . . . And there was the reputation of lovely, leafy Cherokee County being dragged through the muck . . . And there were close-ups of deeds of transfer showing that Charlie Croker had now been able to assemble his land in this viciously slandered county for about $200,000, one-twentieth of what it would have cost before André Fleet and Darwell Scruggs did their duet.

Then this Zale's face grew larger on the screen, and his eyes seemed to pierce Charlie's. "As far as we can tell, Mr. Croker, there is nothing illegal about any action you took. You merely manipulated public opinion. Happens every day in this free country of ours. Congratulations. The citizens of Cherokee County will no doubt marvel at your cleverness." He smiled broadly and, as the camera pulled back, opened the jacket of his suit in order to adjust his belt where it went through the belt loops on the sides. And now you could see his suspenders. Death's-heads ran up and down a black road on either side. *BOOM boom BOOM boom BOOM*—and the music reached its finale as the picture of that impudent gladiola faded out on the screen.

Charlie felt as if he had just been kicked in the abdomen by a horse. His head and shoulders keeled forward and he shut his eyes and slumped over. How did they *know*? Who could have possibly *told* them? There were a few people who knew he had been "friendly with" André Fleet at one time. But nobody knew about Darwell Scruggs. Nobody would see it as just a shrewd move by a developer, would they . . . They'd want his head. They'd want his very hide. It would be worth his life to step across the county line—or to show up at the Piedmont Driving Club, as far as that went. Just let this tape circulate and he'd be finished. How did they *know*! Too late to even ask. The fact was, they *knew*!

Slumped over like a dead man, he opened his eyes and let them pan around the room. The Great Man's Library . . . by the celebrated Mr. Ronald Vine of New York . . . all the carved wood, the $250-a-yard fabrics, the custom-made carpet from What-the-hell-was-the-name-of-that-place-in-New-York . . . He was precisely where he had dreamed of being as a young man: living in a mansion in Buckhead, the master builder of metro Atlanta, creator of a gleaming tower named after himself, a man whose footsteps made the halls of the mighty vibrate . . . and how hollow it all was! It meant only that when your egomania and the defects in your character finally plunged you into ruin, your collapse would provoke more and tastier gloating. That would be it! They'd chuckle, rub their hands together, and smack their lips—and that would be the great Charlie Croker's entire legacy. What a fraud he was!—sitting here in his oxblood leather throne as if any of it were still . . . his . . . Why couldn't he put an end to it all by . . . disintegrating, by vanishing, by walking out into the woods and never coming back? . . . Oh sure . . . With his knee, he'd be lucky to walk a hundred yards . . . Why couldn't he—

Dear Lord—take me away! Take me away in the night! I go to bed and never wake up, and it's all over . . . But shit, *never wake up?*—never wake up, *how*? I have total insomnia, I never go to sleep in the first place! . . . Besides, just how could the Lord take him away? Via a heart attack—or what? He was a logical enough candidate for a heart attack. He was way too heavy, and he hadn't taken care of himself when it came to diet or exercise, and his was what they call a type—what the hell kind of type was it?—he had that type of personality. But if he just lay down at night and waited for God to call him across the river Jordan via coronary ischemia, he might have a long wait. Maybe he could *induce* a heart attack. He would start running, sprinting the way they used to sprint in training at Tech, and his heart couldn't take it—but neither could his knee. Jesus Christ . . . he could see it now . . . He's running like hell in order to kill himself . . . and he has to discontinue killing himself because his knee hurts . . . Reminded him of the story he had read somewhere of the man who decided to kill himself by swimming out to sea until he was utterly exhausted and then would have no choice but to sink and drown. So he starts out—and all of fifteen yards from shore he runs into a flotilla of stinging nettles and can't stand it and turns back. Well—why not the sea? And in that moment he understood for the first time the death of Robert Maxwell, whose body had been found in the sea near where his yacht was moored. No one had ever been able to figure it out, but now Charlie . . . *knew*. Maxwell had faced bankruptcy, humiliation, and, likely as not, a prison sentence. So he climbed over the railing of the yacht one night and hung from the edge of the deck by his fingertips. He hung on until he couldn't hang on anymore. He hung on until his immense weight, almost three hundred pounds, began to tear the muscles of his shoulders and his upper back. Then he let loose and hit the water and swallowed the ocean and drowned. The torn muscles made it look as if he had slipped overboard and had struggled mightily to clamber back to safety. That way *he didn't let the bastards have the satisfaction of knowing he had taken his own life*. But he, Charlie, didn't have a yacht. Maybe—a shotgun. He handled shotguns all the time, and a shotgun could blow you away at short range. Fontaine Perry! Fontaine Perry had owned a big plantation near Thomasville, and one day he was out hunting wild turkey. So he winged one, and the bird led him on one of those wild chases through the underbrush such as only turkeys can do. Fontaine is plunging down a slope after the turkey, and he stumbles, and a vine rips the shotgun out of his hands and twists it about so that he falls on the muzzle, and the gun discharges right into his belly. You don't survive a load of buckshot in your intestines, and the accident would be easy enough to simulate. But Jesus Christ, how Fontaine suffered! Hung on for three days—in mortal agony! And suppose, through some "miracle," you *didn't* die, and you had to live as a cripple with a colostomy bag—and you still had all your problems . . . and all the vultures were still circling . . . There *had* to be *some* way to do it the way Maxwell did it . . . What was he thinking—

Christ, why didn't he just put the shotgun in his mouth and be done with it? But then he would be right back where he started. The bastards would . . . *gloat* . . . and who was supposed to have the nice surprise of coming upon your body with your head exploded like a melon and your brains all over the wallpaper?

So there really was only one hope. It would be hard to look Inman in the eye afterward—it would be hard to look *anybody* in the eye afterward—but they'd get over it. He, Charlie, would call it "saving the city at a critical moment." Maybe he'd call Inman ahead of time and tell him what he was going to do, and Inman would understand . . . *Oh yeah, tell me another one!* . . . *But*—this was his only hope, and maybe it *would* be good for the city in the long run . . . *Stop kidding yourself!* . . . He swiveled toward the credenza by his desk and picked up the telephone book, which had been outfitted with a stiff oxblood leather cover Ronald got from someplace in New York—Anthony's or something like that?—and looked for the number . . . Wringer Fleasom & Tick . . . Wringer Fleasom & Tick . . . Wringer Fleasom & Tick . . . Here it was . . . Well . . . Here goes . . . Christ . . . He didn't know whether he wanted that sonofabitch with the British clothes to still be at the office . . . or not . . . He picked up the receiver and punched in the numbers.

AT THAT VERY moment, it so happened, Conrad Hensley was making a telephone call of his own. He had walked over to Asian Square, on the Buford Highway, and gone into a Cambodian bank and had ten dollars of his remaining stash of cash changed into rolls of quarters, which he put into his overnight bag. What time was it in California? About 3:30. That should be about right. He went to a telephone booth near the Vietnamese music store, punched in the numbers, and started pumping in quarters when the automated voice told him to. Three rings, four rings, five rings. Damn. Would he be up and out already? Six rings—and then someone picked up.

"*Hel*lo." The fact that this consummate Okie pronounced even *hello* on the first syllable blipped through Conrad's mind, but all he said was:

"Kenny?"

"Yeah."

"This is Conrad."

A pause; then: "I'll be damned! Crash'n'burn! Where you—naw, don't tell me where—I don't even wanna know. A couple neckties came by here last week asking if I knew where you were."

"Neckties?"

"FBI."

A wave of neural alarm went through Conrad's solar plexus. "The FBI? Are you sure?" His voice was suddenly hoarse.

"That's what they said. I can't think of why anybody'd fake it."

"Where was this?"

"Here. My house."

"What did they want?"

"They wanted to know if I knew where you're at. So don't tell me."

"How did they connect you with me?"

"I don't know. Maybe somebody at the freezer. Maybe somebody you know."

"What did you tell them?"

"I told them the truth. I said I hadn't seen you since the night you got laid off. I said didn't even know you'd been in jail until I saw it on the *tee*vee after the earthquake."

Kenny's "I told them the truth" made Conrad wary. "You think they might be bugging your telephone?"

"I doubt it. I mean, shit, this is a fucking nickel-and-dime case except for the fact that you're the only one at Santa Rita still unaccounted for. But you never know. So you might as well be careful what you say."

"Look, Kenny, the last thing in the world I want is for you to get in trouble over me."

"Fuck it. Crash'n'burn, old buddy! Sooner or later they'll hang me from the necktie on the bald man the same way they did you."

"All the same, I wouldn't want it to be because of me."

"Fuck it, old buddy. You can't spend your whole fucking life cringing."

"How much has there been on television about"—he started to say *me* but changed his mind—"all this?"

Kenny laughed. "Aw man, for six or seven days there, I'm telling you, you were a media celebrity! My old buddy. I never knew you were such an evil sonofabitch. They said you were in Santa Rita for 'aggravated assault,' for beating up a repair shop employee and causing him to suffer a nearly fatal heart attack. There you were, in a mug shot, my old buddy, the only Ice Humper in the whole Suicidal Freezer Unit who still had his head on straight enough to wrestle eighty-pound blocks a ice and worry about his wife and kids at the same time. I had to fucking laugh."

"Did they say I'd escaped, or what?"

"Well, lemme see . . . At first there musta been twenty or thirty inmates unaccounted for. They were going through the rubble and every other goddamned thing. I mean, Santa Rita was like . . . wiped out. Pretty soon they'd found or captured all but nine, I think it was, and that was when they started showing the mug shots. There you were. You were the only white man in the lineup. I think there was one Chinese guy with these big eyeglasses. The rest of 'em, they were East Oakland all the way. Then they caught three *uv*'em hiding out in Pleasanton. Man, how three Oakland homeboys could hide out for two days in Pleasanton I don't fucking know, but that's what they did. Then they caught the Chinaman in Martinez and four homeboys in Oakland. So that left you. You were the *star*, man! I mean, I about—"

A mechanical voice interrupted and asked for more money. Conrad pumped in more quarters.

"Like I was saying," said Kenny, "I about cracked up! If I'da hadda pick out the last Ice Humper at Croker Global Foods who was going to end up as an underworld escape artist, idda been you, bro! Man, we talked about you in the freezer for musta been three weeks straight."

"What'd the guys think?"

"We were *proud* a you, Conrad! One a our mates had *done* it! We were rooting for you! We're *still* rooting for you!"

"God . . ." said Conrad. "Well, tell our friend in Oakland she's great. Everything's worked out just the way she said it would. Her people were the best—straight shooters. And tell the guy who introduced me to her he's great, too. Without the . . . assets . . . he gave me, I couldn't have made it."

"You in the place she was talking about now?"

"Yeah. I'll move soon, but everything's fine. Soon's I get work, I'm gonna pay that guy back."

"Aw, forget about it, Conrad. I don't think the guy's lost any sleep over it. Crash'n'burn."

"Kenny . . . were you able to reach Jill?"

"Yeah. I called her as soon as you—as soon as possible. I told her—everything I figured she'd need to know."

"Did she seem to know who you were?"

"I guess so. I think she said you'd mentioned me."

"What did she say? How did she take it?"

"She didn't say much. I think she was so surprised, she didn't know *what* to say. I remember she said, 'Is he coming home?' "

"So what'd you say?"

"I said to her, 'Probably not right away.' "

"Did she say anything about the kids?"

"Naw, but you got to remember it was a pretty short conversation."

"Listen, Kenny . . . just one other thing. If you can call her again—just tell her I'm okay, and I *am* gonna come home when things are a little better. Tell her I think of her and Carl and Christy all the time. But you wanna know something, Kenny? I can't even remember what my kids look like. In my mind it's like the sun's gone down and it's twilight, and all I can see is these two dim, blurred little children. Well—don't let me get started on all the things . . ." He didn't finish the sentence. "But one thing I've gotta tell you. I used to think about you guys, you and Light Bulb and Herbie Honda and Dom and Nick Necktie and Tony when I was in Santa Rita. You remember how we used to hump product for Santa Rita?"

"*Aw* yeah," said Kenny. "Nobody was sorry when the quake demolished that fucking place. I used to hate those orders."

"Remember all those eighty-pound cartons of frozen chicken parts?"

"*Aw* yeah."

"Well, at Santa Rita we used to practically live on pancakes and chicken. Every time a trusty passed a paper plate with a chicken leg through a porthole in the door a the cell, I could feel it all over again, what it felt like squatting down in the upper bin of Row W, Slot 9, and humping one a those eighty-pound blocks a ice."

"You know, Conrad," said Kenny, "this may sound crazy, but I envy you. I'm not kidding. At least you're out there—living. I'm always talking about crashing and burning, but all I'm really doing is humping blocks of ice all night. What you're doing is cool, no matter how it turns out."

Conrad said, "You were right the first time—you sound crazy. One thing I can tell you, being down in Santa Rita was not cool."

"At least you're—"

"At least *nothing,* Kenny. Santa Rita was a lunatic asylum where you live like an animal in the wild, except that all the animals are cooped up in the same pod. Half a them are literally lunatics. They're sitting around in their cells moaning, 'Mehhhhds . . . mehhhhds . . . mehhhhds . . .' That's what they called medicine, *meds.* These guys are so far gone, they need pills all day just to cool off enough to make it to lights-out, and then they scream and moan all night. What you need isn't something cool. What you need is a plan. You need to look down the road five years and say to yourself—"

Kenny broke in: "Hey! You're your old self, Conrad! You're still looking down my road for me! I was afraid all this shit had fucked you up—but you're normal! You're my old buddy!"

All the way back to Meadow Lark Terrace the smile stayed on Conrad's face.

"GLADYS?"

Only after he said it did it occur to Roger that he had never called her by her first name before. But he was too excited to worry about that now. His left hand, which held the receiver, was shaking so badly he could feel it rocking on his ear. Nerves; but a *good* case of nerves.

"Yes?" said Gladys Caesar.

"This is Roger White. I'd like to speak to the Mayor. I think this is one call he'll want to take."

"Oh, hi, Mr. White. Let me see if I can get him."

In due course: "Brother Roger?"

"Brother Wes. We're in business. I just got a call from our friend the Sixty-Minute Man. He'll do it."

"Way to go, Brother Roger! That's great. You're a mighty warrior! What was his mood?"

"He sounded awful, if you want to know the truth. He sounded . . . *mighty low*." Roger said it in a put-on basso profundo. "But he hasn't forgotten how to bargain. He said the deal isn't on until we prove that we can get PlannersBanc off his case."

"Well, it's too late to do anything today. But I can make a phone call in the morning. You sure he'll do what we say?"

"Positive, Wes. The press conference—everything."

"Great, great, great. I'm not just saying this, Roger: you've done this city a great service."

"Thanks."

Roger hung up the telephone and gazed out over South Atlanta from his high perch at Wringer Fleasom on Peachtree Street. Without even knowing he was doing it, he inhaled and expanded his chest. The mighty warrior, fresh from the fray.

Chapter

XXVI

Holding Hands

HOW COULD HARRY ACCEPT IT SO NONCHALANTLY? WAS THIS some kind of practical joke? Was Jack Shellnutt suddenly going to pop in from out in the corridor and say, "Just kidding, Ray!"? Peepgass actually flicked a glance toward Harry's interior glass wall, which looked out upon the corridor. Meantime, Harry continued to lounge back in the chair behind his desk with his hands interlaced behind his head and his elbows sticking out on either side and the skulls and crossbones on his suspenders parading up and down his chesty torso. There was no way Peepgass could have struck a relaxed pose like that, even if his desk chair had had leather upholstery as plush and creamy smooth as Harry's, which looked edible. He wasn't that good an actor.

"What did he mean, 'lay off Croker for now'?" said Peepgass, who was standing on the other side of Harry's desk and lifting both hands in front of him, palms up, in the gesture that says "Give me . . . a . . . *break*! That's incredible." Aloud: "What did he give as a reason?"

Harry, still totally at ease, said in his rasping voice, "I'm sure you know Plyers by now. He's a courier. He's not a great one for explanations." On the organizational chart Morgan Plyers was a vice president; in point of fact, he was Arthur Lomprey's aide-de-camp and frequently relayed the maximum leader's instructions. "He said it was a 'macro-decision.' "

"A *macro*-decision?" said Peepgass. "What's that supposed to mean?"

"You never heard Arthur talk about macro-decisions?" said Harry. "That means it doesn't have anything to do with the specific issue at hand. It's part of some larger strategy."

Peepgass shook his head. "I'd sure like to know what *larger strategy* he's talking about, unless from now on we're supposed to let the shit-heads take their sweet time paying us back in the hope that our kindness will stir them to dig deeper."

Harry smiled. "Ray! You really get worked up over this Croker case, don't you! We may have to conscript you into the workout department! That's what we need here, guys like you and Shellnutt who see TRAITOR branded on the brow of every shithead."

"Not every shithead, Harry, but Croker has lied, cheated, stolen, stalled us, laughed at us, played us for suckers—this particular shithead thinks he's too big to play by the rules."

"I don't think he's been feeling all that big, not since we took his G-5 away from him," said Harry.

"That may be—what's Arthur mean, 'lay off for now'? How long is 'for now'?"

"Plyers didn't say," said Harry. "Between you and me, I doubt that Arthur lets him in on the answer to most of these things."

Peepgass just stood there, speechless, incredulous. He couldn't believe Lomprey could have actually issued such an order, he couldn't believe Croker was off the hook, regardless of what "for now" meant, and he couldn't believe Harry, he who maintained he liked to see the cinders dance, could take it with such equanimity. Peepgass could already look two steps ahead. If "for now" dragged on very long, his whole campaign to squeeze Croker into handing over his properties would lose its momentum. Croker might get his brute aggressiveness back. And . . . how long could he, Peepgass, let "for now" go on without informing Herb Richman and the other members of the syndicate about it?

Harry continued to sit reared back, with his elbows winged up in the air. He was beginning to look at Peepgass the way you'd look at a curiosity.

Peepgass said, "Well—I'm going to go talk to Arthur about it. This thing is too important to just let slide like this."

"Good luck," said Harry with a dubious arching of his eyebrows, "but it's been my experience that when Arthur sends Plyers out with one of his 'macro-decisions,' it's something he's not dying to discuss."

It was late afternoon by the time Arthur Lomprey finally deigned to see Peepgass. Lomprey's office was on a corner from which you could look north toward Buckhead, east toward Decatur, and south toward Downtown and, assuming you wanted to, the vague expanse of the lower half of the city. Lomprey's office was so big, it had three seating areas: around a couch, around a table, and around his own gigantic desk. The decorators had been hard at work in here, with all sorts of leathers, fruitwoods, geometric carpeting, and fabrics that looked as lugubriously grand as old tapestries. Lomprey, seated at his desk with his head jutting forward like a dog's, looked up as Peepgass entered, but he didn't rise.

"Come in, Ray," he said pleasantly enough. But as Peepgass came walking toward him across the great expanse of carpet, which looked oddly like rows of campaign ribbons, the little eyes in the maximum leader's jutting head returned to some reading matter on his desk. Why should he waste valuable time waiting for a mere Raymond Peepgass to traverse twenty or thirty feet of carpet? Peepgass knew then, if not before, that whatever he could do to euchre PlannersBanc out of Croker's remains was justified.

In due course Lomprey looked up again and gestured toward an armchair and said, "Sit down." Then he leaned forward and put both elbows on top of his desk and began drumming his left palm with a gold ballpoint pen he held between the thumb and forefinger of his right hand and eyed Peepgass with a smile that was hard to interpret. It was a smile either of amusement, over his underling's puzzlement, or of wonder, at this ant's insistence on seeing the maximum leader face-to-face. In any event, it wasn't friendly.

"So—what's on your mind, Ray?" Lomprey beamed once more, and Peepgass now had it figured out. It was a smile of simple contempt.

"Charlie Croker's on my mind, Arthur," he said so forcefully, in such an un-Peepgass manner, that Lomprey's smile faded quickly. "Harry tells me you want us to put everything on hold where Croker is concerned."

"That's correct," said Lomprey.

Peepgass waited for some amplification, but all he got was a renewed smile. This one had little twists of irritation in the corners. Peepgass said, "Well, Arthur, I hope it wouldn't be out of place for me to ask why. I mean, we have that particular shithead right where we want him. We've got him right on the edge of handing over everything he's got, deeds in lieu of foreclosure. But if we let up now, he's liable to dig his heels in. Dragging this thing out is so unnecessary."

The smile, patient *and* irritated: "I'm surprised Harry didn't explain it to you. This is a macro-decision, Ray. It has to do with matters over and above what we do in the short term with the Croker workout."

In the conversational vacuum that followed . . . nothing more than the smile.

Did he dare prod the maximum leader further? Such irritation *and* contempt were in that smile! But given what was at stake—he dared:

"Do you mind if I ask you *what* matters, Arthur?"

"I mind," snapped Lomprey, lowering his head still farther and eyeing Peepgass carnivorously. "I hope it won't astonish you unduly to know that I am from time to time called upon to deal with problems broader in scope than what you and Harry would like to do with Charlie Croker."

"Oh, I know!" said Peepgass, backing down as quickly as he could. "I realize that! It's just that here we have such a large asset in question and a workout that's matured to such a point—" He kept searching Lomprey's face, hoping for some glimmer of fellow feeling, and found none. "I completely understand . . . I completely understand . . . I just wanted to make sure all the parameters—" He never could remember what one did with parameters.

He retreated from Lomprey's office in a daze.

ON THE PROGRAM of the Atlanta Symphony at the Woodruff Arts Center that evening were Tchaikovsky's Piano Concerto No. 1, Beethoven's Symphony No. 6 ("the Pastorale"), Stravinsky's *Rite of Spring*, and Scott Joplin's "Maple Leaf Rag"—none of which had anything to do with the obvious excitement in the lobby of Symphony Hall. The ordinary buzz of the hive had reached the threshold of a roar. Such looks these concertgoers gave one another! Such high beams they flicked on! How they showed their teeth when they smiled! And on all sides, on the crests of the waves of sound, Martha and Peepgass could hear the same names: Armholster . . . Inman . . . Elizabeth . . . Fanon . . . Fareek . . . Fareek "the Cannon" . . .

Martha and Peepgass had been talking about precisely the same thing on the way down from Buckhead in Peepgass's rented Volvo 960. To Peepgass, even though he understood Inman Armholster's eminence in the scheme of things in Atlanta, it was no more than any other piece of lush gossip. Martha took it far more personally. Ellen! It was Ellen Armholster she kept thinking about. Imagine being in her place! The fact that Ellen had treated her like a non-person ever since her divorce from Charlie made no difference. Poor Ellen!

Martha had very little appetite for talk of other people's misfortunes, and yet she felt rooted to this spot, here in the lobby, where all the frenzied talk was.

"Martha!"

A beaming woman had materialized before her, a fortyish woman with the usual pineapple-blond Palm Beach Crash Helmet—Maria—pronounced the Southern way, Ma-*rye*-a—Maria Bunting. She flicked a glance—and Martha noticed it—at Ray Peepgass before she embraced Martha and swung her head past hers in a social kiss.

"Maria, I'd like for you to meet Ray Peepgass. Ray, this is Maria Bunting."

"Hello, Ray!" said the woman, giving him a big smile and extending her hand.

"It's very nice to meet you," said Peepgass, taking her hand. He started to call her Maria but thought better of it.

Maria Bunting turned back toward Martha and said, "Have you heard the dreadful news about Elizabeth Armholster?" Halfway through the question she flicked her eyes toward Peepgass for a split second before returning to Martha's face for a reply.

"I certainly have," said Martha. "I was at Paolo's and some woman got a call about it on her cell phone. I was bowled over! Poor Ellen—that was all I could think about." Paolo's was a Buckhead hair salon.

"You mean poor Elizabeth!" said Maria Bunting.

Martha said, "I know—" But by now Maria's eyes had settled on Peepgass.

"I didn't know a thing about it until Martha mentioned it on the way over," said Peepgass. "What are they saying on the news?"

"All I've heard—well, Ed and I—my husband, Ed—we listened to the radio on the way over, and they didn't use the name. All they said was that this Web site on the Internet—what is it called?"

"Chasing the Dragon?" said Peepgass.

"I think that's it. I remember the Dragon part. Anyway, they'd broken the rules and used the name, and the girl's father's one of the most prominent businessmen in Atlanta. They were nice and pious about not using the name themselves." She gave in to a smile beneath her ecstatic eyes, but quickly turned down the corners of her mouth.

All three of them gave the lobby a quick survey. Martha saw a black couple over there near the wall. But they were light-skinned, and the man made you wonder if he was from England, the way he dressed.

"Well, I think it's just awful," said Martha. "I don't care whether it's the Internet or what. I think they ought to be ashamed."

"Well, at least it looks like the newspapers and the television stations won't use it," said Maria Bunting.

"They don't have to," said Martha. A weary little gesture. "Just look around this place. That's all anybody's talking about, me included. Everybody whose opinion Ellen and Inman care about already knows. I couldn't believe it. Somebody actually called somebody else at *Paolo's* on a cell phone—for no other reason than to spread the word."

Peepgass and Maria Bunting shook their heads. Peepgass, in his heart of hearts, couldn't have cared less one way or the other. But Maria Bunting's eyes shone more ecstatically than ever.

By the time the lobby lights had dimmed and brightened, dimmed and brightened, dimmed and brightened to show the crowd it was time to get to their seats, three other grand dames—Lettie Withers, Lenore Knox, and Betty Morrissey—had made their way over to Martha to say hello and cluck and fume over the dreadful news concerning Elizabeth Armholster. As for Martha, it was her considered and satisfied opinion that her becoming socially visible again had nothing to do with the Armholster affair and everything to do with the fact that this thatchy-haired, youngish, and presentable man, Mr. Ray Peepgass, was once again by her side. Now they could *see* her again!

As for Peepgass, what rang a bell with him was the fact that he knew all these names—the names of the rich and influential—Bunting, Withers, Knox, Morrissey—only from afar, a far far far distance from the world of Mr. Ray Peepgass of Unit XXX-A, Normandy Lea. In Martha Croker's company he was a mere snap of the fingers away from a first-name familiarity with that world. If Lomprey knew that, he'd change his insulting tune. *Macro-decision—meeeyahhh.*

DEEP INTO BEETHOVEN'S SIXTH they were, this huge arc of human beings up on the stage, all laboring so earnestly with their cellos and oboes and English horns and flutes and whatnot. One moment they'd be working away down deep in a cellar, and then suddenly a shower of notes would rise up and come drizzling down on the audience. The deep sounds resonated in Peepgass's belly, and then the drizzle began again, and his mind wandered. It gave him a mildly headachy feeling. It reminded him of church. His mother had trundled him off to Sunday school and the worship service at the Lutheran church right up to the time he was ten and they moved from St. Paul, Minnesota, to San Jose, California. Somehow religion never survived the trip, or maybe there was no Lutheran church to be had out there. Whatever it was, he remembered the heavy headachy feeling that used to come over him. His mind used to wander just the way it was wandering now. They would be teaching them the catechism in Sunday school, and he'd be thinking about the time he was four years old and he was going to demonstrate to a boy and a girl from the neighborhood that you could walk on ice and he took three steps out on a pond and fell straight through into freezing water and if his friends hadn't been there he would have drowned or frozen to death. Oh, he was the smart one then, the smartest in every class he ever took, even if he hadn't known about the relative thicknesses of ice at age four. He was the brightest, the most promising, every step of the way. And so why was he in the spot he found himself in tonight?—wildly into debt, and into the most childish form of debt, at that, credit-card debt, strapped for cash, unable to go to the Symphony or a High Museum opening unless some female benefactor treated him to a ticket, barely able to assemble a pressed suit, a laundered shirt, and a decent necktie at one and the same time, going nowhere in his career, scorned by that top layer of humanity who make the macro-decisions, thwarted—"for now"—in the most ambitious scheme of his entire life by a macro-decisionmaker whose neck was thrust forward like a dog's . . . Why was it so many "business leaders" were tall men like Lomprey, who was six-foot-four or -five even with his scoliotic dog's posture? Was that one of the host of things the aptitude tests didn't measure that had done Raymond Peepgass in? How could he climb up out of this hole and save himself? Here in the darkness it wasn't so bad . . . The cellos, the oboes, the bassoons, and a viola were sawing and moaning and bassooning away in his midsection—then a huge precipitation by the flutes, the trumpets, the clarinets, the violins, and the piano, which came raining down, like a sudden afternoon shower in the Bahamas . . . but all under the cozy cover of darkness. In the darkness the woman beside him was not a thickset fifty-three-year-old. She was a nice woman with tickets to all sorts of things.

Martha's mind wandered onto the stage. Who on earth were these people up there, playing their instruments with such dedication? That one, the third violinist from the end, must be very close to her own age, a little bit heavy, pleasant-looking, didn't know what to do with her hair . . . What was her story? A sad story, she decided. Had seemed like such a virtuoso when she was a girl, a slender, confident, vivacious girl who seemed to have all the talent in the world, the sort of free spirit who has an unerring instinct for falling for the wrong man . . . and now she's in her fifties and one of a row of men and women playing the violin in Atlanta, Georgia. But at least she has her talent! She can fill up even the loneliest house with music! . . . Or maybe she, Martha, had it all wrong. She'd love for them to put the music on hold, just a low, slightly melancholy symphonic background, and have the musicians rise up, one by one, and tell their stories . . . the dazzling promise of youth, the sag of middle age, and at the end . . . At the end of the row of violinists was a crumpled old man with wisps of hair and gray flesh that seemed to have melted over the end of the violin where he had tucked it under his chin. He lived alone, she decided. He and his wife had lived solely for one another, but she had died. Every stroke of the bow became a cry of sorrow. He eked out a living giving violin lessons, but to what end was all this would-be music? Meanwhile, his bow sobbed and sobbed. The thought brought a mist to Martha's eyes. Two or three thousand people in this one hall . . . and so much loneliness . . . and who besides herself paused long enough to pity the lonely? No one that she knew of. They all saw loneliness as a stigma, as a sign of failure, as a gaffe. It was a violation of etiquette, loneliness was, a source of embarrassment. That was what she had become as soon as Charlie walked out on her, an embarrassment. Maria Bunting, Lettie Withers, Lenore Knox, Betty Morrissey—not one of them had the faintest notion who Ray Peepgass was. Nevertheless, he had rendered her visible again. The violin section was now still. The middle-aged violinist over here and the old man over there had lifted their cheeks and chins from their instruments. Their eyes were downcast, following the progress of the scores—or were their minds drifting? What would be left for them after the music stopped? What would they have to go home to? It was no picnic for Beethoven himself, from what little she could remember.

The drizzle was continuing steadily. In fact, it had become a regular downpour. When Beethoven really got himself worked up, there was no end to it. Peepgass tried to imagine himself as a composer, sitting at a desk in front of those lines, those staffs, and trying to think up notes . . . It was beyond him. Most of them had a bad time of it, even the great ones, as nearly as he could recall. But at least they left something, something their children could point to . . . If he got run over by a Lincoln Navigator tomorrow, what could they write about him? What *they*?—as far as that went. *They* would have to be some loved ones who sent in a paid obituary to the *Journal-Constitution*—and just who was going to do that? Betty? Sirja? Master P. P. Peepgass? The boys? For one reason or another, he had hardly seen the boys since his separation from Betty. Wonder if they ever use the basketball backboard out in the driveway anymore? Forty-six years old, and he hadn't left so much as a footprint . . . whereas somebody like Edward I. Bunting gives five million dollars he doesn't need to the hospital and they name a whole pavilion for him and he's the great philanthropist and nobody remembers that he made his money as an agricultural insecticide broker. They liked to talk about "family" here in the South, but money was what it all came down to at the end of the day. You could talk about family until you were hoarse, but if you were living in a starter rental in Collier Hills instead of a mansion in the West Paces Ferry section of Buckhead, who cared about your "family"? What good was a great chain of being that led straight down a thirty-degree slope to a gully at the base of the cliff that supported I-75?

Wellllllll . . . hmmmmmmmmmmmm . . . she worked out, didn't she? She was always talking about DefinitionAmerica and a class taught by some Turk named Mustafa Somethingorother. So maybe she—what was it Mickey Mantle said? The first thing he looked for in a woman was good calves? If the calves were in good shape, then chances were the thighs were in good shape; and if the thighs were in good shape, how bad could the abdominals and the rest of her be? And Martha had good calves . . . But she's still fifty-three years old, for Chrissake! . . . Relax, Peepgass . . . Think of it as a kind of arranged union. She's not stupid. At her age it's not about children. She'll give you some room, and you'll give her some room, assuming she has anything to do in that big space you'll give her . . . But what would people say?—a woman seven years older than himself! Welllllllll . . . what do they say now? Harry Zale mocks him to his face for getting excited about the Croker case, and when he asks Arthur if he minds him asking a question, Arthur snaps, "I mind"—as if he, Peepgass, has no business poking his nose into matters that are settled only on the forty-ninth floor. As a matter of fact, he'd like to see the looks on their ugly mugs. Right now they treat him like a worker bee, don't they . . . Well—all that's going to change, one way or the other!

The bows of the violins were swooping up and down like . . . cricket legs. Why that image suddenly popped into her mind, she hadn't the foggiest idea. She looked to see if the old man could keep up with the lead violinist . . . Seemed to be holding his own . . . Ray was younger than she was. She didn't know by how much, but there was something about his looks that was still a little babyish. There was something a little too soft and passive about him. He was the kind of man any formidable woman, formidable from ambition or just plain meanness, would run right over. His wife had chucked him out of the house! Just told him to scat, and he scatted! Not that Martha considered herself formidable. It had been hard to be formidable when you had been in the company of Charlie Croker for twenty-nine years. But a woman might *have to be* formidable where Ray was concerned. He was bright, quick, but not at all tough. He would require a lot of maintenance. But he was good company, relaxing company, considerate company. Charlie could be embarrassing, especially when he was off on one of his tears. Ray would never be embarrassing. Not that this was a decision she would even have to make. This was the fifth time they had gone out, and Ray had never been anything other than what he was right now . . . there. She could make out only the vaguest of contours with her peripheral vision here in the darkness. It was entirely possible that he was interested only in getting a gold star at PlannersBanc for creating his beloved syndicate.

Beethoven was going all-out now, bassooning and celloing and drumming away in his belly and sending up a heavy drizzle of notes at the same time. Made him slightly woozy, foggy, and, come to think of it, affectionate. Where would it lead? Hadn't the vaguest notion. What would it cost? Not much. After all, how angry could she get? Not very. It would be a compliment. He was a young man. In fact, as far as he could see, his appearance hadn't changed in twenty years. A couple of extra pounds. Still had his jawline. Something happened to men when they got up into their fifties and sixties; their jawlines collapsed, melted, so that their cheeks began to puddle into their necks. No, the worst that could happen would be that she would feel complimented. The best that could happen? That he didn't have any clear picture of—since he had no real picture of where he wanted this to go. He'd have to wing it. Boom boom boom drizzle drizzle drizzle went Beethoven, and yet more drizzle drizzle drizzle. He felt warm and narcoleptic. He surveyed her out of the corner of his eye. The light from the stage created soft, indistinct highlights, which made her look roundish, as if she were made of ice cream. But that was just the play of light and shadow, the distortions of chiaroscuro. The woman had good calves. Good calves, good calves. Her hands were in her lap, which presented a problem. If he tried to reach *over* her hand and engage it that way and reached too far, it might seem as if he was going after her crotch, which would turn the whole thing into abject farce. He turned his head ever so slightly and swiveled both eyes toward her. A gloss of light went down her forearm and stood at attention when it hit the gold of her wristwatch and her bracelets. Christ . . . she probably had more money on her one wrist than he could get his hands on in the form of discretionary income in two years. Anyway, the glistening gave him something visible to aim for. So—should I?—why not?—here goes. He kept looking only long enough to make sure his hand would be heading directly toward her wrist. He didn't want to be looking at her when his hand touched hers. Why? It wasn't a question he had an answer for, beyond the fact that he had no idea in the world what he would have wanted such a look to say. His fingertips perceived all the highly wrought metal on her wrist, and in the next moment they found the palm of her hand and slid up the fingers. She had her chance—and that hand was not flying away. Nor was she turning toward him with a jerk of incredulity. Her hand yielded as he interlaced his fingers with hers.

Oho! Well—there he is. What, exactly, is he up to? Her mind spun, not with emotion but with sheerly logical computations. I'm not sixteen any longer. If I accept this bit of handholding, I'm implying a whole lot more, even though of what I can't be sure. But if I withdraw my hand, even with a lighthearted jest, then I'm saying no to whatever Ray can do for me by being at my side. If the lights suddenly came on, and all the world could see me holding hands with Mr. Raymond Peepgass of

PlannersBanc, I'd be mortified. Why? That I can't quite figure out. By now his hand seemed terribly big and warm. Should she give it a slight squeeze? She decided . . . no; for the simple reason that she had no idea what that squeeze would mean. Should she look at him? In what way? Warmly? Gratefully? Tenderly? Or with an ironic arching of the eyebrows, as if to say, "All in fun—okay, Ray?" The truth was, she had no idea what she even *wanted* to convey. She cut her eyes as far in his direction as she could without turning her head. With peripheral vision she could see that he wasn't looking at her, either. There they sat, holding hands in the darkness of Symphony Hall at the Woodruff Center. All the lonely violinists were pumping away like grasshoppers.

AT THE END of the concert, as he and Henrietta were caught up in the tide of humanity in the lobby, Roger Too White put a big confident smile on his face and said to her, "I have to laugh. You know why they tacked Scott Joplin on at the end?" Talking about serious music, even to Henrietta, always made the dread nickname, Roger Too White, pop into his head.

"Why?" asked Henrietta.

"It was a nice little piece of chocolate—" He broke it off. He didn't want Henrietta to attach a double meaning to "chocolate." "—dessert, sweets, candy, a little reward to all these folks"—he swung his head about to indicate the crowd about them—"for sitting through the Stravinsky."

He beamed at her, as if this was a terrifically amusing observation and he was enjoying himself hugely. Being the only black folks in the place, so far as he could tell, he didn't want any of these folks, these white folks, thinking that he and Henrietta felt in any way ill at ease, out of place, subdued, intimidated.

Henrietta said, "A nice little piece of chocolate, hunh?"

"I didn't mean it that way," said Roger Too White. Once again he beamed grandly. "I don't think they tacked him on because he's bl—African-American"—Henrietta had become so with-it, he had begun to be careful with his terminology around her—"I think it's because 'The Maple Leaf Rag' is familiar and happy, bouncy, good-humored. That was their reward for enduring *Rite of Spring*. You'd've seen some long faces if all these people got at the end was a big dose of Stravinsky." He put another hundred watts into his smile.

"Oh, I don't know—"

"In Atlanta, Stravinsky's still terribly modern, cutting edge."

"Oh, I don't know about—"

"In Atlanta, it's as if this was the opening performance of *Le Sacre du Printemps*. The only difference is that they're not courageous enough to boo. I don't know what they'd do if it was Schoenberg. Cut a wrist or make somebody resign, maybe."

"I'm not sure they'd do anything different from what they're doing right now," said Henrietta. Then she drew closer to him, so as not to have to raise her voice. "They're not even thinking about the music. All they're thinking about is Fareek and the Armholster girl."

"How do you know?"

"Because I *listen*. That's all they were talking about when we got here, and that's all they're talking about now."

Roger looked about . . . I'll be damned . . . There was no doubt about it . . . After all, his picture had been in the paper three times, and he'd been on every television channel you could think of after the press conference . . . These people . . . *recognized* him! He stood as tall as he could. Over there, thirty or forty feet away—a white woman with puffed-up blond hair was staring right at him. Then she smiled. He didn't know whether to smile back or what. Without turning her face away, the woman tugged on the arm of a tall white man next to her and said something to him, and *he* looked at Roger. Roger looked away, because it was getting embarrassing to be looking at these people without knowing how to respond or even if he should . . . He sighed. He guessed he had the virus, publicity, but he wouldn't let it affect him. He had built up his career in an entirely different way. He wanted to mention it to Henrietta, the way these people were staring at him. He wanted to ask her, "Do you think some of these white people you see whispering—don't you think it's possibly because they recognize . . . *me*?" But he wasn't fool enough to actually ask her. What a horselaugh she'd give him!

As they moved ever so slowly in the tide of white people heading for the exits, he cut his eyes this way and that . . . and now he was *sure* people were looking at him . . . They *recognized* him. It was a feeling he had never known before. He couldn't hold back any longer. He began chuckling.

"What's funny?" said Henrietta.

He looked at her and suddenly felt even happier because of how pretty she was. He put his arm around her shoulder. He could feel the warmth of Fate smiling upon him. Not a *pretty* wife—a *gorgeous* wife! Those big brown eyes of hers, set against her light tan skin, the soft lushness of her *Bout en Train* hairdo—and all at once he was . . . *famous*, too.

He leaned over and whispered into her ear: "Don't look now, but I'm afraid there are a lot of people in here who recognize the Defender of Fareek Fanon!"

Henrietta pulled back from him and gave him a look of the most sardonic bewilderment he had ever seen. "Excuse *me*?" she said. "They're doing *what* to the Defender of Fareek Fanon?"

Feebly: "Recognize . . ."

"Are you *serious*?"

"Well, I only—"

"I don't doubt they're looking at you, Roger, but would you like to know the *real* reason, by any chance?"

"It's not a case of—"

"It's because you're an *African American*."

He was bewildered.

"We're an oddity to them, a curiosity. African Americans don't *go* to the Symphony in Atlanta. These folks do everything but give away tickets at the MARTA stops to get African Americans to come here, so they can feel better about themselves—and they *still don't come*. Just take a look around. They're looking at us as . . . as . . . as aliens, to give it the kindest word I can think of."

"I don't believe . . ." He didn't bother finishing the sentence. He was crestfallen.

Henrietta must have realized some of that, because she now took his arm and snuggled up against him and said, "I'm sorry. I didn't mean that the way it sounded. It's just that you're doing so well, and I don't want you to delude yourself. I'm very proud of you."

Roger didn't say anything. For the first time he realized how much Henrietta detested these trips of theirs to the Woodruff Arts Center. It made him feel like a blind fool—dragging her off to these white "cultural" events the way he had.

But she was wrong about one thing. They *did* recognize him, damn it.

XXVII

Chapter

The Screen

SOMEHOW CHARLIE HAD THOUGHT THE OPERATING ROOM would be a white amphitheater, blazingly bright, with a large oval floor and a white wall six or seven feet high around the oval and, above the wall, high-banked theater seats where doctors in white coats would sit to observe this important operation, or "procedure," as Emmo Nuchols called it. Instead, it looked like one of those small leftover pieces of modern office space where office machines on casters are stored. It reminded him of the room at PlannersBanc where they had held the first workout session, and yet there was no feeling attached to the thought. It was as if all that . . . terrible stuff . . . was being held back by a dam or a levee . . . whatever . . .

Not that he could see a great deal. He was lying on his back on what seemed to be a narrow padded table, and there was a screen about a yard high that they had placed over his midsection so that he couldn't see what they were doing to his knee. He had no feeling from the waist down. They had given him an epidural anesthetic. He had no idea what "epidural" meant, but that didn't matter . . . There seemed to be numerous tubes, some of which came out of him and some of which went into him . . . There was an oxygen mask over his nose and mouth.

Eeeeeeeyehhhhhhhhhhh . . . a high-pitched whine, like the whine of the rotary saws cutting into wood at the pulp mill where his daddy worked, and a high-frequency vibration ran up his upper spine . . . Emmo—or he assumed it was Emmo—was cutting off the tips of his right thighbone and right shinbone where they came together in the knee to get rid of the "osteoarthritic crud," as Emmo seemed to enjoy calling it; but Charlie no longer cared whether Emmo called it that or not. Then they were supposed to fit pieces of titanic chromium cobalt —or was it cobalt chromium titanium?—it made no particular difference—onto the ends of the bones to create a new knee joint, with a piece of polyethylene heavy molecular . . . whatever-it-was. Couldn't remember, which was all right . . . It was some piece of plastic somethingorother that replaced the cushion of cartilage between the two bones . . . *Eeeeeeeeyehhhhhhhhh* . . . They were sawing away down there, and he actually liked the vibration when it ran up his spine.

He could hear them talking on the other side of the screen, and every now and then Emmo Nuchols would raise his voice, saying, "How's he doing?" A voice behind Charlie's head would say, "He's fine."

Then Emmo himself came out from behind the screen. He had some sort of plastic framework on his head, and over the frame came a pale green tent with a picture window in it. His carpeted face was back behind the window.

"It's going well, Charlie." Emmo's voice was slightly muffled by the tent. "How are we feeling?"

Charlie hated the patronizing medical "we," but now—who cared? Emmo looked like an astronaut.

"Em-mo," said Charlie, conscious that his voice was slowing down, "you look . . . like—"

"An astronaut?" said Emmo.

It wounded Charlie to learn in this manner that he had been about to say something that had obviously been said hundreds of times before, but a moment later he wasn't really bothered by it. "Yeah," he said.

Emmo turned around, and Charlie could see two big accordion-style rubber tubes running down his back. "We have our own air supply, just like the astronauts," he said. "Filtered air. Cuts down the risk of introducing any infectious agent into the incision." Then he turned back toward Charlie and said, "So how are we feeling?"

"I feel good!" said Charlie. "I feel better than I did when I came in this morning." He looked up at the surgeonaut behind his tent window and halfway expected a gold star for being so strong and cheery under the stress of major surgery.

"Now we're going to put in your new parts, your new joint," said the tent-muffled voice. "You'll notice the hammering, but don't worry about it. You won't feel any pain." Then Emmo disappeared on the other side of the screen.

Charlie pondered upon the fact that he felt so . . . *good.* He was flat on his back, he had tubes in the back of his hand, in the tip of a finger, in his spine, in his urethra, a tube feeding him oxygen; he had no feeling in the lower half of his body—but he felt good. He would be perfectly happy to prolong this moment . . . infinitely. Oh yes, not just indefinitely—*in*finitely . . . The screen over his midsection was precisely what he wanted from this operation . . . He couldn't see the world, and the world couldn't see him, and time stood still . . . Oh, what a note of astonishment in Emmo's voice when he had called him and said he wanted the operation . . . now! . . . soon as possible! . . . Surgery would take him out of this world for . . . weeks . . . There'd be nothing he could *do*, nothing he was *expected* to do, no dilemmas he *could* solve, no dilemmas he would *have* to solve . . . No Inman . . . no Zale . . . This was a perfectly honorable and understandable withdrawal from the battle. *Don't look at me! I have abandoned my fate to others!* And if an "infectious agent" were introduced into the incision, if particles of bone marrow caused clots, what was the worst that could happen? God might be so kind as to take him away in the night . . .

Then he could hear the hammering, and then he could feel it. It came in painless dull thuds right up his spine and into the rear of his skull. The hammering was metal upon metal, but upon something bigger than a nail. They were driving the new metal ends of the femur and the tibia straight into the live bones. This operation was like a construction site . . . the *eeeeeeeyehhhhhhhhh* of the electric saws, the *bing! bing! bing! bing! bing!* of the hammer . . . like a construction site, and he, Charlie Croker, knew about construction sites . . . His right knee was a construction site, and he had contracted himself out—but he couldn't complete the comparison. It made his head hurt; and besides, what difference did it make, all this mental activity?

IN THE RECOVERY ROOM Serena and Wally were looking down at him . . . in this horizontal life of his. He was lying on a narrow rolling bed with side rails. His right knee created a mound under the covers. He still couldn't feel a thing below the waist.

Wally said, "You were awake the whole time, Dad?"

"Yeah," said Charlie, "I couldn't . . . feel anything, but I could hear . . . saws . . . hammers . . . regular construction site . . ." He smiled. He felt a compulsion to show that he had been a manly good sport. "Pretty interesting."

"You know how long you were in there?" said Serena.

"No, I guess I sorta . . . lost track of time."

"A little over three hours," said Serena. "Emmo said it went very well."

Serena was gently stroking the side of his right hand, the one with the IV tube inserted into a vein on the back of it. He still had a guilty feeling whenever Wally saw Serena showing him any physical affection, but he guessed this little bit didn't matter. Beneath her corona of black hair her blue eyes had a tender look such as he hadn't seen for a while.

"Did it make you nervous, Dad?"

Whether Wally was truly curious or just making conversation, Charlie couldn't tell. And in that moment he realized he had never come to know his son well enough to tell the difference; and never would; but that was all right; we just do the best we can; whatever.

"Naw," said Charlie, "I actually felt . . . good . . . a little tired . . . Hadda get up so early . . . couldn't have anything to eat . . . or drink, far as that goes . . . but I felt good . . ." All at once he felt generous, magnanimous, appreciative, like a good boy. "I'll tell you one thing . . . they got terrific nurses . . . You hear all these stories . . . but I got no complaints . . . This place, the nurses, they come in every five minutes . . . see if there's anything I want. By the time I went in . . . I was so relaxed, it was like I was taking . . . uh uh . . . a walk in the park."

By and by Emmo Nuchols appeared. He still had on his pale green scrubs, but without the surgeonaut's head frame and tent. It occurred to Charlie that surgeons probably liked to walk around in the hospital with their scrubs, just to show the world that they were surgeons only recently departed from the medical front. But it was just a passing thought. It was all the same to him one way or the other.

Emmo peered down at him with a paternal smile, and then he said, "Well, Charlie, you're a bionic man now."

Charlie said, "I could hear you sawing and hammering away in there. Sounded like a regular construction site." He was vaguely aware that he had just used this line with Serena and Wally—but who cared?

"Had to make sure all the parts were in there for keeps," said Emmo. He still had his fatherly smile on.

"I could feel it in my backbone," said Charlie. "The vibration came right up my backbone and into my head."

"That's normal," said Emmo. "Everything went according to plan. The only surprise was, we found a little more necrotic tissue than we thought was there, but you're going to be fine. We'll have you out jumping rope."

Charlie felt another urge to demonstrate that he was a good boy, a stout fellow, a model patient who was mindful of the contributions of others. "Em-mo," he said in his slow voice, "I want you to . . . do something for me."

"What's that, Charlie?"

"I want you to . . . thank the nurses for me."

"The nurses?"

"Yeah . . . They were in . . . to see me . . . every five minutes before . . . I went into surgery. They made me feel so . . . relaxed . . . by the time I . . . went in there, I thought I was going . . . for a walk in the park. They were fabulous. I want you to . . . tell'em that for me."

Emmo smiled. Then he pursed his lips and cast his eyes downward to one side and began to nod his head as if to agree with the profound sentiment his model patient had just expressed. Then he looked at Charlie and said, "I'll do that, Charlie. They *are* fabulous, and I'll tell'em you said so. But Demerol's pretty fabulous, too."

Wally started laughing. Charlie didn't know why at first. He looked up at Serena, who was trying to suppress a smile. Then Emmo's wisecrack made its way through the Demerol dike in his brain. Wally was laughing, Serena was trying not to laugh, and Emmo was smiling the knowing smile of the fatherly wise man.

There was no reason he, Charlie, had to take that kind of mockery from Emmo Nuchols, but at the same time . . . whatever.

NORTH OF THE MARTA tracks Chamblee still looked like the old country town it had always been. And it was in Old Chamblee that Conrad found himself walking on this warm, bright June morning. He felt groggy from lack of sleep and from tension. He wasn't sure he could spend another night at the Meadow Lark Terrace sweating, sweltering, along with a dozen, two dozen, God knew how many Vietnamese. Lying on the floor curled up with his overnight bag pressed into his midsection for safekeeping, listening to the incessant and incomprehensible *unnnh-click-clack* of the conversations around him, waking up four, five, six times a night with a start.

Soon enough eating would become just as big a problem. He had only $272 left of the $1,500 Kenny had given him. If he continued to eat at restaurants on the Buford Highway, that would melt away all too quickly. Without intending to in the slightest, he thought about how he had commandeered the Jeep at Camp Parks—even in his thoughts he avoided the word *stolen*—and experienced a wave of guilt. One might—Zeus might—forgive taking an Army Jeep in the middle of an earthquake, but no such commandeering, appropriating, or "borrowing" would be forgivable in a quiet little town like Chamblee.

In turn the sense of guilt over something he had only briefly entertained the thought of doing made him wonder just what he must look like to the residents of this little town . . . A young man with short hair, swarthy skin, delicate features, clean-shaven—he had managed to get into the bathroom for that long this morning—wearing blue jeans, a polo shirt, a navy windbreaker, construction boots that still looked new . . . carrying an overnight bag . . . nothing remarkable about his appearance, he concluded with satisfaction . . . *except for one thing!*—there was not another soul walking along these streets—

All at once, as if it had been caused by his own premonition, he could hear a car slowing down behind him. Then he could hear its hushed idle as it coasted closer. Didn't dare look around. Now, in his peripheral vision, he could tell that it was right beside him. Which was the cooler thing to do, ignore it or turn toward it?—since the driver would know you were bound to have noticed the car by now? *Decide!*

He turned his head. Sure enough, a police cruiser, with a gold badge and the legend CHAMBLEE TOWN POLICE painted on a white door. The policeman, thickset, wearing aviator-style glasses, was smiling at him . . . just that, smiling at him and letting the cruiser drift forward at the pace of Conrad's walk. Conrad was already ransacking his memory for the answer to the inevitable question—*Why?* At the same time, another decision: which was cooler, to maintain eye contact and stop, maintain eye contact and keep walking, or break eye contact and keep walking? *Decide!*

He nodded with a neutral and, he devoutly hoped, cool expression on his face, turned his head, and kept walking. The cruiser kept drifting along beside him. What now? Ignore him or not? O Zeus! *Decide—*

"Where you heading?" Whirr ya headin'?

Conrad turned his head and then stopped. The man was still smiling. Conrad fought the urge to swallow and to blink. A scrap of memory—caught it!

"I'm looking for a shop, an antiques shop, called Hello Again."

The policeman, his big neck straining against his shirt collar, kept staring at him and smiling. Conrad fought to keep control of his eyes, his mouth, and his throat. It was precisely *now* that the man was deciding whether to check him out or let him go. Finally:

"Up there at the next street?" Up'irr't the next street? "You take a right?" You take a rat? "And it's two blocks from there, that way." *In it's two blocks fum'irr, 'at way.* He pointed in that direction.

Then he dropped the smile and said, "Have a nice day," and . . . *winked* and pulled away in the cruiser. *Winked*—as if to say, "I don't believe a word of it, but I'm gonna let you be."

Conrad's heart was pounding. He figured he'd better head, for real, to Hello Again, a shop he'd had a single stray glimpse of the first day after he arrived.

The shop was in an exhausted old wooden frame house on a corner. Part of the original clapboard façade had been cut away and framed to create a show window. The merchandise was above the level of a flea market, but not a great deal. The prize item was an old J. C. Higgins balloon-tire bicycle, unfortunately a bit rusty.

Inside, in a room that must not have been painted in a quarter century, were an old man and an old woman. Both were morbidly fat. The old man was sitting at a desk in the rear reading a pamphlet. As he checked out Conrad, he opened his mouth and stuck his big bulbous tongue into a stretch of gums where there was a row of teeth missing. His pants, an old pair of navy serge pants now shiny at the knee and on his fat thighs, were zipped up as far as they would go, which was where his underbelly began bulging out in a thoroughly irreducible way. The old woman, who was standing in the front, wore a capacious shift, apparently homemade, with no sleeves, so that the pitted gobs, the garlands, of fat that jiggled on the backs of her arms were exposed. Her skin was a livid white, and her hair was random wisps of gray, but on her face were red splotches that spread or grew smaller according to how much she exerted herself. All around, on shelves, in freestanding glass cases on the floor was . . . stuff . . . pieces of tarnished silverware, most of them knives and spoons, wrinkled Victorian Christmas cards, a partial set of teacups with handles in the shape of nymphs doing back bends, teetering stacks of old *National Geographics* . . . inkstands with the silver plate wearing off . . . a pair of women's rubber galoshes with scalloped edges where one side closed and snapped over the other . . . a moth-eaten fox stole in which the fox seemed to be holding his tail in his mouth . . . In short, junk. Little as Conrad knew about antiques, the thought of trying to sift for the precious pieces possibly hidden among these heaps was too demoralizing to be attempted. The room had a sharp, slightly sour smell that reminded Conrad of something familiar, but he couldn't name it. A sooty gray-green wallpaper was torn away at the corners, revealing a veritable archaeological dig of various wallpapers underneath.

The old woman sized up Conrad, then cocked her head in a slightly challenging way, and said, "Help you, young man?" Then she resumed chewing her cud.

"I was wondering about the bicycle in the window," said Conrad.

"That old J. C. Higgins?" she said. "Pretty thing."

"I was wondering how much it is," said Conrad.

"One hundred dollars," she said. "Got good tires, too." Got good tars, too. "You can ride it right outta here."

There was a lump in her cheek that she kept moving around with her tongue. Then she took a McDonald's paper cup out from behind a lamp with four glass Ionic columns as a base, held it up to her face so that it covered her mouth, and spat into it. Chewing tobacco.

Conrad shook his head. "Can't afford that much. I need a way to get around, but—" Rather than try to finish the sentence, he shook his head some more.

She said, "How much *can* you afford, son?"

The old man made a hawking sound in his throat. Conrad looked about; the old man also had a McDonald's cup over his mouth. Then he put that one down behind a framed sepia-tone picture of a baseball player named Cecil Travis and picked up another one and tilted it back to his lips. The sweet smell of brown whiskey, bourbon or rye, spread through the room.

It was part of an even ranker odor, which was the odor of poverty. As his eyes got used to the gloom of the place, he noticed a potbellied stove obscured by the great bulk of the old man. An old-fashioned stovepipe rose from the stove and curved into the wall. That no doubt accounted for the sharp, sour smell: coal fumes.

"I don't exactly know," said Conrad, answering the old woman. Somehow—he couldn't have accounted for why—he trusted her. "I need a way to get around, but I also need a place to stay."

The old woman glanced at the old man and then said, "What kinda place you want?"

"A room somewhere, I guess," said Conrad. "I can't afford much."

"Where you staying now?" she asked.

"With some friends over near the highway," said Conrad. "But they don't have enough room."

"Over'n Chambodia?" said the old man with a chortle.

"I don't know," said Conrad, not wanting to get onto that topic. "I think they said it was Chamblee."

"Huh," said the old man, "that's what *we* used to call it."

"We've lived in this house for four generations," said the woman. "Us Mungers I'm talking about. Our granddaddy, Brother'n'mine"—she nodded in the direction of the old man—"fought in the Civil War. He wasn't a drummer boy, either. He was in the infantry, started out as a private, fought at Chickamauga, Atlanta, Jonesboro—finally got wounded at Jonesboro. He was a major by then. Battlefield promotions. Our mother went to Agnes Scott College; for two years."

Conrad could think of no adequate response to these revelations. "Ummmmm," he said, nodding his head as if in pleasant surprise.

"I'll be switched if I know how this town suddenly went Oriental," said the woman.

"You know darn well, Sister," said Brother. "It's'at chicken plant in Knowlton. Won't no white man work there and no black man, either, these days. So they wants the Orientals, but they don't want'em living in Knowlton, so they park'em in Chamblee and Doraville."

"Well, to tell the truth, that's another thing," said Conrad. "I need a job, too. What *about* the chicken plant?"

"Naw, naw, naw," said Brother, who always massaged the toothless part of his gums with his tongue before he spoke. "The smell'll finish you off all by itself."

"What smell?"

"The smell of thousands of chickens—and we're talking about *thousands*—the smell of thousands of chickens with their intestines hanging out."

"You go to church?" said Sister.

Conrad hesitated. He knew from the very question itself that the proper answer was yes. So he took a chance. "I go to the Church of Zeus."

"Church of Zeus?" said Sister. "That's a new one on me."

"You sure it ain't the Church of the Zion Crossroads?" said Brother.

"No, it's Zeus," said Conrad. "Started up about the time of Nero."

"Where you gon' find one around here?" said Sister.

"That's the problem," said Conrad, "not many of'em anywhere."

"Sister'n'me's Methodists," said Brother. "Our mama and papa were UB's, but we're Methodists."

"UB's?" asked Conrad.

"United Brethren," said Brother, "but Sister'n'me's Methodists. The only thing I don't like about the Methodist Church is the hymns. John Wesley wrote half uv'em, and he never had the knack for it, if you ask me. The Episcopalians got the hymns. I'll give'em'at much." He burst into song:

"*Lord God of hosts,*
Be with us yet,
Lest we forget,
Lest we for-get,
Forrrrr-getttttt . . ."

He had a surprisingly good tenor voice, which ranged over two octaves in those few lines. "What kind of hymns your Church of Zeus got?"

"Not much," said Conrad.

"Well, it's like I say. When it comes to your hymns, the Episcopalians are the beatin'est." He burst into song once more:

"*A mighty fortress is our God,*
A bulwark never failing.

Our helper he amid the flood,
O'er mortal ills prevailing."

Then he said, "That's another thing. If you're in the Episcopal Church, they call you Episcopalians. If you're in the Methodist Church, they call you a Methodist. Whatta they call you if you're in the Church of Zeus? A Zeusian?"

"No, a Stoic," said Conrad.

"A Stoic?"

"Yeah. People tend to think of Stoics as people who are long-suffering and don't complain. But it's a whole religion."

"Don't sound Christian," said Brother.

"It's pre-Christian," said Conrad. "The Stoics influenced the early Christians."

"Unh-hunh." Brother gave Conrad a searching gaze. "What kinda work you done before?"

"Trucker's helper, warehouse man, construction—but I don't have a trade. I'll do anything, though."

"Truck loading—you don't look the type," said Brother. "Let me see your hands."

Conrad spread his fingers wide and offered his hands for inspection, palm-first.

"I take it back," said Brother. "Sister, look at—what's your name anyway?"

"Connie," said Conrad. "Connie DeCasi."

"Well, thank the Lord for that," said Sister. "A young man who volunteers his last name! All these kids today, they only have first names. Makes you think they're drug dealers. Well, getting back to what we were saying— By the way, where're your folks?"

Conrad hesitated. "They're both dead."

"Where was you brought up?" said Sister.

"All over the place. Macon most recently."

"Where'd you live in Macon?"

Luckily he remembered the address on his fake driver's license. "Twenty-seven hundred block of Cypress."

"Don't know it," said Brother.

"Getting back to what we were saying," said Sister. "You say you need a room, eh?"

"I sure do," said Conrad.

Sister looked toward Brother and must have gotten a sign of approval, because she said, "Well, we have a room here we rent out sometimes. It's up on the third floor."

"How much is it?" asked Conrad.

"Seventy-five dollars," said Sister.

"A *week*?"

"No, a month. We like the rent in advance."

Sister led Conrad up a gloomy staircase, which had stacks of *Atlantic Monthly*s from God knew back when on every step, next to the wall. On the second floor Conrad got a glimpse of two dismal bedrooms heaped so full of books, magazines, and bric-a-brac, the only part you could see of their floors, which were linoleum, was the pathways they had cleared from the doorways to the beds. In a corner of the hallway was a small bathroom with an old soapstone basin.

By the time Sister headed up the stairway to the third floor, she was breathing loudly. She had a way of moving from step to step by sidling her bulk this way and that. "Stairs in 'is house . . . gon' finish me off . . . 'reckly . . ."

The third floor was underneath the eaves. There were several small rooms with dormer windows, but they were so chockablock with . . . stuff . . . they looked impenetrable. Such light as there was in the tiny hallway came from a bulb screwed into the ceiling with a disintegrating parchment shade clipped to it upside down. Sister led Conrad to a doorway. A narrow dormer window, bereft of curtain or shade, admitted a shaft of light into the room within. In this one the floor was not absolutely choked with Sister'n'Brother Munger's Hello Again collection, merely heavily littered. In a corner beneath an eave was a narrow bed, the narrowest bed Conrad had ever seen, much narrower than an ordinary twin-size, with an old painted metal bedstead and some sort of ornately handworked but dusty and yellowish-white counterpane. Half the counterpane was covered with ceramic lamp bases lying on their sides.

"Things sorta need puttin' away in here," said Sister, panting hard from the climb, "but that's a good old bed, and nobody's made a matelassé counterpane like that one right there in a hundred years." A *hunnut* years. "Gettin' hot out already." She swept a perilously hanging droplet of sweat from the tip of her nose with the back of one hand and the sweat of her brow with the back of the other one.

The little room was stifling, and the eaves were pressing down from both sides. But something told Conrad this was about as good as an exhausted unemployed escaped convict was going to be able to get on short notice for $75 a month. And besides—although this yearning he couldn't have put into words—here he would have . . . *fellow humans to talk to!* . . . even if it was only this pair of old pack rats. Eccentric they were, garrulous they were, inert they were, tobacco chewers they were, and McDonald's cup spitters, but they seemed to have good hearts. He had already lived in a place where everyone was young and bursting with energy to burn and every heart was malevolent. It was called Santa Rita.

After completing his cash transaction with Sister, Conrad set about the task of "puttin' away." Even though it consisted of nothing more than arranging all the sad old rubbish in orderly ranks beneath the eave opposite the bed, it took him more than three hours. Then he took off his boots and lay down on the dusty, yellowing old matelassé counterpane and closed his eyes and listened to his heartbeat and sweated and congratulated himself. A bed of his own!—for the next thirty days! O Zeus!

A bed of his own; and the grand sum of $197 left in his jeans.

DAY 2. NO more Demerol. No more immersion in the mindless sea of narcosis, in the hemisphere of Whatever. Charlie was an enormous aching knee with attachments: his upper and lower right leg, his torso, his other leg, his arms, neck, his tormented head, and his bladder, which required him to undergo the indignity of a bedpan.

As armor against such insults to his status, all of which proceeded from the hospital patient's role as a frightened organism upon which superior beings practiced their medical arts, Charlie insisted on wearing a brilliant blue Thai silk robe with white Paisley designs upon it, as if it were a royal blue that would strike the hearts of one and all with fear of the king. In fact, regiphobia, if any, didn't seem to deter his keepers for a second. Emmo Nuchols kept coming by and treating Charlie, who was twenty years his senior, as if he, Emmo, were a parent who, while patient and forbearing, *would be obeyed*. Specifically, he ordered him to obey his physical therapist, a hawk-faced woman who refused to be charmed or amused. She compelled him to do all sorts of painful things with his knee, even to the point of making him get out of bed and support his weight with his throbbing knee with only an aluminum walker to help him support his weight. The walker clanked and rattled in its aluminum joints with every tiny step he took. By the time he got back in bed, he would be panting like a dog.

He felt deceived. Emmo had always described the operation as if it were a piece of carpentry. All the bones and cartilage in the model on Emmo's desk had seemed so cleanly mechanical. Saw off a bit of this nice white plastic part here, insert a nice gleaming titanium tip there, tuck a nice inert piece of plastic padding between here and there—in fact, the sonofabitch had cut through living tissue!—taken a bloody saw to his thighbone and his shinbone, which were full of living blood, cells, nerves, molecules, DNA—he wasn't sure about DNA; nerves there were, for sure. The incision ran from way up here to way down there, and it looked as if it had a tight red tube running the length of it and held in place by strips of flesh-colored plastic tape that ran crossways. The red tube was actually the flesh and blood where the incision had been closed, and the skin all around it felt as if it were about to burst.

Charlie tried to keep his mind focused on the knee, the suture, the pain—surely the pain would be enough to keep his mind off everything else. There was a little machine called the CPM, for "continual passive motion," which they had placed under his knee, and it flexed your knee for you, whether you wanted it to or not. Hurt like hell. Why endure so much pain when all you wanted was for God to take you away in the night? Somewhere out there, perhaps at this very moment, Fareek Fanon's lawyer, a black man who dressed like a British diplomat, was making plans for a press conference at which he, Charlie, wearing a shabby mask of racial harmony, would hold forth in the insolent Cannon's behalf—in an outright betrayal of Inman Armholster. And if he reneged on that deal, this guy Zell or Zale and PlannersBanc stood ready to strip him of every piece of real estate he had, starting with Turpmtine.

Just then the goddamned CPM under his knee went into action, and his knee joint bent, and the pain shot through his entire nervous system until he grimaced and groaned: "Unghhhh!" But soon they were back . . . Inman, Zell/Zale, and Lawyer Roger White . . . stamping around in his skull demanding attention.

Charlie had private nurses on the 4 p.m. to midnight shift and from midnight to 8 a.m., but not from 8 a.m. to 4 p.m. There was so much activity during the day, what with the doctors, nurses, orderlies, visitors, and a fellow who swept and mopped the floors coming by, he didn't need a private nurse. Not that he truly *needed* one on the other shifts.

But they were like the brilliant blue robe. They showed that he was not just some poor gork stretched out on his back. He couldn't roll over on his side for fear of twisting his knee. If he wanted to shift his position, he could elevate his back by pushing a button that caused the head of the bed to lift, or he could reach up and grab a couple of handles that hung down above his chest and pull hard and shift his weight a few inches this way or that. That soon became his way of greeting visitors, his version of standing up out of politeness. Not that he was anxious to have visitors. He didn't want any more reminders of the world outside than were absolutely necessary, although he wasn't so far gone that he would couch it in those terms. Serena, Wally, the Wiz, Marguerite—they were the only people to be admitted to his room.

Early in the afternoon the Wiz arrived. He looked as gaunt as ever, with his sunken cheeks and his neck that never quite filled up his shirt collar, but he had an un-Wiz-like smile spread out down below the titanium rectangles of his eyeglasses.

Charlie tugged on the handles above the bed, moved himself a fraction of an inch, groaned in a subdued way, and said, "Hello, Wiz." It was a dispirited voice, for in his present state Charlie couldn't imagine anyone being pleased by anything.

The Wiz pulled up an armchair with hospital-plastic upholstery and sat down, the remnants of his smile still playing about the corners of his mouth.

"Well, Charlie, how's it going?"

"Slowly," said Charlie. "They make it sound so simple beforehand."

The Wiz said, "I've always heard it requires a high pain threshold."

"Yeah, or whatever," said Charlie, "that and the patience of a saint."

"Well, I've come to cheer you up, Charlie. Or I guess you could say I have good news and bad news. Which would you like first?"

"Surprise me."

"Okay, I will. For some reason—and I have not called them to ask why—PlannersBanc has suspended its campaign of rationalized harassment. They've called off the dogs. We haven't heard a sound from them all week." He beamed at Charlie.

Charlie knew he ought to register pleasant surprise, if only to indulge the Wiz's excitement. But he couldn't playact. He felt submerged by a wave of guilt. They had called off the dogs because he had agreed to betray Inman Armholster.

"Good," he said in a glum way that sent out the signal *It's too late* or *It's not enough.*

The Wiz's smile receded. "The bad news—it's not specifically bad news for us. I suppose it falls under the heading of sad news. You know the case of Fareek Fanon and the rape charge and so forth?"

Charlie nodded.

"Well, you'll never guess who the girl involved is." The Wiz's bar-code-scanner eyes were lit up with a thousand watts.

"Tell me," said Charlie tonelessly.

"Elizabeth Armholster. Inman Armholster's daughter." Two thousand watts.

Charlie shook his head and compressed his lips. The Wiz no doubt interpreted it as a look of sympathy and regret. "How did you learn that?" said Charlie.

"Some Internet Web site carried her name," said the Wiz. "It's an odd situation, because nobody else is using her name. You don't see it in the *Journal-Constitution*, you don't hear it on television, and yet the name's all over town, and it's all over the Internet. I've heard of plenty of situations where they don't publish a rape victim's name, but I've never heard of one in which the victim was the daughter of such a well-known man."

Charlie looked away and shook his head some more. Wave after wave of guilt.

"You're really not feeling so hot, are you," said the Wiz.

"That's true," said Charlie. In fact, he felt profoundly depressed. He reached for the handles above his chest and pulled himself up a few inches. He wanted the Wiz to see that he still had strength. He wanted him to see more of his brilliant blue robe. But for what earthly reason? He couldn't think of one. "I wouldn't attach too much significance to the PlannersBanc thing. It's hard to say what it means. It may not mean anything."

He couldn't believe he was actually going to betray Inman in order to get a bank off his back.

Just then the telephone on his bedside table rang.

Immediately up and on his feet, the Wiz said, "You want me to get it?"

"Would you?" Wearily: "And find out who it is."

The Wiz answered the telephone, listened a few moments, then put his hand over the receiver's mouthpiece and said to Charlie, "It's Marguerite."

Charlie sighed and nodded and closed his eyes and lifted his hand, as if to say, "I'm tired, and this is an imposition, but I'll take it."

Marguerite's voice said, "I'm really sorry to bother you, Charlie, but —how you feeling?"

"So-so. Not great."

"Listen, I'm really sorry, but that lawyer from Wringer Fleasom called, that—you know, Roger White—and he kept saying it was urgent that he speak to you. Something about an appointment you had, or have, with him next week?"

Charlie could feel his heart speeding up, taking off. "What'd you tell him?"

"What I've been telling everybody. You're away and can't be reached, but you'll be checking in from time to time. Then he wanted to know 'Away—where?' He'd be happy to call you wherever. He was really insistent."

"What'd you say to that?"

"I told him you hadn't made your itinerary available."

"And he said?"

"He said to remind you that this appointment was extremely important. Whattaya want me to do?—if anything."

"Nothing," said Charlie. "You did the right thing. No need to tell anybody any more than that."

He said goodbye, sighed again, closed his eyes, and held the receiver up in the air, thereby implicitly instructing the Wiz to put it back upon the telephone's cradle, which he did.

Charlie kept his eyes closed. Should he open them? If he didn't, the Wiz would think he was in pain or enduring some other form of suffering. But for now he just wanted to . . . vanish. Certainly, somehow, he could stretch this hospital stay on through next week, finesse the press conference—all the while realizing it would be no solution whatsoever. Why would they, whoever *they* were, be so kind as to keep PlannersBanc away from his throat in return for . . . nothing? Had he really become so weak and foolish as to think he could . . . hide?

So he opened his eyes. The Wiz was standing there, looking at him with a puzzled expression. "Don't mind me, Wiz. I think it's the anesthetic. It really wipes you out. Makes you woozy." He hoisted his body up an inch or so by pulling down on the handles. Wanted to show the

Wiz he was still in control of himself. He sank back down on the pillow and involuntarily let out a groan, and sweat broke out on his forehead. He made himself smile, but it was a rueful smile. "My knee feels like it's the size of a basketball, Wiz."

"I'm going to let you get back in the inert mode, Charlie. I just wanted to let you know about the bank and Inman Armholster."

"Thanks," said Charlie. "Keep me posted." He attempted another smile. "You know where I'll be."

XXVIII

Chapter

The Spark of Zeus

IN HIS LITTLE ATTIC ROOM IN OLD CHAMBLEE, CONRAD DIDN'T need an alarm clock to wake up on time in the morning. The one window, the dormer, faced east and had no shade. By 5:30 a.m. the light was already pouring in, even on cloudy days. On sunny days, like this one, the sun shone through the dormer's tunnel as a beam, highlighting this or that promiscuous heap of old books, magazines, knickknacks, and exhausted furniture on the floor.

Conrad threw back the matelassé counterpane, started to get up, yawned, drew in an unhappy lungful of the house's ineradicable sour smell of coal fires, kerosene heaters, and hurricane lamps, lost heart, and idly followed the path of the beam. It lit up an old three-shelf-high maple bookcase. Into the shelves were stuffed old books, most without their dust jackets, and on top of it was laid out his uniform from Carter Home Care, a white polo shirt with the green Carter logo on the left breast pocket, and white ducks with a narrow green piping down the outseam of each leg. There were no closets up here on the third floor, and empty surfaces were hard to come by anywhere in the house. He sat on the edge of the bed in his boxer shorts and yawned some more. Well, this would be his fourth assignment working for Carter. He would be spending the day with an old couple named Gardner in a part of Atlanta called Cabbagetown. According to the Carter office, the old man had been paralyzed on the left side of his body by a stroke. The old woman had heart trouble and couldn't stay on her feet for much more than thirty minutes at a time. Many everyday chores—moving a chair, shopping for groceries—were beyond them. The job paid only seven dollars an hour (Carter charged the customer twelve), but he could get by on it.

One of the polo shirt's short sleeves was somehow drooping down over the edge of the top of the bookcase. It made no difference, of course, but it offended Conrad's sense of orderliness. He stood up and leaned forward and reached his arm out toward it—when he stopped and stared in astonishment. Behind the sleeve, on the top shelf of the bookcase, jammed in horizontally on top of a row of books, was a dark blue book, bereft of dust jacket, with faded letters stamped on the spine: THE STOICS.

His hand trembled violently. Such miracles never—there would be some—

The book was jammed in so tightly that at first he couldn't budge it. So now he placed the heel of his left hand against the top edge of the bookcase and pulled the book with his right. It took every ounce of strength—but finally he got it out. Now both hands were trembling. He closed his eyes before actually opening it, for fear that it would turn out to be a dreadful joke . . . the novel he had originally wanted (*The Stoics' Game*) . . . or God knew what. Since the deputy had torn the cover off his book at Santa Rita, he had no idea of what the binding had looked like. He opened the book to the title page—*and there it was!* In that selfsame type, which he would know as well as his own face: "THE STOICS. The complete extant writings of Epictetus, Marcus Aurelius, C. Musonius Rufus, and Zeno." Dying to cry out with joy, he riffled through the pages . . . Epictetus! . . . precisely where he was supposed to be! . . . Conrad opened the Epictetus section at random and read: "A disciple asked, 'How is it possible for a man who has nothing, naked, without home or hearth, in squalor, without a city, without a slave, to live a tranquil life?'

"Epictetus said, 'Lo, Zeus has sent you one who shall show indeed that it is possible. Look at me, I have no house or property. I sleep on the ground, I have only earth and sky and one poor cloak. Yet what do

I lack? Has any of you seen me with a gloomy face? How do I act towards those of whom you stand in fear and awe? Do they not give way before me as if I were king and master?' "

CONRAD HELD THE book with both hands, and he felt as if a current were flowing straight up his arms and diffusing throughout his body. *Lo, Zeus has sent you one who shall show indeed that it is possible.* He began laughing, but forced himself to stop, for fear of sounding like a lunatic to his new landlords somewhere down below. *The book! The text!* Lit by a sunbeam here in the attic of the Hello Again!

Was there ever a clearer sign—that all this, the earthquake at Santa Rita, Mai's army, Lum Loc, the trip across the continent to this little place he had never heard of, Chamblee, all this was Zeus' design? For what reason? To send forth a messenger who shall show indeed that it is possible. That *what* is possible? To serve Zeus! To speak for Zeus! He had suffered terrible pains, terrible losses—but what were they? Zeus' trials! Zeus' training for the tasks ahead!

By the time he came downstairs to the kitchen, Conrad had on his Carter Home Care uniform, including a pair of white leatherette shoes. He carried *The Stoics* in his hand. Brother, wearing a long nightshirt and an old seersucker bathrobe over his immense bulk, was at the stove cooking up a skillet full of fried apples.

"Good morning, Brother."

Couldn't hear him. The frying apples.

"GOOD MORNING, BROTHER!"

"Oh, Connie! Didn't even know you was there."

"I'm going to work, Brother, but I wanted to show you this book. I found it up in my room. I'd like to buy it."

Brother put the skillet down and picked up the book and looked at the spine. "*The Stoics.*" Then he looked at Conrad. "That's some a you Zeusians, ain't it, Connie?"

Conrad smiled in a bashful fashion and said, "That's pretty much what it is."

"Well, I tell you what," said Brother, "I'll make a deal with you. You can have the book if you'll clean out the cellar for me when you get back from work."

Given the chaos of the upper floors, Conrad hated to think about the condition of the cellar. On the other hand, no price was too high.

CHARLIE HAD LOST track of what time it was. He was lying flat out on his back with his eyes closed, watching eyelid movies and sinking into daydreams in which things, innocuous things, were happening in bizarre locations . . . a Coast Guard office on Sea Island, an empty water cooler, a young man lifting up the cooler's enormous bottle, tinted aqua . . . and yet he knew he really wasn't asleep. His knee felt gigantic and kept throbbing and throbbing. And then—what was it?—a shadow falling across an eyelid movie?—a sound?—he was aware that someone was standing by the bed. He opened his eyes—

A black man, a light-skinned black man, dressed to kill . . . a striped high-collared shirt that made his mauve necktie pop out in a certain way . . . a chalk-striped double-breasted suit . . . leaning against the stainless-steel railings of the bed so that his face seemed to be up above him like an October moon . . . Who the hell was he? What was he doing here—this black man, standing here, looking down at me in my bed? Then it dawned on him. Fareek Fanon's lawyer, Roger White.

"Mr. Croker," said the head above him. "How we doing?"

How we doing? Charlie resented everything about the question, the tone, the tone you used to talk to hopeless, aging invalids; the idiocy, the idiocy of asking someone stroked out on a hospital bed how he's *doing*, and above all the presumption, the presumption that the two of them were intertwined in any way whatsoever. What he resented most of all was the fact that it was true, that he had let it become true, that he *was* intertwined with this man, in a perfidious union. All the same, how dare he come walking into his hospital room like this? Where was the nurse? Always out of the room when he needed her. Wait a minute. She doesn't come on until four.

"How'd you know where I was?" He meant it to be intimidating, but it had a furtive, croaking quality to it. He reached for the handles and pulled himself up a few inches, so that the black man would be aware of his strength. If he were well—if he were himself—if—if—he'd give him a . . . a . . . a good tongue-lashing.

Roger White smiled. "Your office was very protective. Wouldn't even *hint* where you were. Luckily an acquaintance of yours happened to run into somebody in our firm and mention you'd undergone surgery."

"*What* acquaintance?" asked Charlie from deep down in his throat.

He'd gladly strangle whoever it was, if only he didn't feel so tired . . . and inert . . .

"I don't know," said Roger, "he didn't say."

He could tell Croker was not happy. But Wes Jordan was not happy that Charlie Croker had suddenly disappeared on him, either. It was only because one Emory Nuchols, Croker's surgeon, had name-dropped to Zandy Scott the fact that he had sawed away on this eminent knee here—and because Zandy had passed this gossip along in a loud voice to a client named Howell Hendricks within Roger's earshot—that Roger had even gotten wind of where Croker had disappeared to. Croker was no longer the mighty King of the Crackers. He looked weak enough for him, Roger, to berate for pulling a disappearing act, for checking into the hospital without saying a word. But Roger was not a Don Pickett. He was not aggressive by nature, and he was afraid it wouldn't come out right. So what he said was:

"You had us worried, Mr. Croker. Suddenly you . . . disappeared. We're organizing the press conference. We can't wait much longer. We've got the Mayor lined up—but what we need is you. I don't know what the Mayor is going to say, but I feel pretty sure he's going to call for calm, so this thing doesn't spin out of control. Having somebody as prominent as you are, somebody who's a member of the city's business establishment—having somebody like you at the press conference—somebody who happens to have been a great sports star for Georgia Tech in his own day—it's going to make all the difference in the world."

What was that in Croker's eyes? Fear? Pain? Anger?

Charlie was horrified by this twist of fate. The sonofabitch had found him. He couldn't even hide behind his knee. But he could *try*.

"I'm afraid I'm not much good for a while." He gestured toward his knee with his right hand and gave the black man a look of glum resignation.

"You can't make it to a press conference next week?"

Gloom: "I don't see how."

Roger had the strange, not at all unpleasant feeling that he had this supposedly big powerful white man cowering. "Well, I don't see how we can continue to hold PlannersBanc at bay if you don't get up off the sidelines. Or how about this? If you can't come to the press conference, we'll videotape your statement on behalf of Fareek. If we have to, we can do it right here. How does that sound? We'll do it right here at your bed. Might even have a more dramatic effect. How about it?"

"Depends on how it's going," said Croker, mumbling.

"Mr. Croker," said Roger, "no matter how it's going, it's got to *go*. You understand? The Mayor's going to be there, and we've assured him *you'll* be there. The two of you can do something very important for this city—I hope you realize that. One way or the other, you've got to be there, in person or on tape."

Croker, still flat on his back, looked up at him, blinking uncertainly. Roger looked down at him and felt like smiling, although he didn't. He had begun treating the big man, the big developer and Piedmont Driving Club man, like a disobedient child.

Jesus God, thought Charlie, this sonofabitch is jerking my chain. Well, I could change that in an instant, couldn't I . . . All I have to do is say, "The deal's off." One sentence is all it would take. I can salvage my honor—and lose everything I have. Why kid myself? This is Atlanta—where your "honor" *is* the things you possess. Who's going to come visit a man who has salvaged his honor but lost his house on Blackland Road? Nobody. His mind kept spinning, and suddenly there was a flash of hope. He just said something, this sonofabitch did. He said that I—or the Mayor and I—might save the city from . . . from what? A race riot maybe. Anyone objects, I can tell them that. It was a strategy to save the city. It just might go down . . . It just might . . . Is that what I tell Inman, too? But then he lost heart. What would happen to the look on my face if I tried to tell that to Inman: Inman, who's thinking in terms of the . . . the . . . the *animal*—that was what he'd said—the *animal* who raped his daughter? On the other hand—

He became acutely aware of what a wretched, sickly face he was presenting to this black man who had been so insolent as to track him down in his hospital bed. On the other hand, the man had the magic ability to get PlannersBanc off his back—

"I'm tired," he said. He realized he was saying it imploringly. "I'm gonna try to get a little sleep."

"That's fine, Mr. Croker," said Roger, "but when the right time comes, you've got to wake up. You understand?"

Croker nodded a feeble yes.

"Well, just make sure you do," said Roger, "or there's no restraining PlannersBanc. They'll do whatever they want."

Another feeble nod.

"We don't want you to turn forgetful the way you turned hard to find. You know what I'm saying?"

An even feebler nod—and eyes that begged and begged.

CABBAGETOWN, AS IT was universally known, struck Conrad as an entire village of dollhouses, an impression magnified by what he had found inside the Gardners'. The neighborhood had been a mill village for the old Fulton Bag and Cotton plant until about a quarter of a century ago. The houses were little wooden bungalows, set on narrow lots fronting the narrowest streets in all of Atlanta. Many of them, like the Gardners', had no more than four rooms. Most had front porches, and quite a few had gingerbread ornamentation such as was in vogue in the 1890s. Nobody seemed to know for sure where the name came from. It caught on about 1910, and it was true that about that time gangs of young toughs from South Atlanta, white boys, would walk along the railroad tracks and have rock fights with the neighborhood's young toughs, whom they called "cabbage heads." In any event, Cabbagetown it was, a dollhouse village, and the Gardners' dollhouse was a dollhouse squared.

The Gardners were in their late seventies. A therapist from Carter Home Care came once a week, and a nurse's helper—Conrad—would come for half a day, four hours, twice a week. As far as the nurse's helper was concerned, his main task was to do everyday things for the old couple that they couldn't do themselves.

Mrs. Gardner answered the doorbell. She was a slender, erect woman with her white hair pulled back into a bun. She was wearing a summer dress of chiffon with large roses printed on it in swirls so subtle that at first the pattern seemed to be abstract. She wore a lovely fragrance. Conrad found her entire presence startling, although at first he had no idea why. This day and age, to come across a woman (or anyone) who had good posture, who had left her hair white, who wore it pulled back into a bun with hairpins, and who wore a dressy dress and perfume in the middle of the day was enough to make any American twenty-three-year-old blink in astonishment. The only weak points in an otherwise impeccable appearance were her ankles, which were swollen.

"You must be Mr. DeCyasi," she said, extending her hand. "I'm Louise Gyardner."

At first Conrad had taken this to be a speech defect. In fact, as he soon deduced, it was merely an affectation, and a minor one at that.

Anytime a word began with *c* or a *g* before a broad *a,* she inserted a *y* after the consonant. Soon she was telling him about the gyarden out back and the cyar they no longer possessed. She had such a lovely soft Southern voice—the sort of voice he always thought he was going to hear in Atlanta—that Conrad felt like applauding and cheering her on with that or any other affectation she might care to indulge in.

"Come meet Mr. Gyardner, Mr. DeCyasi."

"Thank you," said Conrad, following her, "but please just call me Connie."

The house had an awkward layout. It looked as if someone had been handed a rectangle on a sheet of paper and had drawn one line up and down in the middle of the rectangle and another line from side to side, making four rooms. To get to any room in the house, except the one where you entered, you had to go through another one. But Conrad didn't notice that at first because of the extraordinary decoration of the walls.

On almost every wall surface of the house were . . . dolls and porcelain figurines. There were hundreds of them, possibly thousands. There were wooden knickknack shelves attached to the walls and filled with dolls, old ones, new ones, astronaut dolls, African dolls, Filipino dolls, Polynesian dolls. There were dolls resting on little knickknack shelves that went around each doorframe and every window, all chosen for the matching or harmonious colors of their clothes, dolls of old people as well as children, dolls of famous people such as Mark Twain, Genghis Khan, and Albert Einstein. Still other knickknack shelves were devoted to the porcelain figurines. In every room, up near the ceiling, which was no more than eight feet high, was a white shelf upon which were white figurines arranged so densely that at first you thought you were looking at some sort of frieze in high relief. The most beautifully colored ones—and some were extravagant examples of the porcelain maker's art—were arranged on wooden knickknack shelves, like the dolls. The arrangements were precise. The gradations in size were pleasing. Nothing was out of place. Despite the vast number of objects, you were immediately struck by the unity and good taste of this exhibition of a lifetime of collecting. Conrad had no idea what the dolls might be worth, but he had only to look at the exquisite workmanship of some of the porcelain figures to know they must be valuable. Despite its dreadful layout, the little house's interior seemed like something lavish beyond all normal reckoning.

Mr. Gardner was in the bedroom, which was one of the two rooms in back, the other being the kitchen. He was sitting in an easy chair at the foot of the bed, an old-fashioned four-poster canopy bed with an arched ladder frame covered in a mauve, purple, and yellow ribbon cloth.

"Lewis," said Mrs. Gardner, "this is Mr. DeCyasi. Mr. DeCyasi is from Cyarter Home Care."

"Please call me Connie," said Conrad. He smiled.

"Welcome," said Mr. Gardner with a weary gesture of his right hand that seemed to say "Let's not bother shaking hands." "So you're with Carter . . ."

His speech was not so much slurred as it was slowed to an unnatural drawl. The left side of his lips barely moved when he spoke. He was a handsome man; or no doubt had been. He was tall and lean, but his leanness was not the leanness you would call trim but the one you would call wasted away. He wore a plaid bathrobe over a polo shirt and a pair of black flannel pants. On his feet were a pair of leather bedroom slippers that had dried out and were cracking. There was a small table just to the right of the chair upon which rested seven or eight plastic vials of prescription medicines, a small Kleenex dispenser, and a glass of water with a glass straw. The water had been sitting there in the glass for so long it had begun to form stale bubbles.

Conrad was dying to sweep the medicine vials off the table, toss out the stale water, remove the bathrobe, and take Mr. Gardner for a walk in the sun. What he said instead was:

"Mr. Gardner, Mrs. Gardner, I'm here to help you any way I can. Is there something I can do right now?"

"What I really need are some groceries." Her accent was so soft, sweet, and Southern, this seemed like the most sublime of blandishments. "But I haven't even had time to make out my list yet."

"You go ahead and make your list," said Conrad, "and in the meantime I'll vacuum the house for you."

"You will?"

"I'll be glad to."

The floor and the rugs were filthy, so laden with dust and dustballs and hairballs, it was jarring, given the meticulous care with which the couple had arranged the dolls and figurines and, for that matter, their furniture. Carting their old Electrolux vacuum cleaner around these four rooms was very likely more than Mrs. Gardner was capable of. Her husband, who was probably slightly older than she was, couldn't help out with anything, heavy or light, so far as Conrad could tell.

Both were retired members of the Emory University faculty. He had taught English, with early-nineteenth-century poets and essayists as his specialty. She had taught comparative literature and could read French, Spanish, Portuguese, Italian, and German. Her forte was European literature between 1870 and 1914, which, she told Conrad, was from the Franco-Prussian War to World War I. They had no children. Seven years ago, with their income at its peak, they had bought a big house in Inman Park—with scarcely a thought as to how they would continue to pay off the mortgage once they retired. *Somehow* they would continue to make money; *something* would turn up; they would keep the house *some way*. Two years ago, their backs against the wall, they had sold the house in Inman Park and bought this little box in Cabbagetown with the fond hope that they could now live off the profits of the sale plus their modest pensions and Social Security. Every spare nickel they had ever had must have gone into the dolls and the figurines. They were dreamers, they were children; but very polite and goodhearted children, children you instinctively wanted to protect.

When Conrad brought the vacuum cleaner into the bedroom, he said to Mr. Gardner, "Is it all right if I vacuum in here now?"

"Yes, yes, go ahead," said Mr. Gardner, drawling out of the right-hand corner of his mouth. He didn't even try to look at Conrad. He stared straight ahead, slumping back in the chair, seeming utterly dispirited.

Somehow Conrad couldn't just leave it at that. He felt as if he just had to engage this feeble old gentleman in . . . something . . . He ransacked his memory . . . nothing . . . no, a fragment, part of a poem.

"Mr. Gardner, excuse me. I've had the beginning of a poem running through my head, and I just can't think of who wrote it or what the rest of it is. They gave it to us in school."

He looked at the old man for encouragement in this line of intellectual inquiry, but he was staring straight ahead with his lips slightly parted in their skewed fashion.

Having begun it, Conrad decided to blunder on. "It starts off, 'I strove with none, for none was worth my strife; / Nature I loved; and next to Nature, Art.' That's all I can remember."

Conrad looked at Mr. Gardner again. He still didn't look his way, but finally he said:

"I strove with none, for none was worth my strife;
Nature I loved; and next to Nature, Art.
I warmed both hands before the fire of life;
It sinks, and I am ready to depart.

"Walter Savage Landor, 1853. He was seventy-eight years old when he wrote that."

Conrad was appalled. He had inadvertently brought up a poem about the last embers of life. He was speechless.

Not so, Mr. Gardner: "Landor was a good poet, but not a great one. He was too polite, too proper, too staid, too content with the comfort of what he already had to take a chance on his very best. How old are you?"

"Twenty-three," said Conrad, forgetting that his age according to his recently minted birth certificate and driver's license was twenty-four.

"Twenty-three," said the old man, still not looking at him. "That's a good age to be interested in literature. You have so much time . . . you have so much, it must seem to be spilling out of your pockets. You don't need to worry about what an incalculable luxury literature is. Entire civilizations are founded without any literature at all and without anybody missing it. It's only later on when there's a big enough class of indolent drones to write the stuff and read the stuff that you have literature. When I saw all those eager hands sticking up as I taught, I always wanted to tell them what I've just told you, but what right did I have to try to play the iconoclast after making a living my whole life taking it seriously, or at least with a straight face?"

"I disagree with you, Mr. Gardner," said Conrad. "If anyone has a luxury, it's you. You know so *much* about literature."

"Hah. How do you know how much I know?" But things had improved slightly, at least to the point where Mr. Gardner was looking at him.

"Well, I recited two lines of a poem, and you knew not only who the poet was, you also recited the entire stanza and told me what year the poem was published and how old the poet was that year. I'd love to know that much."

"You're not aiming very high, my friend. Besides, that's a very well-known poem."

"I don't know, Mr. Gardner, I'd love to know what's famous and what isn't—"

"Literature's a sort of dessert." The old man's voice took on a shrill tone, and the left side of his lips began to quiver, and tears flowed from his left eye. "Life's about things you know even less about. Life's about cruelty and intimidation."

Now he was crying openly. His face was terribly contorted. Conrad felt guilty. Had he driven him over the edge by bringing up those morbid verses? Conrad stepped closer to the old man and said:

"I'm sorry, Mr. Gardner, I didn't mean to . . . say the wrong thing."

The old man looked up at him and shook his head, as if to say it wasn't Conrad's fault, and had a real cry for himself, blubbering and boo-hooing. Mrs. Gardner, who was in the kitchen making out her grocery list, stuck her head in the door. Conrad opened his eyes wide and turned his palms up in the look that says "I haven't a ghost of an idea why this happened." Mrs. Gardner nodded, as if to indicate she understood, and then went over to comfort her husband.

About ten minutes later, Conrad was in the kitchen with Mrs. Gardner, going over her grocery list.

"Really," said Conrad, "I have no idea what upset Mr. Gardner in there. We were talking about a poem."

"It happens a lot," she said. "It's the stroke. Emotions that ordinarily you can control—they come right to the surface."

Conrad said, "Then all of a sudden he was telling me about 'cruelty and intimidation' and how that was what life was all about."

Mrs. Gardner said nothing at first, then looked toward the door that led into the bedroom and said, "I think—I think he's talking about the state of things in general, in the world. Did he say anything more to you?"

"No."

"Well, I think he's just talking about the world in general. He gets very pessimistic sometimes." That sweet euphonious Southern quality had gone out of her voice.

Conrad was at the grocery store for close to forty minutes. He returned to the Gardners' little Cabbagetown house with two prodigious white plastic bags full of groceries. Mrs. Gardner answered the doorbell. She seemed highly agitated.

"Connie," she said, "uhhh . . . just set those bags down here and go back to the store and get me some . . . sponges and dishwasher detergent and Brillo."

"I got Brillo, Mrs. Gardner."

"I mean vacuum cleaner bags. Go get vacuum cleaner bags, too, won't you?"

Puzzled, he stared at her for a moment. Then he heard the loud voice of a man, from the bedroom. At first he thought it must be Mr. Gardner with his emotions boiling over. But then he knew it couldn't be. There was no way Mr. Gardner could be that loud or pugnacious.

Conrad put the grocery bags down and started walking through the living room and toward the bedroom.

"Connie—no!" said Mrs. Gardner in a loud whisper.

There was a tremendous crash and the sound of glass breaking. Conrad knew immediately that it was the porcelain figurines on the shelf up near the ceiling.

The loud voice said, "I've had enough excuses!"

Mr. Gardner said something, but it was impossible to make it out, because he was crying. Conrad entered the bedroom. There was Mr. Gardner in his easy chair, blubbering and boo-hooing down the right side of his face and as still as a stone on the left side. All over the floor near the old man were shards of white porcelain, an astonishing amount, many of them jagged with a knife-like, even needle-like, sharpness. Sitting on the bed, insouciantly, with one leg and one shoe cocked up on the counterpane was a beefy red-faced man who was now staring at Conrad in a challenging way. He had a small black beard and mustache and long oily black hair that he combed straight back and then let fall in a wild tangle down the back of his neck. He was probably in his mid-forties. He had a big chest, but also an abdomen the size of a watermelon that protruded so far from beneath his sternum you couldn't see the waist of his blue jeans when he sat down.

Apparently proud of his big arms, he wore a tight white T-shirt with sleeves short enough to reveal a crude black tattoo of a coiled rattlesnake with the letters *B.T.K.* beneath it. A truly botched jailhouse job it was, Conrad could see at once, with colloidal scars all over the place. B.T.K. stood for "born to kill." Across his lap he had the sort of stout cane you see at cattle auctions, thick, unvarnished canes used for prodding the beasts into or out of pens. Conrad looked up at the ceiling. On the cornice shelf an entire battalion of the figurines was missing—and were now nothing more than glassy fragments on the floor. It wasn't hard to figure out how they got there.

The man glowered at Conrad and looked him up and down and

turned to Mrs. Gardner, who had come in the room behind Conrad, and said, "Who's he?"

In a tremulous voice Mrs. Gardner said, "Connie's from the Cyarter Home Care. He helps out."

The man looked back toward Conrad, measured him once more with his eyes, and said, "Helps out, hunh," as if weighing this explanation for rational content, if any. "Well, I tell you what, Connie, we're kinda busy now. Maybe you'd like to help out somewhere else."

"Yes, Connie," said Mrs. Gardner, now highly nervous, "I forgot to ask you to get a couple of things, some . . . uh . . . filters for the vacuum cleaner and . . . uh . . . some Brillo pads, I mean detergent for the dishwasher. If you could just go back—"

Conrad took a deep breath and prayed to Zeus for strength, even though he never thought of what he was now doing as prayer. He crossed his arms over his chest to give the man a good look at his big forearms. He looked at Mrs. Gardner and then at Mr. Gardner, and then he said:

"I heard a crash. How'd all these figurines get broken?"

The old couple turned toward each other with looks of terrifying premonition.

The man on the bed now held the cattle cane in his lap in his right hand and tapped the shaft up and down on the palm of his left hand. He smiled and spoke with a menacing sweetness: "Didn't you hear, Connie, we're a little busy here at the moment. Do what the lady says. Go get some filters and some Brillo pads. Be a good fellow." He motioned toward the front door with his chin and looked at Conrad down his nose.

Conrad had no plan, but he could hear Five-O saying, "Use da mouth." "B.T.K., hunh?" said Conrad. "So you been down? Congratulations."

The man began to rap the shaft of the cattle cane into his palm more forcefully. He stared at Conrad and cocked his head to one side and said, "Look, pal—"

"That downtime tattoo artist a yo's either blind or on crack. You know what I'm sayin'?"

"Okay, buddy—"

"Why you tryin'a run a game on'ese good people?" said Conrad, gesturing toward the old couple. "Caintchoo find nobody better to dog? Whuffo' you be sweatin' the Gardners? Why you wanna be gittin' over on'em?"

With that, the man on the bed pointed the cattle cane toward Conrad and said, "I don't know what—"

Conrad's hands flew toward the cane. He grabbed the shaft and jerked it back with such force that the man lost his grip. Conrad now held it in front of himself as if he were a Dojo stick warrior.

"Now whatchoo gon' do? This game is over, lest you wants to gitcho cap peeled. You unnerstan' what I'm sayin'? Gitcho *cap* peeled."

The man on the bed straightened up a bit and slid his leg partly off the bed, but he didn't dare indicate that he might be getting in a position to fight.

And in that moment Conrad knew he had him. It was as if the spark of Zeus filled the room. "Look, you know what N.B. stands for?" Conrad was only barely aware that his teeth were showing and he was seething. "You know what N.B. stands for?"

The man said nothing, but by the look in his eyes it was obvious that he knew N.B. meant Nordic Bund.

"We got a motto," said Conrad. "All for one and all on one. You unnerstan'? If you ever so much as cast a shadow on this house again, we'll cut your peanuts off with a gelding knife and stuff 'em down your throat. My shot caller from last time down lives two blocks from here. He'd just as soon peel your cap as look at'choo. Fack, he be likin' it better, peelin' yo cap. Now git da hell outta here. You know where the do' is."

Slowly, warily, the man edged off the bed and stood up. Conrad kept the cattle cane in front of him, but no longer stood seething. Now he had a look of cold confidence. The man headed to the front door with Conrad right behind him. The scraggly mane of black hair at the back of his head bounced on the hump of his back as he walked. He began wheezing terribly, as if he were asthmatic. As the man went through the doorway, Conrad said in an exaggerated whisper, "We'll *kill* you, motherfucker. We'll peel yo' fuckin' cap."

The greaser said nothing.

When Conrad returned to the bedroom, the old parties gave him incredulous looks, obviously wondering what sort of creature they had on their hands here.

"I'm sorry," said Conrad. "That's the way you have to talk to these people. They're cheap thugs. It's the only language they'll take seriously."

"But where did you—" Mrs. Gardner didn't quite know how to say it.

"Where did *I* learn all that moronic lingo?" said Conrad. "From a movie, some movie about a prison. I figured this guy was all talk anyway. He's a little old to be out working as a hoodlum."

"But as soon as you're gone," said Mr. Gardner, "he'll be back." The "he'll be back" was a pitiful whine.

"No, he won't," said Conrad. "He thinks I'm part of a gang."

"What gang?" said Mrs. Gardner.

"The Nordic Bund," said Conrad. "And believe me, if I thought the Nordic Bund was after me, I'd be frightened, too."

"You mean it's actually over?" said Mrs. Gardner. She put her face in her hands and looked up with a game smile. Then she recounted how the greaser had first approached them, saying he was a burglar alarm salesman. When they said they weren't interested, he returned, saying he was organizing a neighborhood security patrol. Foolishly they made a contribution, and he began to come back more often. Soon it became obvious that it was pure extortion. He would descend on Louise Gardner when she left the house to go shopping. He would turn up in the house, coming in through the locked front door in ways they couldn't comprehend. They were terrified. He had been collecting $100 a week. Today he had said he was upping it to $150. She said they couldn't possibly, and that was when he took his cattle cane and destroyed thirty or forty figurines.

"I couldn't believe the way you stood up to him," said Mrs. Gardner. "That took such courage." She lowered her head and rubbed her eyes and then looked up again. She was crying. "How did you ever do . . . what you just did?"

"It's hard to believe," said Conrad, "but most hoodlums are all talk. The last thing in the world they want is to go to the trouble of fighting. They specialize in victims who won't fight. As soon as they come up against somebody who *might* fight, they're ready to move off, particularly a guy like that one who's already up in his forties."

"But what do you do if you're confronted by a hoodlum who *will* fight," said Mrs. Gardner, "what do you do then?"

"If you run into one of those—then you better be ready to roll in the dirt," said Conrad, but in his mind he could hear Five-O saying, "Use da mouth, bruddah, use da mouth."

He felt radiant. He had used da mouth, and it had worked. That—and the spark of Zeus.

Chapter XXIX

Epictetus in Buckhead

BROTHER AND SISTER'S HOUSE WAS SO OLD-FASHIONED IT HAD only one bathroom, which was on the second floor. Conrad was at the mirror over the bathroom sink, half-finished shaving, when the telephone call came in. He could barely hear the ring, because the house also had only one telephone, which was in a tiny room downstairs, an office, more or less, practically buried beneath Hello Again's stupefying clutter. To get his attention, Brother or Sister had to stand in the hall and yell up.

This time it was Sister, who had a curious way of singing out his name with a higher note on the second syllable: "Con-NIE!"

He wiped the shaving cream off his face and hurried downstairs. He always knew who was calling, namely, his employer, Carter Home Care. He wasn't about to give the number out to anyone else.

The little office was in fact a windowless cubicle. The telephone was black, the first black telephone Conrad, a child of the 1970s, had ever seen. On the line, sure enough, was his employer, in the person of a middle-aged Chinese, or Chinese-American, woman named Lucy Ng, which was pronounced "Eng." Conrad had only been to the Carter Home Care office once, the day he was hired or, strictly speaking, put on their roster of nursing assistants, to be paid as used. The company, which was one of the biggest home-care companies in Atlanta in terms of hours billed, seemed to consist entirely of Lucy Ng, her husband, Victor, two Chinese bookkeepers and three Chinese secretaries, all of them women, who also answered the telephone, which rang constantly, and five computers, in which was stored the roster of Carter Home Care's uniformed workers, from registered nurses and licensed physical therapists to strong backs, such as Conrad's. Victor Ng had chosen the name Carter because he thought it gave the company the aura of former President Jimmy Carter: American, Georgian, dignified, august, sympathetic, consoling, trustworthy, and old. The office was one flight up on Spring Street.

Lucy Ng, in a very cheery voice: "Connie! How are . . . *you*!"

"I'm fine, Mrs. Ng." He had never heard her so happy to be talking to him.

"I don't know what you do for people, but they love you!"

"Really?"

"Really! Mr. and Mrs. Gardner, they say you do very big things for them! Everybody likes your work, but Mrs. Gardner went on and on."

"They're very nice people, Mrs. Ng—"

"Lucy!"

"Lucy. Thank you. I was glad to do whatever I could."

"They said you were *brave*, Connie, but they don't explain me."

"They're old, Mrs.—Lucy—and things you could do for yourself in a minute, to them it seems very hard."

"Well, anyway, Connie, I have a special assignment for you . . . Are you there?"

"Yes"

"We need a nursing assistant for a man who is coming home from the hospital today, a sixty-year-old man, very prominent, very influential . . . Are you there?"

"Yes. Who is he?"

"He's a very big real estate developer, very well known. He's just had surgery, knee replacement, and he's in a lot of pain. He lives in a big house in Buckhead. His name is Charles Croker."

The name Croker registered with Conrad immediately, but this man was a real estate developer, not somebody in the wholesale food business. So he thought nothing more of it.

"This a very important client for us," said Lucy Ng. "The saying goes,

'Big men have big mouths.' If he has a good experience, it will be very good for us."

"I understand," said Conrad. "I'll do my best."

His new first-name friend, Lucy, went on to describe exactly where the Croker house on Blackland Road was. He could take the MARTA line to Lenox Square and then the number 40 bus west on West Paces Ferry Road and another one north on Northside Drive.

"Could I walk from Lenox Square?" asked Conrad.

"You could, but it's a long way, and today is very hot, and I don't want you go to Crokers' very sweaty. You promise me?"

"All right, I promise."

CHARLIE HAD BECOME a morose, irritable, and, from the nurses', doctors', and therapists' point of view, stunningly ungrateful patient. At first they attributed it to the CPM and the RRM. The RRM, for "respiratory rate monitor," was strapped just beneath the chest. Whenever the patient's breathing became too slow, which was most likely to happen during sleep, the machine sounded an alarm. Thanks to the sedatives he was given, Charlie would begin to drop off to sleep—for the first time in *months*, and—

Brannnnnnng!

—the alarm would go off. Even so, few patients had complained so much about their care and shown so little gratitude to Mercy's archangels (the doctors, notably Emmo Nuchols) and angels (the nurses and physical therapists) as that ornery sonofabitch, Charlie Croker. So then they attributed it to a truism around hospitals, i.e., that it's always the big, authoritative leaders of men who make the most fearful, crotchety, and paranoid patients. None of them seemed to catch on to the fact that he was profoundly depressed. They told him that if he didn't exercise his knee more, in addition to what the CPM did, he ran the risk of clots forming, clots that could lodge in his lungs or his heart. Charlie said to himself, "Good. Let's have some clots. Maybe I can stay in here, insulated from the Roger Whites and PlannersBancs of Atlanta a little longer."

At this moment Charlie, all 235 pounds of him, was slouched over, shell-backed, in a wheelchair, while two orderlies struggled to push it up a ramp into a van provided, for hire, by the SaveWay Ambulance Service. Serena and the Wiz stood by with expressions that reminded

Charlie of pallbearers. Despite all his hopes for clots, infection, fever, bleeding, incomplete flexion, and other pathological conditions, he was going home.

In strict point of fact, there was no reason why he should be going home in a wheelchair or an ambulance. Emmo Nuchols hadn't wanted him to, the physical therapists didn't want him to, the nurses didn't want him to; and least of all, the orderlies who were pushing his bulk up the ramp. Everyone had urged him to use his knee, walk out of the hospital on an aluminum crutch, give his knee a workout, that being the shortest route to recovery after knee replacement surgery. That had let all the air out of Charlie's fondest wish—which was to be submerged beneath his moribund knee, to be laid out flat behind it, to drop out of life . . . until life improved.

"Mr. Croker," said one of the nurses, a twenty-three-year-old number named Stacey, who had accompanied him to the van, "*please* remember what I said. The only way to get well is to *use that knee! Please* do your exercises. If you don't it's going to tighten up on you, and you'll never be able to loosen it up."

Charlie wondered for a moment if a permanently tightened knee would be enough to keep him out of commission and let him drop out of sight . . . but realized pretty quickly that it wouldn't . . .

"Okay," he said to the nurse. It came out as much like a groan as a word, and he didn't look at her. In a former life, not all that long ago, he would have looked at her a lot. But depressed men do not become aroused.

"Charlie," said Serena, "I'm going to drive our car home. I'll try to get there before you do, but Jarmaine and Nina will be there in any case." There was nothing wrong with what she said, but he didn't like the tone. It was the tone of frustration and suppressed rage with which you address a hopeless invalid who insists on making inroads into your free time.

Another cross between a mutter and a moan: "Okay."

By now the orderlies had pushed Charlie all the way onto the level floor of the van. He could hear the Wiz's voice outside:

"So long, Serena. I should get back to the office. Tell Charlie to give me a ring if he thinks of anything."

He has to say all that to *Serena*. It's as if I've been written off with . . . Parkinson's or Huntington's chorea or Wegener's granulomatosis or whatever I heard them talking about in there. An ambulance attendant rode in the back of the van with him and kept asking him, the way you ask a truly feeble old man, if everything was all right.

AT THE HOUSE on Blackland Road the yard had the lushness of summertime in Buckhead (north of West Paces Ferry). The trees, the maples, the oaks, the sycamores, the birch, and the pine provided a canopy up above that created a green-and-gold glow below. The magnolias and the boxwood had never looked fatter or shinier. Fabulous borders of ageratum, thrift, begonias, and anemones ran in waves of color along the edges of the grass that provided the green for the house's sumptuous green breast.

All of that Charlie appreciated in the abstract, but he did not find it the least bit gratifying. Quite the opposite. His lawn, his trees, his grass, his shrubs and flowers had no business putting on such a show when he felt so depressed. The depressed man longs for heavy clouds, fog, mist, chilly weather, downpours, hail.

With a good deal of panting and struggling, the SaveWay Ambulance Service attendant and driver managed to get the wheelchair and its 235-pound load up the two low rises of steps that led to the front door and then up across the threshold. Jarmaine and Nina had opened the door and were waiting with enormous smiles (totally insincere, thought Charlie) and many *Mister Crokers*.

Jarmaine said, "Bed ready in library, like you said."

The ambulance men started to leave, but one of them, the driver, a reedy white man with bad posture, prematurely gray hair, and a mustache that was longer on one side than the other, came around in front of the wheelchair and said to Charlie:

"I don't mean to put my two cents in—"

But you will, thought Charlie.

"Now, I'm no doctor—"

But you're not about to let that stop you, thought Charlie.

"—but I don't think you should stay on the first floor, Mr. Croker. I used to do a lot of physical therapy, and I can tell you, going up and down those stairs"—he gestured toward the grand half-spiral sweep of Charlie's main staircase—"is one of the best things you can do for yourself. I've worked with a lot of patients—"

Charlie cut him off with: "Thank you." He was slumped forward in the wheelchair, and his head was bent forward, and he looked up at

Mr. Almost A. Doctor with as malevolent a look as he could muster.

"I don't mean to be out of line," the man said, beginning to look flustered.

"Thank you," said an utterly unsmiling Charlie, and the man with the mismatched mustache beat a retreat out the front door.

The hell of it was, he knew the man was right. But what difference did it make? Recuperate for—what? Why do a lot of exercises and put yourself through a lot of pain as if you're building toward some sort of future—when you know very well there *is* no future?

The depressed man realizes that all daily routines imply a belief in Tomorrow and are cruel jokes since of course tomorrow no longer exists.

As Jarmaine pushed him toward the library, Charlie became suddenly aware of the fortune—not just in money but also in time and care—that had gone into the first floor of this house. Godalmighty. His eyes roamed. Jarmaine was saying something, and Nina was hovering, as only she could hover, but Charlie paid no attention to either of them. He felt enormously sorry for himself . . . an old man being trundled in a wheelchair to a bed in his library. A sorry old man letting his eyes wander helplessly over his worldly goods . . . Oh Lord, the amboyna-wood breakfront, the eighteenth-century grandfather's clock that didn't come from any grandfather of either of them but cost more than either of *his* grandfathers had made in a lifetime of jookin' at the jook houses and swamp-rattin' in the swamps in Baker County, the—how was it pronounced—fautooies?—the fauteuils, the fabrics from whatever-those-thieves-in-New-York-were-called, the lamps from that place in Nebraska, the cabinets—commodes Bombay—was that what Serena called them? . . . all of these names came flooding back into the brain of the poor old hulk as he was being wheeled across a stretch of carpet, which was another wildly expensive item introduced to North Georgia by Ronald Vine, the decorator. Serena had been experiencing for the first time the ecstasy of having an unlimited budget with which to buy . . . *things* . . . *objects* . . . fabulous *stuff* . . . And what nonsense it all was! How vain and petty it all was, all this exulting over . . . *things*! One day—soon enough!—we'll all be gone, and there'll be people rooting through all this . . . stuff . . . like maggots . . . What are antiques, after all, but objects other maggots went over before you? And what is this whole house . . . in the sacred Buckhead . . . but a place he was renting until the next group of renters, as desperate to live in Buckhead as he was, took over . . . Merely renting! Of course, we think we've *bought* these things, we think we *own* them. What a marvelous piece of self-deception! If you add up the cost of maintaining a place like this plus the interest lost through tying up two or three million dollars in the so-called purchase, then there's your rent. You're only in here for a short time. You're only occupying the space until your mortal hide becomes hopelessly decrepit. Your children aren't going to keep the marvelous old place going. Don't kid yourself! They'll be off living with some dreadful creatures of their own generation in some hovel in Old Town in Chicago or North Beach in San Francisco or TriBeCa in New York or Coral Gables . . . They won't waste two tears thinking about the old manse with all its . . . things . . . except to get their hands on the money that flows from all the new maggots rooting through the remains. He should apprise Wally of all this, tell him how life is actually put together . . . He should . . . but he had the terrible feeling that the breach between him and Wally was already too great. They had long since passed the point when he could have put his arm around Wally's shoulders and had a man-to-man talk. It was this damnable boarding school Martha had packed him off to, Trinian. They stuff these poor kids full of political correctness, and they end up pussies. His own son! Christ, at Turpmtine the other weekend Wally was as . . . big a pussy . . . as Herb Richman. He looks at me as if I'm some sort of . . . barbarian . . . These children have no standards. They only know what they choose to be contemptuous of—

"Mr. Croker, you go to bed now?" It was Jarmaine. She had pushed Charlie's wheelchair as far as the bed in the library. The bed really looked terrible in here. The library looked gloomy enough to start with (a thought that had never occurred to him before), what with all this dark carved wood, and now here's this musty old bed with a painted metal bedstead . . . Christ . . . made him think of Jim Bowie on his deathbed just before the Mexicans ventilated him with their bayonets . . . Not only that, there were a couple of things he had failed to figure out when he gave instructions about putting the bed down here on the first floor. The only toilet was the powder room, a staggeringly expensive little piece of nothing Ronald had fashioned out of marble, enamel, and brass. It was dazzling—and didn't have a shower or tub or even enough shelf space to line up all the vials of pills Emmo had burdened him with, much less anything else. Then there was no place to hang anything, such as a bathrobe or any other article of clothing he might want to wear . . . But what other article of clothing *would* he want to wear?

No other. He was an invalid, an invalid for the duration. He had a nurse's assistant, whatever that was, coming in to do all the physical chores he was too crippled to perform himself. The nurse's assistant could hang up the goddamned bathrobe.

For the time being, he was going to sit in that big leather easy chair. He didn't feel like having Jarmaine or Nina watch him struggle out of his clothes and into pajamas. So they helped him out of the wheelchair, and he sank way back into the easy chair and stared at the library shelves with a hopeless, distracted gaze. The truth was, his knee scarcely hurt at this moment. But it *would*! It *would*! It was his screen against the world!

Such were his sentiments when Serena arrived. He could hear her saying something to Jarmaine or Nina, although he couldn't tell what, and then he could hear the high heels of her shoes clack clack clacking across the marble floor of the entry hall. And now she appeared in the doorway of the library and stopped and put her hands on her hips. Charlie lowered his head like a guilty child who knows he's in for it.

"Charlie! For God's sake! What do you think you're doing? You haven't walked one step since you got home. I was just talking to Nina. She said you went straight from the wheelchair to that easy chair. You know what Emmo told you! You know what the therapists told you!"

What Charlie was thinking about had nothing to do with what she had just said. He could only think of how . . . *young* . . . she was. Because there was more light in the hall behind her than here in the library, she existed mainly as a silhouette, a silhouette of Youth . . . the wild corona of hair . . . the long, straight narrow neck . . . the wide shoulders . . . the tiny waist . . . the little silk dress that stopped a good six inches above her knees in a fashion only a young woman with perfect legs would ever dare attempt . . . and hers were indeed perfect in every detail, even in the athletic way her thighs tapered down to where they inserted into the knees . . . the jaunty set of her hips . . . the curves the calves of her legs made . . . the tiny knobs of her ankles . . . He couldn't really see her breasts, because the light was behind her, but he knew very well they were perfect, too . . . He knew it, but he didn't *feel* it, not for a moment. He knew very well that he was impotent and had been for a while. He had made sure he never had to put it to the test, but he knew it was so . . . an old, decrepit carcass was what he was . . . He was moldering but he hadn't even had the decency to die yet. I'm rotting flesh—and she is the very picture of Youth! And she'll never nurse me. Oh no.

"Charlie, are you with us? Are you listening to me?" The flawless silhouette rearranged its arms akimbo upon the sprockets of its perfect hips.

"Yes," said Charlie, "I was just—just—just a little . . . fatigued . . . after that ride." The penitent child drew his chin in even closer to his collarbone. He no longer thought about his own rule: viz., that a leader never explains to his followers or to women. He was a child enjoying poor health.

"Fatigued?" said the silhouette. "From what? You haven't moved a muscle all morning! Charlie—you've got to get going! You can't do this to yourself!"

Charlie didn't say anything. He knew he could ride this storm out. Serena would get tired of the Invalid, no matter what he did. In minutes, not days. She would persuade herself that it was utterly essential to go shopping, whether he flexed his miserable knee or didn't.

The front doorbell rang, and Serena immediately wheeled about and marched into the entry hall to answer it. See? She doesn't wait for Jarmaine or Nina. She answers it herself. Any excuse to get away from the Invalid.

He could hear her in conversation with someone, but he couldn't make out what she was saying, except for "Come in."

CONRAD WAS STUNNED. She was the most gorgeous woman he had ever seen and not much older than himself, if at all. She wore an apple-green dress with swirling floral patterns in it, a dress of such a light filmy material and so short, it seemed like nothing more than a mist hiding, but only halfway, a lissome young body. Her mouth had an oddly playful smile. Playful about what?

He became terribly self-conscious. What an insignificant mortal he was, standing before this house and this beautiful woman in his Carter Home Care getup, his white polo shirt with the green Carter logo on the breast pocket, his white duck pants with the green piping down the side of each leg, the fake-leather white shoes.

"Hello, I'm Con—" He hesitated. He had come close to saying "Conrad." "I'm Connie DeCasi. I'm from Carter Home Care."

"Oh yes," she said. "Come in." She opened the screen door, and he had taken two or three steps inside when she added, "I'm Serena Croker."

Conrad assumed she was the old man's daughter or daughter-in-law. He looked back to acknowledge her introduction, then looked away immediately, for fear of seeming to want to stare at her, which he did. The entry hall where he stood was enormous.

The beautiful young woman indicated that he should follow her. She led him to a doorway off the entry gallery and, just before entering, said, "My husband will be staying in here temporarily."

My husband—should he take that to mean that this gorgeous young woman was the *wife* of the sixty-year-old man named Croker?

All at once she raised her hand in the gesture that means "Stop" and then motioned to indicate that he should move away from the doorway. In a hushed voice she said:

"The most important thing you can do for my husband is stay nearby and keep an eye on him and help him if he wants to move around or take a shower or whatever. He has his moods. Right now he's pretty low. He doesn't want to move at all, not even for therapy. But he's headstrong. The next thing you know, he's going to want to go charging up and down the stairs. The stairs and the shower are what worry me most. I don't want him to fall. Right now he doesn't even have access to a shower. I *told* him not to set up a bed in the library. There's no shower and no tub down here. But he's headstrong. If he hasn't changed his mind by this evening, I'll be surprised."

"I see," said Conrad. He was very much aware of the young woman's perfume.

"One other thing," she said. "If he gets obstreperous and tries to do something foolish, bark at him. That's the only thing he'll pay attention to. There's no use trying logical persuasion."

"I'll do my best," said Conrad. Somehow he didn't dare look her in the eye. He kept his gaze on the zone of her mouth and her nose.

She beckoned him back to the doorway. Everywhere you looked . . . stately, lugubrious panels, shelves, and moldings of mahogany, and matching leather-bound books that seemed to have been bought by the yard. There was an enormous waist-high globe, supported by a dark wooden cradle inlaid with some other kind of wood that was lighter. In the next instant Conrad saw the bed, set up awkwardly in the middle of the room. Only then did he see the big old man. He was slumped back in a leather easy chair. The old man didn't even look at him until his young wife went over to him and said, "Charlie, here's the, uh, the young man from the Carter people—you remember that? He's come to help out."

Then she looked at Conrad in a rather anxious way. It took a moment before he realized that she hadn't caught his name.

"I'm Connie DeCasi, Mr. Croker," he said. "But please call me Connie."

Nothing. The old man was staring between his knees at the floor, apparently thinking of something unpleasant and a thousand miles away. Conrad thought he must be senile. But then he looked up slowly and said:

"Well, Connie, I'm going to bed. Maybe you can help me with that."

"Certainly."

"Please, Charlie," said his wife, "don't just go from a bed in the hospital to a bed here. You're supposed to exercise your knee. You know that."

"I know something else, too. I'm tired." Came out closer to *tarred* than *tired*.

"Well, I'm afraid my husband's in a mood to be difficult, Connie. I wish you good luck." She tried to make it light without succeeding a hundred percent.

"Who's had the knee operation around here?" said Charlie Croker, also with a pretense of keeping it light, although anybody could see how much he was fuming.

Serena Croker departed the room, and now there were just the two of them.

"Help me up out of this chair, son," said the old man. "This knee a mine hurts like a sonofabitch."

"Which knee is it?" asked Conrad.

"The right one."

"Okay," said Conrad, standing to the old man's left, "I'm going to put both hands under this arm"—the old man's left arm—"and you take hold of my arm here"—Conrad indicated his left forearm—"with your other hand, and on three we'll both pull up."

The old man hooked his hand over Conrad's forearm, and then Conrad said, "One, two . . . *three*."

The old man rose, wincing in pain from the stiffness of his knee. Conrad supported him until he got his balance, and then said, "Put your arm around my shoulder. That'll take the weight off your right leg, and we'll walk over to the bed"—which was all of three steps away.

As the old man leaned against Conrad and hobbled, he said, "I didn't think you could do it."

"Do what, sir?"

"Pull me up. I weigh 235 pounds. You must have a lot of arm strength."

"You did half the pulling, Mr. Croker, don't forget that."

With considerable puffing and groaning, plus Conrad's help, Mr. Croker managed to get into bed. He sighed profoundly and sank back into the pillow with his chin up in the air.

"Sir," said Conrad, "you want me to bring you the newspaper or anything?"

A long-drawn-out "Nooooooo." The old man's eyes were closed. Conrad had no idea how little interest a depressed man has in the daily newspaper.

"Well, I'll be here when you need me, Mr. Croker," said Conrad. No reply.

Conrad sat down in a straight-backed chair near the doorway, where he could steal enough light from the entry gallery to read, and opened *The Stoics*.

Epictetus says, "Your poor body, then, is it slavish or free?"

One of his students says, "We know not."

"Do you not know that it is a slave to fever, gout, ophthalmia, dysentery, the tyrant, fire, sword, everything stronger than itself?"

"Yes, it is a slave."

"How then can any part of the body be still free from hindrance? How can that which is naturally dead—earth and clay—be great or precious? What then? Have you no element of freedom?"

"Perhaps none."

"Why, who can compel you to assent to what appears false?"

"No one."

"And who to refuse assent to what appears true?"

"No one."

"Here, too, then you have free and unhindered action. Miserable men, develop this, set your minds on this, seek your good *here*."

Conrad cast a glance at old Mr. Croker. He would love to read to him what he had just read. The body! A slave to all sorts of things, including surgeons and their knives! How can that which is naturally dead—earth and clay—be great or precious? But he would resist that impulse. What could the wisdom of Epictetus possibly mean to a hard-bitten old real estate developer?

CHARLIE OPENED HIS eyes into slits just big enough to survey the library and make out its occupants. Serena was gone. Good. Nina and

Jarmaine were gone. Also good. Only the boy from the home-care service was here. That was fine. The boy didn't know him and had no way of passing judgment on him for "not being himself." The boy was sitting close to the doorway, bathed by the light fom the hall, reading a book.

What a pair of arms the kid has! His forearms are huge; his forearms and his hands. Kid pulled me right up out of the chair . . . What a time it is when you're that age—what?—twenty?—twenty-one?—and you can build yourself up like an ox . . . like a Jersey bull. . . . But this kid, he doesn't look like a bodybuilder. He looks like he got his muscles from *work*. What's that on the ring finger of his left hand? Like a crevice. Something really bit into the flesh. A ring? A wedding ring? What's it matter? It don't matter. He's polite, and he don't riddle you with questions.

Charlie was curious, in spite of himself. What brought a young man to a job like this?

He turned his head toward the boy, opened his eyes, and said, "Well . . . whattaya reading?"

"Sir?" The boy looked startled and closed the book.

"Whattaya reading?" His voice was so tired.

"It's a book called *The Stoics*, Mr. Croker."

"I see . . . What's it about?"

"It's everything the Stoic philosophers wrote, or everything they said that was written down by other people. Both."

"Hmmmm. Is it interesting?"

"It is to me, Mr. Croker."

"What's the interesting part?"

"Well, most philosophies—or from what I know about them—and I don't know much, Mr. Croker . . . sure you want me to go into all this?"

"Yeah. Tell me what makes it interesting." Charlie managed to shift his bulk and prop his head up against the headboard, so he wouldn't be talking from out of a pillow.

"Well," said the boy, "most philosophies assume that you're free, you've got all these possibilities, and it's like you can design your own life any way you want."

The boy hesitated; so Charlie gave him a little encouragement. "Go ahead."

"The Stoics, they assumed the opposite. They said that in fact you have very few choices. You're probably trapped in some situation, everything from being under somebody's thumb to being a slave to disease to actually being in jail. They assumed that in all likelihood you *weren't* free."

"What were they?" said Charlie. "Greeks?"

"They were Romans," said the boy, "although one of them, Epictetus, was a Greek living in Rome."

"When was all this?"

"About the time of Nero. The first century A.D."

What stuck in Charlie's mind was *probably trapped in some situation.*

"So tell me, do you consider yourself a Stoic?"

"I'm just reading about it," said Conrad, "but I wish there was somebody around today, somebody you could go to, the way students went to Epictetus. Today people think of Stoics—like, you know, like they're people who grit their teeth and tolerate pain and suffering. But that's not it at all. What they are is, they're serene and confident in the face of anything you can throw at them. If you say to a Stoic, 'Look, you do what I tell you or I'll kill you,' he'll look you in the eye and say, 'You do what you have to do, and I'll do what I have to do—and, by the way, when did I ever tell you I was immortal?' "

"And you'd like to be like that?" asked Charlie.

"I—yes."

Charlie could tell that the boy felt he had already said too much.

"All right," said Charlie, "let's suppose somebody is in a dilemma. If he chooses one thing, then he gains something valuable, but he loses something that may be even more valuable. And vice versa. If he chooses the other thing, then it's the same problem. He gains one thing of value and loses another thing that may be even more valuable. What does your Stoic say to that?"

"Well, for him, the Stoic—are you sure I'm not telling you more about Stoicism than you want to know? Honest, I'm not a nut on the subject. I just happen to be reading about it."

"No, no, no," said Charlie. "Please go ahead. You can be sure it's a hell of a lot more interesting than listening to lectures about knee replacements and being a good patient and how important it is to do your therapy. *They're* the ones who tell you to just grit your teeth and take it. Which is easy for *them* to say. So what does your Stoic say about dilemmas?"

There was embarrassment on the boy's face. He hesitated . . . then said: "To a Stoic there are no dilemmas. They don't exist."

"How can they not exist?"

"I'll try to give you an example, Mr. Croker. Are you *sure* you don't mind hearing all this?"

"No, go ahead. I'm interested."

The boy said, "Well, there was a famous Stoic named Agrippinus, if that's the way you pronounce it. I've never heard anybody say his name out loud. Anyway, one day—this was in Rome at the time Nero was the emperor, about 95 A.D.—Nero loved to humiliate prominent Romans by ordering them to put on costumes and make fools of themselves in these plays he used to write. So one day this well-known Roman historian named Florus arrives at Agrippinus' house, and he's sweating and trembling, and he says to Agrippinus:

" 'The most terrible thing has happened. I've been summoned to appear in one of Nero's plays. If I do it, I'll be humiliated before everybody in Rome that I care about. If I don't, I'll be killed.'

" 'I've received the same summons,' says Agrippinus.

" 'My God,' says the historian, 'you, too! What do we do?'

" '*You* go ahead and act in the play,' said Agrippinus. '*I'm* not going to.'

" 'Why me and not you?' said the historian.

" 'Because *you've* con*sid*ered it.' "

"Christalmighty," said Charlie. "That's—" But he decided not to finish the thought.

"I can give you another example from Epictetus' own life."

"Good," said Charlie.

"But if I'm rattling on too long," said the boy, "you've got to say so."

"No, this interests me."

"You sure?"

"I'm sure. Go ahead."

"Well, the emperor after Nero was Domitian, and the way he looked at it, the philosophers, particularly the Stoics, were good for nothing but stirring up trouble. So he issued an ultimatum. All the Roman philosophers either had to cut off their beards—the long beards were the emblem, I guess you'd say, of the philosopher—you either cut off your beard, which was like saying, 'I renounce being a philosopher,' or we'll kill you or send you into exile. A delegation from the emperor comes around to deliver the ultimatum to Epictetus, and he doesn't even say, 'Let me think it over.' He says, right on the spot, 'I'm not removing my beard.' And they say, 'Then we'll execute you.' Epictetus laughs and says, 'Are you talking about this vessel of clay and its quart of blood that is my body? Go ahead. I've only got it on loan for a little while anyway.' "

"Okay," said Charlie, "so what happened to them, Epi-teeter?—"

"Epic*te*tus."

"—and Ah-grippus?"

"Agrippinus."

"Two brave men who say 'Fuck you' to the authorities. What happened to them?"

"It's interesting," said the boy, "or I think it is. Both resisted the authorities head-on, with no negotiation, and neither one of them was executed. Both of them were exiled, which was a terrible punishment in those days, but nobody—I'm only guessing, of course—nobody wanted the death of such powerful spirits on their hands."

Charlie lay there for a moment, trying to fit all this to his situation. Suppose he just said "Fuck you" to everybody who was putting the squeeze on him, the bank, Fareek Fanon's lawyer, what would be the outcome? All he could see as the realistic answer to that question was . . . utter desolation . . . a disgraced Cap'm Charlie with no one to follow his commands . . . and yet he wanted to know more.

"Well, let me ask you something, Connie—"

Suddenly Serena was back in the room. Flustered, she closed the library door and hurried past the boy, Connie, and over to Charlie's bed.

"Charlie," she said, "are you all right?"

"Yeah, I guess," said Charlie.

"Charlie, there's this man who keeps calling. He says he's a lawyer and he insists he has to see you. His name is—"

"Roger White," said Charlie in a weary voice.

"That's it. What do I tell him?"

"Don't tell him anything. Let Jarmaine answer the telephone."

"All right," said Serena with a distracted air, "but he kept saying he had to have an answer from you very soon. That's what he kept saying, over and over. An answer about what, Charlie?"

"He's a lawyer," said Charlie. "He wants me to testify in some case of his."

"What kind of case?"

"Oh, it dud'n matter," said Charlie. He tried to sink deeper, deeper, and yet deeper into the bed.

Chapter XXX

The Bull and the Lion

PEEPGASS LEANED WAY BACK IN THE CHAIR TO GIVE HIMSELF enough room between his abdomen and the table to rustle back the first section of the *Journal-Constitution* from page 1 to page 12—much rustlerustlerustling of the newspaper—so he could continue reading about the latest developments in the case of Fareek Fanon and the as-yet-unnamed-in-print Elizabeth Armholster. In the midst of the big foldback he happened to glance out the window. He couldn't believe it. There was the gardener, Franklin, down on his knees, edging the flower bed with a trowel! Where had he come from? Five minutes ago he wasn't there! Peepgass hadn't seen him arrive and hadn't heard him arrive, even though the window was wide open and Franklin was no more than twelve feet away from him. Martha had opened the window, because it was such a nice cool morning you didn't need the air conditioning. It was as if Franklin had grown up from out of the earth like a tuber in his earth-colored work shirt and vest and his earth-colored skin when neither Peepgass nor Martha was paying attention.

Martha looked up from the part of the *Journal-Constitution* she was reading, Section E, called "Horizon"—the newspaper's euphemism, Peepgass thought ruefully, for "the suburbs," particularly poor old basketball-backboard-and-hoop-in-the-driveway commuterburbs like

Snellville—Martha looked up and smiled and asked, "What on earth is that headline about 'Fanon's Cannons' supposed to mean?"

"Well, it's here," said Peepgass, extending the first section toward her. "Take a look. It's interesting. Politics is rearing its mangy head."

"No, no, no," said Martha, "I don't want to read it right now, I was just hoping it wasn't a double entendre."

"I don't think the *Journal-Constitution* goes in for double entendres, or at least not racy ones. That's r, a, c, y, not r, a, c, e, y."

"Is r, a, c, e, y a word?"

"Please don't get technical on me. It seems that they've—I'm not really sure who *they* are—they've started a defense fund for Fareek Fanon, and a couple of black councilmen are saying that the whole thing is—you'll never guess what—a racist plot to discredit Fanon. They're his 'cannons,' the councilmen. It's become very political. The Mayor has announced he'll be holding a press conference and making a major statement about the whole thing."

That was what Peepgass was saying as he looked toward Martha across this elegant round mahogany table with fruitwood banding, aswarm with hand-crocheted place mats and a veritable flotilla of silver and crystal, including a silver bread gondola, with a damask napkin lining it, currently empty because Peepgass had devoured every last morsel of the toasted Sally Lunn that had been therein along with his scrambled eggs, grits, hot country sausage, and New Orleans coffee. But what he was thinking was:

Does she look any better this morning? What could she do about that . . . thickness in the neck and shoulders and upper back? Anything? Probably not. Would she be presentable? I'm only forty-six. She's fifty-three. Would it be embarrassing to take her places as my wife? She does have fabulous legs, but is there some kind of regimen or diet to get rid of that . . . thickness up top? What happens when she's sixty and I'm only fifty-three? What then? On the other hand . . . look at what's all around me here! This is . . . Buckhead! The *real* thoroughbred Buckhead! Look at this house! Look at that yard! Look at that faithful old Franklin! Look at what's on this table! Enough silver to make a down payment on a four-bedroom house in Snellville, poor old Snellville! Jesus Christ . . . If Sirja wins her goddamned paternity suit, which no doubt she will, and I have to pay Christ knows how much in support payments, I'll be flat as a flounder! Pietari Päivärinta Peepgass—"Pavvy! Pavvy! Pavvy! Pavvy!"—Little Pavvy will get bigger and bigger, he'll eat and eat and eat, thanks to me being squeezed every month like a tube of old toothpaste—for the next eighteen years! I'll be an old man, waiting to get the crystal phoenix from PlannersBanc, before it all ends! I won't have *lived*, f'r Chrissake!

He looked at Martha again, as if he were about to say something more about the Elizabeth Armholster business, but in fact he was studying her and thinking:

She's actually pretty. Not too many lines. Nice hair . . . full . . . dyed? . . . Can't tell . . . Has all her makeup on, even at breakfast . . . Simple, stylish cotton dress, navy with vertical white stripes, high in the hem to show off those legs . . . But that neck . . . thick . . . Chunky gold chain for a necklace . . . Casual, but must be a ton of gold in the damned thing . . . Sirja . . . destroying him as if she's God's avenging angel . . . Kept thinking of Sirja last night . . . Only way he could get it done, wasn't it . . . A vision of Sirja the way she was that very first night at the Grand Tatar. She had stripped down to her stockings, the old-fashioned kind, not pantyhose . . . Medium-brown sheer nylon stockings they were, held up by old-fashioned garters with flowery little yellow and mint green bows on them . . . That was all she had on! Not a stitch more! At first she was standing in the hotel room with only the stockings on, and then she had put one foot up on a chair and tipped her vulva toward him. The labiae were red—red!—with lust. She put her forefinger and her middle finger in her mouth and then took them out and stroked her labiae, while her hooters bulged and bulged and bulged with lubricity, and her face—but he had purposely blanked out her face, cut off her head, in his emergency recollection, because the face was the outer mask of her vile and treacherous mind . . . but he needed those loins of hers, had to bring them alive in his imagination or he couldn't have managed to get it done with Martha here, who's so thick through the shoulders . . . Would he have to think of a beheaded Sirja Tiramaki, mother of Pietari Päivärinta Peepgass . . . *every time* . . . from now on? No use dwelling on that . . .

They were both embarrassed when they got up this morning. What do you say to her at her age? Or his age, for that matter . . . His clothes were rumpled, especially his shirt, and he had no toothbrush or razor. Well, PlannersBanc would just have to take him unshaven for the first time in his loyal dog's career there . . . Fuck it . . . The newspaper had helped. Gave them something to talk about instead of what was on their minds . . . He had offered to go down to get the newspaper, which was delivered to a box at the bottom of the slope of Martha's big-breasted lawn, but she had said no, she'd better do it . . . Not that there were what you could really call next-door neighbors in this part of Buckhead . . . Nevertheless, she had gone down the slope, wearing her striped cotton dress and a pair of navy Belgian slippers, and retrieved the newspaper—

"What's Jordan's opponent—what's his name?—André Fleet?—what's he have to say about the whole thing?"

At first Peepgass had no idea what Martha was talking about. He had totally forgotten that he had just been talking to her about what the Mayor and some councilmen had to say about the Elizabeth Armholster business. It took him a moment to sort it out.

"He's not quoted, I don't think," he said.

All at once you could hear laughs, real cackles and deep, deep bassoon belly laughs, from Valley Road, at the foot of the lawn. You could hear *heh heh hegggghhhhhhs* and then a merry contralto voice that sang out, "Who you think's gon' believe *'at*, girlfriend?" Then more cackles and *heh heh hegggghhhhhhs*.

Peepgass looked quizzically at Martha.

"That's the maids," she said. "They get off the bus down on West Paces Ferry and come walking up the street like a troupe."

Peepgass shrugged. "You think that's what's her name?—Carmen?"

"Probably," said Martha, looking at her watch. "That sounded like her . . . 'girlfriend.' I hear her saying that on the telephone all the time. 'It's know-it time, girlfriend,' 'No glove, no love, girlfriend.' "

Peepgass said, "You want me to—go anywhere? I mean, is it okay if she sees me just—having breakfast with you like this?"

Martha smiled. "I don't think she'll be scandalized, if that's what you mean."

"No, I didn't mean—"

"Carmen is ladylike and polite, and I only hear bits and pieces of her conversations, but something tells me she's got a lot going on out in the real world." She smiled again.

But she was thinking: Carmen doesn't matter, but what *will* people think if I start going around with Mr. Raymond Peepgass? The name is one of those unfortunate names, like Cockburn or Hogg or Fogg, but people soon get over that. I don't dare question him directly about it, but he doesn't seem to have all that important a job at PlannersBanc, although, for whatever reason, he was important enough for somebody to invite him to the Lapeth show, and I know very well how much those table seats cost. Well . . . I think I could . . . *relax* with Ray. I don't think he would be very demanding. I don't think he's the type who constantly has to have things whirling and popping, the way Charlie was.

Then a cloud formed in her frontal lobes . . . Charlie . . . Last night the only way she could go through with it was to visualize that first night with Charlie. She and Nancy King Ambler—everybody called her "Nancy King," Southern-style—were sharing a one-bedroom apartment on Oakdale Road, near the Emory Medical School. Their agreement was that if either one invited a man up, the other would retire to the bedroom. But it was one of those apartments where you could hear *everything*, no matter where you retired to, and Nancy King knew very well that this was her first date with the great strapping, handsome former football hero she had invited up tonight. Martha thought it was a bad idea even to *kiss* a boy on the first date, but with Charlie everything had progressed so fast she could scarcely figure out what was happening, except that it was all too audible for that apartment, all too full of groans and sighs, and after things had reached a certain point—they were lying on the rug on the floor—she had started saying, "No, Charlie, no," in what she had imagined was a whisper that Nancy King couldn't possibly hear. Then Charlie practically *raped* her! She couldn't imagine how it had happened! Martha Starling of Richmond, Virginia, going *all the way* on her first date! Thank God, Nancy King was from Tallahassee and didn't know anybody in Richmond! Me—a slut! She was convinced that Charlie Croker would never invite her out again. Instead, he called her the next morning at eight o'clock. And no matter what Martha Starling's better self thought of what she had done, no matter how much shame flooded her mind, she had a visceral memory of the most intense ecstasy of her life. It was so taboo even to *intimate* that you could be aroused by male physical power that she had never said a word about it to anyone, least of all Nancy King. At first neither she nor Nancy King said a thing to each other, aside from good morning and other routine things. Then, just before she left for the medical school, Nancy King said, "Oh, you didn't tell me what you thought of the famous Sixty-Minute Man." Her eyebrows were lifted high and her eyes were wide-open in what Martha took to be an ironic expression. "He was very nice," said Martha in a tone that precluded any further discussion. She didn't really know Nancy King *all that well*, and even if she did, how could she possibly describe to her how her smooth white body had felt last night? That was thirty-three years ago. But that night three decades ago was what she had to visualize in order to get through last night with Ray. Charlie had betrayed her in the most egregious way, but she had visualized Charlie last night. She visualized his massive muscular body, which had scarcely an extra ounce on it back then. But she had to decapitate him. She couldn't bear to visualize the face behind which he had hidden his perfidy. But for how long would a faceless Charlie Croker from three decades ago work for her?

The next thing Ray heard was somebody walking across the floor of the entry hall. Then a black woman—Carmen—was in the doorway of the library. She was wearing black jeans with silvery metal studs where the side pockets joined the outseams, a bold yellow T-shirt, and an open black nylon windbreaker with silvery metal snaps down the front and on the sleeves.

"Good morning, Miz Croker."

"Good *mor*ning, Carmen!" said Martha with considerable gusto. "Carmen, you remember Mr. Peepgass, don't you?" She made it sound as if it were the most ordinary and customary thing in the world to have Mr. Peepgass stay over for breakfast.

"I surely do," said Carmen.

"Nice to see you again," said Peepgass, immediately wondering if he had said the right thing. He was a lot more flustered than Martha, who in fact didn't seem flustered at all.

Peepgass gave Martha another once-over. What is it with me? he thought. She's just like Betty. Only she's four years older. Another big woman, older than I am, built hefty, who has stronger nerves than I do. Will she be as bossy as Betty? Am I like that character in that book—he couldn't remember the name of it—*Ivan Something*, the one where the man gets a second life—and helplessly repeats the first one?

ROGER TURNED RIGHT off of West Paces Ferry and drove his Lexus up to Blackland Road, begrudging Buckhead every last oak, every last maple, every last hickory and sycamore, every last hardwood tree the lawns were blessed with. *Hardwood* . . . smug bastards . . .

Croker had left the hospital, but he returned no telephone calls, neither to his home nor to his office. Two Federal Express envelopes had brought no replies. Wes Jordan was putting the pressure on him, and he was here to put it on Croker.

God . . . Croker's house looked like something from out of those movies . . . a stone wall, a stone courtyard, a stone façade, a quarry's worth of stone for one family to live amid . . . He pulled right up to the front entrance. Why be diffident? He slammed his car door for emphasis and marched up the two little sets of steps that led to the threshold. Because of the angle of the light, it wasn't until he was right at the doorway that he realized that the door itself, a massive thing with raised panels, was open, and only a screen door was between him and his quarry, probably because it was such a cool, dry morning, for a change. If the screen door was locked, he'd knock it right out of its slot. He knew how these damned screen door locks were made, even in Buckhead. Couldn't really see inside. Damned screen was like a scrim they use onstage; you can only see what's on the lighted side of the scrim. But then his eyes grew accustomed to the dimnesss of the entry hall—

Christalmighty! It was Croker! He was on his feet, wearing a nightshirt and a blue bathrobe, near as Roger could figure out. *Clackclack . . . clackclack . . . clackclack* . . . He was supporting himself on a pair of aluminum crutches that clacked and rattled every time they hit the floor. His back was to Roger. He seemed to be heading for that grand staircase, the one that rose up like something from out of a movie. Beside him was some sort of attendant, in a white uniform.

Roger yelled out, "Mr. Croker!"

Croker stopped but didn't try to look around. The attendant, however, turned about and gave him a squinting look as if to figure out who it could be. Then he leaned in toward Croker and told him something, and Croker said, in a whisper so heavy you could hear it all the way to the front door:

"Tell him I'm in the middle of my therapy."

The young man turned toward Roger and said, "Mr. Croker's in the middle of his therapy."

That made Roger furious. He grasped the screen-door handle, prepared to break the lock—and discovered it was not locked at all. So he opened it and—here goes!—he stepped inside and started walking across a vast expanse of marble floor. Made him think of his first visit to a Buckhead home, the rendezvous with Fareek Fanon at Buck McNutter's.

"Mr. Croker!" he said sharply. "Mr. Croker!"

Now the young attendant stepped between Roger and the old man. He stood there with his arms folded over his chest and his legs wide apart in a stance that seemed to say "You're not coming any closer." There was something in the boy's stare that Roger found unnerving, and his arms suddenly looked terribly big. So he didn't try to get any closer. And now Croker was slowly turning about on his crutches. Unlike the boy's, Croker's expression was that of someone who has been whipped and humbled by disease and Fate.

"I can't talk to you now." It was far from the Charlie Croker voice of yore. "I've just been through surgery." Not three syllables, but two: "*surge*-ry." It came out not as a statement of fact but as a plea. It was pathetic. It made Roger bolder than ever.

"I don't mean to . . . *barge* . . . *in*," said Roger in a tone that converted it into raillery, meaning "I barged in because I felt like it," "but I must have an answer from you. I've called you, I've left innumerable messages, I've faxed you at your office, I've sent you two letters by Federal Express—I don't know of any other way to reach you other than to do what I'm doing right now. This isn't a game, Mr. Croker. Are you going to appear at the press conference or are you going to let us videotape your statement, or neither? If it's neither, then *a lot of things* . . . have to be changed, and I think you know one of them."

Croker said, "Well . . ." and then he seemed to deflate before Roger's very eyes.

"This is not going to be any ordinary press conference," said Roger. "The Mayor's going to be there, and it's going to be more like a State of the City address, or a State of Race Relations in Atlanta, than a press conference. I've been assuring him that you'd be there. If you double-cross me—and him—it won't be pleasant. That much I can guarantee."

With that, he cocked his head and gave Croker the wry look you give some underling who is wavering and quavering in the face of the job he knows he has to do.

"Okay," said the old man. He let his head droop until his chin was on top of his clavicle. He looked like the most thoroughly whipped brute Roger had ever seen. He looked up again, but only long enough to croak out, "I'll be there."

"Good," said Roger. "I'm glad. I'll take that as a commitment. The Mayor's not playing games. There's something dead serious at stake here."

Barely above a whisper: "Yeah."

"All right," said Roger, "it's a commitment, and our other . . . arrangement . . . will remain in place."

Roger was now hearing his own words as if he were in a grandstand watching and hearing himself perform in the arena. Had he *ever* before talked to anyone of this man's stature in such a hectoring, lecturing, patronizing manner? If he had, he couldn't remember it. It was exhilarating. The Sixty-Minute Man, Croker the developer who had helped shape the very skyline of Atlanta, Croker the Croker of Croker Concourse!

"Goodbye, Mr. Croker." He managed to make that one little word, *goodbye*, sound like a thoroughly peremptory statement.

Croker croaked out an exhausted "Goodbye" as he turned around to continue his rattling hobble to the staircase. The last thing Roger could hear from inside the great mansion after he went outside, heading for his car, was *clackclack* . . . *clackclack* . . . *clackclack* . . . *clackclack* . . .

CONRAD FELT TERRIBLY embarrassed for Mr. Croker. He had just been humiliated by a fancy-dressed black man who came barging into the house as if he owned it. Just like *that* he had come in. Conrad was too embarrassed for the old man even to ask what it was all about, athough he was dying to. Finally he figured out a way for the old man to tell him, if it suited him.

He said, "Who was *that*, Mr. Croker?"

"Aw, he's some lawyer," said the old man. "Works for a law firm downtown."

Conrad said nothing, waiting for more, but all he got was the *clackclack clackclack clackclack* of the aluminum crutches as the old man neared the staircase.

"Jesus God," Croker said under his breath, "this thing hurts." Then directly to Conrad: "What's gonna be the best way for me to do this?" He motioned with his head toward the stairs. "These damned staircases look terrific, but every step in the curve is bigger at one end than it is at the other."

Conrad said, "Even so, Mr. Croker, just put your crutches up on the next step and push off your left foot and swing your weight forward. In case anything happens, I'm gonna be right behind you, but nothing's gonna happen, Mr. Croker."

"I'm 235 pounds," said Croker. "Whattaya gonna do if I fall backward?"

"But you won't be falling out of a tree, Mr. Croker, you'd be falling at an angle. When it's at an angle, it isn't so much a matter of size and weight as position, or that's the way it's always seemed to me, Mr. Croker."

Gradually he was able to cajole and jolly the old man up the stairs. He had plenty of strength—he was an ox of a man—and plenty of coordination. But for whatever reason, he didn't want to make the effort.

Mr. Croker had decided to move from the library to a guest bedroom. This room, all by itself, was more luxurious than any room Conrad had ever seen in his life. The centerpiece was a big four-poster bed with silk curtains or something and some sort of frame over the bed, covered in more silk, creating a canopy. At the head of the bed were about a dozen pillows, *at least* a dozen, from big bolsters up against the headboard to little children's pillows covered with lace and ribbons, and a lot of other things Conrad didn't know the name for. Covering the bed was a white counterpane with all kinds of trimmings. The floor was covered in a wall-to-wall carpet that looked like needlepoint and was designed with flowers, tendrils, leaves, and stems that matched the colors of the silk that hung down the four posts of the bed. There were two easy chairs covered in a striped fabric and so many curtains on the windows he gave up trying to figure it all out.

Croker was panting from the exertion of the climb. His face was red, and there was sweat on his forehead.

"I need to go in there," said the old man, nodding his head toward the bathroom. "I gotta take a shower."

Conrad walked with him as he went *clackclack* . . . *clackclack* . . . *clackclack clackclack* . . . on the aluminum crutches, over to the bathroom door.

"Want me to come in with you?" said Conrad.

"I'll be all right," said the old man.

Mr. Croker went inside and began sighing and *clackclacking*, all of which Conrad could hear despite the thick door. Conrad was standing just outside, in case the old man needed him. All at once, out of the corner of his eye, he noticed a form in the doorway to the hall. He turned his head, and there, for an instant, was Mrs. Croker, Serena Croker, wearing nothing but a short silk slip. It barely covered her breasts, whose areolae welled out against the silk, and the hem was somehow tucked between her thighs, creating a shadowy delta beneath her mons veneris. Her black hair was tumbling down over her shoulders.

She immediately ducked back from the doorway and then extended only her head into the opening and said, "I didn't know you were here! I'm very sorry!" Amazing blue eyes she had.

Conrad swallowed and said, "Mr. Croker's . . ." He motioned toward the bathroom.

She looked at Conrad for what seemed like several seconds too long and then pulled her head back and disappeared. A few rogue thoughts bubbled up into Conrad's brain, but he refused to dwell on them.

Now Conrad could hear Mr. Croker calling him from inside the bathroom: "Connie, give me a hand with this!"

Conrad opened the door, and there, on his crutches, was the old man, trying to lean into a shower stall and turn on the water.

"Let me help you off with your robe and your nightshirt," said Conrad.

"Oh, yeah," said Croker.

Conrad slipped the blue robe off, one arm at a time, and then supported Croker by putting his arm around his waist as he pulled his nightshirt off up over his head. Now the old man stepped out of his slippers, and Conrad steadied him as he hobbled over to the shower stall. Croker's chest, arms, shoulders, and back—especially the back—were massive, and yet the sight was not a picture of power but of age and decrepitude. The flesh was *loose*, loose on the bone, grayish, sagging, and nothing was ever going to make it tight again, either. He didn't have a potbelly, but nevertheless the flesh was *loose*, and it sagged, and his belly button was buried somewhere beneath a two-inch-wide fold of skin in that loose, sagging old man's flesh. "I'll never let that happen to me," Conrad vowed to himself. He had no way of knowing that the old man had made the same vow to *him*self thirty-seven years ago.

With a big helping of moaning, groaning, sighing, and wincing, the old man managed to take his shower, and was more than willing to have Conrad steady him and towel him off afterward. Then he wanted a fresh nightshirt, and so Conrad went into the "dressing room," as the old man called it. Conrad had never seen so many closets in one room in his life! It was the size of a living room, a living room lined with closets.

There was even a delicate little desk, chairs, and lamps. Traces of young Mrs. Croker's perfume hung in the air. So agog was Conrad over life lived in this way, he all but forgot why he was in here; but by and by he found the bureau the old man had told him about—you had to open a pair of louvered maple doors to get to it—and took the nightshirt back to the guest room and helped the old man into it and then into bed. Just clearing the unnecessary pillows off the bed seemed to take ten minutes.

Conrad said, "You want me to leave you alone, Mr. Croker, so you can rest?"

With a great sigh and without looking at the boy, Charlie said, "No." He paused and then looked right at him and then said, "You got that book with you?"

"You mean *The Stoics*?" asked the boy.

"Yeah. You got it?"

"Yes, sir, it's down in the library."

"Well—whyn't you go get it."

"Yes, sir." The boy went downstairs.

Once the boy was out of the room, Charlie pushed himself up toward the head of the bed and propped two bolster pillows under his head and neck. He didn't want to be such an invalid in front of the boy. At least now he was sort of halfway sitting up.

The boy returned with the book, and Charlie motioned toward an easy chair and said, "Have a seat. Wait a minute. Close that door over there."

So the boy went over and closed the door to the hall. Then he went back near the bed and sat down in a striped easy chair. Charlie did a double take. It was strange to see him there, this lean, lithe, muscular boy sinking down into this voluptuous, pink-and-green fleshpot's indulgence of an easy chair.

"The Stoics . . ." said Charlie. He looked away from the boy and up toward the canopy overhead. All this *silk*! That and the chair the boy was in made him realize how many fashionable trifles this house was stuffed with.

Then he looked back at the boy and said, "Tell me about yourself, Connie. Where are you from?"

Conrad had known someone would ask him this question sooner or later, and so he was prepared, or so he thought. "Well—there isn't a whole lot to tell, Mr. Croker. I'm twenty-three. I grew up in Madison,

Wisconsin." He could remember enough of what his parents had mentioned about Madison to get by with anybody who hadn't actually lived there. "My mom and dad both went to the University of Wisconsin, and he had an okay job, but when I was sixteen, things went very bad for him, and I had to drop out of high school and go to work."

"Whattaya mean, things went very bad for him?"

"He was an alcoholic, Mr. Croker. He just left us. We never heard from him again."

"Jesus Christ," said the old man. "What kind of job did he have?"

"He was a dispatcher for a paper products company, a small company."

"Paper products?"

"Yes, sir. I remember they used to make these sort of gray cartons that eggs come in." Conrad figured that "paper products" and "these sort of gray cartons that eggs come in" would finish off discussions of his father's curriculum vitae pretty rapidly.

"What kind of work could you get at sixteen?"

"Bagger and delivery boy for a supermarket."

"Your mother couldn't get a job?"

"No, sir. Or rather she *could*, but she couldn't keep one. My mother was not organized. She thought of herself as an artist, and she thought regular jobs were very square. That was a term she used to use, *very square*. Mom used to be a hippie, an actual hippie. They had hippies in Madison."

"Where's your mother now?"

"She died three years ago, from something I'd never heard of before, tuberculosis of the brain."

"Jesus Christ," said Charlie. "So you've been completely on your own ever since?"

"If you really want to know the truth, Mr. Croker, even before then."

"What would you *like* to do, if you had your choice?"

"Finish college. I finally got my high-school equivalency, and I completed my two years at a community college. Right now I'm trying to save enough to finish up at a four-year college and get a degree, Mr. Croker."

"How much can you save on this job?" said the old man.

"Not much, Mr. Croker. But it'll do for now, and the hours are pretty flexible, so I got plenty of time to look for something that pays better."

"Well, hell . . . maybe I could help you," said Charlie, suddenly excited by the prospect of doing something for the boy.

But then he sighed. His spirits deflated. After laying off 15 percent of the workforce at Croker Global Foods, it wouldn't be very bright for him to turn around and order them to hire somebody just because he was a nice kid.

"Nawwwww, I don't think we're hiring, and it's a lousy job anyway." Charlie looked away from the boy as if he had already let him down. Then he turned back toward him. "Tell me something, Connie. Where the hell'd you work to get those arms a yours"—he made a gesture toward the boy—"and those hands?"

That was not a question Conrad had anticipated. His mind spun. The best he could come up with was warehouse work—but he'd change the industry. "For about six months, Mr. Croker, I worked in a wholesale paint warehouse. All day long you'd be lifting cans of paint and drums of spackle and plaster mix that weighed anywhere from ten pounds to eighty pounds. All day long you were giving your hands and your forearms a workout to da max. That was what one of the fellows I used to work with used to say, 'to da max.' "

"Unh-hunh," said Charlie. He paused for five or six seconds, then said, "I can tell you one a lot worse than that."

"One what, sir?" said the boy.

"A warehouse job," said Charlie, "a warehouse job worse than working in a paint warehouse. I own some warehouses myself, food service warehouses, wholesale food distribution. Maybe you've seen one of our trucks. They're all over the place. Croker Global Foods is what it says on the side of them, white trucks with navy and gold lettering."

Charlie couldn't figure out what had happened. The boy was speechless. He stared at Charlie blankly, as if all his lights had gone out.

So Charlie repeated it in the form of a question: "Have you ever seen our trucks?—Croker Global Foods?"

Finally the boy said, "Yes . . . I have."

"It would be hard to miss 'em," said Charlie. "We're all over the country. Anyway, seeing as how we're food distributors, we handle a lot of stuff that's got to be kept frozen, especially meat. So in every warehouse we have a freezer unit about the size of this house. Maybe not quite that big, but big. And we got people who work in there called 'freezer pickers.' They work an eight-hour shift at about zero Fahrenheit, hauling product off these racks, out a these 'slots' they call 'em, sixty-, seventy-, eighty-pound frozen cartons . . ." Charlie averted his eyes again, lying there, and shook his head. Then he looked at the boy once more. "The worst of it is when they come outta the damn things with these *icicles* coming outta their noses. I'm not kidding!" He tossed one hand up in a gesture of helplessness. "Outta their noses!" Once more he turned away. "Jesus . . ." He turned back again. Big sigh. "I'd like to sell the whole damn business, but I've borrowed more money against the damn thing than it's worth, if I tried to sell it now . . . So anyway, you had a job in a paint warehouse. Where was that?"

The boy didn't say anything for the longest time. Finally he said, "Milwaukee, Mr. Croker."

"So how'd you happen to come here?"

"I'd read there were a lot of jobs available in Atlanta, and there *are* a lot of jobs available, but they don't pay much unless you're a college graduate."

The old man said, "So when did you get interested in the Stoics?"

"A few weeks ago. I found this book I showed you in a secondhand store in Chamblee." He held the book up so the old man could see it.

"The Stoics," Mr. Croker said once more. "And what was the man's name again, Eppitetus?"

"E-pic-*te*-tus."

"Oh yeah. Well . . . okay . . . what does Epic*te*tus have to say about bankruptcy?—or is that something too mundane for a philosopher to think about?"

"Not too mundane for Epictetus, Mr. Croker. One place he says, 'You are all nervous and you can't sleep at night for fear you're going to run out of money. You say, "How will I even get enough to eat?" But what you are really afraid of is not starvation but the prospect of not having a cook or somebody to wait on you at the dinner table or somebody to take care of your clothes and your shoes and the laundry and make up the beds and clean up the house. In other words, you're afraid you may no longer be able to lead the life of an invalid.' "

"He really said that?" asked Charlie. "About insomnia and leading the life of an invalid and all that?"

"Yes, sir."

"Okay . . . What else does he say?"

"He says, 'Where does your fear of losing your worldly possessions lead you? To death. When Ulysses was shipwrecked and washed up on shore with nothing left, it never broke his spirit. He approached the fix he was in like a hill-bred lion, trusting in his might. He wasn't depending on his reputation, his money, his official position, but on his own might. What makes you free is what's inside you.' That's what he says, Mr. Croker."

Charlie's lame knee wouldn't allow him to roll over in bed, but he twisted his body as best he could, in order to look the boy squarely in the face, this boy declaiming Stoicism from the downy billows of an easy chair custom-made for one of Serena's visions of luxury. "What's he really getting at? This Epictetus?"

"Well—I'm not the final word on this, Mr. Croker, but what he's saying, it seems to me, he's saying that the only real possession you'll ever have is your character and your 'scheme of life,' he calls it. Zeus has given every person a spark from his own divinity, and no one can take that away from you, not even Zeus, and from that spark comes your character. Everything else is temporary and worthless in the long run, your body included. You know what he calls your possessions? 'Trifles.' You know what he calls the human body? 'A vessel of clay containing a quart of blood.' If you understand that, you won't moan and groan, you won't complain, you won't blame other people for your troubles, and you won't go around flattering people. I think that's what he's saying, Mr. Croker."

Charlie said, "He talked about *flattering* people?"

That caught his attention. The lies he had agreed to recite about Fareek Fanon were flattery elevated to some sort of ultimate.

"Yes, sir," said the boy, "that's what he said. 'The flatterer debases himself and deceives the object of his fawning.' 'Dogs fawn over one another,' he says, 'but throw a piece of meat between them, and see how much friendship remains.' "

For a moment Charlie tried to fit the piece of meat into his own relationship with Fareek Fanon, but he couldn't come up with any real analogy. Then he said to the boy:

"Let me ask you this. What would Epictetus say if a man made a speech praising a prominent public figure—okay?—and he did admire the man's, uh . . . power and skill in his line of work—but he didn't think much of him as a person? Would it be okay to make the speech as long as you stuck pretty much to the man's professional life when you gave the talk?"

"Is this someone the person giving the talk truly does not like?"

Charlie paused, sighed, let out his breath, and said dejectedly, "Yeah. He can't stand the sonofabitch."

"Is the person giving the speech praising this public figure with the idea of gaining something for himself?"

The old man hesitated for a moment, then said, "Yeah. You got it."

"Not much, then," said the boy. "Epictetus says that selling out lowers you to the level of a beast, like the wolf or the fox. For some reason he thought that foxes were the lowest of all."

"He actually says 'selling out'?"

"Practically," said the boy. "Lemme see . . ." He thumbed through the book. "Here it is, Book I, Chapter 2. He says, 'Of one thing beware, O man. See what is the price at which you sell your will. If you do nothing else, do not sell your will cheap.' "

The old man said, "How do you know whether you're selling out too cheap or not?"

"If you're selling out at all, it's too cheap," said Conrad, "or at least that's the way I interpret what he's saying, Mr. Croker, since the true Stoic makes no compromises. Selling out and compromises are not part of his character."

"That's fine," said Charlie, "but how do you know what your character is? Let's say there's a crisis you've got to deal with. How do you know what you're really made of?"

"Epictetus talks about that," said Conrad. "He says, how does a bull, when a lion's coming after him, and he has to protect the whole herd —how does he know what powers he's got? He knows because it has taken him a long time to become powerful. Like the bull, a man doesn't become heroic all of a sudden, either. Epictetus says, 'He must train through the winter and make ready.' "

Like a bull!

Jesus Christ, thought Charlie, of all the animals he could've chosen, he has to pick out the *bull*! The old folk song started ricocheting around in his skull so fast, he couldn't get rid of it:

Charlie Croker was a man in full.
He had a back like a Jersey bull.
Didn't like okra, didn't like pears.
He liked a gal that had no hairs.
Charlie Croker! Charlie Croker! Charlie Croker!

Like a Jersey bull! It was as if the boy, this Connie, could read his mind and knew exactly how to prod him, Charlie Croker—he who would compare himself to a Jersey bull!

"This is all very noble," said Charlie, "in the abstract, all this your man is saying, but what does it have to do with real life? Let's think about real life for a second. Let's think about a situation in which you lose everything . . . you *lose everything*! You see what I'm saying? You lose *everything,* the house where you live, your income, your cars—*everything*. You're out on the street. You don't know where your next meal's coming from. What good do a lot of high-sounding ideals mean then?"

The boy said, "Many of Epictetus' disciples asked him that exact same thing, and you know what he told them?"

"No, what?"

"Have you ever seen an old beggar?" The kid's eyes were boring right into him.

"You're asking *me*?"

"Yes."

"Sure I have," said Charlie, "plenty of them."

"See? *They've* gotten by," said the boy. "*They've* managed to get food to eat, 365 days a year, probably. *They're* not starving. What makes you think they can all find food, and you wouldn't be able to?"

"What kinda consolation is that supposed to be? I'd rather die than go around with a cup in my hand."

The boy smiled, and his eyes brightened. "Epictetus talks about exactly that, Mr. Croker. He says, 'You're not afraid of starving, you're afraid of losing face. He says, 'You don't have to have some high position before you can be a great man. One of the great Stoic philosophers, Cleanthes, hauled water to make a living. He was a day laborer, Mr. Croker. But nobody thought of him as someone who didn't have a respectable job. Why? Because he radiated the power of the spark of Zeus."

Charlie closed his eyes and tried to imagine it. He's out on the street. What street? Blackland Road? All he'd get there would be an occasional puff of BMW fumes or a piece of gravel dislodged from a tire tread. So where? Peachtree Street? Nobody even walks on Peachtree Street, and so who's going to stop his Mercedes or Infiniti to give Charlie Croker a quarter? Maybe he could take his tin cup into the parking lot at the

Lenox Square mall. But they've probably got security personnel to chase hooples who come wandering in on foot out of there before they can hunker down on the pavement and set out their cup and a sign saying, "Please help me. Need $28 more so I can get back home to Mobile. No advice, enlightenment, or root-causes conversations, please." That was a sign Charlie had seen in—where the hell was it? Lenox Square? Downtown near the CNN building? Charlie looked at the boy, Connie, and shook his head and said, "I've tried, but I just can't see it."

"And yet if it happened," said the boy, "it wouldn't be nearly as bad as you think, Mr. Croker. Epictetus would say that you—I'm just saying this for the sake of argument, Mr. Croker—Epictetus would say you've given way to your animal impulses and think of yourself as all belly and flesh and animal desire, at the expense of that which Zeus has given you, that spark of the divine."

There was a knock on the door, and then it opened. It was Serena, with a cross between anger and fear on her face. She wore a plain periwinkle-blue sundress that was demure in concept but showed plenty of her bosom. Her thick black hair seemed to be tumbling down in waves, and her eyes were all the more vivid because they matched her dress.

She came toward the bed, saying, "Charlie! Who is this—this man White? He's—"

Charlie cut her off: "Serena, you remember Connie, don't you?" It seemed terribly important somehow that she acknowledge the boy's presence.

She turned her head distractedly toward the boy, who by now had risen to his feet, and she said, "Yes . . . of course."

Then she turned back toward Charlie. "This Mr. White, he keeps calling, he keeps saying he wants to 'reconfirm your decision.' 'Reconfirm your decision,' he keeps saying, and he doesn't care who he's talking to, Jarmaine, Nina, anybody. What are we supposed to do about him? What's this all about?"

Charlie felt terribly embarrassed that she should be bringing all this up in front of Connie. He wanted to put her in her place, but he felt . . . so tired . . . so vulnerable . . . He felt as if he were sinking into the mattress, into the sanctuary of this bed with its thousands of dollars worth of fabric billowing down the four posters, there, there, there . . . and there . . . He was living the life of an invalid, just as Epictetus had said. And what was the name of the guy? Cleanthes? He hauled water for a living, just like some wage mule's work, and he was still a great man, and everybody knew it.

"Well?" said Serena, who now actually had her hands on her hips. Her eyes were blazing. "What do we do about him?"

Charlie pushed himself up by pressing the heels of his hands into the mattress, so that he was at least halfway sitting—and not such an invalid. "You're right," he said to Serena. "So far I've been a fox, but it's against my nature. I feel lousy, and my knee hurts like hell, but I'm gonna be a . . . a . . . a bull. I'll deal with it."

Withering scorn: "What on earth are you talking about, Charlie?—a *fox* and a *bull* . . ."

Charlie realized he certainly didn't *sound* like a bull. His voice was barely above the level and vitality of a croak, and nowhere in himself could he find the will to even *try* to become a bull.

He looked at Serena, looked right into those eyes of hers, and said, "I've descended"—he decided not to mention the foxes or the wolves—"I've descended to a certain level, but I'm gonna get back up. I'll deal with it all."

Serena, with her hands still on her hips, looked at him as if he were senile and shook her head and spun about and marched out of the room.

No, Charlie was no bull who had grown up with a consciousness of his own powers. He didn't have a back like a Jersey bull any longer, and his only hope of getting one was in that book in the hands of a boy who stood beside the chair in his nurse's-aide outfit, that slim boy who, unaccountably, had the forearms and hands of a man twice his size. The boy was like the man he told him about, Cleanthes, who had a job as a day laborer but impressed all who came in contact with him like "a hill-bred lion, trusting in his might," like Ulysses washed ashore, wherever the hell it was Ulysses was washed ashore, and whoever the hell he was. The name summoned up a flicker of memory, but that was all.

It was humiliating, the way she had talked to him right in front of Connie . . . He had *never* let a woman talk to him that way. So why now? Because the source of his strength had always been his money, his reputation, his success in worldly affairs. But the one true source of strength was his own might, his own will, to get or to avoid, his own divine spark of reason, which enabled him to judge which things were in his power and which were beyond it.

Well, Serena wasn't a rich woman—not without him she wasn't—they had a prenuptial agreement and all the rest of it—and she wasn't exactly a despot, but she sure could be a bitch, and there you had that little performance in front of Connie.

Even though the very thought of it made him feel miserable, he said, "Connie, I think I'm gonna get up and take a walk. Gimme a hand. Get me my bathrobe."

Getting the knee off the bed and upright was a killer, but finally he was out in the hallway clad in his blue robe and supported by his aluminum crutches. The hallway was heavily carpeted, but the crutches went *clackclack* . . . *clackclack* . . . *clackclack* . . . *clackclack* . . . all the same. Connie walked beside him.

Clackclack . . . *clackclack* . . . "Connie?" said the old man.

"Yes, sir."

"Connie, I want you to do me a favor."

"If I can, Mr. Croker."

"You'll be coming back here tomorrow at eight, right?"

"Yes, sir."

"Well, what I want is, I want you to leave the book with me after you finish work today, and I'll do some reading on my own and give it back to you tomorrow morning."

The boy's eyes grew frightened, wary, and startled. He stood there with his mouth open.

He didn't know what to say. There was no way he could explain to the old man that the book was . . . *alive* with the spark of Zeus. Therein were the essential truths that had enabled him to withstand the worst the beasts could throw at him in jail, withstand exile from his own family, alienation from the law, a confrontation with a thug—he could see the sneering face of the greaser at the Gardners'. And in that moment it all came together. He could see it as a foreordained pattern. The Book had arrived, seemingly by accident, at Santa Rita—and introduced him to Zeus, to Epictetus and the truth and the way, and given him the courage to fight and overcome the worst predators in the jail. Then Zeus uprooted the entire jail and cracked it open like a walnut shell so that he could escape. Then he made the Army Reservists' Jeep available and somehow led him to Kenny and Mai and the "underground airline" and sent him to Atlanta. And why Atlanta? Because in a hopelessly cluttered attic room in a little town he had never heard of in his life, Chamblee, there was a copy of the Book. And why should he have a copy of the Book? To continue the work and testify to the glory of Zeus. And now he had a chance—the very scalp of his head grew hot from the thought—now he had a chance to convert a man of money and power and renown. From the moment he was laid off by Croker Global Foods to this moment, standing beside a crippled Charlie Croker, this—but of course!—this had been the pattern his life had been woven into: not to punish Croker for throwing hundreds of people out of work with a snap of his fingers, but to recruit him and all his resources into the service of Zeus.

To Charlie it seemed as if the boy stood there beside him for five minutes without saying a word. He looked as if he were off on a cloud somewhere. What the hell was the big deal about the book?

"All right, Mr. Croker," the boy said finally, "I'll leave it with you when I go. But please look after it. Remember, it's . . . alive."

Alive. Charlie didn't know what the hell that was supposed to mean, but there was no mistaking the drift of what the boy had said.

Chapter XXI

Roger Black

ALL AT ONCE IT OCCURRED TO ROGER THAT THE VERY FIRST time he had come here to City Hall to talk to Wes about Fareek Fanon and Elizabeth Armholster, Wes was the one who hopped up and started pacing this brown-and-white Yoruban phoenix rug with a puzzled but halogen-like gleam in his eye. And this time it was him. Oh yes. Roger Not a Bit Too White.

He couldn't stay seated. He kept marching up and down all those deep-piled, tall-tufted birds, the phoenixes, with the adrenaline flowing. He felt as if his eyes were burning brighter and brighter with his gradually dawning awareness of his new role in life. Not a Bit Too White.

As for Wes, he remained seated in his armchair, his excitement, if any, over the new Roger successfully contained.

"So I just opened the screen door and *walked in*!" said Roger. "Then I walked *right up to him*! He was standing there on his crutches with this attendant, or whatever he was, a white kid, and I was no farther from him than I am from you right now, and I said, 'This isn't a game, my friend. Are you going to appear at the press conference or are we going to videotape your statement, or neither? If it's neither, my friend, a *lot of things* will have to be changed, starting with PlannersBanc.' "

Wes said, "Did you really keep calling him 'my friend'?"

"Well, maybe not quite that often, but that's what I called him."

"Okay," said the Mayor, "go ahead."

"He didn't say anything at first," said Roger, and so I said, 'Do you understand? . . . Do—you—under*stand*?' And finally this little peep comes out of this great big man: 'Yes . . .' That's the way he said it: 'Yes . . .' The great Sixty-Minute Man! Makes you wonder . . . the way some of these so-called powerful business interests turn out to be when you actually confront them. I said to him, 'You've made a commitment to me, and I've been assuring the Mayor you'll be there. This press conference is going to be a crucial moment for the city.' I said, 'You double-cross me—and the Mayor—it won't be pleasant. You know that, don't you?' Meek as a kitten he says, 'I know that . . .' That was the way he was talking! 'I know that.' You had to be there, Wes!"

Even as he spoke, it occurred to Roger that he was embroidering the scene more than a tiny bit. But he decided that a little . . . enhancing . . . of the truth was justified in this instance, since it helped make up for the missing emotion, tension, and drama of the scene as it had actually occurred.

"Christ," said Wes, "I hope the sonofabitch isn't in such bad shape he's a basket case at the press conference."

Uh-oh, he'd gone too far. He hastened to reassure the Mayor: "Not at all, Wes, not at all. It's just that Croker, if you ask me, is your typical bully. When his bluff is called, he folds."

"So you feel sure he'll turn up for the press conference," said the Mayor.

"Oh, absolutely," said Roger. "He knows that if he doesn't, it all goes"—he snapped his fingers—"like *that*, the plantation, the big house in Buckhead—incidentally, I wish you could set foot inside Croker's place. There's this entry . . . hall . . . or lobby . . . or whatever you call it, that's bigger in square feet than most people's entire houses. I really wish you could see it. The house is worth probably three or four million in the current market. He'll sing any song you want before he'll give up the kind of life he's living now. Croker Concourse, the buildings in Midtown, this wholesale food operation he has—it's all going to go if he doesn't come to that press conference."

"All right," said Wes, "but just for good measure keep prodding him and reminding him, because I really do need the sonofabitch."

"Oh, don't worry about that, Wes," said Roger. "He's going to get daily reminders, and if I have to, I'll march right back into his house."

The Mayor looked up at Roger, who was still pacing, and smiled broadly without saying a thing.

Roger stopped and looked down at the Mayor and asked, "What's funny?"

"You're really enjoying politics, aren't you," said the Mayor.

"Politics?"

"That's what all this is, Roger, everything you've been doing—it's politics as it's actually conducted. Please don't get me wrong. I'm immensely grateful for what you've already done. I mean that. All I'm saying is that it gives me pleasure to see you enjoying politics as much as I do. There's nothing else in this world like it."

Roger was busy mining Wes's remarks for irony, but all he said was "I still don't know what you're talking about."

Wes said, "Do you know what politicians really love about politics—what makes politics so hard to give up once you've had a taste of it?"

"Oh, I don't know . . . Power? Fame? Money?"

Wes laughed. "It's certainly not money. Anybody who goes into politics to make money has to be an idiot. I know some idiots have done precisely that, but it's a stupid thing to try. Me, I actually lose money every year, because on my salary I can't do all the things I'm expected to do. And it's not power, if by power you mean the power to get things done, change the life of the city, reduce crime, rehabilitate the South side, all those things. And it's not fame. You quickly get used to publicity. You get used to seeing yourself on television, seeing your picture in the newspaper, even to having a special 'In Depth' segment done about you on the NBC nightly news or articles written about you in national magazines or *The New York Times*. You start to take all that as nothing more than a natural part of your life, your role. You start looking at it as something that's just . . . *there* . . . like the sky, the sun, the clouds, the night, the moon, the stars, the traffic on Georgia 400. No, what really gets you, what really grabs you, what really turns you into a political junkie is . . . seein'em jump."

"Seeing them jump?"

"Exactly. Seein'em jump. Sometimes they're literally jumping up. Anytime I walk into a room, at least in Atlanta, everybody who's sitting down is going to jump up, even if it's the so-called business interests, which is our current euphemism for prominent white people. When it's time for me to sit down, somebody is going to jump to get me a chair. People in stores—not that I go shopping very often—they drop whatever else they're doing and jump to see to it I have whatever I want. On that score, white people are no different from African Americans."

"You've started saying 'African American'?" asked Roger.

"*Oh* yes," said the Mayor. "Anyway," he continued, "if I'm going out to the airport to catch a flight, and I'm running late, they'll stop the whole damned airport to make sure I catch my flight, if that's what it takes, and if I'm walking through a public space, whether it's here near City Hall or out at the airport or wherever, people—*white* people—will jump to get near me and coo the sweet nothings of fandom and ask for my autograph. Roger, that's what's addictive about politics: seein'em jump. And that's what you've had a little taste of. Or a *big* taste. Charlie Croker has always been a big player in Atlanta, and you've had him jumping ever since you first went to see him in his office at Croker Concourse. So far you've been a great politician, and you've done something very valuable for me and for your client. That having been said—it's *fun*, isn't it, it's *fun*!"

Roger frowned. That was a skill Wes had, striking close to the bone before you even knew he was about to thrust. And as usual, Roger resented him even more for being right. Wes was always two steps ahead of him when it came to things like understanding human motivation, and Roger was in no mood to forgive him for it.

"I don't know that I'd call it *fun*," he said, more crossly than he meant to.

"Well, anyway, you've done great work, Counselor. Having Croker at that press conference is going to mean more to your client and to this city than you can possibly imagine. I didn't tell you, but we had a riot on our hands last night."

"A *riot*?"

"Exactly. A bunch of the usual homeys are out on the street on English Avenue, and they're talking shit about how their hero, Fareek 'the Cannon' Fanon, has been framed by this wealthy white girl, and their emotions rise, and they start heading over toward the World Congress Center, yelling and breaking windows, and then they made their mistake. They saw a bunch of white men working late on that new construction over there, and so they decided on a little brawling and pillaging. Their mistake was, they went after the wrong white workingmen. These white guys were the wire lathers. They're the white guys you see at these building sites with hard hats, five-day growths of beard, paunches, and sleeveless T-shirts out of which protrude their eighteen-

and twenty-inch biceps. They'd just as soon brawl as drink beer. Either one's okay with them. Five minutes later there was no more riot. The riot had been out-rioted, thank God. I called Elihu Yale"—the police chief—"and told him to put an absolute lid on the whole thing, and nobody in the press ever got wind of it. But that shows you where we are right now. We're nearing the boiling point. Students have been making speeches at Morehouse—and Spelman, for that matter. The so-called Morehouse elite is all for solidarity on an issue like this—if there's ever *been* an issue like this. They're all convinced that Fanon was set up and framed."

"Is that what you believe?"

"Not if you use 'framed' to mean a plot that's hatched ahead of time. If you mean framed in the sense of did she use the R-word as an on-the-spot excuse when her girlfriends find her balling a 225-pound African American, that I find believable. That's Fareek the Cannon's story, and it's believable."

"I'm sorry," said Roger, "but it strikes me as funny, hearing you use the term *African American* after all the things you said about Jesse Jackson."

The Mayor put on his ironic smile. "As I told you, times change and things change. When Jesse hits a home run, there's no use grousing about it. There's nothing to do but record the score. Come on, sit down. You're making me nervous." The Mayor gestured toward the couch.

Roger Not a Bit Too White sat down, but before he knew it, he was on his feet again, pacing the phoenix rug, looking at the patterns that the ivory Yoruban ceremonial swords made against the ebony paneling, and musing to Wes about Charlie Croker and how he wouldn't be happy until he saw him jump straight through the hoop.

CHARLIE HAD ALWAYS used the term *below the gnat line* as a piece of Down Home humor. But this time it didn't strike him as funny. As he hobbled on his aluminum crutches from the Cadillac toward the Big House, black gnats were dive-bombing his eyes in waves, without any letup. Why the eyes? Probably the water. They wanted to drink the water out of his eyes. Because of the crutches he couldn't lift his hands high enough to shoo them away. Now he could hear them singing in his ears. Turpmtine was not the place to be in the summertime. In the summertime South Georgia bowed down, helplessly, abjectly, to her rulers, the insects.

"Owooooh!" That was Serena, who was just behind him. "Charlie! A bee stung me!"

"Wasn't a bee," said Charlie, without looking around. " 'Sa fly."

Probably a black fly, thought Charlie. Mean little bastards. They were mottled, mostly black, in an unhealthy-looking way, and their wings were swept back like a jet fighter's or a Stealth bomber's. They never missed. But it could have been a yellow fly or a horsefly. All three of them stung, but there was no need to go into all that with Serena. He turned his head about and said:

"Heidi! Cover up the baby's face with something." He almost never referred to her as Kingsley.

"You don't worry, Mr. Croker," said Heidi. "I hold her—*whuhhhhh whuhhhhh whuhhhhh whuhhhhh*—close to me—*whuhhhhh whuhhhhh whuhhhhh whuhhhhh*—and I have chiffon."

Serena again: "Charlie! Damn it! Another one! How can a fly—*whuhhhhh whuhhhhh whuhhhhh whuhhhhh*—how can a—damn it, Charlie, *another* one!"

Charlie knew that *whuhhhhhh whuhhhhh* sound from way back before the first word he ever knew. It was the sound of a human being, a hopelessly slow species, trying to blow the gnat swarms away from her eyes in Baker County in the summertime.

"Ughhhh!" That was Connie, carrying the bags and bringing up the rear, muttering to himself. No doubt the flies attacked him, too, but he was the Stoic.

Shit! One of them got Charlie in the back of the neck, and they still had another thirty feet to go before they reached the front door.

"Charlie!" said Serena. "What are these little—*whuhhhhh whuhhhhh whuhhhhh whuhhhhh*—white things? They're disgusting!"

Charlie saw them, too: another mottled fly, but mottled white instead of black. "They're privy flies," he said. "They won't hurt you."

"What are privy flies?"

"They swarm around—*whuhhhhh whuhhhhh whuhhhhh whuhhhhh*—privies."

"What's a privy?"

"An outhouse."

"That's—*whuhhhhh whuhhhhh whuhhhhh whuhhhhh*—disgusting! *Uckkkkkkkkkkk*—I just *stepped* on something disgusting, too!"

A foul odor rose from the path as these wayfarers struggled through the badlands in the kingdom of the insects.

"There's millipedes on the walkway. That's what you smell there. Try not to step on 'em."

"Mr. Croker!" said Heidi. "What happen to tree?"

Charlie craned his head about and saw her holding the baby with one arm and pointing with the other toward a maple tree. The branches appeared to be festering with some dreadful disease.

"Tent caterpillars," said Charlie.

They had infested the entire tree. They would strip it bare of leaves before they were through.

"That sound," said Serena, "is that the—*whuhhhhh whuhhhhh whuhhhhh whuhhhhh*—sound of them eating?"

"Yep," said Charlie. They did make a sort of *crunch crunch* sound. In fact, it was the sound of them defecating, the sound of the droppings of tens of thousands of tent caterpillars hitting the ground. But no use introducing that piece of information when there's still fifteen feet to go before reaching the front door. And no use mentioning that now, in June, in Baker County, right over there, in the shade beneath the live oaks and the magnolias, there'll be mosquitoes, jumbo mosquitoes, thoroughbreds of the family Culicidae, right in the middle of the day. It wasn't far from here to Jookers Swamp, where the mosquitoes multiplied by the billions in June and grew up looking for blood to suck. And no use calling attention to that old live-oak stump over there in the shade. Try sitting on that for a moment to rest your weary bones and get a little respite from the sun, or try lying down on this nice soft bed of pine tags over here. The mosquitoes, yellow flies, horseflies, black flies, and gnats will attack from above—and the chiggers will be after your ankles, your thighs, your neck, and your big unsuspecting bottom faster than you can pronounce the word. June was the chiggers' month. For the chiggers, June was Thanksgiving, Christmas, and the Fourth of July all rolled into one. Nothing those vicious, fiery red mites liked better than a human bottom sitting on a tree stump in June. A single chigger bite would give you a red welt that would burn and itch for a week.

Godalmighty it was hot. The cicadas were up in the trees rattling away. They were big, as bugs went, the cicadas were; an inch and a half long, some of them; and ugly, too; and noisy. In Baker County, when the sun reaches its zenith in June, and the cicadas descend on the trees and start that damned rattle of theirs, and you can't get the vibrations out of your eardrums, that's when you start "seeing the monkey," as the field hands used to say. That was Charlie right now. The black gnats and three kinds of sweptwing flies were after him, and it was hot as hell, and he was seeing the monkey.

He glanced over his shoulder, and Connie was right behind him, carrying in the bags. Connie had done the driving, and he, Charlie, had sat in the back seat with Serena. Frankly, Connie had made him half-crazy, because he wouldn't go more than five miles an hour over the speed limit, or maybe ten. Christ, it was bad enough to have to drive all the way from Atlanta. Durwood and the boys would start buzzing about that, all right. Cap'm Charlie *always* came to Turpmtine by airplane; not always the G-5, sometimes the Beechjet, but always by airplane. What could he say? The bad leg made it too hard to go up and down the Beechjet's stairs? Aw, the hell with it. He wasn't obliged to explain anything to anybody . . . although he felt a tremendous need to.

The Big House was set in a grove of live oaks, magnolias, and dogwoods. The white blossoms of the magnolias had never been more profuse or more lush. But with the magnolias, it wasn't just the blossoms that got you. There were also the leaves, long, thick, deep green leaves, each one of which shone as if it had been waxed and polished by hand. The branches came all the way down to the ground, and the tops rose to a point, like a Christmas tree, and when you saw a dozen of them, arranged on either side of the Big House like this, it made you catch your breath, no matter how many times you had seen them before. The porch, which went almost all the way around the house, was about four feet above the ground, and the Confederate roses had grown on the trellises below the porch in such masses of blossoms, it seemed as if the house had been built atop a vast mound of flowers. Inside the house it was liable to be musty, since he hadn't used it for several weeks, and no place on earth was hotter and more humid than Baker County, Georgia, in the summertime. Thank God he had put in central air conditioning ten—or was it eleven?—years ago, back when a $110,000 HVAC system seemed like nothing, a mere routine expense. Now he couldn't put together $110,000 to buy anything. God . . . if only he didn't feel so tired. He never slept anymore. He was dead tired from the moment he got up in the morning. He didn't want to get up. Not for a minute. He only got up because he knew Serena would break his balls if he didn't—that and the fact that he would look bad in Connie's eyes. So . . . *clackclack* . . . *clackclack* . . . *clackclack* . . . *clackclack* . . . he made his way to the front stairs that led up to the porch. He looked at the stairs and delivered himself of a great sigh.

"Want me to give you a hand, Mr. Croker?" asked Connie.

"Nawwww," said Charlie, "I was jes . . . jes . . ." Great weariness. "I was jes . . . I don't know what I was jes doin'," said Charlie.

"You were *jes* feeling sorry for yourself, Charlie," said Serena. "That's what you were *jes* doing. If you'd put that much energy into doing your therapy, you could be over all this."

By now she was right beside him. She wore a pair of white linen slacks that tapered down to a narrow cuff over the ankle and a white silk blouse with yellow candy stripes. She was trying to chase the gnats away from her big blue eyes. She didn't have to say another word. It was plain that she resented this escape to Turpmtine. This was the last place in the world she would choose to be in the summer.

Charlie started up the stairs, unaided. *Clackclack* . . . *clackclack* . . .

"Why do they make that noise, Charlie?" she said with exasperation, brushing her hand in front of her eyes about ninety times a minute.

"Why does who make which noise?" asked Charlie.

Obviously peeved: "That *clackclack* . . . *clackclack*."

"Well, that's jes the—"

"It's not *jes* anything, Charlie. It's those crutches."

"There's nothing—"

"Are they loose? Were they clattering that way when you got them?"

"I don't know, I s'pose—"

"Well, let's just get inside before we all get bitten to death." By now Serena was flailing her hand before her eyes and screwing her face up into a Serena epitome of frustrated anger.

So Charlie headed up the stairs. *Clackclack* . . . *clackclack* . . . *clackclack* . . . Every *clackclack* now sounded to Charlie like a pair of rifle shots. He was dead tired, his knee hurt like hell, his brain felt as if it were the black part of a tornado, he was seeing the monkey, and his wife didn't like the way his crutches sounded. His *crutches*! If he had had the energy and the confidence he used to have, he would have cut off that line of remarks in an instant. As it was, her observations about aluminum crutches became yet more trash sucked up by the tornado in his skull.

THE BIG HOUSE had always had a decor that was more feminine than not. There were a lot of Chinese-yellow walls with delicate, spidery white plaster moldings, in the "Adam mode," as Ronald Vine had called it, whatever that actually meant. These were apparently the original decorations of the house, so much a part of a bygone era that no one, not even Ronald, had ever dared alter them. After all, Bygone Era was very much on the mind of anyone who bought a South Georgia quail plantation. As a result the house also still had things such as sliding pocket doors with elaborately etched glass windows, with which you could close off the dining room from the back parlor, and bays in the front and back parlors with four windows each, two of which had curved frames with curved glass to match. The interior of the Big House was where the woman, presumably the wife, could express her taste and refinement. The rest of the place was given over to Man the Hunter.

Even though it was on no more than four hours' notice, Durwood had managed to soldier up a house staff for Cap'm Charlie. Auntie Bella would be there, along with two assistant cooks, and Mason would be there with a couple of the boys to help out with errands, lifting, and suchlike, and of course Durwood himself would be around, and Connie would be there. So it wasn't exactly that Cap'm Charlie had been left to his own devices.

With Connie's help, he had had himself ensconced in an easy chair in the Big House's "den," as it was called, the room that had been the Big House's male redoubt before Charlie had built the Gun House. Compared to the big room of the Gun House, the den looked positively effete. No boars' heads, no stuffed snakes, no battalions of upright guns; instead, a rather subtle form of paneling: heart of virgin pine with some School of Audubon paintings of quail adorning it. Charlie found the den peaceful. The roof of the porch outside shielded you from the sun. It was soothing. Heart of virgin pine and quail paintings were fine. He didn't particularly want to be reminded of tusks and fangs right now. He picked up the Book. Connie was off with Durwood, with Charlie's blessing, taking a look at the plantation, or at least the outbuildings and the kennels and the horses.

He opened the Book at random to a passage that said: "Just as every skill is strengthened by practice, so is every bad habit made worse by repetition. If you lie in bed for ten days, and then get up and try to take a walk, you will see how quickly your legs have lost their strength." Christalmighty, Epictetus had been reading his mail! He had come as close to lying in bed for ten days as they'd let him, and it was true: his legs had no strength left!

His eyes came to rest on a painting of a covey of quail hiding in a huddle in tall grass. The artist had managed to make it look as if the birds were all crouching, frightened, ready to explode upward at the first sign of danger. That was what he, Charlie, was like now, hiding, crouched, in the tall grass, panicked to the point of taking off in any direction.

All right, suppose he went to the press conference and told the truth about Fareek Fanon? Suppose he said that Fanon is the epitome of the arrogant, obnoxious, swaggering athlete who thinks he is elevated above ordinary standards of right and wrong? As soon as the words passed his lips his worldly possessions would be gone—*and* he'd be branded as a racist bigot.

He was still staring at the covey of quail when Serena materialized in the doorway. She came toward Charlie with a smile he couldn't decipher. Pleasure? Sarcasm? He couldn't tell.

She sat down in an easy chair near his and said, "So—how does it feel to be back at Turpmtine?"

Charlie couldn't read her expression or weigh her words at all. "It's relaxing," he said finally.

"Relaxing from what?" said Serena. When he made no response, she said, "Do you mind if I ask you something?"

"Go ahead."

"What is going on, this whole business with Mr. Roger White?"

"Well—"

"And don't just tell me that he's trying to get you involved in some case of his. That doesn't make sense, because here is this . . . this *man* who dares—dares!—to come marching into our house uninvited and insisting you give him an answer about something or other. The Charlie Croker I married would have picked him up bodily and thrown him out. I couldn't stand to see you . . . *cringing* like that!"

Charlie stared at her for a moment. "Well, you're right, this is a lot more than . . . than . . . I've made it out to be. In fact, it's a mess."

He didn't trust Serena, didn't trust his own wife, who had married him for better, not for better or for worse, with the information he was about to impart to her. He sighed and then resolved to tell her anyway. After all, she *was* his wife and had a right to know.

He told her step by step. Lawyer Roger White's initial offer to trade him freedom from PlannersBanc's bankruptcy machinery in exchange for a flattering public statement about Fareek Fanon, Georgia Tech's Charlie Croker of today . . . How White had demonstrated his side's power to keep PlannersBanc on a leash . . . His appalling meeting with Fareek Fanon, who got in as many insults and contemptuous snorts as possible . . . How he wrestled with the angels over the whole dilemma . . . How could he betray Inman, especially after volunteering to help in any way he could in having Fanon punished for what he had done? . . . But how could he turn down such a fairly innocuous way of saving his entire empire from certain ruin? Besides, he would be doing something for the entire city by calming troubled waters. The *Journal-Constitution* would no doubt give him a pat on the back for that . . . But *Inman* would be furious, and everybody who knew and *liked* Inman, which was a lot of people, would smell something fishy . . . And did he, Charlie, think Fanon was capable of raping Elizabeth Armholster? He wouldn't put it past him for a minute . . . He told her how he swayed this way and that, wrestled with the angels, and finally called Lawyer White, who had turned out to be pretty obnoxious himself, and said yes, he agreed to the bargain . . . and how ever since then Lawyer White had treated him in the most condescending manner you could imagine . . . how he, Charlie, who used to pride himself on making decisions and then putting the dilemmas behind him, was getting nowhere with this one. On the one hand, if he came out in favor of Fanon, he would save all his possessions and be safe from the bank but lose all his friends, the Piedmont Driving Club set and every other set. But if he refused, he would lose all his possessions, right down to the house they lived in and the cars they drove—and they would still lose all their friends, because the sort of friends they had made were the sort who couldn't stand people who couldn't afford to go out and blow $300 on dinner for four at Mordecai's. His dilemma was just as hopeless as it had ever been.

All the while, as he told the story, Serena stared at him, with her left elbow resting on an arm of the chair and one side of her face resting on the heel of her hand. She scarcely even blinked. But toward the end she began to smile ever so slightly. It was a benign smile, however.

When at last he finished, Serena surprised him. Instead of acting angry, sarcastic, or put out, she took the heel of her hand away from her face and rested her weight on her forearm and smiled—sweetly—and said in a sweet, low voice:

"Charlie, I only wish you'd told me all this before. This is a terrible thing to have bottled up inside yourself."

"Well—"

"Really it is. And you probably thought there was no one who could possibly help you and therefore you didn't want anyone to know."

"That's true," said Charlie. "When I think how I told Inman I'd do anything I could to help him—shook his hand—practically swore a blood oath—on the other hand, I'm sixty years old and I'm about to be wiped out."

"Charlie—"

"—they've already taken the airplanes, three of the cars, and you know what would—"

"Charlie—"

"—would be next—"

"*Charlie!*"

"What?"

Once she had his attention, she returned to the small, soft, intimate voice. "I have something to tell you that may make it easier for you."

Charlie looked at her, seriously doubting that what she said was true, but all he said was: "What is it?"

"Elizabeth made me swear I wouldn't tell anyone, not even you."

"Elizabeth?"

"Elizabeth Armholster. I told her—but I don't care, Charlie, this is something you have to know."

He just stared at her.

"You remember that night at the Driving Club, the night you and Inman went off into the ballroom and had a talk?"

"Yeah," said Charlie with a resigned twist to his lips, "I remember. That was the night I swore to Inman I'd back him up in this thing." He shook his head.

"Well, before you start thinking you're bound by some sacred oath—did you know I had a talk with Elizabeth that same night, at the Driving Club?"

"I remember you going off into the Bamboo Room with her."

"Exactly. And you want to know what she told me?"

"What?"

"About that night? That Friday night of Freaknik? She *hooked up* with Fanon."

"She what?"

"*Hooked up* with him." She gave Charlie the sort of stare, accompanied by a slight parting of the lips, that you give people when you're unveiling a major revelation.

"What's *hooked up*?"

"You don't know *hooked up*? That's something boys and girls do now. You really never heard of it?"

"No."

"Well, today they don't talk about 'dates' anymore. They go out in groups, a group of girls over here and a group of boys over there, all looking for a party. To find a party you go to places where boys and girls hang out, such as the Wreck Room."

"What's that?"

"It's a restaurant near the Tech campus. The Wreck Room, as in 'the Ramblin' Wreck.' So here are five girls, including Elizabeth, squeezed into a booth, and it's after eleven and they're still looking for a party. The next thing they know, four black students slide into the booth opposite them, and everybody in the restaurant knows who one of them is: Fareek Fanon. Pretty soon Fanon and his friends are hitting on the white girls, but it's all very playful, not crude or suggestive."

"Hitting on?"

"Flirting with, coming on to. That's what they say now, 'hitting on.' Elizabeth said they—she and her friends—didn't want to appear standoffish, since everybody in the restaurant is looking at them and Fanon is Tech's poster boy, and so forth and so on. Anyway, Fanon says there's a party going on at his apartment, which isn't all that far away. Naturally, you can say in hindsight, that should have started the girls thinking. If there's a party going on at his apartment, what's he doing here? But the fact is, Elizabeth and two of the girls decided to go to the party."

"What about the other two?" said Charlie.

"They said, 'Unh-unh, not me,' and went home. One thing you ought to realize, Charlie. Elizabeth's not a bashful girl. She'll take you up on a dare. In certain ways she's like Inman or, for that matter, Ellen, who I think is a holy terror. So the three girls arrive at Fanon's apartment, and of course there's nobody there. Elizabeth says, 'I thought you said there's a party.' To which Fanon says, 'Well, *now* there *is*!' So now the boys and the girls have found a party, and that's when the hooking up can begin."

"But what the hell does it *mean*?" said Charlie.

"That's what I'm getting to. The party's in progress, people are drinking, and a boy is attracted to a particular girl—or a girl is attracted to a particular boy—remember one thing, Charlie, it can happen that way, too—the girl can start it—and one of them nods toward the back or wherever there's an empty room, and right there, on the spur of the moment, the two of them go to that room and hook up."

"But what—"

"I'm *telling* you," said Serena in the same soft, confidential voice. "It always refers to sex, but it can be anything from kissing, along with, you know, some 'feeling up,' to going all the way, in which case it's called 'majorly hooking up.' Now, I'd heard of all that, but Elizabeth introduced me to a term I'd never heard of. She's ten years younger than I am—so I'd never heard of it. And that's *score*."

"*Score?*"

"Not *scored with* but just *score*. It used to be that boys would brag about 'scoring with' some girl, meaning getting her to go all the way. But *score* is a word girls use. A girl will say, 'I scored Jack last night, as if she's 'gotten' the guy to go all the way and it's a terrific accomplishment. So anyway, Elizabeth *hooked up* with Fanon. They went into his bedroom."

"Jesus Christ!" said Charlie. "He asked her or she asked him?"

"She says he asked her, but, Charlie, I'm not so sure."

"Godalmighty. What did she say went on?"

"She *says* she didn't have anything but a little mild hooking up on her mind. But she'd been drinking, and things progressed a lot more majorly than she'd intended. Meanwhile, the other two girls, her friends, they're not having a very terrific time. They want to go home, but they don't want to leave Elizabeth behind. By now, according to Elizabeth, her underpants are off and Fanon is trying to get on top of her and she's protesting, she's saying no, she doesn't want to go all the way. But Fanon—this is Elizabeth talking—Fanon used his superior strength and shoved her back flat on the bed and had his way with her. Just about that time the door opens, and it's the other two girls looking for her, and she starts saying, 'Make him stop! Get him off me!' "

"Jesus God," said Charlie, "had the guy actually . . . penetrated?"

"I don't know," said Serena. "I couldn't bring myself to ask her that. But I don't believe her version of how it happened in the first place. I think she was just drunk enough to decide she wanted to *score* Fareek Fanon. I can't think of any other reason why a girl would let a man remove her underpants."

"You mean—"

"If you want to know what I think, I think *she* was the one who gave *him* the eye to hook up, and she ended up doing exactly what she had in mind."

"Are you saying—"

"Exactly," said Serena. "I think the only reason this whole 'rape' business got started was she was surprised by those two girls and had to come up with a quick explanation, and so she said, 'Make him stop!' and 'Get him off me!' or whatever it was she said. You'll notice she didn't say anything to Inman and Ellen, not at first she didn't."

"She didn't?"

"Not at first. It was one of the girls' mothers, Tanya Baehr's mother, who called Ellen and Inman and got them so crazed. Tanya Baehr had told her mother about it. So now Elizabeth was stuck with her story—but she didn't want her parents to tell anybody, not the police, not the university, not anybody. And why? She said she was too traumatized to talk to anybody about it. If you want my opinion, she knew that she had concocted on the spur of the moment something that was turning into a gigantic lie. She was afraid to even try filling in the details for a rape charge and actually bring it before the police or a court or somebody. What she was really telling her parents and everybody else was 'Let's forget about it. *Please* let's forget about it.' But she has the wrong father, if that's what she thought was going to happen. So Inman's going around furiously trying to pull his troops together—but he can't bring any charges because his daughter's so 'traumatized.' Some 'traumatized.' She wasn't acting traumatized that night at the Driving Club."

"I thought you said you liked Elizabeth."

"I do," said Serena. "She's fun. We get along well. She confides in me. But do I think she's an angel? No, I don't. You don't understand women, Charlie, you really don't. Man at his most conniving is no match for Woman at hers. From the very beginning Elizabeth has tried to put a lid on this whole affair without ever admitting to Inman and Ellen that she was anything other than Little Miss Innocent. And now it's gotten totally out of hand. Fanon's name is all over television and the newspapers. You don't see Elizabeth's name, you just see 'daughter of one of Atlanta's most powerful businessmen,' but her name's all over the Internet, thanks to this Web site, 'Chasing the Dragon,' and I don't know anybody who can't tell you right off the bat that it's Elizabeth Armholster."

Serena's eyes were boring into Charlie's.

"All right," he said, "let's assume all this is true. Where does it leave me?"

"It's more 'where does it leave Fanon,' " said Serena. "He's the one who stands to lose everything over some trumped-up accusations."

"So I should—"

"You should give him a break, Charlie! You don't have to attack Elizabeth. You don't even have to mention her, not even as the daughter of a prominent whatever. You just tell everybody to give Fanon the benefit of the doubt, because you know the hazards of sports celebrity, which you do."

Charlie turned his head and stared up at the old pine paneling of the den and sighed.

"Charlie!" said Serena in order to get him looking at her once more. "It's not a question of making Fanon and his side happy. It's a question of coming down on the side of the truth! I'm telling you, I know Elizabeth, and she's perfectly capable of hooking up with any boy as famous as Fareek Fanon, black or not, and *scoring* him. You can't *say* that, of course, you just give Fanon a little bit of a shield. It would be true, and it would be the right thing to do."

Charlie leaned back in the chair and put his head down and began breathing audibly through his mouth. The dilemma now roared in his head more furiously than ever. He wanted to *believe* what Serena had just told him. He wanted to be on the side of righteousness as well as the side of Charlie Croker's bankrupt empire. He wanted to believe that Serena was devoted to truth and fair play and only incidentally to the preservation of Mr. and Mrs. Charles Croker's assets.

As if sensing she almost had him, Serena leaned toward him and said, "Right now this is a hot piece of gossip. But six months, a year from now, who's going to remember the details? Who's going to remember that Charlie Croker made a generic statement about athletes and the pressure put upon them? Nobody."

Charlie could think of somebody. He could see that swarthy fat face and that black hair combed straight back from low on his forehead and plastered down like a swath of asphalt. He could hear that low, angry, Camels-cured voice. He could see those small, unforgiving eyes.

"I know they've got their own agenda," said Serena, "but this Roger White is absolutely right when he says you will be doing something for the city of Atlanta—doing a *lot* for it—if you stand up and say, 'Let's hold on a second. Let's take a breath. Let's not have a rush to judgment.'

That's all you'll really be saying: 'Let's not have a rush to judgment.' And given what I know about Elizabeth—and what a lot of other people know about her—Elizabeth's not exactly tight-lipped—somebody needs to say that, somebody like you. The Mayor can't do it all by himself. But the two of you together, you'd be making an appeal across racial lines. In the long run, people will praise you. Most people, no matter what they knew about Elizabeth, would take the easy way out and say nothing. It takes courage to do what you're going to do. You won't be taking sides, you'll just be leveling out the playing field a little bit."

Yes, thought Charlie, black people will praise me, the Herb Richmans of Atlanta will praise me. At the Piedmont Driving Club—he could see the porte cochere and the front entrance and the doorman, Gates, helping some tall, teetering white man out of his Mercedes 600—maybe Lomprey: just as if he were right in front of him, he could see Arthur Lomprey's great height and bent-over dog's neck—and Lomprey would know that *something* smelled high in this situation, since he had been pressured—by whom?—by someone—into calling the dogs off Charlie and his holdings. But what would Lomprey say? What *could* he say? Just how much did he know?

Suddenly Charlie had an inspiration. He'd *call* Inman or go see him. He'd tell him the dangers presented by this whole business. Elizabeth herself might be at risk. He was going to make an appearance with the Mayor at a press conference to defuse the situation until a real investigation could be made. What he would be doing would be as much for Elizabeth, Ellen, and him, Inman, as anybody else. The high road . . . the Business Interests' way in a town like Atlanta . . . the *Atlanta Way* . . .

The only trouble was—as he made this little speech inside his head, he tried to picture Inman right in front of him . . . He tried to picture Inman judiciously taking this all into account and finally nodding yes . . . The only trouble was, he *couldn't* picture Inman doing *anything* judicious in this situation . . . He might get as far as "defuse the situation"—and then he'd learn something about fuses and explosions, all right.

So the tornado spun and spun and spun inside his skull.

"Charlie," asked Serena in a sweet, reasonable voice, "how bad can it be to tell the truth?"

EVEN WITH DURWOOD as his guide—Durwood was so taciturn, it came across as a bitterness toward life—Conrad immediately sensed the staggering scale upon which life was lived at Turpmtine. The stable, which was grander than any building in the entire city of Pittsburg, California, housed fifty-nine horses. What could anybody do with fifty-nine horses? There was a snake house for snakes and a breeding barn just for mating horses. There were kennels for forty dogs. There were employees all over the place; and if the subject of Charlie Croker came up, they invariably referred to him as "Cap'm Charlie."

Once he returned to the Big House, he helped the old man upstairs to a bedroom, another guest room by the looks of it. The old man was already getting around much better on his aluminum crutches, so much so that Conrad suggested that he try just an aluminum cane, but he wasn't having any of that. He was determined to stick with the crutches . . . *clackclack* . . . *clackclack* . . . *clackclack* . . . *clackclack* . . .

With Conrad's help, Mr. Croker deposited himself in an easy chair near the bed. He was breathing too rapidly, and sweat had broken out on his forehead. He looked up at Conrad the way a disobedient student might look up at a teacher.

"I think I did too much," he said.

"Well, remember what we were talking about, Mr. Croker," said Conrad. "Much as you've been in bed, you're gonna be weak when you try to walk."

"Pour me a glass of water there, if you don't mind," said the old man.

He downed almost half the tumbler at one gulp and went "Whewwwww." Then he looked up at Conrad again. "I'll tell you something I need worse than water." He paused. "I'm talking about the Book."

"All right," said Conrad, "where is it?" He looked about and then spotted it. It was on a bureau. Conrad picked up *The Stoics* and then stood facing Mr. Croker, who had by now sunk so deeply into the easy chair, he was all but supine.

"What would you like to know, Mr. Croker?"

"All right," said Mr. Croker, "suppose you've been asked to say something publicly that isn't literally true but is more nearly true than if you said the opposite." He hesitated and looked at Conrad and said, "Do you follow me so far?"

"Not completely," said Conrad. "But go ahead."

"But if you say this, you're going to lose a lot of friends. Maybe all your friends. But if you don't say it, you're going to lose all your money—and you'll *still* lose your friends, because there's no way you can separate their friendship toward you from the fact that you have a certain place in society, which you wouldn't have in the first place without your money."

"I can tell you what Epictetus says," said Conrad. "He says, 'No one can make progress facing both ways.' "

"Where does he say that?" The old man began to sit up straighter.

"I can't remember exactly, Mr. Croker. I think it's in Book IV. But anyway, he says you can't be both a Stoic and a man who's liked by all his old friends. Half the time they like you because you share their bad habits. Now, if you exercise self-control and self-respect, they'll shake their heads and say, 'He's just not himself anymore.' "

The old man was nodding his head in vigorous assent. "That's exactly it," he said in a low voice, "that's exactly it."

"But, Mr. Croker, do you mind if I ask you something?"

"No, go ahead."

"This is the second time you've mentioned making a public statement about somebody. Could you be a little more specific? I'm sort of confused, Mr. Croker. You were talking about 'something that isn't literally true but is more nearly true than if you said the opposite.' Can you give me an example?"

The old man hung his head forward and then looked up again at Conrad. "All right," he said, "I'm gonna tell you exactly what's going on. You're not gonna believe it, but I swear to God it's true. Incidentally, or not so incidentally, this is just between us. Okay, Connie?"

"Yes, sir. You have my word."

"I don't even know you," said the old man. "All the same, I trust you. Maybe it's because you don't know my friends. Anyway, I trust you. Do you remember the first time we talked about Epictetus and the Stoics and I said something to you about dilemmas?"

Conrad nodded yes.

"And you told me a story about Agrippinus and what was his name, the historian?"

"Florus," said Conrad.

"Florus. Well, now I'm gonna tell you about a *dilemma*. My own. You're gonna be surprised. I'm gonna tell you everything."

The boy cocked his head and looked at Charlie in such a curious way, for so long, Charlie snapped his fingers in front of his face, as if to say "Snap out of it."

"Well—Mr. Croker," said the boy, "in that case I'm gonna tell *you* everything, and you're gonna be even *more* surprised. I don't know any more about you than you know about me, but I trust you, too. If I can't, I'm in a lot of trouble."

They started talking, both of them, and they held nothing back, nothing at all. It turned dark outside, and still they talked. Twice Mason came up and knocked on the door and told them dinner was ready, and then Serena came up to tell them, but they kept on talking.

It was about quarter of ten when Charlie said, "Connie—by the way, I'm gonna have to keep on calling you Connie. 'Conrad' just don't fit. I couldna had nobody named Conrad working in one of those damn freezer units. I'm sorry. Anyway, I've made a decision. I'm going to the press conference. That's my test."

"I'm glad," said Conrad. "Remember Agrippinus, the Stoic who refused to act in Nero's play?"

"Yeah."

"I don't think I ever mentioned what happened to him. Several friends came by his house and they told him, 'Your trial's going on right now in the Senate.' Agrippinus says, 'Oh? That's their business. It's time for me to take my exercise.' Then he singles out one of his friends and says, 'Come on, let's go exercise and then take a cold bath.' So that's what he does. When he gets back to the house, more people are there, and they're saying, 'They've reached a verdict!' And Agrippinus says, 'Which is?' 'Guilty.' Agrippinus says, 'What's the sentence, death or exile?' They answer, 'Exile.' Agrippinus says, 'My property—confiscated or not?' They answer, 'Confiscated.' 'Thank you,' says Agrippinus. Then he turns to his friend. 'It's time for dinner. Let's go dine at Acicia.' Which they did.

"Charlie—*there* was a man."

Chapter XXII

The Manager

THE CAMERA PULLED WAY, WAY, WAY BACK—HOW DO THEY DO these things? Peepgass wondered—until on the television screen in Martha's library appeared a long shot of the City Hall rotunda from above . . . all the gray-and-white marble . . . the marble walls . . . the marble balcony with its gleaming brass railing . . . the lower part of the rotunda's great Pantheon-like marble dome . . . the marble floor . . . in the middle of the floor, a marble fountain . . . off to the left, the window where you could pay your utility bills, if you had to . . . and Peepgass had had to do exactly that more than once, scramble to that damned window with cash, at the eleventh hour, to avoid having his electricity cut off . . . Beyond the fountain was an enormous crescent, almost a semicircle, of television cameras, looked like two or three dozen of them . . . and beyond the cameras, a mass of chairs filled with journalists . . . and beyond the journalists, a short flight of stairs leading up to a marble landing from whence the rotunda's two grand marble staircases led up to the second level . . . More masses of humanity were sitting on the stairs, as if they were tiers at a stadium . . . The landing itself was like a stage or a dais . . . On it were a modernistic blond wood podium . . . looked like maple or ash . . . and behind the podium, one on each side, a pair of stout banker's chairs, apparently made of the same wood

. . . The podium was no doubt where the Mayor would be holding forth.

Peepgass looked at his watch. "It's already 11:05," he said to Martha. And then to Wallace: "Have you seen one of these before, one of these press conferences?"

"No, I haven't," Wallace said dully.

When he moved in here, Peepgass had never considered the fact that now that it was June, the boy, Wallace, would be home from school. It was damned awkward. Peepgass never knew what to say to the boy, and the boy never seemed to want to say anything to him. For a flickering instant he thought of his own two boys, whom he hardly ever saw anymore. But quickly enough he returned to Martha, young Wallace, and Valley Road, in the real Buckhead. Only Martha seemed comfortable about it all.

Without taking her eyes off the screen, she said, "Oh, these things never start on time," but she was thinking of something else. To watch television Ray always gravitated to the same easy chair that had been Charlie's favorite. That was the only way she could think of in which the two men were alike.

Now no more rotunda on the TV screen; instead, a man and a woman seated side by side behind some sort of futuristic TV news desk. An inch or so of coiled translucent wire was unfortunately visible behind the left ear of the man, whose name was Roland Barris. He also had a hair problem. His hair had receded badly on either side, leaving a forelock at the front of his pate separated like an island from the mainland. The forelock had been artfully teased and brushed back and then sprayed so that it reconnected with the mainland, if only for the duration of a broadcast.

You poor bastard, thought Peepgass with a satisfying *Schadenfreude*, you'll never make it to the network nightly news anchor desk, not with that scarce-haired skull of yours. He decided not to mention it to Martha, however, for fear of underscoring the fact that his own career in banking had nowhere to go, either.

The poor man, thought Martha, studying Roland Barris, he's had a complete dye job, every hair on his head. That always looks awful on a man, because it's so obvious. She decided not to mention it to Ray, however, since it was not in her interest, as an eternal blonde, to bring up the matter of who did or didn't have a complete dye job.

The woman on the screen, the anchorette or whatever, Lynn Hinkle, was a good fifteen years younger than Roland Barris. Her main journalistic assets, thought Martha, were her pretty face and her head of straight blond hair, naturally blond no doubt—and how fast it goes, my dear, you just wait.

". . . waiting for Mayor Jordan," Roland Barris was saying, "who has never held a press conference that has aroused more intense speculation. But then this is an unusual situation all the way round, wouldn't you say so, Lynn?"

"I certainly would," said Blondie, smiling instinctively and utterly inappropriately. "No one we've talked to at City Hall can remember a mayor of Atlanta ever holding a press conference to address an alleged sexual assault, particularly in a case where no charges have been filed, Roland."

"That's a good point, Lynn," said Roland, without so much as a glance toward Lynn, as if his eyes had been magnetized by the camera. "Sources close to the Mayor have told us that what the Mayor has been concerned about has been a mini-riot that erupted in Fareek Fanon's old neighborhood, English Avenue, last week. Over on English Avenue and much of South Atlanta many people look upon Fareek Fanon as one of their own who has risen to national prominence as an all-American running back, and now they feel he's been set up and framed, or that's what many people believe, Lynn."

"That's about the size of it, Roland," said Lynn, without looking at Roland. "And of course the entire case has taken on racial overtones, and that's what must be paramount—" She broke off the sentence and cocked her head slightly, and for a moment appeared to be gazing toward someplace far, far away. "I think the Mayor has appeared, and so we now rejoin Joe Mundy at City Hall."

For just an instant there was Joe Mundy talking into a microphone up on the balcony of the rotunda. "That's right, Lynn, Mayor Jordan—"

Joe Mundy was younger than Roland Barris, but he had an unfortunate pair of ears that stuck way out on either side. You loser! thought Peepgass, stroking his own full head of thatchy light brown hair. You'll never even make it into the studio in Atlanta. They'll leave you out there "in the field" until you get an ear job.

On the screen was a medium shot of Mayor Wesley Dobbs Jordan walking up the short flight of stairs toward the landing. The camera angle was from the rear.

"—and toward the podium," the voice of Joe Mundy was saying. The camera stayed on the Mayor, then suddenly returned to the stairs. Now you saw the back of a big, bald white man laboriously climbing the stairs by leaning upon the shoulder of a slender young white man, wearing a navy polo shirt and khaki pants, who walked at his side.

There was an awkward pause on the telecast, as the camera stayed fixed upon the gimping old man's progress. Not a peep from Mr. Joe Mundy, who evidently didn't know who this burly old man was.

"Look, Mom!" said Wallace. "That's Dad!"

ROGER'S SEAT IN the front row had been assigned so that he would be looking directly at Croker as he sat in his banker's chair on the landing waiting for Wes to introduce him. Roger intended to give Croker the eye, the accusing, threatening, bankrupting eye, the entire time, to make sure he came through with his part of the morning's recitation. Two seats away from Roger, here in the front row, was Croker's wife, Serena. I wonder if she's even half his age, thought Roger. She's a number, and I bet she's trouble. With her short skirt she had a way of crossing her legs that was enough to drive you crazy . . . But practically every other seat in the place was given over to the Press, the usual pack of shaggy mutts. At this moment a tremendous buzz was running through the pack. Some wondered why on earth the big developer Charlie Croker had come in gimping from the wings, unannounced, to accompany the Mayor as he delivered some sort of homily on racial unrest in Atlanta. Others saw this big, hulking white man using a young white man as a crutch and wondered who these people were and why they were here.

Croker leaned heavily on the boy's shoulder and grimaced as he climbed the stairs up to the landing. He clung tightly to the boy's hand for support as he lowered himself into one of the ash-wood banker's chairs. He sat there panting and red in the face, with his bad leg, the right leg, stiff as a length of lumber. The boy left the landing and went back down the stairs and stood on the side with the rest of the overflow crowd.

Now Wes was at the podium. Standing there in his standard-issue gray single-breasted suit and his white shirt and his dark red tie, he didn't look like much at first glance. He was about half the size of Croker. If he had a muscle in his plump body, it wasn't obvious. But when Wes seized you with his glittering eye—Coleridge, thought Roger—he had you. He had a stare that radiated sternness and irony all at once. He was now busy panning the members of the Press with that glittering eye, and they grew quiet. Wes faced them down a little longer, allowed just a hint of his familiar ironic smile to cross his lips, then looked serious, serious to the point of stern, and said:

"I want to thank the members of the Press for coming here in such numbers this morning, because I want to enlist your help—the city of Atlanta wants to enlist your help—in dealing with a situation that has been festering for two weeks now. I refer, as I'm sure you're aware, to the reports, the *reports*, that Georgia Tech's all-American running back, Fareek Fanon, has been accused, *accused*, of sexual assault.

"I want to emphasize here at the outset that we are talking about 'reports' of an 'accusation' . . . *reports* of an *accusation* . . . As of this moment no one has filed any charges with the Atlanta Police Department or any other governmental department, organ, or bureau, or with Georgia Tech's administration or student government. We have only *reports* of an *accusation* . . . *reports* of an *accusation* . . . and yet these reports have now been published in every medium of the Press, including the Internet. Now, what is the danger here? I'm sure you know. If a false rumor about you is printed once, you can shrug it off as gossip. But if it's printed twice, it becomes an accepted fact. That's the age we live in. That is what has now happened in the case of Fareek Fanon, except that in his case we aren't talking about 'twice,' we're talking about a thousandfold. Naturally every society is protective of a woman reputed to have been sexually assaulted. But let me remind you that men have rights, too. Even celebrated young athletes have rights. A young man like Fareek Fanon should not have had to endure the rumors that he has had to endure over the past two weeks. Rumors of sexual crime cannot simply be washed away, whereupon you're clean again. Of course, I have no firsthand knowledge of what, if anything, if anything, if *any*thing did or didn't happen on the night in question in this 'report' of an 'accusation,' but I do have firsthand knowledge of Fareek Fanon, and I want you to think about him for a moment before anyone is tempted to continue to relish in this . . . report of an accusation of sexual crime . . . Fareek grew up on English Avenue at a time—I think we have to be frank about this—at a time when English Avenue was one of the most unfortunate, most run-down neighborhoods in Atlanta. Today English Avenue is turning itself around and is fast becoming the vibrant neighborhood it used to be. But it was a difficult time when Fareek was coming up, so much so that parents on English Avenue used to brag about it if they had a teenage boy who didn't have a police record. That was considered an achievement . . . an achievement . . . Well, that was an early achievement of Fareek's. At the age of fourteen he was already a powerful athlete, six foot one and 190 pounds, but he confined that power to constructive pursuits in the arena of sports. And I know of someone who can take credit for this constructive side of Fareek Fanon. I'm talking about his mother, Thelma Fanon. She set herself against every obstacle a boy can run into in the ghetto, and she prevailed. There's one thing everybody who gets to know Fareek remarks upon: not his size and power, not his talent, not his determination, but his thoughtfulness . . . his thoughtfulness . . . a precious gift that only a mother like Thelma Fanon can bestow."

Jesus God, thought Roger, no more, Wes! You're gonna drown!

"The career of Fareek Fanon," the Mayor continued, "is testimony to a mother's love and a son's refusal to be frightened by the odds against him. I urge you to think about that before allowing this young man's reputation to be besmirched any further. The young woman whose name is being mentioned behind the hand, as it were"—the Mayor brought the back of his hand up to his mouth—"is due the same consideration. The most sinister element in this entire 'reported accusation,' however—let's face it and call it by its right name: race. There are those who have immediately seized upon the most heinous and long-ago-discredited forms of racial stereotyping to explain this incident whose actual occurrence has never even been established. Would Fareek Fanon be capable of playing the role that the stereotype-mongers have dreamed up for him? Not the Fareek Fanon I know . . . not the Fareek Fanon I know . . . *not* the Fareek Fanon *I* know . . ." Wes leaned forward on the podium as he repeated this phrase and slowly swept the audience with his eyes, until he seemed to be right across an intimate little table from them, telling them the gospel truth at last. "Nothing, least of all a vile canard like that, should be allowed to tear this city asunder along racial lines. We have all come too far together for that. This *is* . . . a city too busy to hate. There *is* . . . an Atlanta Way. We do *not* . . . give credence to hateful rumors—rumors full of hate—and let them destroy the mutual respect that has brought Atlanta this far. And we do *not* . . . allow them to snuff out the hopes, the dreams, the shining successes of fine young men like Fareek Fanon. Now, I am not alone in my concerns, I am happy to say." He turned toward Croker, then back toward the microphones. "One of Atlanta's outstanding business leaders"—synonymous with "rich white people," thought Roger—"Charles E. Croker, has joined us. It's hard to say what Charlie Croker is more famous for, his success as a real estate developer and creator of the Croker Global Corporation or his exploits as a running back and linebacker for the Georgia Tech football team. In his college years he was what Fareek is today: a gridiron star for the Yellow Jackets. He was known as 'the Sixty-Minute Man': the man who played entire games on both offense and defense. Now, it's true that some things change in sports, but other things don't. The pressures on a successful young athlete, the exploitation of a successful young athlete, the resentment against a successful young athlete—these are all things Charlie Croker can recall vividly. Furthermore, he knows Fareek Fanon and, in fact, has visited him recently. I think we can all learn a lot about this situation from his unique perspective. One of Atlanta's greatest builders of all time, one of Atlanta's greatest athletes of all time, a man from one generation who knows the young man from another whose name has been propelled into this 'reported accusation' "—he gestured toward the hulking white man sitting in the banker's chair—"Charlie Croker."

There was a smattering of applause, thanks to the elaborate tricolon with which the Mayor had introduced the man, but it quickly died down. Soon enough everybody's attention was riveted upon Croker's struggle to rise up from his chair. His right leg wouldn't bend enough at the knee. The boy, his attendant, started toward him from the side, but Croker motioned him back with a faint gesture, a low downward pumping of his hand. Then he put his hands on the arms of the banker's chair and pushed down with all his might. Slowly his massive body rose from the chair, and he managed to support himself on his good leg and start hobbling over to the podium. It seemed to take forever. Roger was afraid he was going to collapse before he could ever get there. But finally he made it, grasping both sides of the podium's top surface in order to steady himself. He looked down at the surface, and the moment began to lengthen, lengthen, lengthen. He looked out at the shaggy mutts and then this way and that way at the assorted lawyers, city officials, and politicians sitting on the stairs, and he smiled—rather sadly, it seemed to Roger—and said:

"Thank you, Mr. Mayor. You're generous . . . to a fault. That wasn't much of an athlete you just saw staggering from that chair over to here. It's *rust*. If you live long enough, your body starts to rust, and so do your ideas."

Roger didn't know what Croker was talking about, but his voice was strong and he had made a seemly sortie out onto the terrain of self-deprecation.

"As Mayor Jordan just mentioned," said Croker, "I have met Mr. Fareek Fanon." He pronounced Fareek *Fai*reek.

The use of "Mister," a genteel honorific that did not fit Fareek Fanon under any circumstances whatsoever, put Roger on guard and on edge.

"But before I talk about that," said Croker, "I oughta tell you how I happened to meet Mr. Fanon, because it's sort of an interesting story all by itself. Mayor Jordan just called me a 'great builder' or sump'm like'at. I s'pose'at's a polite name for real estate developer, and I'm not even feeling like a great real estate developer along about right now." *Rat now.* "There *is* a great developer, from Chicago, named Sam Zell, and he once said, 'Real estate development is a good business to get into—and it's a good business to get out of,' meaning that most *uv*'us don't know when to take our winnings off the table and stop betting. We're always determined to build one more office tower, one more mall, one more tower plus mall plus hotel plus apartments—like the one I built in Cherokee County—and named after myself—no Atlanta developer ever had the nerve"—*the nuv*—"to name a building after himself before—anyway, the time always comes when that *one more* development *does* it, and you wind up just one more bleeding bankrupt son of a gun."

Roger looked at Wes, who was seated expressionless in one of the banker's chairs, and then Wes glanced toward him and arched his eyebrows, and they both wondered, What in God's name is the man doing?

"WHAT'S HE DOING?" asked Peepgass. He glanced over at Martha. Wallace looked at her, too, as if wondering the same thing. But Martha continued to look straight ahead at the screen . . . here in deepest, lushest Buckhead.

"I don't know," she said, but in a dreamy, distracted way that indicated she hadn't really absorbed the question. In fact, she was afraid for Charlie, though she couldn't have told Ray or anybody else exactly why.

"RIGHT NOW," SAID CROKER, up on the landing in the rotunda, "I'm about this far from bankruptcy." He raised his right hand and put his forefinger a fraction of an inch from his thumb. "Now, I'm telling you all this for a reason. One day 'bout . . . oh . . . two weeks ago . . . a lawyer representing Mr. Faireek Fanon came to me with a right interesting proposition." *Rat innerestin'*.

Roger's heart began banging away. He looked to Wes up on the landing for—for—for—for help. And Wes was looking at *him*. His expression was impassive, but his eyes started darting all over the room. He seemed to be searching for someone, some henchman, some minion, some worker of wonders who could step up and put a hook around Croker and haul this great gimping hulk off the landing. Roger began looking about, too. He caught the eye of Don Pickett and Julian Salisbury, who were seated on the stairs. They looked as bewildered as he was.

"This lawyer," said Croker, "he told me he could work some magic. He told me he could make my troubles with the bank disappear, overnight prack'ly. All I had to do, in return"—*retun*—"was grant him a simple favor, a very easy favor." *Veh easy favuh.* "All I had to do was go meet Mr. Faireek Fanon and come away from that meeting testifying—not in a court of law"—*a coat a law*—"but right here at this press conference right now"—*ratcheer at this press con'frence rat now*—"testifying that he's a fine young man who's getting dogged by all the things that can dog you when you're a sports celebrity. Well, I wrestled with the angels . . . for a little while. Then I said to myself, 'Well, hell' "—*wale, hale*—"what's the big deal? I won't be swearing anything on the Bible. I'll just be indulging"—*in*-dulgin'—"in a little harmless flattery at a press conference. Who's gonna care? So I met Faireek Fanon. I met him at the home of Coach Buck McNutter. Oh, by then, *hehhhhhh*"—Croker chuckled morosely—"I was *sump'm.* I was so eager to please, I started flattering Mr. Faireek Fanon right off the bat." *Rat off the bat.* "One thing I got to give Faireek Fanon credit for. *He* didn' bother flattering *me*, even though there was sump'm I could do for him. I could show up at this press conference and create the impression that the business interests—everybody's always talking about the 'business interests' in Atlanta—that the 'business interests' were on Faireek Fanon's side, or at least they weren't"—*wunt*—"lined up against him. Nevertheless, Faireek Fanon's eagerness to please the Sixty-Minute Man here"—Croker paused; a smile ran across his face and disappeared, as if he had thought of something amusing and then decided not to mention it—"his eagerness to please measured about zero, or maybe it was down in minus territory, because I think I detected more than a little contempt. I congratulate him for that, because he was in the presence of a man who was undertaking a contemptible thing. Mr. Faireek Fanon struck me as a typical sports hero. I know the type, because I was once one myself, or so the sports pages kept informing me. You get to the point where you *expect* people to do whatever you want because they've been lucky enough to breathe the same air you breathe. When you pass by people who are talking, you assume they're talking about *you*. You think you're exempt from the rules of ordinary conduct, since the world has been handed you on a platter, and therefore it's all yours. Money? There wasn't much money in football forty years ago, the way there is now, although then, like now, you were likely to take the money mainly to show everybody how wonderful you were. Sex? That hasn't changed much. It was yours for the asking. It was set at your feet like an offering. Did Faireek Fanon take part in the kind of incident that everybody's" —*evuhbuddy's*—"talking about? I ain't got a ghost of an idea. Would he be *capable* of such a thing? Well, Faireek, he's arrogant, he's obnoxious, he's impertinent, he thinks the world owes him whatever he wants—but you can't necessarily jump from that to say he'd *do* whatever he wants. Besides, my information is that sexual customs are a lot different today from what they were when I was young."

Charlie took a deep breath and lifted his eyes and looked about the rotunda . . . the journalists in the seats just below him . . . the great crescent of television cameras at the rear of the seats . . . the gray-and-white marble fountain in the middle of the rotunda and the tons of curved marble that created the rotunda wall . . . the people sitting shank to flank on the stairs to either side of the landing . . . and in the first row of the seats, Serena, slumped back on her chair, giving him the same look of social horror as when he and Billy Bass and the others had gone on about AIDS benefits that night down at Turpmtine—*Lawdy me, I got de HIV!*—and Lawyer Roger White, who seemed to be trying to look daggers through him . . . but in fact Charlie had never felt so impervious to criticism in his life. He felt like a man free of all encumbrances. He felt whole again, as if he could stride up and down those stairs without the slightest limp.

Conrad could tell that Charlie was about to get to the message. He felt exhilarated as he watched him. It was for this that he had undergone the trials of Hercules and traveled all the way across America. *Exhilarated!* Yet dangers remained. He could see the Mayor looking this way and that. He was looking for someone to come up with a stratagem for getting the old man away from the podium. Conrad bent his knees slightly and centered his weight over the balls of his feet. If anyone tried to move Charlie so much as an inch, he was ready to intervene, even if it meant ending up in the hands of the police.

"So I accepted the deal," Charlie was saying, "and they delivered on their end of it right away. Every bit a pressure from a bank we owed hundreds of millions to—*hundreds* of *millions*—stopped all of a sudden, and on the day they said it would. How they did it, I don't know, but they did it. Like I was saying, it was like magic . . . All I had to do was . . ."

IN BUCKHEAD, on Valley Road, in Martha Croker's house, in the library, Peepgass sprang to his feet from the easy chair—or for Peepgass it qualified as springing—and stared at the TV screen with his two hands raised before him as if he were about to strangle somebody.

"I knew it!" he exclaimed. "I knew the whole damned thing was strange! Nobody ignores a defalcatory loan of that magnitude unless something *very* strange is going on!"

Martha looked at him, but said nothing. Inwardly she prayed that he wouldn't spell out this whole situation in front of Wallace. Ray gave way to his emotions too easily. He wasn't very dependable in that sense.

"For Christ's sake," Peepgass said bitterly, "Arthur Lomprey and his *macro-decisions*. *Meeee-yahh!* A humpbacked macro-weakling is all he is if you ask me!"

". . . SAY THE RIGHT THINGS at this press conference," Croker continued. "But I haven't done that and I can't do that. One of the few freedoms that we have as human beings that cannot be taken away from us is the freedom to assent to what is true and to deny what is false. Nothing you can give me is worth surrendering that freedom for. At this moment I'm a man with complete tranquillity. After all, what is tranquillity? Tranquillity is a mind in accord with nature . . . a mind in accord with nature . . . I've been a real estate developer for most of my life, and I can tell you that a developer lives with the opposite of tranquillity, which is perturbation. You're perturbed about something all the time. You build your first development, and right away you want to build a bigger one, and you want a bigger house to live in, and if it ain't in Buckhead, you might as well cut your wrists. Soon's you got that, you want a plantation, tens of thousands of acres devoted solely to shooting quail, because you know of four or five developers who've already got that. And soon's you get *that,* you want a place on Sea Island and a Hatteras cruiser and a spread northwest of Buckhead, near the Chattahoochee, where you can ride a horse during the week, when you're not down at the plantation, plus a ranch in Wyoming, Colorado, or Montana, because *truly* successful men in Atlanta and New York all got their ranches, and of course now you need a private plane, a big one, too, a jet, a Gulfstream Five, because who's got the patience and the time and the humility to fly commercially, even to the plantation, much less out West to a ranch? What is it you're looking for in this endless quest? Tranquillity. You think if only you can acquire *enough* worldly goods, *enough* recognition, *enough* eminence, you will be free, there'll be nothing more to worry about, and instead you become a bigger and bigger slave to how you think others are judging you. 'You have priceless silver and goblets of gold,' said the philosopher, 'but your reason is of common clay.' As of this morning, I am as rich as the richest of you, for I am hereby handing over everything I own, the Croker Global Corporation, every last branch of it, my houses, my plantation, my horses, my car, if anybody wants it—I'm handing them all over to my creditors. They can rummage through these trifles any way they see fit. My keys are on the table, boys. Go to it. They're all yours. I'm happily turning over these trifles to whoever wants to claim them. I won't try to hold you back in Chapter 11 or any other chapter of the bankruptcy code, either."

PEEPGASS WAS ON his feet again, this time in a state of exultation. He held both fists over his head, pumping them for all he was worth, his eyes pinned on the screen.

"Yes! Yes! Yes!" he said. It was close to being a shout. Then he looked at Martha and said, "He's handing'em over! The buildings! Croker Concourse! Deeds in lieu of foreclosure! I can't believe it—the syndicate lives!"

Martha tried to join in his happiness, but she couldn't. What she was watching on that screen made her inexpressibly sad.

"I DON'T KNOW what you're like," Croker was saying, "but if you're like most *uv*'us here in Atlanta, you're driving yourself crazy over possessions. Just think about that for a second."

Despite himself, Roger thought of his gorgeous house on Niskey Lake, that and his Lexus and the suit he had on today, a fabulous single-breasted blue-and-gray Glen plaid, which Gus Carroll had charged $3,500 to make.

"I'm older than mosta you," Croker continued, "and I can tell you that the only real possession you'll ever have is your character, that and your 'scheme of life,' you might say. The Manager has given every person a spark from His own divinity, and no one can take that away from you, not even the Manager himself, and from that spark comes your character. Everything else is temporary and worthless in the long run, including your body. What is the human body? It's a clever piece a crockery containing a quart a blood. And it's not even yours! One day you're gonna have to give it back! And where are your possessions then? They're gonna be picked over by one bunch a buzzards or another. What man's ever been remembered as great because of the possessions he devoted his life to 'cumulating? I can't think of any. So why don't we pay more attention to the one precious thing we possess, the spark the Manager has placed in our souls?"

Roger looked at the Mayor, and the Mayor was looking at Roger. The Mayor twisted his lips in a way that as much as said "This dishonest bastard! Double-crossing us isn't enough! Now he's got to preach a sermon!"

Meantime, a low buzz had started in the ranks of those shaggy mutts, the Press. Roger turned his head and looked about. The journalists were pulling faces at one another and whispering. Maybe they knew of the treachery Croker had been guilty of in this performance of his, calling Fareek Fanon arrogant, obnoxious, impertinent, and voracious, and maybe they didn't. But they could all tell he'd turned into some kind of religious nut. The Manager. The Manager, *indeed*!

"But you say, 'Be serious, Croker. With no money, no possessions, how am I supposed to eat? Where can I stay? Well—have you ever seen an old beggar? Of course you have. We've all seen'em. How'd they get to be so old? They all ate somehow, 365 days a year, most likely, and they all stayed somewhere, too. But you say, 'I'd rather die than sit down beside the road with a Dixie cup, begging.' Do you realize what you're really saying? You're saying, 'It ain't what I'm gonna eat or where I'm gonna stay I'm worrying about, it's saving face, it's what everybody in Buckhead's gon' think about me, that's what I'm worrying about . . ."

Charlie's voice trailed off. He realized something was going terribly wrong. Far from winning his audience with the words of Epictetus and Zeus, he was losing them. They were restless, they were whispering, they were smiling and sniggering. He looked over to the side. Connie had a look of grave concern and was slightly crouched, as if ready to spring into action. In the first row Serena looked petrified. She had shrunk back alarmingly into her chair. If there had been a crack in the marble, she would have gladly slipped through it. The black lawyer, Roger White, was glaring pitchforks at him. Charlie's voice faltered as he tried to resume:

"What are we? We are born with two elements: the body, which we share with the animals, including the lowest animals, the weasel and the snake, and the mind and reason, which comes from that spark the Manager has given us. Now, which—"

Charlie was suddenly aware of a firm, steady pressure against his left arm and elbow. He glanced over—and there was Mayor Wesley Dobbs Jordan. The Mayor was elbowing him aside! Amazed, Charlie gave way slightly—and that was all the Mayor needed. He leaned over the podium and put his head between Charlie and the microphone and said, "Thank you, Mr. Croker. Thank you very much, thank you, Mr. Croker"—all without looking at him even once.

The audience erupted with sniggers and ironic applause.

Stupefied, Charlie began limping away from the podium. He felt no pain yet. He was aware only of the crowd's scorn and the Mayor's scorn.

Connie was by his side. "Lean on my shoulder, Charlie, and watch out, we got some stairs coming up."

Now people seemed to be rushing in from all over, blurting out questions.

"You said Fareek Fanon is obnoxious, arrogant, and a couple other things like that. Then why wouldn't—"

"You say somebody put pressure on your creditors in exchange for your appearance here today. Why do you *think*—"

"What did you tell—"

"You really *mean* you're giving away—"

"Mr. Croker, are you saying that Fareek—"

"Hey, Charlie, Sam Frye, Channel 9!"

"Charlie! Over here! Just one!"

The press . . . not yet capable of asking about the Manager and the message. And now Charlie could hear the voice of the Mayor over a speaker:

"Thank you very much, Mr. Croker. I can't say I detected the voice of the Manager. So it must have been one of the creatures you mentioned that just spoke here. Was it the weasel or the snake . . . the weasel or the snake . . . the *weasel* or the *snake* that just delivered that sneak attack on Fareek Fanon? What sort of creature was it that would come here under one guise and then vilify that beleaguered young man under another? Why would—" Now the crush of the press around Charlie was so great, he couldn't even hear the Mayor over the speakers. The reporters, or whatever they were, were all yelling at him at once.

"—say actually happened?"

"—didn't get along?"

"—have any doubt that Fanon—"

"—then what did you tell—"

"—the one who set up—"

And Connie was saying into his ear: "Don't worry, Charlie, you delivered the message! They're not going to understand it all at once!"

When Connie said that, Charlie knew he had failed as a speaker. But he didn't care, for the spark *had* been *in* him as he stood at that podium. That's what he wanted to tell them, but he couldn't, not yet, although the day would come. He could see that much already. He held his chin high. He looked *through* the mob, the blur of people around him, looked beyond this marble rotunda to a horizon more distant than these people, with their earnest questions of this moment, could possibly imagine.

Charlie's arm rested on Conrad's shoulder as they made their way slowly through the crowd, and Conrad was filled with pity. They had laughed at him, mocked him. And yet he had *done* it. It was only a matter of time before thousands, millions, would know and understand. Epictetus had once spoken as Charlie spoke now. "I have not yet confidence in what I have learned and assented to. Only let me gain confidence, and then I will show you the statue as it is when it is finished and polished. In such a way will I show myself to you—faithful, self-respecting, noble, free from tumult." Charlie *did* have the spark within him! Only another couple of weeks, or maybe a month, Conrad would stay with him, and his work would be done. He was only Zeus' courier. After that he could return to California, to Pittsburg or Walnut Creek or wherever Jill and his children were. He didn't have the slightest fear. He'd turn himself in to the authorities. In the very first chapter of the Book: "I will imprison you," says Caesar. Epictetus says, "What say you, fellow? Imprison me? My bit of a body you will imprison—yes, but my will—no, not even Zeus can conquer that."

What was there to be afraid of, then? Epictetus and Agrippinus had been through much worse. No, he would not groan or whine. He would go with a smile, good courage, and tranquillity.

ROGER WAS STUNNED but on his feet, torn between anger and guilt, guilt at having failed to deliver to Wes the fully broken Charlie Croker he had promised, anger at Croker himself. The snake! Wes had that part right. Croker had *attacked* Fareek! Roger was so furious, he headed toward that 235-pound reptile. The old man was going to get a tongue-lashing he'd never forget! But he couldn't get close enough to be heard. The crush of reporters was too great.

"Counselor!" A big, hearty, cheery voice.

Roger turned around. It was the congressman from the 5th District, a rotund young man, very dark, named Gibley Berm. Roger had never met him; he knew him only from his pictures.

"You're doing great work, brother! Oh, they're *after* Fareek now! They'll try any trick! Oh yeah. Don't let up! You're doing great things!"

"Thanks, Mr. Congressman!" said Roger, genuinely surprised. "I won't!"

"Gotcha back, Counselor!" said Gibley Berm with the warmest smile imaginable.

Gotcha back! You're doing great work, brother! From Representative Gibley Berm, out of the blue! *Gotcha back!*

There had never been sweeter music—not from Mahler, not from Stravinsky, not from Bach, Haydn, or Mozart—to Roger White's ears.

Gotcha back! Gib Berm had said. *Gotcha back!*

For the first time in his life Roger entertained the thought of running for office.

THERE SEEMED TO BE a thousand people jammed in around him, and yet Charlie felt serene. He no longer felt pain in his knee. He still had his arm on Connie's shoulder, but only the way one comrade might have his arm on another. Despite the shouts, which ricocheted off the marble walls of the rotunda and doubled, tripled in volume, Charlie felt . . . tranquil. That was exactly what he had found: tranquillity. That was exactly what he was blessed with: a mind in accord with nature. He was not yet a good speaker, but that would come with time, for as Epictetus had said, "Like the bull, the man of noble nature does not become noble all of a sudden; he must train through the winter and make ready." He felt tranquil and . . . light. His feet only just barely touched the marble and the earth below. He felt as if he could run a hundred yards just the way he had forty years ago. Wouldn't *that* amaze them all! He had shed all the shabby baggage of this life. He had become a vessel of the Divine.

PEEPGASS WAS STILL on his feet, watching the television screen and rocking back and forth nervously, from his heels to his toes to his heels to his toes. *The syndicate lives!*

"He's gone gaga, Martha! Round the bend! Did you ever see anything like that in your life?"

"No," said Martha, all too quietly. Her eyes were misting. She fought to keep the mist from turning into tears.

"What's Dad talking about, Mom?" asked Wallace. "What's gotten into him? He sounded . . . crazy."

Peepgass said, "That spark the Manager has given us? Did you get that part, Martha? . . . What's the matter, Martha?" Peepgass hurried over to the easy chair where she sat. "What's wrong?" She didn't reply.

"It's Charlie, isn't it," said Peepgass. "You still have that much feeling for him, don't you?"

"No, it's not that," said Martha, bringing a lacy little handkerchief to her eyes. "It's just that I know what he used to be. It's hard to watch the disintegration of a human being who . . . who . . ."

She didn't dare try to finish the sentence, for fear she would actually break down and cry.

Epilogue

A Man of the World

"I WON'T STAY LONG, WES," SAID ROGER. "I KNOW YOU'VE GOT A whole waiting room full of people who want to see you, but I just had to come by and shake your hand. It's just great. Congratulations. I couldn't be happier if it was me who had done it."

"But you *did* do it," said the Mayor. The two of them were standing in the mayoral salon, and Wes gestured toward the familiar white couch. "Come on, sit down, have a seat."

"Are you sure?"

"Of course I am." He gestured again. "I've been thinking about you all morning."

"Me?" said Roger as he took a seat. "How do I rate that on this day of all days?"

At first Wes just smiled, and not ironically, either. His face looked ashen, despite his black-as-thou suntan. There were deep dark circles under his eyes, which were bloodshot. He probably hadn't had a real night's sleep for a week, maybe two weeks, and he must have been up all night last night, since the final tally hadn't come in until 4 a.m. He had defeated André Fleet by less than one percentage point.

For a moment Wes gazed pensively out the big plate-glass window behind the couch. It was a miserable November day with dark, low clouds, fog, and a dreadful level of humidity that made it seem warm one minute and cold and clammy the next. Then he pulled up his armchair and sat down and smiled some more and said:

"I hope Gladys or Miss Beasley offered you something to drink. We've even got champagne. You may not see champagne in here again, unless *you* run for mayor."

Roger gave a laughing snort, as if the idea were preposterous. In fact, he regarded it as merely unlikely. "No, they were very hospitable. But I'm not sure I can take champagne at eleven o'clock in the morning."

The Mayor raised his right hand as if it held a glass. "Then I'll toast you, one teetotaler to another. You were the turning point, brother."

"How so?"

"The way you got the most hidebound Cracker in town to come to that press conference. Charlie Croker. That turned this election around."

"Are you being funny? We've talked about this many times, but I still feel terrible about what happened. I thought I was being so shrewd. I thought I had Croker right where we wanted him. And then he double-crosses us! He as much as calls Fareek the sort of young black man who thinks with his groin and goes about deflowering the sweet young white flowers of the Piedmont Driving Club set. Frankly, I thought I'd managed to blow the election for you."

"Quite the opposite," said Wes. "We now know—from the exit polling yesterday—we now know that every voter, or every African-American voter—"

Roger interrupted. "You're sticking with *African American*, even now that the election's over?"

"I'm sticking with it, brother, I'm sticking with it, sticking with it, sticking with it. In fact, I'm stuck with it."

Roger said, "I'm sorry. I didn't mean to interrupt."

"That's okay. Anyway, we now know that practically every African-American voter looked upon Croker's performance as a betrayal of Fareek. Obviously he had agreed to be at the press conference to say something entirely different, and then, like a snake, he does all he can to destroy Fareek's personal reputation. He calls him arrogant, obnoxious, impertinent, and an animal who grabs whatever he wants. I probably got more sympathy for that than anything else that happened in the whole campaign. It looked as if the white business interests were out to sabotage me. And I don't get much sympathy as a rule, Roger. Oh, I think people look at me in a generally good way, but I strike them as a little too . . . self-confident, or whatever it is."

"Gee," said Roger, "wonder why. Incidentally, I don't know if I ever told you, but that line about the snake—Croker had said something about 'the Manager, the weasel, and the snake'?—and you elbowed him away from the microphone and said you hadn't heard the Manager talking, so it must have been the weasel or the snake?—you remember that?"

"Oh yes."

"Well, that was brilliant, Wes. It was one of the best ad lib lines I ever heard. But now, please explain something else to me. You had thought of getting Croker to support Fareek because you didn't want to alienate your white support by defending Fareek in a rape case involving Armholster's daughter. So what happened to your white vote?"

"I *did* lose some white support. No question about it. But two things softened the blow. First, it brought me so much *more* black support. And Croker's performance was so crazy—all that talk about the Manager and the two elements and how it's better to be a tranquil beggar by the side of the road than a perturbed plutocrat in Buckhead—Godalmighty!—he was so crazy that day. Then he announces he's giving away everything he has—I mean, he sounded so crazy, a lot of white voters ended up discounting everything he said, including his vilification of Fareek. Tens of thousands of people watched that press conference on television, because the subject was race and sex."

"What did happen to Croker? I never hear anything about him."

Wes smiled broadly. "You don't? You've got to put your ear to the ground, Brother Roger. Croker's out there stomping around. He did exactly what he said he was going to do. He said, 'Okay, boys' "—Wes turned his palms up and then lifted them in the gesture that says "empty"—" 'here it is. It's all yours. *You* fight over it.' I mean, he walked away from a corporation worth *hundreds* of *millions*. Of course, his debts were even greater, by another couple of hundred million or so, but still—it was unbelievable. Now he's an evangelist."

"An e*van*gelist?"

"Exactly—and apparently doing very well."

"Oh—come—on! What in God's name is he preaching?"

"Nothing in *God's* name. He's out there talking about the Manager

. . . him and Zeus. Apparently the two names are interchangeable. And there's Epi-something—I can't remember the name. And there's Messenger Connie, who'll soon be returning to Earth from wherever."

"*Zeus?*"

"Yep. Zeus and the Manager—and he calls himself a Stoic."

"Where's he doing all this?"

"He started off down in Baker County," said Wes, "and now he's moved into the Florida Panhandle and southern Alabama. Apparently he's dynamite, at least among white folks who go in for that sort of thing. He can talk your socks off, and the bills out of your wallet, is what I hear. The fact that he gave up everything—and he had a lot—to work for the Manager gives him tremendous credibility. He's about to sign a syndication deal with Fox Broadcasting."

"*Fox Broadcasting?*"

"That's the word. It's going to be called *The Stoic's Hour*."

Roger's mouth hung partway open. "Dear God in heaven . . . The Manager . . . Zeus . . . national television . . . *The Stoic's Hour* . . . I think *I'm* going crazy, Wes."

The Mayor laughed. "I'll tell you something. A lot of white folks look down on the way we worship. They think we're too emotional and demonstrative and so forth. Our choirs sway when they sing and clap their hands to the beat. Our preachers don't just preach, they *o*-rate. Our congregations don't just sit there mumbling, they shout 'Right on!' 'Hallelujah!' 'Say it, brother' and 'Amen.' " But I'll tell you something. At least our people don't turn . . . *weird*. At least they don't start praying to the Manager and Zeus and calling themselves Stoics as soon as some old ox with a deep voice comes to town with a tent. I mean, Godalmighty."

"What about—"

"I don't mean to interrupt," said the Mayor, "but I've just got to show you this little footnote to Croker and Zeus and the Manager and all that." He got up, went into his little inner office, and came back with a small newspaper clipping, which he handed to Roger. "Take a look at the headline."

The headline said: TURN ME LOOSE, ZEUS.

"That's from some paper in Oakland, this summer. Anyway, as you'll see there, it's about a young man named Hensley, a white kid. He escaped from jail in California during that earthquake last whenever it was, and he turns himself in sometime in July, and he's about to be sentenced, and the judge asks him if he has anything to say, and the kid says, 'It's up to you to do your part, Judge, and it's up to me to do mine.' And so the judge says, 'You seem awfully relaxed about the whole thing.' And the kid says, 'I'm completely tranquil.' That's the word he uses, *tranquil*. 'I feel completely in accord with nature,' he says. Then he says, right here"—Wes pointed it out in the clipping—"he says, 'My body, it's nothing but a clay bowl with a quart of blood, and it's only on loan in the first place. But Zeus has given each of us a spark of his divinity, the ability to say yes to what is true, and no to what is false, and no one can take that away from you, not even in prison.' So the judge says, 'Zeus, hunh? Escape from custody is a serious offense, but I'm going to take a chance on you. I'm setting you free on two years' probation, in the custody of Zeus.' You'll never guess who this kid is."

"Zeus. Must be Charlie Croker's son or something. Who is it?"

"Elihu Yale, the police chief, sent the clipping over last week. Seems that last spring the California State Police, or whoever it was, asked our police department to be on the lookout for this kid who had broken out of jail and was believed to be in the Atlanta area. The FBI had done some kind of phone taps. The kid had been in jail for aggravated assault. By the time our department finally got a lead on him, he was long gone from Atlanta. He'd been working here for an outfit called Carter Home Care as a sort of attendant for sick people. One of the people he worked for—are you ready for this?—was Charlie Croker. I don't know if you remember, but he was the kid who helped Croker up to the landing for the press conference."

"I remember *him*!" said Roger. "I saw him at Croker's house, too. He had these huge forearms." He made a gesture over his left forearm with his right hand.

"Oh sure," said Wes. "All these convicts do is lift weights and make license plates. But you can see what happened. Croker converts the poor bastard to this weird Zeus religion of his, and the kid goes and pulls this Zeus stuff on some California judge—and it *works*! Can you believe that? I'll tell you what I said before. You can find fault with our people when it comes to faith, if you want to, but we—do—not—turn—*weird* on you. Isn't that a great headline? TURN ME LOOSE, ZEUS? I don't know how they think up these things. Anyway, I'm sorry, Roger, I interrupted you."

Roger said, "Yeah, uh . . . what the hell *was* I was going to ask you? Oh yeah. What about Croker's wife? You remember that number?"

"*Oh* yes," said the Mayor.

"So is she out on the camp-meeting circuit with Croker, too?" asked Roger.

"Not that I know of," said the Mayor. "I don't think young Mrs. Croker is very spiritual. I think she believes that everything that's sweet in this life ends when we die."

"Didn't they have a child?"

"A little girl," said Wes. "Her name is Kingsley Croker." He pulled a face, as if to say, "Pretty outlandish name, hunh?"

"And she's with her mother, I assume?"

"I couldn't tell you," said Wes. "You know, when these hot little vamps marry their rich old men, they often have a child as fast as they can, as an insurance policy. What happens to the child when there's nothing left to insure, I don't want to think about."

"What *did* happen to all his property?"

"Oh, the creditors—you remember he said, 'The keys are on the table, they're all yours, go to it,' or something like that? Well, PlannersBanc and all the other creditors were ecstatic at first. Croker wasn't going to tie them up in Chapter 11, which could've dragged on for years. So they all had at it—and now they're busy suing each other, the creditors are, and it'll probably drag on for decades. There's been some funny fallout from this thing. You're a lawyer, you've probably heard of 'surrendering a deed in lieu of foreclosure'?"

Roger nodded to show that he had.

"Well, Croker just handed over his deeds, including the deed to the property that ruined him, Croker Concourse. You remember Croker Concourse?"

Roger nodded again.

"If you're handed the deed, in lieu of foreclosure, you don't have to have an auction, but what happened was, Croker and his financial troubles got so much publicity following the press conference, all sorts of vultures and bottom-fishers got interested in Croker Concourse, figuring they could get it on the cheap. So they started bidding against each other, and pretty soon PlannersBanc had an auction going, all the same. They got $130 million for the thing. Some group from Dallas bought it. That was a lot less than they'd lent Croker for it, but at least they got away with their hides. In the middle of the whole thing they discover that one of their loan officers, a guy named Peepgass, has secretly formed a syndicate to buy the thing for $50 million, which he was going to talk his superiors into accepting. Of course they canned the guy—but that isn't the interesting part. The interesting part is that just last month this Peepgass married Charlie Croker's *first wife*! I'm not kidding! And so now he's living in a mansion in Buckhead that Croker paid for, with a woman who has millions Croker had to give her in the divorce settlement. Meantime, the guy's involved in a paternity suit with some woman in Decatur, but that didn't seem to bother the former Mrs. Croker." Wes shook his head and then smiled his best ironic smile and said, "It's a great life, if you don't weaken."

Roger laughed and said, "Wes, I still don't see how that whole thing with Croker turned the election around, or were you speaking in hyperbole?"

Wes maintained his ironic smile, but then looked through the plate-glass window, as if toward the murky clouds outside. He stayed that way for what seemed like a very long time.

Then he turned back toward Roger, smiled faintly, and said, "Do you remember the first time you came in here, and I asked you if I could speak to you as Brother Wes and Brother Roger? I never regretted that, incidentally."

"Oh, I remember."

"Can we do that again, just Brother Wes and Brother Roger?"

"Absolutely."

"Okay. And do you also remember one time I told you that when you enter a citywide race, in the first month you're going to learn 100 percent more about politics than you ever knew before and that in your second month you'll learn 200 percent more, and so on?"

"I sure do."

"Maybe I'm just vain, but I figure that just being privy to my campaign as much as you were, you probably learned about 25 percent more than you knew before. Am I close?"

"No," said Roger, "because I'm sure it was a lot more than that."

"Well now, Brother Roger, I'm going to tell you something that ought to raise your political IQ a little more. The first time you came to see me, you told me about how Inman Armholster was furious, and he was going around to people at Tech saying that Fareek had raped his daughter. Right?"

"Right."

"And I told you Inman Armholster was the one who was putting up André Fleet's get-out-the-vote money."

"Right."

"I knew right away this was important information, but at first I couldn't figure out anything to do with it. The news that Armholster wanted Fareek's hide was spreading pretty fast, but nobody was about to run a newspaper story or something on the television about a rape case in which no charges had been filed, particularly when the male and female were Fareek Fanon and Inman Armholster's daughter. Then from out of nowhere come these two nuts with their 'Chasing the Dragon.' "

"Who *are* they, anyway?"

"A couple of Internet creeps, is my considered opinion," said the Mayor. "They look like two white noodles with hair. Makes you itch when you're in the same room with them. But they *do* put out an Internet gossip column. Atlanta's very short on gossip columns. In New York all sorts of personal things about well-known people get slipped into gossip columns, but in Atlanta there's just these two nutcases."

"It sounds like you *met* them."

"Oh, sure," said Wes. "After their big coup they began showing up at City Hall as *reporters* in search of their due deference."

"For God's sake."

"Well, for about a week, Roger, they had this town humming. Once they published the story, and then the newspapers published it, I knew what I had to do."

"Which was what?" said Roger.

"Call my State of the City press conference. I was genuinely concerned that the whole thing might blow up into something very ugly, and that's exactly what I'd told Armholster when I met with him. But the press conference was sort of a borderline call, to tell the truth. Fareek is an *admired* figure in South Atlanta, but he's not what you'd call a *beloved* figure. Oh, people are for him, and everybody is proud that one of their own has made it big, and I'm sure there are lots of teenage boys who identify with him. But Fareek is not warm, he's not good, he's not kind, he doesn't come back to do good deeds in the community, he's not charming—boy, is he not charming. Our polls showed that African Americans in Atlanta believed Fareek was being railroaded, but it didn't amount to a widespread anger with any real voltage to it. All we had was one halfway riot, the one I told you about. But I had my own reason for having the press conference. It would be my only chance to speak out in behalf of your client."

"What do you mean?"

"No politician can go around taking sides in sex cases, because the facts can come out and blow up in your face at any time. But when the issue is not guilt or innocence but fairness, justice, individual rights, and peace and calm in the city—then you can have your say, and I came down as hard in favor of Fareek Fanon as it was possible to do in that context. And then when Croker turned on Fareek—it looked as if he was proving my point! The 'business interests' were determined to be unfair and unjust! Now I'm Fareek's one defender in public life! Now I'm right on top of what is known as a 'black issue'! And where does that leave André Fleet? André Fleet's off in the bleachers sucking his thumb. He remained practically silent through the whole thing. What could he say? He couldn't very well back Elizabeth Armholster the way I backed Fareek, because that would cost him too much of the South Atlanta vote he was counting on. But that's what Armholster wanted! At the very least he expected Fleet to attack Fareek! But Fleet just sat on his hands. Armholster was so mad, he *cut off Fleet's get-out-the-vote money*! He had *none*! *Zip*!" Wes started laughing as hard as Roger had ever seen him laugh. "Yesterday Fleet's out in the street with his mouth open and his tongue hanging out! He's got nothing to buy votes with! Nothing!" More laughter, to the point of tears. "Roger, when you got Croker to that press conference for me—you *won the election!*"

Roger didn't even smile. "What happened was very nice for you, Wes, but not for Fareek. His name was dragged through the mud for a long time."

"The *mud*?" said Wes sharply. "You don't *know* mud, Brother Roger! Mud is not when some girl's loudmouth father is going around saying you raped his daughter. Mud is when you get arrested, fingerprinted, put in a cell, bailed out, arraigned, indicted, and then you sit in a courtroom, all 225 pounds of you, with a shaved head and a neck the size of a tree trunk, trying to look innocent while a pretty little white girl sobs out the story of how you ravaged her! That's . . . *mud*!"

"Still—"

"*Through the mud*," said Wes sardonically. "But that hasn't happened, has it?"

"No, but—"

"Don't *No, but* me, Brother Roger! No charges have ever been brought, have they. And do you know why? Because the Armholsters got a pretty good taste of just what kind of hell they'd have to go through if they made it a real case."

"Do you know that for a fact?"

"Well . . . I don't know it for a fact, but what other explanation is there? Armholster is a blowhard, but he's not *just* a blowhard. He'll do something to Fareek sooner or later. God knows what. I just hope to hell it isn't within the Atlanta city limits and not on my watch. But he didn't want to do it this way, not with the media going into a frenzy over it. Or that's the way I see it. What I did was the best thing for Fareek Fanon and the best thing for the city."

"Even accepting the part about Fareek, which I don't," said Roger, "why 'the best thing for the city'?"

"Because Atlanta needs me," said Wes. Not a touch of irony in his expression. "Have you any idea of what a catastrophe it would have been if André Fleet had been elected? It would have set Atlanta back two generations. The sum total of André Fleet's knowledge of strategy here at the turn of the century is the pick, the give and go, and the Alley Oop."

Roger smiled reluctantly. "Well, I'll grant you Fareek has come out free and clear of the whole thing. But you know, I don't think he ever lost a moment's sleep over it, even when it all looked very bad. He thinks he lives on Olympus, with all the other gods."

"Like Zeus," said Wes. "And how's he doing on the *gridiron* this season?"

Roger smiled another reluctant smile. "Even better than last year. Barring a complete shutdown, he'll be an all-American again. They're already talking about him as the front-runner for the Heisman Trophy."

"See?" said Wes. "And how about you? How're *you* doing? How're things down at Wringer Fleasom & Tick?"

Roger now smiled the smile of capitulation that says, *Okay, you got me.* "I shouldn't give you the satisfaction, but I guess I have to tell you I got quite a nice dividend at the end of the summer after all the Fareek business."

"Dividend?"

"Bonus."

"Did they say why?"

"No, but it wasn't hard to figure out. The Fanon case made them look good. It's one thing for an old Atlanta firm like that to have a couple of token African-American lawyers. That's better than nothing, but everybody knows it's window dressing. But to get involved, successfully, in a high-profile African-American case—now that's the real thing. Nobody can go around calling you a stuffy, old-fashioned, white-glove firm any longer. 'Old-fashioned' is what gets them. The white lawyers at Wringer Fleasom couldn't care less about African Americans singly or in the aggregate. But in Atlanta not even the bigots want to look old-fashioned, and acting like a bigot makes you *look* old-fashioned. The general partner, Zandy Scott, has been dining out on the Fanon case. He's probably out there somewhere right now, casually referring to Fareek as if he was the one who masterminded his defense. But that doesn't bother me."

"Yeah, and just wait," said the Mayor. "Pretty soon it won't just be public relations. There are plenty of big African-American corporations in Atlanta and plenty of rich African Americans running them, and Wringer Fleasom is going to *like* their business and they're going to get it, all thanks to you, Brother Roger."

Roger smiled in spite of himself. "Well—I can't say you're wrong. We just got the Sweet Auburn account—you know Clarence Harrington's restaurant chain?"

"See?"

"I see that Booker T. was right all along," said Roger, "that's what I see. Wringer Fleasom & Tick, the most solemn old-line white law firm in Atlanta is *overjoyed* to be doing business with a successful African-American entrepreneur like Clarence Harrington."

"So this has all been very good for you," said the Mayor, smiling once more. "Admit it."

"Well, I suppose." Roger paused, opened his mouth to say something else, then thought better of it. He opened his mouth again and finally screwed up his courage and said, "We're still Brother Wes and Brother Roger, right?"

"Right."

"And that applies just as much to what Brother Roger tells Brother Wes as it does the other way around, right?"

"Rest assured, Brother Roger."

"Well then, I'm going to tell you something I haven't even told Henrietta. I first got into this case with great trepidation. Fareek took an instant dislike to me. Obviously I was a Roger Too White for sure, as far as he was concerned. Then I worried that my involvement with Fareek would alienate Wringer Fleasom's white clientele—and I've spent years looking good in the eyes of 'the business interests.' But a funny thing happened. It started right after that press conference we held in the library at Wringer Fleasom. People on the street, our people, African Americans, recognized me, because the press conference had been on TV. They'd smile and say things like 'Right on, brother' and 'Gotcha back.' *Gotcha back!* Gibley Berm—you know Gibley Berm?"

"Sure."

"Well, at the big press conference—*your* press conference, Gibley Berm comes up to me—and you've got to understand, I never saw the man in my life, except in newspaper pictures—and he says, 'You're doing great work, Counselor! Gotcha back!' *Gotcha back.* The big admission I have to make here, Wes, is that . . . I *loved* it! I can't tell you how much I loved it!"

"Of course," the Mayor said softly. "You had just entered the political arena. It's more intoxicating than any drug."

"Well, maybe that's it, but I loved the fact that I was no longer an African American who had risen far above the level of his people. I was *with* my own people at last."

"Welcome to the club," said the Mayor in the same soft way. "That's politics, too."

Now Roger smiled what he realized was a sheepish smile. "Brother Wes, I even have to admit I've entertained thoughts of running for office myself . . . someday. I'm not sure about running for *what*." This he tried to pass off with a bigger, broader, all-in-fun smile.

"Aha! Don't think I didn't notice that you were saying 'African American,' too. Well . . . you'd be good," the Mayor said matter-of-factly. "You have name recognition now, thanks to the Fanon case. You're a family man living in South Atlanta. You can always leave Niskey Lake out of it. Besides, who the hell knows Niskey Lake is all mansions?"

"Well, not really *man*sions . . ."

"Anyway, it's no big deal," said Wes. "And one other thing. Right off the bat you'll have the support of a former mayor of Atlanta."

"Who?"

"Me. As you know, a mayor of Atlanta can't serve but two consecutive terms."

Wes had made it all seem so real, so possible, Roger realized too late that he had allowed a gooey, dreamy smile to spread over his mug.

"Sounds good, hunh, Roger?"

A wave of embarrassment. Why had he revealed so much of himself? He stood up abruptly and smiled and extended his hand to Mayor Wesley Dobbs Jordan. "I didn't mean to come in here and bore you with my daydreams, Brother Wes! Congratulations. I'm so proud of you, and I feel so fortunate, just knowing you. I'm not kidding. You were a great Morehouse Man, and you're a great mayor, and you'll be even greater in the future."

Wes stood up, and they shook hands, and Wes said, "Thanks, but I don't know about the future. There's no place for a black mayor of Atlanta to go. When you start talking about being governor or senator, the white folks' reluctance to appear old-fashioned somehow evaporates. Andy found that out."

"Well," said Roger, "what about Congress?"

"That'd be a step down," said Wes. "Being Mayor of Atlanta is a much bigger job than being Representative from the 5th District."

"Whatever you do, Brother Wes, you're the greatest man"—but he was afraid of sounding sappy, and so he smiled and said—"the greatest man whose time I've ever had the chance to take up too much of after a big election."

"Nonsense, Brother Roger," said Wes. "Just remember one thing. You've got to start making the rounds and shaking hands. The awards dinners, the retirement dinners, the charity dinners, the fund-raisers, the community meetings, the church meetings. You got to get to know the ministers, like Ike Blakey, who has poisoned his own goose, that snake."

Roger felt foolish. He had talked too much. "I was just thinking out loud, Brother Wes."

"That's how we all start, Brother Roger," said the Mayor. "We think out loud and hope the right people are listening."

Brother Roger and Brother Wes embraced, and then Roger turned to go, but his eye was caught by all the ivory Yoruban ceremonial swords on the ebony walls. He gestured toward them. "I've got to tell you, those swords are fabulous. What's going to become of them?"

"I'll have to start sending them back, which is too bad. They were just a sly piece of campaigning when I got them. But now *I* think they're fabulous, too. *Roots*, Brother Roger, *roots*."

By the time Roger emerged into the waiting room, the place looked like a cocktail party. There must have been sixteen or seventeen men standing around, most of them with glasses of champagne, talking up a storm.

"Hey, Rodge!"

It was Julian Salisbury, the one white face in the room other than the usual policeman. Julian was with Don Pickett, and so Roger went over and shook hands with both of them and listened to a couple of war stories from the late Fanon campaign. He was about to leave again when a deep voice said:

"Mr. White!"

It was Elihu Yale, the police chief. Roger had never dreamed the chief even knew who he was. But he did! Roger went over and shook hands with him and exchanged a few observations about the closeness of the election and felt like a man of the world.

Finally he was all but out of the mayoral offices for good when a young woman's voice sang out:

"*Mis*-ter *White!*"

Roger turned around, and there was Miss Beasley, who had been busy serving the champagne. She was really quite lovely, beautiful, in fact, aglow with happiness and champagne and the presence of so many males, all of whom no doubt found her just as gorgeous as he did.

"You can't leave without saying goodbye!" she said.

"Wouldn't think of it," said Roger, "and thanks for everything."

"Don't forget where we are, now!"

"Oh, don't worry," said the man of the world, "I'll be back."